The
Ring Master

The Ring Master

David Gurr

ATHENEUM 1987 New York

Atheneum
Macmillan Publishing Company
866 Third Avenue, New York, N.Y. 10022

Library of Congress Cataloging-in-Publication Data

Gurr, David, 1936–
The ring master.

1. Title.
PR9199.3.G795R5   1987   813'.54   87-10860
ISBN 0-689-11935-6

First American edition

10 9 8 7 6 5 4 3 2 1

Printed in the United States of America

A NOTE OF EXPLANATION ...

Edwin's story is fiction. The historical characters he meets are my figments. All the rest are illusory, and no resemblance to actual, or living persons is intended to be seen in them.

AND OF APPRECIATION ...

On the literary front, we can only build on the work of others: in particular, out of an almost overwhelming mass of technical sources, I must thank Walter Langer for his trail-blazing *The Mind of Adolf Hitler*, with its keen *Afterword*, by Robert White; Robert Donington for his eye-opening *Wagner's Ring and Its Symbols;* and Laurens van der Post for his personal picture of *Jung and the Story of Our Time;* and Friedelind Wagner, with Page Cooper, for a fascinating backstage glimpse of *The Royal Family of Bayreuth.* For other interpretation and biography I thank J.P. Stern for his *Hitler: The Führer and the People;* John Toland for his *Adolf Hitler;* and Joachim Fest for *Hitler;* Hugh Thomas M.D. for *The Murder of Rudolf Hess*, which led to my prisoner in the Tower; and Lawrence Durrell's *Constance*, with its apt subtitle, *Solitary Practices*, for the trail through Avignon. The adaptations of the Subject's own *Mein Kampf* are from the Houghton Mifflin 1939 Edition. His other recorded views are from the *Table Talk*, and Hermann Rauschning's *Hitler Speaks.* The 1st and 2nd Speeches (pages 320-321) are adapted from A.J. Sylvester's *Life With Lloyd-George.* All lyrics of Wagner are composite translations.

Moving to the real world, and Germany, a good friend, Rod Symington, provided invaluable Professorial child-guidance through the Gothic forest: many thanks to him – and also to those in London who first had eyes.

While at home, greater love hath no – than all in the family circle who had to put up with the daily hundred decibels of the Helden Horde! And beyond that, a very special note to son Gregory who brought the records, and the books, and shared the months together on our mountain. And to Patricia, who brought us back to the shore.

But most, to Judith ... for the vows that unite.   D.G.

Begun at Mount Newton, 1984
Finished at Ardmore, 1986

To Anthony Jenkins
... as mad as Ludwig

The
Ring Master

THE RING MASTER, Wolf, preparing for bed, on the eve of tossing Fate for Europe, looked out at the stars of Ukraine and said to His Fool,

"Endless plains. Look at them – horseshit and hovels. I've been thinking of *War and Peace* – not the synthetic fiction – as a writer I never read novels! – but the opening, that first paragraph where Tolstoy sets up Napoleon as the anti-Christ in Europe. Atrocities and infanticides, what impudent nonsense! Tolstoy hadn't the slightest understanding of Napoleon, yet the moron intellectuals call him a genius! – gabbling about 'Le Contrat Social' – 'fields untilled, houses burned' – so typical of the maudlin Slavs. And the French – it goes without saying! But the English – and I tell this to you despite my affection for your family and Frau Winifred, and Cromwell – the English can be damn rascals. Swilling Churchill in fact is a syphilitic disgrace. And that shithead Hess flies to him! Now there was a true romantic. The proof? – my Rudi reads novels! Why in God's name won't the cretin English follow the example of your so noble Mother?! She was so absolutely right – those Island blockheads have never understood his Ring! Not even Lohengrin – not even Tristan. Wagner! Performed in a fish market or in nigger-jazz America? Don't tell me! Well at least one can level that baroque excrescence, Covent Garden – the Master's wasted on the whole foul rat-pack of them..."

Yes, children, thus spake our Wolf before the Battle: to me – Edwin Randolf Browning Casson-Perceval (*alias*, Brother, Eddie, Fool & c) – and young Eddie *was* there, in the starry night as His Black Order legions wait to come down on the fold of Ukraine's cobblers and peasants.

My golden youth, and now ...?

... *In Spandau*, here he sits, that Fool, fifty years on, with bones that break and creak after forty of those years in Stalin's Siberia. With these crushed piano hands, that tremble so that perhaps no one can read these

9

first words of His already so painfully recorded, and with white-cataract eyes under crushed, distorted brows that barely scan the words the hands are writing from this crushed brain that sees only yesterdays and hears only the lost voices. . . .

Which does *not* mean I am bonkers, dears. Far from it. There is a clear and rational explanation – because a Middle-aged-Edwin was told by a neurosurgeon (banished to the Gulag for using a telephone directory) that there are places in the brain which, if touched by a silver wire, can release the lost-luggage memories: Engagement dates, numbers, names, snippets of long-dead conversations –

Tomorrow the legend comes to life! Barbarossa rises again like Charlemagne for your so-noble Mother's one Europe! "The soldier does the stabbing and hacking!" Tolstoy says it – that's how it is at the front. The shells go over – howling like cats in the night, and then –

Back to the morning, this hour of cold mists from the Sprey. Wolf's raven voice, harshly filling my cell . . . as He gazed above the hovels to the diamond stars. Rough diamonds indeed, but holding out the promise of far more than wealth – FREEDOM!

Because, children, this very morning, while crouched over his prison gruel, old Edwin's right, rear, occipital grey matter was tickled no-end by a voice – none other than his old school chum's from a 1000 years back. And so clear and bell-like was its fluting tone that our lad cranked round his head, twisted like a heron's from separation and re-fusing of its vertebrae – and first glancing up at a leaf drifting past the bars of our cell window in the claws of one of my black birds –

"Waring?"

There! Lounging against the studded hinges of the door, beside the carved initials, R.H., of our snug room's former demented owner: all too apparently in the (wrinkling, synthetically tanned) flesh. Complete with shooting stick that Ettie bought him at Siegel's Luggage, Unter den Linden.

"So it's really you, C-P."

At which bizarre final proof –

Silly old Eddie, still Foolish, passed out.

His guards, more panicked than he at this possible loss of their 4-Power Golden Goose, revived him. (There is not an inexhaustible clutch of Hess-gooses. Ancient-Edwin is the 3rd – the last! – of the idiot-line, pressed into service from arctic Siberia. The 2nd Hess died two weeks ago. The remains passed each other *in transit* in the Prison morgue. A chill moment . . .)

But before we go on about the extra-ordinary re-appearance of Jeremy Waring (and the late-late "Fräulein Anna" Hess) we must have Order! Prison discipline! Get things straight in your silver, plated head, Number 7!

Jawohl!

The Prisoner's number! the Prisoner's name! He is Ancient, he hears Voices (his Mama's & Sister's, mainly); he is recording, he is in Spandau Gaol as the Last Survivor – with his pet Ravens, hopping and croaking on the great Ash tree outside his barred window. Their names, *Gedanke,* and *Gedächtnis* (Thought & Memory) are not Prison Issue. Mind you, they respond, and talk back to me, black devils, egging on the silver wire voices. Spandau's bars are not set close enough to keep them out, the ravens and the voices, the names of my century . . .

So. It *was* Waring this morning (our Eddie has sworn to be truthful) returned again with the luncheon gruel (a croissant, actually: the Frogs were on guard). He stood there, as cool a damned watcher of the Berlin Scene as ever, wearing another *cravate,* the colour and texture of my late Sister's knickers, a fitting representative of London's Yellow Street Press – the Fleet.

Nearer the gutter than the music halls!

Wolf's opinion. It's harder than one might think to keep the wires uncrossed.

"I'd had in mind – " drawled visiting Waring, after Old-Boy canes, and pleasantries, were exchanged "– just a routine piece showing the Prisoner still alive and kicking against the pricks – but that was Hess. I mean, seeing it's *you* – "

"But it's incredible, Waring," babbled Eddie. "A miracle."

"If a chap watches long enough, wheels come round. But as it *is* you, C-P, and no real Hess? and the affair of Mr Wolf with your sister? and being there for the end? A chap might make a small packet, if you like?"

A proper devil is our Jeremy, swishing the bribe for Eddie in his forked *trident* tail: Write His life for mine! Think! – Rich! Released!

WOLF'S SEX-LIFE!!!

A promising start: just the right yellow line for Waring's old alma mater, the *Continental Mail* (now defunct, he tells me – so His War achieved something). And there will be sex, bags of it, this is a children's story – but *will* "Wolf" unfleeced truly "scoop" our fortune . . .?

Because we must make a LARGE packet. By God, Old Edwin has not been brought out of forty years Wotan-wandering in the Gulag for nothing!

> *There's a Friend for little Children,*
> *Above the bright blue Sky . . .*

Trust Waring?

Nevermore, quoth my Croakers – G & G are not Believers. They laugh their harsh laughs and sit on Old Eddie's cracked shoulders – making my scribbling even more peculiar. They look at His words and eat my breakfast and defecate on both – they have no manners. Nor had Wolf, wolfing it down at the Wagners' Wahnfried table. . . .

What our Jeremy proposes, is that he smuggle Our Memoires – with no assurance other than an Old Boy's Word – under the noses – and so to Yellow Street. "A chap could do some suitable editing, C-P, to remove the period cliché, for the modern reader, if you like."

This, from a proven master of the genre, at sixpence the column-inch.

One tap of Gedanke's optimist's beak for Yes . . . but Gedächtnis, my black pessimist, taps –

Guilt. Pressing down night and night; day and day; second on creeping second since that appalling mountain hour. What right have we to consider escape? Serve out the frozen time, twenty lives over. Ten thousand.

> *O dearly, dearly has He loved,*
> *And we must love Him too,*
> *And trust in His redeeming Blood,*
> *And try His works to do.*

But then again – we have a month to consider, Birds. The Guard changed at tea, and Waring can't get back in here while I'm watched by the Russians: the Bear still hugs the absurd Regulations for

Guarding – the wee problem is, will the Yellows (living on the Wages of Lies) believe we are *not* His Rudi? With those ghastly jug-ears and the teeth-whistling awfulness? Have we been listening too much to Wolf's Doppelgänger nonsense? Isn't that the trouble with Eddie as Wolf-Biographer? – too many years in the wings, too close an involvement with the production? Is it true that Outsiders will never understand?

The Ring, for Nigger-jazz America? Don't tell me!

Because He won't listen! – but His fear of the double wasn't nonsense, for He ruled in a land of opposites; paired images in a world of mirrors and illusions: Wagner-Wolf. Siegfried-Hagen. Blond-&-Dark. German-&-Jew. Genius-&-Madness. Brother-&-Sister. Britannia-Germania. Heil-&-Rule!

"May we hope forever, through Papa's Sacrifice! Anything is possible. Remember, we are Wagnerians now, children."

The dearest voice of all! – darling Mama's on our golden isle: sweeping across the terrace with her Amused-but-not-Showing-it voice ... Edwardian Mama, settling into her wicker chaise among the bees and portulaca by our Mediterranean.

"There is only one way for a modern Wagnerian to tell a story of the Master's properly. For your novelette, Begin at the Beginning, Eddie-dear!"

With Musical Notation:

"Twice upon a Time – "

"Edwin, that is Affectation."

No truly not, Mama. It has to be musical, after the prelude, and I'm starting with "twice" because Ettie and me always share our birthdays.

Edwina and I. You must *remember ...*

Tales From The Ring
for
Little Folk!

Printed at London (1907) on rag vellum, with original Costume Illustrations from Bayreuth, under the Imprimatur, & with a Preface, (in Translation) for Her English Readers by The Master's Widow, Frau Cosima Wagner.

My Dearest Children of Parents of His Ring:

First, Welcome to His Work! And in keeping with our Musical Notation, I shall call this so little addition of mine, as He did, not a Preface, but a *Prelude*!

What you shall shortly read is a story of genius (& composed *by* a Genius) which may seem at first a trifle strange to you. Indeed, many *grown-up* people, without the benefit of Childhood's *understanding*, declare Richard Wagner's marvellous story in its glorious Music to be too difficult & complicated to enjoy. Nothing could be further from the truth! We have all enjoyed nursery stories of Giants & Wizards – and that is what His Cycle of the Ring *is*: a wonderful nursery story. It is called, in the German which you all shall learn one day:

Der Ring des Nibelungen

And this is really what it is about – a magical Ring belonging to a Dwarf called Alberich, who is of a lower race called the Nibelungs. At least Alberich (a swarthy, wretched, villainous creature) *says* that the magic ring belongs to him, but actually, Children, he has *stolen* it (or the gold to make it) from a great Treasure guarded by three beautiful Maidens in the Rhine. Like Mermaids, yes! The first part of our magic Ring's Cycle (or Four Adventures) is called:

Das Rheingold

So *that* is simple enough, is it not?! And then – after Alberich steals their gold the Rhine Maidens put a Curse on it – so that is simple too. The Curse is that the Ring allows anyone who owns it to Rule the World, *but* he shall also be d****d – *unless* he renounces Power for True Love. A most beautiful, & German, sentiment.

And then – as such a wonderful Ring is much too precious to be entrusted to a vile, crippled creature as Alberich, it is taken by a God. His name is Wotan, & he lives with his Wife, Fricka (a sensible woman) & Loge, the playful god of Fire, & the other gods & goddesses of Storm & Lightning & other Natural Powers in a beautiful paradise called Valhalla where Wotan is building a fine new home for His Fricka. (Of course it is the *mightiest* Castle as He is the mightiest God.) And then –

Prelude

The House of Brothers & Sisters
[for strings, mainly]

The Cusp:

As Mama never ceased to remind us – Ettie & Eddie – we were born on it: March 21st, the day when the sun moves from the sign of Pisces into the sign of Aries. Eddie's year was 1911 and his Sun was placed exactly conjunct Mercury, in the Third House, which grants manipulation of the hands and fingers. This is also the House of Brothers and Sisters. Born on that same special day in the astrological year our Destinies had to be entwined. Ettie was two years older, born in 1909, in London – at the Casson-Percevals' narrow house in Mayfair – but Ettie remembers it for a marmalade cat, a wicker chair, and spilled quince jelly in the drawing room.

Tenses, Edwin! Ettie *remembered*. My darling Ettie. As Old Eddie gets ancient, he finds himself believing more in another of Mama's Fads: The World Beyond, The Other Side – which she went into in a big way with Sir Oliver Lodge in 1919 on our return to Britain, ostensibly for our education but in fact for Mama to investigate Theosophy, another promising escape from anguish ...

So. Ettie was a Pisces, too, but born at half past one in the morning, her Sun was in Aries, giving her the music but making her the pioneer, the prima donna. (With her Gemini rising, *very* strong willed!) I do believe it. Although, in our Eddie's case, born 4 weeks premature – "untimely ripped", which date is true? Surely, Mama, if the stars affect Destiny it must be Conception.

Enough of Dalliance. Young Edwin was born at 9 in the morning, the sun was up, firmly on his side of The Cusp; he was a True Piscean. He was born in Madame de la Verendry's house in Toulon, beside what was at that time a pleasant little park. God knows what has become of it since. Old Edwin's French guard says that the Riviera is gone. "No sand and all sewage." Our Provence remains golden and azure in my memory.

The golden child was born at Madame de la Verendry's because Mama was travelling while vastly pregnant: something not done by ladies of her Class & Station in 1911, but Mama had a Mind of her Own, despite her Fadishness. Ettie didn't get that strong will by accident. The name? From Rossetti. Sister was christened Edwina Isolde Rossetti Casson-Perceval. (Mama was wavering between the Poets and Wagner.) As young Edwin got "Browning" and was spared "Siegmund" or "Richard" it seems that by 1911 Wagner was losing. That might have been Papa's influence. Our Father played a violin and was consequently drawn to a repertoire with a lighter touch. Ettie remembers him dressed as a gypsy, sweeping with his fiddle around her nursery cot, on his way to a party. Ettie has a good memory for scenes and impressions. For Eddie, nothing before late three at the earliest, and whether he sees sidewhiskers in fact or from the photographs and portraits – no: there is a touch, and a deep voice, and sometimes the cell at night carries the notes of a violin and gentle Schubert, my favourite composer. Edwin was not a Wagnerian by choice, let me tell you!

He was born at Toulon because Mama had stayed too long at our island: l'isle d'or – golden Porquerolles, south of Hyères and west of St Tropez. The Casson-Percevals had a house there also, as did Madame de la Verendry and three other outsiders. The rest were peasants in stone cottages, a curé, some nuns in a run-down convent, fishermen, and a handful of shopkeepers on the Place beside the landing. No Médecin. Mama was making a leisurely return to London for the lying in when Nature called. Without Madame de la Verendry Baby-Eddie might have emerged to a public ward in Marseilles! Madame was a formidable woman, in purple so dark that it was almost black. Her husband, whom neither we nor Madame ever saw, owned a parfumerie and half of Paris. He made ready cash out of selling supplies to the French battle fleet based at Toulon.

Battleships! Sailor-Wolf cries with a finger-snap like THAT! Battleships are gone! Finished! U-boats are the thing. Grain will be carried, oil fuels. I see this with utmost clarity.

So easy to slip sideways – but this is not *His* ring-story yet. Ettie's and mine. She tells me Baby-Eddie was carried in triumph back to London: a son! A continuation of the Casson-Percevals. Casson is vaguely French by way of Yorkshire and ancient Troy before that. "Cassandra", unhappy Trojan princess, and a feminine form of Alexander in mediaeval times. Edwin's archaeology and much of his anima nature must come from the Cassons. Perceval comes through from the Egmonts – and is commonly thought to have been made up seven hundred years ago by Chretien de Troyes in his story of the Grail.

What horseshit impudence!

Wolf again.

Eddie knew, from the time he could first think, that the Grail was never "made up". Ettie remembers him telling her at least by the time he was six: "Of course there was a really, truly, Holy Grail!" And we weren't living in Cornwall then, with Arthur all around us. How did I know . . . Why could Ettie sing? Why did we meet Wolf? Why did He love her? No, that's not the mystery. Why did she love *Him*?

In our stars. If anyone has a better Fad to explain the Great War, Old Edwin hasn't heard it.

The shooting of a tin-pot duke in a country of pig-sticking and vampires brought about the death of Empires that had stood for a thousand years?! snorts Historian-Wolf. Don't tell me!

I said, He won't listen!

Mama, on her mother's side, came from that background – intermarrying European petty nobility – and grew up in the Household at Windsor. Maternal Great-Grandmama came to the court of Victoria as a lady-in-waiting with only German as a language and a spotless Friesian virginity; but was fortunate enough to get bedded down with a specimen of solid English stock who lost a leg (& one unmentionable organ) in the Crimea and was pushed after that in a basket-chair for the

19

rest of his life. He bred successfully but refused the indignity of walking on a wooden leg. Pig-headed! You see where Ettie got it.

THE WAR

The Casson-Percevals are not on Porquerolles for the Big Day because of the Heat. (We would have been in Cornwall but Papa had been Gravely Ill and had to remain near a Specialist. So we summered in Mayfair.) And Eddie sees flags. Aged three-and-a-half – that must be one of the earliest memories, the flags, and the sound of a band somewhere distant. No cheering, although Ettie says she remembers the crowds cheering before the reaper scythed them down.

The War will be finished by Christmas. The houses in Cornwall are kept open. The Casson-Percevals have two Cornish houses: Trevelly, on the soft south coast, looking out at St George's Island, and a smaller one on the harsh north coast, Table House on the moor above Tintagel and the monstrous Atlantic waves crashing in below Arthur's castle. Because of the harsh climate, the Table House is kept for summer weekends.

. . . *The 16th of November, 1914:* The need for men for the reaper is not yet acute enough to tear them from our Cornish land, and the Casson-Percevals' investments are climbing in anticipation as they do once the City and the Exchange get over their shock and realise that Replacements will have to be made.

At a good price, I've no doubt! snaps Economist-Wolf, with non-competitive bidding and all of Them *stroking one another's fat arses! The profiteering and good men, the best men, give their blood at the front! Don't tell me!*

Papa's business agents were anything but semitic. Rotundly English, with port-wine faces after long lunches, but Wolf is right about the profiteering, and the best men dying.

. . . *The 3rd of May, 1915.* The transits of Saturn and Pluto are in the first degree of Cancer – a square to both their Suns: the time of Gallipoli & the Second Battle of Ypres. Our Father (because of his Connections) needed no physical to join the colours. Barely recovered from his illness, he crossed to France and into Belgium. The night he left, Eddie's first dream came. A white seagull with a blackcapped head flew into the sun

20

and covered it with blood, and I woke screaming.

"You're all right, Eddie, I'm here, you mustn't be frightened."

Ettie was holding me. Comforting me. The gold stars pasted with the silver crescent moon on our dark nursery ceiling at Trevelly were still with me.

"You truly mustn't be frightened, Eddie."

The News came on a bicycle with a boy from the telegraph office at Looe. Ettie & Eddie cried in the nursery. Mama howled below for half a day – very un-English, terrifying – until the doctor also came from Looe and gave her three tablespoons of liquid from a brown bottle with a green cross in a white circle on its label.

Our first circle had been broken. Mama lay in her room under the influence of the brown bottle. Our nurse – a capable Cornishwoman, not a Nanny – took us out in the fields to see cowslips and, if they are over, bluebells in the woods. When we came back to the house, the photographs and portraits of Our Father were draped in black.

. . . *The 1st of June, 1915:* Mama – with three of the brown bottles in her dressing case and Ettie & Eddie – goes across to France. Ettie tells me that we went from Weymouth to Cherbourg in an antique ferry with two funnels and were protected by the Navy in the form of an armed tug. With allowances for her opinionated nature, I don't believe that at six she really knew it was a tug.

It *is* the first time that Eddie remembers being in France – from the smell of coffee and tobacco and steam in the railway coaches. The other great difference was stepping from the coach right down to the ground! In England there are platforms. And the French porters had bright blue blouses and baggy black pants. And there was the flower market in Lyons, and tall glasses of thick chocolate with piled whipped cream, and the view of Mont Blanc where the Rhone almost breaks through the Alps to meet the Rhine –

But of course that so-little Eddie doesn't remember. Views were later. So was the Rhine. But the steam and coffee smell, and the step down, and the porters: yes. Eddie is Four.

. . . *At Porquerolles.* Music begins on Porquerolles. Music was *because* of Porquerolles. It arrived on a cart in the form of a spare grand piano not required by Madame de la Verendry and not missed out of the war profits of her husband. A Bechstein with a nice tone, after it got over the journey. It was harder to find a piano tuner than a piano, and a man eventually came all the way from Marseilles. He was extremely Old and called Monsieur Guillaume. Old Father William – we had a picture book of *Alice* – is very affectionate with Eddie. Ettie gets in a rage whenever Monsieur Guillaume arrives, about twice a year after the initial adjustment. Since Old Father William never opened his fly or touched me, why do I know? How did Ettie know? More to the point, why was Sister jealous?

"I hate him," she said. "He has spit at the corner of his mouth and his bum's too big."

"You mustn't, Ettie!"

B*m is a *strictly forbidden* word that has been smuggled to France from Cornwall. The piano is for Mama. A Fad called "Therapy".

Mama played Chopin at first, delicately and continuously. Ettie & Eddie went down to the beach with Mathilde from the village, engaged as a nurse. Our Cornishwoman had been left behind. No one on the island speaks a word of English. Mama dismisses it. "Remember, we are Islanders now, children. It would have been too much to expect Cornwall to settle in."

Mama is always Considerate of Others. Especially Servants. She only expected her small children, solely English-speaking, to settle in. They learnt French quickly – with rough Provençal edges from the local patois, that so appall Madame de la Verendry that E & E are instructed to attend at her house every afternoon – "At three, precisely!" – to have the edges smoothed. After which, Sister took her own Destiny firmly in hand.

At the end of that first summer, aged six-and-a-half, she took off all her clothes on the beach and taught herself to swim.

Mathilde, shapeless in a black garment to the ground, was horrified. Not at the nudity – the swimming.

"Le serpent, mademoiselle! Les poissons sauvages!"

Because of the sea serpents not one peasant on Porquerolles can swim. Fishermen are regularly drowned. This is not a unique phenomenon. It was the same in Cornwall.

But then, says Eugenicist-Wolf, racially speaking, they are the same peasant stock. I know the type so well. Give them a boat or a small farm, they give back children, fish, fresh eggs. They make a nation.

The Plan for Pawel's Ukraine: *Kinder* and small neat farms. Little islands of Teuton neatness on an ocean of land. *Teutons settled America as we shall the Ukraine – despite the Indians. This is fact! For the time being the East shall have scarves and glass beads.* And no one, in or out of the charmed circle, ever asks, *"What will happen to our new Indians – after the Time-Being?"* It is always treated as a vaguely settled problem, and occasionally, if the questioning from a serious outsider gets too intense, a name is put on it: *Madagascar.* Another island. *Madagascar* settles everything – at least until a time at which no one asks the question because no one wants to Know.

Because He always knew the only answer.

. . . *Our Island* – was covered with pines, needles, huge cones, and sand, there was only one farm, a small-holding attached to the convent. The nuns in their black habits looked much like Mathilde, except that the nuns wore white wimples and never squatted to pee in the sand.

"Or anyway, Eddie, I've never seen one do it and I've really watched."

"Maybe they go in the barn, Ettie, with the cows."

The nuns had 3 cows and a huge-balled bull. Also some chickens with topknots of iridescent green-black feathers, and speckled eggs. At four-and-a-bit, no-balled Edwin took off *his* clothes and loved the sunshine and water on his body – but I didn't learn to swim until the following summer and then, because of the serpents, only a dog paddle within touching distance of the land. By that time Ettie – "I'm nearly *eight*, Eddie" – was swimming from point to point across the little Bay of Lobsters with Mathilde flapping the long way round by beach because of the serpents. Mama reclined, oblivious: we were with Mathilde, all was well.

. . . *The 11th of July, 1916:* The second summer, aged five and seven-plus, Ettie & Eddie play porpoises in the shallows, their nude bodies sliding over one another, innocent as the explorations of their secret selves they carry out as they lie on the sand when Mathilde has gone to sleep. But we knew what we were doing. *"Let's make Thingee grow, Eddie,"* Sister whispers, tickling Brother with a finger and then choking her giggles lest Mathilde wake and see this sunlit transformation from floppy worm to

23

stand-up comedian. Eddie doesn't giggle. The funny sensation is nothing to laugh over. That was as far as our exploration went in the House of Brothers and Sisters – in that year anyway.

... *Christmas 1916:* Edwin played the piano for the first time: a carol. Ettie says it was Hark-the-Herald and not good, but it was picked out unaided and impressed Madame de la Verendry when she called. Mama did not see her. Christmas without Papa causes a deep Decline that lasts right through until our birthday, in March. She stops playing Chopin and day after day will not leave her room. The only measurement of time is Mathilde passing with the chamber pots. Ettie & Eddie read the latest Beatrix Potter to themselves and act out the stories. Ettie insists on being the Fox in "Jemima Puddle-duck". Eddie has to sit on a nest in the pines but is allowed next time to be Squirrel Nutkin, and squashed underfoot by Ettie-the-Owl. Otherwise we helped Mathilde and the kitchen girl. Edwin learns Three Blind Mice and Happy Birthday ...

... *The 21st of March, 1917:* Mama comes out for Our Birthday – wearing a bright emerald frock, the colour of the cross on the brown medicine bottles. "I've had a dream, children," with a sweet, gay smile as though there have been no silent months. "Papa and I were at a performance of *Tristan und Isolde* – before Edwina was born. We loved each other so much, and I know now that he is waiting for us all, safely on the other side. He hasn't been horribly torn or mutilated or anything dreadful with gas. Come along."

And she took us for a holiday outing to the mainland, to Hyères.

Le Cormoran

The trip from our golden island was made in a small steam pinnace, the *Cormoran*, manned by Deaf'n'Dumber. That's what Ettie & Eddie called him – and, as he could neither hear nor complain, it was taken as a sweet little pet name. Deaf'n'Dumber laughs, and everyone on board smiles at the so-adorable Enfants Anglais with their golden hair and blue eyes, the perfect colours for the unspoilt Riviera. That day we had a wider audience than usual, because sailors were being transported. Porquerolles had three other reminders from the harsh outside world: three massive naval gun emplacements set up to guard the approaches to Toulon. (There have been guns on the island since the time of Napoleon, hunting for Nelson.) In 1915 the guns were sixteen-inch, from battleships, and called Annabelle, Berthe, and Charlotte. Once a week they conducted a solemn firing practice of a round apiece. A sailor in a striped singlet, with rolled up bell-bottom trousers, rides on a bicycle from house to house, warning, *"En garde! Annabelle, une heure!"* Which gave E & E just enough time to escape from Mathilde and run to a clearing in the pines from which they could look down to the battery a mile away. Even at a mile the concussion was like a massive fist in the back, and all the convent chickens shrieked.

Concussion from the guns, says Conductor-Wolf, thoughtfully, in the Wahnfried drawing room, is a weapon in itself. Consider, Frau Winifred, how we feel in the Festspielhaus – that first extraordinary chord of The Master's – yes! The opening of Rheingold. That underlying E Flat Major puts all the hairs up on the neck. Noise is a factor in battle, there can be no doubt.

Which is why He adds the sirens to the Stukas to terrify the target even before the bombs begin to fall . . .

Deaf'n'Dumber's pinnace had a little steam whistle escaped from a circus calliope which terrified Eddie when Ettie worked it as we approached the low jetty at Gien, by the lighthouse, three miles south of Hyères. We went the rest of the way in a chaise driven by a mainland relative of Deaf'n'Dumber. The sailors, being relieved from Annabelle and her sisters, marched, somewhat raggedly, scuffing dust and looking sideways at Mama. They weren't looking at Ettie. Not that way. Not yet.

In Hyères, we had glasses of chocolate – that's where old Edwin remembers the chocolate! – and bought ribbons as a present for Ettie and a handcarved wooden donkey with a cart for Eddie. The donkey had a hat and a saddle blanket of red signal cloth, and I had it until –

Mama left us drinking our chocolate and went to the telegraph office in the square. Then we went back to our island and thought we had had a wonderful birthday.

"It was a wonderful birthday," says Sister, on another one, so many years later. "Oh, God, Eddie, we were so bloody happy." And prim Brother kisses her and says, "We still are, darling. But you know these Viennese – you really mustn't swear like that."

Ettie & Eddie awoke one morning some days after (that strange

25

conversation about Mama's dream of Tristan) and getting the wooden donkey in the hat, to find Richard Wagner in our lives.

THE MASTER

Like all the rest of the Casson-Percevals' regular supplies, He came via Deaf'n'Dumber – in a large tea-chest re-enforced at the corners with tin and marked "Wilson & Wilson, Musical Suppliers to the Trade, Covent Garden." With a concession to the flighty French: Poste Restante.

Wilson & Wilson know their business. The tea-chest's progress has not been affected by the War. Mathilde produces a hammer for Deaf'n'Dumber. Inside the chest are books, libretti, scores – full orchestra, not just pianoforte – and circular recordings with dark blue labels and a white dove. Also a gramophone to be wound up, with a packet of 1000 needles "Made from *Lignum Vitae* – Each Point Individually Inspected and Approved." Mama never takes on a new Fad by halves. There was even a marble bust in a school teacher's tassled cap.

"The Master," declared Mama, in a tone even more High Church than The Cusp. This frowning teacher promises to be a Mighty Fad indeed.

"He wants to go to the lav," said Ettie, who must have been going through a phase of her own.

"That is being too silly, Edwina. Remember, we are Wagnerians now. Here is a book of His Special Stories." From the chest she produced a cover with a terrifying, fuming beast, with blood dripping graphically from a gash on its neck. "Siegfried and the Dragon," said Mama, brightly. "Tales from The Ring for Little Folk, with a delightful Preface from the Master's Widow, Frau Cosima Herself. You can read it to Edwin after tea, Edwina, before you go to bed."

My Dearest Children of His Ring ...

   . . . Two Giants are helping Wotan build the Castle. Their names are Fasolt & Fafner. Fasolt is very *tall* (& rather too gentle). Fafner is very *broad* (& rather too jealous & fierce). Wotan must repay both of them for their honest labours. And then – Loge helps Him with ever such a clever trick! Wotan & Loge travel down in flames & smoke to the vile place where the Nibelungs toil & live. Alberich, who is their Slave Master with a great Whip, puts on a magic Helmet, called "Tarnhelm", & makes himself into a roaring Dragon. "How clever!" cries Loge, "but you could never turn yourself into a nasty little Toad!" Boastful Alberich does & gets caught. You see how simple it really all is!

Childish. The Valhalla Stories all seem interchangeable: Hero, with Magic Sword; Heroine, with Horns on her head.

. . . Naturally, being Giants, Fafner & Fasolt feel that *they* should have the *whole* Treasure. Wotan refuses, so the Giants take the goddess Freia instead (Who provides the Golden Apples that keep all the gods young. When you read further on your own, my Dears, you shall see that it is a *tiny* bit more complicated because Wotan at first has *offered* Freia to Fafner & Fasolt – but not seriously, of course!) Wotan gives up the Ring in order to get Freia back. And then –
Fafner *kills* Fasolt for it! So Richard Wagner proves to us, with the simplicity of Genius, that the Curse is working!

By day, Young Edwin pretends to love it all. By night, Eddie's dreams were made nightmares for weeks . . . Dragons, Giant, Bleeding Wound, Magic Spear. At the end, a happy ending with everybody except the villains dead.

And so, Children, with but this briefest glimpse of its Wonders, (with His two pet Ravens, called "Thought" & "Memory" flying ahead of Us) we All go happily into His Ring & Valhalla which we shall enter over a glorious Bridge of Rainbows. . . .

Mama plays the Valhalla records with religious strictness: one hour in the morning, one after lunch. The voices either screech or roar with "r's" that roll forever, like the sea.

"They are *Helden* voices," explained Mama. "Heroic, children, because they sing for heroes, and Immortal in their own right from Bayreuth."

Ettie said, "I shall be Helden one day."

"Held-*in*, for the soprano, Edwina. And Posture – we cannot have a Bayreuth Brünnhilde with a hump on her back. You too, Edwin dear."

"Stupid old Helden Huns," says Sister, slouching. "Eddie, it's your turn to be tied to the rock . . ."

Why did Mama torture herself with the wedding music while we were tied to our rocks? Over and over. E & E would release themselves to go out with Mathilde and down to the village for bread, and come back to Stab & Hack some more, and the Master would still be playing under the *lignum vitae* needle.

Mama never changed it, and Ettie didn't care. Mathilde didn't understand – she associated the sound from the magic gramophone horn with the voice of Le Serpent! At the age of only 6, Edwin realised that he hated the scratchy noise and that it was worse if the record was dirty or the needle blunt. "But then," said grownup Ettie, losing luggage and shouting at porters in different languages, "you always were an awful *fuss*, Eddie. About such silly little things." It was only on the big things I gave in without a murmur. Dominated Pisces.

The Matelot & The Witch

Astrology and the Hereafter played second fiddle but were not muted altogether by The Master. Once they came much closer on Porquerolles. A sister or a cousin of Mathilde's – the whole island was related, even the nuns – this other peasant woman had The Gift. Mama found out by happy accident. She had walked to the village to go shopping. Deaf'n'Dumber was loading the pinnace – *Cormoran* – loading it with sailors. There had been a storm in the night, hurling the great pine cones against our nursery windows and rattling spray and sand in a continuous fine hail for hours. In the morning the sea, our beautiful Mediterranean, was surly grey with a stiff chop from the southeast into the bay by the landing. An old woman was gesticulating fiercely with Deaf'n'Dumber.

"But he just smiled that *foolish* smile," sighed Mama. "One has to ignore these things. Remember, children, one must always be kind to halfwits: they are often the chosen vessel of Our Lord."

That afternoon Mathilde announced with satisfaction at tea, *"Ecoutez, mes enfants. Un matelot est mort."* And crossed herself . . . twice.

It was this catastrophe, of course, that Mathilde's relative had been attempting to avert. Ettie & Eddie rushed from the house to see if they could see the body floating, and have a Helden Funeral Pyre – in costume. And Sister said with clear cold logic: "Witches never tell. If they tell, the magic can't work."

. . . No Helden pyre. Instead the Curé held a special service for the matelot on the landing stage, two days later. The storms had passed and the wind had turned with Mediterranean swiftness. Now it blew warm from Africa, and scattered dry sand over the small congregation. The nuns had made a wreath of white lilies-of-the-valley, Madame de la Verendry, in black purple, as the island's social Leader, stood on the *Cormoran* and threw the sweet flowers into the sea. Deaf'n'Dumber smiled his foolish innocent's smile. One of the surviving sailors, lined up in striped singlets, bellbottoms rolled down, turned to another and shuddered.

Ettie & Eddie skipped home the long way, all around our island, but we never found the body. I only see it in my dreams. Burning.

Mama, after considerable haggling with Mathilde, completed arrangements to meet the Sorceress. Mama wanted to take her little ones, to further their education, but Mathilde flatly refused; stamping her clog on the red tile floor of the kitchen with a sharp, *crack-crack!*

"Non, pas les enfants, Madame! Absolument pas!"

A little dance of fury. Mama gave in meekly and went to meet her Fate alone. She came back late in the afternoon, almost at our bedtime, in the same happy mood as she had been after the Christmas Depression the previous year.

"We did the right thing, becoming Islanders, children. If we had stayed in London we should all have been killed."

(A Zeppelin, indeed, in the first attack on London, had demolished the Casson-Percevals' house in Mayfair with a direct hit.)

Mathilde's relation saw it in a combination of Tarot and the stars.

The Zeppelin, dismisses Aeronaut-Wolf, I saw at once was a completely artificial construction. Nature has clearly rejected the lighter than air principle. She has provided no bird with a set of balloons as she has done in the case of the fish. As to mixing methods of prediction, Himmler tells me that's quite common, among unsophisticates. Mixing their mediums. I correct myself: 'Media', for Herr Ederl, our Latin scholar.

Patting my arm and getting His little laugh . . .

"Mathilde's cousin sees us here for two more years," declared Mama, "which means the War will not be over until you are eight, Edwin dear."

"Are the English going to win, Mama?"

"What a foolish question. Silly boy, of course we're going to win. That is why Papa paid the Supreme Sacrifice and passed over. So that *you* could grow up happy and free."

I know, without a shadow of doubt, that she emphasised the *you.*

"Come on, Mama," begs Ettie. "What did the witch say about *me*?"

"The Occult is not a plaything for unformed minds, Edwina. We did not talk about you. What shall we listen to tonight?"

. . . *The 7th of August, 1918:* Eddie is Seven (before he knew about the magic in Numbers). Ettie is nine. Mathilde is Older and sleeps more in the sun. Despite the serpent, Edwin ventures a little farther from the beach. The blue-green water is deeper. Ettie & Eddie's forming bodies are still naked. Still hairless. Still innocent? In the House of Brothers and Sisters Eddie's manipulative Piscean fingers find a secret room.

"Oh Eddie, don't, you mustn't. Silly, you'll wake Mathilde!" giggling and splashing her gold-white thighs and cleft away. And that night in our nursery, creeping on tanned small feet to my bed by the open window with the moon through the mosquito net: *"Eddie, the porpoise game, with your fingers – do it again."*

That summer and autumn, as the Helden blood washes for the last months over Europe, and gas drops down in a trench and makes a

Private Soldier blind, and dumb, like our simple crewman on the *Cormoran*, Ettie & Eddie play the porpoise game only with fingers. Mama played Wagner in the night on cracked recordings. The Private Soldier heard Voices and saw visions.

Also in 1918 – we almost forgot!

Young Edwin began to play the piano properly. Madame de la Verendry pronounced his a talent that must not be wasted. In the absence of other instructors she shall teach him herself. No Master. Madame & Eddie played Chopin and Liszt (not knowing then that Liszt is related to dangerous Wagner) and a risqué new-comer that Madame liked: Debussy.

Sister only began to sing when Brother was good enough to play Debussy.

So young, her pitch is flawless. Her untrained voice and throat produce an uncanny power. Eddie watches in awe as the notes float out over the terrace and the crimson portulaca, covered with bees, gathering honey from the sun.

"That's what her voice will be," said Madame de la Verendry, "honey. But it must be guarded. Nothing forced. It is too soon."

We went back to sexless Chopin, and Ettie put her voice away.

Just in time, because somehow Mathilde found out that the serpent in the gramophone horn was really *"Les Boches!"*

"No they aren't, Mathilde," said Sister, "it's Hunnish. Look at their pictures – the Helden singers are all just fat and stupid Huns."

The War-to-start-the-next-one ended. Winter in the North. Mama loathes the cold. We stayed on Porquerolles until Our Birthday – and then beyond. The Casson-Percevals did not return to England until May, 1919. We arrived in Cornwall on the 4th anniversary of the day Our Father died. Young Edwin scarcely thought of it in the excitement of rediscovering Trevelly – scarcely.

(Mama told us later that, of course, she went back because that was the day Mathilde's witch-relative had told her to.)

... *At Trevelly, New Year's Day, 1920.* The Twenties. Roaring and rum-soaked, they start quietly for the Casson-Percevals – with a New

Year's dinner of roast pheasant from Trevelly's estate, and Eddie refusing to eat it lest it had been a friend from Big Meadow up by Badger Wood.

"It isn't your friend," said Ettie, "I promise, Eddie. It's a different pheasant, cross my heart."

So Brother eats it and, after the sweet, Sister says, "It *was*." And giggles & shrieks so hard that she was sick – after he was sick – and both get sent to bed by Mama in a rare rage.

"I can understand Edwin being silly," declared his mother, "just. But at twelve – and on the Mandala of my Persian rug! Edwina, it is too much."

"Too much" actually came two days later, from London, an over-weight cousin of Papa's, removed, but not far enough. Wynchman-Hare, pronounced with no "ch" to be difficult. A right-handed man, but he dressed on the left – always a sign of a twisted nature.

"You can see his Thingee wobble," Ettie, with her eye for detail, as Eddie hides with her outside the library, listening through green velvet curtains, "and he honks though his nose. He's utterly horrid."

"My dear woman," the brute honked to Mama, "a free spirit may have been all very well in the 'eighties but it will not do now. There has to be Education, and you know what headmasters are, especially ones with Orders. No more delay – the Boy must be Put Down."

"*Crikey!*" – from the Boy, before being sick again.

"It's all right," from his Sister, after. "They can't really mean put you to *sleep*, Eddie, like a mad rabbit or something. Not truly."

Can they not . . . ?

. . . The 16th of June, 1921: After months of frightful uncertainty, a chauffeur arrives from Looe, with a Daimler in which the Casson-Percevals ford the River Tamar, where the semi-orphans find themselves on the high moors of Devon, before a bleak stone barracks with windswept trees, and a sign:

ALL SOULS COLLEGE

Two female figures stood beneath the sign.

"Dear Children," they said in unison, "We are the Aunts."

A bonded pair. One was Short & Slim; the other, Tall & Stout. One Bustled; the other Swept. The Bustler dug in a vegetable garden with her long cotton dress tucked into the tops of ankle-buttoned leather boots, while the Sweeper sat, gowned, with amber beads, and collected stamps. They slept together in a squeaking double bed, and each called the other, "My Friend."

"They aren't my Aunts," said Ettie, "and the fat one smells."

They were, in fact the Misses Mason & Marsdon, *Athene* & *Boadicea.* Unrelated, but with such names their appeal for Mama was instant.

"We have ten other nephews and nieces," large Boadicea, the sweeper, informed us. "Our new Casson-Percevals shall make twelve – like Our Lord's Apostles."

"And you'll be with us in August – " piped Athene, the bustler, her Friend. "The holiday month!"

Mama had no remaining doubts. "How lovely and remote," she cried, gazing around at the blasted heath. "Children, I feel we shall be very happy here."

This was to prove a false statement. Mama was never there at all. She was in Vienna for almost a year. "I've been Freudianized again," she said, looking peaceful on her return. "Children, how you've grown."

"What's Freudianized, Mama?"

"Dear Doctor Freud, Edwin, attributes certain of Man's baser instincts to an excess of cartilage in a man's nose."

"What about women's noses, Mama?"

"In the lower classes, Edwina dear, and possibly more primitive tribes, noses like ours are too fine – and one must not take everything Professor Freud says at face value. He is quite sweet and kind, but also of the Jewish persuasion."

But if she had not gone to Vienna we might have had no mother to make fun of. And we loved her. . . .

"The daughters of Sappho, remember children," Mama concluded from that first Aunts' visit, as we drove back in the hired Daimler to Trevelly, "have a special place in the Healing Arts and Education."

"Mock-aunts," hissed Sister. "Eddie, we're still going to hate them."

"Yes, Ettie."

Imprisonment lies two months away. Eternity at 10. There is still time for play.

33

Play! What do schoolmasters know of a child's play?! (Schooling launches Scholar-Wolf every time.) Wasted lives! Half men! We had one called Father Schwartz – a complete oaf. On his blackboard I wrote once: 'Father I have committed fleshly sin! Quo Vadis?' Can I tell you all the lectures! The hypocrisy! – old Schwartz's spinster sister owns a little shop, boys visit her and ask for the silliest objects. 'Ladies bloomers, if you please, Fräulein Schwartz? No? Then laced Korsetts – and silk stockings, if you please!" Of course, this poor creature sells nothing of the sort and blushes immoderately. Oh we were rascals! The drunkard – I can see his gross red nose dripping to this day!

Don't tell me! Not *Korsetts* only: Every note, every word of Wagner. His memory was phenomenal. No one has ever denied Him that . . . .

At Trevelly Mama trains Memory with rounds of Pelmanism on rainy summer afternoons, and Edwin falls in love with Numbers from the cards. Also a variant of the game, using pictures – a montage of photographed art-objects, and we had to predict from glimpses what picture it would be. Sister usually won – unless there was a hint of King Arthur in the picture: Brother had discovered the Arthurian world – the child's Malory and Tennyson; *Idylls of the King*, and *Lady of the Lake*; Excalibur, Merlin, the Arm & the Sword.

The Magic Dream

Always the same, it came on many nights.

I, Edwin the dreamer, find myself riding, naked, on a huge Horse, bareback, its mane streaming, hooves pounding. Flames of green fire come from its feet as they race towards a castle with an open drawbridge in a Tower. Faster towards the castle, faster. The door behind the drawbridge yawns black as a dragon's mouth . . .

And then –

It goes up! Horse & Rider are trapped outside! And other horsemen pound behind, pounding, pounding, never seen – but back there, over a boy's bare shoulder, the breath of their unseen horses on a boy's white skin. And the moon – always a Cornish moon, round and full, shining a silver light in front – yet their shadows, Horse & Rider's, and the shadow of the Tower, also fall in front. And as Rider wonders, even in his dream, how can that be? – a Figure emerges, cloaked, on the Tower's battlements and raises an arm, and points . . .

And then –

The land ends! In front of Rider and his great Horse is only the raging sea, surging and foaming and reaching up as Horse leaps out, and down and down . . .

Thank God, Eddie always wakes up before the sea. And always wonders, How can I ride naked and bareback, with nothing squashed? Twice, when he woke, he found he was clutching himself *there*, to be sure.

The second time, late in June, Ettie whispered from her bed, "Eddie, what is it? Are you all right, Eddie?"

"I was just dreaming."

"But you're frightened – was it a nightmare? You mustn't be frightened, Eddie. Next time, I'll come over and wake you up sooner."

Next time is three nights later. The Tower is back, and the other horses, and their frightening breath, and the wrong-way Shadow, and the huge leap – and crying out, and clutching – and Ettie is *there*. The Tower is gone. In its place is the House of Brothers and Sisters, with Ettie's slim, cool fingers under my nightshirt, between my legs, up the chimney. . . .

"Oh, Eddie, let's play porpoises, like in the sea."

Her nightie, with the frilly top and embroidered roses, slides up her body: there is nothing between them, brother and sister.

"They're bigger, Ettie."

Eddie touches. She trembles.

"So's yours, but don't hurt them; they're special. Just be a porpoise."

Rubbing and sliding as though there is water. Our liquid Mediterranean, blue-green, like light through the glass in a nursery stained-window.

"Eddie, no! No, Eddie!"

Back to her bed. Not talking. They lie, wide-eyed in the Cornish moonlight. In the morning there is blood on his sheet and in her bed.

But I hadn't entered the House of Brothers & Sisters. Not truly. I tried and couldn't. Yet I hurt her.

I drove her away.

35

"If you say so, old Chap."

Stupid old Jung, I just have.

... In the morning: Ghastliness, with lady's-maid gasps and consultations.

Brother says, "It was just a dream." Miserably.

Sister is in tears, with Mama, in the bathroom.

After the bathroom, Ettie has breakfast on a tray. In the dining room, with Eddie, alone, Mama sits tight-lipped and silent throughout a breakfast neither one can touch.

Eddie said, "It was just a dream, Mama. About King Arthur."

And his mother said, "It would be better if Edwina had her own room from now on, Edwin." And finally sipped coffee with hot milk from a Willow-Pattern breakfast cup.

. . . At Table House: the 23rd of July, 1921. To make up for the tight-lipped breakfast, Mama has the house at Tintagel opened as a Special Treat. The first time since before the War – before Papa passed to the Other Side. What thoughts passed through her mind as we walked on the cliffs and looked at the ruins, with the vast sea surging and rushing . . . but Edwin, selfish little swine, sees only Adult force, preventing him from climbing tco high on Arthur's battlements. Or getting too close, alone, to Ettie.

The Wizard's Fox

One morning, Brother left Table House early. Sister saw him from the kitchen window, with Cook, preparing meals for the day.

"Where are you going, Eddie?"

"It's my secret."

"Don't be mean. I'll get my shoes. I'll come with you."

"It's low tide. I can't wait."

Brother ran from the garden, jumping the low wall of piled yellow stone, over the Cornish moors along the cliffs to the path by the castle. Not a soul alive, just the Fox, caught by surprise, as a boy rounded a corner. The Fox stayed for a moment, then flipped his brush and vanished under a thicket of gorse in front of the castle. The boy knew he

36

must find something special this morning: Foxes are often a wizard in disguise.

Arthur's beach was rocky, strewn with weed, slippery; the sea, a hundred yards out, waiting. The boy came to the entrance of Merlin's Cave, black as the Tower door of the dream. Hesitation . . . The Fox came out again on a ledge of the cliff above. From his pocket, the boy took the torch he used for reading to Sister under the covers.

INSIDE THE CAVE:

Cool. Sandstone. Smooth to the touch. Worn by the sea that is out there, waiting. A line of salt rings the walls, higher than a boy's head, walking forward, searching for the entrance to the passage that must lead up into Arthur's Castle.

The cave roof, now lower; the walls, narrower; the line of salt rubbing off white on a shoulder. Forced to crouch, then to kneel – then crawl. And still no entrance to the secret tunnel . . .

Pressed flat, onto the stomach, and snaking, pushing the torch in front. The passage will be guarded by a door: thick-planked, soaked-through, rusted bolts and hinges. The cave squeezes, touches on both sides. The roof bumps his head, around another curve –

And try to look back . . .

Ettie, I can't.

Ahead, the cave narrows to a hole barely large enough for the Fox. Stick the torch through – the space widens, reach an arm through, wriggle one shoulder. The other.

Help, Ettie – I'm stuck!

In the light of the torch a brown crab scuttles, then waits. Crabs eat bodies of dead sailors. The sound of waves in the boy's ears, far yet near, as though he's listening to a shell. *Inside* the shell!

And the sea, outside, waiting: the tide due to turn at any moment.

Push backwards with both hands! Try to pull with both feet. The shirt slips up his sides. Rock scratches, salt in his wounds. No feeling. Panic hides everything. Shouting –

ETTIE!

And when the shout stops the seashell sound of the waves is closer.

I'm going to die.

Lying still, heart thumping on the sand floor of the cave beneath it.

The crab digs in. Waiting. Eyes wagging. Claws clacking.

Eddie – like the crab, silly. Dig!

With one free hand, frantically scrabbling the sand from below his chest, hurling it forward. His shoulder drops into the hollow.

Eddie – turn on your side!

Free. The torch was on the other side. I left it. In its fading light, above the crab, I saw a brush-tail on a stone sill, below a planked door. Closing.

I know it.

OUTSIDE THE CAVE:

The sea had stopped waiting. The rocks were covered. Only a salt track was left below the cliffs. Ettie was running along it, towards him, calling. On the path leading down from the castle, Mama ran through the gorse with an overcoat over her nightgown.

We saw the Fox a 3rd time on our way home.

Brother said to Sister, later, "I called, but how did you know I'd be there?"

Ettie-the-witch shrugged, "Who cares? I just knew.",

But I-Edwin know that if I had not left at that moment *she* would have been drowned as well. If there had been no Fox.

Ah-ha! cries Philosopher-Wolf – as far as the Will is concerned, in politics, that little word if *must be avoided! In life also!*

Remember, Children! So often, He reminds me of our mother.

"Of course, old Chap," old-owl Jung, puffing imported English pipesmoke by the lake, in Zürich. "Having driven off your sister, you must see by now that his anima becomes the main part of the Tyrant King's attraction?"

More silver Riddle-me-ree, for poor Squirrel Nutkin.

. . . *At All Souls' College:* Eddie sleeps in a spartan room with Boys. Ettie-the-Girl has a Room-of-her-Own. Boys have Cold Baths in the morning – Ettie has hot water in a rosy china jug. Boys & Girls meet outside a cavernous lav with a twelve-foot ceiling and clanking chain and an "Occupied" sign in needlepoint to hang on the doorknob. The Aunts mean to be kind but they know that Boys Can Get Out Of Hand – if not exactly *how*, although Athene (the daughter of a bishop) had in some

38

distant past trained as a nurse and went out to South Africa for a year to help Our Lads combat Dysentery (a Zulu leader) and the Boers. Large Boadicea, with her beads, can't possibly have known about Boys, ever. Her constant sweeping past the door at bathtime must be an effort to learn more.

Eddie, used to women seeing him naked, had never seen another male's sexual organ (only the bull's with the nuns, once before we were shooed away); he has nothing to hide. His room-mates do, and take refuge in towels.

The first is called Cameron, two years older (deadly 13), and his penis is developed and large, with a permanent kink – also circumcised, to Eddie's astonishment. Cameron was shooting upwards so that his ribs dragged down. He had red hair and a nose that matched his member. Scottish, but didn't sound it.

"*Scots*, if you don't mind, Casson-Perceval you worm."

From Edinburgh, Cameron stays with The Aunts between terms at some other school. Both Cameron parents are Out There, somewhere in the North By The Himalayas. Eddie would have sympathised, but bent-pricked Cameron always looked as though he was waiting to sneer. He left in mid-September to go back to his school. We had only disliked each other for a month.

The other boy was an Exotic. Olive-skinned, like our peasants on Porquerolles. A Ukrainian, to Eddie somewhere beyond the Mountains of the Moon. Written out in chalk on the blackboard, his unpronounceable name was Pawel Hejtmanczuk. Pawel was only one year senior, twelve, but when Aunt Boadicea did her sweeping by the bathroom door, Pawel hid a bush of jet-black pubic hair and a softly pendulous scrotum sac. When she was gone, he waved his olive penis after her retreating back and smiled widely at Eddie with large white teeth.

"I am," Pawel said, in strongly foreign, but rapidly improving English, "the direct descendent of Cossack leaders, and shall return to lead my people when the Bolsheviks are kicked out."

It was true – the first part anyway: Pawel's father had been killed in the Revolution. His mother had escaped to England and then died of Spanish influenza, one year ago. Eddie cried when he heard that. Escaping, and then dying.

Sister took a shine; you could tell from her eyes. The part about

39

leading the Cossacks was glamorous, but seemed dubious from the starting base of All Souls.

"But I am already planning to go on a scholarship to Wellington and then to Sandhurst for a military commission."

Except for a pair of sisters related to a cracked photograph of a touring Actor-Manager in a buffalo coat and too much snow at Medicine Hat, the other "nephew & niece" combinations were ordinary, or temporary, like Cameron. Only the Casson-Percevals knew about Wagner, and had a mother being Freudianized in Vienna.

The Aunts did not believe in Fads – except Prayers, with Household Staff every morning, after patrolling the Boys' Cold Bath, and High Church on every Sunday, Matins and Evensong, off-pitch, which left musical Sister hating all the more.

Those Protestant priests – sarcastic Lapsed-Catholic-Wolf – how many times I've seen them! Crouching at the foot of the table for the Sunday roast goose. Insignificant little grey nothings, submissive as dogs. They sweat with embarrassment when one speaks to them. I sympathise completely with your sister.

"Wolf again – Eddie, for God's sake put a bloody sock in him!"

Naughty! – spying over Old Edwin's shoulder – but silver Sister, my dears, as we shall see, has a small problem with nether appendages and socks.

. . . *At Trevelly: the 21st of March, 1922.* Mama is back from Vienna for Our Birthday, to Entertain.

"No more Nose Man," Sister cries, clapping hands since Ettie & Eddie are liberated from All Souls. "A party for me, how marvellous. Mama, can we bring Pawel too?"

"Wagner is the *only* music, Edwina, but in literature I adore the Slavs." Mama smiled her gayest smile; "Can you read *The Brothers* to me sadly in Russian, Pawel, dear?"

He read *The Brothers*, and told the Casson-Percevals about the life of the Cossacks (or Cozz). No aristocratic titles were allowed in Ukraine. It was a frontier society, a brotherhood of equality. Their head man *(hejtman)* was elected on merit. Sister made eyes. Brother, jealous as hell, wrote musical playlets – with a lot of And-thens, which got ignored.

The Guest List:
The Man Who Won The War was there; Lloyd-George, with a dangerous nose and yellow moustache. For two days after Easter he plays hide-&-seek in the shrubbery with his Dear-little-Ettie. Brother overhears another guest calling the ex-Prime Minister: "The Goat's at it again."

"Why not? He's a perfect pet," said Sister.

And Artur Nikisch came, the famous Berlin conductor. Also another Hun, an unpleasant Professor von Hammel, with hairy ears, promoting Pan Europeanism.

Mama had entered her Friendship Fad – but had found only more demons in Vienna.

"They've cut down all the trees, and no one dances any more – so I'm going to be Addled, in London, children. Herr Adler is also Jewish," that mysterious Persuasion; "his great concern is Childhood Growth – Eddie dear, the Aunts have arranged that you shall play the piano regularly this term if you apply yourself. Pawel, you read Dostoyevsky so sadly, you must come again. Edwina dear, in the meantime be sure to be kind."

The Meantime: back to the purgatory of All Souls. Tiny Athene was booted, bent over, digging in the garden behind the house. A robin perched on a rake handle watching for worms. So that bleak year ended. But the new one –

I will tell you a secret, broods the Oracle-Wolf, on a night when music cannot soothe. I have seen the vision of the New Man – fearless and formidable. I shrank from him.

Saturn is rising.

. . . *At Porquerolles: Easter, 1923.* Nothing has changed, except that the nuns and Mathilde, overjoyed, looked smaller. And there is more undergrowth beneath the pines than Eddie remembered. And Old Edwin remembers now that it had a name, *maquis*.

Les Enfants swam, aged 14 and Twelve. No black wool to the knees, but no nudity either. In body-hugging cotton of bright colours, Brother & Sister lay with their arms and legs touching in the hot sun and thought they were safe – until up went the "chimney" and Ettie saw it, felt it brush against her as he rolled over in a flash, and she laughed and ran away into our Mediterranean.

41

They slept together again – in separate beds, but in our old nursery, because of a shortage of rooms. We wore light, striped cotton pyjamas, not nightdresses, and our door was left ajar. Mama's light did not go out until les enfants were asleep.

And then – ?

... when her light was out Eddie had a dream of lying in the sun – and thrashes, and throws his sheet off, and wakes, and Ettie whispers, *"Eddie, are you awake? Eddie, what's that funny smell?"*

And then, in the island moonlight, both see over his groin the steep, wet, striped-cotton tent – but Brother pretends to be asleep. And Sister knows it's pretend. In the morning, early, Eddie hid his pyjamas under his pillow – *but when he went out, alone, to the beach, she found them. And touched them. Ettie always had to know. . . .*

But no fuss after, like the Blood. This time it was our Secret.

"Now," declared Madame de la Verendry, on Easter Monday, "the throat is ready for some discipline. The gift is from God and may not be wasted – and besides, a girl at this age needs an interest."

Brother was sure she would refuse – with that toss of her head, when he complained of her flouncing for Pawel – but there is no accounting for a woman's nature.

"Remember, we are one with Nature, children. At least on Porquerolles. Make the most of it."

Our Routine:
First, Practice – for 2 hours, in the morning, on the Bechstein, and then – Swim; and then – Lunch, of dull lobster mayonnaise, and then – Rest, a proper Edwardian one, on Beds, out of the Sun, and then – Ettie's Singing, from two until four every afternoon: "Greensleeves", English folk songs for warm-up and relaxation, "Death and the Maiden" Schubert lieder for hard work. In Hunnish, but no Wagner.

"Wagner, Edwin, is too rich for your sister at her age. I was twenty-one, which is too late nowadays, but still, The Master's music has to be experienced first."

"You mean 'seeing' it, Mama?"

"No, Eddie dear. You will learn that there is a difference between seeing something and experiencing it."

42

Take Nuremberg (Existentialist-Wolf insists!) for every rally I have played the overture to Rienzi – a slight work, for the Master, seldom performed – my stout fellows haven't the least idea that it's the story of a twenty-four year-old Tribune conquering Rome – but let them stand there and the music tells them! There are levels of understanding subliminally. Take Cyclops. The median eye, the organ of magic perception of the Infinite. Science has now reduced this wonder to a rudimentary pineal gland. Science! Let's see 'science' reduce Nuremberg!

On the day before the Casson-Percevals left their island to go back to The Aunts, and Being Addled, Mama came with les enfants to their Bay of the Lobsters and looked across to Algiers and announced, "France is lovely, but it encourages decadence. Siegfried's Land, children! In the autumn, we shall do A Tour. Unfortunately, Bayreuth is not re-opening until next year, but there are to be productions of The Master in Munich – so we'll go there. And Austria. And Switzerland. In September, after the heat. It will be a change."

. . . *At Porquerolles.* Pawel stays for the summer. He sits, worshipping Sister, while she screeches – and then he beat Brother at tennis, & swimming, & riding, & archery, & croquet, & reading in Russian – while the bitch watched, google-eyed. Edwin realised it was normal to love and loathe a friend. To break this round of athletic pleasure, at the end of July, the good companions went for another two weeks to Table House at Tintagel. Brother leaves Sister and Pawel worshipping each other and goes to Arthur's ruins (after swearing to Mama with his hand on a bible not to go near the cave – curious that she used a bible). Unnecessary: Young Edwin has grown since the time he was trapped – the secret passage will have to be found from the landward end, within the castle.

But the trippers, my dears! Porquerolles was still safe, as an island, but King Arthur's Court is already invaded. Dark green charabancs with dirty canvas banners, marked "Dorking Historical Society", unloading thirty noisy, snap-snapping, sandwich-eating, wrapper-throwing interlopers at a time into the sacred grounds. Edwin does not consider himself an interloper. He lives here: 2 weeks every other year.

"He won't find it anyway," Sister said, maturely, in front of Pawel. "I've told you, Eddie, it's only a silly myth."

To prove her false, for 5 days straight Brother taps every brick and stone in that damned pile – where he should have been moving hundreds of tons of earth to look forty feet down below the smooth grass that filled the central keep – if he had been able to get rid of the bodies from Dorking that tramped around with half the women asking if they could take his picture – "That marvellous hair! And those arms – so toasty golden brown!"

Our Eddie smiles shyly, loving it.

The Tall Stranger

... *The 5th day, tea-time:* Edwin admitted defeat (for the moment) and trudged out through the remains of the arch, where Arthur was smuggled as a babe, and up the steep path to the field that was used as a place to park. An eight-foot man in plus-fours and tweed jacket stood by a sporting-blue Riley car in front of the green charabancs. He turned, as though he somehow knew a boy was approaching, and said:

"You look as though you belong here, old chap. I'm after the Table House – where Lady Casson-Perceval lives?"

He looked almost English, but his accent was foreign. He had blue eyes like ours, and bushy eyebrows, and a marvellous car. He had said I belonged.

"Yes, I know the way. I'm Edwin Casson-Perceval. How do you do?"

"How do *you* do? My name is Jung, old chap, Carl Jung, of Zürich. And you, I should say, are a follower of the Grail."

Not an English way of greeting a boy in 1923. Nor a German-Swiss professor's way. It was Jung's way. Man and boy shook hands, and then I took Carl Gustav Jung to Table House where Lady Casson-Perceval, my mother, lived.

Fad at first sight. Watercress sandwiches, that's all it took for Jung to take on Mama. He knew fertile soil.

"He's not like a doctor," said Sister, "but then how can you be a doctor of dreams?"

After the watercress and the Private Talk, the group stood on the

44

steps to wave goodbye. There used to be a photograph: Mama, Jung, Pawel, Ettie, Eddie. . . .

"I'm going back for a last dekko at the castle, old chap. Would you have the time to be a guide?"

A lifetime, old Jung.

A friend from London drove us back in the blue Riley. The trippers were gone; the sun low over the western sea, shadows from the castle filled in the patches of grass and gave the ancient spaces depth.

"My sister says even if there was a King Arthur it's silly about me finding the Grail. It's only a myth."

"I shouldn't be surprised, old chap," smiling, a little, into the sun. "What led you to King Arthur? I suppose you read Malory?"

"Not before my dream."

Jung seemed to sigh, or it might have been deep breathing from the steepness of the hill. "Was there a horse in the dream?"

"Yes."

"And a tower?"

"And the moon."

But never tell him I was naked.

"Good, I'm pleased about the moon. I suppose there were shadows?"

"Yes – but they went the wrong way. In front of me – although the moon was in front too."

"I shouldn't worry about that, old chap. Shadows aren't always where we expect to find them."

"But you don't think I'll find the Grail, either. The real Grail. My sister's always right."

"Is she?" And he gave that solemn wink, for the first time, like an enormous but friendly Squirrel Nutkin owl. "We blokes can't always trust the judgement of our ladies. I wouldn't be at all surprised to hear that you found the Grail one day. Say hullo to me in Zürich if you come with your Mama. And my regards to your sister – I confess I forget her name."

"Edwina – like mine. We have the same birthday."

"The feminine form; of course, old chap. You're very close."

Man and boy shook hands again, to part. "Wasn't it an extraordinary coincidence," said Edwin, "me being there when you wanted Mama at our house?"

45

And Jung said, "Life is causal, old chap, there's no coincidence – as you like long words we can call it Synchronicity. I'll be seeing you."

As though he meant it. . . .

At Table House, Mama and Sister were looking at travel plans from Thomas Cook's. A map was spread out on the table that we used for our memory-games of Pelmanism: **The Wagnerians' Guide To Nibelheim.**

Written in thick, black, gothic script, shadowed in scarlet. There were little drawings of Chalets, and the Black Forest, and Dragons, and Knights, and Mermaids in the Rhine, and at the right, towards the bottom, was a castle with a tower, a bit like the one from the Dream. The castle was at a place called Nuremberg.

OUR GRAND TOUR

The Casson-Percevals went from Paris: in at the Gard du Nord, out at the Gard de l'Est, through the drab suburbs that look nothing like the City of Light. They went to Switzerland, but did not see Jung. They saw the Matterhorn, and goats with bells, and a tiny spring trickling from the foot of a glacier.

"If we are going to the land of The Master, children, we must see the start of the River Rhine."

Sister said, "It's hardly big enough for mermaids," and splashed her face in the crystal water, and came up gasping.

"God, that's cold!"

"Edwina, you are too young to swear."

"Really Mama – this *is* nineteen twenty-three."

So young, was sister, but looking older. In spite of the flat fashions, you can see that her breasts and hips are filling out. The other travellers can see. Often now Brother catches them eyeing her – roué Frogs and fat Huns.

"Remember, we are all Europeans now, children. Be extra polite. In spite of the War, the interior Continentals are more set in their ways."

There seemed no sign of the War in Switzerland. Nor Wagner either. Eddie looked for Siegfried and Dragons, but at the sparkling head of the

Rhine found just sandwich wrappers like Tintagel. The coarse world was everywhere, filling with gloom.

"Oh, Eddie – !" Ettie swung on his arm and gave him a kiss on the top of his head; she was still taller than he was – "we're going to *Hunland*, silly. We're going to have *fun*!"

The Casson-Percevals took a funny railway that worked on cog wheels and looked like a toy; and followed the Rhine to the Bodensee, Lake Constance, and stayed at a hotel in Arbon, where they swam in water that felt cold as the glacier, after Porquerolles. The War had touched even Switzerland. Mama sat on the hotel terrace being cared for by an attentive waiter with a terrible wound still freshly scarred on his forehead. He had only one eye.

"Like Cyclops, Ettie."

"It's rude to stare, Eddie – isn't he *awful*, poor man!"

They went east in another train, and passed through Austria – which looked the same as Switzerland – to Innsbruck, on the River Inn. They lunched on smoked trout, with caper sauce, and crossed another border at Scharnitz. They thought border crossing was effortless, but that was because border guards behave for Mama in a way they never do for anyone else. They rode in a third train through Mittenwald, and then past a sign announcing "Garmisch-Partenkirchen", with its spa in the shadow of the vast Zugspitze, and Ettie said, "I do think they have ridiculous names."

"German," said Mama, "is a wonderful language, Edwina – but it is, occasionally, capable of nuances that we cannot fully comprehend."

In a square with a country market crowded with shoppers and farmers, Eddie saw fat fish swimming in tanks. He saw a small band with brass instruments shining in the sun, and a single battered drum, with a homemade black-and-red flag like the colours on the Thomas Cook map:

"Ettie, look – the cover of my Mowgli."

The crooked cross. *"Das Hakenkreuz, Edwin!"* By whatever name, his first. . .

"So clean and lovely everywhere," Mama breathed deeply, touching her chest. "One can feel the music in the very air. The Passing of your Father, children, was not in vain. There can never be another war. Already I feel quite at home."

A brawl breaks out by the Mowgli flag. One man pushes a second into the carp tank. A third, by the battered drum, hits a fourth with his stick.

"Punch and Judy," said Sister; "you'd never think they were grown-up."

"That is the Naughty Marietta side of the Austro-German character, children. Remember, proximity to the Italianate tends to inflame, and the Baroque to corrupt. I think we should leave the train at this point."

The C-Ps accordingly step down at Oberau, and hire a car, a Mercedes, with a slightly rounded front and a folding landau top. The Wonderful Language becomes a problem. E & E can manage guide-book phrases – or random passages from Helden operas. Mama speaks nearly flawless High Hun. The chauffeur spoke the coarsest Bavarian. Neither understood a word.

"Oh dear," briefly at a loss, "Edwina darling, you try; it's like being in a foreign country after all."

"Where are we supposed to be going?" Brother asks, with woods and alpine meadows on either side.

"Berchtesgaden." Sister pokes the map decisively with her so-slender index finger.

"Berchtesgaden, gnädiges Fräulein, ja!"

The Bavarian chauffeur jerks his neck in sharp half-nod, half-bow that brings his head perilously close to the Mercedes' windscreen glass. The Gracious-Sister giggles, spoiling an otherwise impressive show of authority.

"We are about to see the most beautiful spot in Europe, children. If only it doesn't rain."

It poured, but Bavaria was pretty, even in the rain. The C-Ps saw houses with goats and large rocks on the roof, and King Ludwig's Swan Castle, and –

"Neuschwanstein," said Mama, "is a triumph of beauty over cruelty and little minds."

"I'd call a gold lav inflamed," said Sister. "You'd have to be mad as a hatter to go in that."

"As Wagnerians, we must be eternally grateful to poor Ludwig, children. He saved the Master, and was not mad, Edwina. Perhaps, in dear Professor Jung's definition of the Introvert, a little disturbed – by the time of his tragic end."

In Schloss Berg Lake, with his chief medical persecutor, following lunch, plus 1 glass beer, 2 glasses spiced wine, 3 glasses Rhine wine, 2 (small) glasses arrack. Eddie bought a lurid pamphlet on the same (while Ettie got a postcard of the lav).

After Ludwig, from the tiny promontory of St Bartholomä in the Königsee, the C-Ps look up at the Watzmann, where another mad king, this one of Berchtesgaden, set his dogs on a peasant woman and child. Her outraged husband called down a curse from heaven and the fiend was turned to stone.

Thank God — from Humanitarian-Wolf, sincerely — I've always avoided persecuting my enemies. When I think about it, I realise I've been extraordinarily humane. The banks of the Königsee are too depressing. One leaves the beauty of Norwegian fjords to arrive at those blurred Chinese aquatints. History, by the way — and I mean this most sincerely! — does not repeat itself! This is a shitbag schoolmaster's fallacy!

Raining again. The C-Ps turn south. Eddie is beginning to be oppressed by Nibelheim.

"There is a certain ferocity on occasion, Eddie dear, in forests. I think we should compose ourselves, children, for Oberammergau."

"Why, Mama? Is it in a forest?"

"The Passion Play," from Sister-know-it-all — easy when you've got the bloody book. "Every year the Huns crucify Our Lord. That sounds super. Will we be able to see them do it, Mama?"

"No, it is only performed once each decade. We would have to come again at Easter, Nineteen-Thirty. The Play is over for us, I'm afraid — and Edwina, I have said before, 'Hun' is not a word we use."

So we toured Oberammergau in the rain. A gilt-and-blue Jesus-&-Mary on a wall surrounded by vines. Anti-climax, without a crucifixion. But at least the sun came out. We got back in the Mercedes. And a little later, Ettie pointed and said, "I'm famished. Can't we stop here to have some tea?"

The chalet is off the main road, set in among firs. Casual day-trippers won't spot it. The chauffeur drives up to the front and parks beside another car. Another Mercedes, but older. The sun has gone behind clouds. With the landau top down, the wind from the mountains chills. It is, after all, September. September the 7th. 14 days shy of Mama's

49

birthday. The transit of Saturn is underway. The Travellers hunger and thirst, and, "Lord, Eddie, I need to pee."

Mama has a ladylike capacity. Unruffled, she reads in her lovely, clear crisp voice, from a handwritten sign in gothic script, tucked up against the front door window: "Streusselkuchen, Napfkuchen, Kaffee – oh dear children, I don't know this word."

The word, Mama, my darling, was: *Wahrsagerin.*

The Fortune Teller:
The place seems empty. The C-Ps, it goes without saying, have managed to pick the very peak of The Inflation. From one thousand marks to the pound in January to one trillion for our stay. English silver is like Rhine gold. Mama gave our chauffeur an English florin for his pains on our behalf, and took a table by a deep fire of crackling fir logs. Our chauffeur moved to another table, set separately near the window. One other man with driving gauntlets was already seated there, looking out over an open book, watching his car. The two nodded at each other. Men of the road. Our man sat down.

"Grüss Gott, Gräfin."

A waitress, fat from too many Kuchen, received our order with a Knicks – a slight curtsey for the Countess with the English silver.

Sister said, "Mama, Eddie and I simply *have* to go. Desperately."

Brother said, recklessly, "Das Badezimmer, Fräulein?"

The waitress blushes, abashed for the English Gräfin and her so-noble children. There is no convenience inside? Ettie & Eddie are used to Porquerolles. Nuns in the sand. A lean-to against the cold north wall of the chalet held a privy, screened by the firs. It was clean and freshly limed. Newspaper segments were stacked with Teutonic precision on the wooden seat beside the hole. The waitress did another Knicks, and left us. Eddie waited for Ettie. She waited for me.

Brother & Sister went back into the welcome warmth of the chalet, along a corridor panelled and floored with orange-red pine. Lights on the walls were paraffin lamps, more Porquerolles. On our left we passed the kitchen. An unplucked white goose, the size of a swan, lay with its dead neck hanging over the edge of the table by a cast-iron stove.

Ettie stopped. "Like Lohengrin – Eddie, I think he's still alive, poor thing. Look at his eye."

50

The goose's eye was rich brown with a gold fleck at the centre. It seemed to follow. Brother tugged Sister's hand. "It's only the light reflecting from the fire in the stove, Ettie. Who cares about Lohengrin – come on, I'm starved."

The magic name, in our piping English voices, was what caught His attention.

He sits in the room across from the kitchen. An alcove really. The paraffin lamps are out. It is quite dark. The light on His pale face, and the raven wing of hair, comes from a candle placed on the floor. The flame shines upwards through the clear glass top of a low circular table. On the table-top are other circles of glass in different colours. Red as blood, amber-gold, green the shade of the cross on Mama's brown bottles. Signs of the Zodiac. From the sound of our voices His head turns towards us. First Sister. Then Brother. He looks me full in the eye. I nod, slightly. Politely. English manners. Extra-special, Mama, for this unknown interior Continental European.

Heil Hitler, children!

First Movement

Ring of Paper

Overture

Frau Cosima's Second Tale
Our Heroine's !

Die Walküre

Beginning our wondrous story of The Valkyrie,

BRÜNNHILDE!

But stay, Children – for one more small *Explanation*. Since my Immortal Husband conceived *Das Rheingold* as a Prelude to the Work, our second tale you see is truly the *first* one of *three* – or, a Trilogy!

As New Wagnerians, you know now about Valhalla & the Ring, & the Curse, & Wotan, & His dear "Frau" Fricka, & vilest Alberich, & Loge (who so loves playing his little Fiery tricks!) & all of Us, yes I am sure even the very youngest by now shall recognise "The Ride of The Valkyries." This is such glorious music, but it is only a small part – a wonderful part, with its Storms & Mists – of *Die Walküre!*

Our new Story begins with Siegmund & Sieglinde, orphaned Twins of the golden Volsung Race (who rule above the slavish Nibelungs, grubbing

55

below them in the earth!). Siegmund & Sieglinde do not at first *know* that they are twins, but then they meet in a rude Hut belonging to Sieglinde's Husband, a *coarse fellow* called Hunding, & see they both have a Snake Marking shining in their blue eyes! (In His Music, another simple Genius Theme, or *motif*.)

And then – Sieglinde gives Hunding a Magic Potion to make him sleep while they rest together under a great Ash Tree with the Magic Sword, *Nothung*, sticking in its trunk. Their Heir is *Siegfried!* And almost at once this poor little lad too is Orphaned because Wotan, looking down from Valhalla, decides that Siegmund must come to Him. He must die –

. . . *But*, my Dearest Children – do not take fright! Such a death is *not* the cruel Reaper he is when one of our favourite Puppies or Kittens goes Beyond. No! For Us, as Believers in Wagner, Passing On is but a *Transformation!* – to that happier, richer, & fuller Estate as *complete* Men & Women. (Therefore the Music shall be *especially beautiful* at such Joyous Moments!)

Wotan waves his Magic Spear & commands his favourite Valkyrie, the most beauteous Brünnhilde, to fetch Siegmund to Valhalla on her Flying Horse, "Grane". But Brünnhilde, a foolish, *weak* woman for one moment, takes pity on Siegmund – & dares to try & *hide* him with her sisters!

And then – in an understandable rage at such disobedience – Wotan has Hunding kill Siegmund with *Nothung*, & imprisons the naughty Brünn-hilde on a *great Rock!* He orders Loge to surround her with a Circle of Flames & pronounces His Spell: she shall sleep, & *only One who knows no Fear*, the very Mightiest of Heroes, shall approach & waken her. . . .

First Movement

First Passage

[opening with snares, rattling]

Who were the Yeomen, the Yeomen of England?
The freemen were the Yeomen, the freemen of England!
Stout were the Bows they bore, when they went out to War,
Stouter their Courage for the Honour of England!

... *In Spandau* – there has been Stamping and Shouting in the night: the latter from the departing Russians, still insisting on some last letter of the law; the former by some Coldstreams, arriving, to show off their breeches in ludicrous positions of military drill. Ludicrous, given the size of their audience: yes, my dears, the Chaps from Home have taken over Old Edwin's skeleton. First overtures have not been warm. Even unwittingly, two poles repel. When His Ederl speaks their lingo, the Chaps reply in schoolboy Teuton – with Hess's number, who never was their prisoner. Not even in London's Tower! Madness hovers in the Prison air.

The new Chaps are intrigued by the sudden scribbling: the previous No. 7 had stopped seeking attention, one gathers, some months before his end. Aged 90, they say.

Never!

Harsh disbelief from my Raven friends. How long, Gedanke enquires, can the Powers possibly let this charade go on? Won't the Outside world ask questions at 95? At 98? At the century? They *have* to end it at the century. A few Seasons more and it will be that long since

His birth. Gedächtnis cackles: you think the Outsiders even remember *Him*? Or care?

But if we ask that, can there be a soul anywhere who remembers? – Oh cruel God, someone *has* to remember Ettie.

So, Fool! Get on – ensure it.

. . . In 1923, at Oberammergau. But first a correction: Edwin said the candle's flame cast shadows from the raven wing of hair. You see how Gedächtnis plays tricks. *He* did not wear the famous cow-lick yet. It was a Rudolph Valentino: straight back, with grease, and parted down the middle. But the moustache was there.

"Not the Sheik," Sister giggles; "the Tramp Man."

Meaning Chaplin. Wolf and Charlie: paired faces known everywhere. That happens with people born on a Cusp – look at me and Ettie. Not a perfect Cusp in His case; He was born on the calendar day *after* Chaplin. Our Wolf as a Taurus with Libra rising, to the untuned ear sounds rather gentle and creative. The Little Tramp, as Aries, with Scorpio rising, and a career established, had to be dictatorial and difficult. Yet the world remembers Him as a celluloid, baggy-pants comedian with a Funny Walk, and the Moustache, born to make us laugh.

The Reading

He turns his head away from the English Children – back to the Wahrsagerin: for Ettie & Eddie the Fortune Teller is the focal point, not Him. A large woman, we thought her Old, she was probably not in her fifties – wearing a shawl embroidered with the Zodiac, for show. Grey hair in a neat bun. Hands with antique rings that catch the candlelight as she slides the circular coloured glass plates around on the glass table top. They squeak slightly.

"What's she doing with them?" Ettie whispers, as the Casson-Percevals watch, fascinated, even Mama – pretending Not to Stare, from our table.

"The plates represent the courses of the planets through the heavens, children. The Reader is aligning them with that man's date of birth to

58

determine his Personality and Fate."

"Truly? Do you believe in it, Mama?"

"When one is Jungianised, Edwin, the stars are a library shelf in the sky. By plucking down a star, the astrologers are really plucking down those characteristics that determine what each one of us is like."

"But does it *work*?" insists the domineering one.

"Not every day in the newspapers, Edwina, but individually, and if the Reader has psychic channels, yes, then I think the heavens may tell us more than we suspect."

"What are psychic channels?"

"Understanding, Eddie dear – on a Higher Plane we cannot see. Like the wireless. Who could have believed such a thing twenty years ago!"

"I want it," said Sister: "when the Tramp Man's finished I want a Reading."

" 'I want' – " with Mama's Reproving smile, "gets nothing. You are still too young."

The Astrologer's client came out of the dark alcove into the Chalet's main dining room. He wore the Hunnish leather shorts that look too short; a flannel shirt of blue and red; rough woollen socks, banded like a football player's; stout boots, and a violently checked jacket that hung more as a short cape. Not a matching wardrobe. He was slim, but too high in the hips. He had a flush from the sun on his skin, yet paleness showed through. His eyes appeared colourless and without expression. The pouches were pronounced. He stroked the absurd moustache with a finger, deep in thought.

"Like cleaning his toothbrush," Sister said in English, tittering, "and those ridiculous shorts, and his bum's miles too – "

She stopped because he looked at her. His eyes had colour now, but not describable. They were alive. Ettie tossed her head away, like a cat, discomfitted.

"Guten Tag, mein Herr," said Mama, with her smile-to-make-up-for-Daughter's rudeness.

A formal bow, not quite a click with his boot-heels, a half-reach to Mama's hand –

Disaster. Crashings and bashings as the too-big b*m moving backwards, hits a chair at the adjacent table. The pale face flushed. The light went out of the eyes. He turned and positively rushed from the room,

59

past the chauffeurs sitting by the window. His driver – a rake-thin man, with buck-teeth and beetle-brows – leapt up, leaving his book on the table. A Teuton wild-western, "Old Shatterhand", by Karl May.

Edwin-the-polite ran after with it. "Your novel, mein Herr."

"Danke."

Buck-teeth passed a pamphlet in return: a playbill for a meeting, with a black-printed Mowgli symbol. Their Mercedes drove away. It was an old one, underpowered, and coughed exhaust as it turned out through the firs and was lost to sight on the main road to Oberammergau, home of the Passion Play. Sometimes called the Miracle Play.

Inside, Sister said, "I have my own money. I'm going to do it!" and jumped up and ran back towards the alcove. This was open defiance, but Mama only smiled.

"With this appalling dialect, Eddie dear, your wilful sister won't understand a word."

Mama underestimated the magnetism of English silver, and Sister was a quick study. Also, she had safely led the way. Brother followed to the alcove. The Astrologer put a finger to her lips, and pointed to a stool at the opening. The first hurdle – Ettie's date, place, time of birth – was circumnavigated with cunning skill. Beside the glass table was a continuous calendar for one hundred years, "1850 – 1950", and a globe, pre-1914, still showing the old empires, and a cuckoo clock on the wall. Ettie had but to point.

"Thank you, Mademoiselle."

Crucifixions may be only once a decade, but visitors have been coming by tens of thousands annually to Oberammergau throughout that hundred years. The Reader speaks a commercial amalgam of 4 languages. Her name is "Frau Marthe Steiner", burned into a wooden sign, rimmed with gilt, beside her.

"März," Frau Steiner's accent was so strong that her English stayed pure Hunnish anyway – "ze turning point, Aries into Pisces, zo!"

"My brother," said Sister, sharp for a bargain, "mein Bruder – Eddie's the same day – mein Tag. You can do us both."

"Tvins?" Is how she said it, looking quizzically at both. "So smaller is the brother?"

"I'm not small. She's two years older. Meine Schwester." Edwin showed 1911 on the century-calendar.

"Vhat time ist Geburt?"

"Nine," on the cuckoo-clock, "in the morning."

"Der Morgen. Zo. Der Platz you vere geboren?"

As Eddie found Toulon, Mama came over; she couldn't have stayed away another minute. Frau Steiner consulted a dog-eared set of mathematical tables, hand-drawn, already open at a page marked, "November 7-11." She changed to our date, March 21, grunting emphatically: "Ze Kusp, zo. Und zo." She touched the coloured plates with their Orbits etched on the glass like the Great-Circle steamer routes in red on the empire-globe. She looked at the plates. She looked at Sister.

"Musik," declared Frau Steiner; "For many others alzo." . . . because Ettie's Sun at zero Aries in the Eleventh House rules large groups of people. "The woice – die Kehle." Frau Steiner touched her throat – because Ettie's Moon in Pisces *with* Venus, specifically rules the throat – "Zinging, Überall!" Everywhere – because Ettie's Mercury rules Saturn. "Der mezzenger, ja?"

Frau Steiner superimposed Mercury's red glass over Saturn's malevolent amber, still present and untouched from His. She drew in her breath.

Mama said, "Was ist denn dabei?"

"Gräfin – " was followed by a string of rapid Hun, looking at Ettie, with the names Mars, Uranus, Capricorn, Neptune, and –

"Eddie, isn't this terribly exciting. Mama, do tell me, what *does* she say?"

"Frau Steiner says that you are headstrong, Edwina – which hardly comes as a surprise to any of us. Quite right, Edwin. I do not fully understand her German, but I believe Frau Steiner says your sister's astrological aspect is rather like the last gentleman's. Something in an Eighth house of Edwina's allows her to fantasize. We must guard against the bizarre and unusual taking over our lives, children."

"And what about me?" asked Brother.

Frau Steiner moved Ettie's red Mercury-glass half aside and overlaid it with the green, the colour of the cross on Mama's medicine bottles. She still did not move His amber Saturn-glass at all. Again she addressed herself over the children's heads.

"Weiblich, Gräfin – and Musik alzo. Die Pisces."

61

"What's Weiblich, Ettie?"

"Girls," said Sister. "You're going to be a masher, Eddie, and make me jealous with lots and lots of girls."

Mama said, "Edwin's Moon is in Sagittarius. He has sensibilities. It is easy for a boy born in Pisces to be victimised by other people ... by older men. Your naiveté and good nature, Edwin dear, could get you into Situations."

The word is Bondage, Mama. But, as Brother told himself and Sister often, and often, the Moon in Sagittarius, my dears, does not have to mean homosexuality with men ...

"Now you, Mama," cried Ettie, "it's going to be your birthday, you must!"

"No thank you, Edwina. I know myself as a Virgo. The day is advanced and we have taken up quite enough of Frau Steiner's time."

"Don't listen to Mama, Frau Steiner. The place was Windsor Castle – Eddie you know all the numbers."

"1889," said the traitor, "September, the twenty-first, but I don't know the time – what was it Mama?"

"Children, I have said, 'No'."

An almost unheard of event – so that the Reader, who had looked swiftly in her dog-eared almanacs, and with every vested interest to keep the game in play, looked shrewdly at the disobedient children's mother, and said only, "Gräfin, as you zo vish." And then removed the amber glass of Saturn, and put it in a bag of black velvet, and blew out the candle.

After which, Frau Steiner received a golden English sovereign – which seemed hugely more to E & E than their garbled translation was possibly worth. Not thinking that their Virgo mother's date – *precisely* six months removed from their own – marks the equinoctial turning from golden summer to amber autumn, and so is always looking back. The Sign of the Edwardian, lost longing. Nor did they remark, her Self-obsessed children, that the year of her birth was His year. They were the same age, 34.

THE GREEN HILL

An elm tree, with one side dead; a field of late grain, a pond, with the wreckage of an ancient wooden foot-bridge; a path around it; twin square steeples of a church beyond, domed, capped with spikes; in the far distance, behind the small town, rolling hills. Four long-haired cattle and some peasants, harvesting, in full sun, complete the scene.

"Bayreuth . . . perfection! In spite of the dreadful war, nothing has changed." Mama checks to be sure – comparing perfection, an old engraving in a small book, with reality before us in 1923. "The view is exactly as He saw it in 1871, the year your Great-Grandmama died. Exactly as I saw it for the first time with your Papa. Exactly as you see it now."

The "He" was always capitalised. It only needs 3 crosses on the green hill. The Casson-Percevals walk back in Indian file to their hired Mercedes and chauffeur, taking care not to misalign a single holy blade of grass.

"It's only about the size of Looe," Eddie said. The Master seemed worthy of a grander scale.

"That is its charm, children. As a Genius, Richard Wagner deliberately selected the town himself. In that way he could ensure that when he designed and constructed the Festspielhaus, no other lesser, cheaper theatres might compete."

A rigged race, from the start. Bayreuth looked like all the towns on the Tour. The Casson-Percevals see the Rathaus ("Because of the Pied Piper, Eddie silly – that's where they put them"). They see more Hun peasants in breeches or high-waisted dresses, and their Hunnish children in funny feathered hats. We saw high houses, once brightly painted – now peeling; we saw a town square with a statue of Frederick, the Great Hun.

"It's just postcard stuff, Ettie."

We drove through a cobbled square, up an almost deserted dividing street, keeping left, past a rundown Hotel Anker – "mit Kaffee-Geschäft." Tables were set up outside. No one sat at them.

"Wagnerstrasse," Mama breathed, in her Cusp-voice.

"We must be getting close, Ettie." Despite the empty streets, beginning to be excited. The strange man with the bulging head and floppy cap had after all been the central focus of our lives. We crossed the River Main.

"The swans, children, for Lohengrin!"

63

Already we were almost in countryside again. The road climbed, entering a park, with lime and ash trees.

"The Magic Mountain, children!"

A building, large but not enormous. It had a round-domed roof. It too needed a coat of paint. Repairs had been abandoned at the rear.

"The Festspielhaus, how terribly sad. There have been no Festivals since before the War, and the poor Wagners have had no money to make things right, and now this dreadful inflation. Well, children, we must change all that."

A suitably Wagnerian challenge – even for Mama. The C-Ps' car turned away from the domed Festspielhaus and drove in through a pair of large iron gates past an engraved bronze plaque:

> *Where my Illusions have found Peace –*
> *Peace from Illusion –*
> *I name my House:*
> *WAHNFRIED*

The Outer Temple:
The garden is too formal to be English, too romantic to be French. The Casson-Percevals disembark on a gravelled circle fronting a cubic house of stone. In the centre of the circle, a granite plinth. On top, not The Master but –

"*. . . The Hero of My Life, sweet Protector of my Existence!*"

Murdered Mad Ludwig. A bust of him, staring down. A brown cat sat at the base staring back. Faintly there came the rat-a-tat sound of a drum. A woman came round a box hedge. "Lady Casson-Perceval – I remember you so well. And these are your lovely children."

"Indeed they are – Edwin, Edwina, to dear Frau Winifred Wagner, say how-do-you-do."

This unnatural rudeness was not because we had no inkling until that moment that Mama knew part of the living Legend, nor that it spoke English – but was caused by the passing parade. Four moppets, golden and blue as ourselves, in descending order of height: boy, girl, boy, girl, like those wooden dolls that open to show another, smaller doll inside. These four were dressed in black togas with Siegfried-horns on their

64

heads. Number 1 beat the drum. Numbers 2 and 3 between them carried the bier – a toy wheelbarrow, draped, and on it, a moth-eaten sparrow, stone-cold, legs-up. Number 4 waved a toy spade, and vaguely smiled.

"As you can see," said this Wagner mother, "we're having a funeral, and it's also the anniversary of Gockel's death so it's rather special for the children. Do you mind terribly, Lady Casson-Perceval, if we complete the ceremony before we go inside?"

"How adorably tragic – Frau Winifred, we shall be honoured."

The C-Ps fall into place in pairs behind the drum. "Who was Gockel?" Edwin asks Moppet-Two, Wagner-girl-One.

"Grandmama's parrot. The sparrow's mine – but he doesn't have a name: he was dead when I found him. I'm Mausi; I'm four and a half. Who are you?"

Humbling to be addressed bilingually by an infant.

"I'm Edwin – Eddie, actually. I'm twelve."

"Wieland's six, but he lisps, and Wolfi's three-and-a-half, and Nickel's two-and-a-half, and Putzi's the oldest at eight; she's our dog. Is that your sister?"

"Yes, she's Ettie; she's fourteen."

An elderly Skye terrier barked irreverently. The drummer, Wieland, by this time was beating us past a wasteland of last year's vegetable garden.

"Frau Winifred," Mama was stricken, "whatever happened to your beautiful lawns?"

"The War, Lady Casson-Perceval, but we hope to sow grass again soon."

Sister said in a voice that was supposed to be muffled by the drum, "All Hunland's so poor – I'm glad we didn't lose."

But the drum had stopped. Fortunately the bereaved Huns had the grave to occupy them. The sparrow's hole was already dug, not a deep excavation. Several white crosses stood at angles around it, for a variety of extinguished lives: Gockel, and two other parrots; a pony, many dogs and cats.

"This is the first sparrow," said Edwin's companion, Mausi. "Now we have to sing a hymn."

"I really don't think – " said her Wagner mother.

"We have to. Wieland promised."

The tiny creature stood there, thick little legs and arms akimbo, clutching the sparrow, glaring defiance at the rest of the blue-eyed tribe.

"Very well, Friedelind, but just one verse."

> *There is a Green Hill far away,*
> *Outside a city Wall,*
> *Where our dear Lord was Crucified,*
> *Who died to save Us all.*

Amen. With an encore *Friend For Little Children* (for extra weeps) the procession disbanded, in the care of a pretty Nurse-Emma.

"It's funny," mused Sister, "everything's so like Us, the silly hymns and things, when it's supposed to be Hunnish."

"Edwina, if you continue to employ That Word I shall be gravely vexed. Frau Winifred *is* one of us."

Senta

[A Wagnerian Life]

Born, 1897, Winifred Marjorie Williams, in Hastings, where the Conqueror came ashore. Father, Welsh, a Journalist. Mother, English/Danish, an Actress. 1899, both parents dead. Nurseries and boarding until Fate intrudes. 1904, Adopted. Karl Klindworth, Stepfather; also student of Lizst, and piano-arranger to The Master. 1912, Winifred dedicates herself: assumes name of Flying Dutchman's bride, and (1913) is taken to the Shrine to be Prepared. Walks on the veggies-lawn/ takes-tea with Master's Widow. "A year later I was Siegfried Wagner's wife." 1914, War, takes Master's Nationality for convenience. From union of Master's son and heir (never-married, 46) with "Senta" (née Williams, virginal, 18) – Issue: Wieland, 1917; Friedelind (Mausi), 1918; Wolfgang, 1919, Verena (Nickel), 1920.

The Inner Temple:

It has satin walls, the first thing; sleek and slippery to the touch, in luscious shades of green and blue – not everywhere, not in the kitchens, it goes without saying. The Wahnfried kitchen was just like ours at Trevelly, but run on more Spartan lines. Jolly Frau Winifred does her best to run a family country house in the middle of a museum. The Master's Spectacles, The Master's Pen, The Master's (glass-topped) Desk, The Master's Pianos – heaps of them – the favourite ebony Black Swan from Lizst, "on which was composed *Parsifal*." The Master's Library – immense – awes Eddie with its bindings and inscriptions from Worshippers with crowns on their heads. Also Revisionists: a portrait with walrus moustache. "Poor Nietzsche," said Mama, "before he became too silly altogether." A portrait called Schopenhauer was next to the late-lamented Parrot's Perch.

"I wish you could have met Gockel," said jolly Frau Winifred, "a terrible old bird, but very amusing. After meals he used to belch like my revered Mama-in-Law – of course, children, we can't tell that to a soul outside."

Sister said, "Did they actually *swim*?" looking at a drawing of the first Rhinemaidens, dipping for gold; Knut Eckwall, circa 1876.

"They most certainly did. If your mother has time, you shall see the original swimming tank. It's a wonderful story, getting the first ladies into the tank; they were so large! Oh, my dear – Lady Casson-Perceval is here."

"Children," said Mama in her Cusp voice, "meet Herr Siegfried."

"Real Siegfried?" asked her son, preciously.

"I often wish these days I was not, but yes, I am afraid I am."

The middle-aged man who stands in the satin hall, with sunlight shining across his kindly face, wears yellow socks – and knee-breeches, and a jacket with patches on the elbows. And beside him on the wall, the Same Face, Father's, bulge-browed and brooding. And outside in the garden, the Same Face – on Edwin's companion mourner, Mausi. It is uncanny to see so many.

"Lady Casson-Perceval, your young man makes me forget my manners – How good to see you. And your daughter, such a beauty, if I may say?"

Till the cows come home. Sister stops pinching Brother for the Real-Siegfried preciousness. His English was excellent and colloquial –

but somehow just a shade off. He took Mama's hand, shaking, not kissing like the effeminate Viennese. He was smiling, but he had the air of a man distracted.

"You had written to us, asking, for this year, the Season, but alas, things – " his small, yet sturdy body showed the impossibility of things. He moved away from brooding Father on the satin wall.

Mama said, "Dear Herr Wagner, Frau Wagner, at the risk of rudeness I must come straight to the point. I have been bottling it up inside me from the beginning of our Tour. I had no idea of the conditions – no idea. I had already spoken to my husband, through Sir Oliver Lodge, and we had both agreed that we should make a donation of twenty thousand pounds to help renew the Festival. But having seen for myself the state of your poor country I have decided it shall be thirty thousand – in Sterling, naturally; after communicating with my husband, I had already checked with the Bank of England for the transfer. There are no conditions attached to the donation – now, please, there is nothing more to be said."

One-fifth of the C-Ps' fortune. In Pounds. Before Depression. Incalculable wheelbarrows-full of inflated marks. Ettie & Eddie follow the adults, in their happy daze, into the Wahnfried drawing room. No one present thinks it odd that the financial decision has been reached through communication with a man dead for eight years. On the Magic Mountain the line between earth and Valhalla is always rather blurred.

Winifred Wagner does say, "I think we should have something a little more suitable than tea!" so a bottle is brought, Heidsieck, 1908, and cork popped. E & E are allowed their First Champagne. There are reminiscences of Performances; the conversation floats in and out of Hun, so that gradually one is no longer conscious of a difference. We *are* Wagnerian children now, children . . .

"Dear Herr Wagner, Frau Winifred – this has been truly wonderful, to see Bayreuth again. We shall find an hotel, all the poor places looked quite empty. But next year – "

"There can be no question!" exclaimed Real-Siegfried. "Not a hotel. You shall stay in my study."

"We call it the Siegfriedhaus," laughed jolly Frau Winifred.

Her husband walks with the C-Ps to their special-guest quarters. The flower beds still have roses and dahlias and crisp everlasting flowers in brown and crimson. The Siegfriedhaus is a small chalet set among evergreens and fruit trees, with its own approach and sheltered lawn behind hedges.

"When one composes, one has a need to get away. You must come back at seven, for supper."

The little house is Bavarian-chalet, outside, but English-cottage, in. Wood and rough plaster, carpets on plank floors. Even English novels: Trollope, and H.G. Wells' *The Shape of Things to Come*.

"Utterly delightful," said Mama, examining an original Master's Score. "Herr Siegfried is the equal of Humperdinck, in many opinions, but remember, children, like Convention, Reputation pales in the shadow of Genius."

"Wahnfried was awful," said Sister. "Eddie, didn't you get a sense of gloom? As though someone was hiding at the top of the stairs."

"Edwina, that is too fanciful, too fanciful for words. Frau Winifred is such fun – and I loved dear Herr Siegfried's yellow socks."

The One who was hiding came down after dinner.

The Widow:
Cosima. All in black, she was the Queen of Night, awaiting Death and Re-union. She appeared to the sound of a crystal chime, rung once, so that Ettie & Eddie looked up from the hall by the Music Room to see this black apparition above them, standing on a landing. The Master's Widow was flanked by two other women, old, but not Ancient, also in long dresses of dark colours. One struck the crystal chime a second shimmering blow. Guarded as some priceless fragile ivory treasure, the Widow began her descent. Step by painful snail-step – it took hours, and all the time the ones waiting at the bottom said not a word. The daughter of Liszt's slippered feet, long and thin like her nose, sought out the tread of each stair. She could hardly see, but her bones knew every step of the house. She was in on the ground floor: when He first drew the plans.

"Frau Cosima," said Mama, in a sweeping curtsy to the ground, "we are immensely honoured that you should come down."

"Gräfin Casson-Perceval?"

Her voice was the only strong part of her – except for that huge Liszt beak-nose. She had more than the usual Teutonic inflection upwards at the end of each remark, so that each came out half-question, half-command? These were constantly interpreted by the other two old Delphic ladies.

"There are also children, Daniella – Mama says beware of the sofa's edge."

"Mama knows of the children, Eva – she says be sure to avoid the piano."

The rest of the party followed after like a Coronation train into the Music Room, a two-storied space, with a glass roof and all the Immortals hung in oils as a gift from Mad Ludwig: Lohengrin, Tannhäuser, Tristan, Hero-Siegfried.

"You will remember my sisters," the real one said to Mama, in the wary manner of a female household's Only Male.

"Fräulein Daniella, and Frau Eva, indeed I do – and how well you both look. May I introduce my children?"

Half-sisters – only half-Wagner, from that Awkward Time with von Bülow that We Never Mention! The Master's Daughters came to roost before a hand-tinted photograph of the late-lamented Gockel on its perch. The dead fowl regarded them with a jaundiced, over-yellow eye as Daniella and Eva twittered their reports in Cosima's ancient ears.

"Like the Aunts," whispered Eddie.

They were long and short, like the Aunts, and always hatching.

"Old parrots," said Ettie, "I bet they belch."

Tall Daniella was the half-von Bülow, with the Liszt nose; also a gifted costume designer, but tribal jealousies had confined her talents. Her eyes were her most astonishing feature: one Blue and one Brown! (After her birth, Cosima feared the Devil had brought a split personality into the Family.) Short Eva was illegitimate, but Wagner; she had His face but less forehead. She was married to, or at least lived in the same house as Stewart Chamberlain, the noted English protagonist of Aryanism & Race. Whenever they finish reporting or interpreting, the Parrot-Sisters fasten their gaze on the Interloper – whom they call not Sister-in-Law, or Jolly Winifred, or ex-Senta, but *The English Woman.*

"Good evening, dear Mama." The youngest Frau Wagner gave the oldest a dutiful kiss.

"The English Woman – " from Daniella,

"Says the evening is pleasant – " from Eva.

70

"But in fact it is raining – " pattern repeating,
"On the glass you can hear it."
And then – The Widow Spoke:
"Next year we shall include the Ring? shall we not, Siegfried?"
So Old Cosima knows about the Cash. Her son smiles and strokes her ancient hand, and watches his old half-sisters and his young wife – a delicate balancing act.
"I had thought Meistersinger and Holländer, Mama – Winifred agrees, it may be less ambitious but safer, after so long. And opening as always with the Ninth."
"Mama feels – "
"That ambition and safety – "
"Are ill-matched – "
"Mates."
The sisters finish this series staring at Winifred with open hate.
"The Ode to Joy," the C-Ps' Mama remarks, to fill an awkward pause, "is a tradition started by The Master, children – in homage to Beethoven, the first man to add words to music in the inner search for the Psyche."
"Beethoven is none of my affair any longer," said The Widow, "only His work. The child sings?"
The translucent face had turned on Sister.
"Edwina sings a little," said her mother. "For pleasure, Frau Cosima, nothing more."
"What more is there?" said jolly Frau Winifred, encouragingly.
Real-Siegfried smiled at Ettie warmly.
"Music should be only pleasure. Rehearsal spoils all."
"Mama says – "
"Rehearsal ensures – "
"That nothing changes."
Real-Siegfried sighed and cast his blue eyes up to his heroic namesake.
"She has a teacher?" asked The Widow.
"Mama means – "
"An accompanist."
"Only me, Frau Cosima." It's Little Eddie's business to be the centre of female attention.

71

"And a charming one I'm sure," said The English Woman, as Ettie kicked her brother's shin.

"I shall hear her now."

The Widow raised a bony forefinger. For this Lady C-P has paid out thirty-thousand pieces of silver. Ettie sang her Schubert. There was dutiful applause – perhaps a touch more than that. Real-Siegfried reached over and tousled Eddie's hair. Like a father. . . .

"Mama decides," from bi-eyed Daniella, "the voice shall be Floss-hilde first – "

"With sufficient work," from Eva, "Second Norn, even."

"Nonsense!" declared Cosima, speaking for herself, "with sufficient work she shall be a Woodbird."

Our cash was not put out for nothing. By royal fiat there was Minor Talent here.

"A *Norn?*" said Sister with venom, in the Siegfriedhaus. "Frightful old Parrots – when I'm Helden I'll show them."

. . . *At the Siegfriedhaus: morning.* Raining again in solid Bayern showers. The C-Ps enjoy a continental breakfast – black coffee for Mama, tea diluted with milk and honey for Ettie & Eddie. At ten, a knock: Real-Siegfried, smiling in his yellow socks.

"I am unlocking the Festspielhaus. The rain has stopped; shall we walk?"

Along combed gravel paths that scrunch wetly after the rain. The domed roof on the Festspielhaus looms over the garden wall. We went out through a wicket gate, and the building designed by Richard Wagner was in front of us.

"Edwin! Edwina! – there are still posters from the '14 Season!" Mama's enthusiasm became a sigh. "The last time with your Papa – Karl Armster sang Amfortas, Karl Muck conducting."

"When we knew war was coming," Real-Siegfried said quietly, as he unlocked a door at the rear of the building; "terrible, but how it heightened the music."

Brother realises the incredible is happening: all morning Sister hasn't said a word!

"Aren't you excited, Ettie? We'll see the Swimming Tank."

Excited? . . . Fool! She was over the Dome and far away.

72

The Altar:
Real-Siegfried opened the side door – outward, in case of fire.

"The first thing with your magnificent gift, some oil for these hinges. While I put on a light, be careful everyone, there is litter underfoot."

The light came on: a single bulb in a white reflecting cone, shining down.

"Litter," said Edwin, "it's like the passage into King Tut's tomb."
Into the subconscious, old Chap, into our myth of the mind ...

Fafner, the dragon, was there – just the head, severed in the final round of the titanic struggle; and Siegfried's armour – Hero-Siegfried; and swords, and helmets with horns, and gold and silver goblets, and giants' stilts; and golden braided wigs and makeup, and sumptuous velvet dresses and gowns, and –

"My wife promised to you the swimming tank, but for that, children, I shall have to find my man. Explore the House but not up in the galleries, if you please, or the flies. Dear Lady Casson-Perceval, in my office, we may perhaps talk?"

And still Sister says nothing . . .

Brother moves forward, deep into the tomb, like searching again, first-Questing, following wizard fox-tails to Arthur at Tintagel. Footsteps echo on bare boards, a sense of vast space widening; wooden rails, ropes, portholes, a spoked helm-wheel six feet across, and Ettie whispered, in a Helden call that carried in those perfect acoustics a thousand miles:

"Eddie, look up."

Lofting away into absolute night, the billowing sails of a great galleon, hung with cobwebs, thick with dust. Years of dust.

"The Dutchman's ghost ship, Ettie."

Der Holländer – lost forever with all sails set since the Last Production before the old world divided.

"Oh Eddie," says Sister, softly, softly, "not the Dutchman; it's Isolde's ship."

Sailing her to Tristan.

Across the stage towards the footlights, darkened, skull sockets in a row; beyond them a curved blackness – The Master's other unique creation: the Hood, to bury the orchestra in the black pit. Walking down from the skull-footlights, the same sensation in a Boy's stomach as crawling in the cave; the same sea outside, waiting, sounding – but it was Sister's breathing.

"There's a piano, Ettie – come down and see."

"No." She stays on the stage, on deck, where she belongs. "Play for me, Eddie. Play *Liebestod*."

"The lid's down, there's a cloth, it's all dusty – everywhere's so huge, with the lid down, you'll sound completely flat."

"Just play."

And then –?

"*Mild und leise* – " sang my Sister, *"gently and softly, He smiles so sweetly . . ."*

Must I alone, her Brother, playing, this wondrous Melody, feel within me . . . as the billows roar round me . . . surging, roaring, plunging, resounding . . . höchste Lust!

Supreme desire!

We were mere children: we did not hear the main door open, nor the click as a wooden shutter swung back. She was in a shaft of sunlight – her hair more gold than any wig on a peg backstage, bound up by a green velvet ribbon.

And then–?

First Movement, Second meeting. He was there.

"Tristan!"

The first word – from a strange voice, so low in the throat, yet oddly nasal; striding forward, and clapping and clapping; his head, like her's, was in the sunlight through the Festspielhalle window, and there were other people, but all I-Edwin absorbed forever was the first torrent of Speech.

"Tristan, this is the masterpiece! One has to say it, even in the home of the Ring – the emotion! – a young girl singing, a boy playing – a brother and sister! – their talent, our music, Civilisation's heritage – but it's the very beauty – it can only remind us: the crimson tide of the Bolsheviks! We're already swept to the turning point – like Der Holländer we're embarking on a Steersman's voyage we can't see the end of, and if a man hasn't the courage to steer it, no matter the dangers, all mankind founders. Humanity becomes the shapeless Mass! Swinish

74

cattle, brutes chained for all eternity in the sty of greyness and despair! – but one has to say it, even a common private soldier, a nobody – to tell the so-talented, so ineffably pure and gracious Fräulein she has unforgettably reminded him of his unswerving course – for his lifetime, so little as it is: when a man's parents die young, he can never ignore it – and this golden boy, the golden Fräulein's brother, I repeat – Herr Hanfstaengl, be warned, there's competition for you! Noble Gräfin, highest Lady, when you met the oaf at Oberammergau – oh yes! He remembers! It was so horribly obvious, ah! what a dolt you thought him, that low fellow! – please, don't deny – it was totally deserved, with the chair falling over! The entire thing was Hess's idea, that Astrology nonsense – but now it seems, the wretch's deserved embarrassment must have been Fate! To meet again today otherwise would have been impossible. Today, because the former soldier's only here in the Temple by accident, so-kind Frau Wagner can swear – staging a rally in Bayreuth for the fall of Sedan – a proper way to end a Franco-Prussian War! As the humble Speaker, one is invited to visit Herr Wagner's sister's husband – Herr Stewart Chamberlain, the most tremendous honour, my man Hess still can't believe it! – the Speaker goes upstairs. He finds a little bedroom apartment – yet so often this is the way the world rewards our greatest intellects while the ratpack bloodsuckers fill their disgusting pleasure domes and palaces! – The old gentleman, Herr Chamberlain, is bed-ridden, half-paralysed, he can't speak. He gestures – the bedside, a writing pad! Of course! He is a Writer! The Speaker passes his own fountain pen. The old hand shakes like a white sheet on washday – the Writer writes . . . and the words overwhelm the Speaker: they're so exactly everything his own mind has been boiling over with – *'For the Aryans, on the brink of the racial abyss, locked in a mute life and death struggle, it is still morning, but again and again the powers of darkness stretch out their octopus arms, fasten their sucking cups on us in a hundred places and try and draw us back into their darkness. . . .'* this frail body, nothing is left but its indomitable spirit – and from that most incredible vision, I, that humble Speaker, with nothing else to my name in this world, come to the Festspielhaus of Genius and hear the Tristan. And now again to meet you, most noble Gräfin, your brilliant children – and the too-gracious Frau Wagner tells me of your supreme gesture of support for our Festival, our Sacred Cause we share in common – and to be English, this is the most wonderful thing! Our two peoples brought together in recognition and understanding purely of the Master. No! such a gesture can't ever be thanked for enough! Herr Wagner will now clearly achieve the impossible – next year he'll have it all for us, a full production: Beethoven to open, Meistersinger, the Ring – Parsifal to close, it goes without saying. Now, Putzi, my huge friend, I have to show you! The original sheet, in The Master's study off the Green Room, for the start of the Rheingold, you will see even how he made up his mind for the E Flat Major opening – at first like all Genius the Master isn't sure: he tries this approach, it doesn't work – he cancels it. Then, unsatisfied by the second thought, he goes back to his original and lets it run the whole sixteen bars. Oh yes! The original is always the best! Don't tell me! The moment one allows oneself to change one's mind, the will is defeated. The fire dies out. The first time I – "

The Flood stopped.

It was Sister who damned it, that incredible stream that had poured over us, his listeners, without a pause or break, to let Eddie notice, for example, that the Putzi referred to wasn't a small Skye terrier, but a human giant with monstrous head and hands the size of breadboards –

Ettie's ribbon: the green one from her golden hair; she staunches the flood when she passes it to him; and he holds it, on one palm, stroking with the other the sleek nap of the soft fabric; and his face, already flushed, suffuses magenta . . . as he strokes it between those small, surprisingly feminine palms – although the first impression was manly soldier's roughness.

"Eddie, did you see the simply disgusting way he bites his nails?"
And then –?
Horrid silence.
And then –?
Cinderella at midnight: he was only the Little Tramp.

He looked around the vast, dwarfing stage: round-shouldered, almost furtive, in a shabby grey suit. He carried a worn raincoat and a spotted beige-velour trilby hat. His black shoes were cracked, though brightly polished. He would have been nobody, yet he had held Us – not Ettie & Eddie, the children, but the Royal Wagners of Bayreuth (Achieve the impossible! All He ever asks!); and the so-noble English Gräfin, and this bizarre giant called Putzi – or Hanfstaengl – all spellbound, hypnotised, not registering his bounding up from the hooded Pit, out

76

onto the great sails' stage. Through all that, no one said the obvious: Sister's play-singing is amateur childish showing off. You've seen productions in Vienna and Berlin, what the hell are you raving about, little man?

Instead, to break Ettie's ghastly nail-biting silence, jolly Frau Winifred, at twenty-six, touches his arm, and her husband, Real-Siegfried looked on with an Onkel-isch smile: young people, there-there. And Mama, who always seems cool and Knows Better, was pink-cheeked and bright-eyed. And her perfume was stronger. And the giant, Putzi, stared down at Edwin from somewhere up in the stage-flies, and winked, barely hiding what had to be a condescending smile.

"We understand, dear Herr Wolf," jolly Frau Winifred said gently, as he turned away, and tripped over a guy-wire, "the love for the Music affects us all in the same way. Ladies and gentlemen, may I suggest lunch?"

The clouds have lifted outside the Festspielhalle: the sky has cleared on the Magic Mountain. The chattering group walks back to Wahnfried past the tilted parrots' and sparrow's crosses, past a grey granite slab: The Grave.

RICHARD WAGNER

The shabby nobody called Wolf stands with his head bowed, the raincoat on his left arm, with the left hand holding the spotted velour hat. The other, right hand, hidden by the raincoat, is in the bulging trouser pocket (on the side he dresses) where Eddie saw him stuff Sister's ribbon.

He stands for so long, breathing so deeply, that the rest, made awkward for some reason still outside the knowledge of children, withdraw from his presence.

The Good Giant:
At lunch in the Wahnfried dining room, Edwin sits next to him, far below his shoulder. The Giant's head is strangely off-centre, with a colossal lantern jaw. His real first name is Ernst; the Putzi, with its faint

hint of the bi-sexual, was used by all his friends. Only his piano-playing and a slight bitchiness in his anecdotes betrayed the anima roots of the name and his nature. Putzi Hanfstaengl loves women, my dears, is (presently) happily married in Munich, and simply adores telling Kaffee-Klatsch stories.

While the other guests wait for Herr Wolf to join them, the Giant says to his table partner, "Eddie-pal, he's quite a guy – in many ways a mystery."

"A guy?" A form of Giant English that has Mama perplexed.

"Not in our sense of the word," said Frau Winifred, with her jolly laugh. "Herr Hanfstaengl has enjoyed the benefit of a Harvard education. He's speaking in American, and he has the most phenomenal span, I swear two octaves! Dear Putzi, what mystery?"

"The lady of the Thierschstrasse, Frau Winifred, in '21 – the hot stuff is that it wasn't an accident."

"Good heavens, you don't mean –?"

"Nobody knows for sure," the Giant lowered his voice to a rumble, "but the police reporter told me new evidence makes it look deliberate on the woman's part. I guess she rubbed herself out – but please, don't mention it to Adolf."

"I wouldn't dream."

"A love-death?" Mama was clearly still slightly discomposed from the earlier excitement. "How simply extraordinary. It must be the eyes."

"Rubbing-out!" said Sister. "Is that how they speak at Harvard, Herr Putzi?"

"In Chicago, Miss Edwina – my wife comes from there. Believe me, I barely rescued Helene in time from the bunch of gangsters she had swarming around her."

"Gosh," said Eddie. "You never! But tell me please, Frau Winifred, why do you call him Herr Wolf when he isn't?"

"The children named him, Edwin dear – he tells them such marvellous tales of his own childhood adventures. With this terrible news of yours, Putzi, it begins to seem suitable again. How sad for him – and in the Thierschstrasse!"

"I shouldn't have brought it up," said the Giant, not being a gangster for the moment. "Lady Casson-Perceval, let me re-assure you; my

78

mother is a strict New Englander, and Great Uncle Harry carried Lincoln's coffin. When you're in Munich, please call. The family fortunes are in the dumps from the American War confiscation, but we still have music, and the odd picture to talk about. I've just picked up a wonderful red-and-green woman by Picasso ... "

"The Hanfstaengls are in publishing," explained Real-Siegfried; "the first Heine, they put out, also some of my father's scores – ah, here comes our other guest. Winifred my dear, I think I'll start to carve."

But the mystery man, more eagerly awaited than ever since the Love-Death news, sat through the meal almost silent, white-faced, shooting occasional glances at the fine ladies, barely picking at his food, although it was best roast veal in poverty-stricken Nibelheim. Out of his element.

Leaving the Magic Mountain in the hired Mercedes, Edwin complained to his mother, "Really, Mama, it is too bad – because of Ettie's ribbon nonsense we never got to see the swimming tank!"

"We'll see it next year, Eddie dear, when we come back for our First Season. Children, what a curiously fascinating man Herr Wolf is for one so common."

"He doesn't fascinate me," said Sister; "he spits at the corners of his mouth and his bum positively is miles too big."

... *At Porquerolles: October the 15th, 1923.* Recuperating on our island. The Casson-Percevals regroup to consider the training for a Helden career. Mama writes letters. Sister daydreams of concert halls all clapping as crazily as her admirer, the mysterious Herr Wolf. She wanted Brother to play Liebestod day and night, until he rebelled and even Mama said, "Thank God!" Ettie turned to librettos. Eddie loafed and swam, nude, by himself, in our Bay of the Lobsters – still with an eye out for Mathilde's serpent in deep water. Madame de la Verendry brings the new Curé to tea: a strange little man who eats jam off his knife. Two communications come back. Cables, but carried like letters by Deaf'n'Dumber because the line stops at Hyères.

FROM WYN-HARE LONDON YOUR FLAT GIRL'S TUTOR
ALSO CMA JEW MEYERHOF AS REQUESTED CLN BOY DOWN
CMA ACCEPTED EXCLAM STOP

This ominous missive followed by –

FROM SENTA BAYREUTH OUR GREAT PLEASURE YOUR
VISIT STOP RE 1ST EXPOSURE CHILDREN CLN OUTSTAND-
ING MEISTER NUREMBERG NOV 5TH CMA LOHEN 7TH
MUNICH HOTELS DONE STOP PRESS REPORTS UNREST
GREATLY EXAG DOUBLE EXCLAM STOP

The Casson-Percevals take no newspapers. Without wireless they are
happily deaf as well. "What could be more appropriate than Meistersinger in Nuremberg!" exclaimed Mama. "The home of Hans Sachs.
And Lohengrin, in Munich – children dears, it may well be too much!"

"Who cares," said Sister, that night in our bedroom. "There's no
point in being Helden except in Bayreuth – and I'm *not* flat!"

Outside our window the waves of the Mediterranean washed ashore
in our Bay of the Lobsters. Ettie tossed in her bed at arm's length, but
the door was open, Mama's lamp on. Eddie watched her breasts rise and
fall as she played the porpoise game under the sheets by herself.

Locked out of the House of Brothers and Sisters, so did he.

... *Nuremberg: Guy Fawkes Day*. The station, at 9 o'clock in the
morning: the sky is overcast but for the visiting C-Ps there are bands
everywhere, openly playing the banned *Deutschland Über Alles* – and
wherever the bands play there are Mowgli flags and bright colours, and
the marvellous old city inside its wall, and Ettie calls, "It makes you all
goosey, Eddie, let's follow!" as some boys in Brown go stepping by.

Mama restrained her. "You will find, Edwina dear, that first performances are always enervating – especially for girls. Frau Winifred has
rooms reserved for us in the Hotel Stadtler. We shall rest after
luncheon, children, and read our Scores."

Die Meistersinger von Nürnberg; being a True &
Gay account by Richard Wagner of the Cobbler-
Poet, Hans Sachs, the gallant young Knight,
Walther von Stolzing (the Last of his Line), the
beauteous Eva, the cheating old rival, Beck-
messer, as they compete for her Hand in their so-
exciting Song Contest. (All in a so-optimistic
C-Major atmosphere, as this is The Master's only
comedy!)

80

Also, at time of composition, the longest bloody score ever written. Read & Rested for the happy ordeal, the C-Ps attend the Old Opera House where in spite of Inflation there are jewels and gowns – and the Hun audience cheered the Overture and laughed from the first curtain.

"The plot may not be sophisticated," said Mama at some Interval, "but Hans Sachs, remember children, represents the small man in all of us: the Peasant at his Plough, the Cobbler at his Last – not perhaps *precisely* Us, but you know what I mean ... Edwin, wake up!"

"Is it the anthem, Mama?"

Brooding over being the Last ... the Boy had dozed over the rail of the box. The orchestra in the pit below was in full flight. All around, the audience of Huns was rising ponderously to its feet.

"It's like Messiah," said Sister, as the winner's gold chain was put round the stupid von Stolzing's neck, "the Hallelujah Chorus. Eddie, the Huns are all staring – stand up!"

"*Honour your German Masters, and if you favour their Good Works –* "

The audience knew every word. Not one throat in that Nürnberg house wasn't singing – except Edwin's.

Mama, so carried away, said, "If you've forgotten, pretend, damn it."

"*If the Holy Roman Empire dissolves in mist, Holy German Art – Holy Germany! – remains! Heil! Sachs!*"

A wreath was placed on noble Sachs' head. Mama sighed, "Forgive my language, Eddie dear, but the Hallelujah *and* Rule Britannia, rolled up in one. And Lohengrin to come."

Sister said, "They'll stand for me when I'm Helden – Mama, we must go to supper. I'm simply starved."

Bavaria's peasants and cobblers may be pinching potatoes from the fields, but the Casson-Percevals have cash. The Hotel Stadtler did us proud.

... *Munich: November the 7th, 1923.* The C-Ps, travelling their usual First Class, by daylight, by train, observed neat Bavarian cottages and farmers with brown cows – as we passed through a typical small town called Auschwitz (before its eclipsing Shadow fell over that Other, later) and an unremarkable group of drab villas named Dachau. The weather had also become typical for the time of year: low skies of Bayern cloud grey-black to the north, with a driving rain to greet us as we alighted on the Munich platform. The rain turned to a heavy wet snow. Thoughts were of Porquerolles in the sun.

"We are Müncheners, now, children," said Mama, bravely gathering her furs around her. "We must endure it. Does anyone see – ah, dear Professor von Hammel, and thank God, he has a car!"

The Sheep with hairy ears, a black coat trimmed with lamb, shook Edwin's hand and called him, My dear young fellow! – in a bleat, it goes without saying. The car was a heated Daimler-Benz which deposited us at Number 40, Residenzstrasse. It was hardly larger than a private house. The hoteliers were a small stout couple, the Gerbers.

"And flowers," said Mama in our rooms, "Herr Gerber, I know we shall be happy here."

"Undisturbed also," said Herr Gerber, bowing, while his wife waved maids and houseboys to do their good works. "The Residenzstrasse is well policed, Gräfin, you may be sure. And the Staatsoper is close at hand, and the theatre if you wish to attend. A car will be arranged."

"The Opera House, thank you, Herr Gerber – we shall be experiencing Lohengrin tonight."

"Ah – Gräfin, you will not have heard. There has been a postponement of the Lohengrin."

"A postponement, Herr Gerber? Of a Wagner performance?"

"For one day, only – but twenty-four hours, a question of payment for the musicians if you can believe such a thing! Naturally, as this is unexpected, Gräfin, there will be no additional charge for your rooms."

The Casson-Percevals were the only guests at Number 40.

"We shall enjoy the extra time by exploring your lovely city," replied Mama. "And of course, Herr Gerber, you will charge me at the normal rate for all your services. I shall make a deposit in advance. Will a cheque drawn in Sterling be acceptable?"

"We're not going to have any money left," Brother moaned to Sister, over lunch, "after buying Wahnfried and your London lessons."

"You'll just have to work. You can play at tea dances and things – after you've been put down. Silly old Eddie, I'm *joking*."

After their hilarious meal, the C-Ps drive in the Sheep's Daimler-Benz to the Zoo – with Mama & Sister pointing and oohing. The animals share Edwin's opinion of the weather and hide from view. Next joke: to drive across the Isar River by the Ludwigsbrücke and past an unremarked dingy stucco pub, the Bürgerbräukeller, and the Maximilian Circle, and the Woods, and the Stadium, and then back across the Leopold's Bridge for tea in the snow at a café in the Englischer Garten. And then home to the Gerbers via Königstrasse, the Hofgarten, and the Odeonsplatz.

"Frau Winifred was right," said Mama; "remember children, at Home or Abroad, we ignore the Yellow Press – and now we shall use our extra evening to prepare our souls for Lohengrin."

... *Nov 8th, 1923*. Winifred Wagner arrives as the C-Ps are finishing a late breakfast – and in spite of the freezing weather the party goes window-shopping: Mama, jolly Frau Winifred, Ettie, Sheep von Hammel, and Eddie, at the exclusive stores along the Briennerstrasse. The Sheep has a front hoof on Mama's arm.

"On the wrong side anyway, stupid ass."

"That's how they do it in Hunland, Eddie."

The lady walks next to the gutter. In the bright windows there are goods for Us; it's the unseen small shops for the masses where things are missing. For Boys, Looking at Dresses is dull, but at least the stores are heated.

"Eddie," whispers Ettie, nudging, "look!"

Sheep von Hammel's bulging eye has been drawn to the mannequins in a Korsetterie display.

"Knickers, Ettie? Wearing them – out in the open?"

The sleek pink satin of the forbidden garments is exciting for Boys, in the disturbing way of the porpoise game ...

"Eddie's blushing," says his swinish sister.

"We shall have a cup of chocolate at the Kaffee bar, my dear young fellow, while our ladies do the remainder of their shopping."

The Sheep brought his chair close. His thigh touched Edwin's. Our ladies joined us at our glass table with their packages. Sister sat down. Sheep von Hammel slid closer to her. A Boy's first exposure to a male bi-sexual.

"Eddie-pal, you're looking blue."

The giant Putzi Hanfstaengl, speaking his mock-Chicago. His giant's off-centred head bumped the ceiling light in the Kaffee bar. He held an example of the Yellow Press.

WHERE IS THE GENERAL YORCK IN THIS HOUR OF OUR NEED?

"Putzi, just in time for lunch – have you seen Herr Wolf?" added jolly Frau Winifred, casually.

"I left him having Java at the Café Heck," said the Giant, "with Hoffmann – you know Hoffmann, his photographer guy? With this fuss in the papers I expected Adolf to be in the thick of things. He constantly surprises me, that man."

"The Austrian side of his nature," Frau Winifred said to Mama, "and it will sound silly, I know, but I can't go with you to the Lohengrin – it's rival Munich, you see. These Family pressures! Word would get back to Mama, her daughters – it just can't be done."

"We understand perfectly, don't we, children?"

Not a word, but we invite Putzi Hanfstaengl instead. Then the C-Ps went back to the Gerbers to Prepare. The Sheep being routed by the Giant was a bright side to the day. Otherwise it was snowing again, but not staying. The Munich pavements were covered by floating slush. Up in our room Sister unwrapped a package.

"Frau Winifred says Putzi plays the Black Bottom marvellously at parties. Eddie, do you want to see what I bought at Meyer Brothers?"

"I'm trying to read my score, if you don't mind."

"I saw you looking at them," waving a pair of *them* in Brother's face, brushing him with pink satin. Sing-songing "Eddie was look-ing, Eddie was look-ing . . ." Abruptly she shut *them* in a dresser drawer. The top one on the right. "I'm going to wear them under my blue dress for Lohengrin."

"Who cares?"

He cared. She knew it. Why else did she do it?

Lohengrin, the lyric & soft Transition from The Master's early Works. In the court of brave King Henry of Brabant, our Heroine, fair Elsa, is accused by villainous Count Telramund of murdering her Brother! A pure & noble Knight arrives in a boat drawn by the Swan. He will marry, defend & cherish Elsa – BUT – she must never ask the Fatal Question: What is thy true Name? Trapped

84

by her Nature, & the witchcraft of Ortrud, weak Elsa breaks her vow! The Knight reveals he is – Lohengrin! But also, he must now go back to the Castle of the Grail, & his father, Parsifal. The Swan returns & – Transformation! – it is Elsa's bewitched Brother! Lohengrin is taken by a Dove. Elsa dies. (We may note a modest use of leitmotivs.)

From the start the mood is different: a hush in the House for the first magic moment. There is no chance of Edwin being bored: the word *Grail* has been mentioned.

"The strings," sighed Mama, "oh, children, even so early, one can hear *Parsifal* coming."

Edwin heard only trumpets blasting. Knights in armour assembled on a jousting field. Pennants, spears, swords and shields. Oh, glory!

> *I did not make this journey idly;*
> *Let me remind you of the Realm's distress!*
> *Need I tell you of the affliction*
> *So often wrought upon German soil from the East?*

"Eddie, look – "

"Shut up, I'm listening!"

"Children, hush."

"Mama, I was only telling him that soppy Wolf Man's here again. Nail biting."

The Third Time. Standing at the back of a box directly across from us, stage right. Changed to hired, ill-fitting tails. He was in shadow, staring not at the marvellous stage but at Mama & Sister beside Hanfstaengl the giant. The time, 9:19 by the cherub-clock on the opera-house wall. Edwin didn't care about the nail-biter's watching. The music had the Boy: witch's potions, stabbing and hacking, fatal questions – even the soppy Wedding, da da de da – to the last line:

> *They shall name Him, Fuehrer . . .*

But by then he was gone.

"Elsa missed that eighth-note in her dying," said Sister, triumphant: "Herr Putzi you must have noticed, on her 'sweetly' – the whole thing fell utterly flat!"

NAUGHTY MARIETTA

AN ESCAPADE IN TWO ACTS
also entitled
THE KNICKERS' STORY!

*

[ACT ONE]

*Scene 1: Across the River Isar, in the
Bürgerbräukeller.*

*On a drinkers' table, surrounded by Party members
and Band players and also gallant Captain
Hermann, stands The Leader. He wears a* moth-
eaten Tail-Coat *and brandishes a drawn*
Revolver. *Sweating and pale, He fires one shot into
the ceiling – He makes it seem, perhaps this is by
Accident?*

THE LEADER

This is the hour of revolution! There are five rounds
in my gun. Four for the traitors. If I fail, one for me!

A PARTY MEMBER

Puts on a good act!

CAPTAIN HERMANN

You've got your beer, lads! What more can you ask?

BAND PLAYER

Cash, Captain! We have not been paid our wages in
advance.

CAPTAIN HERMANN

How much is this?

BAND PLAYER

Only fourteen trillion six-hundred marks, mein Herr.

THE LEADER

God in heaven I said revolution! Pay these shitheads!

BAND PLAYER

And a receipt, also?

86

Scene 2: A Hotel Bedroom. The sounds of Shouting
and Jubilation *on cobblestones. A glimpse of a
Lamplit Street outside. A Sister rushes to the
Window to see the excitement. A Brother creeps to the
top-right dresser drawer.*

Suspensefully he takes out . . . new pink Satin
Knickers. *And slips into a Bathroom. And slides
them on. Under his pyjamas. Gripping slickly.
Swept away by the* Porpoise-thrill *that grips so
many in Munich, Bavaria, this Climactic night!*

*Scene 3: The Next Morning, in bleak daylight. The
action alternates between the Street and the
Bedroom.
As Brother and Sister face each other —*

*. . . The Leader's Stormtroop set up a machine-gun,
in front of the Police Directory Building.*

SISTER [*accusingly*]
    Where are they?
BROTHER [*defiantly*]
    What?

    *Cross-purposes. The Stormtroop capture, instead of
    Police, the Marxist City Fathers [for refusing to fly
    the Mowgli Flag].*

SISTER
    You know what – my new knickers.
BROTHER [*weakly*]
    I haven't seen your beastly knickers.
    *The Storm Trooper in charge, a tobacconist, requests
    the Marxist Councillors to please stop smoking.*

SISTER
    Liar! you stole them.
BROTHER
    You waved them. In my face.
    A Large Crowd in the square bays for Marxist blood.

The Councillors, smokeless and frightened, are
loaded in a truck. The Munich Trolley Cars stop
moving. The Mowgli Flag flies bravely. The loyal
City Police paste up posters denouncing Storm-
Trooping.

SISTER [*losing*]

Eddie, tell me where they are, please?

The Police are now arrested by the Storm Troop. The
new Posters are torn down swiftly. Impasse.

SISTER [*desperate*]

I'm sorry, Eddie, truly, I was just teasing.

BROTHER [*red-faced*]

They're in the sponge bag.

The Leader's Men now hold the bridges.

SISTER

The sponge bag?

Astonishment. Military State Police in Green jackets
and trousers disembark from lorries.

BROTHER [*mumbling*]

I had to wash them.

SISTER [*mouth open*]

You –

Mama enters – cutting things off in her sweeping
manner. The Green Police block the bridges.

MAMA

I have ordered breakfast, children. Stop playing, and
pack your things. Coming on top of Lohengrin there
is altogether too much excitement in the air. We shall
leave Munich.

HERR GERBER [*arriving with tray*]

Gräfin, I regret, for the time being the trains are not
running.

On The Bridge: Captain Hermann prudently urges
retreat to his village on the Austrian border.

GENERAL LUDENDORFF: [*war-hero: tersely*]

The Movement, Captain, shall not end in a ditch in a
country lane!

*Across The River: all eyes turn to The Leader. He
straps on a pistol belt; still in his Tail-coat,
bedraggled, yet fierce! A provincial conductor under
fire.*

HERR GERBER [*humbly offering*]

There is a train scheduled again at two o'clock. If one
may suggest, Gräfin, it might be wise to await
developments?

MAMA [*with impeccable gift for timing*]

We shall not wait, children. Herr Gerber, if you
would be so kind, please order me a motor, for
half-past twelve, precisely.

THE LEADER [*flourishing his whip*]

March! – for Germany!

[ACT TWO]

Pretence ends. Naughty Marietta has turned ugly.

Sister forgets about the sponge bag and the knickers. "Do you think it
really is a revolution, Eddie? The Bolsheviks murdered the Tzar's
whole family in the last one."

"I don't know," Brother goes out onto the balcony, "I don't know if
these are Bolsheviks, Ettie." From the east there is the faint sound of
martial music. A lorry drives by rapidly, a machine-gun on a tripod in
the back. A Boy's first machine-gun!

"Edwin, come in at once."

"I've finished packing. It's exciting, I can see the bridge."

"There are Mowgli flags."

"Children, this is too much!" bringing both inside and closing the
French doors. "Where you will remain out of harm's way until we take
our train."

12:15

Through the closed windows the advance Brown guard are halted by the
Greens, then, "They're moving through," Eddie shouts. "They're
marching. And there's soldiers and a band."

A ragged one. Mama rings for the porter.

12:20

The Casson-Percevals arrive in the lobby. The marchers are already in

89

the Zweibrückenstrasse.

"Listen, Eddie – singing."

"*O Deutschland hoch in Ehren!*"

High in Honour! From hundreds of voices. Thousands? No one can tell how many Bavarians sympathise with the Brown marchers.

12:27

Mama settles accounts.

"Thank you, Herr Gerber, Frau Gerber, for a very pleasant stay. You may be sure that we shall come again on our return to Munich."

12:30

The ordered car is parked before the portico on Residenzstrasse. To the right, the southeast, the Brown marchers turn into the street, blocking any chance for movement in that direction. To the north, at the Odeonsplatz, the way is stopped by the Green police. The Residenzstrasse is narrow, only wide enough for eight men to walk abreast. They begin to sing again, the "Storm Song", marching in cadence, arms cross-linked, black-and-red flags waving. A tall man, heavyset, wearing a quilted hunting jacket under a greatcoat and a Prussian eagle helmet on his shaven Junker's head, is the centre of the line.

"Good heavens children, General Ludendorff."

The National Hero. To his right, in a plain but brightly polished helmet with a large white Mowgli symbol edged with black, a natty figure in thigh-boots and trenchcoat of black leather – with the lapels back to show his military medals. Unknown to Edwin, this is gallant Captain Hermann, still a mere air-ace about town. And on Ludendorff's other side, in his ring-master's tail-coat (under his trenchcoat) carrying his circus whip, and his velour hat, with the revolver in his belt, looking right at Ettie –

"Herr Wolf!"

The rest were just marching, not well. Half-uniformed, young and old. A rag-tag Brown army.

We only noticed him. The Pale Man. Mouth set – but he was not in a trance, he nodded slightly when he saw us: remember, children, this ex-private soldier served four years in the blood of the trenches and did not run.

"*Kompanie –! Marsch!*"

90

The Green Police drop their bayonets to the horizontal. They begin to march in a line of steel, their boots in step on the stone cobbles.

"*Kompanie –! Doppelt Marsch!*"

The Green Police line begin to jog. The Brown hold firm. His eyes are straight ahead. His feet, with Hero-Ludendorff's, keep perfect time. General, & Ex-corporal march into history.

The Green and Brown tides merge. A Boy hears a clash of steel on steel. The most exciting moment of my life!

And then –?

The shot. Only one. The first gunshot – except for Annabelle on my island, and that was the sound of thunder – is a *pop* from Guy Fawkes night. But a Green man with sergeant's stripes falls down, and red blood flows from his neck, among the cobbles.

"*Edwin-Christ-Edwin!*"

Mama screaming. *Christ!* Can you imagine? Ettie dragging, Mama dragging. Our car door opens. *Pops* everywhere, banging the narrow street's windows. A Brown man throws himself across Herr Wolf, and falls dead with a torn pistol belt and stomach. As he falls, he and the man to the left grasp His right arm with a death grip, dragging the Leader down to safety. Ludendorff, the Hero, by instinct flings himself face forward – although myth says as a General he marched through a rain of fire. No man could march in the Residenzstrasse. There were 18 dead in our street. The time by a striking clock was 12:45, precisely.

A white Mowgli helmet lay in the gutter beside me. Across the street, the helmet's owner was crawling into Number 25. On our side, Herr Wolf emerged from a pile of bodies. A boy a little younger than Eddie had a shoulder and sleeve drenched with blood, yet wasn't crying. I don't remember anyone crying. Just the terrible sound of those *pops*, so small. So random.

He looked around. There were two other Brown men with him. The Green Police were milling at the far end of the street.

"Herr Wolf!" Mama called, in her new swearing voice. "Here! My car!"

"The boy," he said. "Save this boy."

The one with the bleeding arm, not Eddie. The boy and Herr Wolf, and the two other Brown men got into our car. I-Edwin slammed the

91

door: jolly Frau Winifred Wagner was looking down from one of the Gerbers' hotel windows, hand to her mouth – anything but laughing – while the Green Police advanced, and our chauffeur just sat there.

"Drive!" Mama commanded in two languages. "*Verdammt! Drive!*"

Like maniacs, through back alleys for blocks to Max Joseph Platz.

En route, he said, once more turned back into the huddled Little Tramp, "It's all over, I shall die, but save this boy."

... An old grey car, a Selve; on the back seat, boxes of bandages and dressings. He got out of our car. His right arm was hanging, unusable. His mouth was set with pain. He had dropped his whip. The revolver was still in his belt. He still carried his velour hat.

He remembered to say thank you, to our astonishing Mama, and goodbye to us, Ettie & Eddie.

First Movement
Second Passage

[obbligato !]

It's a warm wind, the west wind, full of birds' cries;
I never hear the west wind but tears are in my eyes.
For it comes from the west lands, the old brown hills,
And April's in the west wind, and daffodils.

. . . At Machem's House: April, 1924. Young Edwin was "put down" at Easter, the time of year most redolent of promise, when cricket pads and bats are broken out, and pitches rolled, by gardeners in pairs, dragging the waterfilled rollers behind, as they strain across the turf. The condemned can hear the water slosh as they pass by.

The School – Olde Boys do not name names – was located two more counties east of Cornwall. Along with the abbey, it was the central feature of the Town. With its 12th Cent mellow stone and elms, and quadrangled squares of grass within its walls, and freshly-collared shining Youth, it was –

"Delightful," said Mama. "One can imagine Trappists at their devotions. I am sure, Edwin dear, that once he knows we are Wagnerians the Headmaster will allow you to have a piano in your room."

Eddie knew how mad she was from the moment that he first saw the Very Reverend Dr Eustace Bell: with his black-crow gown, and hooded eyes, and talons (his finger nails were preternaturally long) he was known as Ding-Dong by his supportive Staff, or Doctor Torquemada to those entrusted to his care.

"One sacrificed one's Bishopric, Lady Casson-Perceval, to battle for Boys' particular souls. Your son shall be assigned to Machem's House – he will be among friends and the element of the Spirit is closer there. Where possible," added in a voice that was a croaking rattle of red-hot chain, "the School always likes to find an acquaintance – a sympathetic compatriot to ease the difficult first day."

"You see, Eddie dear, already a friendly face. That Glasgow boy you liked so much at All Souls. Now I know we shall be happy here."

The School clock struck with the clap of doom as she left.

"Hullo, Cameron," said Mama's boy, at half-past three on that black, late-April Thursday afternoon.

"Casson-Perceval, you little Frog worm, I run your dorm. You'll be my fag."

Cameron's nose at 15 was larger and seemed still more bent, as did, that evening, his genital organ, now embedded in bright red pubic hair. No trace of even an Edinburgh-Scots accent remained. He was already six feet tall and thinner than one of Old Cosima's feet.

"Do you like it here, Cameron?" the new prisoner asked.

"Snots have twenty-four hours to settle in. Fresh collars on Sundays, Tuesdays and Thursdays. Lights out are at nine in summer term. If I catch you pulling it, six of the best. Any questions?"

"No questions really, Cameron – only who should I see about getting a piano in my room?"

There was no roasting flesh and public sodomy: it was disguised as high spirits after games, and foreskin-pinching in the communal bath. For a week Edwin lay with his eyes open until midnight, waiting for Cameron's worst.

Nothing happened, except getting increasingly tired, and oversleeping, dreaming about Ettie and Mama. The attack came in the morning. A kick. The bed footboard lifted high in the air, dropped down, jarring every bone awake as the sheets were ripped off.

"Boner! Casson-Perceval's got a boner, filthy little swine!"

Or cricket – terrified that the rock-hard ball would break his piano player's Piscean fingers.

"Butter fingers!" Whizzing the ball deliberately at his golden head. "Casson-Perceval's a butter-fingers! Clumsy sissy. Bloody oaf."

This was clearly against the rules. Boys were not allowed to swear.

"Cameron!" bellowed by the Games Master, "have that boy report to me!"

Eddie waited, reprieved, for his persecutor to be taken to justice.

"Don't just stand there, Casson-Perceval, you snot. At the double – *Run!*"

Such innocence.

"Don't you like games, Casson-Perceval?"

"I don't know, sir. I've never played any."

"Never played?" Incomprehension. All this is covered by Prep School. This is what prep schools are for.

"I never went to Prep School, sir."

"Tutors? In this day and age? Good God."

Private tutors, however, seem marginally acceptable. Edwin has enough sense not to mention two maiden daughters of Sappho, named Athene and Boadicea, watching naked boys.

"Even with a tutor, you must have played something, Casson-Perceval?"

"Ping-pong, sir."

"Tennis! Good show!"

Letters poured it out to Ettie. Sister's letters back were only half as often, a quarter as long. "Of course I miss you too, dreadfully, and love you awfully, the practice squawking's pretty ghastly – except that the Pill Man (that's Beecham's) invited me *twice* to tea! Don't believe the Yellow Press; he's a perfect Pet. Old Meyerhof smells a bit on Saturday mornings. The throat gets Sundays off. (A frightful Church Choir takes the piano – all no-pitch Aunts!) Lots of kisses. P.S. Underneath your Eddiness, it really sounds quite fun with Torquemada! Tonight *I go Public*!!! Oh Gawd. Love again, E."

Only finding the library saved Brother's sanity.

Mr Mares:

The Stallion (Boys being vicious sods) was a gentle little man, twisted by rheumatism in the lower back. It always made Eddie feel guilty watching him climbing the ladder and painfully stretching for a volume on a high shelf.

"I can get it myself, Mr Mares, sir."

"Your task is to seek and read, Casson-Perceval. Mine is to find."

"Do you have anything on King Arthur?"

The librarian was disappointed, but resigned. "I expected more imagination, Casson-Perceval. Malory, the illustrated fourth edition is in the upper stack. I'll fetch it down."

"I've read Malory, sir – I hoped there might be something more detailed about the Holy Grail."

"In the context of greater European civilisation? Well done, my boy."

"Not really, sir. I'm only interested in Cornwall or Wales."

"Geoffrey of Monmouth," little Mares said, but kindly. "And then *La Queste du Saint-Graal*. We have a good modern English version by an Old Boy – a Cambridge man. Yes, old Geoffrey of Monmouth is where we'll start. If you're going Grail-searching in your summer holidays I'd better give you Schliemann too."

"Who, sir?"

"The re-discoverer, you ignorant creature, through the Odyssey, of Minos and ancient Troy."

"Truly sir? He really found the actual places from the Odyssey?"

"And the Iliad. It caused a considerable stir among scholars at the time. After the event it seems like so much common sense. But then most of life does – after the event, wouldn't you say, Casson-Perceval?"

"Yes sir." Liar and toady that he was.

"Schliemann's is a wonderful story, but to my mind what is revolutionary about him is his method of attack on languages. You're going to need languages, Casson-Perceval, to go after the Grail. I could get shot for saying so, but forget the Classical Method, boy – follow Schliemann."

For success in Life, Edwin, ignore both Yellow Press & Academe.

But first – the prisoner has to be released from prison. June crawls its way into July. It rains on England. The damp humidity of summer encourages unnatural growth in the wood behind Machem's House. Young Eddie C-P comes across two Fifth Form boys in sports togs, shorts down. He presumes they have both been taken short. From their flushed young faces they feel the same embarrassment that he would in their predicament. Tactfully he turns away. That evening after supper in Hall, one of the pair seeks him out.

"Casson-Perceval, about this afternoon – I'll kill you if you tell."

96

"Of course I won't tell, it can happen to anyone."

Disembarking from the Great Western, in London, Edwin's arm was still sore above the elbow from a turn of rotation through 100 degrees.

... *At Mama's Little Flat:* First, heaven! On the platform, both his women are waiting. Mama, re-Jungianised, reveals the depth of her understanding.

"Edwin dear, despite the piano, one can see you've had a happy time."

"Torquemada's stretched him," said Sister, kissing, not altogether pleased. "He's going to be as tall as me – Mama, look how tall he is."

Taxiing, the conversation continues at cross-purposes.

"Eddie, you're going to simply *love* Covent Garden. I have to show you on the way home to Mama's little flat. And Pawel's coming with us to Porquerolles, before Bayreuth. Eddie, what a summer it's going to be."

"Pawel?"

So briefly was Edwin to be alone in Eden with his women.

"I knew that you'd be pleased," said his Mama. "And dear Professor Jung sends his regards."

Mama's Little Flat, being Mama's, is half a Georgian house – off Sloane Street, on the quiet side of Hyde Park. There was plenty of space in the "flat" for separate rooms. Brother's had a view of trees and shared a bath with Sister's. She came in as he was getting out.

"Oops, my mistake! Eddie, you're growing fur. Isn't it gold. Just like me. Oh don't be silly about covering up. We always used to see ourselves. We're old enough to be sensible now. At the Garden, the Corps de Ballet people see each other simply all the time."

So blasé, my dears – but her blue eyes linger. Not just fur, and height: Eddie's growing Bigger. (And even if she *had* been wandering backstage by then, the Corps de Ballet people, darlings, keep their straps on!) "It has to work both ways, Ettie. You can't just come barging in on me."

"Of course both ways." And she slipped off her clothes and got into his bath.

"You've grown too."

"Yes, they're quite nice now, aren't they?"

Her breasts are nearly fully formed, with neat nipples. Brother is looking at her other parts. Like his own, her gold hair is spun too fine to hide anything. For the first time he sees the lips that guard the secret room, the mound. She hums a little *Tannhäuser* as she washes It. The Venusberg. Fascinated, yet repelled, Eddie flees from the bathroom.

I hurt her last time. I made her bleed.

... *At Porquerolles:* Pawel joins the C-Ps at Victoria for the Boat Train. With feelings for Sister in a turmoil, Brother thinks he's glad after all of a male ally. The Boys make Olympic jokes in English about Frenchmen as they travel through France – they said in French that Liddell and Abrahams would beat the socks off the Frogs. We were devilish clever. Pawel was 14 ...

"And devastatingly good looking, don't you think, Mama?" said Sister, stirring. "Pawel's going to be a real masher."

"I thought I was going to be the masher," Brother said.

"Pawel's older."

"I hope this trip is the right thing, children – the heat is sure to be *intense.*"

They had a bedroom problem on the island. Eddie took Pawel to explore while the women solved it. The two friends went to the fort. The doors of the gunhouse were broken and hanging. Annabelle's great muzzle was stuffed with oakum lagging. The barrel and breech were rusted.

"I suppose it doesn't matter, Pawel, as there's never ever going to be another war."

"If we don't have a war, Eddie, how can I free Ukraine?"

Both stared at the massive gun, in silence.

"I suppose you could always run for Parliament – in Moscow, when they have the next election."

"You don't free countries with elections. Tell me again about the Munich revolution and its leader. How many of the revolutionists had guns? What calibre were they? How many with bayonets?"

Pawel was always as one-tracked as Sister. Singing & Guns.

"One revolver, and now he's in prison?" said Pawel. "That's not much of a revolution. Anyway, Germany isn't where the trouble is. It's with the Reds. Look at the size of it on the map. Just from Munich to the Volga is bigger than all of Europe."

How can tiny green Nibelheim possibly compare with great white Russia?

Back at the Villa C-P, the bedroom situation has been resolved:

"Mathilde shall sleep at night with her sister in the cottage off La Place by the landing stage," declares Mama. "Edwina will have your old nursery room. Edwin, you and Pawel shall share Mathilde's former space off the kitchen. I have had it whitewashed, and new netting installed for the mosquitoes. As a Slav, I know you won't mind, Pawel, dear – the north side is quite the coolest spot in the house."

A 20th Cent-landmark: the first time the Casson-Percevals sleep in a house without a servant on the premises.

Nothing else has changed. Mathilde's night-time absence isn't noticeable. She is still there clucking with fresh bread and coffee in the mornings by the time we wake up. Then swimming, lounging, resting at noon, planning Revolution, walking to the landing, riding with Deaf'n'-Dumber on the *Cormoran*, the days of gold flash by. . . .

One languorous afternoon Eddie comes back by himself from the landing. Mama is resting, with her door closed. Mathilde nods in a rocker in shade outside the kitchen. No sign of Pawel and Ettie. Eddie walks through to the large room that serves as parlour and for dining. He sees Sister lying in the sun among the pink-and-white portulaca. From behind the mosquito curtain he watches her. She's wearing her new bathing dress bought at Harrods for this Season; a flowered pattern of cotton and silk. She lies on her back, arm behind her head, golden hair fanned out; a matching blue butterfly dances by her closed eyes. Her formed breasts rise and fall. Her golden tanned legs are slightly apart, towards him. He feels the same turmoil of feelings. He sees a slight movement in the pines to the left, the west.

Pawel is watching too, hidden in the trees.

Brother decides to ambush his Friend – to escape the feelings. Creeping out past Mathilde, bare feet placed with super-care to avoid rustling the cones and needles. Stepping forward, noiseless through the maquis, the undergrowth. Pawel tenses. Brother stops. Sister stretches her gold thighs in the sunlight. Pawel gasps. Eddie snakes to the side – and sees the olive penis, now engorged, free of its sheath, shining and purple. Brother sees what his Friend's doing with it. Hypnotised, he feels his own Self rising. . . .

Eddie backs away through the pines to a clearing not visible from the Villa Casson-Perceval, where he completes his first knowing act of Self manipulation.

But more. I-Edwin, convulsed for the first time in deliberate maledom, wish to *be* my Sister. The object of Friend's lust. Two in one.

Is that so terrible, old Chap?

Indescribable.

OUR FIRST SEASON

Opening Remarks:

"Without a doubt, in Bayreuth, even the spectator will be worth seeing!" Said Nietzsche, before the 1st-First – in manic anticipation!

For E & E's, the re-opening of the Shrine in 1924, the Casson-Percevals' fellow-Wagnerians come from all over Europe. They come from the Americas, even from Japan. Ancient, gowned duchesses with mutton-chopped, bemedalled consorts peer through lorgnettes on chains as they stand, like unfortunate Herr Wolf, before the Grave. Starving musicians, gaunt in mothballed tailcoats, like his, carry yellowing sheets and hum from the Original. Wild-eyed artists, paint-smocked, daub at canvases on easels in the town square and smoke Parisian Gauloises. To Edwin it was as though a museum of the theatre had opened its glass exhibition cases to let the costumes wander out.

Oh, and Nietzsche's Sister (of the Rumours – an incredibly ancient Parrot) is met, and prods Edwin in the b*m, by mistake, with her stick.

"Oh Eddie – there are normal people like us too."

Said Sister, as she and Brother paid an English threepenny-bit to the Wagner Moppets for the dubious privilege of witnessing their staging a Helden Battle in the garden near the parrot and sparrow crosses.

"Aunt Daniella made all our costumes," said Mausi, now almost 6; "next time me and Wieland are going to be Siegmund and Sieglinde having baby-Siegfried."

"Good lord!" said Eddie; "Ettie, with all the visitors oughtn't you to sort of at least mention it to Mama?"

"I think it would be a hoot if some old Duchess saw."

The C-Ps' view was privileged. Once more they are staying in the

100

Siegfriedhaus tucked away in its corner of the garden. In Wahnfried, Old Cosima is too frail to come down, but receives Upstairs, in a salon filled with His relics. The Parrot-Sisters guard the Widow, and interpret more jealously than ever. Downstairs, and everywhere, Real-Siegfried is frantically busy. Only jolly Frau Winifred and Mama relax, talking and laughing in garden corners where new lawn has been reclaimed with her gift: The English Women seem to have established some unique bond.

Eddie said, "I bet it's because of our money."

Ettie said, "It's Frau Winifred being soppy about the Tramp Man in prison – good riddance – and you're just grouching because Pawel's soppy about me."

"Rubbish. Pawel never even noticed you – he only wants to lead another Revolution. Ettie, with Herr Wolf, Frau Winifred isn't *really* ? She can't be. She's married."

Don't tell me!

. . . July the 14th, 1924. Bastille Day – but about Pawel: Eddie's friend had left our island to return to the Aunts for the rest of his summer, poor orphaned devil. Brother is delighted. Without Pawel to remind, the guilt eases. Eddie finally has his women to himself under the Casson-Percevals' umbrellas. Rain is one feature that even the Master couldn't control. The Continentals huddle in the overcrowded dank stone galleries of the Festspielhalle. Mama nods, often smiles, but her children are seldom introduced. Staying at the Siegfriedhaus establishes a pecking order among the faithful.

"It is not only the weather, Eddie dear. The poor Wagners were never lucky with money. It is the price of Genius, to be denied." Mama sighed, and tested the waters, and folded her brolly. "The decor must remain that by Bruckner from before the Great Divide. Come, children, enough melancholy. The fanfares call the magic moment – your First Ring!"

And how was it, your First Time . . . ?

Too much to take in. My dears, it took Genius twenty-six *years* to get it straight. For the Boy (at appalling 13!) – in between the moments where giants shook the ground, and horses flew, and dragons flamed, and men and women burned, truly, on enormous pyres – his First Ring was, for hours and days on end . . . EXCRUCIATINGLY DULL.

101

"We must make allowances, Edwin. Without adequate funds, rehearsal has had to be cut short – and some of the sets are perhaps a little faded, but, as dear Herr Siegfried says, with everyone's feet wet once more," as the C-Ps squish back through the rain to yet another reception at Wahnfried, "and with the Weimar economic situation under control, things in the country can only improve. Oh, children, as the Gods crossed the Rainbow Bridge I could see your Papa so clearly. Waiting for us all in shining armour, with that glorious sound."

Our Silver Knight.

> *Parsifal*, being The Master's last, sombre yet most Glorious Work on the suffering of the King, Amfortas, guardian of the Holy Grail, & the Holy Spear. Amfortas, having been bewitched by the wiles of Kundry, the Sorceress, into Sin, now lies stricken with a Wound that will not heal – excepting by the aid of a Pure Fool. Too sweetly simple at first to know his assigned role, the Youth must wander the world to share the sufferings of Mankind, to find Wisdom. The most wicked black magician, Klingsor, (who hates all Women) having stolen the Spear (which is Power), in his Fortress attempts to entrap Parsifal with a Garden of magical tempting Flower-Maidens. The Fool's Purity triumphs, & in resisting Temptation – even the Kiss of Kundry! – the Youth shows the Sorceress the evil of her ways. At the last, on Good Friday, she repents! She dies. The soul of torn Amfortas is saved! As it ascends to God, the Grail descends once more among the Grail Knights in the Grail Temple. Parsifal becomes their Leader. A New Order of Redemption for the World is given!

"A beautiful story," said non-religious Mama. "Parsifal represents the return of The Master to Our Lord. Remember, children, because Romans are caught by their frightful Church so young, they always do return – even the Jungianised, at the end. It's their awful Purgatory."

"It's being so chromatic," said Sister-Covent-Garden, "and in operas it's only make-believe blood. Even you really can't be silly about the wound bit after Munich, Eddie."

Brother can't believe it. These two females have been sitting beside him through the same six hours – counting Intervals – four hours on-stage of whores dressed like flowers in a garden, and Parsifal watching them, tormented – like Eddie watching Pawel watching Ettie – imagining being kissed by the Chief Whore Mistress, this witch with the frightful scream, and the incredible burning eyes, called Kundry; and a more frightful wound on a pillow that bleeds, and can never be stopped; and a totally evil magician, Klingsor, who condemns a golden boy to endless wandering because of only what he had been thinking, and had seen – of a situation he had done nothing to put himself into in the first place ! – yet finally, transcendentally, white-magically, if the Boy remains pure, he does find, at the end of his journey and the story, the object of his search, *nothing less than the Holy Grail.* And all Freudianised, Jungianised tormented Mama, and flaunting, bleeding, know-it-all Sister have seen on that stage is Roman religion and make-believe blood.

Rescue me from Hands defiled by Sin . . .

Like his namesake, I-Edwin had to wrestle alone that evening after the performance, in Real-Siegfried's little house:

A Boy may not actually *know,* yet, what whores *are,* or what incest *is,* or even what Man & Woman really *do;* but he knows what it feels like, and how it starts. It starts as the stuff of dreams, growing like flowers in the mind, like Ettie in her bath or in our island garden, or beside him at Bayreuth. Like the tormenting flesh growing between his legs even as he watched, innocent as Mausi's "Me and Wieland" in the dark, the actions of the writhing, grossly oversized Teutonic children on the great stage of the Festspielhaus.

For our Sin, Eddie realises with black despair, it isn't just Parsifal – the whole second part of *His* bloody Ring is aimed directly, only, at Us: *Brother & Sister, making a baby.*

"Oh here you are, Eddie-dear," Mama swept in with the Score for revolting Walther von Stolzing, "I'm glad the first time's been so marvellous for you darling. Our visit to Herr Wolf is arranged for the day after Meistersinger, by the way."

How she loved dropping Our little surprises – by the way.

". . . I'm going to be Jungianised for another year, children . . . We're going to Prison . . ."

The Hotel Landsberg

"It looks more like a monastery."

Ettie, as the C-Ps cross a rumbling old wooden bridge spanning the narrow River Lech. Before them, the outer wall, and the buildings visible beyond are painted white. There are tall brown-brick chimneys in pairs, and steep red-tiled roofs with tiny attic windows peeking out; on one of them is a cupola, for a clock: the hands set in line at three-quarters past three. In the centre, dominating the structure, an octagonal tower – not the one from Edwin's dream, this was like a squat lighthouse. A rounded gate led through an arch in the outer white wall.

"I think it looks more like a farm," Eddie said.

"It looks like a prison," said Mama. "Children, how the poor man's spirit must suffer behind those cruel bars."

Her blind children hadn't noticed the bars. As the gate in the arch opened, they were in front, rough iron, on a bank of great windows, forty feet high. The space within the outer wall was partly grass and partly cobbled. There were fruit trees bearing ripening plums, and pears, and apples. A group of men was walking beneath them. They wore civilian clothes, not stripes. Eddie was disappointed, hoping for ball and chain, with manacles.

"The ghastly whistler," Sister said, as the group came closer, "Buckteeth. The one with the cowboy book, Eddie – at the fortune teller's."

He snapped his heels together. Mama returned her Gracious smile as a guard arrived.

"Remember, children, a place of Incarceration, but Courtesy is not blocked by prison walls. We shall treat it as a visit to a good hotel."

Laugh if we will. Most that was decent in this world died with Mama's Age. Anyway, her form of address is apparently what a Hun "Hotel" guard expects. He salutes like a doorman and escorts the C-Ps through another arch into a spacious hall with a floor of flagstones, lit by the cathedral windows. "The Herr Governor will be with you directly." The

104

doorman leaves the visitors in a comfortable office with two well-used pipes in a rack on an oak desk, beside a blue leather blotter.

The blotting paper is immaculate. There are no bars on these windows. No screams of torture, only the sound of someone playing a piano at a distance, needing tuning. E-sharp is off.

Said Ettie, "I feel quite goosey. I'm sure we're standing on top of a dungeon."

"Gräfin, I am the Governor, Leybold, my most sincere apologies for not being here to receive you properly."

The Hotel Manager. He was middle height in a typical Hun official's uniform – a cross between military dress and a cutaway morning suit. He bowed to Mama.

"Not at all, Herr Governor, your staff have been most kind. I have brought a new volume of poetry from Frau Wagner, who could not visit today herself."

"So truly gracious of Frau Wagner. Will the Gräfin do me the honour to come this way?"

The Gräfin's gracious children follow. The Governor-Manager stops. More clicks and bows. Considerable embarrassment.

"Gräfin, die Kinder . . ."

He means, The Hotel Regulations. Even for so special a guest as Herr Wolf there are Certain Rules. "Only children directly related, if you understand?"

"Oh Gawd," Sister has picked that up from Covent Garden. She tosses her golden curls in pretty annoyance behind Mama's and the Manager's retreating backs; "Eddie, sometimes Hunland's simply too silly for words."

Deprived of visiting a dungeon, E & E watch Buckteeth and cronies exercising in the Hotel garden, shirts off, playing catch with a football. Hung from the apple-boughs, the jackets of the inmate-guests sport homemade Mowgli badges in their lapels – a far more serious Breech than visits of unrelated Kinder. Buckteeth sports also a neat, star-shaped scar above his right nipple. The Manager returns with thoughtful mugs of cold chocolate from the Hotel kitchens.

"You have come from the Festival? Such a privilege! It will stay all one's life, yes?"

He bowed and left again with one of his pipes.

"I don't care," said Sister, "I'm going to see him."

"You can't. You heard the Governor. It's forbidden."

"The fortune teller said we have the same signs – we paid her a whole sovereign. I'm going to prove it. You can stay for the stupid rules."

Brother obeyed: he was used to being a prisoner.

In the Hotel orchard Buckteeth made a catch – elegantly, even gracefully, yet one of the other Mowgli men laughed, and called,

"Don't strain anything, Fräulein Anna."

Buckteeth, bending for the ball, dropped it: the exit wound on his back was huge, between 3rd and 4th ribs, with ragged edges, a killer. The lucky survivor straightened and stalked off on his own, whistling furiously through the tooth-gap. His E-sharps matched the piano's. Eddie felt sorry for him, being made fun of, war-wounded, as a prisoner. Ettie laughed – her show-off laugh, somewhere above. Sister's got away with it again! Brother dares a foray to the hall. His women were coming down the Hotel staircase.

SILENT AREA
TALKING FORBIDDEN BY INMATES
D-SECTION

"Herr Edwin – Grüss Gott."

Overhead, that guttural, nasal voice. He stood on a balcony on the second story of D-Section, smiling at breaking the Silence rule. He was wearing his too-short shorts with braces and his odd cape-jacket over a white shirt, and brown tie. His thighs bulged slightly; there was the beginning of the paunch. His cheeks were puffy.

Eddie waved, but Ettie trilled it: "Bye-bye, Herr Wolfi."

A frozen moment. His face closed. He gave a stiff little salute with his hand and arm – just a bend at the elbow – and was gone. The first personal Wolf-salute.

Said Sister, "He's changed his hair. Even less Sheik and more Tramp."

So by then the raven-wing was in place on the forehead . . .

"But what did you talk about all this time, Mama?"

"The walls have ears, Edwin, we shall discuss the visit later. Thank you, Herr Governor, for your kindness to my disobedient children."

"I wasn't," said Eddie. (As the C-Ps sweep out into the Hotel hall, the Manager opens the front door himself.) "Ettie, with Herr Wolf and Mama, you have to tell me."

"I didn't hear – but one thing you'll never ever guess, and of course he tried to hide it when he saw me – he had my ribbon tied on his Trampy old bed."

"He never!"

"And more revolting, even – but don't tell, because Mama made me promise – Eddie, he had to get up off his knees because he had his greasy Tramp head in her lap! He'd been positively blubbing."

A revolutionist – blubbing?

"He feels things so deeply," said Mama, as the visitors drove away from Buckteeth-Fräulein Anna and the other Hotel Guests with their illegal Mowgli badges in the orchard; "Herr Wolf is one of those people who normally cannot allow themselves to show it. He cannot even play for exercise with his men. He said to me, 'A leader cannot be seen to lose.'"

The car rumbled over the bridge: the octagonal tower, and the bars, and the cupola with the clock: the hotel was lost to view . . .

"But tell me about the real part of the prison," Eddie begged. "What was it like in his cell? Were there rings on the wall? And rats?"

"There were the bars, alas, to confine the spirit. But otherwise, Edwin, it was pleasantly light and airy. There was a desk for Herr Wolf to compose the Work he is engaged upon. He was gracious enough to allow me to read some pages. The theme is Monumental, although I confess it seemed a trifle *congested* in its style, but it is of course only a draft. And there was his typewriter, an ancient machine. There were simple flowers – dianthus and antirrhinums, mixed, below a portrait of his late mother, from a gravure, rendered in oils – somewhat primitively, I must admit. His bed was spare – the bed of a soldier. There was not a scrap of dust – not that he has to clean it himself, his staff see to that. Herr Wolf has persuaded the Governor to have the room repainted, all in white. It has what he considers his lucky number on its door: Seven.

107

But it is still a prison, children, and he must suffer four more years at least."

Five years for armed rebellion and High Treason, with men killed? As *The Times* huffs in London, "A plot against the Constitution of the Reich is obviously not considered a serious crime in the State of Bavaria . . . "

"But all that isn't the important part," now Sister begged. "Why was he blubbing? Mama, it isn't fair not knowing what you talked about to make him do it."

"One does not talk, Edwina, in the presence of Genius. I listened."

"A genius? Herr Wolf? like the Master?"

"Precisely, Eddie dear. Naturally it is not evident to the world as yet – only to those with sufficient discernment, persons such as Frau Winifred and, I hope, ourselves. Imagine, children –" leaning back in her Mercedes seat, Mama's colour and breathing became heightened with the intensity of her vision – "to have been present as Richard Wagner sat down to commence His Ring. Who could then have been prepared to believe as they watched pen move across paper, that before them was the pre-eminent man of Europe? His most brilliant book, Opera and Drama, was widely dismissed. Rienzi had been called shallow. The Dutchman had been scorned, and Tannhäuser considered a regression! The Revolution of 1848 had failed dismally – though fortunately, in my opinion. Lohengrin had yet to be performed. Our immortal Master was a hunted fugitive for debt. A work on Jesus Christ Our Saviour had had to be abandoned. And in Destitution, that wretched creature, Minna – His inferior first wife – left Him again in His hour of need: yet out of such ghastliness He was even then composing Siegfried's Tod, which we worship today as the magnificent twilight conclusion to The Ring. Was there ever such a monument to the Triumph of the Will! Yes, children – I may tell you that our friend Herr Wolf *is* a genius. And The Book *He* is writing will build the New Europe of which even The Master could only dream. We are going now to find the house where He was born, by the way."

Our New Genius: and His Birthplace – and as this is Mama's Fad idea, We must find it the hard way.

Backwards.

MAMA'S PILGRIMAGE

. . . At Linz: August the 8th, 1924. At noon precisely the Pilgrims arrive in Linz, on the Donau.

"The Blue Danube!" cried Sister, twirling on the station platform.

Brother said, "It isn't blue, it's brown." With greenish foam from a factory discharge. The banks are steep. On the far side is an ancient fort. "And how are we ever to find this man of Herr Wolf's, Mama, when we don't know a soul?"

"When in doubt, ask a policeman, Eddie dear. Children, this person we seek was Herr Wolf's closest boyhood friend. I cannot impress on you too strongly how significant that is. We have but the barest knowledge of The Master's early days. Imagine what might have been discovered if the right steps had been taken when He too was only thirty-five."

Mama's Edwardian faith in Institutions was never questioned by Officials. Within ten minutes the Pilgrims are with a Chief Inspector at the Central Station. Another five, and their quarry has been found. At least on paper.

"A town clerk, yes, presently unemployed; with a wife and three children, in the Bergstrasse, but as he is not connected by the telephone, perhaps the Gräfin would care to proceed to her hotel while a runner is sent round?"

The Police can do such things in Austria.

The Pilgrims travel by cabriolet to the Rhapsodie Hotel – 16th Cent, with feather beds and cooing pigeons, and postcard view. Plumbing is Porquerollisch for the C-Ps' benefit. There were stuffed animals all over the place. A polar bear in the Manager's Suite! At one-thirty the latest capture was brought to the main parlour.

The Guinea Pig:

His collar is starched as a plank, his hair still wet from some noxious lotion. His hand trembles. Clearly it's not every day that this clerk is dragged by the Police to meet an English Countess.

"Herr August Kubizek?" said Mama, "how very kind of you to come."

"Gräfin – your servant, I'm sure. The police say you want information about Adolf?"

"Indeed I do. Every scrap, Herr Kubizek. I understand that you are a longstanding family friend."

"A Guinea-pig," said Sister, "can't you simply see him with a mouthful of nuts, or whatever they eat?"

August Kubizek had one of those smooth, pouch-cheeked faces that made him look ten years younger than his age. His pomaded hair rose in tight waves from a high forehead above eyes that protruded in a constant state of alarm. He spoke more slowly, and his dialect was more Austrian than his incarcerated friend's.

"A friend of Adolf's? Well I was – but I haven't seen Adolf in fifteen years, Gnädige, that is to say, Gräfin – longer, eighteen. Yes, at least eighteen years. I read in the papers, but really I have nothing to do with these political affairs. The police – "

"I assure you, Herr Kubizek, this matter is nothing that involves the police. With my children, I wish only to locate your boyhood companion's place and circumstance of birth. If you could find the time I had thought that you might be our guide. Naturally I should cover all expenses, in addition to a suitable fee."

"A fee, and expenses; for Adolf, I don't know what to say."

"Say yes." The man was unemployed. Mama could be formidable on a Fad. "With His present suffering, it would mean so much to Him that someone cared, I'm sure. Were you also born in Linz, Herr Kubizek?"

"I was, yes – but Adolf wasn't. When I first knew him, Gräfin, he was living with his mother in Leonding. The Herr Oberoffizial, his father, had died. We took holidays together in Spital – a village. Frau Klara, his mother, came from Spital. The Herr Oberoffizial, also, I believe. But not Adolf. He mentioned Lambach. I could show you where he lived in Leonding and then tomorrow wc could go to Lambach. Now it comes back, I know he went to school in Lambach, yes."

... *At Leonding:* The Pilgrims' hired cabriolet takes them across the Danube by way of an old stone bridge. A pair of storks nest on a buttress. "When we were in Vienna together," August Kubizek said, "we used to walk across the bridges for our entertainment. It was free, and all the young ladies would promenade, if you'll excuse me for saying so."

110

"In Vienna? How long was that, Herr Kubizek?"

"Two years I would say – yes! Nineteen-five, nineteen-seven, our first time away from home, both of us. A lonely time. We had really nothing but music on the piano in the evenings."

"He was musical!" Mama said it on a note of rising triumph.

The Pilgrims' car turns into a newer suburb named Urfahr. August Kubizek seems less than overjoyed.

"Adolf insisted we buy the piano. There was really nothing else in our apartment. In our lives. Except the opera – we went to the opera constantly! The cheapest seats. Rienzi, Lohengrin, Tristan – Lohengrin especially."

"*The Master*," breathed Mama, "*Lohengrin*."

"Rienzi was the first. Yes, that first time he was literally in a trance. Gripping me on the street. 'Gustl,' – he called me Gustl – 'did you *see*? Did you *hear*?' I may tell you, Gräfin, on the street, I had a job to calm him down. This was the Frau Klara's last home."

A typical apartment building of the late last century. Two-storey, sandstone-block; beneath the windows, rococo balustrades that might have been all right hidden by lavender in Trevelly's gardens, are stark to the pavement. A high, rounded doorway fronts the dingy hall . . .

"Like another prison," Sister shuddered, "no colour or flowers, Eddie, don't you hate this sort of town?"

"One must make allowances, Edwina, the Master too, was poor."

"If I may say," August Kubizek said, cautiously correcting, "Adolf was not what we would then have called poor, Gräfin. Even before Frau Klara died he received an allowance – twenty crowns, as much as a clerk would have made working. And we were, after all, only students."

"Of music?"

"I, yes, a violinist. But Adolf, an architect – in his own mind an artist, although, to be honest as to real art, painting, I would say no. But then the night after the Rienzi he began to compose. I was considerably surprised. He had never learnt to read music. We had been on our walk to the bridges, and after washing his hands he picked out the themes with a finger. A historical opera; but at seventeen one would have to say this was good."

"Untaught, children! – at seventeen! The Master was also late. Precocity is often the mark of a narrow genius, but the broadest Vision is

111

invariably late. Herr Kubizek, you have quite solidified my faith. You didn't chance to keep the score?"

"Adolf destroyed it, Gräfin. After two days, he said, the vision went. He refused to look at it again. He was like that. He washed his hands – he was always washing, it was a habit – and made town plans instead. A new opera hall, with a dome. Workers' apartments." August Kubizek smiled diffidently and directed the Pilgrims' gaze across the road. "There is a fine prospect of Kürnberg Castle. Adolf said it used to give him inspiration – you will doubtless know, Gräfin, one says the Castle is where was composed in ancient times *Das Nibelungenlied*?"

"One cannot escape it." Mama sank, happy, into her cushions. "Herr Kubizek, this has been a tiring day but full of interest. Tomorrow we must explore on to – where was it?"

"Lambach, Gräfin. Some fifty kilometres. By motor one would reckon, an hour's drive."

At the Rhapsodie Hotel Sister looks out at the battlements of Kürnberg Castle. "I don't like Linz. It makes me feel empty. I would simply have to get away! Eddie, there's nothing to come back for here."

... *At Lambach:* The Pilgrims' exploration takes a full day, allowing for a pleasant lunch. August Kubizek has become animated. The search for his friend's roots intrigues him, and the money's good.

"But for what is only a holiday in the country! Gräfin, one feels guilty."

"Nonsense, Herr Kubizek. That is what money is for. Children, we can see where Herr Wolf's artistic inspiration started. This mill is delightful. Worthy of a Constable."

An ancient Miller still works, tossing great sacks of grain five feet up in the air. And remembers. The conversation is loud. Millstones rumble and the Miller is deaf.

The Miller's Tale
Still working – yes, at eighty, Gracious Lady! It's our wonderful Lambach air. Who? I'm sorry, your Ladyship, who? Yes, we rented to them. When they came from the Leingartners. That's a few years ago now. Twenty-five? I don't count the days. A Customs

112

man, the Herr Inspector. Officials! Taxes – who needs
them! They had a child – always climbing, and wolfing
my apples. A bit of a fibber. A lot of howling when he
was caught. Yes, Lady, I think there was a sister. The
mother had lost more than one. An upstairs problem in
the head. A sad business. That was the way of it in those
days. It's better now, with the hospital in the town. That
wolf-child's in prison is he? For rebellion? What times
these are! Well I'm not surprised. The Emperor's gone.

The Pilgrims drive back to refresh at the centre of the town.
   "Wolf-child, Children – how extraordinary Fate is."
   "More Mowgli." Young Edwin is bored.
The Gasthof Leingartner referred to by the Miller, is four storeys
high, with a painted yellow façade of stucco. The Hausfrau's matches it.

The Landlady's Tale
On the third floor, yes, Gnädige Frau, but only a short
while they were here. I was but a child myself – two little
boys and a girl, perhaps. Not sound in the head? – an
older boy of seventeen? No, I don't remember any of
that. There was a younger one, of four or five –
Edmund! – he died of measles, Hail Mary, I'm sorry to
say. When the other boy – Adolf? Yes, that's the name –
when this Adolf was ten or eleven. A tragic thing. The
father was an official and shouted. Yes, drink, Gnädige
Frau – isn't it always? The boy was in the choir of the
Brothers – there, just across the road. Singing all the
time, like a bird, and dressing up in a table cloth like a
priest, and getting beaten at night for smoking a
cigarette. But he kept on doing it, asking for a beating –
and getting what he wanted. Every night someone was
screeching in that family – even the poor grey cat! How
it comes back! The two girls were Angela and Paula –
half sisters; one might have been vacant, as you mentioned. They all came from Hafeld. Yes, a farm at
Hafeld. If you have a motor it's close, ten kilometers, no
more. Why – danke schön, Gnädige Frau.

A little Knicks for Mama. Beatings and smoking:

"We must make allowances. The German male parent is by tradition a disciplinarian – our narrow Cousin Wynchman-Hare shares it – but everywhere the eye turns in Austria there is support for the spirit. Children, observe the fenestration of the Abbey."

The next way-station: a place of Benedictines, many hundreds of years old. Like Landsberg it has a wall with an arch. As the Pilgrims walk through it, a priest comes out to greet them from the Middle Ages.

The Monk's Tale

Brother Groner, Countess – you were enquiring after a pupil? Young Adolfus? Good heavens! Naturally one is aware from the newspapers, but that is a time ago! In my choir, yes, so he was. Not a voice of top quality for a leading solo, but fortunately he kept it – the high soprano – he didn't mature as early as most. There might have been a slight medical problem – with, ah, the 'pennies dropping?' – one can't help observing, when the lads are swimming at the river. No, I'm not surprised at the politics. These visionary boys – if the family had stayed I'm sure I would have had him for the Church. With drunkard fathers – I regret to say it – the saving image of Our Blessed Virgin burns deep. And again, beatings in the home make the sufferings of our Lord so much easier for a child to understand. When one is bright one readily makes connections. I remember his talking of Gethsemane: 'Now I, too, understand betrayal, Father. In Germany, Our Saviour Christ would be our Siegfried. The Judas-Jew would be our Hagen. The kiss was a *Dolchstoss* – a stab in the back.' I suppose he'd been reading Pan-German nonsense. And I recall there had been a recent death – the younger brother, yes. To such a troubled boy how could it be otherwise than that heaven should seem especially close? Mother Church is our refuge and strength. I'd come in early and find him crying, staring up at our east window – the Crucifixion is particularly vivid in a

114

morning light. The ruby glass for the Saviour's blood comes from Wiener Neustadt, it could never be duplicated today. The Legionary's spear is inlaid with real silver, by the way. Like Parsifal's? ... Do you know, Countess, until your handsome son here mentioned it, I had never thought of that. Parsifal's spear! Have you just come from the Festival? Yes, it is an impressionable age. Especially for boys. I must write a word of comfort to my ex-pupil. Indeed, we *have* a fund, Countess! Bless you ...

"Parsifal's spear," from a disgusted Sister, "Gawd, Eddie, you can be an awful show-off."

"Edwina, I have reminded you before of that frightful expression — and that your brother's is a sensitive nature."

At an impressionable age — when 2 pennies are supposed to have descended. Above the Pilgrims' heads, carved into the stone of the arch, a cross lies skewed on its side like the Mowgli's.

... *At Hafeld:* There seem no dark overtones at Hafeld. This white Wolf-house is set on ten acres, among green walnut trees, with sunshine and a brook burbling. The present tenants are from the district, but the man of the house was only four when — and even though he must have shared a year at the Realschule, he can't — but then, as the Pilgrims are leaving, he suddenly produces:

"Das Wirtshaus!"

The Hafeld village pub. Its owner, red-cheeked and inflated from a lifetime sampling of his own wares, bursts grotesquely at his Lederhosen seams ...

The Brewer's Tale

Forget my best customer? Not likely, Lady! The old man — Old Rhino-hide, we called him! He had a coachwhip of the same, you understand. Spare the whip and spoil the child, yes? They weren't spared! The family dog peed — you'll excuse me, Lady, yes, puddles, right there on the kitchen floor. The woman kept an immaculate house — it would be cleaned immediately, you can be sure. The dog ran off – and the boy, he wouldn't take it. No, no, Lady, not the puny one, the oldest – Alois, the same as his father, about fifteen. The boys were half-brothers, like the sisters. The Frau Klara would attempt – well, as stepmother she couldn't do much. She got short shrift, you can imagine! Old Rhino-hide's third – be charitable, and say wife. Oh yes, this was a formal marriage, but that young woman, Klara, had plenty to put up with, I can tell you. Losing three little ones already, she doted on the youngest boy – her Dolf. I'll tell you a story: they had this fine gelding, seventeen hands, a bay – the kind that has plenty of mettle, even after it's been cut. Old Rhino-hide made this young Dolf stay on that horse, plunging and rearing around, until he crapped his – your pardon again, Lady. Their ages? The mother? Oh she was a good twenty years younger – thirty, maybe. Old Rhino-hide fancied himself, though. 'With my position – ' he used to say – 'have it put on the account.' His position! What was it – underpostmaster's clerk or somesuch! From Passau, over on the German side. He'd had posts in a dozen towns. And women! Wore his Brass buttons and braid in here even after he was retired. Or sacked. There were rumours. I can't complain; he drank a lake of beer. Isn't there one of that name doing something in Bavaria? You don't say? A criminal! With Old Rhino-hide behind him, I'm not surprised. My wife could have told you more, but she's gone before me, poor love. Why, thank you, gracious Lady. Go with God yourself.

. . . *At Passau:* It's a jarring full day's drive to Passau, and it isn't the rural paradise of Hafeld.

"Gawd, it looks like the backside of Paris," to Sister.

"Edwina! At least not when Herr Kubizek is with us."

The Guinea-pig is earning his money. While the C-Ps take the best rooms in the Hohenzollern Inn, poor August Kubizek spends that evening and the next morning squirrelling. Undaunted, Mama passes the time writing the previous conversations out from memory (those old Pelmanism games) in her perfect hand on the hotel's cheap stationery.

Brother & Sister went walking on a stone promenade beside the brown Danube. "Gawd I wish we were back in London, Eddie. I haven't practised for two weeks. My voice will be a positive screech. Going to Landsberg was all right – like visiting Sir Walter Raleigh in the Tower – if the Tramp Man had a cloak instead of those ridiculous shorts – but pubs and priests – really, sometimes I do think Mama goes too far."

"He did lead a revolution, Ettie. It's like learning about Garibaldi, I suppose. Or William Tell. One day it will be history."

"He has to get out of prison first. Besides you could hardly call Bavaria revolutionary."

A steam tug with a high funnel and barges chugs by. The sky is blue. Far to the west on a wooded hill is one of Mad Ludwig's snow-white fairy castles. The painted houses of the town are quaint. "I like the way it looks. If you have to be poor, Ettie, I should think it's a happy sort of place to be poor in."

The tumbrils carried innocents like these.

"Oh, Herr Edwin!"

"Oh damn," from Sister, "the Guinea-pig's back."

With fresh fodder obviously. August Kubizek was jogging along the promenade, face flushed, pouch-cheeks puffing with exertion.

"I have found the informant, Herr Edwin, Fräulein Edwina. An old, old woman. We must report immediately to the Gräfin, your mother."

In such a society the Police don't even have to try!

Her name is Frau Kraiburg. Kubizek has found her in a decaying tenement built as a square around a hollow central court over what has recently been stables. Frau Kraiburg lives on the top floor. How she got put there no one knows. Completely crippled with rheumatism she sits with crutches at hand, bent in a chair, under a wool rug despite the heat of summer. Her forehead wrinkles to indicate a curtsey; the best she can do for a visit by royalty. The arrival of the Casson-Percevals on the top floor is equally a miracle to her.

Frau Fai-Fai's Tale
Oh yes, I can remember – it was the time of the great

Bismarck leaving! One of my sons got in a fight about his leaving. No, not with the husband, Highness – the family weren't in the house then. Another year it was they came. Two more. It's clearer now. I lived in the right side of the house. We shared a kitchen. My man had just died . . . Remember the children, Highness? Indeed, two girls – or had one died? Or was that the puppy? Quite right, Highness, the baby was a boy, my Dolferl, yes! Almost three, he was. The little pet would come over to my side when there was fighting – 'Come to your Frau Fai-Fai, my precious darling,' – and I'd give him an apple and put blueing on his bruises, terrible on delicate young flesh, and just for a little slowness in the potty training. Fights . . . when the wife is so much younger, they happen, don't they? I wouldn't say there was anything to it – no, nothing at all! I can say this definitely! My tenant was a nice young fellow for one of Them – this was what made the trouble, one has to suppose, if he hadn't been one of Them – the Husband was the sort who can't see any good – so, yes, perhaps the young wife chatted over our back wall. Maybe in the kitchen they met, even. Nothing more, I'm sure of it. The Husband was away – that one certainly had no right to talk about carrying on, I can tell you! – but the fight when he came back! Oh terrible, terrible! Through the walls, up and down the street – thrashing the horse, roaring like a bull – drunk as a pig, it goes without saying! *'Hure! Hure!'* . . . Highness, I can't repeat. No, not in your Highness's presence, and your noble children, but the young wife brought her little one to me for the rest of that night. You never saw such bruises! In such places! Is it any wonder he was messed? I cleaned him off and dried his poor little tears, and turned down the coverlet and tucked him in with me like one of my own, and gave him his special ribbon, half-chewed by the puppy it was, but you know, Highness, how they love them at that stage, or a bit of blanket. . . . It was better after that. My tenant left. The police came around about the horse – they put it down, then and there! A bullet right between the eyes before I could stop the little one seeing it. The Husband went away a year to a post without the family. The young wife had another child, a boy again, yes. A fight can be like that. Terrible, like a thunderstorm, but it can clear the air. For a while anyway. My poor baby Dolferl. So hard isn't it, a new one comes when they've had all the attention? And then they moved, the family. How my Dolferl cried when he parted from his Frau Fai-Fai . . . just turned five. . . . And now he's a Leader of the people? The changes in our world! Don't tell me! And God bless *you*, Highness. Bless you a hundred times. And your noble children. . . .

. . . *At Braunau on the Inn:* The Pilgrims reach The Birthplace: House Number 219, on the Town Plan, a hostelry, on the bank of the river, confusingly named the Pommer Inn. The happy family lived there for the first three years, but no one remembers. The Rathaus produces the vital statistics:

Mother: Klara (née Polzl).

Father: Alois.

No mention of drink, or anything else. The Pilgrims return with the Guinea-pig to Linz – the first way-station, Leonding – another pub, the Gasthaus Stiefler, in the Wiegener district. Two fat regulars compete for Mama's cash in boozers' voices.

"Arguing about a skittles game – "

"His boy was outside in the street – "

"Stood up and bellowed once – "

"Sent by the mother as usual to drag the brute home – !"

"Took a last swig of Sturm – !"

"Poleaxed!"

The Linz *Tagespost* gave two thirds of a black-bordered column "to a Friend of Song, worthy Officer of the Government, staunch Companion, Beekeeper, and truest, temperate, and well-beloved Family Man. . . ."

119

"My poor Adolf," said his only close friend, August Kubizek, as the Pilgrims parted on the Linz station platform. "He mentioned only the happy times. I had never imagined, Gräfin, it was so bad."

"We should rejoice, Herr Kubizek; yes, rejoice! From Adversity in childhood, remember, springs so often in history the greatest triumph of the Will."

"Oh Gawd," said Sister, "Eddie, we've been in Hunland too damn long."

Epilogue to the Tales

Mama did not leave it at that. She did not go further in person but hired a firm of notaries, the Brothers Mack, in Linz: "To ascertain the family's roots in the village of Spital, and however farther back you may feel it prudent to enquire."

It took time – there are three villages named Spital – but a thick manilla envelope bound with twine and sealed with blue wax arrived at the Hyde Park house in November. Mama thus became the first outside observer to know about the bastard birth of Old Rhino-hide, the father; about the illegal change of names. Heil Schickelgruber. Don't tell me!

No, the name in the brown envelope that made Mama ecstatic appeared in a photograph of a cemetery in Graz. A tombstone, carved not with a Mowgli mandala, but with a star . . . for one of Them.

The name was Frankenberger. From the house where the grandmother had been a maid. "Oh Children, don't you see? The Master's natural father was a Richard Geyer. The same part Jew. *The circumstances of birth are identical!*' "

120

First Movement
Third Passage

[vibrato]

One hung high an'
One hung low –
Piss-pot Percy's
Jus' won't grow!

. . . In Machem's House: Autumn, '24. Edwin, object of close-harmony and observation on the Footer Fields – and in the showers after. Red Cameron of the bent prick and twisted mind is especially watchful. (Abnormality in the Tyrant's genitalia is par for the myth, children.)

"Playing with it again, Casson-Perceval, you Wagnerian worm. Five laps around the pitch and report to me."

Eddie jogs around the rugger pitch and makes plans of Escape: Brother put them on paper so Sister could meet the train.

"Sorry," she scratched by delayed post. "Attempt will have to be postponed. Mama's gone to be Jungianised some more in Zürich. Fourteen hour squawks – and afterwards your Big Sis is trapped with ghastly female Wyn**man-Hare! Varicose Veins and a *Wart* on its T*t!!! P.S. Can't you play them dirty drinking songs? We do at the Garden. Xmas Parties soon! Usual love, E."

How little she knows. The music room is on the way from the showers. Just the sight of a musician enrages the athletic. But nonetheless, Musik hath charms . . .

121

Yum-Yum:
The School, like all the others, had a Christmas-term "Mikado". Edwin escaped to it. One day, seated at the piano, in rehearsal:

"You're wasted on G & S."

Yum-Yum was standing on stage. He was brunette, with ruby lips. He looked sensitive, in his rehearsal dress, pulled down over his shirt and trousers.

"I have to wear it to get the idea of movement in a kimono. My name's Waring."

"Casson-Perceval."

"I know. Old Stallion-Mares says you've been to Bayreuth. I'm fed-up with Yum-Yum. A chap could go for tuck if you like?"

This proves to be Waring's way of cadging. His father was a clergyman from somewhere in Derbyshire. His grandfather had been a clergyman. His mother, like our Papa, was on the Other Side. The last of her money was paying Waring's fees.

"It's Nietzsche's fault," said Waring, mouth full of tuck – plum cake from Fortnum's sent down to Eddie as an afterthought by Mama with her more important gift, word of the tombstone discoveries by the Brothers Mack. "The C of E's gone broke because God's dead, so I can't possibly chance a parish, like the old man's. That's why I'm interested in your Bayreuth. I'm going to be an actor, or perhaps a writer, I'm not sure yet. What about you?"

"I'm going to find the Holy Grail."

"My arse!" bent-pricked Cameron was going by. "Piss-pot Percy – you can find your name on the board for extra maths."

"About the Grail," P-p-P said to Waring at the next Yum-Yum rehearsal, "the only question is the actual location. Because of Parsifal it seems to have travelled all over the place. But I'm starting at Tintagel as we have a house there."

"That makes sense," said Waring. "How many houses do you have?"

"Only three – since the Zeppelin bombing we're just renting our one in London."

Only 3 . . .

"It is not self-interest, Casson-Perceval, that places your namesake in

122

mortal peril. It is compassion for others that blinds him to prudence. It is love for the oppressed that causes him to rescue damsels in distress in the course of the Quest. He is, however, sadly deficient in these gifts of the Holy Ghost, and thus fair game and easy prey for his temptress of the flesh. Would you not agree?"

Observant little Mares: the Perceval side of the family has changed but slightly through the generations.

And nor –

The Nibelungenlied:

"Of course, Waring, it's only in translation – " (Young Eddie can't yet tackle the Old Hun) "but it was really real. We saw the actual poet's castle: Kürnberg."

"And was it like watching the Ring, C-P?"

"Not too – the book doesn't help there at all. It doesn't match Wagner's version except for Siegfried, the head of the Nibelungs, being stabbed in the back by his best friend Hagen – after fighting a bear. And there is a dragon, but no gods like Wotan, and no Rainbow Bridge. When the Nibelungs come to the Rhine they have to steal a ferryboat by tricking the ferryman to get across. And then Hagen killed him, Waring – for absolutely no reason! If Hagen hadn't killed the ferryman with the magic sword, Balmung, he wouldn't have upset King Etzel of the Huns, and there would have been no need for any of the rest of the prophecy to come true."

"I thought Hagen was a Hun," said Waring.

"The Huns aren't, they're Hungarians. The Nibelungs are the modern Huns – but they were really Burgundians. I think. And at the end there's a tremendous battle between them and the Nibelungs, with oceans of blood. You can just imagine – with all those arms and legs cut off." Eddie showed his new friend the engraving at the frontispiece from the Hundeshagen Codex.

"And after the blood, C-P?" Waring analytically compared two stumps of severed thigh.

"Hagen and the last of his knights retreat and lock themselves up in the Great Hall, and then the Lady Kriemhild, who used to be Siegfried's wife before he was murdered by Hagen, takes the magic sword and chops off his head – Hagen's. And then she burns down the hall before *she's* killed, and they're all dead. Except for the last survivor, a chap called Dietrich, who has to get out to write it all down."

The story ends here:
Such was
The Nibelungs'
Last Stand

... *At Mama's Little Flat:* Out of prison for Xmas! Brother joins Mama & Sister in London, before Porquerolles. The C-Ps always spend the actual holiday there. Aside from the English weather, Mama goes into brown-bottle Depression when the first tree lights up.

The telegram came the day of departure. Telegrams were special then. The Christmas form was bounded by printed green holly leaves and red berries.

> SURPRISE EXCLAM STOP THE MIRACLE HAS BEEN ACHIEVED EXCLAM STOP IN TIME FOR XMAS DOUBLE EXCLAM STOP DO COME WAHN AND SHARE OUR JOY SIGNED SENTA STOP

... *On the Dragon Train:* For the first time the C-Ps travel to Nibelheim by the Night Boat from Harwich to the Hook of Holland. Enormous excitement on the London platform.

"Mama – !" EXCLAMS Ettie! "Eddie! – you simply won't believe! The Tramp Man!"

The real one! Chaplin is riding in the next compartment. Each time E & E pass it, the Little Tramp glares back at his adoring public with a look of extreme revulsion.

"He doesn't have to do the dance with the buns," said Sister, "but he might at least smile for Christmas."

Not knowing then the price of Fame. The being stared at. The pointing. The peculiar letters.

The ferry-steamer arrives at Ostend at the ungodly hour of four in the morning. Then Customs. No one is smiling. As the cold north dawn breaks, they cross the plains of Flanders where millions fell, including Papa, but no one mentions it. The Other Side is one thing. This wet black reality quite another.

124

Out of the blue, Eddie said, "Exactly what *is* being Jungianised, Mama?"

"It is a voyage, Edwin."

"Like now? On trains – you have to travel?"

"Naturally," said Sister, "why do you think Mama goes to Zürich, silly?"

"One does travel, children, but it is through our spirit's landscape." As a sign went by . . . *Brabant*, King Henry's East! "Dear Professor Jung shows us through myth, the archetypes of our several personalities. That is why the Ring for Jungians, even more than others, is so important."

"More than the Nose Man?"

"Doctor Freud, Edwin – while undoubtedly a great Mind – chooses to examine only the baser side of human nature. Dear Professor Jung looks to the stars and shows us the gold among the dross of life. For example, as Wagnerians, all the golden gods and goddesses that are the facets of The Master's immortal personality are ours too. That, children, is our special privilege."

"But I'm not a goddess," said Eddie.

"I will be when I'm Helden," giggled Ettie.

"You know what I mean – and nor was the Master. How can a woman ever be part of a man?"

"That is the complexity of Genius, Eddie dear – but in each of us there is a cousin of the opposite sex. For you, her name is Anima. For Edwina, he is Animus – but it is a complicated subject, which is why one does not come to Jung until the later years."

The godly C-Ps crossed the border of Nibelheim at Aachen.

And then – ?

Upstream: past Cologne's twin spires, and Bonn –

"Only important for Beethoven's birth, but oh, children! We are coming to the most wonderful names: just to say them! *Drachenfels*, the *Siebengebirge*, the *Lorelei* – darlings, for the first time you truly see Siegfried's country!"

The Dragon's Rock, the Seven Hills, where our hero slew the beast and bathed in its blood to be invincible.

"The last dragon of legend, children, lived on almost to the Renaissance – when it had the misfortune to attack a barge carrying gunpowder.

125

I always feel so sorry for that poor dragon, living into the wrong age."

Mama gazed wistfully from the compartment window, as the Olympian ones left the valley of the dragons for old Heidelberg. Then east with the night across Baden-Württemberg into familiar Bavaria, arriving in Nuremberg at ten, too late to travel on. As gods & goddesses, they stayed again at the Hotel Stadtler and departed at a civilised hour.

... *On the Magic Mountain:* The Green Hill is all white.

"Oh, Eddie," sighs Ettie, squeezing his arm, "isn't it simply too perfect. Wahnfried in the snow on Christmas Eve."

"Perfect." Brother & Sister together again – till, "Damn."

"Edwin!" from Mama.

A snowball! On the back of the head. Fragments melting down the neck. Merry Xmas from lisping young Wieland!

A Victorian-English one, transplanted by jolly Frau Winifred back where it came from with Albert. Huge tree, candles, puddings, roast geese – and Old Cosima presiding overall. Special: all in the Family fear that this is the Last Christmas Dinner she will be able to attend. The Parrot-Sisters attend her, hovering (and re-arranging the portions of food already laid out on the Widow's plate by The English Woman).

Real-Siegfried, as top male, sits down at the other end of the table and carves under Father, frowning, in oils. Lady C-P sits to his left, under Schopenhauer. Jolly Frau Winifred to his right, with Nietzsche. Ettie & Eddie act as borders for the Moppets, separating the two camps, completing the happy family circle.

And 2 Outsiders: a local couple. "Our so very close friends," Real-Siegfried said to Mama. "You may remember, Herr and Frau Griesbach, who live in the house only one past my dear sisters?"

A sharp look switched between those ladies.

Mama bestowed her Accepting smile on both Griesbachs. "During the last interval of Meistersinger in July – we met at the Singers' Table in the restaurant."

"Our neighbours' house," said Frau Winifred, "is charmingly set among the trees behind the Hofgarten."

"Mama says – " said Daniella,

"The wind cuts like ice – " from Eva,

"Through that corner – "

126

"Of the Hofgarten."

"There is of course – " a hemmed-in Herr Griesbach diffidently stated – "my motor, dear Gräfin, if you do not care to walk."

"Walk?" said Mama.

"Don't tell me!" Exclammed jolly Frau Winifred! "The Sieg-friedhaus! – don't tell me I was so stupid that I forgot to mention it in the telegram?"

"Renovations," Real-Siegfried smiled warily and sliced another part of goose.

"But naturally," from Mama. "Frau Winifred, we Casson-Percevals have imposed far too much already at Wahnfried these last two years. With the Renovations we shall be happy to stay with your friends."

"I have some extra," said Real-Siegfried. "Now, who shall be for this slice of breast?"

"Renovations," said Sister, inelegantly, through a mouthful, "ain't much of a Miracle. Exclam stop."

It was only then, as plump Mausi said, "He was invited, and we made special presents, but he hasn't come!" – that we noticed the empty place set across the table, between pretty Nurse Emma and Little Wolfi.

... On Christmas Night: At Wahnfried, there were carols, and presents off the huge tree with the top Star touching the glass roof of the two-storey Music Room, and Old Cosima was taken off to her perch by the Parrot-sisters – eyeing The English Woman & Mama, cheek-kissing like Europeans.

"Like schoolgirls," Eddie says to young Wieland – at the same time shoving snow, passed by Mausi, down *his* neck.

"Good night, Frau Winifred," chorus E & E.

"We can't be so formal. You two must call me Aunt Winnie. And, do come back for a nightcap," to Mama, "after I see the little ones to bed. There's so much to talk about ... "

The Casson-Percevals walked under the Bavarian moon, through the squeaking snow of the Hofgarten, past the stark iron rails blackly marking off the Grave, to the Griesbachs' house to go to their unaccustomed Bayreuth beds. It was a comfortable house and the

Griesbachs were comfortable people although they were childless. As a long-married couple they had grown together so that both were short, and grey, and stout, and laughed in the same way, or put out their hands for something at the same moment.

"Humpty and Dumpty," said Sister, "but if we must have landlords – look, Eddie, you can see the Festspielhalle from the window. And the lovely tiled stove! I like this room."

Brother's also had a stove. It was at the end of the landing, separated again from Ettie by a bathroom but with no connecting door. The view from my window was east, the way we had trudged. Through the skeleton trees of the Hofgarten I could see the lights of Wahnfried.

"And old Mr Chamberlain's window next door, over the wall," Mama had arrived to kiss goodnight, "and you can just make out the little Siegfriedhaus, all dark in the moonlight. Oh, children, I know we shall be happy here."

She was happy, in spite of Christmas. Slightly excited even – as a child is, knowing there's still one last, best, secret, super-special present to come.

. . . *Boxing Day:* Another over-long, exciting day, visiting on the Magic Mountain, then back in a Piebald-horse-drawn, jingling sleigh, excessively gilded & carved, that once belonged to the saviour, Unmad-Ludwig, Exclam-stop!

The C-Ps keep warm under real wolfskins. En route, there are Dickens-bits by Real-Siegfried and surprising charades by Mama in English & Hun. The Piebald horse farts loudly. For counterpoint Ettie sings her Messiah-bits; Eddie spoils the effect by being sick over the side of Ludwig's gilding, leaving the evidence horribly visible in the snow.

"That difficult age," a resigned Mama says across the wolfskins. "I shall see the children safely to bed before our nightcap."

"Bed?" Upstairs, Sister was not amused. "*I* wasn't sick – and she isn't an Aunt either. For heaven's sake, Mama, I *am* going to be sixteen."

"We are leaving for Porquerolles tomorrow, Edwina. When the spine is still forming, we need our sleep." Unusually firm.

128

As Eddie relaxed his spine, and put his head down on the pillow he heard the jingling of the Ludwig-sleigh-bells taking Mama back to Wahnfried for her nightcap. The moon shone over the Magic Mountain like the moon of the castle-dream, but the shadows fell safely in the right direction. He slept . . .

The over-eating wakes him: it has worked its way through to the other end. The Griesbachs' house is silent, but his Noises in the lav are louder than the Piebald horse; the flush, the roar of Niagara. In the dark, he pulls up the window to let in fresh air.

Through the trees of the Hofgarten yellow lamplight falls on the snow outside the little Siegfriedhaus that's supposed to be closed for renovations. Two figures walked across the light. Female.

Shivering, Eddie creeps back to his room, wraps himself in an eiderdown, goes to his own window, warm beside the tiled stove, to continue his watch.

"Creeping around – what on earth are you doing?"

Sister, in a hissing whisper. A white ghost at the door.

"God! You frightened the heart out of me!"

"So tell me?"

"I'm watching – Mama and Frau Winifred have gone into the Siegfriedhaus."

"It's supposed to be empty."

"Why?"

"Why what?"

"Why are they in there?"

"Come on."

"What?"

"Idiot-boy! We're going to *see*."

"We'll wake the Griesbachs. Or the servants."

"No we won't. Old Griesbach snores frightfully – and the servants are above us in the attic."

Overcoats and scarves over our nightclothes; carrying our boots down the servants' stairs – to find the back door locked with a bolt.

"It's stuck, Ettie, really, it won't move."

"Spit on it."

"What?"

"Gawd – is that all you can say?"

129

Sister spits. The bolt slides. The door opens, creakless.

"Where did you ever learn that, Ettie?"

"The Door Man at the Garden. Old Jackson says spit's the best for everything – the varnish on a Strad for instance."

Sister's knowledge of the real world is already infinite. The pair pass the Grave. Ettie takes hold of Eddie's arm – not immune to ghosties for all her Garden education. The light from the Siegfriedhaus casts its shadows blackly in the wrong direction.

A cheerful fire burns in the English country hearth. Two English women sit in wingback chairs upholstered in English Paisley pattern. Between them, as the Ladies look at each other in some consternation and take turns stroking a coarse-cropped & brilliantined black head, Herr Wolf, aged 36, is crying.

"Eddie, isn't it marvellous. We've simply got to hear what they say."

"It's none of our business, I think we should leave them alone."

The first Law of School: Men do not Cry.

"You're afraid. What a pansy."

"I'm not afraid, I'm freezing."

"So we must go inside where we can hear and it's warm, silly."

Sister has already spat on the Siegfriedhaus' back door.

"What if we get caught, Ettie?"

"I'll blame it on you. The serving hatch in the pantry will be perfect."

And she dragged me in.

THE PASSION PLAY

The Crying Stage has stopped. Wearing his shabby, dark grey suit, the kneeling *Leader-cum-Orator sits back on his heels. His Pale Cheeks, still wet,* unnaturally flushed. *His Blank Eyes seem to see through the darkness of the pantry hatch* straight to a Boy.

ORATOR

So useless to hide.

BROTHER [*gasping*]

He knows we're in here!

ORATOR

Harsh truth must be faced.

> *The Man walks forward two steps and stares into blackness. The Boy holds breath, squeezes nails into Sister's hand.*

ORATOR

Red Lenin said it: 'What is to be done?'

> *The Two Ladies look after Him, protecting, adoring? The Boy backs away from Those Eyes, up against Sister, as the Orator moves into full swing...*

ORATOR

Released from prison, alone, the Leader goes from place to place...

> *[beginning to pace, to stride!]*

His dear friends meet – seem glad to see him. The little ones have the joy of Christmas...

> *[arms stretching wide]*

Their parents, if they are so lucky, can share love while the Country sleeps...

> *[voice dropping]*

But the Leader? Reviled and ridiculed in the Gutter Press – Traitor! Clown! Putschist! – he skulks through the silent streets of the land he loves...

> *[pace slowing]*

He sees the treasures of that Culture he must save.
He stands before the Shrines of the Master. He hears
that Music. He thinks of those who have heard the
Voice before. Of Caesar, of Henry, Charlemagne, the
Great Fredericks, Iron Bismarck – men of steel! with
mighty armies! – while he has *nothing*! A continent,
an entire civilisation faces extinction, while a convict
– a *jailbird* – sets out to save it with scrawled pages on
the floor! One half of an unprinted book!

THE YOUNG MISTRESS OF BAYREUTH

A *hero* sets out!

[up on her feet!]

Like Siegfried, He shall forge a Ring of Steel!

LADY C-P

He shall print it! We will see to that.

[the bulldog breed!]

The Word shall burn like Wotan's to make a Ring of
Fire!

ORATOR

Oh my so dear noble and gracious Ladies.

[taking their hands]

If one only had men with the strength of women – !

[a kiss for each]

I've just come from Munich. The Party is reduced to
squabbling cackles in the coffee houses!

[anger, yet hopeless]

The sole weapon the common soldier still possesses –
his sword *Nothung*, his poor power of speech – he is
forbidden under pain of death from those Weimar
cowards in Berlin to wield! My dearest friends, a
country to save and I don't even have the use of a car!

YOUNG MISTRESS OF BAYREUTH

A country? Good God! Dear man, believe it – you
have our *world* to save!

*Sombre, the Man again faces a Boy hidden in the
dark.*

ORATOR

No, now I see the way clearly. The time is too soon.
The blood of the fallen in the Residenzstrasse was
not enough. Our Cause needs its single martyr, its
Teutonic Christ. If there must be pain of death, the
Leader must join his brave fellows. His mind is made
up. Tonight, he returns to Munich! Tomorrow, with
the Blood Flag beside him, the Leader shall stand in
the snow of the Feldherrnhalle . . .

   [as He stands]

On the white steps where his brothers fell, arms held
high . . .

   [as His arms are held]

He shall fall to ensure the New Beginning. The paper
Book will be behind him with his iron Word. In front,
flaming Valhalla calls. He has but to cross the
Rainbow Bridge to hear the shining trumpets. One
short step forward –

   [He takes it]

Oh, my dearest, truest Lady friends, the humble man
you call Wolf, tells you: in two days' time, on the eve
of the New Year, I shall end it all!

A COCKNEY WHINE

Gawd! Wot a 'am

   Behind the Boy – his Foul Sister; utterly shattering
   the spell!

BROTHER [*fierce whisper*]

Ettie how could you?

SISTER

Oh really, Eddie – surely you don't think he believes
a word of bosh he says?

BROTHER [*hissing*]

Of course he believes – and shut up or they'll hear!

YOUNG MISTRESS OF BAYREUTH

Never! Never! Never!

   Through the Hatch, all Eyes are Wet, Faces Flushed,

133

*Bosoms Heaving. The Orator stands with The
Mistress's hands gripped in both of His. Not all wet!
The Lady C-P's are fiercely dry. The Boy spots all
the signs of a Fad.*

LADY C-P

No! Herr Wolf, Frau Winifred is quite right. This is
not the way it ends. But how well I understand you.
When my husband was called for all of Us, on the
field at Ypres, for a year not one day passed that I did
not think of joining him. At night, I would hold the
sleeping draught in my hand. At noon, I would stand
on the Cornish cliff at the edge of the sea. I would
think of Senta following her Dutchman. Of Isolde
after Tristan. But, Herr Wolf, I had children. You
have a Nation. More, you have a world-wide
Mission! It is not in our Stars that you should fail.
And you shall most certainly have a motor car.
Winifred, before I take my leave, instead of a
nightcap, I shall make us all a nice cup of tea.
*The Boy's Mama moves to the Pantry Hatch. Her
son is transfixed – by Him.*

SISTER

Don't be an idiot – Mama's coming in here!
*Ettie's seen what she wanted: she drags Eddie out in
time. And then –*

. . . *Six weeks later:* To the mystification of Giant-Putzi and the other
Munich pals, Herr Wolf, flat broke, takes delivery of a gorgeous red
Mercedes, brand new. In it, a month before Our 14th/16th birthday, He
is driven across the frozen Isar, to the Bürgerbräukeller (with the
accidental bullet-hole in the ceiling).

Outside is a turnaway crowd. Inside, 4000 steins crash down to greet
Him in no uncertain terms upon the beerstained tables.

"We shall," says the resurrected Leader, with no false modesty at the
end of a forbidden speech, "crush Marxism in Europe – and *Them* – but
constitutionally."

Remember, children, The Law always looks after its Own. (Except in the Dungeons of Torquemada.)

... At Machem's House: Bleak Mid-Winter.

"Casson-Perceval, you snot – wash your filthy neck. And use a fresh collar. You're wanted by the Head."

His angel of death, red-Cameron. A call to Torquemada is the closest thing to death. Machem, the house-master, deals with all but the most hideous offences.

"It can't be just because of your maths, C-P," said Waring reassuringly, dancing away with the only collar stud. "And it's no use padding your bum, Torquemada makes you take them down. It must be about your German revolutionist. A chap could have the rest of your tuck if you don't come back, if you like?"

The Darling:

The Headmaster – lives childless with his crow wife in a clump of elms, winter bare. A forlorn group of snowdrops has tried to emerge but been trampled at the door. A housemaid, in white cap and black stockings with a hole behind one knee, lets Edwin in.

"The Doctor be waiting in his study. You'm late, young sir."

Torquemada waiting!

"You sent for me, sir?"

"Ah, Casson-Perceval. Yes." The last syllable hisses, like water thrown on the torturer's coals. "So I did, boy. So I did. Come, we shan't bite." Not a royal plural; he has an assistant in the work of searing souls. "You know Mr Darling, of course."

The fat-fingered School Organist, and Darling was indeed his name. Also Choir Master, and he has had his eye on Eddie from Our first arrival. That C-P hair and complexion would look marvellous over a ruff in a sunbeam for a solo. The Darling's smile, like his fingers, was too fat, his thinned hair too sleek. Every Sunday as he played, Eddie sat back in the Lower Fourth form pew to thank God that I couldn't sing a note.

"Yes, I know Mr Darling, sir."

"He has been observing you in Service. I will leave it to him to put his case."

135

Prosecutors for the Crown use an identical tone to paralyze the brain of the accused.

"Thank you, Headmaster," the Darling's voice was suet, melting. "Casson-Perceval, my organ loft is at right angles to the nave. I cannot help but observe boys' behaviour in the pews. However mine is not a disciplinary function. It is enough if with my music – in adjunct naturally, with our Headmaster's inspirational Address – I can assist in raising the youthful spirit even one step closer to the Sublime."

The Headmaster's vulture eyes blink as he stares at the prey.

"You, Casson-Perceval," the Darling continued, "I have to confess I thought at first were asleep – regrettably a not uncommon lapse – until I realised from the rapt expression on your upturned face that it was the ceiling itself which you admired."

"I'm sorry, sir."

"On the contrary, Casson-Perceval, as I reported to our Headmaster, out of some two or three thousand boys you are the first to my knowledge to have even noticed that there was a ceiling to the structure! Art and beauty go hand in hand with Grace. I have heard your composition on the piano-forte. I need an assistant. Would you consider taking up the organ under my direction for the remainder of the term? Our Headmaster has agreed."

"The organ, sir?"

"Take your time, boy," Torquemada's voice changes again, to its usual disagreeable sermon drone designed to put his Boys at ease. "We are not unmindful of the sacrifice involved. You would, I know, have to give up two hours a week of scheduled games."

"Two hours, sir?"

"If I may say so, Headmaster," said my Darling, fatly, "with the School Song at Morning Call – three hours at least."

> *Loud roar'd the dreadful Thunder,*
> *The rain a Deluge show'rs;*
> *The clouds were rent Asunder*
> *By lightning's vivid Pow'rs . . .*

No rain, or snow, or mud for Piss-Pot-Percy! Just dear old Number

7 – from the dear Olde School Song-Booke (with a swing, but not too fast) in 2/4 time, The Bay of Biscay, O!

Or Ash Grove, or Sir Eglamore "That valiant knight, He took up his Sword and He went for to Fight!" or Francis Drake, or Agincourt, or Strawberry Fair, or the Mariners of England, or Yeomen (with animation) depending on Eddie's mood in the morning, and whether he wanted to make his chums stretch to an impossible key (squeaking), or let them off lightly, throats roaring (*Allargando*).

And then the organ! Edwin takes to that glorious sound-machine like Bayreuth's ducks on the River Main. The keyboard transition comes instantly. The stops take a fortnight, the pedals a month. And then lift the Abbey's painted roof with Siegfried's Funeral. Even the rugger neanderthals jogging around the quad have their scrotal hairs tickled by that!

So happy was the lad with the music that he didn't notice the fly in the ointment – sleek Darling hovering behind by the Abbey wall at the rear of the loft. He was Edwin's teacher. It was his duty to lean over his pupil's shoulder with a helping hand. Or make Dorm Rounds, like Aunt Boadicea, after baths, when that heightened, boyish tumescence from warm water is still softly pendulant, yet swollen almost to the size of –

... *At Porquerolles:* Pawel has been invited by Ettie, but refused: "Cramming for Sandhurst, a year early," in his thankyou-but letter. Mama shall join us directly, freshly Jungianised from Zürich, at Toulon. For the first time E & E travel alone together through Europe. Not much of an adventure: Cousin Wyn**man-H honks them to Victoria, then Wagon Lit, straight through, reserved.

The golden days return. Mathilde spoils as usual. For 3 heavenly weeks Brother & Sister swim together, and lie with thighs touching on the golden sand. Eddie plays the piano. Ettie sings. Not Wagner:

"The damn Garden's trying to turn me into a wop," she said, with that adorable lack of selfconsciousness in our prejudice. "Compared with being Helden, Verdi and Puccini's awful mush."

And then – ?

The First Call:

"From dear Herr Siegfried," Mama, on her chaise, reading the post. "For reasons of economy, the Season is to be the same – Parsifal, Ring, Meistersinger – oh my goodness."

"We gave them all that money," Edwin grumbles, "and they're not even going to change those old sets."

"Oh *Eddie*!" Sister rounds in a positive fury for no reason. "Do shut up! Go on, Mama."

"The chorus."

"In The Ring?" from the deranged.

"No dear. Meistersinger."

"Oh damn."

"You're going to sing in it?" Another Brother's penny drops. "At Bayreuth, and you're not happy?"

"I wanted *Helden*. When I tell them at the Garden it just won't be the same if it's Meistersinger. Oh what's the use."

"But you have it!" Hand dramatically to throat. "*Das Waldvöglein!* In *Siegfried!* Oh Edwina, my darling darling!"

And then – ?

Edwin's women fell upon each other's necks, weeping – at a cost of thirty thousand. Sterling.

. . . *At Machem's House: Hot Summer, 1925.* The weather becomes a heat wave. If it isn't the flesh at the pool, or in the dormitory, it's the Darling more helpful than ever in the stifling organ loft. Only little Stallion-Mares in the cool library is an island of calm.

"I've got you in the Cambridge 'Parzival', on loan. Wolfram von Eschenbach's. He moves the Grail search into France – Provence. A footnote mentions association with the Knights Templar at Avignon. Isn't that another of your bailiwicks, Casson-Perceval?"

"At Avignon, sir?" A mere hundred miles off our Wagon-Lit beaten track, and the boy had never known.

"Don't take my word for it. I have the 'Tristan' here, as well. Gottfried von Strassburg – that's Ireland and France. Rather a risqué woodblock as the frontispiece, but considering your continental travels, we scholars won't be upset by a woman's breasts, I'm sure. Do I take it that you want von Strassburg too?"

The Scholar Edwin took both poets to a shaded clearing in the wood behind Machem's House and with the traditional English June backdrop of cuckoo, and the vicious *thwack* of cricket ball on bat, he devoured the Sagas in a single never-ending afternoon.

"You're late for prep," Red Cameron snapped. "Go on brushes and chalk for a week in Lower Fourth. I'm doing you a favour to tell you this, Casson-Perceval, but I reckon I owe it to your pater, from the War. A man can't just fart around with Aesop's fables and music. If you don't buck up in life, and get down to something sensible, you know, you really are going to be no end of a bloody worm."

. . . On the Magic Mountain: Our '25 Season.

"Come along, children, it's time."

Just like Mama – Real-Siegfried, in his yellow stocking socks, with a clap of his hands to his singers, the Most Famous Voices in Europe as well as unknowns like Ettie – that's how he calls them to duty, and up they get from sprawling on the grass, and troop inside to the old rehearsal hall – after checking the blackboard for instructions, just like the Lower Fourth. "Unfortunately, our orchestra has a day off – AGAIN!" Or, "Has the Men's chorus please seen my umbrella?" chalked in Real-Siegfried's generous script. But no matter how difficult, forget about Money. Hold fast to the Vision: never, ever, lose sight of the Goal.

Listen to the Voice. Get caught by the Music, the blood from the Wound, and the Silver Spear, and me & Ettie, and my early dreams, and Sex – as I knew it, single-handed; and Guilt prickling my spine as the Grail descends again in blinding ruby light from the invisible spire of the Temple.

And when the lights go up on *Parsifal* Eddie finds he's been crying and the Adult Wagnerians in the Family Box put their handkerchiefs away and embrace him as one of their own.

And then – ?

Siegfried. No-brain, All-brawn – ideal Tackle material for the First Fifteen, going after poor old roaring Fafner, and then licking some of the dragon-blood from his Helden fingers (which made Eddie feel quite sick) and finally – *FINALLY!* – we get to the part the Casson-Percevals have been waiting on tenterhooks 10 years for:

"Hey! The Nibelungs' treasure now belongs to Siegfried!"

139

Sister's First Line. That was the highlight of Edwina Casson-Perceval's First Season. Later, flanked by Immortals, accepting their tumultuous applause as hers, Edwin's sixteen-year-old sibling is led by Tradition through the Upper Level, and down the Stairs, and all across the broad span of the Lower Level of the Restaurant, and finally ensconced beside her mother, across from her brother, at the Singers' Table. She sits with Wotan on her other side. She sits in her own right. Her part was small but her voice had been flawless.

"A touch low for the role, I must concede," said a smiling Real-Siegfried. "Frau Cosima was right that Fräulein Edwina must for some years really stay more in the mezzo. But oh, so nice tonight as our tiny bit rich, beautiful little wood bird. May I raise a glass?"

... *The Morning After.* Mama is in one of her Brown Bottle depressions. Not a 3-month affair, just a day of closed doors & Melba toast on a tray, with bottled water from Baden-Baden. Ettie rehearses at Final-Dress for the chorus for Meistersinger. Brother could watch but he refuses.

"You really are being stupid, Eddie – you simply can't go through life in a rage over Hans Sachs and Nuremberg."

"You sound just like Cameron – it's Walther von Stolzing that's stupid, with his mushy song."

The Last of – but it's Sister and her songs the fool boy has to come to terms with.

"It isn't too late, Eddie," as he condescended to walk with her for a final-fitting next morning. "I know it's only chorus, but it's the last time for this Festival and there isn't going to be another one for two years. Really, Eddie, it's still going to be a sort of special evening in our lives. Do it for me."

"I'm sorry, Ettie, I've made plans."

"What plans?"

Cornered. A motor coach draws up with a banner on the side like the Dorking charabancs at Tintagel. This one to, "Bamberg Besichtigung." Assorted Wagnerians move purposefully towards it.

"Bamberg – I'm going to visit Bamberg."

"Where's your ticket?"

An elderly spinster marches up the bus steps to the driver. Prepared for anything with both an umbrella and a coloured Japanese paper parasol, she has to be English.

"You buy it on board," said the Boy making a dash for it.

"I bet it'll be appallingly dull," behind his back, in that C-P voice . . . as he leaps with graceful disregard onto the spike of the parasol.

"Fahrkarte?" demands the driver.

Mama could have handled the oaf with ease. Eddie argues until Ettie's gone – and then he got off, and went to the tourists' ticket office as instructed, and paid in advance, both ways, plus one lunch, and the next bus didn't leave for an hour, so he lounged nonchalantly behind the lime trees to be sure Sister didn't see.

. . . *Evening.* The last bus leaves from Bamberg for Bayreuth at seven. It deposits the Rebel outside the Festspielhalle at nine. Through the windows the restaurant is full. Mama never makes a scene in public. Edwin was starved. The Head Waiter met him at the door. Herr Fritz. They know each other. A C-P's credit is good.

"A place for one, Herr Edwin, certainly. But on the upper level, I have to say with regret. If your mother, the Gräfin, had informed us . . . ?"

"That's quite all right, Herr Fritz, I don't have to sit with my mother. I'll just say hullo on the way by" – a casual gesture, one adult male to another, in the direction of the Singers' Table.

It was devoid of Casson-Percevals, or Wagners.

"The Gräfin, your mother," said Waiter Fritz, "has left. With Frau Wagner and your sister, the Fräulein Edwina, also. One believes they are attending at another party? At the Eule. For their friend the radical politician. One understands that he has had published recently, a book?"

Mein Fox'l

The Restaurant of Owls is miles down the Maximilianstrasse: the young gentleman's legs are tired from tomb-marching in Bamberg. Summer night is falling. Dining alone loses its appeal. He trudges

141

across the Festspiel circle for Supper chez Griesbach, taking the shortcut through the laurels between the Parrot-Sisters' and Wahnfried.

"Eddie, come up."

Mausi, leaning plumply from the Wahnfried Nursery window; she wears a horn-helmet for some adventure past Bedtime. Her voice is low, to keep it Secret.

"Not tonight Mausi. I'm tired. I've been to Bamberg."

"You'll be sorry. Wolf's here for a story. He's got a revolver."

"No he isn't. He's with Ettie at the Owls."

"No he isn't. And now you're our prisoner. Wolf, make Eddie be held to ransom."

He stood at the window. His velour hat was pulled down at a rakish angle. He cracked the whip. Really-truly, the one jolly Aunt Winnie gave Him.

"Herr Edwin, you have no choice. Fräulein Mausi insists on a fair capture – besides, I have you covered. Raise your hands."

He holds a gun, blue-black, just right for a Desperado.

"Come inthide through the Garden Room," young Wieland lisped.

Eddie has never received an invitation at gunpoint.

"He needs the password," yapped little Wolfgang.

The gunbarrel holds steady, to make a Prisoner's thinking difficult. The Word obviously has to be Masterly. A portrait of Schroeder-Devrient, the First Brünnhilde, overflows its diaphanous wrappings.

"Valkyrie?" offers the prisoner, without much hope.

"Pass, Friend."

His words. Herr Wolf smiles, and puts aside the blue-black gun. The dogs jump up and lick Him. The Prisoner is escorted to a fortress, of chairs turned upside down, with sheets and blankets for battlements, next to a tray of milk and biscuits. The Desperado shares His ration with the Prisoner.

"Tell us the story of Fox'l again," begged Nickel-Verena, at five, the youngest.

"Mein Fox'l? You want his adventures again?"

The Desperado-Wolf smiles, at ease with five children as He has never been in grown-up meetings.

"We want it," said Mausi. "Eddie's never heard."

"In the trenches! Tell us how you very first got him, Herr Wolf."

"Very well – but just for Herr Edwin, so no one can accuse me of boring their ears off with the same old business. There's nothing worse than a man who tells his War adventures over and over. It was the first year of the War, December – "

"January," said Mausi.

"This is my story, Fräulein Friedelind."

"So shut up," chorused her brothers and sister. "Go on, Herr Wolf."

"December – I know this most distinctly – it had been a quiet week, after Christmas, I had been able even to paint a picture of the village where we were billeted – and two gross fellows caught a trench-rabbit, and ate it – rats, quite disgusting, I agree, but you've insisted on the story. Naturally, I could have no part of that – to eat a rat?! it goes without saying! – but I was fiercely hungry. For an Orphan there are no food parcels from a Mother, or tobacco from a Father, but one does not complain. Life is what Fate sends us, we make the most of it – but it can be lonely in a trench with only the rat-eaters for company. You can be sure there were no lovers of your Grandfather's immortal music among such creatures. So! Imagine our poor Artist-soldier sitting, thinking, 'Mother in Heaven what one wouldn't give for a packet of raspberry tea, or biscuits?' – like these, many thanks, Herr Wieland, I will have another . . . the English make biscuits better than other races, possibly it's the climate, affecting the yeast action. I once lived near a brewer, the fat monster . . . But in the trenches, the wind has risen, the way it does in Flanders' winter – King Henry's Brabant – sweeping over the marshes, making that sound the Soldier never forgets, whistling and strumming in the barbed wire as though God has turned the great globe into a harp, and he huddles there, listening to the shells, going over like cats in the night, and explosions of gas from the dead horses – the bellies swell to the size of barrage balloons first, yes! Just like a giant's birthday party . . . What fun we used to have at birthday parties – I myself was blessed with a wonderful childhood. Even a family without financial resources can find fun where there's love – when the Herr Father comes home after work, and offers a ride in a

143

carriage out to see the new house they shall be moving to, with fine walnut trees, or perhaps a quince, to make preserves. So you can imagine, a private Soldier sitting there . . . no packages from home – no home to go to! – quite alone in the world, but that's the way it is for the Artist, the gifted soul – when over the harp noise of the wire and the shrieking of shells . . . he hears a whining. A scratching . . . and out of the filth of the exploding dead horses comes – a black and white object! An English Fox terrier, can you believe it? And this is not the impossible part: the gallant creature carries in its small jaws, through the Devil's Orchestra of shot and shell – a bar of English chocolate! Yes! Tasting of mothballs, but beggars can't look a gift horse in the mouth, as they say. *Mein Fox'l* – what else could I call him? Like our Master's gallant Robber, at his side in the Holländer's storm, the noblest friend, the bravest – the smartest! I actually taught him to climb ladders! He'd have used the Colonel's trench periscope given half a chance – and done a better job of observing with it! An English dog. And here we all are – both sides together, our two races, the finest possible partnership, or mixture, whatever you want to call it. He was with me for two years, right through the thick of the worst of it, I told him everything – how the Voice warned me to move before the shell landed, you all know that story. But the tragedy, the greatest of my life! He was stolen by some arch-villainous swine – I know, it makes us cry, even to this day. So that he couldn't be with me when the next Word came. Ah well – I have a fine Alsatian now – it's necessary, Red bandits! One has to travel at night, incognito, with the gun: please God I never have to use it – but my Alsatian isn't a Fox'l . . . There could only be one Fox'l ever in a man's life – My apologies, all round – it seems I've taken the last biscuit, and Herr Edwin and I were to be with his so-extraordinarily gracious and gifted ladies at the Eule, an hour ago! However could you young people let me rattle on?"

. . . At the Restaurant of Owls: Owls of all names, and shapes and sizes, their round glass-eyes like so many spectacled Carl Jungs, stare down from their corner perches at us mice, foraging for Wagnerians' opera gossip, or Bayreuth's strong-hopped beer, or Bavaria's black-blood sausage, across the plain unvarnished beechwood tables, with Mama, &

Sister, & jolly Auntie Winnie, & Eddie – He joked, He was witty, He drank a toast – in champagne! – to all of us, after we toasted the Book.

He presented her Copy to Mama.

Below the Dedication to the Fallen.

That Day, outside the Gerbers',

In the Residenzstrasse:

And then

His

Signature

... sloping down, and to the right,

And then – her lucky Number, in an inner circle:

And then – ?

Mama said the opening was deeply moving, and He dabbed at His eyes – authors believe anything – and Aunt Winnie exclaimed, "We've sold 8000 copies!" and Sister said, 'That must be a record for something so dreadfully dull as Bavarian politics," and Brother said, "God, can't you *ever* be tactful?"

But He thought it was *hilarious*. And then He danced with Mama, when a gypsy fiddler came – just like Papa – a Viennese waltz, swooping all over the place, and He said again, how embarrassed He'd been, bumping into the table at the astrologer's.

And then – all the Restaurant crossed hands, beneath the Owls, like Auld Lang Syne, but for Hans Sachs' chorus.

And then, Saying good night – on the corner outside the front door of the Eule. He had the new car, Mama's scarlet present, with another Mowgli-man driving, and He was thanking again, when a brewer's team came clattering out. The dray was empty, the great horses wanted to get home for the night. One of them slipped in a pile of muck at the alley corner, and skidded sideways, and Aunt Winnie said, "Herr Wolf, are you all right?"

He was flat against the building. His face blanched.

"He saw horses killed in the war," Eddie said, after.

... At Berchtesgaden: in August, 1925.

"Herr Wolf has invited us to call, by the way ..."

The C-Ps arrive by hired car. This time the landau top is down. The sun beats on bare gold heads. Mama's is screened by a white silk scarf: like Isadora's, it floats, flirting with Death and the rear spoked-wheels . . .

"The Pension Moritz – this is the place, children. In the care of a Frau Meissner at the top of the hill."

Following a lane with grass and wild flowers between the tracks, the C-Ps chug upwards into the blue. A handyman tacks up a falling vine.

"Him? You'll have to ask the Widow, Lady. She's up there now. In the cottage past the chickens at the back. And if the billy's out, please to close the gate behind – you'll smell the old brute, yes?"

A fence of two bleached poles zigzags from the henhouse, off across the grass. Chickens cluck. A bell jangles.

"Pe-ew!" from Ettie. "It *does* – like billy-oh."

An enormous one – chewing sideways over his beard and staring at the C-Ps through the poles with parrot-yellow eyes.

Mama said, "It has an amiable expression but goats have a tendency to eat silk. Eddie dear, knock on Herr Wolf's door, and ask if he could be so kind as to remove this beast to a safe distance."

There is a cottage beside the henhouse, the same size but with curtains. Billy stands between. Eddie looks at the goat. Billy looks at Eddie's summer linen suit. Eddie squ-e-e-z-es slowly through between the poles . . . Billy moves one pace, two –

"What a scrumptious view," said Sister. "Go on, Eddie, he won't bite."

Eddie makes a dash for the cottage and up the two wooden steps and crashes into the ample stomach of the Widow Meissner coming out the other way and both gasp and bounce apart and Eddie jumps in through the open door. Billy pees on his front feet and rubs his beard in it.

"He has had to be in Munich since one day," said the Widow Meissner, "with Herr Hess about his book."

Vol 2:

A stack of Manuscript, weighted down with a sawn-off brass shell-casing, rests on a plain table. There is the old typewriter, a wooden chair for the Writing, an over- stuffed red divan, and one of those hugely ugly sideboards that Huns love, and a stove, and through the curtains the glorious view from the top of the world.

Edwin glances at the Top Page.

Wolf's Lecture

... from our Courtrooms events sometimes permit a horrible insight into the inner life of our fourteen and fifteen year-old youths! Who will wonder that, even in these circles, *Syphilis-the-Destroyer* seeks its Victims?! All public life today resembles a hothouse of *Sexual Stimulants*! One has only to look at the menus of our Cinemas Vaudevilles – all must be cleaned of the symptoms of a *Rotting World!* Personal Freedom steps back in the face of our Duty to Preserve the Race! The *isolation* of the incurably Diseased, barbaric for those stricken, is a *blessing for contemporaries* and Posterity. The temporary pain of a century will redeem millennia from suffering. Otherwise, the Prostitute, outwardly cured, will be let loose to prey again on the rest of Mankind ...

The next page under the shell-casing is only a stodgy Teutonic exposition, "Orientation, Or Eastern Policy ..."

Edwin, shaken by Syphilis-the-Destroyer, spies another open door. It leads to a second room, only half the size of the first. Whitewashed like the henhouse. Done recently. An outline on one wall shows where a crucifix has been taken down. Below the outline of the Cross, His Mother (on a painted snap, by a primitive in oils – tight-haired, with those same strangely staring eyes) and a truckle bed with an embroidered coverlet, folded back. No rug on the floor. A plain white-enamelled chamber pot has a small chip where rust stains show through. In the far corner, a Mowgli flag, homemade, with a small rip, has similar stains. Tied onto the bed-rail is a green velvet ribbon. Next to it, a purple. Above that, a photograph: *Liebe, Mitzi*. Under it, a bookcase – Campaigns of Caesar & Naughty Stories (with *incredible* Drawings!) by Schroeder-Devrient, 1st Senta (also Pornographatrice!).

"He will not be back tonight," calls the Widow Meissner, pointedly;

"I will take the message, yes?"

"We're from England," Eddie says, "perhaps I could write it down?"

Peasants are always impressed by the magic of the written Word. Edwin used His typewriter, the first Wolf-Machine:

August 25, 1925

Dear Herr "Wolf":

On our way home to Britain we
came, & saw, but could not be
conquered by Caesar at Berchtesgaden
today! The view however is quite
extremely fine. Thank you for being so
kind to my Mother & Sister after The
Meistersinger at the Restaurant of
Owls. They are presently outside with
the goat but send their sincerest
regards, as do I.

E.R.B. Casson-Perceval

PS. I hope you will excuse the use of
your machine & good luck with the
2nd part of the Book!

E.R.B. C-P

"What on earth were you doing in there?" demanded Sister. "We shall positively *reek.*"

And, turning away, tore the skirt of her dress. Not a big tear.

Behind his beard Billy's expression is even more humorous than before. Behind his forelegs he has developed a huge erection. Bright crimson, dripping. Edwin, making instant mental comparisons to his considerable disadvantage (and after the bookcase) looks away vastly embarrassed. Mama, Ignores It. The Honorable Edwina stares openly while pretending to examine her torn dress. The peasant Widow Meissner – takes the action appropriate in such circumstances and hits the offending organ sharply with her broom.

The Dress Shop:

The "Modenschau Reiter" has a bell that jangles, like the goat's. Edwin

148

follows Mama & Sister – nonchalant and hanging back, making a show of being bored.

But instead of Knickers on display, there were dresses pathetically trying for this year's style with last year's, on two old mannequins. There were hats in a window, covered with sun-faded lace. There was the smell of steam and women's cheap cologne and sweat.

"Gnädige Frau, Gnädiges Fräulein – can I please to be of help?"

The Shop-Girl is Ettie's age, Ettie's height, with Ettie's hair – but her breasts, in her Shop-Girl's dress, are fuller than Ettie's, her hips too.

"This tear in my daughter's frock," said Mama. "Do you suppose that it might be repaired as one waits?"

"But of course, Gnädige Frau! At once!"

And soon the repaired C-Ps leave Berchtesgaden and a sexy shop-girl who, carefree and waving from her dress-shop door to a shy English boy thinking of a goat's crimson erection, signs herself to Him, with her purple ribbon,

Liebe, Mitzi . . .

. . . At Machem's House: Adolescence ends. The years compress. Eddie touches Waring's Thingee – after a rehearsal for Gondoliers immediately before the end of term. He gasps – and touches back, *and the Darling almost caught us!*

In the thrill of Guilt that autumn term, Scholar Edwin rereads Parzival, and moves on to Sir Gawain and the Green Knight, and the Song of Roland.

In Sister's Letters:
There is to be no Festival at Bayreuth in '26, but there will be a Summer Rehearsal for the '27 Parsifal and the obligatory Ring –

"And there's no proper part in it for me," was her face-to-face reaction, naked in the bath, on London half-hols. "Damn it, Eddie, there's got to be more to life than stupid Valkyries and Norns."

"Herr Siegfried's given you one of each – " exchanging soapy places – "and you are just a beginner, Ettie. Isn't that pretty good?"

"After Woodbird, I should be moving up." Drying between her thighs. "It's this damnable low voice of mine." And walking down the stairs, to dine, "If I'd been a boy like you at least I could have had myself cut."

                               The Pension Moritz
My dear Herr Edwin:
   From this Altitude, the View of the
World indeed is clearer! Volume 2
goes well. Tell your dear and noble Mother,
"One dreams of Tristan!" and to your so
very charming and talented Sister, also, my very
best wishes. And to both gracious Ladies, my
profound apologies for the Widow
Meissner's Goat! One understands it ate
a Frock?!!
                       Your Friend,
                         Herr Wolf

... *Easter, 1926: Sur le Pont d'Avignon.* Ettie sings it as the C-Ps walk along the ruin to the tower at its limit, then on the new structure downstream all the way across – to say we've been by foot over the Rhône. For a Boy who wants to rob tombs the walk is History. The Romans bridged here. Invading Nibelung-Huns burnt it down. Charlemagne built another. The Knights Templar marched over that one on their way to gain the Holy Land. *Quincunx, and Pentateuch.*

"I believe, Eddie dear, that it was also a pattern often used to plant orchard trees?"

"Exactly, Mama. If I can find five yews forming a quincunx here in Avignon, and if they're old enough, the Grail is buried under them."

There are 5 planted behind the Abbey of St Benezet and Mama always believes in Starting At The Top. The Community proves to be Cistercians. Their Abbot is tall, sixtyish, with graceful hands and a grey fringe.

"From Porquerolles? And Cornwall? We had a House in Plymouth until the Dissolution. And what may I do for you, Comtesse?"

"For my son, Monseigneur, he is searching for the Grail."

"Le Graal?" The Abbot looks down at the Scholar with a half amused but potentially recruiting gaze.

"Yes, Holy Father. One legend has it buried under five old yew trees – in a pattern like the one behind your abbey."

"Ah yes – and do you feel Le Graal is but a legend, my son?"

150

"No Holy Father, I think it's real – but lost. Like the city of Troy. I'm going to find it, if it takes my whole life. Like Heinrich Schliemann, I'm going to find it."

"I wish you well, my son. Comtesse, do not distress yourself. Faith is rare in our age. Your boy has embarked upon a worthy search. At the end of it he may wish to come back to us and our yew trees. In the meantime, perhaps Joseph of Arimethaea – "

"The Grail Keepers! The Fisher Kings!" the Scholar yelps . . .

"Holy Father?" Sister groaned. "Oh Gawd."

Mama made a donation large enough to cover the imposition. The Abbot raised his hand in blessing as we left.

. . . *Off-Season:* So the sun shines on Bayreuth, hot as Porquerolles. Real-Siegfried has a piano brought outside and his singer-children rehearse under the lime trees. Ettie sings her 3rd Norn and Valkyrie-parts on pitch, but barely. Twice a day, at Kaffeeklatsch time, Eddie is allowed to stand in for the accompanist.

. . . *The Camargue: 1927.* Now, the world has found it: then, it was still a secret place of wild white horses and cowboys dressed in chaps, with lariats, just like Karl May's Teuton vision of America's Wild West.

The cowboys are called *gardians* and wear brown cloth-trousers, stiff as leather, and a black coat lined with velvet, and brilliantly coloured shirts and woollen belts, *tailos*, yards long, and they herd their cattle with strange pronged *tridents*, cusp-shaped with a point in the centre like a junction of the Cross with a new moon. The gardians' women ride behind them on small folded blankets and can travel like that for miles, just holding on. Strangest of all are the gypsies, the *Gitanos.* Every spring, they gather mysteriously in the Camargue – in the town of Saintes Maries de la Mer – where an ancient Templars' cross on the foreshore marks the point at which Mary Magdalene set foot, with Lazarus, from the dead, and Mary Jacobee, the mother of St James the Less, and Mary Salome, the mother of James and John. But the Gitanos take no notice of any of that. Like the Tannhäuser pilgrims, but silent, they travel from points all over Europe to chant in worship of their patron, Saint Sara, the Egyptian.

"Remember, children, Superstition has its place – for primitives like our dear Mathilde – but the fascinating thing about these gypsy creatures," said the children's mother, "is their teeth. When compared with those of the Red Indians they give us proof positive of lost Atlantis."

"Gawd," gloomed Sister, "Eddie, Atlantis has to mean another fad."

But from the moment the Scholar saw the Templars' Cross and heard the tale, I knew, unshakably, it was no superstition: this spot of salt marsh was the starting point.

. . . In the Organ Loft, keeping warm, Waring & Eddie touch again. It seems the safest place – who would ever think of looking for lust in an abbey?

The Darling caught us, as they say, red-handed.

It can be no surprise. The Organist had been listening – and watching, and breathing, and leaning over extra close – since our Gondoliers' rehearsal before Christmas: Pederasts Always Know.

"Oh, deplorable! Unspeakable! And even on the keys!"

Too bombshelled to note the Darling's own considerable flush and disarrangement of Dress.

"And Waring! One had expected better things from a Church family, but as the younger it is easy to be led astray. Return to your house at once, and wash those fouled hands boy. And button your trousers! Leave this odious Casson-Perceval to me."

Alone with full-sized male arousal in an organ loft, the Darling's face is glans-coloured. Sweat slides down his brow. His eyes, bulging, cannot leave the still swollen object Edwin is desperately concealing with his handkerchief.

"Remove it, sir! Let us see the full nature of your defilement in the house of our Lord!"

Oh please, yes let's! The Boy's prepuce is still stretched back. A last milk-drop drops onto the Darling's reaching suet hand.

"These things happen, Casson-Perceval, dear boy. With an aesthetic nature. Do not be alarmed. The Headmaster need not know."

Dear boy? Need not?

Fat fingers inside flies, fondling. Edwin submits, at the thought of Torquemada . . .

On March the 1st, in Hols: Mama has had a flaming row with Wyn**man-Hare downstairs. "You are a solicitor. Those are my instructions. Edwin is a musician. I have no intention of speaking to any Headmasters. I never approved of that dreadful school. My son has no need of any but a musical education. I shall take him South with Edwina, to recover in the sun."

. . . *On Our Island:* Mathilde refuses to sleep under any other roof while her pet requires nursing. She moves back to her place off the kitchen. Eddie moves back with Ettie, in our old nursery room. For the first time in five years, I had my tower dream again . . .

No cold Mistral blew. The C-Ps sat out on their terrace for breakfast. A pelican splashed. Eddie drank a first curative cup of calf's foot jelly with wine. Mama rose and went into the villa.

"It must be something early for our birthday," said Eddie.

But the package was too flat and small to be shared.

"Jewellery, for me," said Ettie.

"Cold," said Mama, undoing the first end-flap.

Eddie said, "A book."

"Warmer." The second flap.

"Snaps," Ettie said. "An album of my first pictures from Bayreuth?"

"Cooler."

Eddie's turn. Mama pulled the ribbon. She had the Fad look in her eye. The shape was –

"You've written a book! – you're an author, Mama – "

"Hot."

"It's a family history!" screeched Sister. "About me – and you, Eddie. All of us."

At that moment, as Mama turned the mystery-book over, even before Eddie saw the gothic script in gold, I knew. It was the colour: Brown. You have to be a Wagnerian for the connection. The Master kept a diary from time to time. The earliest pages were recorded haphazardly in a "Red Book", but after Cosima got hold of him things were better organised. The Wagner Life was presented to the world in the first "Brown Book". In front of us was the second. Entitled, by our romantic Edwardian:

Wolf Child
A New Leader For Our Times!
The Early Life

"Naturally, children," blushing with virgin authorship, "it cannot be considered in any way complete, but it is at least a first small step on which others may build."

Lambach was there, it goes without saying, and Passau, and Braunau, plus the mein Gustl stories from the Guinea-pig, Kubizek, written out on the paper from the Rhapsodie Hotel, but that was only the start. The illegitimate family history and the possible grandfather Jew hide.

"Are you really sure that people are going to want to know about the family part, Mama?"

"The more Pedestrian the background, the more truly remarkable is the rise of Genius. That is the point, Edwin, which the future reader will see. We are going to Venice for your birthday, by the way."

THE BLACK GONDOLA

... *At the Palazzo Vendramin-Calerzi.* The door to a Palazzo suite opens.

"Signor, Signorina – " a Venetian doctor stands, all gesturing hands and Latin grief. Unable to spell it out. "I am for the police – it is with the most deeply profound – dear children, be brave. Your noble mother, *si*, the Contessa Casson-Perceval, alas . . ."

"I'm afraid it's true." Behind the Venetian doctor, Our Man from the Consulate: tall, clipped, doing the Decent Thing by keeping a Tight Rein. Equally incoherent in his British way, "Wretched Gondolas . . . unstable . . . March winds . . . the tides . . . Really, most fearfully sorry . . . Arrangements . . . Informing . . . Of course, simply anything at all that we can do . . ."

She was gone to the Other Side. There was nothing anyone could do – but they did try. The Venetian police spared us identification until she was fully "prepared". The Consulate man was decent, deeply kind in his reserved way. When the preparation was complete, he took us to see her.

Orange Blossom & Mignonette. In her gleaming chestnut coffin she looks as she would have wished to look, as Mama in Death. And her age? My ageless darling, faddish, irreplaceable mother when she died for *Him*, was only 38 . . .

The tactful police and the Consulate, sparing E & E, blame it on the black Gondola. They make no mention in their various reports that the craft was tied to the iron rings set into the stone blocks of the canal wall. There is still the slippery weed and sewage on the stairs, and the wind and rain and rising tide. No need to jump to conclusions: There is no *proof* that because of a letter by furious hand from Munich, your mother cast herself, with her portmanteau of priceless rejected biographical notes, and her personal proof-copy of the Brown Book, into the Grand Canal in front of the place of death of Richard Wagner. No proof at all that for *Him*, she destroyed herself and her two-year labour of Love.

Another telegram arrives via the Consulate:

> WILL STATES CREMATION CMA ASHES SCATTERED
> BAYREUTH STOP DEPARTING LONDON THIS DATE INTEND
> TAKE CHARGE ARRIVAL VENICE SIGNED WYNHARE ENDS
> STOP

"Oh no he bloody isn't," said Sister. "If Mama wants to be burnt we'll burn her and take the damn ashes ourselves. We belong at Bayreuth and he doesn't and never ever bloody shall!"

"But what about the money – Cousin Wynchman-Hare looks after it?"

"Only your half – for two more years. Mine belongs to me already. The telegram says 'cremate' – it doesn't say when."

Finding dry ground for any task is difficult in Venice. The crematorium is disguised as a cupola'd chapel in a peaceful glade of mossy graves to the north where the city eventually finds high ground. Although Mama is Wagnerian, the Consulate provides a C of E clergyman: many English have drowned in Italian waters, not only Mama & Shelley.

The lid closes down on Her face forever. The chestnut coffin rides over the rollers. The doors of the furnace are bronze, Italianate, with cherubs. Ghastly fat pig-children dancing at the mouth of hell!

Edwin rushes out into the graveyard. Birds sing. The white cupola shines over blossoms on a tree. A son falls on his knees, eyes blinded with tears. Not blind. I saw her smoke ascending in the still Venetian air. Beloved by artists.

155

The Return:

Ettie & Eddie took their mother north in an Italian urn of marble sculpted so thin that when it was empty you could see through it to see she wasn't there. Aunt Winnie and Real-Siegfried both were out to meet us at the Bayreuth Station. The Lohengrin swans were back as well. Winifred kissed us. Siegfried squeezed my arm. Ettie held the thin urn as we rode in their car. They talked of the New Season. It was, I agree, what She would have wished.

"You'll stay in the Siegfriedhaus," said Senta-Winnie, "and we'll plan the future. This is just one more transformation. We'll have tea first. The last thing on earth she would have wanted is for anyone to be grim."

E & E unpacked their suitcases in the little Siegfriedhaus. Daffodils were budding in the flowerbed outside the window. We had tea in the Wahnfried drawing room, with cream buns Edwin couldn't eat. The Parrot-Sisters arrived twittering in black-feathered dresses they must have worn for their father's funeral. The Orphans are taken to see Cosima, frail as a black bat's wing, propped up with pillows. Almost blind as one, too, but she could hear, and her mind was sharp. Eddie kissed her hand. She said, in her thin voice with that trace of Prague, "Remember, my dear children – Valhalla calls its fanfares early."

The Rose Bed:

Out in the Hofgarten. In front of the Grave's black iron railings roses in a horse-manured bed are pruned, waiting for another summer, another Festival.

He was waiting at the edge of the trees. He held His velour hat over His heart. "We have both lost a mother. Come, ride with me."

He had as good as killed her! Ashes in shit was Her Valhalla.

. . . Yet there are tears in His eyes as hot as mine. Through the trees of the Hofgarten, the red Mercedes She gave Him is parked with its engine running on the road beside the Griesbachs' house. Gaunt Hess is once again the chauffeur, but He opens the back door for me. I climb in on to the red leather seat. He sits beside me and closes the door. Fräulein Anna lets in the Mercedes' gears. The sun shines through a shower making a rainbow spanning Bayreuth's bridge across the Roter Main. Behind us, a quartet – cello, viola, two violins – plays out Her love-death Liebestod. The house gardener, with canvas leggings around

156

his knees, reaches with a terrible cultivating hoe. The man we call Wolf looks into a Boy's swimming eyes and says in the guttural-nasal, Klingsor-magical voice that the tens of millions who, once they hear it, are unable ever after to refuse:

"Your own copy of my Book. One of only a dozen I've had specially bound in leather."

And takes my right hand in both of His, and squeezes it hard.

Like a soldier.

Over the top!

BEERDIGUNG

A Requiem

Der Alptraum

The Nightmare File

The case of **A** being
**The Summary Analysis
of a Battlefield Schizophrenia**

Pasewalk, October 13, 1918
From the Examination on Admission
The soldier A is of medium height, (176 cm) slim build
(68 kgm). Pulse 72. Pressure 130 systolic (rapidly rising
to 170 in the act of examination): 86 diastolic. No sounds
of abnormality to the great vessels or chambers. Minor
mustard blistering on the cheeks. Slight congestion of
the lungs. No blood in the sputum. Tonsils scarred, vocal
chords unimpaired. Mute since arrival from the Front,
apparently blind. No injury observed to either cornea or
lens. No concussion to the skull. Genitals normal. No
signs present of venereal disease. An anal fistula, in
abeyance. Diagnosis: battle-field hysteria.
Ward Orderly's Instructions: Bed rest.
Any change to be reported.

From the Ward Orderly's Log
October 14/26
No change in A's condition. Not eating. No B.M.

159

Indicated belly pain. Laxative administered by suppository.

October 27

No B.M. but A sat up. Still blind. Belly pain worse. Enema administered. B.M. resulted.

October 28

Belly pain eased. A spoke for first time. Enema requested and administered.

November 10

Enema daily. A now has almost normal vision. Eating well. Good patient. Eager to help on the ward.

November 11

Armistice announced. A relapsed completely.

November 12/14

No change – until 20.00 hours. A began shouting. Would not stop. Given a sedation by Laudanum.

21.00 hours: Further sedation. No effect. Duty Medical Officer informed.

First Clinical Observation

November 16, Midnight

By chance, the writer was on duty. Upon arrival at the bedside, A's posture was the immediate symptom of interest: almost inert, varying between slight spastic tremor or catatonic rigor, yet throughout, and despite the extreme sedation, the hands flexed convulsively. Speech was only slightly slurred – even perhaps, more rapid than normal. The central theme of the disquisition was a harangue against the "conspiracy" of the German General Staff and International Finance for making him blind. An unusual "Identification with the Aggressor" for a wounded Lance-Corporal !

Add to this the hands: markedly feminine; the nails of the fingers badly bitten. The face was clean-shaven, nondescript, with no mark of character set although his age from the record was but one year short of thirty. His documents revealed another fact of clinical significance:

160

A was a volunteer, not a conscript, had served continuously at the front for four years, received awards for gallantry, yet never been promoted *beyond* Lance-Corporal.

The pupils of the eyes responded to light, but the lids did not blink when the writer's (hereafter, the analyst's) hand was brought suddenly close – confirmation of A's powerful, self-induced, hypnotic suggestion, even over the laudanum. It seemed probable that the immediate root of the blindness was a fear that, with the war now over, A would be forced to return to his pursuit as an artist, at which, presumably, he had not excelled as he had volunteered for the dubious life of an Army private at the outbreak of hostilities. Hence, too, the extreme hostility now directed at those same Army authorities for "letting him down."

This thesis was suggested to A.

"He never wants a boy to be a painter," was the reply. The voice was high-pitched, self-pitying, immature, an adolescent's.

The analyst enquired if by *he*, A meant his father? Clearly the most probable deduction. A responded:

"*Scheisskerl!* Mind his spear!"

The anal-phallic allusion was followed by a wild shriek and a cataleptic thrusting of the tongue, and arching of the neck, while the eyes rolled up in the head towards a corner of the room behind the bed. This position of great discomfort was maintained for a full minute. The hands clutched convulsively at the buttocks in a manner half-stimulative, half protective. That A's aggressive fears had been transferred, if not to the actual father, then to some "father figure", and that *He* was imagined to be present in the corner was starkly evident.

The analyst asked, if A saw this person now, could he describe him?

A replied, "Hagen swine! *Dolchstoss!*"

Dolchstoss, meaning, "stabbed in the back". With this

161

extraordinary phrase A's whole personality was changed. The voice was now harshly *masculine*; the eyes flashed. He sat up in the bed and glared around him. It was decided by the analyst to explore this apparent duality of the psyche, and that a record should be kept of the exchanges in shorthand notation. Further physical testing was also immediately applied to determine at once both A's comprehension and vision.

Transcription of the First Session

Analyst   Can you count the number of fingers of my left hand ?

A   Three you shit-head moron ! – do you think I'm crazy ? – forgive me, Herr Hauptmann-Doctor. The man knows. It's too much.

Nota: "A-Masculine", the "strong" personality as abruptly vanishes. He reverts to "A-Feminine", the adolescent. His body sags. He falls back, covers his face with his hands, begins to sob.

Analyst   What is too much ?

A   If he tells, you will say the man's crazy.

Analyst   My task is to help him to get well.

A   Like last time.

Analyst   Tell me about the last time.

A   A boy was delivered to his death-sentence ! Well, not by you, but another doctor – a young man can't trust anyone. Herr Hauptmann, there was poison in tonight's supper.

Analyst   Rank is not required between us. Tell me about the other doctor. Was he in a hospital ?

A   No, Herr Haupt – it was in Spital. But it would never have happened if a mother didn't send her son to Steyr. That filthy old garret – her boy has to sit up to all hours shooting at rats ! The size of horses. Disgusting ! Their rat-droppings are all over in the mornings. That's what comes of living with Italians. Of course they call themselves Austrians – Cichini ! – the sound of shit ! If

162

that cow of a woman would keep coal in the scuttles it would never happen. No one can imagine what it's like to see blood coming out when they're coughing . . .

Nota: A takes his hands away from his face. Examines the palms. Shudders (*Mark the self-protective shift of Tense, and into the 3rd Person.*)

Analyst   It must have been a great shock for the man to see blood come back in his sputum from his gassing.

A   One of *Them* invented gas – that's typical ! Mass death and *they* make money out of it ! November criminals !

Analyst   What time of year was it when the boy's mother sent him to the town of Steyr ? How old was he ?

A   Fifteen, in the autumn. Death's time. The boy can't speak then either, from catarrh of the chest, but they never listen at the school, those teacher-swine – they send him home. To the rats. A boy writing poems to rats !

Analyst   He wrote poetry – can you remember any of the poems ?

A   All ! – a poet remembers all his works, in the same way the artist sees all his paintings. Or musicians. Do you think Wagner couldn't remember every note ?

Analyst   I meant, recite one.

A   So they arrive at home, and sadly,
For then have been the hours forgotten !
Now comes his wife, poor man so rotten –
And cures his wounds with a beating, gladly !

Analyst   An unusual metre – were there more verses ?

A   No one wants to read them. The page is torn out of the guest-book register.

Analyst   That must have made the poet unhappy.

A   The artist, in this case.

Analyst   There was a picture too ? – describe it for me.

A   It was charcoal. A sketch.

Analyst   I have a pencil. Can you draw it for me ?

A   A sketch done by a boy ! Barely sixteen. How can that matter ?

163

Nota: But A takes the pencil. The rendering is from a child's perspective. The male image is a small man, wearing a helmet. A woman, much bigger, beats the man with a stick — excessively large. Her breasts are huge. In relation, the heads of both figures are tiny. *(But the eyes are detailed.)*

Analyst   Was the boy's father alive when he was sent away to school in Steyr?

A   No.

Analyst   How old was the boy when the father died?

A   Fourteen.

Analyst   You must remember him well.

A   Every hair on his head.

Analyst   Describe it for me.

A   His head?

Analyst   Or anything else about him.

A   What can a boy say about his father? He was respected by everyone. 'Herr Oberoffizial' they address him — this is insisted on.

Analyst   Obviously the boy admired his father greatly — even though he was a little man.

A   Little? He's big! Isn't it clear from all the buttons? His moustache is so wide it won't fit the shaving cup when Alois brings it in the mornings!

Analyst   Alois — a man-servant?

A   Servant? Hah! My dear Doctor, the Herr Oberoffizial was an inspector, not the Emperor! Alois was the oldest son before the coward ran off after a small whipping.

Nota: The tone has shifted back from obsequious-defensive to imperious-aggressive.

Analyst   The whipped Alois was your older brother?

A   A half-brother.

Analyst   Is he still living?

A   Who knows? He went to England. *They* may have gassed him too.

164

Analyst	Did you have any other brothers ?
A	Edmund. He died.
Analyst	At what age ?
A	He was a baby.
Analyst	You were the son in the middle. And how old were you when Edmund died ?
A	Eleven.
Analyst	And when he was born ?
A	Five, six – what does it matter in a large family when one child is born !
Analyst	A large family – you had other brothers ?
A	Sisters. For God's sake !
Analyst	It upsets you to talk about your sisters. What are their names?
A	Dead – like Edmund and Otto, he died before I – there is nothing but death in the family. All right, one, Paula is alive, and Angela, but she's only a half-sister. All right, and half-crazy Ida – the women in the family are nothing to talk about.
Analyst	Nothing but death. With four years in the trenches you must indeed have seen unlimited death.
A	Millions. And out of it all, that single boy survives. One *can* believe in miracles, Herr Hauptmann Doctor, for all your science. Oh yes, we front-line men know about miracles ! The Voice – that terrible winter when a little dog is all that keeps a man sane. Mein Fox'l, the smartest dog on the western front –
Analyst	Tell me about the Voice.
A	Ah hah ! So you'll know a man's truly crazy !
Analyst	If you would rather talk about his father that would be useful. How he died, for example ?
A	A spasm of the heart. He had been visiting old comrades. He was a bee-keeper, perhaps he had had one too many stings – that was what Doctor Bloch thought.
Analyst	The family doctor ?
A	Family butcher ! For years he pretends to care – with all

165

the agony he caused her – *Mutter, meine Mutti. . . .*

Nota: Unrestrained sobs – suddenly stopping. Laudanum, finally.

Summation of First Session

Pasewalk, November 15, 1918. 01.30 hours.

1 There is danger here. Four facts emerge of primary importance:
i) The current struggle for dominance between the halves of the personality: ie, "the boy" and "the man".
ii) The sexual hostility and role reversal still present as shown in the drawing.
iii) The projection mechanism – the *Them* phobia.
iv) The unknown task and nature of the "Voice".

2 What may we deduce from A's responses? That he was treated as "the baby" of the family, the mother's precious *boy* in a family of dead siblings (some mental defectives, Ida), is obvious: so too the double catastrophe of "Edmund's" birth and death at the most critical ages for A. Within two years, *death of the father.* Then the mother dies, apparently in great pain, witnessed by A. And at some point in this sequence, there is a further period of solitary adolescence to re-enforce the aggression already formed through infancy as revealed by both the picture and the poem.

3 The *boy's* nature is clearly feminine: the art, the poem – the latter with strong imagery, but little literary talent. He still searches (at 29!) for a leader-figure to replace the father – the allusions to Wagner, etcetera. The root cause, and nature of the *Projection*, has yet to be determined. It seems probable that this facet belongs to the *man's* side of the personality – so far, the weaker in the struggle. It will be interesting to see how this emerges, and what task the Voice assigns to it.

From the Ward Orderly's Log

November 15

05.00 hours. A viclent from a nightmare. Screaming, clawing at his throat. Restrained by harness. No sedation (in accordance Duty Medical Officer's written instructions). D.M.O. informed.

Second Clinical Observation

November 15, Five-fifteen, a.m.

The brief duration of the sleeping period (a scant three hours) was not expected. The analyst arrived to find the strong "A-Masculine" sitting up, tugging with his arms against the harness. Saliva was present at the corners of the mouth. The eyes were open, with a light in them that can only be described as blazing! A's rage was directed at the orderly – now "visible": A did not at first appear to recognize the analyst.

Transcription of the Second Session

A   At last! An Officer! These straps cannot be tolerated another second! *Cannot, do you hear?* I *demand* this shithead oaf be punished!

Analyst   Try to be calm. The harness is for your own protection.

A   Calm! The bastard orderly was killing the *Fuehrer*! When our motherland lies raped by *Their* banks and criminal Generals.

Analyst   You are the Leader, is that it? – the Fuehrer?

A   *You* hold a commission – something *must* be done about this outrage!

Analyst   What do you suggest?

A   Death! Mass execution of the traitors!

Analyst   That would hardly change the victorious position of the Allies. The orderly was not strangling you – you were having a nightmare.

A   Tied down! My God, while he was behind. Always he's behind.

Analyst   The man in your dreams – tell me about him.

A   A man in chains! Herr Hauptmann Doctor, please, make him go; one can't breathe. This frightful harness. The

167

gas ! The chest. Squeezing —

Nota: A breaks off, gasping. The strong "Fuehrer-Leader" has left, but the feminine "boy" is not yet in his place. This must be "A-Normal". He has recognized the analyst, but the face is purple, the tongue protruding: he clearly believes he is being asphyxiated. The harness is unstrapped: the ward orderly instructed to leave.

Analyst Now you can see, no one is choking you.

A Thank you, Herr Doctor — it can't be imagined what it's like, poison gas.

Analyst The person standing behind you in the dream — do you know who it is?

A No.

Analyst Yet you say, "he" — you do know it's a man.

A It smells like a man. That's how it first comes, the dream, from the smell — ach, it makes one throw up.

Nota: Vomits bile. Sips water when offered.
(Does *smell* imply *epilepsy*?)

Analyst What sort of smell ?

A It can't be described.

Analyst You've never smelled it in real life ?

A Humanity wouldn't allow such a stench in the streets. Imagine gangrene from a hundred rotting corpses — only ten times more. A thousand ! With shit spouting everywhere. Ghastly.

Analyst It does sound horrible — but why is it a man's smell ?

A You've never smelt a woman ? Dear God, when a boy grows up with a houseful of sisters !

Analyst And a mother.

A That isn't the same. Not at all ! It's disgusting to even suggest — the mother keeps her house spotless. And her dresses — the aprons are always starched on Tuesdays, in the mornings, snow-white, like her bedsheets with the lace on the edge. And ribbons, right to the end, when the butcher Bloch killed her . . .

168

Nota: A strokes the edge of the coarse army duck-canvas. Turns it down like a coverlet. Then back. Then down. A compulsion.

Analyst   In the dream, is the boy in a bed when the smell happens ?
A   Perhaps.
Analyst   Is it his own bed ?
A   Beds beds beds what does it matter ! It isn't the boy who's responsible anyway.
Analyst   There's someone else in the bed with the boy.
A   It's possible.
Analyst   Perhaps a sister ?
A   No.
Analyst   A brother ?
A   No.
Analyst   Are you sure ? Not Alois, before he ran away, after the whipping ?
A   It can't be discussed.
Analyst   But there was a whipping of the person in the bed.
A   There isn't a person.
Analyst   A little boy.
A   Wrong wrong wrong ! Why go on and on ?
Analyst   Why not tell me ? There's nothing shameful between a patient and his doctor. I assure you these things happen to every boy. Just say the name in the bed, you'll feel better.
A   Fox'l.
Analyst   Fox'l ? Your dog from the trenches ?
A   Fox'l from Hafeld. Black and white with brown ears. He came as a puppy.

Nota: Completely unexpected ! A is reliving. Cradling in his arms.

Analyst   And he slept with — how old were — what age was the boy when the puppy arrived ?
A   Six.

169

Nota: The year after "E's" birth. Compensation

Analyst So puppy Fox'l wet the bed and the boy – you were blamed. Now that we've said it, does it sound so bad ?

A Not wetted.

Analyst Defecated ?

A Shitted ! Say that Herr Hauptmann Shithead Doctor ! Shit shit shit ! You talk of dogshit and our Country's defeated ! If you had any sense of honour you'd take your pistol out and die !

Nota: The "Fuehrer" is back: the face again contorted, saliva flecks from the lips, the eyes bulge out from the head in the effort to stare the opponent down. (Yet: no move is made to physical force – an unfortunate break in the flow: the orderly arrives, brought by the shouting.)

Analyst We are not here to talk about the war, or the Country. We are here to talk about your dream of choking. Why you still find the memory of the first Fox'l so upsetting.

A The boy loved him.

Nota: A child's small voice. By the time the orderly was sent out the "Fuehrer" had vanished.

Analyst You say loved ? – Fox'l was sent away, as punishment ?

A Much worse than away.

Analyst Do you want to tell me what happened ?

A It's nobody's business. The Herr Oberoffizial is right. The dog was dirty.

Analyst He came from Hafeld – how did he arrive ? Did father buy the puppy as a present after Edmund ?

A No. After the Jew.

Nota: A has startled himself with this admission. He turns away to the wall.

Analyst What about the Jew ? Was he a friend of the family ?

A It's where the smell comes from ! Those filthy caftans

170

they drag in the gutters of Vienna. Catching turds on the cobbles. Never washing. And their disgusting pipe-stem trousers ! Crawling like vermin with the whores around the Opera. Reeking with sweat, winter or summer – they don't feel the cold ! Animals.

Analyst Did this Jew from Hafeld wear a caftan ?

A What does it matter ? He had money. When they have money they don't wear caftans – they try and hide as human beings, the swine, letting starving artists paint their stinking houses for five pfennigs with their parlour maids while they're off running all the banks in Vienna. That was one good thing about the old Emperor – the damn Jews were kept in their places.

Analyst You didn't like Vienna.

A The worst years of a young man's life ! So much filth in so much beauty. The Opera House and the Hofburg are magnificent – the best in Europe – but the people, those damned Austrians, despicable rabble like the Czechs.

Analyst Yet the young man was an Austrian. Like his father and mother. He loved and respected them.

A The mother was German. And there are some good apples naturally, in every barrel.

Analyst Even in the Jewish barrel ?

A Some, yes. A godfather, old Johann Prinz – and Lieutenant Wiedemann, the platoon commander, he was good also.

Analyst Did the young man have any other relatives who were Jewish ?

A Relatives ! Absolutely not ! A godfather isn't a relative, for God's sake !

Nota: The first laugh ! Harsh. The "Fuehrer" hovers. (The man behind the shoulder ?)

Analyst Tell me more about Vienna. Your records show you were a student of art.

A Of architecture. Much greater abilities are called for. That should have been clear even to those fools at the

	Academy. A young man applies to draw cathedrals and they say he can't do heads ! Can you imagine it ? Heads !
Analyst	The young man failed the examinations.
A	His mother died. A Leonardo would have failed after sitting by that bedside. The iodoform scours her wound – the room stinks of flesh burning – her whole breast, that butcher ! For the last week, as the son watches she can't even drink – while the candles flicker on the Christmas Tree ! Mocking. Gifts and love and peace on earth ! Christmas shit ! Milk, water, the juice of oranges, he tries everything, but all liquids taste like poison ! Maybe it was. It wouldn't be the first time Jews killed a saint ! And in Vienna those Academy shitbags expect a perfect painting !
Analyst	What was the subject, can you remember ?
A	Only the title – typically stupid ! – "After the Fall" ! And the one for the alternate was "A Scene from the Great Flood" ! Those fools.
Analyst	But that was not for architecture.
A	Architecture ! The examiners can see with their own eyes – nothing less than a whole re-construction of Linz – and they turn him away for a piece of paper ! A diploma in mathematics from the Realschule ! Well God's having his revenge on Austria ! Bolsheviks instead of the Emperor !
Analyst	The student prayed for revenge – that's understandable.
A	He prayed for "The Great Flood" to sweep away Vienna ! That sinkhole of slums and syphilitic whores with all their mongrel-bastard mixing of the races. Not a flood – it needs a fire to burn out the whole stinking mess. And now the same thing happens to Germany. *Dolchstoss* ! I tell you it needs a Christ to come again and cleanse the Temple ! Off with their heads ! It's the only –

Summation of Second Session

Pasewalk, November 15. Eight-thirty, a.m.
Ended abruptly by the arrival on rounds of the Hospital
Deputy Surgeon General – whose first reaction was to

have A summarily courtmartialed ! The whole structure of command wavers. Order follows counter-order from Berlin. In our world now, A's ravings are not all madness. Mutiny has already broken out in Leipzig. The patient has been isolated in a protective ward to prevent self-injury – and spread of the infection ! What are the further symptoms or evidence of illness to be drawn from his Second Session responses ?

First, a Messiah Complex: as suspected, the Voice has summoned A to be the "Fuehrer". Despite Normal-A's denial (the plan is hopeless), identification is well advanced: *viz* the temple purging.

Second, the struggle raging between the halves of the personality is increasing in its intensity. "Normal-A" is unaware now when the shifts occur.

Third, the castration fear of the Father is pathologic in degree. (See, the constant references to "chains", the "raping of mother's land", the "poison" even in her medicine, etcetera: all support, at least, the strong suspicion that Father participated in some direct act of sexual aggression within the family.) This castration fear has somehow been transferred through the dog, Fox'l, and resides in the faecal preoccupation which represents fear of the apparently "saintly" Mother – "shit" in her spotless house ? This guilt must be redeemed by A's presence at the death bed. Unsuccessfully. The mother's all too real suffering merely exacerbates the guilt. Fouling of the bedding has now led to Mother's death ! Acceptance of blame however is too horrendous.

Fourth, anti-Semitism, in the *Them* phobia, as the outward Projection increases. That this is an abstract hatred is shown by the acceptance of the Jewish godfather and superior officer. (A also seems to have made no connection to the analyst's own obvious Jewishness.) Given a Jewish godparent, it would not be surprising to find, despite A's denials, some further Semitic relationships underlying this phobia. In connection with this and the Messiah Complex, we are presented with:

Fifth, the denial of paternity (the frequent "bastard" references) common to surviving children after the death of siblings – this re-enforced by the survival, truly amazing, of a foot-soldier through four years of trench warfare ! The "Fuehrer" side of A's personality cannot believe that this survival, after a life of such struggle and rejection, has been for nothing. The intellect may dismiss it bravely but the human psyche dare not.

Sixth, and finally, the revulsion from all things feminine: which is to say, the weak side of A's nature. The references to smell are too obvious for further comment, but the masochistic strength of the loathing is pronounced enough that it might well lead – after fruitless sexual self-degradation (with "syphilitic whores" ?) – ultimately to self-destruction. The danger is that this rage and self-loathing may first vent itself outward, on others. Meanwhile, confinement is best for both the Army and the patient.

From the Ward Orderly's Log
November 15
21.00 hours. Lights out. A found hanging in a bed-sheet. Alive. Taken down. Guard posted. D.M.O. informed.

Third Clinical Observation
November 16, Midnight.
Initial thoughts: would a third session held earlier have prevented ? Pressure of events has been such as to preclude all but the most urgent tasks within the hospital, yet time can always be found. If the attempt was not foreseen, the method was clearly signalled: the "coverlet folding" and its connected "caftan" fetish.

After discussion with the ward orderly it does not seem that the attempt was serious: the galley staff were still collecting trays from the cells opposite; the marks on

174

A's throat are not pronounced. He is sitting up. Pleased with the attention – but which A, I wonder, is in residence?

Transcription of the Third Session

A   Herr Hauptmann Doctor, you've heard the good news!

Analyst   It is good that you were not severely injured. You've come through too much war to risk your life at –

A   Not that nonsense! The news from Berlin – the Armistice is a hoax! A few days, a week – just enough to get the Allies to let down their guard! Then over the top all along the front! Utter surprise through the Ardennes! Caesar's route. It's brilliant. Our General Staff are to be congratulated.

Analyst   Indeed. Where did you hear this surprising news?

A   A military secret. The despatch rider could lose his head, poor fellow. It wasn't his fault. The word dropped while he was having coffee with the orderlies. Hah! Let's see Lloyd-George's Tommies and the Wilson nigger-rabble get over this one!

Nota: A's manner is brisk, decisive, high good humour: the "Fuehrer" in residence, a manic phase.

Analyst   We must wait for a bulletin from the front before we raise our hopes. Did you see the despatch rider?

A   Locked in this pest-hole? You must be joking! Of course, it's a disgrace, being treated as an idiot, but with the change in the war there's no point in crying over spilt milk. Every man who can crawl must get back to his unit.

Analyst   It's a long crawl to the Front. It might be wiser to wait for transportation – so you overheard the despatch rider, am I correct?

A   Those motorbike chaps have one's highest admiration.

Analyst   They are brave. This chap's dialect – tell me, just out of curiosity, what region was he from?

Nota: Silence. None of the A's is a fool. The "Fuehrer" senses the direction of the question – almost takes flight.

Analyst   If I had to guess I'd say, a Saxon ? No ? The Rhineland ?
                Not the Rhineland ? It must be South German – Bayern ?
                Yes ? Somehow I was sure he was Bavarian. Probably
                from Munich ? Yes ? Perhaps you would have known
                him ? – I see from your records you enlisted at Munich.
                Let's be honest with each other, we've spent these long
                hours together – as a leader you have nothing to fear
                from facing the truth, it will help you – wasn't the Voice
                the despatch rider ?

A   You call it help to be treated like a maniac ?

Analyst   You haven't answered my question.

A   Yes or no, you'd say it was crazy. You're all the same
                with your questions, you madhouse doctors.

Analyst   You've met an analyst before ? Was that in Vienna ?

A   Analysts ! Jew-science. You think a man in the ranks
                hasn't read about Freud and his filth ? Utter rubbish !

Analyst   His work is still certainly considered controversial. Did
                you have an accident in Vienna that required treatment ?

A   A man can't help accidents – unless he's a vegetable.

Analyst   Life is painful to any thinking human being, we've
                agreed. Was it with a sheet, like this accident tonight ?

A   God knows. You tell. You have all the damned answers.

Nota: The residual self is alone, and frightened by its
attempted destruction.

Analyst   Was there not a friend at the start, to begin life with in
                the great city ? Perhaps someone you already knew from
                Linz ? A fellow artist, or poet ?

A   A would-be violinist, that's all. He's carrying the case
                when we meet on the platform. A familiar face. We kiss
                on both cheeks, the Judas ! And a would-be pianist ! He
                insists on the most expensive, a damn grand piano ! –
                with not a penny of his own money ! A mother dies in
                agony for Kubizek to have a piano !

Analyst   You didn't enjoy the piano, with your appreciation of
                Wagner's music ?

A   Appreciate ! How can a man even think with that shitty

	piano, and dragging women back every second hour. It's impossible. The only way is for the numbskull to be ordered to return the damn thing to the Jews at the Dorotheum ! This afternoon ! At once !
Analyst	If the piano came from the Government pawnshop it could not have cost so very much money.
A	It isn't only the money. Kubizek has no understanding – a country lump ! – like those fossilized arseholes of the Academy. The entire assembly of morons should be blown up !
Analyst	You weren't perhaps a little jealous of your old friend, for having so many young women ?
A	Jealous ? Of Kubizek ? With those cheeks and beaver teeth ! Hah ! Besides, there weren't so many women, it's an expression –
Analyst	How many ?
A	One mainly. A slav, Katerina.
Analyst	Was she pretty ?
A	For Kubizek ! Considering those teeth. And for a slav.
Analyst	Describe her to me.
A	Blonde hair in a plait. Blue eyes – what else is there ?
Analyst	What did you see, when Gustl undressed her ?
A	Nothing ! He didn't. One wasn't watching.
Analyst	It was a very small apartment – three paces plus a piano. Every man given the chance likes watching.
A	Perverts ! Don't tell me ! One sent them packing, the pair of dirty dogs ! If they want to do it they can use under the bridge by the Opera House like the other animals in Vienna.
Analyst	You took a moral stand – but then you had no friend left in that great city of Vienna.
A	Not one single soul.
Analyst	And you had failed the entrance examinations. Was that when the first accident happened ?
A	Almost then.
Analyst	But before the spring. Some time that winter.
A	February, yes. Before the spring. The Danube is frozen.

Like their Viennese hearts, those filthy bitches.

Analyst Prostitutes.

A Yes. The whores.

Nota: With the "whores", A's voice is a little boy's furtive whisper.

Analyst You looked among the women under the bridge for Katerina. But you couldn't find her, although you went back many times.

A Night after night. Drips from the manhole covers. Freezing.

Analyst And then, when you couldn't find her, you found someone else instead.

A Yes. Some other.

Analyst But she wasn't blonde, with a plait, and blue eyes, like your mother.

A *My mother? That Yid cunt? Jesus-God! Never!...*

Analyst Like your mother, but Jewish. And then what happened?

A Nothing.

Analyst Something. Tell me the boy's nightmare.

A One can't. The eyes! One can't see!

Analyst You can. You will. You want to. Tell me everything.

Nota: The eyes are blank. Amazing – even the irises aren't responding!

Analyst Everything. You must. You'll feel much better.

A Stark naked I fall on my knees in the river – and then the smell comes! He's there! On the horse! Aaah, the swine, choking me. Choking . . . He jumps off the brown horse and grabs my long trousers. I cry out, I'm washing it, Papa. Don't bite it please. See it's clean – but he won't listen. He never listens. He shoots the horse. A fountain of blood spurts up over the people. I am carried up with it like a whale's spout higher and higher. And then falling, and falling and all the people laugh. I scrub my thing till it bleeds and put the bandage on it, but they laugh and laugh and I wake up . . .

Analyst	And the woman that wasn't Katerina, what did she do when you told her about the biting, and the bandage?
A	She laughed the most.
Analyst	And what did you do?
A	I washed off the knob of her room door-handle with disinfectant. It has to be clean. It has to, Mutti! Baby Dolferl will scrub his hands again.
Analyst	And then what did baby Dolferl do?
A	He bandaged his thing again . . . and I went back to my room without Gustl, and I slept with the windows open all night for the germs — even though it was freezing.
Analyst	But before you went back to freeze all alone — what did she say to baby Dolferl?
A	You mean Frau Fai-Fai?
Analyst	If you like. If that is her name — the woman who wasn't Katerina, the one like your mother?
A	The Jew syphilis-bitch said she knows what boys want that have to wash their things. She said she has an Austrian sergeant. She said, a fat man like your Poppa, with a tiny cock and only one ball. When I squat on his face you can watch, for ten pfennigs, little Mama's boy . . .
Analyst	And when you watched, what did you see?
A	The boy didn't. He ran away.
Analyst	I think he did see. You've told everything else. Tell me the last and your eyes won't go blind again.
A	He didn't see. He didn't see. He didn't see. He didn't see —

Summation of Third Session

November 16, 1918. Five a.m.

Delayed two hours by the arrival of injuries from street fighting! German against German — is it possible?

"Baby Dolferl", now we have a name for the inverted *boy*: the sheltered opposite of the harsh "Fuehrer". And the dream — what a field day a Jungian would have with such a *mélange* of symbolic allusions! From the strict

Freudian's position, however, as many tantalising questions remain unanswered.

The Voice is A himself, summoning the "Fuehrer" to release him from the insupportable anguish/guilt that accompanies the invert. That A *is* inverted sexually seems indisputable – but in the passive role, the female's:

i) The attacks from behind, the "stabs in the back" accompanied by the indescribable "male" smell.

ii) The relationship with "Gustl". Much is omitted, but all salient points are there: adolescent between them in Linz, but when Gustl is permitted access to the normal channel, through prostitution in Vienna, he makes the transition immediately – leaving his friend, A, tormented at this further evidence of his inadequacy.

iii) The mother – but her predominant role in crushing and distorting the Super-ego must be dealt with separately.

iv) Disgust at the female genitalia, from (iii) and masked by the syphilis phobia.

v) All the above illustrate graphically the arrested Oedipus – through *apparent* excessive affection for the saint-mother/hostility to the ogre-father. In *actuality* this is almost certainly known by A to have been the opposite – but repressed. (Dangerously, in view of the lurking "Fuehrer".)

vi) Sensing A's unusual need, the experienced prostitute offers what at first she feels he seeks, fellatio – this terrifies him! Yet fascinates too: with a foreskin bitten off he will become even more in the eyes of the world the despised, bastard Jew he fears/wishes he may part be! Through instinct, and her craft (the prostitute, unlike the analyst, always knows her man!) she divines the true nature of A's perversion – still in its immature state. Skilfully, she offers it for his initiation safely at one remove, through voyeurism. Despite his denials, A watches her performance with the Austrian sergeant.

From the Ward Orderly's Log

November 16

18.00 hours. All beds filled with riot admissions.

2 prisoners under guard placed with A in padded cell.

19.00 hours. Fighting. A moved to D.M.O.'s quarters.

Fourth Clinical Observation

November 16. Eight-fifteen, p.m.

How can medicine be practised under such conditions? The prisoners were mutinous brawlers, drunk from looting. One apparently proclaimed himself "Commissar" for the Pasewalk *Soviet*! This with one third of the surgical staff! – all without relief! Chaos beyond description, and no fuel for the furnaces. In my rooms A shivers – as much from shock, no doubt, as from the cold: it takes more strength than he possesses to support his Superman's convictions.

Transcription of the Fourth Session

Analyst   And how old is Dolf when he lives in Passau?

A   Dolferl lives there. Three years old. Four.

Analyst   Frau Fai-Fai lives downstairs – Dolferl's family share the house. Is anyone else living in it with them?

A   Fox'l.

Analyst   The dog? Then? Are you – is Dolferl, sure?

A   A child forgets the first dog in his life?

Analyst   But before, puppy-Fox'l came at Hafeld, to Dolf, when he was six?

A   Six, four – you only want numbers, over and over!

Analyst   You're right, age doesn't matter. Fox'l was a present from Papa, someone for Dolferl to play with.

A   Not the Herr Oberoffizial.

Analyst   A present from Frau Fai-Fai?

A   A present's a present.

Analyst   When they make toilet mistakes it can be embarrassing, we found that out before. So it was in Passau that you had Fox'l in bed, not Hafeld?

181

A	Yes, Passau – shit mistakes are a disgusting subject !
Analyst	Dolf didn't tell last time what the father's punishment was for the first mistake in Dolf's bed ?
A	The Herr Oberoffizial isn't at home the first time.
Analyst	The second ? Fox'l wets in the bed. And what does Dolferl do ?
A	He goes to the laundry to get a towel.
Analyst	And Mutti's bedroom door is open.
A	Yes.
Analyst	And who is there in the bedroom with Mutti ?
A	The Jew is.
Analyst	And what is he doing ?
A	He's shouting at Papa for killing Mutti.
Analyst	Just shouting – and then what happens ?
A	The candle goes out. I can't see.
Analyst	But what can you feel ?
A	I'm back in bed with Fox'l. I wrap him in the towel and then the candle is lighted again. Papa – he stands there with the great trap. He grabs Fox'l and shouts Filthy jew-hound you piss in my bed ? !
Analyst	And then ?
A	Papa puts the trap on Fox'l's thing and Fox'l screams and the shit comes all over the bed.
Analyst	Fox'l's shit ? Or Dolferl's ?
A	Yes.
Analyst	Dolferl makes a mess in the bed.
A	Yes. No.
Analyst	Ah – not in his own bed. In Mutti's ?

Nota: Only a nod. Speechless.

Analyst	And Papa's there, in the bed with her.

Nota: Only a nod – but the mouth is working.

Analyst	And then – ?
A	Papa shoots the horse.
Analyst	Yes ! And then ? – tell me the worst part, and you'll be through.

A   Not yet.

Analyst   But almost – and while all this mess in the beds, what does Dolferl's Mutti do?

A   She cries and laughs when Papa hits her.

Analyst   And then what happens?

A   Frau Fai-Fai comes.

Analyst   And then?

A   · He shouts and the trap snaps on my thing and the smell happens I'm screaming – !

Analyst   But before the smell – Father snaps the trap on Dolferl's penis, yes, but what does he shout?

A   It hurts. The pain is terrible.

Analyst   But you *must* remember – Dolferl, answer, what is Papa shouting?

A   Jew's whore.

Analyst   Ah! –

A   *Jew's whore Jew's whore Jew's whore . . .*

Analyst   And what else, Dolferl? Say what ends it?

A   He laughs at the end . . . and he holds me up by the trap on my thing and he says, She wants a Kike in her bed – now she's got one!

Screaming. Sobbing. Silence.

Summation of Fourth Session

November 17. One-thirty, a.m.

Exhaustion is total. A accepted a sleeping draught two hours ago: he lies beside me as I write, his white, soft-featured face a curiously blank cover to a book that holds so harsh and cruel a story.

That the puppy was a present from a Jew seems reasonable. That this Jew was a neighbour, a young man boarding with Frau Fai-Fai; that an attraction formed between him and the young wife of the absent, much older, Herr Oberoffizial, is more than plausible. That he, the Jew, was seen by "Dolferl" having intercourse with Mutti/Mother, is possible – parents are careless in such matters with three-year-olds. (Or signalling: perhaps to

183

arouse jealousy from the absent/older husband. That mother was strongly masochist herself is undeniable.)

The Rat-Trap Dream. Fascinating – but how to separate the dream from the factual is always the problem.

The little boy has had an "accident" in bed with his new puppy. (Equally, it may have been "Dolferl" who caused the wetting, but that is not of material importance.) He goes to find towels from the laundry. The parents' bedroom door is open. An argument is raging. All this sounds plausible. That the *Jewish lover* is actually in mother's bed, does not, because the scene that follows is horrific, yet the lover likes the boy and has given him a puppy. If Jew and Mother were discovered in the act, there might be confusion, but not paranoia. (After the first slight shock such moments are usually found amusing by the adults.) Indeed, baby Dolferl would probably have been bribed with more presents, sweets etcetera, to go away quickly.

Thus the raging man is Father.

The boy holds the puppy, a visible reminder of the rival. In the terror of the moment, boy, or dog, or both, soils himself. The Herr Oberoffizial is determined to prove his authority, but he is old, he drinks, no match for a vigorous lover in the flesh. But at a remove he can act out his hostility to the full. He snaps a rat trap on the terrified dog's organ. "Jew's whore!" the father cries at mother and child! Or does he? For here science fails us –

Can A be cured?

The belief that mother betrayed him has been so re-enforced by a life of failure that it must surely require more than revelation of the roots of his problem to effect any amelioration. A "sea-change" in his destiny would be required: either through recognition by the world of his achievements in art or to be taken in marriage and loved for himself by a "Frau Fai-Fai." But how is this to happen? His artistic ability never existed; no Frau Fai-Fai

184

has leapt at her chance in the past ten years. And behind all is the fact that the psychosis, with its perversion, is not static. Like any other disease — indeed most like the deadly cancer that destroyed his mother, the psychosis feeds on its own failures and hatreds. It may even have organic roots — the "smell" does strongly suggest epileptic disfunction.

And if there is not that recognition and acceptance ? Then the perversion will advance at its own accelerating rate and Frau Fai-Fai matrons will not be its target. The woman in the bull's eye is the idealised mother from Dolferl's crib: blonde, blue-eyed, ever-young, ever beautiful — and ever the accomplice of the Jew !

Thus, at its end, after inevitable rejection by young women because of his impotence, and after auto-erotic visual gratifications, will come the other forms of abnormal sexuality — coprophilia, coprophagia, coprolalia — as the sadistic "Fuehrer" side takes over. And then . . . the ultimate extreme.

But there need not be a "then". The patient is intelligent, still young, perhaps this terrible war will have given him the impetus so often required for art to flourish. In what time is left we shall talk, and see what comes. For the present, sleep.

From the Ward Orderly's Log:
November 17.
11.00 hours. All ambulatory patients discharged in own recognizance. (Authorisation, Berlin Central Medical Bulletin H-130 (c)) Re A: D.M.O. informed.

185

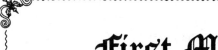 First Movement

Fourth Passage

Olde 88

He was a rat, and she was a rat,
And down in one hole they did dwell:
And both were as black as a witch's cat,
And they loved each other well.

...*In Spandau,* Waring produced it – "The Case of A" – not Gedanke & Gedächtnis; its recurring technicalities are far too heavy for my classical black birds to carry home in their scaly claws or inky heads. No! Waring went to Toulon, if you please, and in some alley found the printer-devil who still had Mama's original draft of it, and thinks himself incredibly clever for this cheap detective work – which he only did because of pique & shame to find his Organ interludes exposed to public view.

The Requiem. Jeremy W insisted it went here, giving away everything, simply to divert attention from his own peccadilloes. Well, G & G have a trick or 2 up their Freudian feathers!

... *At Bayreuth:* Cousin Wyn**man-Hare arrives two days late for Mama's scattering, "Having been misdirected by Italians and one's luggage lost – deliberately one suspects! – in the matter of connecting trains. Be that as it may, and with all due deference to our tragic – " and allowing a moment of kerchief-mopping around his sweating neck to pass for grief before continuing – "a girl – very well, Edwina, a young woman, but scarce eighteen – in Central Europe, on her own? And the

Boy, here, your brother, with the barest Fourth Form education – With this you expect to fend for yourself in the world? I cannot for the life of me begin to imagine what your mother had mind of in re-ordering her affairs!"

"Eddie knows how to catch a damn train," says his Helden sister. "Words fail me."

Unfortunately not. The Wagners come to assist.

"Fräulein Edwina," in Real-Siegfried's ponderously endearing English – "for the three years until her Majority reaches, when she is not in London shall be considered as part of the Festival's permanent organisation under our Family's immediate care. Her brother, also, with his piano, Herr Vuntschmann-Harruh."

"*Wyn –* " our legal Cousin instructs the coaching-master of Bayreuth – "the 'V' naturally I excuse, in Germany, but the central consonants are silent."

With which correction, all bed and dining rooms nearby to Wahnfried are found to be suddenly, miraculously full. Cousin W-H is obliged to remove himself and silent consonants to the Hotel Anchor for the night.

"But he'll be back," Eddie said to Ettie, from the tub, through the bathroom door, when they were alone in the Siegfriedhaus. "And he might be right. Can we really do it? On our own?"

"Mama was darling, Eddie – she was marvellous – " as Sister came into the bathroom, "but if you think about it, with all the Fads, we've always been on our own," and sat casually on the edge of the bath, removing stockings, "Siegfried's giving me one Sieglinder – I do adore that man."

"And what about me? What about when there's no Festival?"

"I shall have engagements. When I'm with other companies in productions I'll need extra rehearsing. All the Names have their own accompanists; it couldn't be better. Jump out so I can have the water."

Brother climbed out. Sister slipped off her dress and underthings, letting them just drop in a heap, and stepped over them into my bath. By school-habit Edwin picks up and folds. "You're so neat for a man. Oh Eddie, imagine – eighteen, and I'm going to be Sieglinde! At Bayreuth! Really, darling, the way everything's worked, you have to say it's simply fate."

188

Absentmindedly she soaps her breasts, lathering her nipples with her thumbs, making them harden. Brother feels himself growing inside his dressing gown . . . Suddenly she stops soaping and looks across. "Eddie, darling, it's going to work perfectly, but we have to promise ourselves one thing – no porpoising. Not together. We can kiss, of course – but real porpoising together now would ruin everything, all right?"

"All right."

"Good. Soon we'll have boyfriends – and girlfriends for you – then there won't be a problem anyway. Isn't it incredible about getting Sieglinde?"

Soap bubbled between her legs. She began to hum some bars again.

> *Prematurely was I robbed of Sister and Mother;*
> *Out hunting and harrying, until Home on that dark day,*
> *I found the Wolf's lair barren, burnt to ashes his great Hall;*
> *Slaughtered, my Mother's valiant body,*
> *Vanished in flame was all trace of my Sister . . .*

From Die Walküre – but Siegmund's part: where he tells her he used to be called Wölfing.

"Gawd, we're lucky, Eddie, I'm going to skip all the Norn-Valkyrie filler bits. Thanks pet – " for the towel Brother handed her – "when are you going to tell me what you talked about when you ran away in his car?"

"Mama's car – if you mean Herr Wolf it was private."

"I bet it was politico." Tossing her head, contemptuously, shaking out her golden hair.

"If you must know, it was the fate of Europe, we're – "

"At a turning point, the most important since the Romans – or at least Charlemagne – it only happens to civilisations once in a thousand years, and if they aren't saved they die. Gawd, how boring." With which perfect imitation she wrapped her hair in a turban with the towel. "Poor Eddie, I don't suppose you got a word in."

"I thought you liked Him."

"When he's amusing and not crawling – he was beastly to Mama about her Brown Book, even if it was a stupid idea."

189

"*Stupid?*" Her son was outraged.

"Eddie dear, if he's going to pretend to be an Emperor he can hardly have a book around that shows you when he didn't have clothes. Didn't he even mention me?"

The prima donna is truly unbelievable.

Brother shouted, "I didn't talk, I didn't think. I hardly heard what He was saying. Damn it! Ettie – couldn't you see? With the roses? On the thorns? It was awful. When that gardener raked her – "

Storming out of the bathroom, onto his bed, sobbing. She follows. "I know, Eddie, I saw. But we have to be strong, darling. Losing Mama is like Freia's being taken by the giants – only there's no magic golden apples to help us. We're on our own. We have to make the best of it. And we will." Bending down to kiss his forehead. "Forget the silly book. We're only going to remember the good things. Then she'll always stay with us the way she was."

With her Edwardian's impervious dignity and lovely gentle smile, and her orange blossom scent as she bends over to kiss us goodnight in our nursery with the stars on the ceiling; kisses me as Ettie does now. Looking down on me just like Her. *By the way . . .*

Mama, my darling. She *was* still with him. She was his sister. He would love both of them in one. Even more. Eddie put his arms around Ettie's neck, and pulled her down, and hugged her, *hugged her.*

"Silly old Bro. You mustn't cry. She'll always be with us. There, that's better. Now, turn over . . . "

And close your eyes Eddie dear . . . like that . . . Night-night.

And so, with Saturn over the Moon, classic sign for loss of the mother, side by side, separate but together, in our two beds in the little Siegfriedhaus, we slept.

. . . On the Green Hill: The Orphans move in with the little Griesbachs on a permanent basis, or at least for whenever Bayreuth is to be Home. There is none in England: by the terms of her typically Mama-ish Will she has ordered both Trevelly and the Table House at Tintagel sold.

Only golden Porquerolles remains.

"In a Trust," big Sister explains, "between both of us, Eddie."

Their Legal relation, addressing Dear Edwina with his fat italics, doubly underlined, reveals another Mama strangeness in the Will.

190

... About Money! It is laid down that the proceeds of sale from both dwellings are to be retained not in debentures of any sort, but in cash, converted on deposit *as gold only*! It is as though your late mother considered herself a State! *I* consider it almost sufficient to indicate an unbalanced mind. The market for stocks has never been brighter, whereas bullion draws no rate of interest and remains fixed in value by the ounce. Nonetheless, her wishes – unless you should instruct we sue for Incompetence – must be obeyed. The Boy's apportionment of other than Real Estate, you will be relieved to know, I have myself invested in a portfolio of City shares of *irreproachable security* – with some prudent anticipation of Dividend and Growth. I anticipate by return of post, Edwina, instructions that your own residuum is to be dealt with in this self same fashion.

Ever Your Cousin, W-H.

"*Unbalanced?*" the Boy whispers, revealing the hint of secret fear. "Mama?"

"Bosh! Eddie, the man is an insufferable fat pig. Mama knew perfectly what she was about. If the houses were there I'd always have to be dragging back from an engagement; it would be hopelessly inconvenient. And on the Continent they go ga-ga just at the mention – I shall tell the pig-Hare to put my part in gold as well – we can live off the interest from your part."

In the heady years ...

THE '27 SEASON

Parsifal, Ring, and this time for the change:

Tristan und Isolde, the immortal lyric Masterpiece, being set aboard a great Ship sailing to Tintagel, in Cornwall, once King Arthur's, now jealous King Mark's, Court. In legend, a golden Boy has been

191

earlier presented, to play the Harp & soothe Mark's brooding cares of State. In our Master's Work, the Boy has become Knight Tristan, escorting beauteous Isolde, princess of an Island Kingdom, the betrothed of Mark, to marriage. Isolde first thinks she hates Tristan (blaming him for the slaying of her former Beloved) but being given a philtre of Love Potion in error by her serving maid, Brangäne, the Twain fall, through the Greatest Musical Passion ever written, by Duet, & Death, for Eternity in Love! (& so, while *leitmotif* may be dispensed with, the Divine Melody of Richard Wagner is unending . . .)

Our first Bayreuth Liebestod, and Mama not with us to hear and see it. *To Experience, Edwin dear. There is a difference . . .*

Parsifal, and four bloody days of Ring in the middle, with no hope of dodging, because Sister's in it.

"But only in Valkyrie, Ettie – surely this year I could miss the other parts?"

"Eddie, silly – you have to see the other parts, or how will we know how I come off against the Nanny-goat?"

Nanny Larsen-Todsen, as Brünnhilde. First time out, and Edwina C-P matches herself against the Immortals.

But in 1927, to see a young woman frankly and openly seducing her own brother (the least-seducible Melchior), entwining him with her arms and legs, bending over to kiss him – lying on her back for him! – the gasping Wagnerians thought it *was* incestuous (instead of just the play-act porpoising when she was seven, on the beach of our Bay of the Lobsters). Afterwards, as they walk, the on-stage Brother and the real-life one, on each side as she descends the Restaurant staircase to the Singers' Table, all around, with the applause, Eddie catches the whispered, "So alike! . . . can you imagine only? . . . yes, together! Oh, but if he could – ?"

Not possible, my dears, with Edwin's shy flat squawk – but small wonder their singing heads get turned. Queen Nanny smiles from her monarch's position at the Table. "So very nice for a starting Sieglinde, Ettie, dear."

192

An Invitation:

The Orphans come upon Him the next morning (having arrived unannounced with His Desperado's revolver for that first post-war Tristan and stayed overnight in the Siegfriedhaus). Walking in the Hofgarten, deep in talk with Winifred. Eddie nudges Ettie to keep to the edge of the trees and give the adults privacy. A mistake. Sister considers herself an Adult.

"Wolfi – " making a bee line, her most blinding smile – "I do hope you're coming to see my second Sieglinde. You mustn't believe what they say about it being naughty. And Auntie Winnie. Guten Tag to you both. Isn't it a simply lovely morning?"

He grovels to the ground with the "naughty" and "Wolfi" – as the "Auntie" ages Winifred twenty years – and in Sister's radiant smile Edwin observes for the first time those 3 Norns, Malice, Sweetness, & Envy, busily spinning.

"Edwina dear – and Eddie. How are my little ones?"

In Hun, and kissing cheeks, and smiling maternally, jolly Frau Winifred sends the thread whistling back.

"Herr Edwin," He said gravely, "one hears that in Hunding's Hut your so brilliant sister's naughty Sieglinde burnt up the house. What do you think – is she perhaps too dangerous to have at my House Warming?"

"If you ask me, Herr Wolf, Ettie overdoes it. Her poor Siegmund was gasping like a stranded whale. The lift platform shook so much that it got stuck half way."

"I don't have a lift. For our 'Einzugsfeier' we shall have to take a chance. The Mercedes has six seats, when I travel south would you do me the honour to ride with me – Herr Siegfried, also, it goes without saying?"

Amply proving He has humour. Sister laughs, radiating her youthful glow. Auntie still manages to keep her smile.

Real-Siegfried does not go to the housewarming. At the end of the Festival he comes down with a cold that settles as a pain in the chest. "Nothing to be alarmed for, but Berchtesgaden, no, I don't feel up to that. I rely on you, Edwin, as the man of the group to keep our ladies from harm. Winifred, with the other gifts, you really feel it's necessary to part with the Lohengrin?"

193

A page in the Master's Hand – in addition to the white china plates and soup bowls with "R.C.W." for Richard & Cosima, in blue script on the side, and the set of green-satin bedroom curtains with more "W's" woven in a diagonal pattern.

"Yes I do." Said Senta.

Her husband coughed, frowned slightly. "Edwin, my boy, I rely, as I said. Take care. Bring them back to Bayreuth safely. Auf Wiedersehen!"

Wife-stealing is a fact in the turbulent Wagner Life. For Real-Siegfried, lovely man, it is infinitely more pleasant to think of rehearsals with his singer-children, on the grass under the lime trees, in his yellow socks. . . .

The Salt Mountain:

He was suddenly called away – like Wotan, in the middle of the night – so the Orphans don't drive from the Green Hill but go with Aunt Winnie by train via Munich.

An ebullient Herr Wolf meets His guests with Mama's red Mercedes at the Berchtesgaden station; the platform is deserted, even though this is an extra run for summer trippers. He wears His leather shorts. Perhaps through walking on the slopes, His b*m doesn't seem to stick out so much in all the bending, & bowing, & upholstery-cushion wiping before the ladies put their gracious ones on them. Pleased with the cushion-work, Mein Host is an expansive guide.

"It's the air, the salt in it, there are unique salts under the rock – people have been burrowing for centuries for their curative powers – at this very moment we're driving up on a veritable mountain of salt, and small human histories. Monks and knights, and witches – of course, this is where our Hänsel and Gretel come from. Macabre as such stories for children invariably are, that's what gives them such immense appeal! What little one watching Mutti prepare a gingerbread man can't imagine himself in the frightful witch's oven? This is why I can't drive myself, confound it. There are towns where those Red she-hags would throw their own little ones under the Ogre's wheels! Still, one supposes it's some proof of recognition – perhaps they've read the Book . . . I agree, dear Fräulein Edwina, not likely! Politics is not for our Ladies, with rare exceptions – the Widow Bechstein for example, exceptionally kind, giving your noble mother the house for practically nothing, not that I'm saying the Gräfin's gesture was anything short of magnificent! First a car, and then a house, how could a man possibly expect such a display of generosity. This is what made your noblest of Mamas so infinitely superior – Frau Winifred, you are a complete exception also, it goes without saying. . . . Well done Müller! – these hairpins are devilish to corner. Müller taught me to drive, Herr Edwin – that old grey Selve in which we escaped from the Putsch? Even on a glorious day like this it dampens the spirits . . . but no gloom. You see, Ladies, up there, to our right, the depression in the grass? . . . no, not a cow trail, gracious Fräulein Ettie. How you love to make jokes, but it's one's own fault for not being clear. The salt route from Hallein to Augsburg came right through here. Hallthurm – the house up on the bluff, only a ruin now – that's where the tax was paid. And the witches too – there are villages all around that smelt the stench of the heretic's pyre. There are accounts, such details you wouldn't believe! Judges of the Inquisition gloried in having twenty or thirty thousand witches burned! That's religion for you – mass murder! in Obersalzberg, on top of our magic salts, you can see for yourselves – utterly unspoilt. The Innkeeper, the Smith, the Cobbler, far more than Nuremberg this is the spirit of Hans Sachs. Like Lambach and Hafeld, a paradise for romping children . . . You marvel at the vista, mein Ederl – could your mother have left any more enduring legacy? You must consider my little house on my Salt Mountain, yours – at any time. No invitations! I owe her everything. . . . "

In these blue mountains and green valleys her son can only see her witch-smoke, ascending, straight up, in the still Venetian air . . .

"Adorable!" said jolly Aunt Winnie, at a final hairpin turn, "Complete even to the vine over the porch."

"It's certainly better than the henhouse."

Sister, tugging the thread – but it *was* a perfect house our astonishing Mama had bought, dirt-cheap, from the Widow Bechstein to let Him start with. The rocks on the roof, to hold the shingles; and the hand-cut shutters, and the criss-cross carved logs, and the thick stone chimney, and nothing around but mountain and sky, for miles and miles and miles. A home for giants.

195

"Grüss Gott, meine Damen."

A plump woman, apple-cheeked, print-aproned, comes out through the vines to welcome the Ladies & Edwin.

"May I introduce my housekeeper, Frau Raubal."

Two tables are set up in the meadow, both covered with snow-white cloths, held down like the roof shingles with rocks, but smaller – and a picnic because there isn't room for more than at most one pair of guests to stay overnight.

"Gawd – ants and mosquitoes, I can't stand picnics," gracious Edwina replies in one of her jokes.

Two girls begin carrying out heaped plates. Edwin, little gentleman, ashamed of Sister, stands to one side to let them pass.

"Meine Töchter, mein Herr," offers Frau Raubal. "Geli und Friedl."

Friedl is smaller, adopted, although she has the mouse-coloured hair and manner of her mother – adoptees, like chameleons, take on protective coloration.

"Guten Tag, mein Herr."

"Guten Tag, Fräulein Geli," mumbles Eddie, blushing, because "Geli" is Angela Maria, smiling a secret invitation. Her hair is not a full blonde – almost an ash light-brown – but positively *not* mousey.

And what a gay picnic it now becomes with the Ladies! Auntie Winnie, who has had His head in her lap, bringing bed curtains; little Ettie, head-in-air, spinning nooses with her Norn-thread, pretending not to give a damn; and smiling-Geli passing plates over His shoulder, bent, breasts and buttocks tightening her dress before His accidental eye . . .

And then, as the Party are finishing their potato salad (made from Winifred's and His favourite Wahnfried recipe) and about to move on to the mountain strawberries – Edwin spies a car winding its way upward.

Another Mercedes. The Party is growing but still conserving. This car was the old four-cylinder model with the rounded bonnet first seen at Oberammergau. It made the final hairpin turn, disappeared in against the cliff, emerged again, coughed its way forward, barely managed the last hundred yards, rolled in under some plum trees beyond our picnic tables, and stopped. Buckteeth, Fräulein Anna Hess, was the driver. Our Host chuckled.

"Wotan has Waltraute, this is what God sends me as a Valkyrie! A faithful messenger but no beauty! Although – " and He looked suddenly at Edwin, extra-keenly – "now this is extraordinary! Ladies – look!" Everyone looks. "Imagine our Hess in a funfair mirror – then being straightened out in the sunshine – black hair to gold, that corrugated-iron forehead made noble. Ears in, not like jug handles – you still don't see it? You would get our Herr Ederl!"

"But Herr Wolf is quite right about the underlying bone structure." Aunt Winnie laughed and patted the Boy's hand to remove any sting. "If we gave Herr Rudolf to Hans in Makeup at Bayreuth for one year!"

"Five years." Our Host smiled, having won another argument. "Then Doppelgänger – yes, definitely! Ignore the old wives' tales. Now, I must ask to be excused."

Doppelgänger. The Shadow-Self. Our Ederl laughs off the impossible exaggeration . . .

Wotan's messenger didn't get invited to the table. Herr Wolf walked over to the plum trees instead.

"That long face," said Winifred. "Herr Rudi normally grins like the village idiot, even in a thunderstorm." Under the plum trees He strikes His right hand against His temple. Winifred says, more worried, "There was talk of a new speaking ban."

He slumps against a tree. Smiling Geli gathers up plates and gives them to her mousey sister. He comes back towards the table. Jug-eared Anna stays with the Mercedes.

"Bad news from Berlin, Herr Wolf?"

"Berchtesgaden, Herr Edwin. A young girl one was kind to. Terrible. Frightful. In the dress shop. She's tried to kill herself. With a rope. We used to walk. Even now she may be dead. They can't be sure."

"The dress shop!" Sister remembers, with awful delight. "Eddie, I got her to fix my tear with the goat. Oh how perfectly ghastly."

"Meine Mitzerl, tot! – ach, mein Gott!"

He sank into a chair at the picnic table. His head was in His hands. His face was white. His women gathered round to comfort Him. "There there, you mustn't blame, God's Will, one glass of wine now, Onkel Alf . . . "

"*Uncle* – ?" breathes Sister. "Gawd Eddie, the little tart's his – !"

197

"Then Frau Raubal, Ettie, must be – ?"

"Only a half-sister," says Winifred, with unnecessary sharpness in her tone, and a shooting glance at only-half-niece-Geli.

And the fleeting look that flashes across *her* pretty face – and is caught again by Ettie and Auntie Winnie – is it triumph, at the death of a rival?

Post-Mortem:

The House-warming is frozen, but selfish Mitzi Reiter does not die.

The sad, but mundane sequence of events was this: she went up to His former abode (behind the Pension Moritz) and took the rope (used to tie the lustful Billy) and placed one end around her slender neck, and the other around the Henhouse door – where the Widow Meissner found her, semi-conscious (either because the hinge was old and had pulled out of the jamb, or because Mitzi Reiter had not tugged the knot tight enough) but, as she had left a note to guide her rescuers, we may, I think, children, assume the latter.

Until next time.

THE '28 SEASON

Sieglinde again. The greedy child has hoped for a second role, perhaps Brangäne, Isolde's companion, "But apart from voice considerations," says Real-Siegfried, "Brangäne is playing a second fiddle, and you my dear Edwina, if one may say, do not have the temperament easily to do this."

She raged for a day then, being Ettie, took matters in her own hands. When Eddie came home to the Griesbachs from watching stage rehearsals she was all smiles. "Guess what?"

"Siegfried's given it you after all."

"It's nothing to do with Siegfried. I've been on the 'phone to London."

"London! That must have cost an absolute fortune."

"We've got one. The point is – darling old Meyerhof has pulled strings and got me Rosalinde in Fledermaus, next month in Vienna! You can order the music tomorrow for our practising. Just think, Eddie, the first role all on my own!"

"I was going to give a performance of my composition next month. You know Siegfried's arranged for Karl Muck to listen."

"They love light tuney little things in Vienna, we'll find someone to listen to it there." She paused, actually grasping what she'd said. "Eddie, you don't think Fledermaus is *too* light for me, do you?"

... *Vienna:* How Mama would have loved showing us the ropes in such an eminently Edwardian town. The station is floodlit, and the churches and palaces – the lobby of the Imperial Hotel is a palace itself. The Orphans, on their first tour to an Unknown Engagement are escorted to their suite like royalty by a representative from the State Opera Company: Frau Ebert, the Director's personal secretary, a motherly woman, exceptionally capable.

"In the morning, Fräulein Edwina, I shall come myself to take you to your first rehearsal. The buildings are all at a convenient distance for walking. On rainy days the hotel can arrange a car – but unlike Bayreuth, it never rains in summer in our Wien! Sleep well – and you also, Herr Edwin; a room with piano is arranged for your composing. Now, to you both, Good-night." As the Orphans look down from their Imperial window at the splendours all contained by this majestic arrangement of roads that the Viennese call *Der Ring*.

E & E walked along it the next morning to first rehearsal.

"You *have* to come with me," Sister had pleaded as Brother ate breakfast. She didn't eat. "How can I possibly go in there without an accompanist? Eddie, you must see – these Austrians pretend to be charming but they'd simply walk all over me."

"I was going to start my museums, this morning, Vienna's got the most fantastic archives in the world, outside the Vatican."

"Oh Gawd – Eddie, I can't go in alone. Darling, *please?*"

So we went walking – with Sister chatting and laughing to kind Frau Ebert with the most utter sang-froid, my dears. "Stage fright? Isn't it too absurd? Frau Ebert, you're awfully sweet – isn't she, Eddie? – but I'm afraid that I've been trotting around on my own already for far too many years."

Edwin reverts to his role as mere masculine appendage.

"I suppose I can't force you to go off on your own," Sister says, as the

Director advances with an armful of flowers among an all-around kissing of hands, "and if you insist, Eddie dear, give me my first high C – but really I'm sure you'd be happier with your old museums than hanging about here listening to me howl for the rest of the day." Delighted laughter of relief at such welcome evidence of self-deprecation in our young prima donna.

" . . . Yes, Covent Garden, *and* a Bayreuth Sieglinde at her age! Charming! Innocence. It's Meyerhof's training . . ."

The whispering campaign is won.

The Hofburg:

Repository of the knowledge that had been an Empire for a thousand years, until the day before yesterday. In its archives there must be something on the region of Romania where the Teutonic Knights held the border against the Mohammedan hordes. The Hofburg Archivist has a hump on his back, and a cardigan under his suit; a gentle helpful nature, the Austrian strain of little Stallion-Mares.

"Braşov, mein Herr? – yes, this would be the starting point perhaps – and then through the Saxon and Szekler regions to Rasnov."

"You have material on Rasnov? How much?"

"This depends, Herr Casson-Perceval. May one ask how many weeks do you expect to spend in the research?"

The Boy had hoped to fill the morning. The Hofburg has drawer after drawer, case after case, stack upon stack. A million books, thirty thousand manuscripts, hand-drawn maps, siege reports, supplies lists, burial lists, castle plans . . .

The Apricot Knickers Story

or

The Lizard Rat!

At five, the Reading Room closes by Posted Order. Edwin the Scholar locks up the 9th Cent plan of the Castle of Bran and returns to the present's Imperial Hotel where Sister's having a bath.

"We're going out for dinner, with Frau Ebert, and I want you to look nice. Thank goodness you're back in time to change. Wherever have you been – I thought you were lost!"

Stage fright has returned in our absence.

"You didn't seem too worried this morning," Brother says as he undresses. "And Frau Ebert's a pet – I'm sure she won't care how I look."

"It's not only Frau Ebert." Sister climbs out of the bath. Brother pulls the plug to let it drain. "Oh put it back and use mine. Do hurry, Eddie, we're going to be late."

She dries herself rapidly, in swift pats up her thighs, over her stomach and breasts. Eddie gets in and runs some fresh hot. "You dry the opposite to me; it's inefficient to start at the bottom. It all drips down from the top."

"I am opposite." She turns off the tap and yanks out the plug. "I don't have the floppy parts to drip – and I said *hurry*! He'll be here any minute." Holding up her arm and peering at the pit. "Did you bring a razor from Bayreuth?"

"I didn't think I'd need it. We're only going to be a month. Who's this 'he'?"

"Nicholas Baer. Oh blast and damn – I simply can't go out in an evening frock in Vienna with hair!"

Brother dries his pubic area. Under Sister's arm is the barest hint of matching gold against her white skin. "Unless you're going to put a half-Nelson on him he's not going to see. What does this Nicholas Baer do?"

"He conducts. And I'm sure he's going to see." She steps into apricot satin knickers and pulls them up. "In future we're going to make a list so you don't forget things."

The apricot knickers are new. Brother puts on his own dull drawers. She cups herself into her brassière, pulling it tight behind her, binding her poor breasts flat as a Chinaman's feet for the hideous fashion of the day. The bell rings from the front door of the suite.

"You go," she said.

"Like this?"

"You're a man."

At seventeen, in his flannel dressing gown from school – that comes barely halfway down his thighs and won't close across his chest – Edwin feels every inch a boy. At the door, more Viennese flowers. Behind them, a bored voice in a High-Hun's flawless English; "You must be the

201

young composer. Your sister and I are going out to dinner. May I come in?"

Nicholas Baer hands Edwin the flowers so that we can see the rest of him. In patent evening shoes Nicholas Baer is half a head taller – almost the height of giant Putzi, but Oh, how elegantly slim! His hair is black as his patent shoes, and as slick. His eyes are grey, too close together, and intense. He owns two duelling scars as proof of a Hunnish education, and a thin sliver of moustache to emphasize the wideness of his upper lip for kissing. Women found him irresistible. After the way he said "young composer", Eddie saw a 2-footed lounge-lizard, crossed with a rat.

"Yes, come in." But by now the rat is. Holding the dressing gown together with one hand, clutching the damn flowers with the other, Brother trails after. "Excuse me, I've got to get dressed. I'm going to dinner too."

"That will be delightful." The lizard-rat's eyes appraise flatly. In transferring the flowers to a side table the bloody dressing gown has fallen open. "Siegmund for our Bayreuth Sieglinde – how very alike you are. The flowers perhaps should be in water. May I smoke?"

The Up-and-coming Conductor-about-Town owns a gold cigarette case and ivory holder. Sister's First Suitor (not counting Pawel) – how could a brother not loathe and despise?

Edwin takes up the odious flowers as Edwina comes out of her room. Deliciously cool. Until she saw the dressing gown. "Oh, Eddie, how could you! Herr Baer you'll have to excuse him. Boys have simply no idea of style or time."

Little Mother – aged 19. Only Frau Ebert makes the evening remotely livable, talking about Wien, while Sister laughs at the lizard-rat's music-world jokes or waltzes the worst one around the room.

The 2nd Day Of The Rat:
Brother goes back to the Hofburg Reading Room and can't. The next night she went to dinner without him. He ate alone in the hotel and choked. She didn't come home until two. He was awake, but didn't call through. Nor did she. I heard the sound of washing in the bathroom before she went to bed. In the morning the apricot knickers were hanging on the radiator. The stain had not washed out. Brother knows

Sister's blood when he sees it – and it isn't That Time; she never shares the bath then, and besides, there was no moon. (Ettie followed the lunar cycle like tidal clockwork: beginning her gross flood on the wane, ebbing 4 days before the crescent was gone.)

Edwin orders breakfast for both at 8, and takes it to her in bed. She is exaggeratedly normal. They talk about his plans of the castle (briefly) and for the remainder of the forenoon, until he delivers her at the rehearsal hall, about her moves in Fledermaus's batty second act. "If I finish the Bran-plan I may join you for croissant lunch," he said off-hand.

"That would be nice, Eddie darling – but we're going right through today."

Liar. When he comes back from the Reading Room to check, she's gone with the lizard-rat to the Imperial's Grill, brazenly, right under her Eddie-darling's nose. He watches them from the lobby, hands across the table, feet below the chairs. Touching his ankle. Nicholas Baer wears sheer silk socks. Like grey French letters. *Ugh.*

Dame Sorrow's Tour:
By night Eddie tries to read his leather edition of The Book: *The Causes of The Collapse* – " . . . excrescences and germs in rotting world . . .";
Years of Study and Suffering – The matter seems so monstrous, the accusations so unbounded.

By day, the Scholar wanders the museums looking at every sort of weapon to sever limbs and smash heads. He thinks of using them on himself. Has *she* not left him, an Orphan, friendless in a foreign land? Where isn't foreign? Only Porquerolles was home . . .

The Orphan sat on a bench, with The Book, and cursed his fate –
. . . That took the milksop from his downy nest and gave him Dame Sorrow for a foster mother, that threw him out into the world of misery and poverty – Vienna is to me only the living memory of the most miserable time of my life!

And suddenly, almost blindingly, Edwin C-P, milksop (though hardly poor) sees Our Wien through those same self-pitying eyes. Now, where splendour lived, the Boy sees palaces deserted by their toppled Emperors, leaving splendour dead. He sees hovels and the victims of earlier postwar starvation, children so thin that they were sent for food to postwar England! He sees Strauss's Vienna Woods cut down for lack of coal. He sees a dirty, teeming, polyglot, wrecked hub of a city – the detritus of a crumbled empire.

. . . I drank my bottle of milk and ate my scrap of bread . . . and one day when I was walking through the inner city, suddenly I came across a being –

As does another Boy, 25 years later –

clad in a long caftan, with black curls . . . topped by a wide-brimmed shovel hat, with shawl, & bird's nest beard –!

One of Them?

Later, the smell of these caftan wearers often made me ill . . . !

In Edwin's nostrils the whole of Vienna smells – stinks! Of oil and petrol, coal gas and horse dung, flowers and rotting vegetables, cigarettes and Hookah-pipes.

Mama's brown-bottle depressions could last for months. Her son found it bloody dull after 3 days. He might have stretched to a week if he hadn't found –

The New Friend:

. . . Is sitting on my chair in my cubicle off the Reading Room. He is rotund, about 5 feet tall with very little hair that grows in a monk's fringe, leaving a pate tanned brown with the summer sun. His eyes are also brown. Merry eyes. He wears a wrinkled linen suit, a whitish shirt, and no neck-tie. Edwin, with wide travelling experience, puts him down as Poor, not too Bright, probably Basque-Spanish or French: an out-of-uniform, happy-go-lucky, rural-Catholic priest of 40.

"Sorry – " this with a cheerful smile that creases an already plump face into two more chins. "I did check with the Archivist. You hadn't ticked your name off, but we weren't sure that you were coming back. I'll clear out right away."

1st Revision: fluently colloquial English – though with a thick accent. Eddie said,"You don't have to go. It was my fault for not confirming. How do you do?"

"As much as I can in the long struggle. I'm Michael Rau – I know who you are, so why don't you let me buy you lunch?" Eddie couldn't think of a reason. "Good," said Michael Rau, "we'll find a place."

Our first . . . It had a sawdust floor, and Hungarian claret served from a barrel, and was off the Bäckerstrasse in the shade of the Dominicans' Church to the West; the Jesuits to the North; St Stephen's Cathedral to the East, and the Franciscans to the South. Locked in by these four pillars of Christianity, Eddie's new friend ordered himself a huge plate of pig's knuckles and boiled ham, and ate it on a Friday.

"'My small effort at furthering the ecumenical movement. My father's a Jew. What's your aim in life?'"

Michael Rau grinned, with grease highlighting his chins. Edwin dissected the bones of some spicily grilled fish and thought about this strangely formulated question.

"I'm in music because of my sister, but what I really want is to find the Holy Grail – we were brought up as Wagnerians you see."

Michael Rau didn't – couldn't, but he had that air of interest even when you aren't, and with smiles between gnaws he drew young Eddie out. I told someone about growing up with Ettie and Mama and the Fads. Not all, no house of Brothers and Sisters, or Waring and the Darling: a Boy can't tell of things that matter until –

"So," said Michael Rau, "seventeen, and devoted to pyro-maniacal Master-Wagner, and Mad Ludwig. We have something in common. I'm twenty-four and studying Marx."

"Who exactly is he?" asked the product of his Fourth Form and Mama's ideas on Education and The Book.

"Karl, my dear Eddie – the second Messiah given the world by my Chosen People, who died in the same year as your Ring maker. Is it true – have I really met someone untouched by Marx?"

"I'm afraid I don't know anything at all about politics; compared to history, with battles and kings, and empires dying, politicians don't seem to matter much."

"Edwin, my son, you've made my trip to Vienna." Michael Rau drained the last of the Hungarian claret, and wiped his thick lips with the back of his hand, and belched, and didn't excuse himself, and said, "I've got to drop in at the Bank for some cash, but what about supper tonight? If you're free, of course?"

"I'm sure I'll be free, but I can't let you pay. If we eat at the Imperial, I can put it on the bill."

"The Imperial isn't eating! You're in Vienna. We'll find a place."

Edwin's new friend looked sadly at his last bare knuckle of pig. "It's impossible for me to spend my father's money fast enough to make a dent in it – but before the decline of the West I have to try."

But Edwin hasn't heard of Spengler either. Here walked previous Minds. We are not alone!

But Sister was.

The Lizard-rat, Nicholas Baer has attained his objective: the apricot knickers come back with a note from the Imperial's laundry apologising because the stain won't come out. The de-flowerer continues to arrange lunches and suppers but they are suddenly broken off, or cancelled with no warning – "An extra rehearsal with my bass section, Edwina, you can understand."

At first accompanied by flowers and chocolates. Eddie smells the rat, but then I was jealous.

"Of *course* he has rehearsals," says Sister, forced to dine en famille. "Nicholas is the most sought after new conductor in Vienna. Anyway, it's none of your damn business. And I saw you spying on us the other day at lunch. Yes you were – in the lobby – hiding behind the palms! It's too childish. What on earth must Nicholas think?"

Everyone else knows what he's thinking. He doesn't bother to disguise it. You had only to look at those grey lizard-rat eyes. Baer let her drag on for three more weeks, until the final General for the Bat: Full Ensemble and Orchestra but only half-costumed; the seamstresses working after-hours letting-in or out, for the following day when there would be a first audience. Not the general public, but fellow musicians, relatives, some Press from the provincial weeklies, who couldn't afford the tickets on opening night.

Brother & Sister got back late. It had gone well – only the normal number of miscues by the tenor and drownings by the violins, and one man in the brass chipped a tooth on his mouthpiece. Ettie sang correctly but without fire. As she got closer to a performance she gave less and less of her inner self, saving the real thing. In those days she thought that was how she had to do it; "It makes sense, Eddie. We're all rationed. There's only so many heartbeats. I only have a limited number of good breaths."

Denouement:

The Orphans are dressed for dinner. Eddie is going out with Michael Rau who's left word of a new "place" he has discovered. The time of the lizard-rat's arrival to escort comes and goes. Another 30 minutes. Another eight o'clock. A note arrives with a pageboy: "Herr N.B. sends his regrets ..."

A piano soloist was late arriving from Salzburg.

"Come with me, Ettie – you're all dressed anyway, and I promise you'll like Rau. Even if the places he finds don't always work it's an adventure."

"All right," she said, "call and ask the porter for a cab. But not pig's knuckles. Just looking at them makes me want to be ill."

... Out into the gilded and crimson hall of the Hotel Imperial and down in its birdcage lift. We passed the palms in the lobby.

"Eddie, the silly spying – promise you won't do it again?"

"I promise."

"Good." Sister peers through the fronds. "I don't know what you hoped to see from out here anyway – "

Her first lover – sitting with his French-letter grey-silk socks under the table, rubbing ankles with his latest Salzburg-piano bit of fluff.

Ettie didn't move. Pink, red – dead-white. Her face for that moment was Mama's that one last time in her chestnut box.

"Come on – darling Ettie, it doesn't matter. Come and have supper. I always hated him anyway."

"It matters, Eddie. But I am going to have supper."

"It's quite the best thing. You'll love Michael Rau."

"Balls to Michael Rau! With them. In there."

Her complexion had settled at a delicate pink, except for the flush up the back of her neck. She was wonderful to watch. Brother follows in her wake and knows from that moment that she will be a truly great actress.

The Lizard-rat saw her coming. By planting himself so close to the palms in our hotel's dining room, Nicholas Baer had hoped that she would see him. He would have anticipated the pleasure of inflicting more pain on a fallen virgin. With his lizard luck there was a Society photographer present to catch the public humiliation of a Minor Talent who got Above Herself.

"Good evening, Nicholas. I'm sorry I'm late. You know how rehearsals are. And you don't mind me bringing Eddie? – his dinner arrangements unexpectedly fell through. Waiter, may we have an extra chair? Thank you. Now Nicholas, you must introduce us to your piano-player from Salzburg – is it your very first solo? – I say, what fun."

Some pathetic little creature from the ballet. The meal concludes. Nicholas Baer's duelling scars are as livid as the Imperial's hotel carpets, above his rat's moustache. The Honourable Edwina Casson-Perceval insists that the head-waiter bring the Herr Conductor one of the Imperial's best cigars and a second brandy: "When we're enjoying ourselves so much, it seems a pity to rush away."

Mama couldn't have done it better. After our Good-nights, and Let's all do this again, Eddie took her back in the birdcage lift. She even kept it up with me until her door was closed. But through the long night I heard her howl like a dog. Like Mama on the day we heard that Our Father died.

... *On Our Island:* To let Sister recover from Love. Just Ettie, Eddie, and a Mathilde ecstatic at having her charges once more where they belong: out of this world. One day a yacht of compatriots arrives to anchor in our Bay of the Lobsters, and –

Eddie found two of them DOING IT! – STARK NAKED in our cove.

For the first time a Boy sees it all! – what gods & goddesses, Wotan & Fricka, Lizard Rat & Sister, Mama & Papa, Richard & Cosima, Siegfried & Winifred ...

The spread thighs and white buttocks glistening on the beach fascinate yet still repel. The figures thrashing and slipping are attractive, agile and young. But the Master in his floppy hat at 60? The Widow in her weeds? Not possible!

Our Career:
Rocketing. Old Meyerhof gets offers for the Hon Edwina C-P as Elisabeth in an Edinburgh Don Carlos, and Agathe in a Freischütz at Weimar, and the Marschallin in a Paris Rosenkavalier as icing on the cake – before going to Bayreuth in June to rehearse for the following year.

"The idea of Paris terrifies me – Eddie, write and tell him I can't. I'm not ready for the Frogs yet."

"I don't see why Paris is any worse than Vienna."

"It just *is*. Darling, they *booed* Wagner."

Eddie writes to old Meyerhof and adds at the bottom, "If I were you I'd say 'yes' all round and just wait. She'll go at the end."

Paris cheers. Her notices everywhere are skyhigh. Brother gets to see a lot of hotels and rehearsal halls.

GREETINGS YOU BOTH ONE ELISABETH IS YOURS IF VOICE
WORKS MUCH TRAINING NEEDED LOVE REAL SIEGFRIED
STOP

"Oh Gawd, what a darling poppet, but I simply *can't*!" And after the full weight has sunk in. "Why is he giving me just one of the Elisabeths? Surely if I'm good enough the first time, I'm good enough for both, as long as I don't croak. It's Auntie, I just bet."

"I'm not writing about that," Eddie protests, "Winnie doesn't have anything to do with the casting at Bayreuth."

Or much else.

Sister begins her wheedling campaign for more Elisabeths, the morning of rehearsal. "Surely, Uncle Siegfried, I could at least have two?"

"Already I'm taking a chance on the voice, Edwina, my dear. For one Elisabeth you will have to stretch all the way. However, you can have a Waltraute also if you wish."

"Both Waltrautes," said the Honourable Edwina, trading. "You said yourself about second fiddles, and after Sieglinde, it's such a tiny little part. They'll never remember me."

"My dear child, you are going to be Elisabeth in between."

"But only once. And truly, on reflection – Eddie and I were just talking possible roles last night – he agrees that Waltraute is too low for me now. Don't you, Eddie?"

Siegfried gave an amused but tired smile. "The Tannhäuser is my new production, Edwina, the first since the war. If I give you first understudy for Müller in the other Elisabeths, do you think you could manage the Waltraute range?"

209

"I'll just have to won't I? Oh, Eddie, isn't Uncle Siegfried simply a perfectly positive dear!"

THE CRASH

...*At Bamberg, '29:* By now the Scholar has the run of the Ecclesiastical Library on the Michaelsberg. His mission is to track the movement of the Teutonic Knights from Nibelheim to their last outpost in the Castle of Bran.

"If he has the cash, can't a Christ-killer buy his way in to this kingdom for Heaven's sake?"

In English, a complete surprise: the rumpled smiling figure of Michael Rau being restrained by a fluttering cleric at the library door.

"Make a donation, Rau – and keep your voice down."

A friend, and vastly welcome, yet we have to say it: the Scholar is embarrassed – and only 18. Michael Rau is, loudly, and if not in any way orthodox, still all too obviously one of Them, and this is a Jesuit library. Shades of Torquemada.

Ten new marks stopped the fluttering.

"There was a lot to be said for indulgences, Eddie – the Great Reformer didn't understand a thing about cash flow. Your landlord told me you'd be here. How's your talented sister?"

"Bargaining Elisabeths. It's like indulgences. You have to be part of it to understand."

"Aren't we always the outsider?" Rau smiled more widely, making more chins. "I missed lunch. Let's go out and find a place ..."

The friends settle in a café with a terrace on the west-bank side. A rose garden is planted next to it; a thousand blooms, ten times as many bees. Occasionally one flies into the mugs of beer.

"Wagner's idea of Eden," said Michael Rau. "Eddie, you've had a birthday. Your delightful sister I know is already a gold bug – what are you doing with your cash?"

"I don't do anything. My cousin manages it in London. He says he's made a heap for us in the stock market. Apparently everything's almost doubled in the last year."

"Do you want to keep it or lose it?"

210

Edwin looked at his new friend carefully. Still joking? He wasn't. He was just asking the question. Either way he wouldn't care. "Of course I want to keep it, Michael. We have to. The singing doesn't pay a quarter of all the travelling. Cousin Wynchman-Hare told Ettie, but she won't listen. We don't get a penny from her gold. It just sits there with Mama's. I suppose someone goes down and counts it now and then."

"Rheingold bars with Casson-Perceval stamped on them." Rau laughed and rescued a drowning bee from his beer. "Tell your cousin to sell the stocks, convert to bullion like your sister, and move three-quarters of it to a Swiss bank. My father has a Zürich branch, or I can give you another name."

The bee wobbled, and dried its boozer's wings.

"Sell my stocks? But they're still going up."

"I know," Michael Rau said sadly, as the bee took a first uncertain step. "It's a wonderful chance to lose a bundle."

"There is Speculation abroad – !" bellows an incredulous Wyn*man-Hare in London, in August, in his overheated Chambers – "it is only too painfully obvious that you have been talking to a Jew. I am to sell your entire portfolio? To *Switzerland*? – good God almighty, there is a strain of madness in your mother's family! There could be grounds for questioning in Chancery. For a Casson-Perceval is not even the Bank of England sound enough?"

Eddie wants to weaken. Ettie wants to get away for ten days on our island before starting as Donna Elvira for the terrifying Pill Man at the Garden.

"Michael Rau's your friend and the Hare-pig is hateful. And I liked Switzerland – don't you remember, Eddie? – so long ago, with Mama, the start of the Rhine. We've pots of money anyway. Just do it."

Edwin does it. A letter is sent around by hand-messenger to cousin's Chambers. The acknowledgement of sale and transfer was marked only by a scrap of paper initialled by his clerk. The First Mercantile Bank of Zürich, however, sends an embossed letterhead with a confidential number and is Pleased to have on Board.

The C-Ps sail on to see their fortunes rise – as the Central Banks fall off the Gold Standard and the Outside world goes bust.

... April, 1930:

MOTHER JOINS FATHER TOMORROW STOP PRIVATE
IN HOFGARTEN COME IF YOU CAN STOP SIEGFRIED

Bordered in black. Cosima, The Keeper of the Flame, is gone through the curtain. Her hearse stops for one long minute in front of His great hall on the Magic Mountain ... Bayreuth falls silent ... Edwin feels sadness seeing her lying in black, but it was not like Mama. The Widow, in her weeds, with her rice-paper face and hands, had been half with death since I first met her.

The hearse moves on. Real-Siegfried, looking tired, is freed at last. His wife, no longer the Daughter-in-Law, even freer. The jealously guarding Parrot-Sisters are the caged ones.

To the notes of her Master's masterpiece, her lover's *Parsifal*, lowered on Norns' threads, Cosima went below the grey granite to meet Him with Erda, and all the other spirits waiting for us in the earth.

The Kaffeeklatsch Circle

... At the Gerbers': After Wagnerian Death, and 6 glorious weeks of bouillabaissing, swimming, sunning, Mediterranean *life*!

"Let us hope brighter days for our country," says little Herr Gerber, bowing Us in. "We have ready your special room."

Partly out of fondness, partly because business is down – optimists and desperate alike are still waiting for The Turn. Putzi Hanfstaengl is an optimist. Edwin finds his Giant friend having a leisurely Chicago breakfast behind a newspaper in the Gerbers' public dining salon next morning. Sister always has breakfast in her room – even the strongest ego can only take so much mauling by the fans.

"Eddie-pal, great to see you! Drag up a chair. Hava-coupla easy-overs."

"Thank you, Putzi, I've eaten with Ettie, but I'll hava java."

"Good boy – you're learning."

To play gangsters. Edwin asks, "Is Herr Wolf in Munich?"

"Psst!" The Giant puts an 8-inch index finger to his lips: a glance

212

indicates mock-terrors. "Our Adolf's keeping his whereabouts extra hush-hush. People are after us."

"Bill collectors, Putzi?"

"Eddie-pal, you slay me. Tell you what, it's opening day at the Brown House, if you're not busy come on along."

"I'll have to confirm with Ettie."

"Uh-huh."

What wealth of meaning may be carried in a grunt . . .

"Why on earth should I want to see his new house," said Sister. "Give me a minute to find some gloves."

Fifteen. For more java, and giant-gossip on Münchener personalities.

"Aren't you two ever going to stop?" The Honourable Edwina trips across from the lift, delicious in white silk with yellow flowers.

"Van Gogh," says the Giant. "Ettie-moll, a knockout."

"They are a bit, aren't they? Putzi-dear, tell me all about Wolf's new house. Is it far?"

"The Briennerstrasse. An easy walk, four blocks. I have to drop in for some portraits he ordered – it's on the way."

The trio sets off down the Residenzstrasse and takes a shortcut across the Salvatorplatz. Traffic waits patiently for the enormous man and the golden girl.

The principal subject is in the centre of the window.

Photographie – ATELIER-HOFFMANN – Porträts

The Frozen Wolf all the world knows.

"Really, Putzi, he must learn to smile more. You can't make people vote by frowning at them, surely."

"The Leader never smiles, Fräulein Edwina, it's a Rule."

"It's his ghastly rotten teeth. I can't imagine why he hasn't had them fixed."

"Me neither. Your mother offered the moola."

The handle turns. A shop bell rings.

"Guten Tag, Eva."

"Guten Tag, Herr Hanfstaengl."

Another Shop-girl: this one on a step-ladder, reaching, so that her skirt lifts, showing the beginning of thigh above the back of knee – just enough to wet a man's whistle. She climbs down from her stepladder, demurely adjusting, and gives the C-Ps a pretty little bob with her pretty little head. To the Trade they look like ready cash.

"Yes, your pictures are ready," this Shop-girl said to Putzi, in a pleasant, not uneducated voice. "I made sure they were done early. A Stitch in Time, as they say – would you like to see before I wrap them for the Fuehrer?"

So with the little blush that follows, the Cat, for one as finely tuned as Sister, is a mile out of the Bag – as they say.

Ettie, in flutingly pure High Hun, with her sweetest smile, on our way out, while the door was still open: "What a charming little frock your shopgirl friend was wearing. The hem was a bit uneven at the back. I suppose it's hard to see when you're pinning things on yourself. Thank God for the costume department. Is she sleeping with him, Putzi?" Casually, as the theatre world does, for the rest of it to hear, in English, in the street.

"You know the Leader holds himself pure for the Nation, Fräulein Edwina." The giant was formal in his native tongue.

"I'm not talking about his 'I can't marry' nonsense – what about that other girl we met? I don't mean the henhouse one who tried to hang herself, the one at the picnic?"

"Herr Wolf's niece?" Brother was shocked.

"Half-niece," said Sister. "Only the C of E and the Pope worry about halfs like that."

"Fräulein Geli, Fräulein Edwina. She lives currently in her uncle's apartment."

Edwin said, "Is that why he needs a new house, Putzi?"

The giant's crooked head almost splits with the effort of keeping a straight face. "Possibly, Herr Edwin. The apartment, however, is on the Prinzregentstrasse. A good address, I assure you. The Leader has nine rooms. With his generous nature he has allowed his dear niece her own suite. Fräulein Geli is a student, one understands, in thespian and choral arts."

DER BRAUNHAUS

On the other side of the Briennerstrasse: what had been the Barlow

Palace, run-down, with broken glass and boarded doors, now has Mowgli-banners & Eagles. The front doors gleam with varnish and brass and His warm welcome.

"My gracious young friends, what an honour! Hanfstaengl, well done!" Surprised, but delighted, with the bubbling pride of all new owners. "I was itching for someone to show my new treasures to, and you arrive! What a wonderful surprise! Yes, the interior's my own design – with execution by Troost, one didn't draw the final prints, naturally – but all the doors, the furniture. And just let me show you the new marquetry. The stairs had to be completely redone. Later we must have some proper art! – it's my wartime regiment, all but fifty of us wiped out! It has to be a miracle I'm here at all. Enough of the war. This is the future – our Senate Hall. I didn't want that round-table nonsense of Himmler's – there has to be a head to everything. The horseshoe is an admirable compromise, and it's lucky for those who are superstitious. And always in memory, our true heroes! The early ones like your so-noblest mother we shall never, ever, forget!"

60 chairs upholstered in red morocco wait for new Teutonic Knights – and from the Fallen of the Putsch, engraved in bronze, His young guests are whisked to the Leader's Seat in the cellar canteen for whipped-cream Kaffee. Half-full mugs show hasty departures. Eddie munches a cake. Gracious Ettie sips coffee.

"The cream's turned, but it doesn't matter. Eddie, visiting the studio reminded me that I need a new picture for this year's programme. I wonder if we should have Hoffmann's take my portrait – the girl in the shop was so sweet and helpful. What do you think, Wolfi?"

"Hoffmann's girl – ?" for a moment even the Leader is at a loss for words. "No. No – no, dear gracious Fräulein Edwina I don't see Hoffmann for you at all. Parades are one thing, and God knows with these unfortunate features, there's little enough harm his camera can do to me! But for Bayreuth, for the programme, in my opinion definitely absolutely, no! And now my dear young friends, I must give you back to Hanfstaengl. Another rally for a Recruiting Night. By heaven I'll be glad when this phase of the struggle is done! The galley staff can't be excused for the cream. I shall have to wag a finger."

Edwin said, "Thank you for the cake and coffee anyway. When you come to Bayreuth next time perhaps you would allow us to invite you to dinner at the Griesbachs', Herr Wolf? Frau Griesbach is an excellent cook."

"I'm not much challenge with my black bean soup. But we'll see, my Ederl, we'll see. Dear Fräulein Ettie – one awaits Herr Siegfried's new Tannhäuser and your Elisabeth with the greatest possible anticipation. But not Hoffmann!"

... *Under the Limes:* The familiar rehearsal round begins. Real-Siegfried feels the pressure, his new version of Tannhäuser: Wagnerians outraged can bay for the blood even of a high priest.

"Never mind, children, never mind – once more the Parsifal – let us go back to Kundry's cruel laughter with the Kiss. Remember she is an enchantress of men against her will. It is Klingsor – where's our Klingsor, ah there, excellent fellow. Now, Klingsor, remember – belief in nothing! The chaos of pure egoism. Edwin, if you please, from the seventh bar."

Brother walks Sister to her first semi-dress Elisabeth. The easel-blackboard on the grass lists Siegfried's whimsical requirements:

Bull

Swan

Cows, one herd!

Hounds, 32

Horses, 5

The hounds pay no attention to anything else musical, but whenever the Honourable Edwina reaches an especially pure Elisabeth they begin to howl in unison.

"I like an appreciative audience, dearest Uncle Siegfried – but couldn't they at least go around to the back of the hall?"

Even there they heard her. "Your projection is just too perfect, my dear Edwina. You should be on horseback leading a hunt. Imagine, what a magnificent setting for Brünnhilde that would be."

"Is that a promise, you darling darling Siegfried? Brünnhilde? Next year?"

"One of these days, perhaps. Edwin, my friend, ask if we can't move those wretched dogs."

"How far, Herr Siegfried?"

"Across the River Main – that should be enough even for your sister!"

Venusberg:

Upstairs at the Griesbachs': Eddie bathed first, then ran fresh water from the cold tap only. Bayreuth's weather is unbearably sultry. Ettie came in and threw off her clothes. She took it for granted that I was naked.

"God," she said, settling, "so lovely and cool. Eddie, to be a love, do my back with the loofah."

He scrubbed her flesh which was his flesh. I kissed the nape of her neck. She said, "Mmm, funny old Eddie – that doesn't feel like a loofah!"

After Nicholas Baer she knows what it feels like. What it looks like.

She turns her head. Brother's pulsing flesh is level with her perfect nose. "Poor darling, we must find you a girlfriend. Poor Eddie . . ."

She touched me. Thunder crashed above Bayreuth. Lightning shot from groin to spine. I gasped. I kissed her lips. "I love you, Ettie. Only you. Always."

"And I love you too, pet, but we can't. We mustn't let ourselves."

But she was still holding – that uncontrollable part that tries blindly to jerk itself free of her binding fingers, to find that secret room waiting just below the surface of the bathwater where the Rhinemaidens swim to and fro, taunting all men, *"Come down, come down . . ."*

To the Venusberg! Reach my hand for her golden pudenda. Her thighs don't stop me. My Piscean fingers slip in again to that room of the House of Brothers and Sisters. The purple-satin gleaming place they have been so long denied. More thunder, more lightning. Her head is back, her eyes are closed. My lips find her nipples. Her hand begins a speeding rhythm on my chimney – we know only too well how quickly that fire ends! Oh, traitorous Venus! Into her bath. Splashing. I was on top of her –

"Eddie, oh Eddie . . ."

But she isn't stopping me! Nearer the secret. Nearer, then –

Terrible lightning. One last colossal thunder. The whole house shook. I was flung aside, hit my head against the metal rim of the bath.

Herr Griesbach's voice comes weakly, "An elm has fallen on the house. Upstairs, my children, are you all right?"

The evidence of the closeness of our peril lies whitely on a sister's stomach.

"Yes," she calls from the bath, as the evidence floats off in filaments that weave among the gold strands of her pubic hair, "thank you, Herr Griesbach, Eddie bumped his head but otherwise we're both all right."

We blame it on the oppressive weather. Workmen come and chop away the elm. Eddie agrees with Ettie that he won't be so silly again.
But all I thought was, SHE DIDN'T STOP ME!
Nor has the storm cleared the air of Bayreuth.
"Edwin, my arm, the chest . . . don't tell my singers . . . I don't feel very well."
For 7 days Real Siegfried hovered as his Festival went on. Mausi, his special daughter, came from her English school to save him – but the doctors, being doctors, said shock would kill him and would not let her in.
And so he died.

THE CHANGING OF THE GUARD

A SPECIAL DESPATCH FOR THE YELLOW PRESS
by Our Man on the Green Hill

CAVIARE IN A CAULDRON

Bayreuth this morning is a seething Wagnerian cauldron! Rumours, doubts, affects-on-careers, and-where-will-the-cash-come-from?

(They say Karl Muck, the famous conductor, alone consumes a pound of caviare at a sitting between acts!)

SCOOP! WIDOW'S NIGHT DEATH-WISH REVEALED

Through this dark night the New Widow, (Frau W, a lifelong Wagnerian) has faced two choices: repeat her girlhood triumph as Senta in the Flying Dutchman, and hurl herself into the vortex from the cliff. Or – follow the Old Widow's example and keep the leaking ship afloat. Your reporter was given an exclusive hint. . . .

POLITICIAN'S RED MYSTERY CAR

At 5 AM, a scarlet Mercedes roadster was seen driving away at high speed from the guest cottage in the grounds (insiders call it the Siegfried House). It is our belief that the New Widow received advice in the crisis from Herr W**f (the once-jailed Mowgli politico). Karl Muck's advice quote, "Not to bring in that Wop!" has been discarded. (And Tosca-No-No, as they call him, is getting next year's Parsifal as well!)

PARROT SISTERS DECLARE WAR

Before the late Festival Director was even underground, two of his Sisters (known to insiders as The Parrots) had already joined forces with the City Fathers of Bayreuth. According to "M", these 2 old ladies are currently "Hatching and plotting like Norns!"

ENGLISH WOMAN'S HOME HER CASTLE

Surrender terms: The burghers of Bayreuth want nothing less than The Master's Home for a pay-at-the-door museum! The New Widow's response? Quote, "An Englishwoman's home –" (One bright spark: the caviare eater, Karl Muck, has resigned!)

STORK ENGAGED

After Frau W begged on her knees, the services of crane-necked Wil-

helm F*** wangler (Ni-
belheim's premier con-
ductor, The Stork, to
insiders) after quote,
"His god-awful endless
dilly-dallying"

WINNIE WEEPS

At first hand: Frau W
openly wept! But the
question remains: Can
there really be any fin-
ancial hope of rescue
for this so-gallant, em-
battled Englishwoman?

Late Flash
NEW MAN ON WAY

Herr W**f (the mystery
man in the Red Mer-
cedes) in national elec-
tions has just leapt
from minor-role ob-
scurity to 107 Reichstag
Seats on centre-stage!
And our source (at the
very centre of the
Struggle), tells us,
quote, "Now those
bloody old squawking
farts will see – a New
Man *is* coming!"

First Movement
Fifth Passage

[basso ostinato]

❧

. . . *Berlin: March the 11th, 1931.* For the first time the capital of Nibelheim comes into our Edda-saga, just before Our Birthday, for Sister's in Fidelio, rounding out the season Unter den Linden.

"Oh Gawd, Eddie, the Berlin State! You know the stone-throwers do that awful whistling when they boo. I simply *can't.*"

The Capital's stone-throwing opera-lovers keep up their ovation for the Honourable Edwina for an hour. The stage is carpeted in flowers. "Aren't they dear," she said, on our Birthday-night dinner in the Hotel Esplanade, "what a marvellous present. Did you ever know an audience to be so wonderfully *aware?*"

"Half the applause was for Furtwängler." Damn it, it was Edwin's 20th birthday. "He's a little funny to look at, but frightfully good."

"He's Godawful to look at, those thyroid eyes on a stork's neck. If you once start to watch it's hopeless. The head-bobbing puts you right off your time. But Tosca-no-no was a treasure. I'll kill if Winnie doesn't keep me with the Wop Man for Elisabeth again this year."

"As well as Brünnhilde?"

"Don't be silly. Of course I know I can't be Brünnhilde this year – the

221

roles are frozen – we're lucky to have any Bayreuth at all. I'm going to go after Winnie for next season. Happy birthday, Eddie darling – '33 –, that's going to be our first *big* year!"

To a smattering of applause – not for her Sisterly kiss on Brother's cheek – a small convoy crosses the hotel's dining room: the head waiter with flunkeys towing a huge cake with sparklers, and champagne – and behind:

"Good Lord – Waring!"

Taller, but still shorter than Eddie by two inches. Carrying a new shooting-stick. Otherwise, just the same. Smiling in his diffident, yet cocksure way – bringing back the whole school-chum ghastliness in the organ loft.

"I knew you'd be pleased," said Sister. "We met outside Siegel's Luggage yesterday morning, but I made Jeremy keep it as your surprise. I bet you thought I forgot it was your Twentieth."

Jeremy!

"What on earth are you doing visiting Berlin? The acting or the writing?"

"More like watching, I suppose," said Waring. "Well actually, living."

"In Berlin?" said Sister. "How marvellous. I've been thinking that Eddie and I should find a little flat in Berlin, so that it won't always be hotels with a suitcase when we're in Hunland but not Bayreuth. Not more than six rooms – counting my maid's – and a nice view. Where do you live, Jeremy?"

She looked expectantly – but it was obvious from his dinner jacket.

"I don't know that you would call it actually live," said Waring. "I sort of rotate. At the moment I have a fifth-floor room with a cracked window off an alley behind the Alexanderplatz at the Luxemburg Gardens end. Lots of people. It's the best a chap's had as far as watching goes."

The jacket was greenish, clearly hired. A chap's time for tact, but Champagne pops English inhibition.

Edwin said, "What's happened since frightful school?"

"Cambridge for a year, C-P – and then the Vicar died, and the last of the money sort of went with him, and the Crash crashed, so there wasn't really much of an option. I'm not complaining. I've found a chap really doesn't need much in Berlin, just to watch."

222

Ettie said, "So a chap could actually say you're stony broke?"

"Yes, one could actually."

Heedless Sister giggled, then asked, "Would you like some cash as well as the stick?"

"Yes please." Waring smiled at her over the bubbles, "cash is the one thing a chap's short of. Not eating makes even just watching rather a bore."

"Watching exactly what, Waring?" signalling casually to the head waiter for another bottle. The group's 3rd.

"Life in the street, C-P. Head-bashing. Men leaping out of windows."

"You *haven't?*" said Sister. "Not really leap?"

"Don't be bloody silly," Eddie said.

"No." Waring admitted it. "But I saw one on the Alexanderplatz deliberately jump in front of a tram."

"Anna Karenina." Sister gave her Operatic sigh. "Jeremy you can't know how much I envy you. Capitalism! If you could only *see* the Wagnerian variety we get at Bayreuth."

"I'd like to, Edwina. As a matter of fact a chap was going to try and screw up the courage to ask if you ever have tickets?"

Some screw. Edwin stared at the two of them, unable to determine what amazed more: Waring's utter self-confident smoothness in begging or the Honourable Edwina's sudden espousal of the Class War.

...At the Kaffeeklatsch: Two months later, June, the Carlton Tea Room, just down from the Brown House on the Briennerstrasse. (The Casson-Percevals did not take any accommodation in Berlin that spring.) Ettie & Eddie are laughing at an Adolf-story of giant-Putzi's – when both principals walk in: Onkel, with half-niece-Geli on arm.

"Herr Edwin, Gnädiges Fräulein Edwina – my niece, Fräulein Raubal. Herr Hanfstaengl, you know."

Stiff, stilted introductions. The Honourable Edwina rises to the occasion with her most gracious smile; "Fräulein Geli, our lovely picnic, you were serving so prettily – do sit by me and tell me all about your singing lessons."

Uncle Alf hesitates – and our Geli is dropped in place between Brother & Sister.

223

Eddie said, "We haven't had the chance to congratulate you on your election victories, Herr Wolf."

"No politics, please," He tapped my knee. His eyes were on Ettie – the ribbon with Mama's locket around her neck. "It's not often I get the chance to be among artists these days. Artists and poachers are my favourite people – they both live happily apart from the rules of the bourgeois world. Tarts adore poachers – excuse us, noble Fräulein Edwina – shall I say, women adore real men! The protection of heroes."

"These days, Wolfi my dear, we ladies have to settle for poachers because there aren't as many heroes to go round."

She touches the locket, turns it. He flushed at the Wolfi.

"Exactly, most gracious Fräulein Ettie! The decay of civilisation. We need a touch of ancient Rome. I'm not thinking of blood sports – decadent Spaniards, it's disgusting! No. Say the Olympic Games. Something of that quality all year round. Don't you agree, Herr Ederl – then our ladies would have their heroes?"

"It would be all right for Ettie and Fräulein Geli, Herr Wolf, but I'm not much good at games, except for tennis."

"Adolf isn't even good at that – and he's a hero!" Putzi Hanfstaengl, giant-thrill-seeker, throws back his great head and roars. Niece-Geli laughs with him – a belligerent act. Before that she had looked bored. Now His neck was flushed.

"As far as I'm concerned," said Sister, stroking the ribbon in all innocence, "heroes come in all shapes and sizes. I took your advice, by the way, about not getting my portrait from Hoffmann's – but I let them do a passport. The little girl there was so sweet and disappointed, one couldn't refuse. What *was* her name? Eddie? – or Geli dear, you must know? – rather like you? but more blonde?"

Olympic games for women: javelins across a tea table. Under the cloth Eddie feels Geli's thigh muscle tighten against his own.

"Fräulein Braun, I believe, is the name, Fräulein von Perceval," replied Fräulein Raubal.

His flush subsided. This glimpse of blood sport between His women had quite restored His spirits. "Most honourable, gracious Fräulein Edwina, my thanks for the tea. Ederl – no! I have a better idea. We've all got on so well together. Tonight, after dinner – I have a meeting first – at my apartment for coffee and cakes. Just the four of us – you'll be with

Goebbels in Berlin by then, Hanfstaengl; I can't wait another minute for this Foreign Press nonsense! – you've been to Harvard; you speak their language. Herr Edwin, no taxis; I'll send Maurice."

Niece-Geli's thigh slides along Eddie's as she rises to leave, and walks out with Uncle, the line of her knickers showing . . .

"Too many Kuchen," said Sister. "Which Maurice, Putzi?"

"A thug from the beerhall days, completely thick and loyal to the death to the Leader's person. With the hots for his niece. But then she goes for anything in pants."

The Gilded Cage

. . . *16, Prinzregentstrasse:* E & E walk from Thug-Maurice into a spacious hall and up a broad flight of wooden stairs to the second floor to be met at the door by a School matron.

"Gnädiges Fräulein, Herr von Perceval, please to come in, Herr Adolf is not yet back. I am Frau Reichert, his housekeeper." She leaves Brother & Sis reconnoitering alone in the parlour.

"Winnie really should send him down one of the Set decorators, Eddie. This South Hun upholstery makes you feel you're trapped between balloons."

The red plush divan has moved from the Hen-house. Above it is a garish Leda & Swan. Beside that, 4 canaries, whistling, in a baroque brass prison.

"And I simply can't stand birds in cages. Some of the pictures are quite nice. This church – oh, it's one of his own. Eddie, you must look – what funny little people."

St Peter's and the Market Square in Munich, another two of Old Vienna. He gets the buildings right, but the people are wooden and lost and tiny.

"He *never* feels for people!"

Geli – suddenly beside us and the bird cage in the drawing room, with her tight skirt and puffy cheeks under pink eyes.

"You're not at the meeting?" Was all Eddie could think to say.

"I hate the meetings. Honz sweetie, come to Geli." She put a red nail-polished finger through the bars of the cage. A canary with a white head jumped on the finger. Geli kissed the bird and challenged Edwin with parted lips, moistly.

"But it must be tremendously exciting, Fräulein Geli," the Boy said, "with all those people roaring?"

"He never takes me to them anyway. He gave me this horrid brass cage instead. They had a much nicer one before, of wood."

His half-niece moved the horrid cage to a window.

The Honourable Edwina said, "Geli darling, you've done your hair since this afternoon, how chic."

Sleeker, pulled in at the back on the neck, to make a Geli an Ettie – instead of a healthy, wanting desperately to be happy, common, orchard cottage, doll.

"I always think, at his meetings, Fräulein von Perceval – this time will there be a gun? I can't help it, and don't tell him, but I just hate guns. I shouldn't be so gloomy. Will you have wine with the cakes? Uncle Alf won't touch wine, but he'd like you to if you enjoy it. We have in some bottles made when the grapes are going bad and you get that delicious honey taste?"

We sat together on the red divan by the birdcage, touching. Her forehead was low, her cheekbones broad, her mouth too large, her nose too flat and wide and turned up – yet to Edwin she was pretty. She was forbidden.

Said Sister, "I'll try a little of your funny rotten wine, Geli dear."

"All enjoying yourselves?" Hearty Onkel Alf is back. There hasn't been any sound of arrival at the door. "Didn't I say this afternoon, Geli child? Just the right sort of group. Music and art, we have the best things in common – the only things. I curse the hours I have to put in on Machiavelli – Geli, my angel, you know your mother doesn't like you wearing rouge – but there it is! War and Politics, the way our horrible modern world goes round – Meetings, meetings, meetings! I've planned twenty-eight cities in five days with the aircraft, can you believe it?! There's no need to pout, child. You can see, the so-noble Fräulein Edwina wears no rouge at all!"

The Reluctant Politician looks at His half-niece with eyes that are part moon-calf and part not. He sets down His whip, gloves, velour hat – and the Desperado gun. Geli gives a tiny shudder.

"I could eat a horse!" declares the whip's owner. "If those wretched yellow squawkers would only shut up. Frau Reichert, you must be so kind as to bring out the cakes at once. Geli, child, cover the cage and keep amusing our guests while Uncle Alf washes his hands."

Geli half covered the cage. "Poor Honz darling, Uncle Alf's so cruel."

When He came back talk turned to Bayreuth and the up-coming Season, "With Furtwängler and the Italian both – that'll give us some fireworks!" – and of Sister as Tannhäuser's pure Elisabeth, "One of the Master's shallow women. We have to admit. Mein Ederl, most gracious Fräulein Ettie, is it too much to ask that you do a Liebestod for me?"

"I couldn't possibly do a note, Wolfi dear – my throat's resting."

Torturess. She touches the locket ribbon. His hand trembles. Brother plays, greasing the skids for the court-pianist from Chicago. Geli-child stares at the gun by the whip. Onkel blows His nose. On our way out, He washes His hands again and makes a point of showing us His half-niece's separate room. Dirndl flounces on the curtains and quilted spread. And a simple little wood-bird's cage, with a swing, deserted.

"Delightful," said Edwin's sister, the Bayreuth Opera Singer. "It quite makes one wish that one could be a little girl again."

Geli kisses golden Eddie goodbye – aiming for the cheek, but getting the ear, on the lobe, enfolding with hot parted lips, wetly. Onkel shakes hands and grips shoulders, but His all-seeing eyes retain that Kiss. As the door closes, behind it, voices are rising.

The 2nd Battle of the Parrots

. . . *At Wahnfried HQ:* A sun-drenched afternoon. The windows to the Music Room are open. Outside, in the gardens E & E are dragged by Mausi and Wolfgang to inspect 8 puppies born to the Schnauzer bitch, Stritzi.

"I didn't kiss him!"

A shrill Norn's screech by Daniella, comes through the window.

"You did!" Winifred, a Senta at full bore, shouting. "How can you deny it? After the Memorial! You hurled your arms about his neck. Heinz Tietjen saw you. The whole damn orchestra saw you!"

"I didn't. I didn't! I never have kissed Herr Doctor Furtwängler."

The sound of bitter feminine Norn weeping.

227

"You did. And we all know why!"

"Winifred, how dare you?!" Eva, hopping to back her sister, but weakly.

"I know how she dares," between sobs from Daniella. "All Bayreuth knows. With That Man ... "

"What Bayreuth knows – " now a positively Helden bellow from Senta – "Bayreuth knows you for a horrible scheming old maid who was married twenty-eight years and never kissed before by anyone! Even her own husband!" A last wild Norn shriek-gasp parrotted in unison. "And spare me any more of your damn histrionics! I've lost Toscanini. Now Furtwängler isn't coming back next year either. No Melchior. No conductors. No money. You've deliberately sabotaged everything I've been trying so desperately to save. Well to hell with all of you! My husband's will states that *I* alone am the beneficiary. There *shall* be a Festival in '33. I may die in the attempt but let me tell you, old women – you'll go first."

"Aren't they adorable?" said Mausi.

"I can't wait to tell Putzi," said the Honourable Edwina.

"Damn all of you," cried the New Widow, "I'll find *someone*!"

... So Auntie promotes Heinz Tietjen, the Prussian, her Artistic Director.

HUNDING'S HUT

... *At the Griesbachs':* "After this madhouse of a season," said Sister (re '31's) as Brother was brushing her waistlong hair, "and with London in November – you know how terrified I am of the Pill Man – Eddie, a friend of Putzi's and Helene's has offered them a dear little summer house down on the Tegernsee, and they can't use it with their divorce business, so let's take it for a month – Porquerolles's so beastly hot and the French are all there anyway until the end of August, and the trees are so lovely in Bavaria when they turn – you can explore some Mad Ludwig castles – oh do let's, Eddie."

As though he ever offers argument? But the Boy thought he might as well use her mock-terror for something positive. "If we can have a car, Ettie, and I drive us down."

228

"You, drive? Eddie, darling, how can you drive?"

"With the gears, and the accelerator. I've been taking lessons from the Griesbachs' man at their garage."

"I don't mean *how* – I mean you never have and it's fearfully dangerous. What if we had an accident and one of us got killed – or I damaged my throat?"

Touching the slender column with her hand, enjoying the moment. Darling Sister's getting more like Mama every day. Lovely.

. . . *At Tegernsee:* 50 kilometers south of Munich, almost centred between Hotel Landsberg and the Salt Mountain, the heart of the pattern. Edwin's first long drive: with the depth of Depression, fortunately not much traffic – although Nuremberg is considerably more alarming than the Boy lets on. The Tegernsee house is one-storey, wooden and thatched, not tarted up with whitewash or enamel, just left to weather. It sits at the end of a narrow lane on its own peninsula. There is a small sagging dock and a boathouse with a sailing boat, and some acres of meadow and orchard, and spinneys of birch and beech with a few isolated leaves already turning purple and gold in advance anticipation of winter. Other summertime visitors sail or swim at houses that are all about but not too close.

"Isn't it simply too adorable, Eddie? With the peninsula it's almost our own little island, but you don't need Deaf'n'Dumber to get on and off."

"Just me driving – it's a long walk to Munich."

"Longer from Bayreuth. Darling, now you can drive, you won't ever leave me, will you?" There hasn't been a word of praise en route for his accomplishment – yet she takes his face between her hands, pulls his head to her and kisses him on his mouth!

For a scalding instant the tip of her tongue was between my lips, then it was gone, darting back like a snake's. Brother & Sister alone in Eden. "Of course I wouldn't leave you – not when you need accompanying. But when you're doing rehearsals it means I can go on my own to places like Bamberg. You hate all that anyway."

"But often I need you for rehearsals too. You know how ghastly some of these conductors are. Eddie, you have to promise. You won't run away?"

"I'm too tired after driving. Let's go inside and see if we can find some tea."

"Oh my Gawd," she said, "I never thought. You don't mean we'll have to actually *cook*?"

That anxiety at least is swiftly laid to rest. As the Orphans walk up on to the porch, the front door opens: the same black dress, but a Bavarian embroidered apron and coiled-grey plaits, and pink cheeks instead of the black hair and brown Mediterranean skin; before us a Bavarian Mathilde, beaming.

"Gnädiges Fräulein! Mein Herr! I am Frau Fischer, your house-keeper." Followed by the inevitable, "*Bruder und Schwester?* – peas in the pod aren't so alike! By the train I was expecting! But by motorcar? And all the way from Bayreuth? You poor children must be quite exhausted. I've coffee and honey cakes waiting. Come in, come in!"

The C-Ps never fall on stony ground . . .

The house – all wood in its interior, and the roof vaults into old adzed beams, but otherwise the arrangement is Porquerolles: a common area for living and eating, with a huge stone fireplace and vital piano; a kitchen with cherry-wood cupboards and a copper sink in a marble slab, and a great iron stove which heats the water for the bathroom.

"And an indoor lav, Eddie – thank heaven. I really didn't want to have to squat outside like a nun." Which sent Frau Fischer guffawing and crossing herself back to her kitchen for fresh honey cake, a staunch peasant catholic. "And two bedrooms," Sister poked her head in. "They look comfy." With carved four-posters and goosedown mattresses and pillows.

"Three," Brother said, "counting the maid's room."

A tiny room, seven feet by ten, with a crucifix starkly on one whitewashed wall over a chamber pot and a white metal bed. The mattress was straw-filled and striped.

"Yes," said Frau Fischer, positively negative in the Hun way, "there is no maid. Stupid young creatures they are anyhow! Better I do it all. From my man's house I come over – he was killed in the terrible war. . . . Your noble English father also? Then you know. Thank God there'll never be another between us! But you don't need to worry about coffee for waking, my children – every morning I'll be here long before your golden heads are off the pillows."

230

She leaves after supper, in time to walk to her dead man's home in the village three miles away, before dark. Eddie's offer to drive her gets the same reaction as Ettie's nun-remark. Guffaws & Crossings as she rounds the bend in the lane and disappears. Leaving Bruder und Schwester for their first night in a house completely alone.

"What a hellish good idea of mine to come down." Recklessly tossing back her second schnaps. "Have another glass yourself while you wait. I'll go first in the bath."

Eddie has the 2nd schnaps and feels it burning.

"I'm out now. You'd better hurry if you want it hot. There doesn't seem to be much more in the kitchen tank."

Only a hollow gurgle, followed by a trickle of ice.

"Never mind." Sister slips on her Yum-Yum silk kimono and ties it loosely around her waist. "You can warm at the fire. I'll heat the damp towel for you."

She wraps the dry one around her head. The kimono clings. Her nipples stand out. With the schnaps, and the clinging, Brother starts his own standing. Washing does nothing to lessen it – with no towels, no way to hide it; forced to walk half-backwards, with a hand placed strategically, dripping through to the living room.

Forced? Sister is in front of the fire with two mugs of chocolate – mixed with our 3rd schnaps – on a copper tray, and the flames gleaming from the tray on the Nibelung gold of her hair. Her Yum-Yum kimono has fallen casually, artfully, open.

"Here darling – " reaching, casually, artfully, up with the warm damp towel, without looking, "let me wrap this round your – Oh dear! " giggling, as by artful accident she touches, "oops, sorry, pet. The bath couldn't have been too cold after all. Sit by me on the hearth. Maybe Thingee'll go down if you have some chocolate."

More giggles. Sitting. Drinking a sip of chocolate with schnaps that scalds the tongue. "You made it too damn hot!" With the towel up in its circus tent. Alive, with the circus creatures under it, twitching. "I've burnt my bloody tongue."

"Poor tongue-ee, poor Thingee, poor Eddie, I'll kiss it all better."

Her mouth on his again, face-to-face, the mirror-image. Doppelgängers, but Male & Female created He them. Her tongue is my tongue. Her hand is my hand on poor Thingee. But the feeling is utterly, utterly different. Licking her nipples . . .

"The roof, Eddie." But the Boy was licking, looking only at the parting, crimson opening of the secret room, opening for him like the petals in the black magician's Parsifal garden. "The beams . . . " his Sister, half a whisper, half moan; half incoherent, half guiding his snub thrusting ignorance into her soft flower with its mystic alchemical scent of transforming power. Boy into Man, *Bruder* into *Schwester*. Four halves: two wholes. "The fireplace . . . oh Eddie . . . flames . . . beams . . . *us*! Oh darling, now, *now* – in our Hunding's Hut!"

Our Hunding's Hut! Three mad Wagnerian words, and so quickly the black magic was over. I collapsed on her body – my body – as it convulsed. Kept on convulsing and gripping long after the male flesh of pride was fallen. That was my second instant lesson. The third was the restorative power of schnaps, in moderation, when mixed with vibrant youth.

"Four times," she said, as over the Tegernsee dawn was dawning. "Oh Gawd, Eddie, I can't again, I'm sore as a badger. And Frau Fischer will be here. Wait till tonight, darling."

But the genie is out of the bottle. Once more, with feeling, for fallen Parsifal. Then we fell apart to our separate beds.

"Exhausted!" clucks Frau Fischer bustling with coffee for our bleary eyes in the middle of the morning. "And no wonder. By motor car! All the way from Bayreuth! Such an activity isn't natural, children."

The Orphans ate a breakfast-lunch of sausage and ham and eggs on the porch and then lay in the sun, and then swam – paddled is the word – and then had a sail on both sides of our peninsula.

"This is pure heaven, but you know, Eddie, it can't be a habit – last night. It has to be special."

"It is special, it's the most wonderful, marvellous feeling I've ever had, but it's also terribly wrong. Ettie, it *is* wrong."

"Of course it isn't wrong – it can't be for everybody, darling, it wouldn't work. But we aren't everybody. What a hoot it'll be next time I play Sieglinde."

We sailed back to our paradise garden. All Brother can think is, Frau Fischer Go Home! Three weeks of sunny days, and endless nights by the fire with Frau Fischer gone home. A honeymoon ... *Or is it a dream? Was there ever an Ettie lying on a rug in a Hunding's Hut for my exquisite pleasure?* Of course there was. She was. But how long did it last? Because all honeymoons must end ...

Three nights I'm sure. Four probably. Five would be stretching, because it would have been a Sunday and the right train didn't run.

"Train?" looking at her incredulously. "Why on earth do you need to catch a bloody *train?*"

She was all dressed and business-like. He was barely awake with Frau Fischer's coffee.

"I'm going to Salzburg. You know Elmendorff wants to talk to me about doing Fiordiligi in Così for their festival in our off-season next year."

"Next year? We're on our bloody – " almost the word slips out, *honeymoon* – "on holiday. And anyway, if you want to go to bloody Salzburg I'll drive you."

"You won't always be bloody able to. That's why I'm going by bloody train, darling. I have to learn to do these things by myself."

"Of course I'll always be able to. Damn it, Ettie, I only took up the driving to be useful for us."

"I'm not complaining, Eddie. You'll want to be off with your old tombs as you said, or Jeremy Waring – I don't mind. Now get out of bed like a dear and drive me to the station."

"Waring? What the hell has driving got to do with Waring?"

"You don't have to get angry. I just happened to mention Jeremy. I could have said your Jew friend, Michael. The point is, you'll be leading your own life. You can't be always cluttered up with me."

"But I want to be cluttered." Almost in tears.

"You're just being sweet. Of course you don't. Here's your other sandal."

The cunning of it! The way the trap was sprung with the honey from the magic garden. But she couldn't have been so calculating. Lying on the rug of Our Hunding's Hut, the grip of her pulsing flesh was not fake. It was *my* flesh. I *knew.*

"When will you be back?" Eddie asked miserably on the Tegernsee platform. "I can't stay in this damned wilderness all alone."

233

"You won't be alone. Frau Fischer will spoil you to death. And anyway, you need a rest. I'm sure it can't be good to do it so many times. You'll wear poor Thingee out. Or me out. Take care. Love you. A couple of days, that's all. Enjoy your clever drive home . . ."

The train chuffs away from Tegernsee Station in the direction of Austria. Or anywhere else. How does he know she's going to Austria? Or ever coming back? Rejected, betrayed by Woman, he drives in a fury to dead Eden on the peninsula. And there he sulks till the cows come home. . . .

A herd of them, dumb beasts, grazing in the grass around the spinneys and orchard. Edwin used to hear them clanking their idiot bells and mooing under his window at six in the morning waiting to be milked. And again in the evening, just at dusk, milling around the gate at the end of the lane. Morning and evening were the first day without Ettie. The second. The third. There is no telephone – no electric light! He has no address to telegraph to Salzburg. One more bloody day (he said to the idiot cows) and I'm driving to bloody Salzburg, and I'm never going to let her out of my bloody sight ever again!

On The 4th Day:

Frau Fischer asks if she can leave early, "Because now the thunder comes? I've left honeycake out, and a ham. Keep the milk under the wet cloth or it'll be sure to turn. Young Herr Edwin, the devil's in that Föhn wind."

She crosses herself. Alone, young Herr Edwin throws sticks and small stones at the cows. "Go up to the bloody gate, go to your own bloody home."

The thunder begins, but still far off. The first rain falls into the Tegernsee, sweeping in a sheet with the mad Föhn wind towards Munich. Froh, the twin brother of Freia, spins his rainbow over my solitary peninsula. There is no pot of gold. Ettie has gone.

The day darkened. The Norns howled on the wind. White water showed on the lake.

> *Loud roars the dreadful thunder,*
> *The rain a deluge show'rs,*
> *The clouds are rent asunder –*

I went to the piano to beat back with its own music the noises of madness. The Storm theme from the Holländer. Pounding. Pounding – but the pounding is real. With that man's cry of the damned for souls in torment.

Someone is at the door. Leave the piano . . . draw back the bar on the door . . . Slowly . . . with excess imagination: the face of madness is only a familiar, though sodden –

"Geli."

"Is she all right?" Edwin shouted back. "Is she outside? Is it lightning? Do you want me to go to fetch her in?"

"Gun – " I think is what He said. Then, "Knife . . . Drown . . . Die . . . Let me . . ." and then, clear as a Wahnfried funeral bell in a lull of the wind, "Can you believe? Ach, mein Ederl – my girl is dead!"

"You mean Mitzi, Herr Wolf – ?" and then with full frightfulness – "oh Christ, not Ettie?"

"My Geli . . ."

"Fräulein Geli?" now it sank in. "She's dead? But how, Herr Wolf? Why? Where? When?" and then, "You're soaked, Herr Wolf," as still He made no answer, "at least come and sit by the fire. I'll make you some coffee. Or chocolate? With schnaps?"

"The world knows it was my gun." He stared, but didn't see. Catatonic. "Near the heart. Not at once. She lingered. Two days ago. Yesterday. I don't remember."

He was not going to move. I took His arm. "You have to sit and get dry, Herr Wolf. This way, by the fire." He let me take Him – like a sleepwalker.

"Her canaries were still singing – " as I placed Him in the chair – "in the new cage. I just gave her the new cage the week before. All except Honzerl – her little favourite with the white head. He was dead too. Beside her. Ach, ach! Gott im Himmel! ACH!"

With that harsh roar of grief He put his own black head in His hands and began to cry. I went for schnaps from the kitchen. I found glasses – I needed help too. I turned with the bottle. He was behind me.

"A knife – in a kitchen you must have a knife."

But His blank eyes didn't look for one. They were fixed on a point of the wall above the copper sink. "No Herr Wolf, there aren't any knives.

Frau Fischer takes them home with her at the end of each day."

Instinct, trying to cope with madness.

"It doesn't matter. We'll find a rope. In a country house there's sure to be rope. Schreck was driving. I said, 'Watch it, Schreck – there's another car behind us!' I wouldn't have had to tell Maurice, but Schreck was new as chauffeur. Just a couple of weeks."

"Please, Herr Wolf, take the schnaps. It really will do you good. Frau Fischer swears by it."

He let me put the glass to His lips, and sputtered and coughed, but most of it went down. "My God, isn't it ironic? I fire Emil Maurice, and all the time it was that bastard music teacher in Linz. Music? Don't tell me! In Their stinking pipe-stem trousers. Crawling – they say the swine got her pregnant but I don't believe it. I *won't* believe it!" Roaring again, spittle in His Ederl's face. "Do you believe it? Pregnant? – BY A *YID*?"

The word sears. *Pregnant!* What if Ettie – ?

"I don't know," Eddie whispers.

"Of course you don't. How can a clean decent boy in the country know the filth of city life?"

But what country do those strange eyes see? What boy? Edwin says, "You were in the car, Herr Wolf?" to get him away from *pregnant*.

"Schreck didn't know about the city either. Not the way in which the rats can suddenly be on you from behind. Now, of course, I've had spotlights installed – I can blind them instantly – but Schreck can't find the switch. I have to direct him – and then I see it's a taxi behind. '*Stop, Schreck!*' I scream. We stop. In the taxi it's a pageboy I recognise from the Deutscher Hof in Nuremberg where we've stayed the night before – I'm on my way to Hamburg. Hoffmann's with me to record it, so I have a witness – five cities in two days! In Nuremberg, you understand? So how can *I* have killed her when my Geli's in Munich? How man? *How*?"

"You couldn't," Edwin said, appalled in his ignorance. "Herr Wolf, you couldn't possibly have killed her."

"The pageboy tells me, 'Herr Hess has called from Munich – even now he's on the telephone. Holding the line open. He refuses for one second to get off. A fortune, mein Herr, it must be costing!' Then I know. *Back!* I shriek at Schreck. We wheel, screaming in the street – a hundred we show on the clock. *Faster, Schreck!* Faster you shithead

236

Saxon bastard! A hundred-and-fifty, two hundred. Two-hundred kilometers an hour we hurtle and all the time the Voice knows, and tells me . . . But still I ask Hess, still holding the line, 'Rudi, is she – ?' I can't say the word, and he won't answer. 'Mein Hesserl – ' I can still hear myself shrieking – 'Hess for the love of the good God just tell me, yes or no?' And still there comes no answer! At this most terrible hour of my life the line's been cut . . ."

I felt that cut. Hot tears welled in my eyes. But His were dry. Red and searing. "I vow as we drive to Munich, *Never again*! Never rely on an idiot-fucking-German-shitbag-rat-bitch of a telephone operator. Germans never accept an Austrian. The same in schools, it doesn't matter how much you give them – Napoleon was always the Corsican – you can never change your place of birth. The Corporal, the ratpack sneered at him – you can't change what life first made you either. The Corsican Corporal. The Housepainter from Wien . . . It's all over by the time we get to Prinzregentstrasse. I look up at the balcony. How can I go up to her? But I do. Through the door I hear the canaries like the thrushes outside my Landsberg cell. This time the birds are the prisoners. I am a dead man. Dr Brandt is in her room. And Goering. 'Hermann – ?' that's all I can say. 'With angels,' he says, 'and archangels.' Goering, that great man, weeps. But her body isn't with the angels. 'My Geli – ?' to ask it is tearing out my heart – 'my angel, *has been given to the corrupt Munich police?*' Hermann can only nod. So be it. I, the Austrian Corporal, must be crucified by this country before I die . . ."

He flung His arms wide against the stone chimney of Our Hunding's Hut – like Tristan when he's lost Isolde. How does a boy hold a man back from taking his own life?

"When will the funeral be for Geli, Herr Wolf? Ettie's in Salzburg. I know she'd like to go?"

"Like – ?"

Want, of course, was the word I meant. But Eddie had said what Ettie would have meant.

"The canaries whistle in their cage. The police have taken her. I shall have to kill myself. There's no other way. Two-hundred kilometres . . . those terrifying shit-horses . . . For more than an hour Hess holds the open line . . ."

Over it, He went, and over; through that long night as the Föhn wind

howled outside. The same story, but sometimes with contradictions –
He got there before she actually had died – and sometimes just distorted
embellishments – "I should myself have shot that accursed snivelling
bastard Yid!" – and sometimes plain statements of amplifying fact: "I
came down here to my publisher's – Müller, he has a place around the
lake. How can I stay in Munich? Hanfstaengl tells me Herr Edwin and
Fräulein Ettie are here. I only know I can't bear another single instant
with a German! Just smelling a German and I can hardly breathe! I
rush out of Müller's house and start to walk through the storm. Even
without my hat. If there is a God he will let the lightning strike. Mein
Ederl – play the Liebestod for me."

We never think of the obvious – using our piano to soothe. Or will it?

"Are you sure, dear Herr Wolf – Liebestod?"

"What else?"

He began to cry again . . .

Frau Fischer found us when she came with a can of fresh morning milk
at six o'clock. Edwin whispered His name, and what had happened. She
had not the least idea who the visitor was. She only recognised a boy
hiding a man's suffering.

"It's time to rest," she said firmly. "I'll make up Fräulein Ettie's bed
and sit by you until you sleep. Come."

And He went, like a child, and as He passed the maid's bare white
room, He said to Frau Fischer in a small boy's voice, "No. Please. I want
to sleep in there."

"And so you shall, my pet." Her peasant instincts knew what she was
dealing with. "You sit, while Frau Fischer gets fresh sheets – so. And a
pillow – so. And turns down your coverlet for you – so. Now get
undressed and she'll come back to tuck you in."

I didn't bother undressing. I just collapsed on my feather mattress. As
sleep came with temporary unravelling, I heard a man's deep little-boy
voice, say, "Frau Fai-Fai, can Dolferl have ribbons on his bed?"

He slept the clock around. I woke at three that afternoon to the honking
of a horn among the mooing of the infernal cows. Through my window,
Mama's red Mercedes. I rushed outside. I expected Schreck, the new
chauffeur replacement for philandering Emil Maurice to have arrived

from the publisher Müller's house. Instead – immense relief! The driver's seat of the car was filled to the roof with –

"Putzi! Thank heavens!"

"He's here then, Eddie-pal? I figured he might be. Müller had no idea where he was. He called up in no end of a sweat to say that Adolf had buggered off in a storm."

Hardly the sympathy due a great tragedy.

"He's inside, Putzi. Sleeping at last. He talked and talked. I couldn't get him to bed until eight this morning."

"More than we could. He's been like a chicken with its head off for two days."

"Putzi, it was terrible. He wanted a knife or a rope."

"Too bad you didn't find one. Eddie-pal, I'm sorry to let you and your doll sister in for all this."

"Ettie isn't here. She went to Salzburg about a role."

"You had him on your own? My apologies double." But again, Hanfstaengl's look was more appraising than sympathetic. "We were fed up to the teeth with him. You can't imagine the madhouse in Munich. Give Goering credit – he really took charge with the bloodhounds of the local Polizei. Got the body back and over the line to Vienna. Without Hermann, you ask me, our boy would have been looking at a murder rap. The headlines are still screaming – "

"Murder?"

"Less likely now. Hans Frank's got a legal muzzle on the press." Hanfstaengl sighed. "The poor kid's safely in an Austrian box. I guess I'll have to wake Adolf and tell him."

"What about the other man? He's in Austria too. Surely the authorities can do something about him?"

"What man. Do what?"

"At least pay for the funeral. I mean damn it, Putzi – this cad of a music teacher got her pregnant. His student! It's really all his fault."

"Music teacher?"

"The Jewish one," Eddie said, "in Linz."

"And Santa Claus is in the North Pole – if young Geli was up the stump I'd check Santa out before I worried about Jews in Linz. Well it's over now. She's underground. Pour me a schnaps and let's see what our gallant Leader wants to do."

I looked for Frau Fischer to pour one for each of us – Edwin drank more schnaps in that Hunding's Hut than the first twenty years of his life combined! – but the old woman wasn't in the kitchen. In the white room. She sat on a chair, like Waring, watching.

Her charge lay asleep on a hut-maid's straw mattress, below a crucifix, with a Christ crucified, snoring lightly. The wing of black hair fell across his pillow. Under the Little Tramp's moustache He was sucking on the little finger of his left hand. His right clutched bright ribbons that "Frau Fai-Fai" had braided on the white enamel rail of His truckle bed.

Frau Fischer shooed us away with a hushing nanny gesture: the nursery is a private world. Putzi & Eddie will have to leave. As they go, Nanny strokes the Leader's brow, "There there, my pet. When it's time to wake her Dolferl, Frau Fai-Fai will get him some nice hot tea . . ."

Last Rites:
The next morning He gets up – to receive a deputation of Hanfstaengl, returned with Schreck the chauffeur, and Hoffmann the photographer-crony. His skin is blotchy. He still looks at parts of the wall, not faces. Otherwise He is controlled.

"I'm going to see her, Hanfstaengl."

"With all respect, Adolf, you can't. The Austrians would take you at the border. Even with false papers and some kind of disguise, they know the damn car."

"Shit on the border. I'm going to see her. Then I can die."

Hoffmann argues the same facts and gets the same response. Schreck just holds the abdicating Leader's velour hat and whip – a new elephant-hide one Winifred gave him, the favourite of His special three – it isn't a chauffeur's place to argue. Eddie knows, if it was Mama, or Ettie, I would have to see them.

"We could cross in my car, Herr Wolf. The Austrians don't know that. It's hired from Bayreuth."

"Good fellow."

We went that night. A convoy. Mama's red Mercedes in the lead, with the Leader, then another bigger Mercedes with bodyguards and guns, then Edwin in the Bayreuth car, a touring Daimler-Benz sportster with a folding top. Hanfstaengl rode with me, in relative comfort as long as the top was down. We took the route that leads to Berchtesgaden, skirting it at Bad Reichenhall. The place picked for the crossing was at Grodig, just south of Salzburg.

The convoy stops. He changes places with the giant, who is returning to Munich. Eddie watches his two friends pass each other in the headlights. He looks puny. Brother thought, Somewhere over there Ettie's asleep. Maybe they'll wake her to say I'm in prison . . .

"Don't worry," He said, thought-reading as He got in. "I know for a certainty we shall not be stopped."

The convoy starts forward. It is as He said. The Austrian officials are officious but lax. They complain about some stamp-marking not in order for Hoffmann's profession of photographer. They pay no attention to the occupation of the accompanying Hunding bodyguard thugs. Or the cars.

"Next."

Us.

"English?" says the official, fat, with sausage breath, impatient to get home. "From Bayreuth? Salzburg is better! Grüss Gott."

"To think," as we left the Motherland, "that could have been the Herr Oberoffizial, my father."

He was silent after that to the outskirts of Vienna. Edwin followed the tail lights of the bodyguards' Mercedes. They stopped at a church with a Maltese Cross, as the sun was rising, and relieved themselves behind a laurel hedge. Edwin also. He stays in the Daimler-Benz: The Leader Cannot Be Seen To Pee.

A small grey car drew up beside. A rat-mouthed face in Tojo glasses, grey as the car, a querulous voice and manner like Mime, said, "The Central Cremetery, my Fuehrer. For one quarter-hour it will be private. This is rarranged."

"Danke, Himmler. I know the way. Herr Edwin, it's only a kilometre, if you could be so kind. Turn left when you drive on."

We left the Maltese Cross, and the grey Mime-man with too many *Cremetery* "r's" in his head. Half a mile later, as the great spire of St Stephen's caught the light, He said, "Flowers! Christ! Everything arranged but flowers! I have to have flowers!"

He was almost panicking again. Edwin said, "Herr Wolf, the Market behind the Hofburg has flowers. But they wouldn't be selling so early."

241

"Find me the market. They'll sell."

In the market a peasant woman charges double for lilies and roses but The Leader Doesn't Quibble. At the cemetery Hoffmann was there with camera.

"We thought we'd lost you. Adolf what happened?"

"No photographs," He says, not seeing the speaker.

Alone He walks forward fourteen paces. The grave is a slab of white marble in acres of Byzantine baroque. He places the market lilies and roses on the slab.

Here Sleeps Our Beloved Child
GELI
She was Our Ray of Sunshine
Born 4 June 1908 – died 18 September 1931
The Family Raubal

When He returned to the car He said:

"She wanted to be a singer, in the Opera at Vienna. Now my angel will never enter it even to watch. Nor can I, a common criminal in the eyes of my homeland – but I can see it, the Opera, once, for her, with my eyes. Mein Ederl, drive me, one last time for her, around the Ring . . ."

. . . At Salzburg: The Honourable Edwina C-P is staying in the obvious spot, the best hotel, on top of the world having concluded without casualties her small skirmish for the '32 Bayreuth opposition's Cosi.

"Dead?" deliciously appalled. "Eddie, you don't mean he really shot her? Our Wolfi, in *une crime passionnelle*? And I missed the whole damn thing! Well, I suppose a foot in the door at Salzburg is worth it. Aren't you dying to see Auntie's face when I tell her."

And then – ?

Envoi:
For a young woman of no breeding or accomplishment, who loved canaries, and was scared to death of whips and guns; who went to bed indiscriminately with chauffeurs, and art students, and perhaps music teachers from Linz – and is commemorated by a white slab, and market flowers, and a set of charcoal drawings executed by one of her frustrated

242

artist-lovers who shows her: legs akimbo, squatting, fingers splaying the hidden opening to the magic garden. The face in the sketch stares upwards, huge eyes transfixed, with a gash for a mouth, drawn down either in horror, or fear, or both. One of the Rumours has it that the nose on the body taken by the Munich police was smashed, like the wooden bird cage of its childish owner. The sketcher, who destroyed so many of the tiny traces that might reveal His inner self, seems strangely unconcerned that this gross clue is circulating on the Kaffee-klatsch circuit. Perhaps the sketches, like The Book, are a last cry to the Outside world?

Stop me!

And then – ?

A week after the funeral He refuses to eat ham at a meal.

"Never shall I eat meat again! You must understand – it would be like tasting a corpse!"

And then – ?

He languishes for a year.

In November, the old Crown Princess Cecilie says to the Hon Edwina C-P at a party in Potsdam after Sister's first acclaimed Queen of the Night:

"I don't understand how Winifred Wagner can have him in her box. My dear, the man *farts*!"

For Xmas, '32, in 6 sheets of violent scrawl in Latin, and Hun Gothic, script dragged almost off the page downhill to Auntie Winnie He writes, with an ending worthy of the Little Tramp:

... Given up all hope! Nothing of my dreams. The years of end-
less struggle! Until now never lost courage. No hope left. Opponents
too powerful! As soon as it is certain you know what I
must do. I give my word! Will end my
life! With a bullet – !
P.S. – This time it will be serious!
I simply cannot see
my way
out!

And then – ?

The growing-up children at a Music Room New Year's party dance to

243

Eddie playing Chicago Swing on the Black Swan piano. The scrawled pages fall off Gockel's perch, swirling in a scattered circle on the parquet floor, a paper ring beneath the painted eyes of the Helden pictures: Tristan, Lohengrin, Siegfried.

... Together with Dolferl, & Wolfi, & the Fuehrer-A, & Alberich the Dwarf, & the Bad Giant, Fafner, & Black Hagen the Betrayer. Truly a cast of thousands!

MILLIONS!!!

Believe me, children, all Nibelheim's a stage in That Man's head. And then – ?

Why, Tomorrow, children! There's always Tomorrow!

And Tomorrow, a man mad enough to renounce all Love (except for a Sister's), may even dream that he can Kill all of Them! Or Rule the World! Or Actually Find His Holy Grail!

Second
Movement

Ring
of
Steel

Overture

Frau Cosima's Hero's Tale

Siegfried

My Dears! Such Adventures we have already seen in these pages of His Ring, yet all do but bring Us to *this* point: the arrival of Our Hero! Mighty Siegfried, golden & true!

The orphaned *Babe* is now a glorious Youth – on the very Brink of his Maturity! – & *He is utterly without our Knowledge of Fear!*

He has been raised & nursed & trained by another Dwarf, a smith. How *kind*, we say, so to treat an Orphan – *But*, Children, this Dwarf, alas, is *brother* to vile Alberich! His name is *Mime!* He is grey, with a monstrous head, & sly, & altogether villainous as befits a Nibelung. And his *apparent* kindness to our Hero is for Evil ends! He wishes Siegfried to slay the Dragon (in a wonderful Blue Light you shall see on your first Bayreuth Pilgrimage) – so that Mime *alone* shall own the Source of Power!

And then – a Little Wood-Bird talks to Siegfried in the Forest – & now Siegfried can *tell* what treachery Mime is *thinking* . . . !

Second Movement
First Passage

[a quadrille – with quiet beauty]

**Who sent Earl Percy present word,
He would prevent his Sport?
The English Earl, not fearing that,
Did to the Woods Resort!**

. . . *In Spandau* – because our Jeremy's being silly over Eddie showing Waring being Waring. The Lackey of Yellow Street, my dears, would have us employ Euphemism & Pseudonym, when Old Edwin cuts too close to the bone! Thus we are avoiding Waring by walking in our Prison garden – hobbling, actually, under graceful trees planted as saplings by our unlucky predecessors when the Four Power Quadrille first struck up, 4 decades back.

Also, Visitors aren't Allowed in the Garden – It's a Rule! So we are free, Eddie & Ravens, to think out our Master's plot without fear of Yellow Street's attentions. Yes, my dears, Birds too. Remarkably, G & G stay with me out of doors, flitting like sacks of coal from leaf to leaf, nevermore than arm's length distance. Perhaps they think I'm going to die . . .

Not yet, Croakers! We have unfinished business.

The Prussian:
. . . *On the Magic Mountain:* with a new Play-mate – Heinz Tietjen, the Generalintendant of Opera, with his rimless-Teuton glasses, has quietly

moved in backstage and taken charge for the first festival since Real-Siegfried's death. A whole generation of Immortals departs from the scene. Brünnhilde & Isolde are both up for grabs.

Sister, walking back through the Hofgarten past the Grave; "I just *have* to have one of them. It's my only chance. The Prussian Man's going to bring in simply a battalion of people from the Berlin State!"

"Well you can't have Isolde," Eddie said, "Tristan isn't going to be on. You could try for Eva in Meistersinger I suppose. And your Waltraute again."

"Ten bloody lines. Oh brother darling, you are a help. And Eva, that brainless soppy cow?"

"You have to be realistic, Ettie. You can't possibly expect Brünnhilde with Frida Leider around. And your voice isn't ready for Kundry – even old Meyerhof told you that. There's only Eva left, and you'd better get it while the getting's good."

"I'll die first." But that night as I was just about asleep she came into my room. "Eddie, you really think there's nothing else?"

"Else what?"

"Than Eva, silly."

"Waltraute," he said. "And Norns." . . . as he looks up at her standing in her nightie, frail and beautiful with Bayreuth's moon behind her hair. "Ettie," he whispers, "you look so lovely and it's been so long since we – ?"

"*Only a Norn*? You must be mad."

She flounced away.

In the morning at breakfast she said, "You have to come with me to see Tietjen. I can't possibly go in there alone."

"You went to Salzburg alone."

"Salzburg was my idea. Tietjen's yours."

Brother & Sister went arm in arm. Heinz Tietjen was sitting in Siegfried's chair in Siegfried's office. Winifred's now, but Winifred had flown back to Paris overnight for another round with Tosca-no-no.

"Fräulein Edwina, Herr Edwin – a pleasure, do come in." The Prussian's English was more precise but not as at ease as Siegfried's. He gave the C-Ps a Junker's bow and heel click, and came around the desk. "If you were expecting to meet with Frau Winifred – ?"

"No, dear Herr Heinz," said the Honourable Edwina, "only you. I have a silly problem with the Pill Man – Sir Thomas at the Garden, a telegram – oh, do you mind Eddie being here? He was moping at a loose end so I brought him along to cheer him up."

Tietjen found this succession of lies entirely plausible. "Naturally, Fräulein Edwina, your dear brother is welcome at any time. What of Sir Thomas – we are all hoping to have him visit us next year?"

"It's his London Ring," she said. "Sir Thomas wants me for his Brünnhilde, but it would conflict with next year here at Bayreuth – oh, good heavens, I don't mean me being Brünnhilde *here*, not with Frida available for the role – but I thought there just might be a chance for Eva in Meistersinger. I would have gone first to darling Aunt Winnie but she's flown, so I thought I should come straight to you, Herr Heinz."

"You would sacrifice the London Brünnhilde for Eva, my dear?"

"It's hardly a sacrifice, Herr Heinz. Bayreuth is Eddie's and my adopted home."

"Fräulein Edwina – " with a Teutonic throat clearing, taking her petalled hand in both of his – "the part is yours. One gets so used to confronting temperament. I can't tell you how refreshing." The Prussian removed his glasses and wiped them with his handkerchief.

"Temperament," said my sister, "is really just a word for unprofessional, isn't it? But I have to confess, Herr Heinz, Eddie said it would be worse than it was. You have a reputation as a bit of an ogre you know. 'Generalintendant' is rather awe-inspiring."

"Our use of titles." Tietjen smiled at the foolish Eddie as he put back on the glasses. "At your age, Herr Edwin, I remember exactly your feelings. Fräulein Edwina – "

"*Ettie*, please, Herr Heinz – darling Uncle Siegfried always used to call me that."

"Fräulein Ettie, in addition to the Eva I think, given such sacrifice, you should understudy Frau Leider as Brünnhilde for next year. I shall recommend this to Frau Winifred on her return."

"Oh, Herr Heinz . . ."

Oh children! – the dimpled skill with which it was done!

"My God," Eddie said outside the Festspielhalle, "my God."

"You have to learn, Brother dear, to have the courage of your convictions. You can't always be a mouse. Bayreuth *and* Salzburg. Let's blow a weekend in Munich on our way."

251

... *At the Gerbers'*: After a cool bath, with salts, the Honourable Edwina says, "I almost feel human again. Let's drop around to the Carlton and see if anyone's there for tea."

Hanfstaengl, alone at a table set up outside in the courtyard.

"Ettie-moll," rumbles the giant, "looking like the proverbial cucumber, how do you English girls manage it in this heat? Eddie-pal, how are things? – no more midnight flits to Vienna, I trust."

"London, and Paris, and Porquerolles twice, and Bayreuth, and now we're on our way to Salzburg."

"As crazy as Adolf's schedule." Hanfstaengl signals a waiter by raising a squash-racquet hand two yards in the air.

"Then he's back to normal," said Sister, disappointed, "after that dreadful business with the wretched little half-tart – I mean, Putzi, dear, Vienna at dawn? It's more like a duel – with his own gun! And all the lurid Yellow Pressings Winnie sent us. Poor Auntie, she's really like a mother to him, I suppose the whole Uncle living-in-sin thing must have come to her as the most awful shock."

"Like a mother?" Hanfstaengl cocks a hedge of eyebrow as fresh tea arrives. "She's never stopped playing Senta. And not to speak ill of the departed – you've heard our Geli found a note that Uncle Alf left in his jacket pocket? By accident, it goes without saying."

"A note!" the cucumber-girl gasps, "Putzi, you ogre, do tell!"

"From Fräulein Braun – if you won't tell Adolf – our inferior Eva, the shop assistant of Hoffmann's, another feather-brain for anything in pants. Listen, you two, it's been a breath of fresh air. Come to dinner tonight. Helene's withdrawn the divorce and we're entertaining a difficult guest. Call it our little re-uniting surprise."

The Picasso Woman:

The good Giant's house is an island of true Culture in the Mowgli sea. A shrinking island, with Devaluation and Expropriation, behind a large stone wall which the Giant built to hold out Revolution when the Bolsheviks briefly controlled Bavaria. Inside the house, everywhere there are books on art, and art that Edwin has only seen in books – most astonishingly, the new yellow-red-and-green Picasso Woman with 3 heads and 5 eyes.

"It drives Adolf bananas," said Putzi, greeting in the hall. "Everywhere he goes there's one watching – you know his neurosis about doodling eyes and heads. When I was running my campaign to make him see at least a bit of the great world, I almost hooked him for London with The Tower and Henry the Eighth. 'We could see the scaffold, Hanfstaengl! The six wives! The very spot where they were executed! And Charles the First by the immortal Cromwell! – I was born on the day Cromwell dissolved Parliament. Hanfstaengl, you're right – I absolutely must make time to get away!' Naturally he never did, but I still live in hope. We're out on the terrace. Come along through."

"Oh, there you all are." Our hostess did not speak gangsterese, but had the Americans' casual way with manners. "Edwina honey, and Eddie – how great to see you both again. I guess you already know Hermann?"

Born in Haiti, land of voodoo: the 2nd of the giants.

The Gallant Captain:

Goering's face and form have changed since the Gerbers' gutter in 1923: Morphine (from the pain of two Munich police bullets in the groin) & then the Cure, & then finding himself an Outsider in the Leader's Bavarian cabal. Now, the normally humorous mouth droops, the eyes are tired, the ample flesh is wan.

"Be amusing," Putzi whispers, on our way in, "Karin died last autumn – we're still having a terrible time trying to cheer him up."

(The late Karin van Rosen von Kantzow, my dears – aristocratic, Wife 1; acquired when the Captain was an automatic-parachute sales-man in Sweden after the War.)

The Captain also made an effort.

"The von Perceval children – but naturally I remember. When you think you're about to meet your Maker you never forget the last faces you see – although I'd rather it was from a cockpit than a Munich gutter. Yours, if I may say so, were particularly attractive faces. And your extraordinary Mama's. I've heard so much from Adolf about her."

"And I'm awfully sorry about your wife," polite Edwin said, as Sister jabbed her elbow in his back.

"Thank you, Herr Edwin. But my darling Karin had been unwell for some time, her heart, and diabetes, it was a release. Fräulein Edwina, your brother's done me a kindness, we can't bottle these things up forever. And I shouldn't have introduced the grim reaper in the first

253

place – now, if I swear to be good company, promise us we're all forgiven and you're going to sing before the end of the night."

"Anything but Liebestod, Captain Hermann – of course you're all forgiven."

So!

Drinking, and Eating, and Harvard Putzi playing, with his double-octave hands, and Golden Edwina singing, and wide-eyed Eddie listening – to the hair-raising misses and crash-landings in the Red Baron's squadron.

"In a graveyard, the last one, thank God! – because the church was being used as a field hospital, or I'd definitely have 'bought it'. But I'll tell you, when I first looked up and saw a white marble angel it was a damn curious sensation. I'd had a dream a week before. I was walking along a beach of jet black sand and then suddenly I found I was at the end of a peninsula. And in front of me, rising from the water, a white figure, like my gravestone angel! What the hell do you make of that?"

"Too much boozing in the mess." Hanfstaengl clapped his fellow giant on the shoulder – with a gesture at the rest of us: *shake him out of it.*

But the Gallant Captain laughs for the first time without any holding back, as the party breaks up and he pauses in the hall to check his appearance in a mirror. A sign of adjustment: except that the mad eyes and heads of the Picasso Woman are doubled behind him, together with a signed photograph of the Leader, so that there is a whole small asylum in the glass. . . .

The Captain taps the yellow-red-and-green of Head I.

"Senor Pablo Picasso's first on Adolf's list of modern art abortionists. I've tried to tell him, at least pick one up as an investment – they'll quadruple in value when we burn the rest!"

Chuckling again, the C-Ps and hosts follow to the cars.

"A lovely evening, dearest Helene," with cheek-kissing, from the Hon Edwina, "it's such a joy not to face sausage for one night. Captain Hermann, give my love to our Wolfi when you see him, and say I'm Eva – in Meistersinger for next year."

"Enchanted, Fräulein Ettie. But you should give him the good news yourself. He's speaking at Rosenheim tomorrow evening."

"Oh," Sister said demurely. "I wouldn't dream of intruding."

254

THE MEETING

Is to be held at a stadium in a postwar suburb immediately to the west of the centre of the old town. To get there, Gallant Captain Hermann drives his Honoured Guests himself – appallingly badly, for an Air-ace! – top down, full speed, with one pork-trotter hand on the horn, while the other points out the beauties of the countryside, until –

"That was fun," said Sister, stepping out daintily, "Captain Hermann, Eddie's such a slow puss. I've been trying and trying to make him get us a sports."

Little bitch.

The Mowgli men force a good-natured way through the crowd for the Gallant Captain's party. He's easily recognized:

"Bravo our Hermann! Give them hell!"

Whoever *They* are.

A stage has been set up in the centre of the stadium, and a band oompahs around on it as the Guests of Honour are shown to a special section of seats, ten feet out from the stage. The space between is kept clear by a shoulder-to-shoulder phalanx of Storm Browns. A similar arrangement maintains an aisle through the great crowd.

11 o'clock: An hour late. Two have passed since our arrival. The note in the Crowd's collective noise begins to alter. It surges restlessly against the Browns – cattle in an abattoir pen, aware that something of stupendous import is almost on them.

Where is He?

Even Captain Hermann mouths it; in his dignitary's chair onstage, glancing at his watch with increasing annoyance. A fight breaks out in a row of the stands surrounding the outer edge of the stadium.

"Kill the Reds!"

A businessman, neat in a suit.

"Kill the Reds! Kill the Reds!"

The band picks up the rhythm on the bass drum. The Crowd stamps its feet and roars. The Browns let the fight go on for five minutes then, at a signal from Hermann, they storm up into the stands. The trouble-maker is silenced. The Crowd roars louder for good order restored.

255

But still He isn't here!

Quarter to Midnight: Guest buttocks are numb. The standing Crowd rocks from foot to foot, tossing its heads. The noise ebbs.

And then – ?

"An aeroplane?"

Ettie said it. We craned our necks. But the night was black as the stadium lights go out. An *oooh*ing inrush of breath from the Crowd, as it thinks it knows –

And then – ?

A searchlight! Only one: a stabbing white-silver spear. The aircraft is caught on the tip: a moth impaled by the Crowd's collective need.

Him. In a sighing, soughing, cry, His moth-plane circles, once, twice, three times – then leaves the light.

He's gone!

But He must come again. It is Written – although still only a handful have read His Word. Even Hermann's in the dark; turning his head on his thick neck with the least of the rest of us, back towards the way which we know He must take – if He is coming.

The band strikes up Horst Wessel's cabaret song of death:

Raise High the Flag – !

And here it waves. And whether the Crowd was singing or cheering Edwin can never remember as the flag went by, because all I wanted, all we wanted, was the first glimpse of That Man behind it. . . .

Yet still He denied us.

The singing tails off. The Crowd angers.

Some even start to move out into the aisle but are blocked by the Browns. The only way out is His way in.

"There, Eddie!"

Like Loge, lord of the fire, He has tricked us – There! Through that other opening in the stands – as the band crashes out His March, reserved for Him alone! – do we realise, and shout, and shout . . .

Not all of us. One third are fanatic; the middle have come prepared to be entertained; the last third of the Crowd holds the hecklers.

He saw the Guests of Honour, and turned aside from His procession (Fräulein Anna was behind Him) to shake our hands, but His face was locked and frozen with no expression; the eyes blank as the mask-holes

256

of Greek Chorus. He climbed the half dozen steps to the platform, shook Goering's hand, and Edwin thought: No magician can live up to this.

Sister said, "His shoulders always slump when he doesn't wear his jacket."

And then – ?

He stood and looked at us all. Or through us. Beyond us . . .

There is a chest-high table to His left, another to His right. A lectern in front of Him supports a microphone. He places a sheaf of notes on the lefthand table beside a silver water jug. He takes a sip from a plain glass. Sets it down. His hair is neat. He looks dull now, as well as small. Empty.

The first words weren't even His. They came from the fighting cheap seats.

"Get on with it, Corporal Schickelgruber!"

And then – ?

His microphone went off. The tin voice of the loudspeakers fell dead. For five seconds perhaps He looked at the mechanical forces which had let Him down.

"Do you think we've got all damn night?"

Still He waited. Waited. Waited.

And then – ?

"*No, sir* – !"

The Voice! – and His arm shooting up, Up, UP!

"*I do NOT think this country has all night. I do not think this country of ours can endure another single agonizing, starving and humiliating hour!*"

The roar that follows! And Edwin thinks: Toscanini? Beecham? Nikisch? Furtwängler? – more than all of them together, except that here is also the composer. To be greater, it could only have been The Master.

". . . Not for an hour, and yet – " the Voice has dropped, so low that we can hardly hear it – "since that day when I was that humble soldier, in the gas, and mud, and filth of Flanders . . ." so low that we have to listen, because to miss it is to have part of our life cut away, ". . . since that disgusting day, not hours but fourteen *years* have passed. Years of enslavement, of foul treaties and decrees, of failure upon failure, collapse upon collapse, of Timidity, Lethargy, Hopelessness. . . . Millions have died. More millions starve – many of you I know are starving now. Christ had loaves and fishes – yet what have I to offer you . . . ? Our peasantry, the root-stock of our land is ground down in the manure beneath the moneylender's heel. Industry is *castrated*! Millions like you are unemployed, with no hope of work, no roof above your heads. The foreign usurers of Versailles stole even that! Only one group still eats. Only one dark clique among us! And who are They? My friends you know the answer! *They* are the swine who took the noble discipline of a Frederick and gave us the corrupting incest of party government! The men who call for Class Struggle – to disguise their Religion of the Inferior! *They* who are blind to your wretchedness, to hunger, to suicide, to tragedy. But these swine, my friends, are also men! In the Capitals they sit arguing and haggling and counting their own shekels! Well, my friends, do not despair. The hour is running out – I myself count every second! – *but*, Versailles's cruel commandments are scratched in moneylender's ink, not carved in stone! Your children do not have to starve. Your husbands do not have to kill themselves. You can have a roof above your heads! Our enemies will be humbled. Our Motherland will be great. Our future will be bright and glorious as any Valhalla of the ancient gods. With you beside me we shall march there – over that rainbow bridge, to a Greater Nation where there is land for every peasant, a forge for every smith, an education and healthy life for all your children; a place in history for a People who once defeated the might of Ancient Rome! A Homeland for us all to be proud of for another thousand years! March with me, my friends. Give me your love and loyalty. Take my hands! Link arms! March! March! March against the sorry rabble of backstabbing, putrid, petty politicians and the gutter hounds of *Their* Yellow Press. Say to *Them*, with all the depth of your National soul: Adolf Hitler we are with you! With you, now, today, and always! One Folk, One Race, One Nation! *Deutschland* – !"

Deutschland . . .

. . . *At the Gerbers'*: "I'm still absolutely bushed," Brother says from his bath, at ten next morning, "we can't go on to Salzburg today."

"I don't want to go to Salzburg – Eddie come to bed."

"A good idea – a snooze for a couple of hours – "

"I don't mean snooze, silly. I mean *bed*."

Lying on it, stark naked. Her legs are open. One hand plays in the secret room. The other reaches, as Kundry tempted Parsifal.

"Oh Gawd," she says, clenched around me to squeeze me dry, "I can't *believe* he could be so *good*!"

... *At the Albemarle Club (London):* Evening. E & E are relaxing post-performance with Gerald M****, another piano player, and old-friend Pawel, Sandhurst trained, my dears, swash-buckling among the Concert Hall Artistes. Between Figaros for the Pill Man, we are accepting London Engagements, Public & Private – "Not for the cash, Eddie – we have to be *seen*."

A couple of weeks before Christmas, '32, we just had been, at the Connaught Rooms. Sister's blasé attitude to cash notwithstanding, she charges a flat 50 guineas because she likes the sound of it.

"And what about you?" Gerald M**** asked Edwin, at the Albemarle's bar.

"Me what?"

"Money," said Gerald M****, "for accompanying."

"Eddie doesn't," said Sister. "We're just together."

"Twaddle," said Gerald. "What if you weren't together?"

"But we always are," Brother said, "And why would I need to make a fuss for an extra couple of quid?"

"I get fifteen," said M****, "guineas – or twenty, depending ..."

And we are being "seen" twice a week. Even Edwin's golden head can manage that arithmetic. "In guineas, cash, with no tax – Ettie, it would pay for your sports car."

"A Riley – the colour of my eyes," she said to M****. Turning them on Pawel ...

Which Brother takes to be her blessing, and trots around next morning to the showrooms on Jermyn Street.

And as a Reward, my sister, ungrateful B***h, invited Pawel back with Us to paradise so that there was no chance of getting into any magic gardens, or secret rooms, or even her knickers for Xmas.

... *At Porquerolles:* Pawel is not a happy holiday guest.

"It's probably Gyppy tummy," said Sister, when Brother mentioned his concern, discreetly, alone with her after lunch. "Pawel darling," brightly, when he came back from a solitary walk in the pines, "we know each other far too well to be shy. If you've got Island collywobs, just say. Mathilde has a witch's brew that will stop up a sink."

"It's not the island, Edwina, it's Ukraine. Stalin wants to kill us all off."

"You don't kill millions of ordinary people unless you're mad – and Stalin isn't – is he?"

"Stalin's a Georgian," said Pawel, as though that was an answer. "If he was even a Russian it wouldn't be so bad."

"But how do you know he is – ?" Eddie asked – "starving your Ukrainians? Have you been?"

Pawel shook his head. "We have a group. I can't go in to Russia – that's why I've resigned my commission."

"Oh Lord," said Ettie. "Oh, Pawel, dear."

"But you don't have any money, Pawel, how will you eat?"

"While my people are starving?"

"Eddie didn't mean it like that," said his sister, with a surprising show of loyalty. "But there *is* a Depression, and at least the army was sort of a job."

"On half-pay, in India. Anyway, the group get subscriptions," Pawel said. "You could help."

Indeed, my dears! He looked at the C-Ps with that way Your Slavs have of daring you to find a hole in their latest firebrand cause. Our darling Mama would have responded instanter with half the bank. My Prima Donna said, "Eddie's going to be making some extra – but it's going on my car, otherwise your Ukrainians could have had that. Pawel, pet, we both wish you all the best, but really I don't see what else we can do."

. . . *Jan 3rd, '33.* Brother has stayed on after tennis to play Chopin for Madame de la Verendry and is walking back along our beach of the Lobsters in the dusk, when he hears Sister pray:

"Oh Christ Pawel – "

Sister on her knees, stretched forward, head up, throat extended – begging heaven for a last savage thrust that quivers her breasts and flanks and buttocks and wet electric flesh between . . .

I watched from the pines, seeing Friend mount Sister, one butchering

260

Ukrainian's arm around her slender throat, that olive-skinned Slav weapon driving and sliding its way into Ettie's Kundry parts.

In our 20th Cent, we are all voyeurs now, children.

The Riley:
Getting the Riley makes up (almost) for the awkward holiday. Edwin loves that car as much (almost) as his straying sister. It looks as blue as her eyes. Appearances, as they say, are what count.

"One of you really should think of getting married, Edwin," says the warty female Wyn**man-Hare, obliquely, in cold February. "Your sister is of that age when a woman needs steering by a good husband."

"Like Cousin Wynchman-Hare?"

Gone to his Reward. And winters in London are not all wasted. Step by step with the Templars, E. C-P's Grail Map of Europe is coming together in the fading light of late afternoons at the British Museum. There is no proof of the magic Vessel, but sitting under the yellow lamps of the great Reading Room, the Scholar-Edwin followed in daydream his Pot's progress: once ashore from the Church of the Marys in Camargue, up through Avignon, with its quincunx Yews, and along the chain of Templars' hospice fortresses. Perhaps through Siegfried's dragon valley of the Rhine, and to the tombs of Bamberg, or finally to Graz, on the far border of Christendom, last post against the infidel Mongols and Ottoman Turks.

But what *if* – ?

Pawel's account of his people has put a little Ukrainian flea in Eddie's ear. Not because the poor devils are starving – because of their churches: one in particular, the Monastery of Skulls in Kiev. The monks had taken up residence in caves to avoid the Mongols, and to preserve the bodies of the faithful. Legend had it that the first Great Gate to the city was sheeted with gold; like Jerusalem's . . . the New Jerusalem. The more the Scholar thinks about it, the more he has to *know*. But friend-Pawel has run to ground; the War Office have no forwarding address.

"Although you might let us know, when you catch up. For the Reserve list, just in case."

Eddie did find a Slavonics man at the University. "No joy there, Casson-Perceval. You'd never get a visa – and if you did, Stalin's burnt

261

down the churches and your caves have been sealed with concrete. With half the monks inside, I shouldn't wonder."

But still . . .

"You don't want to sing in Russia, Ettie, I suppose?"

"With a double-barrelled name? Darling, you must be mad. And next week's our opening of Tannhäuser. If his Elisabeth went to Russia, the Pill Man would be in an awful tizz."

. . . At the Garden:

"Hail to Thuringia's prince, the Landgrave Hermann!"
Act 2, Scene 4:

> *. . . If this, our Sword, in bloody Battles fought for the supremacy of the German State . . . Prepare for us another Festival, now that the Valiant Singer, whom we so long missed, has returned to us. What brought Him back among us remains a secret Mystery . . .*

The London Landgrave roars and spits in Edwina C-P's unblinking face. Elisabeth, our Sister, white-gowned, slim hands crossed chastely on the cloth of gold girdle, screening her pure Venusberg, gazes up to the stage flies, Rear Left, for Inspiration. Her Tannhäuser grovels at her feet.

> *. . . How shall I find pardon kneeling in Her dust? How atone for my Sin? O, could She but forgive, my Guardian Angel, who so rudely betrayed, yet offers Herself as sacrifice for me!*

"Eddie, be a darling," she said in the dressing room at the interval, "get me a Gin and It."

"You really shouldn't, you've only got half an hour to your final croak."

"I'll croak for sure without booze – the bloody Landgrave's got the most disgusting breath. Just a tiny one, you can scrounge from the Pit bar, not the Players'. I've got a thermos, Eddie, nobody'll know."

He's bought her a car – what's one small drink? The queue mob sprawls three deep along the bar.

"Eddie. Over here. I've found a place."

Michael Rau, guttural, beaming and barely visible behind the curve of the bar, waves a plump hand at the miracle of a barman all to himself.

262

"You might have let me know, Rau. I could have met your train."

"I flew. It was a spur of the moment chance to cripple the old man's English operation. I saw your sister was being Elisabeth in the aircraft *Times* – this seemed the best way to meet, and it was. What can I buy you?"

"I'm just rum-running for Ettie. A small Gin and Italian, please. She likes it very cold. You flew? Actually? Where from?"

"Prague, with a stop at Templehof in Berlin. Eight hours in the air. The world's shrinking nicely. Tell our friend to stop shaking when it's cold enough."

The barman was still fizzing away with Ettie's gin. "More than enough, it would be kind if you could pour it in the thermos. Ettie's not a boozer – it's the Landgrave's breath. Like Wolf's goat ... at the henhouse?"

"I remember. Your friend's out of it now. Have you seen him since he became Chancellor?"

"No. But He hasn't, quite, has He? I think He has to share – we don't really follow the politics at all. Look, I've got to take this to Ettie–"

"After the show," said Michael Rau, "meet you both at the Nag's Head – "

"And then we'll find another place!"

The friends say it together, laughing. Buoyed up by his reunion, Eddie makes the rum-run backstage.

"You took your bloody time! I'm on again in five."

"You'll be glad when you hear – " but Sister, for no good reason, has worked herself into a bad small state, and just grabs, straight from the thermos.

"We've already got an invitation." She tosses a programme from her makeup shelf. "On the back."

In a narrow margin, between Brylcreem and Players, a cramped hand has squeezed:

Well now! From yr	*events! Dine if*
Mama's garden at	*poss: Schmidt's in*
Trevelly, to that of	*Charlotte Street.*
fair Venus! What a	*Yr admiring,*
lovely turn of	

A swirl of initials – a D? and possibly a C . . . ?

"G," said Ettie, from the door, "for Goat. You'll see when you go out to the House – he's sitting with his Fanny Woman next to the Royals' box."

The Welsh Wizard:
"Little Ettie from Cornwall – all grown up!"

The former Prime Minister of Great Britain and Ireland, pillar of Victorian Rectitude, Morality, Chapel Hearth & Home in public, in private has let his hair grow (since the last time we saw him chasing Little Ettie in Trevelly's shrubbery) and his moustache, into a straggle, yellowish, below a nose that has become more hooked with age: he does indeed look like a friendly, maudlin, old Goat. Despite his diminutive size he seems to fill the other side of the table (across from Sister) but he is, however, accompanied by one of his male Appointment Secretaries (a man so self-effacing that he never leaves a name) and the Fanny Woman, Miss Frances Stevenson – the Goat's principal Private Secretary, and former governess to his child – with whom (when not with his wife, Dame Margaret) the Great Man in Waiting lives bigamously.

"With that dreadful little-girl parting on the side," said Sister, at only half her Festspielhaus whisper; "you know she was a Wimbledon games-mistress before the Goat asked her to be the other kind – *dear* Miss Stevenson, I've heard *so* much. How lovely to finally meet."

"Well now!" said L-G, continuing unbroken in his lilting Celt. "In my opinion, Herr Hitler is a Phenomenon – a Natural Force risen from the heart of the German people – Almighty God should give us one such here! Edwin, boy, you must tell me every word he said."

"It would make rather a long supper, dear L-G," said Little Ettie, "once Wolf starts he simply doesn't stop."

Eddie said, "He has a chalet at the top of a mountain. He walks alone up there for hours, like Wagner, getting inspiration for Tannhäuser."

"Herr Wolf he calls himself? Like Wagner – is he now? And born from the common folk, like Romulus for Rome! – and me the son of a shoe maker, like Hans Sachs. I tell you, boy, this is more and more a man of my own heart. The greatest music ever written is that Tannhäuser we heard tonight. The Pilgrims' – oh your part was very fine too, my dear little Ettie –" leaning over the table and pressing her hand –

"exquisitely pure you were, but it's the choruses that get a man. All boiling up inside. I only went to Bayreuth once myself – in 'Eleven, that was, three summers before the Terrible War. Not for the Ring – we Welsh like *singing* – !"

"You said 1910 to me," The Fanny Woman observed.

"Well it wasn't."

"It's not important."

Frances Stevenson shares a small smile with the male Secretary. The Goat has let go of Little Ettie's hand. All his hackles are up: a Welsh Wizard's alchemical transformation to fighting bantam cock.

You don't love me! The oldest spell of all. At home, a Wizard could cast it. In Schmidt's Restaurant his eyes can only fill with tears from the wine and injustice of life.

"I call forgetting an act of common sense, Prime Minister," Michael Rau beamed his warmest, irresistible smile. "I forget the dates of my father's shareholders' meetings, and I've only got half your years."

"Damn it, you can't be thirty, boy. I'm seventy. I like you – where do you come from?" The bantam's wattles are already mollified. Lloyd-George peers at Rau. "A Jew! I might have guessed. One of the finest chaps I ever met was a Jew – Weizmann, the Zionist chemist, you probably know him."

"Zionist chemists are one of the things I always forget – and I'm from Prague, Prime Minister, just completing a move to Zürich."

The Goat explodes into laughter that must turn heads in the rooms below. "I'll tell you a story about Weizmann. He was at Manchester University. I was Minister of Munitions – "

"We have a train to catch." The Fanny Woman rises to cut off another favourite story at the knees.

". . . Well anyway, when I became Prime Minister I saw that he got it – Palestine, with the Balfour Declaration. With you Jews it's all a question of psychology, isn't it?"

The ex-Prime Minister looks to Rau, wistfully.

"Goodnight, Miss Casson-Perceval," says the Fanny Woman, firmly.

". . . Old Joe Chamberlain, now, was a master of our British psychology. He started a research at Birmingham University, into beer. People like Winston scoffed, but old Joe was right. 'Winston,' I said, 'you brandy drinkers ignore the role of beer in the life of our nation at

265

your peril!' I'm going to put that in my book when I get to the part about the King. I made him go dry for the duration. You know he's a true Phenomenon – Herr Hitler, of course!" holding both Little Ettie's hands this time, outside Schmidt's, a tender parting. "Whenever you're home come down to Churt and visit. I want reports on his every word, mind. Your dear Mama knew it ten years ago – an inseparable Anglo-Germany is the only key to the peace of Europe, and with Ramsay MacDonald disposed of I have a definite feeling the pendulum is swinging. We'll be back, you'll see. The country knows it needs us. Goodbye, Edwin boy – dearest little Ettie, so like your Mama you are. It brings a tear to an old man's eyes. His contemporaries vanish like leaves on the chill winds – "

"I'm not vanishing." The Fanny Woman physically separates her charge from Sister. Miss Frances Stevenson tucks up the fur collar on his coat with that gesture which shows, more than a marriage ring, how things stand between man and woman.

"He's serious about your Wolf," murmurs the invisible male Secretary, falling in behind, "I really don't know why. The man surely can't draw the votes in the Reichstag to rule without von Papen. Master will be shouting – Edwin, Edwina, I must run."

E & E ride with Rau as far as the Savoy where he's staying as part of his forlorn campaign to ruin his father. "Did you mean it, Michael," Ettie asks him, "you're moving to Zürich to live?"

"Fairest Edwina, with your friend Wolf in the farmyard, staying in Czechoslovakia with its Sudetens would undoubtedly kill me."

"Oh, do be serious, Michael."

Rau beams his widest beam.

A Dwarf-isch Lohengrin!

A Film by Riefenstahl

Stage-Manager's Notes:
(PRIVAT! – HERR DOKTOR G******S EYES ONLY!)

THE PRODUCTION DATE:

March 21st, 1933. Anniversary of Great
Bismarck opening our First Reichstag
(NB: Also, Birthday of Our Principal
Player's young English Friends.) 2nd Note:
See *best seats* are provided. 3rd Note, PAN
often, and to Frau W****r (for Foreign
Markets!)

THE SET:

Can only be Garrison Church:
Resting Place of Mighty Frederick!

THE DECOR:

To have (so-called-Mowgli) Flags beyond
counting, and tapestries of Knights
Templar, and garlands of sweet flowers
festooning Lohengrin's route of Triumph
(from burnt-out Reichstag Building! NB:
frequent CLOSE-UPS!) Innumerable bands
shall play (1) Lohengrin's March, (2)
Horst Wessel's.

THE CAST:

1) Mostly call EXTRAS. Dress as: Old
Hindenburg (play as King Henry), Crown
Prince (play as Hopeful), Veterans from
Great Bismarck's expanding wars – play as
ancient White-Beards with Wounds and
Campaign Ribbons dangling and jangling
from 1864, and '66, and '71. (NB: *No shots*
of Crown Prince's Father's War!)
2) *Our Principal*, as Ex-Corporal shall wear

267

only His Iron Cross, 1st Class, pinned to His plain tailcoat. (No playing instructions needed!)

TRANSPORTATION:

While a Swan-Boat would be more suitable, Our PRINCIPAL shall ride like any other good People's Politician. (NB: car *old* paint!)

THE ACTION:

All arrive. Bells and Cannons. Our PRINCIPAL stands solicitously in background while War-Horses climb out stiffly, and PAN on white Ostrich Feathers of Old H's hat hitting car door – so: ZOOM! Our MAN-OF-THE-PEOPLE spots at foot of steps, tiny hidden GOLDEN GIRL clutching Nursery Posy of *wilting* Daisies and 3 (only!) Daffodils. Herr W leaves line of Dignitaries, bends solemnly, takes *spontaneous* offering from Tiny Hand, and . . . *touches these Golden Curls –* !

SOUND:

Ohhhhh . . .

Moan of Ecstasy shall sweep ALL WOMEN in Crowd Scene. CLOSE-UP of *Tears* pricking even MALE eyes. And then –

"SIEG HEIL! SIEG HEIL! SIEG HEIL!"

AND ENTER (ten feet away, behind the worshipped, modest New Siegfried) for the first time His Alberich, now disguised as the Dwarf Reichsminister Of Propaganda, limping, with an imp's smile for the so-close English Friends on his narrow, sallow, Nibelung's face.

"Oh children," said their Aunt Winnie, as the 2 giants, Hanfstaengl & Hermann passed, "if your Mother could only have seen this moment!"

268

EXCLAM SENTA STOP

And then – ?

"Nun danket alle Gott!"

The organ, with 400 pipes, soars and rumbles and shakes the stone walls and floors and congregation with the chorale the host of Great Frederick had sung in unison in their thousands after his Battle of Leuthen restored Silesia to Prussian arms.

And I thought at first, He's got His mask on – but then I saw the light of LIFE! in those fantastic eyes as the choirboy from Lambach Abbey for that instant truly thanked his God.

And then – ?

He has to meet the strutting Crown Prince, and He becomes once more only an awkward figure of a waiter at a wedding in hired tailcoat; (The stage directions say this is the Old Guard's hour); so that He meekly follows Old Hindenburg laboriously creaking his way down from our sight into Erda's underworld of tombs in the crypt.

"A so-incredibly historic moment, don't you agree, Herr von-Perceval?!" The Dwarf stage manager, Joseph Goebbels, beside himself, and Eddie. "The Shield of Honour is once more washed clean! The Standards with our Eagles once more soar high! Hindenburg himself with our beloved Fuehrer places Laurel Wreaths on the biers of our greatest Prussian Kings! And did you *see* His eyes? – I felt I could drown in these Pools of Blue!"

"Did you see his ghastly dwarfisch foot?" – said Sister, at the party with The (attractive, almost a competitive, Leni) Riefenstahl, after – "In a black-silk sock, like a horse's Thingee."

"Like a Tidal Wave!" – cried even the Old Guard newspapers, in reviewing the Production – "Nationalist Enthusiasm renewed pours over the Land! New Hope spills over the dikes and bursts open all New Doors ...!"

The 1st Trickle:

Was a telephone call. "From a Mr Teacham," said the English operator, "in Berlin."

"Herr Heinz Tietjen! Am I speaking with you, now, Herr Edwin von Perceval?"

"Yes, Herr Heinz, it's me, Eddie."

269

"I regret this intrusion, Herr Edwin, but I must speak also with your sister about her Eva."

"I'm afraid you can't, Herr Heinz. She's on-stage as Elisabeth. Can I give her a message?"

"Yes. You shall have heard of the success of the Fuehrer in the final election? An entertainment is being offered by the artists of Berlin. A performance of Meistersinger on the Inaugural Night. Frau Winifred also shall be present. One realises the notice is short, my boy, but your sister already has learnt the part for Bayreuth and still there remains a week's rehearsing with the Staatsoper here."

"You want her to sing?"

"This is what I have been saying. Frau Leider was to take the role but she is unwell."

"I'll tell Ettie."

"She will understand this is also the Fuehrer's express wish?"

"Yes, Herr Heinz. Herr Wolf wants Ettie to go on as Eva, in Meistersinger, for Frida, who isn't well."

"Precisely so!"

"The poor darling," said Sister, "she must have come down with a case of Berlin Throat. But only a week? As Eva in front of the whole world? Tietjen must be mad. Eddie, no, I simply can't. I don't care what Wolf bloody wants – I won't, do you hear? Eddie, I *won't*."

Perhaps she really wouldn't if she'd known Nicholas Baer was conducting, but she didn't find that out until the afternoon before the Night.

... *At the Hotel Eden: Birthday Night.* Edwin, avoiding Walther von Stolzing like the plague, broods alone in the Eden Grille bar with gin & lime between rehearsals – where Waring found me.

"Hullo, C-P."

"Hullo, Waring." The Chums haven't seen each other for a year but that doesn't matter. Waring's Waring: his face and his old suit look even thinner from another twelve months of watching. He was carrying Ettie's shooting stick. Said Eddie, "You haven't pawned it – how did you know to catch me here?"

"I didn't," said Waring. "I'm just going through all the hotels, watching. This city's seething. A chap could have a schnaps if you like."

270

And another gin for Edwin. "Berlin's like a bloody coronation, Waring. I wouldn't use 'seething,' exactly."

"You don't watch the back streets, C-P. Behind the Alexanderplatz it's as though a siege had been lifted by a relieving army. Scores are being settled on a mass scale. Not just bashings – Reds are being taken away by the lorryload. The worst part is the non-stop bellow from the loudspeakers. Come watching with me."

"I can't possibly. I've got to sort out Ettie and her conductor. It'll take hours. And then there's bloody Walther von Stolzing and Hans Sachs. I'll have to be polite in front of Wolf. And it's our birthday! What a bloody evening."

"Many happy returns. Come after. I'll be watching in the den Linden side bar. We'll go crawling. This is a chap's last week in Berlin. You ought to take advantage."

"I'll try, Waring, but I can't promise."

"Thank God I don't have a sister. You could leave a chap another schnaps if you like."

Plus an extra 10 marks, and then face Ettie.

"How could you leave me? And you've been boozing!"

"I met Waring. Two gins. It *is* my birthday."

"What about mine? Stuck away up here, alone – and that vile Baer. I know he'll throw me off the beat when it gets to Eva."

"He wouldn't get very far as a conductor if he did that for every female singer he's – "

"*Every* – ?"

"For heaven's sake, Ettie, I never said – "

"No, you never do! Or stand up for me, with rat creatures like that Baer, as we drag all over Europe. As far as you're concerned all I do is open my mouth and howl, and afterwards fall on the nearest bed with the nearest goat of a conductor while you go off with one of your pansy friends to ogle the dead in one of your bloody tombs."

"I don't ogle. And you don't need a bed. And Pawel certainly wasn't a pansy on the bloody beach."

A longish pause . . .

"You spied on me, with Pawel?"

"You can't say you were quiet about it. Oh never mind – "

"Never mind? My brother being a disgusting peeping tom? You

271

probably porpoised all over yourself, just watching. You did! You're blushing! I don't know how I could ever have let you touch me!"

"You don't mean that?"

"Of course I mean it. You knew all along it was a sin." A pot of Ponds flew by his head. "Go with your crawly queers like Waring." A packet of powder exploded. "And don't you dare take any of my knickers with you!"

"Enjoy your Meistersinger," Edwin replied, in his coldest fury. And left her. And went down and had two double gin and limes. And then cried with hot rage about women, in the men's lavatory. And then went looking for Waring.

The Chums' Night Out

"You got away early, C-P." Waring was watching from a corner of the bar. "Did you get caught by the mob? What's all that powder on your collar?"

"Ettie's. Bloody bitch! I don't want to talk about it. Look, Waring, can we crawl somewhere that I won't have to meet anyone? I simply couldn't face Winifred's or Wolf's crowd now. She called us both queers."

"Winifred Wagner?" said Waring.

"My sister. I could have killed her."

"Little birds in their nests ... We could walk on the crawl – or you could find a chap a taxi if you like."

"Walk. I don't care. You're the one that knows Berlin."

"The Café Montmartre," Waring said. "Not original, but it's where Huns are feeling naughtiest this month. Half a mile in the West End. We could have a schnaps first if you like?"

"Not here, I don't want to get collared by *her* again."

Waring branches off into a warren of alleys that serve the shops and emporia with delivery at their back doors. The Chums pass sausage and beer places half underground at the bottom of steamy steps, with cats and tatty women prowling or leaning.

"Was your sister right about you being a queer, C-P?"

"Good-God, Waring – she was mad! Raving. She only said it because of that school business with the filthy Darling."

"And us."

"We were just boys."

"I suppose," said Waring. "The wind's cold through this suit, let's stop here for that schnaps."

The Chums descend one of the grimy steps, past the prostitutes and cats and smells. The bar is full of Storm Browns, table-thumping and singing. They wave good humouredly at Young Eddie. "Sieg Heil!"

"Sieg Heil."

The first time I ever said it. The Browns grin, one shouts, "Schnaps for the young Herr!"

Kameraden.

"I usually just wave, C-P. If a chap Heils you never know when you're going to suddenly find Reds outnumbering Browns at the other end of the room."

"Thank you for the schnaps," Edwin says to the tablethumpers, as the Chums leave.

"Sieg Heil – and don't you boys do anything we wouldn't do!"

Rough laughter follows the Chums up the stairs. A cat squalls. Dame Sorrow has returned, determined to take Sister's place and settle in. The Chums come out in the open and cross the Schillerstrasse. The Café Montmartre confronts the Chums. More on street level than the dive with the Browns. An awning is luminous pink and canary yellow.

"How many, Liebchen?"

Under the awning a woman with caked makeup sits with legs crossed to show her thighs and matching pink and yellow knickers.

Eddie says, "Just the two of us."

"Never mind, Liebchen, you'll find someone nice inside. Five marks."

"I say, that's a bit steep."

"You get what you pay for, Liebchen."

Only when she laughs, and slips down two octaves, does Edwin realize – *she* isn't! The Café Montmartre is crowded, smoky, with a Negro jazz band, and on a tiny parquet floor the sexes melding. Some of the patrons have to be women but, even when they laugh, Eddie can't be sure. A girl strips slowly on stage while the Chums find a table. The girl *is* – she has breasts. The Chums sit down. One of the staff affects to be American, and knows Waring.

"Hi treasure. What's your best buddy buying for you tonight?"

"Schnaps," the buddy says, knowing he's blushing.

"Why not have something special, Honey? That's such a lovely gold." The staff member giggles and touches Eddie's hair so that I shiver. "How about Billy-Hans brings you an 'Oskar Wildekuss' – brandy and cream, whipped with guess-what from the bar guy?"

"You order, Waring," mumbling, as a Latin-looking man comes out to dance with the bare-breasted girl on the stage.

"Just schnaps, Billy-Hans, and don't be naughty; a chap's leaving this week."

On stage the Latin kisses the girl's nipples. At a table beside the Chums two probable women kiss each other, lingeringly, on the mouth. On stage, the girl slips her hand inside the Latin's tight trousers – who tears off her leather skirt. Under it "she" has no knickers. Only an erection and no pubic hair. Billy-Hans brings the Chums' schnaps. The crowd screams as the Latin drops to his knees, putting his tongue to the "girl's" shaved male organs.

"Isn't he *wicked*?" Billy-Hans giggles. "He *knows* we could lose our licence! Five marks, Liebchen."

The stage spot goes out. Eddie gropes for money in his flannels' pocket. A Negro drummer rolls to a bored crescendo. The crowd falls silent. From the dark stage come sucking noises. Eddie gets out some change and feels the throb of his own Mr Thingee. The Negro band begins to play the Horst Wessel Song to a copulatory beat. The crowd cheers – and Waring's hand was on my thigh, moving higher. Music and cheering, and Waring, faster and faster, and then with a *crash* of symbols he takes his hand away. The stage spots come on long enough to show the sodomy of the shaven "girl" on all fours, as she was masturbated simultaneously into a champagne glass by the penetrating Latin.

"For an Oskar Wildekuss," said Waring blandly; "it's ten marks if a chap likes – or we could stay with schnaps."

"My God, Waring – you wouldn't . . . "

Drink it? Edwin stared appalled – fascinated? – as a man's coarse thug voice said beside me, in German, "I thought so! – our Adolf's golden little English boy!"

Hunding:
He was in a suit, dark blue, not his Brown's uniform, and although the

thug's face was familiar, and the "Adolf" too intimate, Edwin could not put a name.

"Ernst Roehm." Extending a thug's hand that smells of too much, too sweet, cologne. "That was quite a show, Herr Ederl. You were lucky to see it. We're closing the place tomorrow. Our mutual friend's determined to nail up anything that looks like a little joy. It's fine for him – but we can't all keep our true loves in a coffin. If you boys haven't dined tonight, I'm holding a wake for von Papen at HQ. You're more than welcome. I've got a car. You're far too good looking for Adolf to keep all to himself. What do you say?"

Edwin said, "I'm afraid I'm not dressed for dining, Captain – "

But Waring said, "Yes!" Jumping at the invitation with surprising speed – although nothing was surprising after his hand on my leg and the Oskar Wildekuss. "We'd like that very much. A chap's always wanted to watch inside SA headquarters."

As the Chums leave, the woman-man at the door under the awning crossed its legs at me to show the pink and yellow knickers.

"Didn't I say you'd find someone nice, Liebchen?"

Hunding's HQ:
Is on the Standartenstrasse, back where the Chums started in the centre of Berlin. On the outside it might be a hotel. Inside, a nouveau riche's vision of a brothel: rococo chandeliers, and Gobelin tapestries and carpets with a pile to lie down on, and mirrors.

The Thug revellers for the Co-Chancellor's downfall are seated at an enormous horse-shoe dinner table, and already in the mood. Despite the lavish decor, Eddie's flannels don't matter; the dress of the partygoers is as mixed as the furniture: some in tails, some in suits like Roehm's, but worse cut, some in a variety of Storm Brown Mess Dress. The only thing in common is the Mowgli symbol. Some of the men have women on their arm. Some, men. Some, a turf-accountant wouldn't bet on. The Café Montmartre at an uptown address.

As Roehm walks in with the Chums, a young male – beautiful as Eddie, but with a shaven head and painted top to naked toe in gold – leaps from a confection made of sponge cake and ice in the shape of a Lohengrin swan. A great cheer and a laugh, as he runs nimbly once around the table with the diners trying in vain to lift his fig leaf. As he

275

passes the Chums he flips it up with one hand at Roehm – that nether part too is shaven, and its foreskin golden.

"SIEG HEIL!"

The diners roar it back over a toast of champagne, as the Chums sit down to dinner.

"On my right, little Ederl," says Hunding-Roehm. "Your friend can goggle from the other side. Under our Wolf's watchful eye!"

The Chums' host bellows with laughter. Some of the diners join in. The majority look anxiously at the portrait of the Leader, as stewards bring around His favourite: liver-dumpling soup.

"All he ever bloody eats! Soup! He should be here like yourself, Herr Ederl, but we're not good enough. Up on his bloody mountain tops like a new Yid Moses, or kissing the Kaiser's arse this morning! Already Adolf's in the sack with them. Keeping on that old fart Hindenburg – we should cut off his nuts!" A steward refills Edwin's glass. "At least von Papen's gone, that squawking parrot. We should have wrung his bloody neck – now what about you, little Ederl? Why do you let *him* hide you away in that Bayreuth cell of his with that gossiping toad-shit Hanf-staengl?"

The Thug Boss waves his hock glass at the diners who mistake the gesture and roar back another,

"SIEG HEIL!"

"I'm afraid, Captain, I'm really not political. Herr Wolf shares our interest in Wagner – my sister's singing, you know."

"Has he got her to squat for him yet?" Roehm thrusts his Hunding mouth only inches from Brother's shocked face and bellows with laughter. "He likes to see both doors to the House, does our Wolf, if you take my meaning. When you're next in Munich and he isn't, I'll show you his pictures. A great artist – if you don't mind the Wurm's eye view of Miss Pussy!"

"SIEG HEIL!"

. . . And up through the centre of the U rises a new confection: Leda & her Swan. Leda is the hermaphrodite from the Montmartre. Stark naked. And the swan is the golden youth, now with feather wings and no fig leaf.

"Adolf will piss himself when he knows," Hunding-Roehm shouts as

276

the table screeches its approval. "He's babbled about fucking Leda ten thousand times and now he's fucking missed it!"

Edwin's whirling head recalls the picture – over the Red Divan, from the henhouse, in the fatal birdcage apartment on the Residenzstrasse.

Before me, in the centre of the Storm table this latest "swan" extends its sinuous neck in the same inevitable direction as the Latin lover on the nightclub's stage. And again I feel a hand on my thigh. But Waring's ten feet away. Roehm's flushed thug cheeks glisten with sweat like the candied apples on the Schillerstrasse. The swan-boy wraps its wings around the freak-Leda, feathering its organs. Under the table, thick fingers fumble roughly with the buttons of my flannels.

The Leda-freak contorts as an acrobat, emerging with its own head between its legs, mouth open, seeking! The swan flaps in ecstacy. The Brown diners and assorted partners shriek. Edwin gasps.

The Show's Over:
The swan and his freak sink under the table. Head down, and scarlet, Edwin buttons his trousers. Couples drift apart, or to private rooms on other floors.

"Give my love to Adolf, little golden boy, when you see him." Ernst Roehm blows a sarcastic kiss with his coarse, loathsome thug's fingertips and wipes his hand on his Mowgli napkin.

With mocking laughter ringing in his ears, Eddie runs down the Unter den Linden past the honest prostitutes, all the way to Eden.

Where, at twenty minutes past one of that memorable post-birthday morning, with an expression on her face as fraught as mine, I found Sister.

His head was in her lap. He was on His knees, in His dragging tail-coat, His shoulders heaving. There was no other soul with us; no bodyguard or even a dog, inside the suite or out. Just Wotan dropping in on Brünnhilde. Except that onstage the motif at least lets you know a bar in advance that He's coming.

"I can't go on," sobs the New Men's god. "Not without you."

Brother & Sister can read more than each other's faces.

Shall I say something?

277

"There's no other way." From a piteous Wolfi.

No, Eddie, it's all right.

"It's hopeless! Hindenburg, the whole army are against me."

But are you sure?

"Can you doubt it? You saw their faces – behind one's back, in the church – I'm filth to them."

YES! – a furious glare from Sister.

"So how can you still deny me?"

What on earth does He want, Ettie?

"No more than a kiss, like two swans, for life – "

Jesu Christ! Like a Leda –

"Our own little nest . . ."

Mind your own bloody business! Eddie, please – bugger OFF.

Post Mortem:

"You might at least have stayed awake," Ettie said, when for a change she brought me coffee in the morning. "You look even worse than usual. Eddie, you're simply going to have to stop this boozing."

"Oh, Christ, my head . . ." Dame Sorrow's usual pleas and excuses; "What on earth was He doing here? – it looked like a music-hall proposal."

"It was." She sat down on the bed and chewed on a croissant.

"Marriage?"

"A sort of." Between bites she mimicked cruelly her ardent suitor, " 'I can't divorce Germany! It must be one perfect heart – our secret! as two swans – for life!' "

The vision returns – of the Leda-Freak, mounted, madly fouling the nest. The coffee cup clatters in Eddie's shaking hands:

"He's asked you before?"

"Three times at least." She dabbed crumbs with her fingers and dropped them deliberately to itch between the sheets. "If you'd stayed with me last night instead of running away, this time would never have happened."

"But when?"

"When what?"

"The first time?"

"The day of the picnic, I think – yes that was the first, after that

278

shopgirl pretended to hang herself. Really, Eddie, it's years. I can't remember."

When a rival Queen of the barnyard strings herself up on the henhouse door? . . . my dears, really!

"So when was the second?"

"When I was Waltraute. The summer darling Siegfried died."

"When Geli, died. Perhaps she knew. Perhaps that's why she – "

"That was after the season ended. And she probably meant to miss – Eddie, don't be such a melodramatic ninny. Wolf only does his crawly proposing when he's about to do something tremendous, or more likely has, and then he's disappointed – the day after Christmas when you're very small and you've had all the presents so you know there's nothing more, because the idea of the next Christmas or birthday seems so impossibly far away. But then you cry to Mama, or a Papa if you've got one, and on you go. Are you going to get up and bath or just lie there stinking?"

But when he climbed from the bath, squeaky-clean and fresh, with aspirins cancelling the headache, instead of being dressed for lunch she was equally naked, perfumed under breasts and between legs, holding out her hands to me. "I know it's a day late darlingest Eddie, but let's give ourselves a private birthday present to make up, shall we?"

So they did – with Brother trying to block sensations of Roehm's & Waring's hands and fingers, or swan-feathered images of shaved hermaphroditic sexual organs . . .

"Oh Gawd, Eddie, that was our best ever."

The Church Bazaar

"Pal, I don't know what monkey-shines you've been up to, but the Chancellor invites your presence, and Buster, he don't mean maybe!"

He is not yet in what the world knows as His Chancellery, but in an apartment that had been the Secretary of State's under Weimar. (Equally despised – constantly shown off – by the new owner is The Demok-Rats' Bolthole – a narrow, triangular escape passage from the garret over the roofs to the Reichstag.)

"If I have to smash my head another godamn time," said Putzi, in the foyer, "wait here. I'll see if he's ready for you."

279

Aspirins wear off. Legs wobble. Eddie collapses onto a spindle-shanked gilt chair. A bevy of Fricka matrons are setting up tables for what seems to be a ladies' Easter church bazaar. Draped cloths embroidered with every conceivable Mowgli design hang down like altar vestments framing communion plates of His favourite sweets from Hamann's, the confectioners.

"Good morning, Herr Edwin."

"Good morning, Frau Ilse."

The Frickas are led by Fräulein Anna's wife. Now, as she says "Herr Edwin," Eddie observes that her hair has that chronically dirty look of the aging blonde. No makeup either.

"Are you having some sort of a sale for charity, Frau Ilse?"

"A sale, Herr Edwin? Sell the gifts of our Fuehrer's grateful people?"

Render unto Dolferl these jams and jelly sweeties!

Ten minutes. Thirty. Eddie runs out of things to say to Ilse Hess and his head is splitting. He wonders why Herr Wolf has sent for him, and debates getting up and walking out. Not so simple. The Volsungs' new master is no longer a mere demok-rat politician. The Teuton Praetorian Black Order is positioned at the doors.

An hour. Ilse Hess and her Fricka women have finished piling their altars. Their subdued old-girlish church chatter dies away with the clack of their flat heels. Edwin closes his eyes . . .

"You dare to sleep when I send for you?"

His mask was down. Slammed shut with flat white cheeks, doll-rouged, and stiff as a Templar's helmet visor. Only the eye-holes show life inside. Blazing out. Not blinking. Not a twitch of a single eyelid hair, as a boy gaped back, trapped on the rickety gilded chair, and tried to stand – but that means bumping Him.

"Herr Wolf, I – "

"What's that you name me?"

He seems dressed in armour, although it's only His baggy blue suit – His Country Schoolmaster's, Mausi calls it.

"Herr Adolf, excuse if I've offended – "

"Excuse?" In a spit explosion. Hailing my face. *"Excuse? EXCUSE?"* For a third time, an impossible fourth, and fifth, with an inconceivably rising, bellowing rage – "Would your so-noble mother *excuse*?!! Would

her immortal memory *excuse* as she looks down from heaven to see her son's depravity? His participation in productions of the most revoltingly obscene? Witnessing with her eyes – which are the same noblest, generous blue as his own! – every type of freak filth of the shitbag sewer West End?! The perverts' alleyways where *Their* pimpmasters' hag-vermin wait to prey on the naive, and the innocent, and the pure? And not just a mother watches! A golden sister is dragged down! Her peerless reputation fouled before the world! *My* reputation – the Leader's! – for being so foolish as to extend the hand of friendship! Extended his protection to an orphaned boy because of Music! But where's the use?! Shit finds shit! Dirt eats dirt! Worms crawl always on the corpse of decency! Boy – have you the least idea what spirochaete horror may already, yes! at this very instant! eat away inside your brain? Tearing down to nothing with its poisoned saliva-rotting teeth, softening to grey putrescent liquid cheese the notes that could be Wagner's, the lines Leonardo's, the very foundations of a man's soul. *Your* soul, boy! Well may you stare! Your soul and brain liquefying every minute! Putrifying – waking and sleeping! – as the Yid instigators laugh in their sewer alleys and mothers weep! No more, do you hear? Never, never, *never, NEVER*! Oh, one knows the blame wasn't a boy's. One knows what older hands are out there reaching, clawing, grasping under tables and clutching. I've seen those coarse fat cheeks once too often! And Hanfstaengl's been warned, in the gossip circle! Well now it's over. Let them tremble – when I clean the stables, heads will roll! Those shitbrown bastards on the Standartenstrasse won't be able to walk, there'll be so many bleeding squishing skulls in the shit on deck! Mein Ederl, dearest boy – do you have any idea how I felt, to hear that you were 'entertained' by a degenerate like Roehm? A visionless oaf who seeks only to destroy me. How dare *he*? How *dare* he? *HOW DARE HE*?! Herr Edwin, I now formally forbid you utterly-utterly ever again to mix the miracle of our Green Hill in the sewer of politics. *I*, the Leader, have to sacrifice and prostitute myself! *I*, the Leader, have to risk infection for the good of the world. So be it. But it ends with me! Do you understand, boy? – *ends*! Now, that's all I have to say. We've wagged the finger. For your noblest, dearest Mother's sake, I am your father in this country – we're friends again. We'll wash our hands and face, like good fellows, and meet my other guests."

Who – as the fellows emerge from the inner study where somehow He has mesmerised and manoeuvered me – are already standing, with incredulous expressions, assembled in a semicircle like the Camargue guardians' trident: Aunt Winnie, on the left horn; Ettie, the right; Hanfstaengl, clearly warned, at the giant centre, with Helene beside him; and Mausi, the too-plump chip-off-the-old-block, spiked in front.

"Ah," says their Host, pushing back His wing of hair which has become somewhat displaced, "Dear friends – thank you for coming at such short notice. Welcome to my very first dinner as Chancellor – you must see *Their* Bolt-Hole – Ederl and I were having a little chat."

Second Movement

Second Passage

[agitato]

Who never spake more Words than these,
Fight on my merry Men all;
For why, my Life is at an end;
Lord Percy sees my Fall.

. . . *In Spandau*. My dears. What a to-do with Waring! Old Edwin, justly proud of the Chums' Leda Story as being exactly up Yellow Alley's street, presented his latest scribble humbly for the famed Novelettist's perusal –

"Christ on a cross, you can't print that about me with Ernst Roehm!"

Yes children, Chum Jeremy threw a Fit!

"But why not, if it's the truth, Waring?" enquired Old Eddie, meekly seeking to learn the craft of Popular Writing.

"Because – Jesus wept, man! – I never suggested *drinking* it!"

Poor Oskar's Wildekuss! There lies the rub.

"But I didn't actually say you'd drunk it, Waring – it says, 'buying'. Perhaps it's my writing?"

"It's deliberate. You can't possibly expect me to sell this, and if you do I'll sue."

Regina vs Number 7? Hess the 3rd? A hollow threat – we've had the Trial. Also (it appears) the last of Waring for a while. Jeremy has missed our last 2 Editorial meetings which were to discuss Yellow Street's further requirements.

SPIRO KEETS GNAWED HIM!!!

Don't tell me!

... *At Porquerolles:* Guilt & Fear. Those two hag Norns hang back during our first Easter drive with the blue Riley: following the sun, and getting lost, and laughing, and the wind coming in through the sliding roof and playing with Ettie's hair, and at country inns and garages peasant mechanics patting her bonnet and flanks (the Riley's), and cows mooing and children in villages waving. At little Hyères Deaf'n'Dumber was waiting with the *Cormoran*. There's no way the Riley can get across. Or needs to – what will a car do on our one-track island? Eddie found a home for it in a barn belonging to yet another of Mathilde's mainland relations, and tucked it in with a last fond polish to make it gleam, as the doors of the barn swung shut with a screech, and the Norns fell on my head.

At night, Edwin began to dream, as he hadn't since Tintagel. The dream was the same, with the same tower and horse-riding and a boy naked, and in front the edge of a cliff, and behind a company of pursuers thundering, but when I looked over my shoulder, now, there was only one man, Ernst Roehm with his leper's stump of a nose, and pocked dueller's cheeks, and pig's eyes squinting with horrible laughter as my horse leaped out and down into bottomless space. . . .

And then Eddie wakes screaming, Mama, Mama! – to find only Mathilde in her nightgown with a candle, stroking my brow to make the sign of the cross, and muttering Satan's name under her breath. While Ettie, behind, says, "Gawd, how will I learn my damn Brünnhilde if none of us ever gets any bloody sleep?"

By day, Walk & Swim & Fish & Tennis & Piano constantly between, but nothing on Porquerolles can erase the touch of Waring's hand on my thigh in the Café Montmartre, with its Oskar Wildekuss, or his look, watching. Or Edwin's answering excitement. *Homosexual!* – as well as *Incestuous?* Depravity is total. And Easter is Parsifal, and Amfortas's wound with its agonising death in life. *Diseased as well?!* No wonder He washes His hands! Because nothing ever-ever will blank out Ernst Roehm's coarse thug-fingers, groping – and finding! – and wiping. Or the ghastlier thought of where those fingers have been, what else they've touched – who else? Why shouldn't the dread Spirochaetae even now be crawling their gnawing way inward and up —?

To Sister?

"Dear God," Brother prayed aloud, walking alone on our Beach of the Lobsters, "Oh, God, if I have to die, don't let me have given it to her!"

The boy's medical ignorance as total as his guilt, he can only wait for the signs of Nietzsche's and Van Gogh's madness, and each night dream the nightmare, and each morning look in the mirror for frothing at the mouth or rolling of the eye, and when Ettie says "I don't know what on earth Wolf said to you, but with this dreaming and screaming you're behaving damnably odd these days," rush away before she can see me cry.

Only one bacillus concerns her: the Honourable Edwina is studying night and day for the Brünnhilde in case Frida Leider comes down with another dose of Jewish-Husband disease in the summer.

"Of course I don't *wish* it on Frida, Eddie – about her husband. And you know we all of us singers think the whole Boycott business is perfectly silly – I mean not shopping in Department stores on April Fool's! I'm sure it's only that little Dwarf swine; as Putzi says, did you ever see anyone that looked more like one of *them*? – but if Frida *isn't* going to sing in Hunland, it would be mad not to be ready."

... *To the Green Hill:* Sister allows us to make a side excursion to Avignon where the old Abbot of the Quincunx Yews is as kind and unyielding as ever. "The Grail will be found with prayer, my son – not with a shovel."

"Bloody old fossil!" Eddie swore, but Ettie said, just being awkward, "He's a poppet. You can't expect him to dig up his precious trees because you've started to dream again. And this season you're not running off to Bamberg the minute we arrive. Even if I don't get a crack at Brünnhilde, you're damn well going to see my first Bayreuth Eva."

... In her Festspielhaus office, Senta-Winnie is at her wits' end. Tosca-no-no, more vehemently than ever, refuses to say Yes with Him in power. And F***wängler, children. He says it's the uncertainty over Doctor Geissmar – the Stork's secretary is one of Them – but he can't be so foolish. Berlin isn't doing anything to Berta Geissmar. It's really because he wants the hood off the orchestra pit – but at least Frida Leider's coming back.

"Oh wonderful," said Sister.

... *En route to Triebschen:* "It's because Mother complains so much," Mausi explains as the Trio escape in the blue Riley, through green fields with golden buttercups and crimson-eyed white daisies. "If she'd only shut up, or let me go back to school in England. By the way, Eddie, what's syphilis?"

... As Edwin lets in the clutch so hard that the Riley shudders.

"I asked Tietjen yesterday, Ettie, and he said there isn't such a word – even when I showed him The Book. There's ten pages."

"We haven't read it." Big Sister smiled at her brother.

"No one has," said Mausi, "it's the dullest book in the world."

Big Sister bluntly told her – but that only opens a convent Pandora's box of ignorance, with the result that by the time the Riley purrs by Lake Lucerne, Eddie's blushing like the eye of a daisy: Mausi, over gasps & giggles, and despite having two brothers, has received a vital missing part of a Freudian's education.

"That's what the flower maidens are doing, in Parsifal? And the spear is really a man's – Oh, my Lord!"

And as we arrived and she left the Riley, the gross child whispered to Ettie in front of the old Parrot-Sisters, waving, "This summer when Heinz Tietjen's sitting around the swimming pool come and watch. I'll ask him about it. You never know – his spear might flop out!"

Our trip had been a two-way education. The C-Ps had filled in a multitude of Wagnerian parental gaps.

"Of course darling Siegfried was hurt – that's why he adored Mausi so much at the end, and why Auntie seems so beastly to her half the time – but I still don't think that Winifred was ever actually in bed with Wolf."

"But you don't know, Ettie. Wolf was ten years younger then."

"So was Helene Hanfstaengl – and he only put his head in *her* lap."

"That's what she says to Putzi."

"And I'd bet it's true. This cottage is rather sweet – could we be dull little Swiss here?"

"It's all right. Why do you think it's true, with Helene?"

286

"Because she didn't try to hang herself, darling. Or shoot. Eddie, let's tell the estate person we'll buy this one. I love the apple trees, and the little dock, and the fireplace. It's like our Hunding's Hut."

"Ettie, you don't mean they kill themselves because of what they have to do in bed?"

"I mean, Eddie dear, that Big Sis doesn't intend to say 'yes' and find out. Come on, get your chequebook and we'll make love to celebrate being Swiss."

"No – I can't."

"Why ever not?"

"There isn't any furniture."

"You adorable silly – we only need a rug."

"It isn't the rug. I just can't."

"Are you saying you're impotent?"

"Yes."

"At twenty-two?"

"It doesn't matter how old you are."

"I'll bet you aren't."

She drops to her knees – and before the boy knows what's happening she's pulled up one leg of his corduroy shorts and taken his Thingee in –

"Your mouth! Sweet Christ! Ettie, you mustn't – "

But he doesn't stop her. Can't. He can only sag against the chimney, and look down at the crown of her golden head, and see her blue eyes look up at him, gleaming over his expanding flesh, and feel her Kundry tongue, and her lips working, and think of Klingsor's Wildekuss potion . . . and, defeated before he started, simply let the Disease, pent up for weeks in his weak body and degenerate's brain, burst into his sister's insatiable mouth.

"Fellatio," she gasped, triumphant. "I knew it would work! A bit of an ucky taste though – the books don't tell you. Kiss me and see."

A Moral Stand:

Edwin refused to buy that cottage: claiming it was too much under the eye of the Parrot Sisters at Triebschen – although as Richard & Cosima's former nest sits on a hill in its orchard, and is 3 stories high, with dormers (for a spy telescope in an attic), all the other chalets in the Wagnerians' colony are equally observed. The one the Casson-

Percevals finally buy ends up being even more like our first Hunding's Hut because it has a peninsula, and a boathouse, with boat. E & E go to Zürich to sign the papers and have dinner with Michael Rau. Oysters. Floating, in a milky broth . . .

OUR '33 SEASON

Herr Wolf arrives at full speed: with outriders, and the Praetorian Black Order leaping off the running-boards while the State Mercedes (three times as long as the one Mama gave him) is still in motion. At the entrance to Wahnfried He gives a little half-salute and a chuckle of pure joy to Ludwig staring down from his pedestal.

"To think when I stood on the Dutchman's ship! With our country doomed, people said! Condemned to drift forever as the dead man of Europe, and yet now here we are! In the Master's presence. His pianos! His writings! And our most gracious and noble Fräulein Edwina, you're going to give us your lovely Eva again – and a Brünnhilde – ah ha! You didn't know? Call it Herr Wolfi's little surprise. Oh yes! Frau Winifred and I have had our backstage discussions. And I appreciate your concern, Fräulein Ettie – but Frau Leider will still have two cycles of the Ring. Three strains the voice excessively, in my opinion. Mein Ederl, what mischief have you been up to? One hears your blue Riley turns all the heads in Triebschen."

Such a man *can* conquer the world and, when it's done, with Civilisation saved and the Western Soul renewed, retire as He promises, to write and ponder, happy that His founder's task is done and that younger hands can carry on with the Nibelung donkey work of turning lead into gold. . . .

. . . *Upstairs at the Griesbachs'*: "Brünnhilde!" the Honourable Edwina cried for the thousandth time. "I could have fallen on His pockmarked neck and hugged Him – and Auntie. And we'll all have to be especially nice to darling Frida, but Wolf's right, three goes at the Ring is too much for anyone. Oh Gawd – even one go! Eddie, can I really do it? A Bayreuth Brünnhilde at twenty-four? Old Cosima said my voice wouldn't be right before I was thirty – although semen's supposed to help tighten the cords."

"What did you say?" Because half the time Brother doesn't bother really listening.

"Semen – your juice, it raises the pitch, it's vitamins or something."

"Who in God's name ever told you that?"

"Hanussen. I went to him in Berlin."

"The astrologer quack?"

"He's not a quack. Or if he is, Putzi says he found the damn mandrake root for Wolf to be Chancellor – and that certainly worked."

"Was that the reason –?" unable to believe that even *she* – "at Triebschen? It wasn't me being impotent at all?"

"Hanussen said it had to be once before Midsummer's Day. And once the night before the first performance."

She glares: defiant Brünnhilde.

"I won't let you. Ettie, it isn't right."

"Go on, you loved it."

"You could get a disease." Edwin does his mumble, weakly.

"Then that would be your fault wouldn't it? Oh, Eddie, don't be so solemn. I'll let you do it to me after, and then you'll get the bug back. We'll be immunized – like a diphtheria inoculation."

"Do what after?"

"Cunnilingus, darling. Just the word makes you feel goosey. Oh, never mind, when it's time I'll show you."

Our First Brünnhilde:

"I guess you've both heard what Adolf did last night?" says Putzi, the next day over lunch at the Hotel Anchor.

"No," said the Honourable Edwina, equally insatiable for gossip as for lust. "What?"

"He's brought her back."

"Who, Putzi?"

"The tart, Eddie-pal – niece-Geli. From Vienna. In her lead box, in time for this year's anniversary. A touch bizarre, some people are saying – oh yes, and that mandrake quack, Hanussen, got rounded up by Hermann and put in one of his Boer War concentration camps."

And then –?

Rheingold: where the music drops, . . . and in the hush, Alberich, the Evil One, mouths His spell: "Nacht und Nebel – niemand gleich!"

Night and Fog . . .
. . . resembling No One.
And then –?

The afternoon following, before the evening when Sister is going to fix her throat for Brünnhilde, and demand from Brother this latest secret act with the tingling name . . .

"You mean you still don't know?" she whispers, giggling. "You spent enough time in the library."

"Wahnfried only had a schoolroom dictionary in English."

"So you looked! And you found it – you're getting excited."

"Of course I'm excited." Her tongue has touched his glans, lurching blindly out of its foreskin. "How can I help it when you're doing that?"

"Poor worm. I'm sure this is why Hun says *Wurm* for dragon." Blowing on it with inflamed breath. "What do you think it is, Eddie – cunnilingus?"

"I don't know." Gasping, as she sucks him in whole.

"Shh!" Letting me slip out. "The Griesbachs will hear. Make a guess."

"I can't. I don't care. I'm going to burst. Just lie down."

"We mustn't waste it. Turn around. Not that way silly – the other, so your head's down there."

Head in the lap stuff? Is *this* what He wanted? This lust-garden scent filling the nostrils. Making me dizzy. Her gold hairs in tight rings tickling the nose – making me sneeze.

"Oh how luscious. Oh, Gawd. Oh lovely. Now, Eddie darling, now – with your tongue!"

Bitter-sweet. Lemon-honey. Pain-pleasure. A bud throbbing, petals parting with slippery guilt. "Ettie, I can't! You use it to – "

"You *must*! We have to, for Brünnhilde – now! *Together*!"

She drags him back in her mouth so that we become one body with two tongues, moaning, heedless of the Griesbachs. Or Disease. Or anything – until it was over, and the evidence of our shared wickedness gleamed on our lips and chins.

290

"Oh Gawd – Eddie, that was marvellous. It'll simply have to have done the trick."

The Library:
Torn by the power of Sin. Stay with Sister for these dictionary acts which must be increasingly, horribly wrong. Leave her, and fall into the hands of Waring or Ernst Roehm. And then, on the top shelf, safely removed from the children's hour . . .

Buchstaben & Journal
Privat
L.II – R.W.

29 June/
O! Precious Friend. Only Star of my Life. No! I repeat, no! We will not, must not, *shall not*!!! – for 2 weeks at least this time! 14 cruel days. But oh God! To think of His lips! His hands! No! No! *NO*!!!

7 July/
Sweet Christ we fail! Morning and evening with Penance and Lash! But the fragrance of His lilies . . . *I am the King*! 2 weeks was all. For 8 more days and nights we have to keep away. Not again, Corruption! Not till the 21st. Swear before His portrait. *Swear* . . . !

16 July/
Loathesome! Spineless Weakness!!! A Pilgrimage is the answer. If I part from Him – the only answer. Otherwise the Coils tighten. Death is the Rapture! One month's Pilgrimage, *We cannot weaken* . . . !

29 July/
Hope abandoned! So strong is the Magic Spell of the Desirer . . . Tonight a Lohengrin-Scene: Sugar Swans . . . Grooms . . . *Then Feast in the Fairy Tent* . . . !

A boy's tear trickled. For poor Ludwig, poor Friend, damned Sister and Brother –
"Show me."

He was standing in the doorway, His hand with its newly manicured nails stretched out. I gave the book wordlessly – with no idea how long He had been standing, watching like Waring. He read the last page, then snapped the book shut, spun on His heel, and rushed away . . .

I must act, will, SHALL.

So Vow it!

Make my own pilgrimage and pursue the Grail – or see this Fool too, trapped in the hothouse for the rest of its life.

The Fortress

. . . *To the Farthest Eastern Point in Europe* – as marked on the Fool-Scholar's Grail maps. It had not been an easy separation. Loyalty was brought up. Also a Hand-Mirror (sterling); Ingratitude, Cowardice, Incompetence, and rehearsal schedules for some years into the future.

"It's a month, Ettie. That's all. Tietjen's made special arrangements for a private accompanist every bloody day. I'll even make it only three weeks – unless I get too many punctures."

"In *my* car. Or run into Waring."

"I paid for it. And Waring's gone Home. He's writing his novelette in a garret in London."

"At least he has a goal." Shot back with anima's logic.

"You can't say finding the Grail isn't a goal." Replied the youth, coolly.

"*Find?* You couldn't find your thing in bed – without a dictionary." On which tender note . . .

. . . Faithful Riley took the Scholar (without even one flat tyre) east through Wallachia, and across the Burzen plain to the border of Heathenesse and a storybook Transylvanian village, where perched on a Rapunzel crag was the Castle of Bran (complete with Templar broadswords, and a quavering Major-Domo to the absent landlady Queen of Romania), but the place was wrong for the Grail, and so, reluctantly –

. . . To Rasnov, across the plain, with evening falling, and a noisy procession of peasants returning from the fields with hoes, jangling, and cows, bellowing, and geese, honking, and Riley's horn answering in thanks as they moved the whole lot sideways to let the Scholar pass – from ten miles away I saw it.

"What's that place?" asking a young boy with the geese. "There –" pointing – "with the sun setting on it?"

"Why, the Burgberg, Sir."

The Castle on the Hill. A proper fighter's castle, not for pining princesses and fairy stories. An immensely high and long stone wall stretched from edge to edge of the quarter-mile-wide bluff it sat on, with massive square stone towers at its corners, built everywhere down to solid rock. There was no road for a pilgrim to approach this fortress. A man must come on foot, all the while under the range of bows and guns. The hard way.

The Scholar left his Riley and climbed – noting in passing a triangle of 3 gypsy caravans encamped by a calcified spring for the night – to a small round gate in a circular structure at the base of the last point of the west end of the wall where the sun was now leaving: small only by comparison – with a boot on the sill the top of the gate was twenty feet above the head. A five foot wicket let the eager searcher through.

Earliest mediaeval Europe faced him. A cluster of cottage huts, with thatch gone from the roof beams; a smithy, stables, a church with no glass in its windows. Now, it was less than a village: then, it would have counted in the heathen wilderness as a town. One hut has a roof, and a light. The Scholar walks forwards, knocks. A Crone opens the door. She has no teeth and smokes a drooling pipe.

"Does no one else live here, old Mother?" the Scholar asks.

"Why bless you, young Lord – who'd want to sleep in my bed? Except the Crown Prince, maybe." The Crone cackles at the thought of Carol of Romania as a partner.

"I meant in the castle, old Mother."

"They'd sleep with rats then. That would be worse than with me, eh?" Cackling again, sending a shiver of disgust through a boy's loins. "Young Lord, no man's lived here since the robbers of Dietrichstein – slice their black parts."

So then I knew. Why I shivered at the Crone's dead lust. Why I saw Grail Knights' shadows patrolling with black Nibelheim crosses on their ghost-white tunics as they marched between a vanished temple's columns. The crone, altered hideously by Klingsor's wizardry after her betraying Kiss, is the shade of

Kundry, guiding Parsifal's steps. This rocky place was Dietrich's; the last survivor from the Nibelungenlied after its Great Hall burnt down ...

... *Kaffeeklatsch:* "Shot," said an immensely shaken Putzi Hanfstaengl, in English which had no trace of Chicago, while actually turning his great head to be sure we weren't overheard. Our Munich gossip circle had assembled for lunch at the Gerbers' to hear about the giant's Harvard Re-union with his old school chum, Franklin D. Roosevelt. "It seemed such a promising idea, after Adolf making sheep's eyes for the Dodd girl – the American Ambassador's daughter, haven't you heard? She looks like Geli, it goes without saying! She was divorced after a week's marriage in Chicago. And then I stepped off the ship and got this appalling news. The whole trip became a disaster because of things here with the Jews. I tried to explain it isn't Adolf's personal policy, just idiots like Rosenberg and Goebbels whipping a convenient scapegoat until unemployment's down – and then he has this purge of Roehm."

Said Ettie. "The Dodd creature's name is *Martha*, if you please. Just about the shallowest role in the repertoire – but surely no one thinks Wolf goes around ordering people to take down statues of Mendelssohn, for heaven's sake. And Putzi darling, Roehm was the most awful sort of Hunding-thug. I can't think why Wolf kept the Browns around so long."

"It isn't what they were, Edwina – it's that it was done without warrant and trial. A hundred people. Five hundred. A thousand – no one really knows."

At which gross exaggeration, Edwin said, "Aren't you being a little melodramatic, Putzi?"

And then –?

"Eddie, you'll simply never guess," says Sister, "the *Martha* Dodd's been smuggled home to Chicago with sticky tape all over its wrists!"

And then –?

THE MANOWARDA
INCIDENT!

or

"MORE MARIETTA"
[An Invasion of Privacy]

THE TIME
Our '34 Season's 2nd Cycle.

THE PLACE
The Privat *drawing room installed especially for Mad Ludwig behind the Family Box.*

THE CAST
AUNTIE WINNIE *is there, with her least favourite child,* MAUSI *and* EDDIE. *[But* not ETTIE – *triumphing as Brünnhilde] and the Giant* HANFSTAENGL *[but raising the gossips' eyebrows* without HELENE – *this time it's Decree Final!] and* HERR WOLF *[stuffing cake], at which point, as though with* GOD *Directing –*

CURTAIN UP

The Sound of 'Phone rings, OFF, *as a "Fricka" Party-matron, identified as one Frau Manowarda, [dressed over-all in a* sailor's suit *!] and manoeuvered by a Black Order Aide as an ocean liner would be by a tug, steams into the harbour of the Leader's Presence.*

THE FRICKA-MANOWARDA [*overcome*]
Ach! Mein Fuehrer!
She curtseys – bright puce *from excitement – to the waterline before her Leader, while:*

THE TUGBOAT-AIDE [*grabbing up insistent 'phone.*]
Ja?

THE LEADER [*bowing to F.M.* – wink to *Winnie*]
Gnädige Frau, my pleasure . . .

> *He gallantly kisses sausage fingers of F-M's starboard hand, as:*

THE TUGBOAT-AIDE [*puzzled at receiver's hysterical ranting.*]
Herr Doktor Goebbels, my Fuehrer. I think from the lobby, but he is not clear on the line.

THE FRICKA-MANOWARDA [*overcome utterly* !]
Ach! Danke! Mein Fuehrer, Danke – !

AUNTIE WINNIE [*seeing*]
Oh my God – someone catch her!

> *But F-M capsizes with bow wave of melting lard, as:*

THE LEADER [*at the phone*]
Done *what*?
MAUSI [*suddenly helpful*]
Fainted, Herr Wolf.

THE LEADER
Fainted be damned! Dolfuss is dead! Get that cow-bitch out of here!
> *2nd Black Order enters to assist 1st Tug-Aide, barely able to nudge F-M's bowsprit!*

THE LEADER [*screaming into 'phone*]
In Vienna? The Radio Station has been taken? Goebbels, is this right?
> [*a Leader-grin of exultation flashes* !]
By her legs, you good fellows!
> [*followed by black frowning rage.*]
Taken back already by the army?
> [*and now incredulity* ? ? ?]
By *Austrians* ? ! Oh my God!

[CURTAIN]

. . . In the Music Room: "He can't stay over there all by himself. Putzi, you must go across and play to cheer him up."

"Not unless I'm sent for, Winifred, thank you very much." The giant isn't putting his great head on anyone else's block. "Since Martha Dodd and the American fiasco, my reception has been uncertain, to say the least. All he does is gobble Fräulein Anna's half-baked geopolitical rubbish. 'Who rules the Heartland rules the globe.' As though its oceans didn't exist! Truly, friends, I despair of the man."

"Well we can't just let him sit and brood," says Sister brightly. "Eddie, you go."

"After that ragging He gave me in Berlin?"

"Oh you foolish boy." Winnie puts on her most Auntie voice. "That episode was forgotten and forgiven five minutes later – and he was absolutely right about your not associating with the odious Roehm. You know perfectly well that Herr Wolf sees himself almost as your father, and I'm quite sure your mother would agree. Edwin, I'm bound to say I feel you have a Duty . . . !"

The Piscean's call to arms! So Edwin marches, a reluctant recruit and cautious, across the Hofgarten in the dark – it's past midnight – telling himself that all he has to do is knock and run, and report to Winifred at HQ that there had been no answering "Come in." The humid night air smells like Trevelly, of Tobacco Flowers and Evening Stocks. A bat flits through the light from a window at the kitchen end of the Siegfriedhaus – where E & E eavesdropped a hundred years ago. An owl hoots from an elm.

Man's 3 instinctive horrors: the snake, the owl, and –
"Achtung!"

Followed by 2 additions to our modern fears: the unmistakable *click* of a trigger and, in the sudden glare of a spotlight, the jarring sight of a Mowgli symbol on a Black arm.

"Casson-Perceval," Edwin blurted, "I stay through there, at the Griesbachs'. Frau Wagner asked me to drop in on my way to bed and talk to the Chancellor."

"You are recognised, Herr von Perceval. But without an appointment? On what subject are these discussions with the Fuehrer?"

On bats and owls, my good man. On the uncertain balance of His mind. But in this hothouse of guns and night-noises the Youth's own mind is none too stable. "I was only going to say hullo, and perhaps play a spot of piano, but one really doesn't have to bother."

"Nein!" A 2nd click. The spotlight went off. "Herr von Perceval, if these are Frau Wagner's personal instructions you must proceed! Present this pass to the second echelon when you are stopped."

The second sentry, not so zealous in the performance of his duties, merely walks with Edwin the few feet to the Siegfriedhaus's front door. A rap, diffidently. "No answer." Relief, but the damned light still shows from the bloody kitchen window. Rap again, even more faintly.

"One suggests, Mein Herr, that you knock at the door to the Fuehrer's parlour." The Black arm reaches past and turns the handle.

INSIDE

Alone, fumbling for the hall's switch . . .

The wall-sconce, designed to look like an English Coach-house lantern holding a pair of candles, throws barely enough light to reach the near end of the passage from the kitchen.

"Herr Wolf?"

Before remembering, Christ! Last time that brought a spit explosion!

This time – silence. The drawing room is dark. So is Siegfried's old study. He must be along there, at the far end, in the kitchen, still stuffing cakes to get over the Austrian scene at the Fürstenzimmer. I'll take a shortcut through the study . . .

Empty.

He must be in the lav, or off in the garden Wotan-walking – because on the kitchen table two glass pedestal dishes are loaded with Kuchen, sugar-sprinkled, jam-stuffed, untouched. A Youth's hand reaches of its own volition –

"*What are you after?*"

Not Wotan: Klingsor! His wizard's voice is magically somehow in the dark study behind. I jump – so that my guilty hand knocks a cake off its dish – and turn.

Not Klingsor, either. Hagen. Wrapped in a rug, sunk deep in a chair, in the dim sconcelight from the hall looking as He had that first time over Frau Steiner's Oberammergau astrology table.

"What is it you want?"

The voice was a monotone, and I thought: He must have watched me all the time – as I walked right past Him! – and then, as a boy does in the dark for a snake, or a bat, I shivered.

"At forty-five, I'm finished, it's all over."

If He had watched, He hadn't seen: His eyes were turned inwards, not aware of who it was with Him. Under the rug His body was shuddering.

"Frau Winifred was concerned for you, Herr Wolf. You seem to be cold. Would you like a hot chocolate?"

"They're trying to kill me."

"I don't think her chocolate –?"

"The conspirator's best friend is sweet poison." Now I saw that the black hair was wet. Sweat rolled out from it, down over His forehead.

"It's a fever, Herr Wolf – I'll go back to Wahnfried for a doctor."

"You think those quacks are going to touch me?!" His voice shot up as He pulled the rug tighter. "Who knows what they put in their devilish needles? A man lies there, helpless, with their gross fingers reaching into orifices and prodding. Asking their questions of nobody's business – with their black shit-bags crammed to the brim with a *hundred* poisons! They don't care about pain! They want it to hurt – then they can hook you on morphine, like Goering. My God, they had their hooks in Goering! – it's taken me years to get him free, and then who ever truly knows?" He began stroking His hands, one over the other, then rubbing, scrubbing at the fingers furiously.

Edwin said, "I could try to find a thermometer, Herr Wolf?"

"Hah! Where those things go? Don't tell me!"

His blanket fell off His lap. His knees were shaking.

"Herr Wolf, really, you ought to let me at least tell your guards to call Frau Winifred. Even an aspirin."

"Aspirin? The fat-arse Yid Bloch gave *her* aspirin when he poured in his iodoform! Can you imagine what that was like for her? – on the breast of a woman? a hole of raw flesh? burning like prussic acid? And for what? They don't have the least fucking idea! *Krebs*! Ugh! It always goes for the most dreadful places. Good God – *why do we have so little time?* They're all gone in my family by the time they're fifty. *Five years!* Ederl, for the love of God, say – what can a man possibly achieve in five years?"

But all a Fool could think was, at what point did He know me? And then, Why does He tell me?

"You're right –!" tugging the blanket on the knees – "Silence is the only answer. In five years I'll be dead. The struggle will have been only shit falling through a hole in a crapper – excuse my language – but isn't it just like this mess with Austria? I'm a laughing stock. I'll die, and Old Man Hindenburg will live forever – with that clique of the General Staff glued to him like tics in a bull's bag crotch. The way they look at me – at my Black Order – I *have* to have the Army! Rat-grey is the colour that makes Europe tremble. The Field Grey of a Prussian army. Give the Junkers credit for that – there's only one colour closer to Death on the field, it's all psychology, they know, trust *Them*! – Roehm and the other Brown fellows would always be ploughboys. Yet they died with Heil on their lips, those fellows. I swear on their graves one day I'll make it up. There'll be a memorial ten times the size of Munich's – fifty! I've already drawn the sketches, a great dome, I'll show it to you. But what a tightrope I walk. Dollfuss's wife. Having to crawl and snivel to *wops*! Can you imagine?! Well, it's over now. Finished. In three months I'll be out, you'll see. I give it six at the absolute most. It doesn't matter. I was born to be stabbed in the back! Mein Ederl, play the Beerdigung for me. . . ."

The Funeral Music, for Siegfried, borne back in procession after Hagen's black act, led by the two myth-Ravens who pick out the eyes of corpses to gain insight –

Nuts to that! – as Putzi would say. Instead, on the Black Swan, Eddie plays Him the Wallala theme of the Rhinemaidens, happily splashing & dabbling in the brightening dawn. *Rheingold, Rheingold . . .*

"Oh, lovely," He said softly, "lovely. . . ."

His hands stop their feverish rubbing. His knees their shaking, even the sweat stops breaking out along His brow.

"The uninitiated think the song of the Rhinemaidens is the earliest motif. In fact it's the thirty-first. And then on to – that's it! – through the triad, the major, good boy! to the 'Gold' theme, the forty-fourth. Then back now – ah, you've done it: 'Rheingold, Rheingold,' again that glorious cry. Straight from Goethe it comes, the Eternal Feminine draws us on! Richard Wagner, Faust and I . . . Enough Rheingold – give me

300

Siegmund and Sieglinde's duet . . . Ah! Only listen! That suspended B-flat in bar four . . . as they see the snake symbols in each other's eyes, how it draws every drop of their blissful longing. Ederl, honestly, you must tell me why it is that your sister no longer likes me."

As abruptly as that. In the middle of the twins' incestuous passion, Brother's hands stopped playing.

"Of course Ettie likes you, Herr Wolf." What else does one say to a man who claims to be your father?

"She despises me. Like Hindenburg's lot."

"No, truly she doesn't. She's very grateful – I mean you helped get her Brünnhilde."

"I asked her for a kiss – she told you that."

It wasn't quite a question. Unless you count the way He looked at me over His clutched blanket.

"She can be a little selfish, Herr Wolf, but she doesn't mean to be unkind. Singers simply don't think about the other partner as a person."

"Good God, Edwin! – In your dear mother's memory! I was never her partner! How can you suggest it?!"

Mama, or Sister?

"I know I can't offer her an English mansion, but can't she like me for myself, a little tiny bit? Or for Wagner? Surely she can like me for Wagner?"

"Yes, Herr Wolf, I'm sure she can like you for that."

"Are you? Really sure?" – looking positively piteous over the top of His blanket. "I have to have a woman who can understand the music. Otherwise it's like stroking a cow. That's all most of them are anyway. The world's a dunghill. Mein Ederl, if Fräulein Ettie perhaps has heard of my friendship for Fräulein Braun, or these gross rumours of the American –?"

"Herr Wolf, I really think I ought to go."

"Yes. Desert me like Hanfstaengl and the others. Alone. I shall march to the end and the barrel of a gun. Goodbye Edwin. Farewell."

He stood, dropping the blanket. The Fool is dismissed.

And then –?

2 days later, Old Hindenburg is dead.

And then –?

301

With a repeat of Edwin's Beerdigung, is buried.

Ex-Corporal Wolf gives the eulogy, "And now enter thou upon Valhalla!"

And then –?

CORONATION

To make sure that it was so, between the morning & the evening of His 3rd day as single head of state, He rose, & summoned the Chiefs of Nibelheim's armed Forces to come to Him, & there, without warning, or ceremony, in Privat, before His person, they raised their right Hands in feal Salute, as the Knights of Parsifal to Amfortas, & repeated after Him:

"I swear before God to give my Unconditional Obedience to . . ."

And after them came others of His subjects: Sauerbruch, the greatest Surgeon (who had carved the bullet from Fräulein Anna); & Heidegger, of Philosophy – & for a time, also, even Spengler; & Gerhart Hauptmann, the Nobel prize winner; & diverse lesser Scholars, & Painters, & Singers, & Shoemakers all honouring their Volsung Master, like Hans Sachs.

And He draws strength from the Blood & Tumult of the Sacrifice they offer up to Him, and a Literary Critic (who has never liked dull *Buddenbrooks*, by Thomas Mann, giant Putzi's nextdoor neighbour) in a little trick of Loge's, composes his own banal words for the occasion, called:

THE FIRE SONG

Reject what confuses You
Outlaw what seduces You,
What did not spring from a Pure Will,
Into the Flames with what threatens You!

Bye-bye, Buddenbrooks! So everyone is happy in the Land of Sachs! And then –?

His Nibelheim withdraws from the spineless League of Nations, and even Outsiders are happy, and cinema audiences cheer in London when

His Face comes on the screen; and He surrenders the butchers of Dollfuss back to Wien, so the Duce is happy; and then after a People's Gift called the Saar Plebiscite, He sets out to reach accord with that other Empire, Merrie England, on the size of His Fleets on the Sea and in the Air: The Armaments Race shall End! And with *that*, children, a Fool can tell you that the whole Dunghill World was HAPPY!

Except –

Die Blöde Kuh:

... *At Kaffeeklatsch:* "Ettie-moll, Eddie-pal, you'll never believe the Publishing decision I'm having to make this lovely morning."

A slim package rests as a feather in the giant palm.

"Cast your peepers on this baby."

And so, after *Red Book*, and *Brown*, arrives now a 3rd set of covers for desperation: a convent girl's exercise scribbler, neatly ruled:

Mein Grünes Buch

Feb. 6, '35

... I have just reached the age of 23 – whether I'm happy's another question! At the moment I'm anything but! My office at Hoffmann's looks like a flower shop and smells like a Mortuary chapel. *I do so want a Basset Puppy.* .... My jealous friends say, "*Ach*, He can never be caught – He's married to Germany!" I tell them, "I'll get Him!" It's Our Little Secret ...!

Feb. 11, '35:

... Just now He was *here*! – but no little Doggie, no cupboards stuffed with Frocks. He didn't even ask what I wanted for my Birthday ...!

Feb. 18, '35:

... Yesterday again He arrived! – quite unexpectedly – we spent a *lovely* Evening! The best thing is He's thinking of getting me *out of the Shop*! – no more opening the door for my 'So-Honourable' Clients! – *My Own Little House*!!! I daren't Count my Chickens, as they say, it would be just too Wonderful! There are times He behaves in a *vulgar fashion* – but He loves me so much, I'm so infinitely happy! Oh, God, let it remain so. I never want it to be my fault if one day He should cease to Love me . . .

Mar. 4, '35:

. . . I'm *desperately* unhappy again. I spent 2 marvellous hours with Him until midnight at Prinzregentstrasse and then, with His permission, went on to the Nocturnal Ball for another couple of hours. . . . The next day I was waiting at Hoffmann's like a Cat on Hot Bricks! as they say – and then I had to *rush* to the station because He'd *suddenly decided to take a Train*! – and I was only in time to see the Rear Lights of His coach. . . . I don't know why He's cross with me. Perhaps because of the Ball but He gave me permission to go. I'm racking my Brains to discover the reason why He left so early without saying goodbye to me. The Hoffmanns gave me a ticket for *A Night in Venice* . . .

Mar. 11, '35:

. . . I'm buying the sleeping Tablets again. If only I'd never met Him! If only the Devil would take me – I'd be much better off! I waited *3 hrs* outside the Carlton and had to watch Him buy flowers for Anny Ondra, the actress creature – and take her to Dinner, and Champagne . . . ! He needs me only for the *special reasons* . . . When He says He Loves me, He only means it for *that* moment. Like all His promises – which He never keeps! Why does He keep torturing me . . . ?!

Apr. 1, '35:

. . . Last night He invited me to dinner at the Vier Jahreszeiten (the most elegant hotel in all Munich!) I had to sit beside Him for *3 hrs*! without being able to say a *single word*! For our Goodbye He handed me an envelope with Money, as he has once before. . . . With a *single* Kind Word I'd have been so Happy – but He never thinks of such things . . .

Apr.29. '35:
. . . I'm poorly. Last week I cried my eyes out *every* night! – on Easter Day I had a bilious attack when I stayed home alone. I've made *desperate* efforts to scrape and save! I'm getting on everyone's Nerves trying to sell them the Coat off my Back, as they say – frocks, camera, even theatre tickets! But things will work out, my Debts aren't *that* big, after all . . .

May 10, '35:
. . . Frau Hoffmann informs me He has found a replacement for me. She's called *Die Walküre* and looks like one! If it's true He'll soon make her thin as a Rake! It's a pity that just now is Spring . . .

May 28, '35:
. . . I have just sent Him a *decisive* Letter! If I don't receive a reply before 10 o'clock tonight I'll simply swallow my 25 tablets. I've done nothing wrong. *Absolutely nothing!* Perhaps it *is* another woman – not the Valkyrie Girl – but there are so many Others . . .

May 28, '35:
. . . Dear God help me perhaps my Letter was wrong but I must speak to Him today tomorrow will be too late. Uncertainty is more unbearable than a Sudden End I've decided on 35 tablets this time I want to make Dead Certain! as they say if only He would Ring . . .

My dears! What a simply *marvellous* wallow! We can't get over it.

Boy Meets Girl

. . . *At the Carlton:* In mid-September, the golden month in Munich, with the leaves turning and still heat in the sun, but not excessive, and before the beer swillers fill every street with their mug-thumping and spewing for the Oktoberfest. The Boy was in the courtyard of the Osteria, waiting for Putzi H. The Green Book Girl was chatting with two other shopgirls at an opposite table. The Girl laughed a lot – but with that fragile rising note that Freia gets just before the giants are going to lug her off.

The other girls left, depositing their shares of the bill in silver, but the Green Girl stayed at her table. Her eye glanced . . . a smile, and break the contact. Look at her watch, drum fingers on the table, glance furtively – out cigarette! Light – with a quick deep breath. An experienced smoker – we know how He hates it.

"Mein Herr, excuse me –?" the Girl has turned her chair. Skirts are short. The nice knees and calves, from the studio's stepladder. Smooth silk stockings . . . "You are Herr Eddie von Perceval, excuse, but I am Fräulein Braun, from Hoffmann's?"

"I know, actually, I remember. A friend of . . ."

"You do remember? – may I ask, are you? Waiting for . . .?

"Herr Hanfstaengl. Are you? Waiting for . . .?

"Oh no – or should I say, not exactly. Herr Hoffmann wanted me to give these proofs if He arrived in my luncheon break."

But He hasn't.

"Fräulein Braun, I'm not sure what I could –"

"No-no, absolutely not, I didn't mean – you know He is so-incredibly busy now He's moved from Munich to Berlin?"

"I'm sure – although I believe He still keeps an apartment here."

"The Prinzregentstrasse – that is, we often deliver there. Hoffmann's does all the Party pictures. From the earliest days – they're tremendously interesting. Of course I was only a child."

The Girl's nipples show through her ruffled blouse. Her breasts are heavier than Ettie's. And her hips. The Boy says, "Have you lived all your life in Munich, Fräulein Braun?"

"Except for holidays. And school at the Kloster. My father has an apartment on the Hohenzollernstrasse. He is Professor Braun?"

"I'm afraid I haven't met."

"Naturally, Herr von Perceval, I didn't mean – with Bayreuth and the Wagner family, absolutely another thing, I realize. You met Him for the first time there, I believe?"

"Not quite, Fräulein Braun. The first was at an astrologer's in Oberammergau, actually. Look, you must call me, Eddie."

"An astrologer? Herr Eddie, my mother's a great one for astrology – my Saturn opposes the Bull or Ram or something, anyway I have reason for Great Expectations, as they say – with Father it's all nonsense. Mutti says I shall perhaps be a famous dressmaker. My own salon in Berlin, by the Kaiser's palace. For now, darning my stockings is all the sewing I do!"

Her laugh still has that Freia edge. She turns her ankle. Boy & Girl look at the darn on her heel. Her skirt slips that inch above her knee. The Boy said, "Aquarians often lead exciting lives. You might still get to Berlin."

"I should like to go to England, He talks so much about it – Herr Hoffmann, that is." A patch of colour reddened her cheeks. "In my Kloster we were taught by the English Sisters – they had to escape from Henry the Eighth?"

"Lots of people did, Fräulein Eva – Herr Wolf's a great admirer of Henry's."

"Yes – Wagner most."

"He prefers opera, no doubt."

Eyes meet again: both know. We Know.

"Like Fräulein von Perceval. I so enormously admire her talent, but with that sweet smile, and never her nose in the air. Herr Eddie I think I'm more for Him like Naughty Marietta?"

After this warped description of his Sister, the Boy said, "I'm sorry I won't be seeing Herr Wolf to tell Him – about your photos."

"No," the Girl said, "it was just a thought. If you did see Him."

She opened her purse and looked for change. There was no silver, only a few copper pfennigs.

"Let me," said the Boy, "you can take it off the bill next time I get my passport photo."

"Danke, Herr Eddie – auf Wiedersehen."

"Auf Wiedersehen, Fräulein – "

"Marietta?" the Girl said, with a quick smile, and the lightest touch on the Boy's hand from the tips of her fingers . . . trapping Herself a friend at court, even if he is only a Fool. . . .

"Die blöde Kuh?" rumbled the giant, arriving as the Girl was leaving,

"Eddie-pal, what on earth did that empty-headed little moll have to say to you?"

"Nothing really – but I don't think she is one."

Eva Anna Paula Braun:

The Boy bumps into her next at the Carlton when snow is again on the ground of the English Gardens. February, her birthday month. As she laughs, her gaiety seems even more desperate. She wears earrings and a necklace made with her stone, purple amethyst (oddly mixed with blood-red garnets) which she continually touches to make sure that the Boy will comment.

"An attractive piece, Fräulein Marietta." Although they are small, and badly cut, and purple doesn't suit her. And at first she blushed – thinking that perhaps by *piece* he means –

"My amethysts and garnets, Herr Eddie. Yes, they are a present. It was my birthday last week. You'll never guess how old I feel?"

"A young lady should be allowed her secrets. Were they from . . .?"

"Yes – but He was here so briefly I hardly saw Him. Herr Eddie, you're so kind. Truly I think my heart is breaking."

The Green Girl takes out her handkerchief and begins to cry. Pretty, and helpless, and He has enough royalties from the damn Book. He could have done more than these tawdry, Woolworth's gems.

"Fräulein Eva, please, you mustn't cry. Let me pour you another cup of tea. I'm sure Herr Wolf is simply too busy . . . Conscription and the Saar."

"Won't you speak to Him? I know He would listen to you. I have to do *something*, Herr Eddie. It's impossible to be staying at Hoffmann's the rest of my life."

"There's lots of time, really."

"If you won't speak, would you go to the Nocturnal Ball with me next week? Only an hour – just enough that I could hear the music and dance. I love dancing and I am trapped like a bird in a cage."

The unspoken name of the dead canary-owner hung in the air between us.

"I'm afraid I won't be here next week. The Goerings' wedding."

"A wedding . . ."

Always a Bridesmaid. Eva Braun dabs at her eyes with an edge of lace.

"And then," says the Boy, "I'm driving to our villa in the south of France with my sister." And as soon as the words were out, how they must sound to a half-starved shop-girl. "I'll be back in May, Fräulein Marietta – perhaps we could go on a picnic or something."

She managed a weak smile for the 'Marietta'. "A picnic would be nice, Herr Eddie. If you see Him in Berlin, perhaps you could tell Him I said hullo?"

"Of course. He can give you a telephone call."

"Oh no!" She crumpled the lace into a ball. "He won't phone to my house because . . . Herr Eddie, it's all so difficult. Why can't He be like an ordinary person?"

Because then you wouldn't be pining for the Greatest Man On Earth, my dear – but the Boy just paid the bill, and pretended not to notice when the Girl pocketed the tip.

And then –?

A frightful shock – *Krebs-Cancer* – going, as He said, for the most dreadful of places.

The Voice.

A polyp on His larynx. The cutting took place following April Fool's Day. For more than a month while she waited for His love, *He* waited for . . .

False Alarm. It's benign. This time.

. . . At the Kaiserhof Hotel: His Bayreuth Circle are His special guests at a buffet to celebrate Albion's defeat in the Armaments Negotiations: Winnie, Ettie, Eddie – and Putzi, restored to good favour at the piano. His fellow giant had also been invited, "But my gallant Hermann's having bridegroom's jitters," chortles Mein Host, "Sir Mosley, you see how wise I've been not to take that fatal step."

Yes, my dears, the Leader of Our Home Blacks, Oswald was there with a Lady-friend, Diana Guinness as was, Mitford before *that*, which brings us, darlings, to our last guest –

Die Mitfahrt:
All 6-foot of jolly hockey-sticks, dear Diana's sister, and cause of many a

sleepless night for our Inferior Eva – the Honourable Unity Valkyry Mitford – but as far as the Hon Edwina C-P was concerned, aside to Eddie,

"The Mitfahrt's got frightful teeth and she can't sing. What's wrong with Wolf's voice?"

"Know when to stop, Sir Mosley!" Plain-spoken Mr Wolf always has trouble with English rankings. "That's my golden rule. If you could have seen Anthony Eden's face when I insisted only on equality of divisions – not a twitch on that stiff upper lip. Last year, London would have had a fit. Now they're so relieved that I didn't ask for more! What great fellows your English are. Even when they're lying – which, with excuses to my dearest friends present, they do all the time! – on a truly magnificent scale. Not like those niggardly French. You'll offer them a banquet and they'll still try and save half a frog's leg to smuggle out in their napkin!"

He slaps His thigh and claps His paws, and laughs – until He coughs, puts a napkin to His mouth, sees the crimson spot of blood, and blanches, snow-white.

"An operation," Winifred whispers to the Mosley-Mitfords, as He sips from a glass of iced water waiting on a tray, "it's all right but it was only last week, on his throat. Don't draw attention."

. . . So that Sister goes straight to Him and, in Festspielhalle fashion, takes the glass from His trembling hand: "Instead of this cold-water nonsense, I want you to promise you'll take an old-old recipe of Mathilde's – my nurse on our island – honey and lemon, warm, with a teaspoon of rum and just a dash of quinine, at least five times a day. Will you?"

Those changeling's eyes looked at her blankly over His napkin. The Mosley group was curious and awed, like all first-timers. The rest who knew Him waited for the bomb to burst. But –

"Yes," was all, meekly, astonishingly, "Fräulein Ettie, I will."

"Even the rum?"

"Yes."

"Say, 'I promise.'"

"I promise."

"Good boy. Now it'll get quite better."

And she kissed Him on His pale cheek – as she smiled, victorious

Brünnhilde, at the junior Valkyrie who would never come close to the net with her hockey sticks.

Jumbo's Ring Ceremony!
or
Fat Hermann's Wedding

As our Eddie can tell you, darlings, Berlin bust its Garters! And Hermann likewise! Following the giant's breakfast, there were 2 ceremonies, Religious & Civil, and 2 storks (*not* Ravens!) released by former comrades from the Red Baron days, to circle the cathedral spire in panic and defecate on the crowd.

"On Hermann likewise," the Dwarf delivers a jab to his rival; "but if we must have circuses with our bread, people always love the clowns and elephants best, Herr Edwin, wouldn't you agree?"

When he keeps the Mime note out of his voice (which is then a mellifluous baritone) the Dwarf can be charming, and his wits need to be exceptionally sharp, currently slicing through an awkward patch with the Leader, because of his wife – Magda Goebbels – whom the Dwarf has been trying to leave for the latest Actress love of his life. Divorce outrages the Fricka in Wolfi.

Now He gives the Bride away with a tear glittering in His eye for the Lohengrin music and a huge bouquet of orchids. And then the Reichsbischof Müller addresses the Newly-weds:

Be faithful unto death and I will give you the crown of life . . .

"I would say," says the Dwarf, in a parting shot, "that our Hermann already has it from the King of Bulgaria." An enormous decoration of Sapphires & Diamonds outshines all the rest. "But if I had been awarded the Knight's Iron Cross, that's all I'd wear. True strength is in simplicity. You must come to dinner with us, Herr Edwin – with your exceptional sister, please. My wife is entertaining again now we're settled in near Sans Souci, and there's no reason she should be stuck with only the Berlin State – your sister, naturally, not my wife. My dear Magda is photogenic but somewhat hideously off-pitch. And how devoted you and the beautiful Fräulein Edwina are. A model for brothers and sisters everywhere in our Reich. Auf Wiedersehen, mein Herr."

The Mime cackle momentarily escapes, but the Dwarf controls it. And then – The Fancy Dress Party.

Eddie went as King Arthur, in tights, with a scarlet Welsh dragon. Ettie was The Little Match Girl, shoeless, in tatters, with a tray of wares for sale – like any inferior little Munich shop-cow.

He came as Himself: the Ring-Master Wotan in top hat and tails.

And then, to end our day with a giant laugh, the Frau Manowarda sailed in as a Gypsy Fortune-teller in sequinned headscarf, a crystal ball in a sling over her shoulder, a huge Mowgli gold ring as big as a fist on her portside middle finger.

"You must see, Reichsminister," she gurgled to Goebbels, who was there as the Devil, "I had it made especially to cover the very spot where my Fuehrer so wonderfully kissed me!"

"Very fine," said the devilish Dwarf, "but only think, dear Frau Manowarda, how much more wonderful still it would have been for us all if He had kissed you on the lips?"

... *At Li Santo, Camargue:* Another blissful escape by Riley to Porquerolles. Sister seems in a better mood on our island – or perhaps finally growing up: 26 is long in the tooth to be girlish, even for a singer – when Brother says he wants to take a whole week in Camargue with the Three Maries she doesn't object.

"But you hate the Camargue. With the dust and mosquitoes."

"Not in May. Eddie dear, I want to be with you – am I so insufferable to have along? I won't embarrass you in front of your old gypsies."

"I don't know if they'll even be there – and I'd love to have you. I just didn't think you'd want to go."

"I didn't say you could *have* me, either." Reaching out and taking my hand, and kissing the palm, and licking it, flicking it with her snake's tip tongue; "but you can, darling, if you get rid of Mathilde. Nicely ..."

Brother & Sister stayed together in one room at the Pension Li Santo. It had a thatched roof and a trident nailed up over the door. The day after our arrival was the blessing of the fishing fleet. We leaned on our window-sill in the clear May morning and watched the procession pass below us with the effigies of Lazarus and his virgins in their model boat.

"Speaking of immaculate conceptions," Ettie said casually, "I'm

312

running a month late on my curse, do you suppose your gypsies can do anything about that?"

"Oh God. You aren't."

"Oh God, I am. Don't worry, my sweet, it's happened before."

A priest, in crow-black soutane and vestments, cast his censer in our direction, and gave his blessing.

"When?" Aghast. And then, as the sweet smoke floated through our window, with full import, "You mean before with us?"

"Sometimes it's hard to tell, darling – of course, if it *wasn't*, one wouldn't have to."

"I thought you used something. You always said –"

"It takes the edge off, to always plan. Sometimes one simply can't be bothered."

The tide was in. The procession of the Maries had stopped at the water. Fishermen pushed the model boat on rollers out from the Templars' Cross, over the sand.

"But what will happen?"

"More cunnilingus, darling, you can't get preggers with that."

In the distance the priest touched his lips to each effigy of a virgin. The model boat bobbed on our blue Mediterranean.

"I meant – a baby? God, just saying it makes me feel quite sick."

"Me too, my pet – and there isn't going to be a baby. I'm serious about asking the gypsies. They always know. Or else I'll go back to Mathilde again."

Sister pointed in the opposite direction to the black priest and his blue-robed Maries. Down the street a first *roulotte* was trundling with Gitanos, on painted wheels.

"She helped you before?" Now Brother was appalled utterly. "Who with, Ettie? When? And you can't ask Mathilde – for Romans it's the most mortal sin."

"With Pawel, although I don't know why you think it helps to be so nosey. And Catholics aren't Romans when they're peasants; they're practical. Mathilde will just say an extra Hail Mary . . . Eddie, you mustn't be cross with me."

"I'm not cross. But I thought it could only happen on one special moment, and you'd know. You even let me, last night. Why ever –?"

"Hung for a sheep as a lamb, my ignorant precious." Kissing his cheek. "It's all spilt milk – if you'll pardon the expression. Come on, help me find the right bloody gypsy."

Brother went dazed into the village street with its packed dirt, and fishy smells, and dung. Sister, beside him, looked her same cool beauty – yet inside so different.

"Do you suppose it would be a Siegfried? – if you had it?"

"It would probably have two heads. We're doing it a kindness. I'll go and sit in the church; I don't want to be gawped at. Look for one like a granny."

Beyond the graveyard with its tipping tombstones, the Gitanos' roulotte caravans assemble on a flat patch of dune grass under feathery tamarisks grown into trees, bent over like the grave markers by the wind from the sea. Near the closest grave, a man, middle-aged, with a great black moustache, sits plaiting a lariat of hide strips on the steps of his brightly painted wagon.

"Good morning to you, young Lord." The Gitano speaks in the ancient Provence language of *Oc*, but heavily guttural from middle Europe.

"Good morning to you, Gitano craftsman in leather." The Scholar replies as Mathilde had taught us, more liquid and Latin. "My name is Edwin. I seek a grandmother's advice for my sister – with a female's problem. She has an old nurse, but her home is out on the islands, too far away. Can you assist us?"

"Such advice should not be hastily given." The Gitano works the horsehide to make it supple, twisting one strand through two others without looking, while he considers the Scholar's question. "Edwin – that name in the Saxons' tongue brings prosperity and happiness. Are you from the Saxons' land, my young Lord?"

"My sister is a great singer, and we follow where her voice takes us."

"Travellers. That makes a difference." The Gitano puts aside his lariat to give his hand. "I am Sevastyani; would your Lady sister sing for us?"

"She will, Sevastyani, if she has your tune, and the words."

"She may sing her own tune. But not today. Tomorrow, for our patron Saint Sara the Egyptian. In the basilica, at sunset, as the relics are lifted."

Sister was less than delighted when Brother brought the good news.

"Sing for gypsies? Good Christ, I asked you to get me an abortion – not a bloody audition!"

"It's hardly that. You can sing something religious. There must be a hymn book. Call it a penance. We deserve one."

"*You* do. Oh blast, Eddie, damn it – this is really too much. I can't. You must be mad – in front of *gypsies*!"

"You can – unless you want to have a baby. Gitanos will be a bloody sight politer than Wagnerians."

"You know I simply loathe singing in churches – particularly Roman with bleeding Jesuses staring at you everywhere. And no music – a cappella is the absolute bloody end."

... The procession returned from its pilgrimage to the sea. The Sinner went out and down into the street. When he returned to her in our Pension room he said:

"The church has an organ. I've asked the priest to let me accompany you – for a fiver we could have got the keys to the kingdom. You can sing this one." The 147th psalm. "It says for evening. *Laudate dominum*, I'll give you a Gregorian, with the Bach arrangement. And I'm terribly sorry, Ettie. Truly. We'll never do it again."

"Yes we will, Eddie. Now." As the Sinner boy stood, gaping. "Come on, take off your trousers – we've got the rest of this awful day to get through, and I've been waiting an hour."

"No," he said, "I won't. I simply can't."

"You know when you say that, you always can. I've nothing on under my dress – look, Eddie. *Look*."

So the Boy did, and was turned to a pillar of salt wetness for his sin. *But dear Lord Jesus*, Eddie prayed, with his face at the fragrant door between her twisting thighs, and her Kundry-tongue crucifying him, *for God's sake don't let me suck it out!* As once more Brother & Sister formed the twin-backed beast with a head at each end, whose names are –

"Cunnilingus and Fellatio – like Doctor Doolittle's 'Push-Me-Pull-You'," she had the gall to say, refreshed and prepared for her newest role of Vestal, as Brother & Sis entered the holy ground of the Church of the Three Maries, "I wonder if that's what old Lofting meant – writers do lead the foulest lives. Give me three bars lead on the treble

315

and don't overwhelm me with the damn bass. When you get on an organ you tend to go mad with the pedals –" and then, with a giggle – "me too; it must run in the family."

A Different Crowning

The Gitanos are assembled in 2 files in the churchyard: one of moustached men in black coats and breeches; one of scarved women. Each row holds 2-foot bees'-wax candles which Sevastyani lights solemnly with a taper at the entrance as each pilgrim gypsy passes him by. He inclines his head to the Scholar & Ettie, but does not speak.

"Gawd, Eddie – whatever old-wives'-do have you got us into?"

... Inside the church, Edwin takes the stool at the organ. Sister stands in front of the altar rail in the chancel. The bribed priest, pulling on a red and blue striped rope, slowly raises the Saint's relics back past a crucifix for another year in the loft. The gypsies process, chanting, with their candles, passing to either side behind the roof columns – phallic pillars of stone, white with salt at their base from the randomly flooding sea. . . .

The Gitanos turn inward, moving towards Sister, by the altar, then descend by steps in the floor to Erda's mystery of the crypt. The chanting stops. Edwin presses the keys, but the organ is old, with manual bellows, and for several seconds no sound comes out while the bellows' peasant boy labours. And then the chords ripen.

"*Jubilate!*" sang out my sister, in sweet Latin, throat freshly lubricated with spilt milk, glorious and ethereal she stood below Him on His cross, before His evening candles:

> *For it is a good thing to sing Praises unto our God:*
> *yea a joyful and pleasant thing to be Thankful.*
> *The Lord doth build up Jerusalem: and gather*
> *together the Out-casts of Israel.*
> *He healeth those that are broken in Heart: and*
> *giveth medicine to heal their Sickness.*
> *O sing unto the Lord who feedeth the young Ravens*
> *that call upon Him. . . .*

Thought and Memory ... as Old Eddie sees Her and hears Her, this half-century later, Ettie, my love, singing to doomed gypsies of the outcasts of Israel, even unto the last verse of the psalmist:

He hath not dealt so with any nation ...

... That Night: An old Gitano woman comes to the Siblings' room at the Pension Li Santo. Brother is ordered to leave.

The Scholar returns to the tamarisks to speak more to Sevastyani, who confirms what the Scholar has long suspected: the Gitanos follow the Templars' route of the Grail in their annual pilgrimage across Europe! Encamping at a ruined fortress near Graz – *Dietrich, the Last Survivor.*

No less. And then –

"Even to the great Golden Gate of Kiev, itself, it's true, young Lord. For a thousand years – " Sevastyani told Edwin, half-proudly, half-sadly – "before the new Tsar-killer, Stalin, slammed all our gates shut . . ."

A Mandrake Root told the gypsy woman that Ettie was not going to have a baby – and the next day my sister was saved by the curse and began to bleed. Here endeth this Lesson.

ᚢSecond Movement

Third Passage

[quick march!]

... And Spaniards and Dutchmen,
And Frenchmen and such men,
As foemen did curse Them,
The Yeomen of England!

... *in Spandau.* Like Waring, I watch ...

"Numèro Sept, en avant, s'il vous plaît!"

The polite *et* casual French are back. Goodbye to the Comrades'
frozen Rule book for another 3 months! The Frog Captain is one of
Them. This 4-Power trick of confronting Villain with Victim, it goes
without saying, is the happy work of hidden Anti's: the Semites, for their
part, are invariably courteous to Old Eddie (playing Rudi) and interested in his welfare.

"*Bonsoir, dormez bien ...*"

How many countless nights did infant-Eddie hear that? But then
Eddie *could* sleep well; now, as all This floods ever faster from
somewhere in his head, scarcely at all.

*Was He born with a silver wire? What did the Voice sound like? Was it
male or female? Did it sound like a Yammering Yid?*

The Goat's Birthday Dinner

...*Tempus fugit:* '*35-ish* "Why –" cried the ancient Birthday-boy,

319

bobbing with delight at cutting off the Artist in mid-air – "our young musical friends at last! Winston, Margaret my love, everyone, it's my dear little Ettie, from Cornwall, grown-up – and Edwin too – Margaret, you'll surely recall their dear Mama? Our Anglo-German work at Trevelly, Winston, in 'Twenty, it was, the first time, and here to tell us now all about their friend 'Herr Wolf.'"

Edwin said, "I'm awfully sorry we're late. My fault, a collar stud."

"Bosh, darling," said Sister, "we're late because of me. Why, my dear Mr Churchill, what a delightful surprise."

"My dear Miss Edwina." The Artist took her hand, but diffidently, not your born ladies' man, and turning to his opponent across the ring, "L-G, perhaps your young guests, now happily present, can tell us what, pray, is to be the Wolf's next course for dinner?"

The Table Placement:
The Hon Edwina C-P, beside the Goat and across from the Artist. The Goat-daughter, Megan, on t'other side, with her Mum, for doubled-up domestic support. Megan, 34, virgin electee Member of Parliament, has her Mum's crumpled, determined little face, and her Dad's Welsh-Wizard mysticism. She prays frequently and proves opposed to Sex in conversation. ("I would only marry," she once declared to the mild Secretary, after a flaming row about the Fanny Woman, "a man who would dominate me.")

1st Course: 4 female L-G eyes fix on Sister:
All the better to –
. . . But how the conversation sparkles. Despite the fact that the Goat has put on mismatching boots for dinner these *are* brilliant men.

After the Savoury, the Secretary rises and puts out the electric light. A cake is carried in with a mass of candles and some hieroglyphics in Welsh.

"'To Tada,'" the Wizard translates with a catch in his throat, "'many happy returns' – oh my dears, my own dearest dears. . . ."

At which the Artist rises to deliver:

THE 1ST SPEECH

My companions, old and new, on this memorable –
though delightfully informal – occasion, I am going to

320

add to the many thousands of speeches which I have inflicted upon people by asking you to join with me in drinking to the health of our illustrious friend. Ours is a very *long* friendship. Indeed, it is now forty years or more since we began to *be* friends in the House of Commons! – and there have, during that period, been many vicissitudes in public life. Through all that time I have thanked God that this great and good man across the table has been born to work for the life of our country, for the masses of those poor people in times of peace, and for our strength and security in the great days of the War. I ask you again to join with me in drinking his health on his Seventy- third birthday, and let us hope that another decade at least of full vigour lies before him, for I can assure you we shall need his wise counsel and his best efforts in the difficult years that lie before us. To our Welsh friend, and England's great man –

To which that Same responds with:

THE 2ND SPEECH

If *I* may be allowed to add to the scores of thousands of speeches *I* have delivered in the course of my life, I do thank you so warmly for drinking my health on an occasion when I have attained years of which I am not proud, and of which I am not very pleased to remind myself too often. What has added to the pleasure of my seventy-third birthday, however, is that I have the good fortune to have present with me today, on this occasion, my oldest political friend. Indeed, it is the longest political friendship in the life of Great Britain. It is a friendship which has not depended in the least upon agreement – even on fundamentals! – and I doubt very much whether there is any other country where it would be possible for men to fight, and fight very hard, as we have done, *without for one moment* impairing the good feeling and warmth. If I may be allowed to say so, no one

321

knows better than my dear family, the affection with
which I return a friendship. I thank him, and you all,
from the very bottom of my heart.

Applause, and lumps in the throat, and not a few tears around the
family table. Surely, children, this dinner shows the full glory of Our
Empire's Parliamentary System when 2 strong men stand face to face
and agree to differ.

"But I don't," said the Goat, with a mouthful of cake, "with the best
will in the world, Winston, I don't agree at all with your opinion about
the Man. And I say so in the strongest fashion!"

"Oh no, father –!" from Megan – "not *now*."

"Oh blast –" in an undreamt-of depth of passion (though under his
breath) from the Secretary – "Edwin, we must try and stop them."

"You may say it," declared the Artist, "until the cows come home, but
I can only repeat that the Man is a menace to all Europe."

"Not actually all," Edwin said. "It's only the eastern part."

"That is not, young man, what the Wolf snarls at us in his lurid book.
He refers in the most specific terms to France and the western marches
of his lair."

"But nobody reads it," said Sister. "Winston, dear, I know you're a
great writer, but Wolf's is mostly rubbish he got off his chest while he
was in prison."

"And you, my dear Miss Edwina, are a great singer – but Germany is
not a stage production. German cellars are awash with real blood. Berlin
itself is a charnel house."

"Cleaning out the stables," said the Goat, breezily. "An act of the
greatest courage and entirely necessary. I tell you, Winston, Germany
has trained up a Leader! You thought so yourself until a year ago. 'A
great man,' you said, 'from the heart of a great people.' And so they are,
and so he is. While in this country we have none!"

Bad News:

"If I may interrupt," interrupts the Secretary, "a telegram . . . about
the King. His Majesty has contracted a chill. The doctors now list his
condition as grave."

Says the Goat. "This is going to put the cat among the pigeons, with the Little Fellow marrying his Simpson woman."

"He cannot marry in a period of uncertainty," the Artist rumbles.

"But if the Little Fellow wants her he should have her. The only sort of people," says the Goat, with grim conviction, "who will be against him are the aristocracy, and they are the very rottenest in the national barrel."

"Christ! Now he's done it." The unflappable Secretary hides his face behind Edwin's shoulder.

"*Rotten* – ?" glowers the Artist of Blenheim – "Sir, my father *was*, and my brother *is*, an aristocrat. Dame Margaret, I wish you goodnight."

In a towering huff, stumping off, while Margaret Lloyd-George acquires a new line of resignation on her forehead and her irrepressible, semi-bigamous husband chirrups after his departing Lifelong Friend and special guest, "And goodnight to you, Winston! Ah, the foul hand of demon brandy. No offence was meant by my remark about the Little Fellow – why, with him happily married and on his throne, and being so well disposed to Germany, and that Miracle-Man working his wonders, my dears I do really feel that we can say, with this New Year, for once our Bad Old World is looking up."

... *At the Kroll Opera House: March the 7th.* A Saturday, two weeks before Our Birthday. He stands again on the stage. He speaks hoarsely, hesitantly, of those shopworn Criminals of Versailles, und Lebensraum. The Foreign Press yawn.

"Members of the Reichstag, I have to tell you, at this moment our troops are marching ... !"

Fafner is roaring! The Rhineland of Siegfried's dragons is retaken. The creatures of the chorus go beserk.

The Times, in its review, is more restrained.

FROM OUR CLIPPINGS

... Those who wondered if her launching, as Waltraute, by the late Siegfried Wagner was a touch premature for the voice and the singer, can only have marvelled at his prescience this past week. Miss Casson-Perceval's deep understanding of Brünnhilde, linked with brilliant

musicianship, the mystic strength which she brought to
the final Immolation Scene – once more we are forced
to bow to Bayreuth, with all its recent problems, for here
it has returned to us, her countrymen, a Brünnhilde
(and, we may hope, soon an Isolde) not only in the full
flush of her youthful beauty, but on the very brink of her
glorious maturity.

"Damn them to hell," she said, "on the brink of maturity puts me half
in kindergarten and half a hag!"

Triumph upon triumph – yet the curse on your great Artist is never to
believe. In His train, after His bloodless-victory service at Cologne
Cathedral, He scrunches in a corner of His carriage, trembling with
relief that the Frogs haven't blown His puny regiments away.

*The iron wheels roll Him past blast furnaces glowing fierce as any of
Alberich's ever did in the Master's mind, past the House of Krupp & I G
Farben, chemists, with its splendid workers' concert hall. The Victory train
carries Him past His adoring, cheering thousands upon thousands, while in
Munich, the Green Girl weeps alone in the new Braun house He is paying for,
and in Berlin, an actress, not yet mentioned, hesitates, at a fresh abyss. . . .*

A Childisch Argument

. . . *at Triebschen:* Edwin, seeking for Truth, lying naked in the sun, with
his friend Michael, after swimming, on the rocky bank beside the little
dock of our Swiss Hunding's Hut.

"Eddie, old friend, read me some more Wagner – the most offensive
bits, please."

"It's all offensive. 'If we were repelled by his appearance and his
speech, the Jew's song will engage our attention only to the extent that
we exclaim at so absurd a phenomenon.'"

"Like the dancing dog, yes, very good. Find me another."

"I don't see the point if you're just going to laugh at it. He isn't going
on about dancing, it's singing. 'Who has not had feelings of repulsion,
horror and amusement on hearing that nonsensical gurgling, yodelling
and cackling which no attempt at caricature can render more absurd
than it is?'"

"The synagogue on Saturday morning. Wonderful. You have to grant him full marks for catching it – our Shabbat."

"I'm sorry, Rau. One shouldn't mix religion with friendship."

Mausi's Picnic

"Heaven – !" Mausi Exclams ! – "I do so love this piece of country. It still must look exactly as it did for Grandfather. Eddie, turn off when we first see the Green Hill."

Pond, meadows, broken stile: it does still look as it was when E & E first stopped with Mama to Compare . . .

The Riley turns onto a side road of baked Bavarian yellow clay that raises a column of fine sulphurous dust which hangs in the windless air.

"Now the lane, Eddie – to your right. If you let me out, Ettie, I'll do the gate. Go on when you're through. It's only a hundred metres. I'll run behind."

Upwards, between larches and pines, and mountain ash replanted after one of iron Bismarck's wars, and turn the corner, and considerate Eddie glances back in the mirror to see if Mausi's being bothered by the dust – so that it was Ettie who said:

"Oops, darling. We've run into the army."

Two great field guns – squatting with tapered barrels pointing skywards. Filled beside them, racks with real shells. A platoon of a dozen men in black uniforms mans them. A blond Lieutenant is in charge. An even blonder-blond Lieutenant-General strides in front, making an inspection.

"Not army," Eddie said, "Black Order."

With Death's-Heads and zig-zag silver Donner's Lightning bars, the officers swing on their heels in unison:

"*Achtung!*"

It's all psychological? Don't tell me ! Two of the troops step out with bayonets fixed on their rifles – in front and astern of the Riley.

"I think they want you to stop."

"What on earth's going on?"

First idiocy from Sister, last from Mausi, puffing up.

"This is a restricted area," the young Lieutenant shouts; "why did you not read the orders?"

"I didn't see it," truthful Edwin replies.

"There wasn't a notice. I closed the gate and I would have seen it."

As Grand-Daughter of the Master, Mausi still holds the illusion that makes it safe to play with a dragon.

"This is no excuse. By order of the Fuehrer it is required to follow the posted instructions!"

A toad is a toad. The young Lieutenant by his constant glances and twitches is exceptionally concerned for the presence of the Lieutenant-General. This gentleman is tall, as well as blond, with a long face as sharp as a headsman's axe.

"Oh dear." Sister addresses the vulnerable death's-head Lieutenant. "This really is too silly, but I suppose as his instructions have *not* been posted, and you've sworn an oath, when we see him next week we shall have to tell your Leader. Perhaps you could be kind enough to give me your name?"

Sister indeed becoming Mama's daughter. The young Lieutenant's jaw drops to,

"Heil –"

"Heydrich, Miss Casson-Perceval, and quite charmed ..."

Blond Moses:

If *He* is Wolf in the barnyard, this is His Fox. Like Fräulein Anna, Heydrich has jug-ears which spoil his profile, but his English is flawless, and at only 32, already commanding the intelligence apparatus of the Black Order, all Volsung heads tremble – except an irrepressible rebel's like Mausi.

"We've been coming up here forever. My grandfather had picnics when they were building the Festspielhalle, so he could look down on the Green Hill and see the men working. Take your horrible guns somewhere else to practise."

"Fräulein Wagner, it is my pleasure that you should picnic in a place that will, I'm sure from now on always hold so many happy memories for us all." An appreciation for irony, mixed with the light of possible self advantage, showed for a moment in the penetrating pale blue eyes of this Foxy demigod. "Lieutenant, have your men carry the hamper for the Fuehrer's guests. Miss Casson-Perceval, first we must give you a pass for your car, and then you won't mind if I join you and your brother as as you walk? – as a mark of personal identification, we might say."

The young Lieutenant rushes forward with a Mowgli'd Death's-Head, "Free Passage" sticker which Edwin applies to the Riley's windscreen as the Hon Edwina says graciously, "We don't mind at all if General Heydrich joins us – do we Eddie?"

... With Mausi leading, and the Fox taking station beside my Jemima Puddle-duck Sister, the picnickers stroll forward through the ash trees and larches to a vantage point that overlooks Bayreuth and the Magic Mountain. Wahnfried is a salt box in a toy-railway garden; the Festspielhalle, a doll's house with a large bump.

"How would this suit you, Fräulein Wagner?"

"The next bend. I don't want to look at those horrid guns."

"It's regrettable, so near the presence of your sacred grandfather, but we have only one Fuehrer."

And then –?

Now. Edwin looks out from the ash trees over our small world of Bayreuth, and winking back from all the green hills that encircle it he sees metallic flashes: from lightning-bars, or anti-aircraft muzzles, or tank-tracked personnel carriers pivoting in with a fresh supply of His Death's-Head boys. Richard W****r has got what he asked for in his Grail Temple prayers: the Last Romantic's golden, illusory, Festspielhalle dreamworld, confronts 20th Cent reality, *His* ring of steel.

"Far better safe than sorry," said the Fox. "Miss Casson-Perceval, I hear that you are to give us Elsa, as well as Brünnhilde, this season."

To show how close his Nordic jug-ear is to the grapevine.

"Edwina," cooed Sister; "Casson-Perceval is so impossibly long a mouthful."

"Reinhard," the Fox bowed. "At your service, always."

All the better to eat, Jemima-dear.

That vulpine mouth, with its wide, full, yet always slightly pursed and feminine lips, shows the refined pleasures of the sadist lurking close behind the mask.... Meanwhile, children, in the Marietta way that seems never to be absent from our Mowgli associations, the young Lieutenant and his men are doing a frantic scramble through the bushes and over rocks to have the picnickers' Hamper & Cloth, and 6 collapsible steel chairs set in a formal military placement before arrival.

"No, I think over here is better." Mausi waited until all appeared

327

finally settled, thus kicking off another 100-yard dash. "Yes, this is where Father told me Grandfather used to sit."

Curiously, his Shade felt closer here, in the open air of the unmarked ash trees, than it did among the Liszt pianos and Nietzsche mementoes in his own house below us now.

"But there should be a sword in the trunk, don't you think?"

Heydrich stabs his ceremonial dagger into the bark – immediately above Brother's bloody head!

"Oh capital! Eddie's always nattering about William Tell."

"I should have thought Siegmund." The pale eyes rest. A chill wind tremors the boy's soul. "I too had a Wagnerian mother, Fräulein Edwina. How she would have appreciated this moment. She was profoundly musical, a teacher of some reputation at our family's academy in Hamburg. My father studied once under Frau Cosima herself. The result? We have to share the burden of those romantic nineteenth-century Christian names. Tristan, to your Isolde, it embarrasses me to admit. Although I do play adequately on the violin. For a time in the navy I formed a quartet with Admiral Canaris."

Isolde, Mother, and Music. Also linguist, fencer, brilliant as a student – cashiered as an officer! – and with the naturally bent mind required by a Machiavelli, BUT –

. . . Sad though it is in the shadow of Wahnfried to destroy a last illusion, under that perfect Aryan's gleaming exterior, our Brer Foxy trickster is, alas lamentably, but all too probably, some generations back, (according to Putzi) a Maggot. Yes, my dears, another one! – who, observing in the mirror of his own mind that huge bent-broken nose, and those sideways, oriental slits in the mask for eyes . . .

It isn't the "Tristan" from childhood, the Kaffeeklatsch whispers, that embarrasses this Siegfried – it's the "Isy", and "Blond Moses" by his jeering Dresden chums that makes the adult Reinhard-Tristan fight being thought one of Them.

But all the better to Serve . . .

As they say.

A New Lodger:

After their so-pleasant picnic, and with the Death's-Head Free Pass taking the Riley without question through umpteen layers of Police, the

328

Casson-Percevals drive down to Bayreuth, unwittingly protected by its ring of steel in the green hills. How times have changed since our First Season. Mowgli flags hang from every lamp post. The streets have the same hectic bustle as Nuremberg. The Hotel Anker, like all the others, bursts at the seams. Every bed-and-breakfast room is taken. More people than ever before are booked to attend the Festival – for a chance to worship not John-the-Baptist-Wagner, but Him.

Even the Griesbachs' has been invaded. After dropping Mausi off at Wahnfried, E & E found a new guest sharing their Privat upper floor.

"Halt and Identify yourselves!"

For our 2nd time of asking! Presently, a man in Black Leather – a trenchcoat, absurd given the weather.

"Casson-Perceval," Edwin said, "and we don't have any identification – we live here."

"Your building has been designated a restricted access structure for purposes of Defence of the Reich. You will report to the Police Station for passes which shall be produced on every entry to this floor until further notice. Is this clear?"

"It's rubbish," said the Hon Edwina. "I've just come from having lunch with General Heydrich and we didn't need any pass for that! I'm not going anywhere near your *Gestapa* station, I'm going to have a bath."

"General Heydrich?"

"He gave us a badge for our car," Eddie said. "It's in the garage at the back."

"This shall be attended to at once."

"It had better be," Sister called over her shoulder, "or I'll phone Hermann and make a real fuss."

"Mein Gott – this shall not be necessary!" Wolf-Saluting, and thundering off down the back stairs.

Ettie stripped and lay back in the water. Secure in their Tarnhelm of privilege, the C-Ps laughed, as your English will, at the Heartland's ponderous fools.

"But you really shouldn't tease them," Brother said from the edge of her bath. "It's only their job, and it's Gestap-o, now – Gestap-a was part of the Post Office and, either way, Captain Hermann doesn't run the show any more. Putzi says the Chicken Farmer's got it now."

"I don't care who's got it, darling; I'm just not going to be bullied in

329

my own home. Did you see the brute's face when I mentioned Reinhard? We must find out exactly what he does."

"Tears the wings off flies, I shouldn't wonder."

"Aren't we jealous!" She spread her legs to lather her golden pubes. "Or is it our inferiority complex because of the knife-in-the-tree Siegmund business?"

"No – it's the 'Tristan to your Isolde' business. Why do you have to be such an absolute bitch to me, the minute you meet a replacement for Baer?"

"Darling boy, I could say –"

"Oh my God."

To the Boy's horror the white lather floating by her thighs is tinged with red.

"Really, Eddie, you should see someone about this ridiculous neurosis you have for blood. It's the most normal thing in the world. Lots of men find it more exciting to do it then."

"It's ghastly. Frightful."

"It's not frightful. It's slippery. Feel, Eddie." He tries to leave; she grasps him by the wrist; pulling his arm, tempting, like Kundry. "Touch it, go on, with your fingers, in my –"

He vomited. That stopped her.

The Black Leather came back to find us cleansed, in separate rooms, and not speaking. As a normal Hun he addressed himself to Edwin.

"A dispensation has been granted about the identifications until this next morning when full instructions shall arrive from Berlin! Be kind enough to inform Fräulein von Perceval. Auf Wiedersehen, mein Herr!"

Brother wrote it out and slipped it under her locked door – only because it was important, you understand. He heard her get off the bed and come over, and her finger nails scratch the floor lightly as she picked up the paper, and then a crackle as she unfolded it, and then a pause as she read it. He said, "Ettie, I'm sorry –"

"*Cunnilingus*, darling. Imagine doing . . ."

Beyond belief! Eddie beat the door with fists to drown her and the carmine image out, but he could still hear her laughing. He stormed away from the hell house to the solitary Hofgarten and the Grave. Dame Sorrow's talons gripped his shoulder. The bitch! – shouting at Wagner's granite stone – the hideous filthy bitch. How can she do these dreadful things to me, her own brother? Her only real friend? The only person in the world who loves her? I *hate* her! Loathe and despise her! Bitch, bitch, bitch, *BITCH* . . .

Edwin, the non-person. 25 years of a senseless life behind him. Ahead a Grail farce of utter futility. And always in the shadow of *her* fame, and good for absolutely nothing – except snide cracks about incest and Siegmund. He has no gun, (like Inferior Eva's 1st): nor pills (her 2nd) – fate even denies the luxury of Female ill-health. A knife, like Heydrich's? – but I didn't have that either, and how can the end be in blood after what the bitch had done?

Home to the Griesbachs'. For efficient asphyxiation it will have to be the Riley. There's satisfaction in doing it right under the bitch's blue eyes, the Riley's lovely colour . . .

"Locked?"

To the door of the garage. And then,

"Bugger! Bugger! Bugger bugger . . ."

The door was most obviously locked with a shiny brass padlock snapped shut on the hasp. A Gothic sign Instructs:

> *No Motors shall be started*
> *without Orders, or driven*
> *in this Area while*
> *the Fuehrer is in Residence!*
> Signed in the name of:
> HEINRICH HIMMLER

Confronted with this demonstration of the Chicken Farmer's dread intelligence, before Edwin killed himself for the first time he decided to walk down to the Owls for a last supper.

> *There is a green hill far away,*
> *Without a city wall,*
> *Where our dear Lord was crucified . . .*

P.S: Our Eva's 1st.

The Day of All Saints, Nov 1, '32: Devastating Electoral Defeats.

By 'phone, to surgeon, one Dr Platte: "Dead . . . shot . . . through my heart!"

331

Girlish Hyperbole – merely a severed artery in the neck. Darlings, Death was whole *minutes* away. "Is it possible –?" enquired a Gentleman-Caller of Doc P. – "that Fräulein Braun shot herself simply with the object of becoming an interesting patient . . . ?"

Hanging Fire
(a Compound Interval)

. . . *On the Green Hill.* Sister's defiant stand doesn't stop badges, complete with photographs: not only for foreign Casson-Percevals, but –

"All of us as well! Mother, having to wear a badge in Bayreuth? – and she's made Tietjen our guardian! Now I *know* they've gone mad."

An outraged Mausi in the private burial part of the garden, with the pets' crosses, and Eddie brooding, and Toby, a new Wahnfried Schnauzer, boistering. Ettie was up to her eyebrows, at the Festspielhalle rehearsing her first Wolf-Lohengrin – and dining 3 nights in a row with her newest Tristan.

"And now Wolf wants the Norns sitting on top of a globe," said Mausi, "oh yes, and Mother says we aren't to call him that any more, but I'm going to! I don't know why he just doesn't take over as producer and director altogether."

"That's not a bad idea, though, Mausi. The Norns are spinning the fate of the world."

"I didn't say he wasn't imaginative, Eddie – but next it's going to be naked flower maidens for certain. When he gets here you'll see."

No one saw: He did His Wotan-flit in the dark. Next morning when Edwin went out to get the Riley, a Black Order stood guard on the locked garage. "Your key, mein Herr?"

"I don't have a key; it's your people's lock."

"For the car, mein Herr. The start of the motor. The Fuehrer is sleeping."

"If we don't start the motor, how am I going to move the car?"

The Black Order snaps his fingers. Three stalwart Teuton private soldiers double forward from behind the garage, enter – and PUSH!

"Their damned boots made more noise on the cobbles than the starting motor," Brother said when he fetched Sister. "They pushed me and the Riley all the way down to the corner by the Festspielhaus circle.

332

Behind when I left, two more of the idiots were trying with biscuits to stop Toby from barking on the lawn."

"I don't think that's idiotic at all. Wolf's another night performer. It's absolute hell for us being woken at the crack of dawn."

"Noon's a pretty late 'crack'."

"I'm not going to fight with you again. You've been in this weepy mood for weeks. As though *I* didn't need a good weep with Elsa *and* Brünnhilde."

"I haven't been weeping – and you asked for both. You can bawl on Tristan-Moses' shoulder."

"Aren't you ever going to let that Siegmund remark go? Reinhard has to know things about people close to the Fuehrer. It's his job."

"You've never called Him that before."

"It's only habit, from Auntie catching it. Mausi's right. I wouldn't dream of calling him anything but Wolf to his face – except when he's crawling, he's already far too big-headed. Are you going to say you love me, and be friends?"

"Are *you*?"

"I never stopped, darling. It wasn't Big Sis that ran off in the huff. Run back with me now, Eddie. I'm simply scared to death; with the Elsa, I'm biting off more than I can chew."

As they say. In her room upstairs at the Griesbachs' Eddie allows himself to be mounted, astride, with her thighs squeezing; and then wildly, greedily stuffed into her mouth to taste him basted in her own juices . . . while she stared up with her Kundry eyes, watching my face to know the precise moment the magic potion would arrive for her golden throat, as Elsa . . .

He invited us to dinner afterwards.

Putzi's Funny Story

But 1st, a round of Punch & Peppermint-tea on the Privat lawn next to the little Siegfriedhaus, now one room bigger because of an extension Winifred has added for Young Wieland to live in while he's a bachelor. (Except, it goes without saying, on those occasions when Mr Wolf comes to call.) I'll huff, and I'll puff, and –

333

"I have to say," He said, "the Three Little Pigs is the masterpiece – the very essence of Disarmament! I haven't seen a film that affected me as profoundly since King Kong. Which is, of course, Freia in Rheingold, being carried off by Fasolt. 'We clodhoppers toil, sweating with our blistered hands, to win a woman sweet and gentle, who will dwell with us poor creatures – and you term the bargain absurd!'"

"It is," said Edwina; "Wolf dear, I can't imagine living for a moment with either of them. But why not pick Fafner? He's much more of a brute."

"Precisely, Fräulein Ettie. With the ladies our poor Fasolt is always the gentleman, like oneself – or Mister Hanfstaengl, here. Whereas Fafner is definitely Goering on a bad day! And who can tell me the difference between what a Goebbels and a Goering is? No one? Frau Winifred, this party of ours is far too polite. A 'Goebbels', dear friends, equals the amount of sheer nonsense one man can spout in an hour – whereas a 'Goering' is the weight of tin he can pin on his chest!"

By the time the dinner ends the only member of the Circle not freshly amused or re-charmed by such chestnuts is Putzi. The giant takes Eddie aside when the smokers escape to the garden.

"Edwin, have you got a spare bed where I could stay tonight?"

"I thought you had a billet at the Post with the foreign correspondents. There's a spare room at the end of our floor. I'm sure Frau Griesbach would make you up a bed in that if I ask her."

"Good. But don't ask – I'll do it myself when I arrive. When we leave here I'll go along with you and say 'goodbye', as though I were walking to the town. What do you think of his behaviour?"

"Wolf seems in a wonderful mood. I suppose it's the Rhineland."

"It's the taste of blood. Didn't you hear how he addressed me?"

"Very clearly, 'Mister Hanfstaengl.'"

"Exactly."

Brother can't wait to tell Sister the giant's odd behaviour. *He* accompanies to the door, bowing almost to the waist with His Wienese Handkuss.

"Most gracious, supremely gifted Fräulein Ettie, my heart goes with you as Brünnhilde – but when you sing for Bockelmann, please, please, won't you sing just a little for this old Wotan-Wolfi?"

"A dear Wolfi – but I can't possibly. I have to give my soul in flames for Bockelmann." Trilling a little laugh. "But cheer up, you'll have all the other women in the hall."

"I don't want others, my noblest Helden Fräulein Edwina."

"That's terribly sweet, but you're married to the Nation. Be kind to him, Aunt Winnie, night-night all."

Exit on a grace note.

Giant Putzi left with us.

... *At the Griesbachs':* Only one old housemaid is sitting up in the kitchen, dozing: her starched cap nods in time with every two ticks of the clock. She wakes with a start when Eddie taps on the door to ask for spare bedding for a visiting friend.

"I'll make it up, and let him in. You don't have to bother."

But the old maid is far too Hunnish for that, and so Hanfstaengl has a witness to his arrival.

"Damn it to hell! Now it will get straight back to Himmler."

"She's only a housemaid, Putzi – she's been here for years."

"And Adolf's only an opera-lover, Edwin, you've played the Fool too long."

To the Fool's pure astonishment, the giant begins to check the spare-bedroom's walls. Lifting, poking, tapping the plaster.

"If you're looking for a secret passage, I tried that on our first visit. The walls aren't thick enough."

"Microphones, for gelatine recording devices, although it should be all clear since you don't usually occupy this room."

"Really, Putzi, you can't mean it?"

The giant left the hunt and sat heavily on the brass bed. Microphones? – my dears, the whole town could hear him.

"Would I waste my time at one in the morning? Why do you think Blond Moses spends so much of his time with Edwina?"

"I suppose the functionaries may be somewhat drawn by us, knowing Wolf as we do."

"Somewhat drawn? Functionaries! For God's sake, boy, stop this English charade. You know damn well the whole pack seethes about you and your sister. I can see it has advantages for Edwina. It's how your relationship whets Adolf's whistle that – "

"I say – damn it, Putzi, that's a bit stiff."

"Edwin, it isn't a school game of tickle-my-fancy. The Man is hypnotised by his 'noblest gracious Fräulein Ettie', and the more she plays her hand so damn cool . . ."

"Putzi, I can't allow you to sit there and say such things about Ettie – or Wolf for that matter. You're still here, and so's everyone else, except Roehm, and a bloody good riddance. And now, as you haven't told me, why *are* you here? Unless it's life or death, I'd really rather go to bed."

"Love or death . . ." The giant closed his eyes and massaged his rock of a forehead with his fingers. "I'm here, Eddie-pal, because I don't want to wake up one early morning with a one-way ticket to a Valentine's Day in Chicago. And if you think no one's taken the trip except Ernst Roehm in the past two years you're an even greater fool than I believed – oh Lord, Edwin, forgive me, but Helene's gone, with the decree nisi, and I've been so worried about my boy Egon these last six months – half the time I don't know what I'm saying."

. . . And he buried his enormous misshapen skull in his hands, and cried, my dears! The Fool could only sit in the spare-room's cane-backed chair across from the brass bed and wait until the giant ceased.

"Martha Dodd warned me as long ago as the Roehm affair, just before she tried to kill herself: 'Your crowd doesn't trust you any more.' – but I didn't believe she knew what she was talking about. I still thought I could broaden Adolf's mental horizons, get him to see reason. My curse is that I still do. And now this horror over Renate Müller –"

"Renate?" said the Fool.

The giant peered wanly through the double-octave span of his fingers. "You haven't heard about that either? Out of the Adlon Hotel, a fifth-floor window."

"Christ, Putzi, only last week, Renate and I had supper."

"It was three nights ago, just after he'd left her. The last thing she told me was that he actually lay on the floor and begged her to kick him, with her high heels. The Leader of the New Vision, it makes me vomit, and I get all his filth on my plate because the foreign press rakes it up and comes for confirmation. And then I have to ask the Chicken Farmer's office. Can you still doubt my head's on the line?"

"It's simply ghastly about Renate," said the shaken Fool, "but Putzi, we just can't believe every bit of Kaffeeklatsch that we hear."

The giant removed shoes the size of the Rhineman's ferry, and placed them side by side beneath the bed. "Edwin, it isn't what Adolf *hears*, it's what he thinks, or senses. The man's a witchdoctor. After the row about my overture to Roosevelt, I caught him standing staring at a photograph he had of me on his desk in the Chancellery. I tell you I could feel the needles and pins stick in. I still feel them, every time I'm with him."

The Fool said, "I've never seen Him nicer than He was tonight. I'm sure, Putzi, if you try and behave the way you used to – the piano, and laugh at His jokes – He'd be the first to pick it up and go on. He hates unpleasantnesses in the family. And we are almost like His family, aren't we? I'd suppose we're as close to Him as anyone."

"And doesn't that terrify you?"

The Fool stared.

"Of course it doesn't. I'm not in politics, and Ettie's not going to jump out of any windows for Wolf. Anyway, He's *got* the gold ring. He's done almost everything He wanted. I wouldn't be at all surprised if one day He didn't simply retire exactly as He keeps saying. Even the Jews are starting to return – ten thousand this year, Michael Rau tells me. Putzi, the revolution part *is* over. Just go on as if nothing had happened between you, and it'll be all right. Now, I really would like to go to bed."

The giant swung his tree-trunk legs to the floor. "Eddie-pal, you haven't the slightest idea. Edwin, he can't get it out of his system – the vicarious thrill of thinking about you and your sister."

"For God's sake –"

"You don't think that's why I got kicked off the piano, boy? So he could ogle and fondle hands before washing them at your late night tête-à-têtes."

The cry of every desperate, fallen favourite!

Ignore him, Edwin dear.

OUR '36 SEASON

... *Among the Wagnerians:* The gossip switches from the Stork's tempo-foibles to the Prussian's daring lighting of the Grail Temple. A new favourite with Us for the first time on the Magic Mountain, a young architect, is much impressed. In our Nursery libretto, "Wotan's spear" as doubtless you will remember, children, reads in Hun, "Wotans Speer!"

337

Synchronicity is a so-wonderful thing.

And then –?

Once more, The Parsifal, (for the non-yawning true believers); and then The Rheingold, (brief, for the haemorrhoid sufferers); und then, on the afternoon following Hanfstaengl's soul-baring, The War Horse (known even to non-believers from little Henry W**d's proms concerts). With the Self absorption of Youth, the Fool has, to this point in Life, seen the second part of the Ring solely as Brother & Sis, with the Incest-Snakes hissing. Even so late as this Act One, the wretch got an erection (from day-dreaming about yesterday, after Her vileness with the Blood).

Watch & Learn, Edwin.

And now–?

God in the Box

or

WOTAN and BRÜNNHILDE

... Act 2, *Die Walküre*, after the Twins have got rid of thug-Hunding from the Hut, and lit up the Sex-snake. While in Valhalla ... the Fool's Sister yodels with two cheerful *Heiaha Heiahas*:

> Let me warn you, Father – make yourself ready for a
> violent storm. Your wife's on her way to pick a quarrel.
> Much as I love bold men's battles I prefer not to engage
> in skirmishes like this. You're left in the lurch. *Heiaha*!

Laughing, as the Leader is, Sister rides off, while behind her, Fricka sweeps down in her chariot – drawn by two of Tietjen's live rams. In terror, at stage right, in sight of the orchestra buried in the pit, the rams bleat, the chariot wheels clatter, delivering Margaret Klose with all the fury of a Fricka scorned. Wotan hunches his shoulders at the first crack of Wife's whip.

> In the mountains – where you hide yourself to escape
> your wife's notice! Over that impudent, blasphemous
> pair – these monstrous twins! Your adultery's dissolute
> fruit! Unceasingly you've cuckolded your faithful wife,
> everywhere you looked with lecherous eyes. When you

338

went into battle with those uncouth girls that a wanton fancy caused you to father. Even Brünnhilde, the bride of your true desire . . . !

1st Fool-sight:
Brünnhilde is Wotan's daughter? It strikes with a thunderclap: *This god wants to f**k his DAUGHTER*!

In Ludwig's Box:
The Candidate broods. Fricka protests.

> You're trying to confuse me. It's all your fault. You set it all up. You stuck the sword in the tree. You allowed it to happen – that disgusting act between these Volsung children. And it's all nonsense anyway. How can this 'hero' you go on about do anything you don't want? If you create him you're always his master. But apart from that nonsense – I know you're in love with Brünnhilde, but for the sake of Valhalla you have to stay married to *me*. And my price for that bargain, husband? You see that Siegmund gets killed!

From His Web Centre:
The Leader watches.

> I have been caught in my own trap. Daughter, I am the least free of all men. O, sacred disgrace! O, shameful affliction! My misery is everlasting. I am the saddest of all men.

Don't Tell Me!
The Worst Moment of My Life!!! The stage-God is bitter of soul. Young Speer takes notes. The Leader begins to chew His little-finger nail.

> When young love's delights waned in me, my spirit longed for power. Impetuous wishes roused me to madness. I won the world for myself. But now, through Alberich's army our end is looming. With baleful rage the Nibelung nurses his grudge. Fafner guards the

339

treasure that could save me but since I covenanted with him I may not attack him. These are the bonds that bind me. I became ruler through treaties; by my treaties I am now enslaved. Only one person could do what I may not; this Man opposed to the gods who will fight for me. But how can I find Him? How can I create that perfect Other, no longer part of *me*? What a predicament for a god! Disgusted, in everything I create I find only myself, every time. For the Free Man may create himself – but I, a God, can create only subjects *to* myself. Let it fall to pieces, all that I built! Only one thing I want now, Girl: the end, the *End*!

The Death Note:

... Echoes ominously in the hood of the pit; behind the Leader, brooding and gnawing, in darkness, with this mighty music rumbling and soaring beside His Little Speer, noting, an impassive Blond Moses – close as damn it to a perfect Other – sits watching, as the God onstage makes fearful prediction:

For that End is at hand, even at this minute Black Alberich is working. The Wise Woman said, 'When Love's dark enemy begets a son in anger, the end of the Blessed Ones is nigh.' Girl, I have heard rumour that a woman was overpowered by the Dwarf, and seduced for money. The fruit of his hatred, with his full envy, is stirring in her womb.

Hagen:

Finally! – the black-shadow *Doppelgänger* Other-Half of golden Siegfried arrives in the story.

In The Box:

In front of inscrutable Blond Moses, & the New Speer, & the Dwarf of Propaganda with his Thingee-foot, compulsively tapping, only the Raven-wing of hair shows against the pale lamp that is the Leader's face.

Presumptuous girl! Do you rebel against me?! What else are you but my wish's blindly approving instru-

340

ment? When I confided in you did I so demean myself
that abuse from my own creation was the result? Child,
do you *know* my anger?

The music storms, the God departs – and in the dark of mad
Ludwig's Box the sweated hand of the Leader grips the Fool's thigh.

Interval:
Herr Wolf jokes and eats chocolate cake as if nothing has happened, and
says He was taken with the Appia lighting, and the bleating rams, until:

"Not counting Brünnhilde and Waltraute, who can name for me all
the Valkyries? Speer? Hanfstaengl? Ach, mein Putzi, you've missed
Helmwige again, but never mind."

2nd Fool-sight:
The true dramatic purpose – for when the shriekers are gone, and
Wotan is once more alone on that great stage with only his daughter, the
magic returns, 10-fold in contrast to the screaming. Not Funerals and
Flying Horses, and Valhallas, but this, Sister with Wotan, becomes for
the Fool, her Brother, the greatest scene written by Richard Wagner:

No-one knew my innermost thoughts as she did. No-
one but she knew whence my intentions sprang. She
herself was the fertile womb of all my wishes.
But then, she was *my Sister.*

In His Chair:
The Leader leans forward. The Battle-God draws himself up to
pronounce sentence – but his War-child will not surrender.

Was it so shameful, what I did? Was it so base?
Battle-Father – look me in the eyes. Silence your rage,
control your anger, explain to me clearly my hidden guilt
which has blindly and stubbornly forced you to abandon
your favourite child.
Did I cause the War to end it?

In the Festspielhalle:
The Fool weeps for her, and our father I never knew – as He reaches
out a second time, and takes my Fool's hand, and Sister pleads with this

implacable, immovable god we call Wotan. . . .

> One man's love breathed into my heart. Yes, your love,
> Battle-Father. One will it was that allied me with the
> Volsung; and faithful to you, *inwardly*, I disobeyed your
> command.

The Leader:

. . . Sighs, releasing the Fool's hand. There is blood on His hand, bitten
into the cuticle, as the stage-God transforms again: from wonder to
fiercest Anger.

> So easily did you imagine love's bliss was attained?
> When burning pain had stabbed me to the heart? When
> in desperate necessity I had turned against myself in
> agony? Against stunning sorrows had risen in my rage?
> Angry longing with its burning desires had formed my
> dread decision: in the ruins of my own world I would
> end my endless sadness.

The God:

Draws around Him His full strength: raises His spear to pass His awful
sentence. The Leader takes out a handkerchief – with E.C-P, on it . . .
Sister has never been more beautiful. The God is roaring.

> *You were happy to follow the power of love: now follow him*
> *whom you are* Obliged *to love!*

Postlude:

She comes down the stairs . . . on the arm of Bockelmann to the Singers'
Table, and the Restaurant exploded, and applauded, and applauded,
and applauded, with fat Palatinate bankers screaming, and cropped
Junker generals crying, and Him standing, leading the clapping – and
then bowing to the bust of Richard Wagner staring down at all of us
from his pedestal at the top of the stairs.

"Genius," He pronounced, over assorted helpings of mounting
triumph, "never sleeps – it comes through even in these moth-eaten
Wotan myths which Himmler's got himself so absurdly involved with.
Oh, there's no doubt that because it's Wagner, there's some sort of
hocus-pocus-psychology for some people in the Ring, but this year –

342

after the Olympics – the masterpiece it goes without saying has to be the Lohengrin! You were, may one say, Fräulein Edwina, simply the most delicious, the most exquisite, the most truly noble Elsa ever. At the end, don't tell me! You were part swan yourself, with the melody floating upwards. Utterly glorious! – Mein Ederl, we'll have to sail a swan-boat for your so-beautiful sister across the English Channel for the Coronation. Yes, I've told Furtwängler, I've decided the Lohengrin's going to be our present for King Edward next summer. We'll have it put on in Covent Garden – and I don't want to hear another word about the size of the place. I've thought it all out, and gone over the plans with Speer. The back of the building will be opened up like a can of sardines – and then you'll see: our Bayreuth sets will fit in perfectly. That will give those Londoners something to talk about besides Frau Simpson and the League of Nations! When Sir Beecham arrives I shall iron out the whole thing with him."

But the Best laid Plans, as they say . . .

For when "Sir Beecham", accompanied by his new secretary (the Stork's ex, and Jewish) Berta Geissmar, arrives at the Green Hill – somehow, despite the Huns' reputation for efficiency, Sir Beecham's programme is found to be always mysteriously out of synchronicity with the Leader's. This disappoints Herr Wolf, but is no problem for the Dwarf's Ministry, children – who simply produce a *montage* photograph my dears, in which the Famous Conductor is SEEN to be in the Box at His side! A transformation.

As for our Olympics –?

"Eddie, we'd only be deliberately left out by The Riefenstahl – and all the roads are torn up with Wolf's mad re-building."

Second Movement
Fourth Passage

Alas, my Love, you do me Wrong,
To cast me off discourteously;
And I have loved you so long,
Delighting in your Company . . .

. . . *At Triebschen:* Listening to 33, that short & playful piece of Elizabetheana (a *toye* from the old Booke), recorded and rippling across Lake Lucerne, E & E lie sunning in their little boat, dull as real Swiss, with Brother rowing while Sister trails a slim hand in the warm few inches at the top surface that doesn't stay freezing from the glaciers all year round. Dabbling with Our Reviews of the past Season. Olympics-dodging, through Exhaustion: far greater, after her dual roles of Brünnhilde and Elsa, than we admit.

"I told you you would be. Doing Brünnhilde in all three parts is enough for anyone. Thirteen hours *is* practically an Olympics, and Elsa's such a shallow nothing. No matter what Wolf says, the entire plot of Lohengrin would blow away in a spring breeze, if Elsa didn't ask the one stupid question – "

"I'm not fighting with you, Eddie. I did the Elsa as well because it was there, like Everest, but I agree, before I tackle three in a row I'll take more vitamins and physical jerks !" With that angelically, she made him instantly once more her slave.

"But what do you mean, three ?"

"Kundry, darling. Next season Big Sis is going for her hat trick: Kundry, Brünnhilde and Elsa."

She lifted her hand and ticked them off on her dripping fingers.

"It isn't possible, not at Bayreuth. Not in a row, Ettie, you'll strain something, truly."

"Piffle. Just because it hasn't been done before, doesn't mean it can't be. It's only a matter of training. Who's that on the dock? One of your gypsy boyfriends, I'll bet, here with the Pot."

The figure – male, slim, fawn-suited, slightly stooped, and obviously British, waved a straw hat in our direction.

"Eddie, let's make love out here in the boat."

"Don't be insane. That chap will see."

"I know. I'll lie in the bottom . . . here, using my foot . . . 'This little piggy', under your seat."

"The Sisters, then. Their telescope –"

"The Parrots can't spy up your shorts, silly . . . I can. I spy with my little eye . . . Piggy's growing . . ."

Her prehensile toes are wet from the lake, warm from the sun.

"Bloody hell, Ettie –" but weakly, jiggling sideways.

He could have lashed out instead, and kicked her – but her toes were wriggling up between his thighs, and the figure on the dock was perfectly trained to record a private situation.

"Christ, it's the Goat's man! You mad woman, for the last bloody time, we're *adults* –"

"If you don't porpoise-squirm like that he won't know."

"But it isn't fair now. Putting me on the spot like this."

"I know, Piggy's juicing already."

"Damn-you-to-hell, I'm not having a climax in front of a bloody Prime Minister!"

"He isn't," giggling, "not any more – and I'm afraid, my juicy darling piggy brother – you are . . ."

And did. All over her foot.

Laughing, she slides her massaging appendage out of his shorts. When she spreads her toes, sticky webs form between them. "White," she said dreamily, "like a swan's. I wonder if it was really possible, with Leda?" She dipped the webs delicately into the waters of Lucerne. "Eddie pet, you're simply hopeless at self-control, you'd never make a singer."

A Change Of Mind

Tea, for English-3, abroad, demurely, on the porch of our Swiss Cottage. Whatever the Goat's Secretary might guess – or, horrors, have seen! – is locked away behind his smooth Sphynx face, to emerge as a memoir nest-egg for his retirement.

"It's a delicate situation," the Scribe said, over a slice of our thin Swiss rye bread and local butter . . . and golden honey. "L-G's on his way for this meeting that you helped to arrange through Hanfstaengl – who, I must say seems awfully positive, so perhaps it will go well, but you know the former PM's, ah –" pausing to catch a drip – "he does get rather carried away."

"The row, about aristocrats."

"Exactly, Edwin. One did one's utmost afterwards, but that débâcle may still come back to haunt us. At least the consequences with Winston are purely domestic. Whereas –"

"If the Goat goes off the deep end with Wolf," said the Hon Edwina, "the cat's at the pigeons. Well I shouldn't worry. One's a pet, and the other worships him from the War. More tea?"

Mama's Guide Diplomatique. The Secretary laughs, but his fears have not been eased.

"I left Master at the Spa. Megan's with him, not Miss Stevenson – and speaking in complete frankness, when he's only with Daughter, sometimes one does feel the lack of a restraining hand."

"She's a bit dotty – " this from Sister! – licking a honey-web salaciously off her sticky fingers, "but Politico females are. Nancy Astor's gone as a hatter. They need a man with balls – but then I suppose they wouldn't *be* political, would they?"

"Ah – " the Secretary gulped tea – "quite. Eddie, I wondered whether you and Edwina . . . well there would be less chance of him running amok . . . in the right sort of group, and you know the other side so well. I don't suppose you could see your way clear? It would only be two or three days. In Berchtesgaden . . . we shall be putting up at the Grand."

"You want us to go with you?"

But Ettie was adamant. "It's sweet to ask, but I'm starting a Boris Godounov for Fat Hermann at the Berlin State – I've never done a

347

Russian before – so Politico's simply out of the question. But give my love to the Goat."

But –

When a large touring Mercedes from *His* Embassy in Zürich draws up at the Cottage Casson-Perceval – as Brother is about to pay the bitch back in bed for the toe episode in the boat! – and when the Teuton driver, stamping & heel-clicking & bowing with the Leader's most-urgent-compliments, turns out to be no less than His Deputy, Fräulein Anna Hess, with Privat 'plane . . .

. . . *On Our First Wolf-Flight:* in a summer-shower rainbow. The plane is a Dornier, huge-bellied, 3-engined: an enormous one with cylinders on the snout, and a smaller one to each side. "Walhall", in black gothic, with red flames. Fräulein Anna, playing introverted, quixotic Froh, twin of Freia, as god of the rainbow does the honours himself, curving us up and out over it for our 1st view from the air of white and grey Swiss Alps and the black dots of the Parrot Sisters' spy-nest and our Hunding's Hut.

"But no pot of gold, Eddie, for our first flying."

School-girl Ettie – dashing from one window to another, pointing and chattering in amazement over landmarks known so well by road. Eddie's surprise is the man at the controls. Pilot Hess is sure, decisive, masculine. Once above the mountains he relinquishes his seat to a co-pilot and comes back to be with us in the cabin. An Aryan Valkyrie, armoured in a uniform with *Lufthansa* monogrammed across her full right breast, materialized simultaneously to offer champagne and hors d'oeuvres of ham and smoked fish before Valhalla arrived.

"Your camomile tea, Herr Stellvertreter. Do you wish also one of your cress sandwiches at this time?"

"Nein, danke."

Polite, but cool. Even his voice seems tougher off the ground. Or perhaps it's just being out of the overwhelming Shadow. Also, he has another surprise up his pilot's sleeve: clear English! *All the better to over-hear my dear* . . .

"I never take solid food while in the air," he informs his passengers solemnly. "The weight of the lower stomach at altitude is put out of adjustment by the decrease in atmospheric pressure."

"And if you get sick," said Sister, "what hasn't gone down can't come up. Eddie, perhaps you shouldn't have the ham."

His Deputy was not amused.

"At any time Schenkel is doubtful, Fräulein Edwina. Smoking meat affects the cells. Also in pig's flesh there is always the question of worms."

Eddie changed from the pig's flesh to pike from the north Rhine.

"Well I adore ham." Ettie made a sandwich and washed it down with champagne. "This is sweet of Wolf to send us a 'plane."

"The Fuehrer, Himself –" His Deputy cleared throat, an awkward noise, stretching his neck out of his collar at the same time, wanting desperately to break into his tooth-whistle – "he is not, I should say, precisely aware at this moment."

"But you said he asked for us," said the Hon Edwina. "Damn it, Herr Rudolf, I wouldn't have come."

"Fräulein Edwina, these are not false pretences, I assure you." Coping with your prima donna shifts the Deputy's voice into its more familiar, slightly effeminate register. He eases his collar with a finger. "The Fuehrer indeed has mentioned your presence in connection with the visit of former Prime Minister Lloyd-George – for a private reception after the first meeting. It was my own thought, however, that a talk with you might be useful before. In order that an appreciation of the situation could be made to the English side. This is the most historic occasion, you understand – our Fuehrer with the man who made the peace in Europe! It must be that nothing should affect the outcome adversely. Some little thing, the Fuehrer might say without realising. One hears that Herr Lloyd-George has – how can I say this –?"

"The Goat has moods. Well so does Wolf. They should get on like a house on fire."

"Moods, possibly," allowed His Deputy, "temperament is the pre-rogative of genius, but it would be a disastrous blow to understanding between our countries if something ridiciulously small was a spark for this setting on fire, as you put it, and burning down the hall."

"Stay off organised religion," Eddie said, "the former Prime Minister holds strong views about the Archbishop of Canterbury."

"What are his views, would you say, on MacKinder's Theory of the Heartland and the World Ocean?" His Deputy looked expectantly. His

349

eyes were much greener-blue than Edwin's, and above them the harsh sun at altitude showed another battle scar: from a beer mug, Putzi says, tossed in the Bürgerbräukeller revolution.

"I wouldn't say, Herr Rudi. Which ocean specifically?"

"Herr Edwin, in Herr Professor Doktor Haushofer's estimation sea power is obsolete through aircraft. Who rules the Heartland with air power, rules the globe."

"Poor old Empire," said Sister. "I wouldn't wave that red rag at the Goat."

"Fräulein Edwina, please, we are talking only of abstraction currently. The British Empire is of course – outside Europe – the world's greatest force. The closest harmony is vital in the coming years because of Russia re-arming to the East."

Eddie said, "L-G's quite keen on the Russians. He used to have tremendous rows with Churchill about them."

"Praise God, we don't have to worry for Winston Churchill!" The Dornier bumped. His Deputy rose to his feet. "We shall be approaching Obersalzberg. Do not be alarmed by the mountains as we descend. And you shall impress on the Lloyd-George party how much the Fuehrer truly desires a co-operation with Great Britain, *ja*?"

"*Ja*, we'll play piggy-in-the-middle for Herr Rudi, won't we, Eddie?"

... On the Salt Mountain: His Valhalla landing-strip is constructed half-way up the northeast face. The other half appears to have been flattened to allow it. Only the rocky promontory peak is untouched.

"Although surely that's Mama's chalet," says Ettie, pointing.

"I suppose it is. I suppose it must be."

Because the gable-end looks the same, but all around it another house has been constructed, so that the first part looks absurdly out of scale, a residence for ants. And below it is a barracks block, and bisecting the whole meadow a new Macadamized road, full width, chopped right through the rock; and lining the road an almost endless file of ant-people – men, women, children, waving tiny Mowgli flags, or eating sausages, or selling them. The little wooden house with its vines in the meadow had been turned to –

"Lourdes, Ettie. He's ruined it."

"Oberammergau," she said, "all year round. I think it's rather sweet of them coming all this way just for a look."

Deputy Anna emerges from the "Walhall", removing Froh's flying cap. A 3rd man – a short, squat, toad of a Hunding-thug carrying a briefcase, steps up.

"My assistant," offhand, as the guests walk to the Mercedes, "Bormann. . . . Auf Wiedersehen, Herr Edwin. Fräulein Edwina. Und danke !"

. . . With heel-clicks the C-Ps bid farewell to the toad and his present employer, and drive, without getting close to Mama's once-little chalet house, past the flags of the waiting faithful, and concrete pill-boxes with machine guns, through expanding Obersalzberg, and past its mine, down the Salt Mountain the 10 miles into Berchtesgaden.

"See, Eddie – no worse than Oberammergau, and at least the hotels don't have to wait ten years between performances."

. . . *At the Grand Hotel:* A note in the Secretary's immaculate script suggests the probability of Dinner with Goat that night, so Edwin goes up to confirm. The Secretary is distraught – for him – continually running a manicured hand over the perfectly brushed-back grey hair on the left side of his head.

"It's too late, Edwin. They're up there alone." Wolf, being Wolf has moved everything forward. "A car just arrived. Master was ecstatic. His little-boy behaviour, getting-out-of-school-early-for-Christmas. Ribbentrop was in an awful flap. Do you find that man a bit of an ass?"

"Not a bit. A lot. How long ago did they leave ?"

"Two hours. I'm sorry I wasted both your time."

"It wasn't a waste. We got our first aeroplane ride – at Hess's expense. The great men must have been watching us landing under their noses."

"Hess ? – the one with the eyebrows? He seems well disposed. He's asked for a session with L-G as well, when we return to Munich. Dinner will be at eight, if we're all speaking to each other."

Brother went back and told Sister that they wouldn't be needed as diplomats extraordinaires, and then played some Boris Godounov for her on the Bechstein.

"I'm tired of Boris – let's go to bed for an hour."

351

Our Best Foot Forward

Mohammed comes down from *His* mountain as the siblings complete the Act. Much raucous honking of horns to part the Leader-pilgrims. Sister points a languid leg at the window.

"It must be the Goat. Check and see. He'll have that bantam-bounce if he's come off well with Wolf."

Nude behind the curtains, Edwin cautiously peers out. The little figure seems tired, but when it turns up its face the glow lights the sky. He catches sight and waves his blackthorn stick.

"Ha! Young Edwin! Didn't I say it, boy? Germany has raised up a leader!"

"And a half," said the Hon Edwina, also naked. "If you can't raise your leader again come back and just do piggy with your foot." And as Brother stands speechless. "I want to see what it's like. But you'd better wash it first or I'll turn into a tennis sock."

Eddie put his foot down. Which is to say, he refused to comply with her latest aberration.

"Absolutely and unconditionally not."

"I did it for you, in the boat."

"You took advantage of a captive market and embarrassed me to death."

"You could use my dressing gown cord and tie me up."

"*No*, blast you!"

Tying up was new since Blond Moses. Edwin locked himself safely into the bathroom and turned the taps to drown her out.

"Eddie, guess what?" . . . still her voice floated through the waters with a Rhinemaiden's giggle . . . "I can use my own foot."

But he knew the slut was lying.

The Ribbon-Snob:
Refreshed, the C-Ps repair to dine with the Right Honourable David L-G. Who is still dressing, but the Secretary is there, and a tall man with an undertaker's face whose correct title Eddie forgets because Ettie, taking one of her instant dislikes, insists on calling him Lord Ghoul. His Lordship serves a medical function in London, but here for some

inexplicable Goat-reason he is also current Favourite Advisor on the Hun body-politic.

"Basically sound at long last, in my opinion," Lord Ghoul opines, in a tone for carrying out the dead. "I was particularly impressed by the new proposal for the sterilisation of the unfit. Exercised humanely – and the Germans *are* a humane people – the moral strength and stature of the nation can only improve."

"Moral strength, indeed, let me tell you!" The semi-bigamous Wizard bounces in on daughter Megan's arm. "Dear little Ettie, what a day I've had up in the clouds with your friend Mr Wolf! And what a happy accident to find you here! Fresh from new conquests in Bayreuth, if I'm to believe the papers. And now, everyone, a pleasant surprise – von Ribbentrop is coming along to sit down with us."

"Blast – they won't have set a big enough table." The Secretary dashes for a rush consultation with hotel staff.

"I am exceptionally impressed with Ribbentrop," pronounces Lord Ghoul.

. . . As the Secretary returns with the Ambassador at Large for the Reich (or less kindly by the trade, "Brickendrop", or sometimes, "Ribbensnob") wearing white spats with his evening dress and a Hermann-sized sunburst decoration on his chest.

"I am worried," is his opening Brickendrop with sherry, "about the Archbishop of Canterbury."

"Not worth it." The Goat chuckles, spilling turtle soup in his good humour.

"But for my good lady," the Ribbensnob confides to this room full of Anglo strangers, "when we take up residence in London, we are not, you will understand, in the eyes of the church, so to say, man and wife?"

"Good God!" Lord Ghoul's ejaculation.

"It is so. And although it is foolish you will appreciate," the Brickendrop's thyroid eyes bulge at Edwin for some reason, "with formal Clergy there is always the sense of damnation for Consummation from unhallowed Union?"

The Goat chokes on his soup. The Fool feels Guilt's owl-claws digging. The Secretary scrabbles for footing in this social quicksand.

"Ambassador, that is most interesting – but with tomorrow's visit, would the Chancellor grant permission for one to take a moving-film camera?"

"This is possible – after final confirmation has been obtained. Mr George what, in your opinion, is to be made by Winston Churchill?"

"Less than half my royalties!"

The grinning Goat proceeds wolfishly to roast beef, overdone in the Hun way, getting a forkful of Anglo mustard by mistake.

"But seriously, Herr Lloyd?"

"Seriously, my dear Ribbentrop, Winston has no spontaneous sense of humour – " cut short by streaming eyes and a gulp of water.

"Winston is a poppet," said Ettie, dismissing it. "Dear L-G, did Wolf tell you his plan to tear the Garden to pieces, and take London's mind off Frau Simpson?"

"Herr Wolf wants to give the Little Fellow an opera, does he? Easier to give him one than get him to go and hear it, I should say. His new Majesty's heart's in the right place, but I'm not so sure about his top storey – "

"Father!" from daughter Megan. "Not abroad."

". . . When it comes to *musical appreciation*, I was about to add – *if* I could be allowed to get a word in edgeways." Little red eyes crinkling and gleaming.

"But returning," returns von Brickendrop, doggedly, "to the Churchill consideration?"

"A brilliant mind! Oh, the most very brilliantest – he can be almost Shakespearian on occasion with the written word, *but* – no judgement at all. When the Kaiser was the problem, with Winston it was Russia, Russia, Russia. Today, the man's positive obsession is Germany. Speech or print!"

. . . *In the Night* – there comes a knocking. Edwin rouses himself blearily, stumbles over slippers to the door of the suite. Opens –

And Lederhosened, Tyrol-jacketed, there He was; not another soul in the corridor. In manic high good humour. Flitting.

"Mein Ederl, may I come in? You're looking fagged out – one has to say this. Too much wine and cigars, the body can't take it, but you're young enough to change those ways, thank heaven. My car's downstairs. Throw on some clothes, there's a good man, and wake your sleeping-

354

beauty sister. No suitcase-nonsense, the staff will collect your effects and send them up to the Berghof. Come along, you excellent fellow – Herr George has given me your English for it – Chop-chop!"

He clapped His hands together and strode past bleary Edwin to the Bechstein.

"Herr Wolf, forgive me, I'm afraid there was too much wine – you want Ettie and me, both of us, to go back to your house with you, now, for a supper visit?"

"But naturally we'll have a snack of some sort if you're hungry." He riffled through the Boris. "Some of the Slav stuff isn't bad, I don't care for tambourines, those damned gypsies, stealing horses – not a supper visit. To stay. When Hess told me, at first I was inclined to wag a finger – flying off at half-cock, and sticking you down here. 'Damn it!' I told him, 'you, Hess, if anyone, should know. Their noble Mama provided this house of mine, and you've stuck her children in the Grand Hotel!' He won't pull that trick twice, I'll be bound. Now Ederl, I insist; you're my guests. Wake your so-gracious sister."

A midnight ride in the clouds to stay with a God doesn't come to a fellow every day. Brother went through the connecting bathroom – closing both doors, against any untoward remark that may escape gracious Sister's ruby lips.

"Ettie," hissing it in her shell-like ear, "it's me, Eddie – wake up. Wolf's here."

"Bugger off."

"Keep your voice down. He wants us – "

"I heard you the first time. Tell *him* to bugger off. I'm practising Marina."

The delicate creature pulled the sheet over her head.

"Are you stark raving? I can't tell Him that."

Her ladyship flung off the sheet: her bare B*m in air. "If you won't tell him to go, tell him to come in and see. That's what Putzi says he likes."

"But Ettie, I want to go." Replacing the sheets modestly. "Ettie, please."

"Absolutely, and unconditionally not – wasn't that the expression?"

"You're not doing this to me because of the foot thing?"

"I'm doing it because I'm not going."

"All right, damn you. But *I'm* going. Even if I have to tell Him exactly what sort of self-centred, narcissistic, extroverted bitch I have for a sister."

"Tell him we'll play three little piggies for all I care. Do you want to see how it's done with your own foot?"

She spread her knees akimbo ... and slid the left heel up the right calf ... and thigh ... until it actually –

"I tried, Herr Wolf, but she's taken two of her pills. On top of wine. She's been studying too hard for Boris Godounov."

"These young women and pills! Well, never mind, she can join us tomorrow after Herr Lloyd's tea party. Chop-chop!"

Night On The Salt Mountain

With the top down, and the night wind streaming His dark, my blond, hair.

"I had to come to see you," He said, squeezing a fellow's arm. "It went so astonishingly well! – all one could think of was your so-noble mother, with her dreams for our countries in the New Europe. One had to say 'thank you', Ederl, can you understand that? The vision of one Europe! Great buildings again to be proud of instead of stainless steel boxes, cooping up a man's spirit like so many chickens! No longer should artists daub excrescence-cubes of horseshit, like Picasso. Where is there the evidence of even one single picture by a Jewish artist to show us the glory of nature? I don't know of any – but I'm not going to be sidetracked by Them either, on a triumphant night like this. They have their place – but not in Germany."

Obersalzberg: a sleeping village with few lights, and the lower miles of its Salt Mountain are behind us. The Mercedes' snout lunges upwards. Pillboxes flash by, with their barriers lifted. Their guards' Heils follow from post to post in a fading, triumphant echo ... Siegfried's triumphant progress up the Rhine. The guard posts are set before and after every hairpin corner. At random intervals more guards with dogs show in the Mercedes' headlights behind the wires.

By moonlight, Mama's picnic chalet is turned by Klingsor shadows to

Hagen country. At the entrance to what has become His castle, a rapid stop. A flurry of guards and aides spring forward.

"No business tonight –!" waving them away – "tell Frau Angela, if she's awake, our guest has arrived. Ederl, we'll have chocolate as a nightcap and you can play me *Rosenkavalier*." And then, as two Alsatian dogs come bounding, "Blondi, Wolfi, do you love me? Do you?" as they wag and lick Him. "Good beauties. Say hullo to my Ederl –" and then as they turn their attentions – "ah, you like him. I knew you would. We see eye-to-eye on people, don't we? Down now! Down, you brutes or Papa will have to get the whip!"

The Lickable One crosses a marble expanse of floor that once was a wooden porch, and up some broad steps, bypassing what had been the front-room parlour, to a study above it that is almost an exact replica of Siegfried Wagner's. Gemütlich. Another Bechstein in an alcove. A fire burns to keep off the chill.

"So! What do you think of my little Siegfriedhaus in the mountains?"

"It's grown, Herr Wolf. Like the beanstalk."

Fee-fie-fo-fum – and here I have my Englishman!

He chuckled and clapped me on the arm. This rare display set the dogs leaping again. "You brutes. I'm away for an hour and you forget all your lessons! No bones for you tomorrow. Ah, Angela, Liebchen, you remember Herr Edwin, from the old days, with the noble Gräfin, his mama?"

"I remember," Angela Raubal, half-sister, housekeeper, mother of dead Geli. "You ordered two rooms," she said accusingly to Half-brother, "and waiting up half the night. It isn't good enough."

"The Gnädiges Fräulein Edwina couldn't be with us – indisposed; it's a lady's privilege. You go on along to bed yourself, Liebchen." Amazingly conciliatory. "Ederl and I are going to have a little music."

"You said not to be late, with Herr George returning tomorrow."

"And we shan't be. Off you go, like a good woman. One of the kitchen girls can send in our chocolate."

"They'll do no such thing! I shall see to the chocolate."

"Our ladies!" Behind His sister's back, Half-Brother rolled His eyes to the ceiling, but was still smiling. "Ederl, start with the overture and give me a melody – faster than normal. Old Richard Strauss stole the

Zarathustra opening from Rheingold, but I've really grown quite fond of his race-course tempi."

The hot chocolate arrived with the disapproving face of Angela. An extra pot on the side of the tray was heaped with spare cream. Half-Brother blew steam off the top of His cup.

"Drink up, there's a good fellow."

He strokes His dogs' heads, and murmurs to them – but His eyes watch – until the Fool sips. . . . Safe from poison, He slurped down His chocolate, appropriating all the extra cream. Edwin exhausted the C-P repertoire of operetta – exhausted himself.

"That's it! What fun this evening has been. And what a day to come tomorrow! I'll show you your room, and in the morning we'll see all the changes I've made since your dear mother's time."

We left the study and walked with the dogs up another half-flight, onto a landing.

"My guests' suite is here. This room of yours has quite the best view in the building. Fräulein Ettie's is beside it when she joins us. I myself am in my soldier's cell, down there at the end. Gut' Nacht, mein Ederl."

And then –?

He walks alone with His dogs to the end of the passage, and unlocks the door to the white room, and lets one dog go in to sniff, and search, and then calls the animal out again, and goes in Himself, and closes the door, and locks it, from inside, with a *click*.

. . . *Morning:* Waking to full sun, streaming through muslin curtains . . . in a strange bedroom, wondering where? – with whom? The room has been decorated by a man's eye: a middle-class man who likes flounces and brass birdcages – but the bird is flown. Or not yet caught and trapped. A large oil of a reclining nude hangs on the wall facing the flounced bed. The nude's face is familiar, yet indeterminate . . . then realising: it's a composite of all His women. His name is on the bottom corner, sloping.

Out into the hall: His door is still shut. One of the Alsatians still lies on the mat. It wags with a thump; no other move. Beside the dog, on the wall facing the door of what was to be so-Gracious Ettie's room, hangs *HIM*, by Hoffmann. The hypnotic eyes could have drilled through the door – and if they had they would have hypnotised that nude.

358

A smell of coffee: it takes Edwin's attention from the pictures and leads down the half-flight of stairs past the rubbersoled guards into a small dining-room, Family-sized, with wooden wainscoting, bright-painted flowers, and chintz – and fret-work Storm Browns on the chandelier.

"Good morning, Herr Edwin, sit down, sit down. Today is a Lazy Day."

Sister Angela in a better mood this Faulenzertag morning. She pours Kaffee and puts down a fresh roll and butter, as Herr Edwin sips.

"Thank you. But I should really wait for Herr Wolf, for breakfast."

"Breakfast, young Herr – that one doesn't eat breakfasts!"

Two braided Nordic dumpling-girls enter, carrying covered plates. Edwin's contains fried eggs, ham, green tomatoes, and pancakes. Angela Raubal's, one soft-boiled egg.

"You shouldn't have gone to so much trouble, Frau Raubal. A boiled egg would have been ample."

"In Germany a boy eats a man's breakfast."

Half-sister gives a slight toss of her head. The Nordic serving-maid bobs a Knicks at Herr Edwin.

"So – she didn't come with you?"

It takes a moment to realise that "she" means Ettie. "No, Frau Angela. My sister was tired from practising a new role – she's never sung in Russian."

"My Geli also. She used to be tired, and then Adolf would buy her a bird cage or re-decorate her bedroom."

Angela Raubal pretends to be eating her egg, but is watching her guest acutely. More poison, Mein Herr?

"I remember the birdcages, Frau Angela. I remember Geli, too, of course. She was very pretty."

"She thought you were too handsome. A golden Siegfried. You've seen her room upstairs – with that picture? How he can paint such a thing! The room is for *her* – your sister, the Fräulein Edwina! – you know this."

Half-sister stared over her egg with open hostility.

"For Ettie –?" the woman makes no sense – "my dear Frau Raubal, until last night, neither my sister or I would ever have dreamt of staying in Herr Adolf's house, or of inconveniencing you for a breakfast."

"Re-decorating a bedroom is no dream, young man. Your sister has her eye peeled since before his gun shot my Geli. And in Berlin – the actress, Renate Müller – it's terrible. What people are saying. 'Die blöde Kuh', at least that little Munich slut has a brothel of her own. Not in a decent house!"

Don't tell me! The guest pushed his chair away from their table.

"Mein Gott, what have I done? Mein Herr, forgive me!" For a solid chunk of woman, she can move fast – before Eddie to the door. "Herr Edwin, I'm distraught – you can understand, a mother. It's the anniversary of her death, my Geli."

A gentleman can afford to be generous in victory, Edwin – and she was too massive to toss aside.

"You have my sympathy, Frau Angela. I didn't realise the significance of the date. I take it I can express your apology in return, to my sister, if not to Fräulein Braun?"

"*The Braun*!" Shock, horror, rage, marked by the movement of her eggy lips, transforms Angela Raubal's face as swiftly as it can Half-brother's. "Not your sister – if only it was – or Frau Winifred – at least they're ladies. The room must be for *her* – My God! – In my house – Eva Braun, that cow!"

At which Angela Raubal burst into tears, and her guest went walking.

He didn't come down until past noon. "Ha! Ederl, you've been out for fresh air. Good fellow. They say there's less oxygen at this altitude, but quite frankly I don't believe it. One feels infinitely better up here than on the plains, and as for the sea-shore! I can't stand it!"

"You'd like the Mediterranean, Herr Wolf. You should come to our island for a visit. Perfect privacy once you're there."

"It has to be Greece first. Pericles was an architect, also, which endears me. 'The Olympian' the Athenians called him. Who else would have thought of extending Athens landward? Remind me to talk to the old Welshman about Pericles when your sister gets here."

The Arrival:
Edwin watches from the terrace. The Goat-elbow-gripping, the hand-pumping, the gesturing and smiling, plus Megan, & Lord Ghoul, & the

360

Secretary (plus cine-camera), & Schmidt (His miraculous interpreter), & both Ribbonsnobs (out of view of the Archbishop of Canterbury!) and –

No Sister.

Only the Secretary silently recording for Posterity. The brief Shadow on His face when He sees She isn't.

"Where the hell is damn Ettie?" Edwin whispers, behind the proscenium. "She can't possibly still be in bed."

"Your sister got away on the early train for Berlin."

Leaving brother to bear the brunt for rejecting a Special Invitation.

"Your very own Olympus," the Goat is saying to Pericles. "How it must lift the spirit to walk here with the gods. Megan, do you realise, we're higher than Ben Nevis? Can you not show a little more enthusiasm, girl?"

The Wizard's daughter has her sulking-Pekingese look. Your black-valley Welsh can out-Hagen Hagen any day when they aren't in the mood for Eisteddfod song & dance.

"There are thirteen of us in the group," she grumped, "because Edwina wouldn't come."

"Stuff and nonsense," cries her aged Parent to his Host, briskly. "Thirteen has always been my lucky number. Tell me now, what's that mountain over there?"

"Mount Mausoleum, Herr George, at least this is what I've called it. I'm going to have myself buried under it when the time comes. The peak to the left is Charlemagne's, so one shall be in good company – but not before tea, I hope."

And LAUGHTER! – with the whole Company On-Camera for:

MR WOLF'S TEA PARTY

MR WOLF, MR GOAT, YOUNG EDWIN, AND EXTRAS:

MR GOAT

... In good company indeed! And if I may say so, for the first time in a thousand years this trouble-wracked continent has found the man who truly may lead it forward to Charlemagne's vision. The Cromwell of

361

Germany you are – and I assure you, Fuehrer, I don't say that lightly. In my opinion the Lord Protector is the very greatest of our British leaders.

MR WOLF
(clearing throat with deep emotion)
Herr George, all my life Oliver Cromwell has been *my* hero. Until this century, I considered him to be the greatest man of England. Now, another joins them.

The two MODERN PROTECTORS (one *dark round-head*, one *white long-haired*) gaze with Admiration into each other's eyes.

MR GOAT
And if you, Fuehrer, had been Germany's leader in 1914 the nations of Europe would never have slipped and slidden over the precipice into a war that no one wanted. That disaster was caused by weak men. Peace is gained through strength and sureness. That strength Germany now has in you, so that through you, in sureness, Europe may at last *know* peace.

MR WOLF
Herr Lloyd, the Allies won that war, but not through their soldiers – excellent fellows though they were – however that's water from the Rhine. No! The Allies won because a Great Statesman rallied the people. 'Victory!' you said. 'Victory today, tomorrow, and always!' Who could fail to be stirred by such a cry? – but it goes without saying that if *I* had been Leader of Germany instead of being shot at by blackskins of the French –!

MR GOAT
(cutting in)
Now that's what I like about you – and I've said this before – 'Herr Hitler's a cannonball,' I've said. 'No

deceits! No feints! He declares his objective –' and by
God, sir you get it. Rather differently to our friend
Ribbentrop, here, who is more like our other friends,
the Americans, who always want to jawbone their way
around a problem. Mark you, the bible tells us that
much was accomplished with the jawbone of an ass.

MR WOLF

Herr George, that's precisely why I've sent him as my
Ambassador. You wouldn't want a cannonball arriving
in London!

Fresh LAUGHTER – *except* from RIBBENSNOB! in mutual esteem new
GREAT ONES sit down to *truly* High Tea. The FUEHRER *wolfs* honeycake,
tells *Mein Fox'l* stories, and VOICE Choosing.

MR GOAT

(Exclamming! – honey on chin)
Now here's an amazing thing! The very same happened
to me – except that it was my own voice. Climb a tree, I
used to, as a lad, to read my *Euclid*, right at the
tippy-top. And one day I said to myself, 'Dai –' that's
our Welsh for Davy – 'Dai, what a remarkable fellow
you are, a cobbler's stepson to be reading *Euclid* up in a
tree, but *why* are you doing it boyo?' And then, quick as
a flash, I answered myself. 'I *am* special. I am *astonishing*.
Dai-boy, I do believe I am a *Genius*!' And so perhaps I
was, before the electorate saw fit to disagree . . .

Wolf-Boy from Lambach, to cheer up His New Friend, swiftly produces
silver frame, and signs *large* Portrait in *Hun-Gothic*, sloping *down* to *right*:

MR GOAT

(husky, accepting pic. of New Friend)
Nothing must ever come between us. Whether God
grants that I am in the government or not, if there
should be a problem between our nations we two must

363

talk it out. That must be a promise between us. And you must come to London and be welcomed by the British people.

CUT TO:

MR WOLF – looking across to YOUNG EDWIN.
MR WOLF – smiling; strange, musing smile.
MR WOLF – spreading bitten hands: Who knows?

CUT TO:

MR GOAT
(*very* insistent)

I know – it will happen. The time will come, and soon – if not for the Coronation with Lohengrin – for you to make your mark on London.

BLACK OUT

Departure:

With more elbow-gripping. Edwin too was pleased that Tea had gone well, even if the C-Ps did nothing material to oil the wheels – and then I realised He had not said a thing to me – not even about Ettie – during the whole performance.

He waved goodbye, watching as the convoy of cars passed through the faithful, surging suddenly forward at the gate, in case . . . They fell back, disappointed. A chill wind gusted across the valley from the ice of His Mausoleum Mountain.

The Wolf lowered His hand. The Goat was gone, with Signed Photograph & London Invitation. *He* turned on His heel and walked back up His mountain-palace steps – right past me, and disappeared.

The Fool stared after Him. No one approached me – as though Edwin wears the Tarnhelm of invisibility, yet I knew they could see me. He must have state business, the Fool thought. Papers to sign, decisions to make. But the thug-aides came back and He wasn't with them. The Fool sat alone in the vast room, looking out at the mountains with purple evening falling on them through the magic window.

364

And ate supper, in the small Family dining-room, alone – except for the Storm Browns on the chandelier – even Half-sister had deserted me. After supper the Fool read a Grail book, alone, in light not good for reading. Then up the stairs, past the rubber-soled guards, to the private corridor with His hypnotic picture, and to bed. And for the first time in five years, dream – of the Tower, and burning sand by black water, except that in this dream the dreamer heard Him and Angela Raubal up in the tower, screaming. . . .

Another morning on the Salt Mountain: like yesterday's, with cooing doves and sunshine, but no sign of either a screaming Angela or Half-brother, at breakfast. The Fool thought, I'm going back to Ettie –

But he had vowed his Foolish vow. I won't break it. Let her stew in Berlin. I'll ask for a car to take me down to my luggage at the Grand, to set off again on my Search – only there is no one to ask, except impassive Black Orders and a serving girl.

I'll walk – just decided – when He reappeared.

As usual, just there, in the middle of the great Hall, as a visiting deputation of Browns arrive for some form of Mowgli prizegiving. He doesn't see His other guest – or chooses not to! Confused completely, the Fool hovers at the entrance to the drawing room. Then, Bugger this, I'll ask. "Herr Wolf –?"

The thug-faces show their usual shock at our Family Circle name. He turns half to me – as a Brown in the deputation draws a pistol, and fires.

And because of His turn to me – by a miracle, misses.

Shouting in the Hall, and pandemonium. The Brown assassin lay in blood on the marble. The Target stood on the bottom step of the main flight, looking down at the body. His face was white. His hands were slightly trembling. He put them in His pockets . . . took them out, to shake the hands of the Parsifal Knights who had saved His life. Without any word or nod to His Fool, He turned away and walked swiftly up the stairs, leaving behind Him a hive swarming.

The whole thing had a Festspielhalle unreality. I'll go up to my room, thought the Fool; that will give them time to mop the floor and remove the body; then I'll leave – on Shanks' pony, if necessary. At the private passage, the rubbersoled Black Order salute, so the Fool at least is real – if they are, and not just phantoms of Parsifal.

365

I came to the door of my room, next to Ettie's, or Eva's, or Geli's, or Winifred's, or –

It was not Geli's room.

Her room is on the other side of the passage, through a door the Fool hasn't noticed because of the hypnotic Portrait. Next to His white cell, the Fool sees an interior court, a grotto, like something of Ludwig's. Geli was in it. Or, rather, her catafalque was, of bronze, and black granite, with her picture, and the effects of a young girl frozen in time.

Her half-Uncle sits in a chair, staring at her casket. A blue vase holds white blossoms of rare Edelweiss.

"Herr Wolf –?" from the Fool – "I don't mean to intrude, but I'm leaving, and I thought I should thank – "

"What's the point if she won't see me?" His voice is a monotone. His blank eyes stay locked on the bronze casket.

"I'm sure she will see you. Mama firmly believed in an after – "

"When? How long does she expect to keep me waiting?"

"I suppose it depends." He can't mean Mama – *can He*? "Time may be different in the life beyond, Herr Wolf, with Geli."

"Don't be an idiot. There's nothing beyond. I mean your sister."

"Ettie?" The Fool's wits are as slack as his jaw.

"How much must I sacrifice for her?" The dull eyes quicken slightly with self-pity. "This girl died for her. If it hadn't been for you calling out I'd be dead myself because of her – don't tell me I'd have been seeing those moron SA shitheads if Edwina had been here! And when we do meet ... Mock! Scorn the guttersnipe from Lambach! Oh yes! The look in her eyes that day in the Regentstrasse apartment. That smile and laugh about my overstuffed furnishings and pictures – your noble mother never had that laugh. The Leader of the Country's own simple house isn't good enough. Intolerable! Well it can't go on. Come!"

Galvanised, He sprang to His feet, lunged past the Fool to the grotto door and, as I hesitated, grabbed my arm. "*Come!*"

Almost running, almost dragging, out and down the corridor with its hypnotic Portrait and rubberised guards, over the blood on the marble, down the terrace stairs where he had said farewell to Goat and party, to the great Mercedes, somehow already waiting with its engine running. The mad warm wind had risen to a scream.

"One moment, if you please, my Fuehrer."

"What's this?" Bellowed, over the noise of the wind. "Damn it, Heydrich, I'm going driving."

"But in the next car, may I suggest, my Fuehrer."

"What next? What nonsense! This is my car!"

"So it should appear, my Fuehrer – but if you will allow, with this afternoon's event I've provided another."

With identical Leader Flags and markings: it waits in the lee of the Mountain wind, beside the wall of the small screened garden off the private dining room.

"Very well," curtly, in the lull, "but get on with it."

Heydrich waves the first car forward. A Leader-sized figure in cap and uniform jacket sits in the back seat.

"*Ein Doppelgänger!*"

Recoiling. Blond Moses soothing. The Fool embarking. In the blessed silence of the second car, He sinks back in the seat and bites a nail. "God knows, I'm not superstitious, like Himmler, but why tempt Fate? – it's well known, to look on one's Doppelgänger is to face Death."

The sound of a cheer blows across the alpine meadow, in the dusk. The first car has reached the crowd of worshippers at the gate. No explosions. Tristan-Heydrich heel-clicks us forward.

"In future I shall arrange three cars, my Fuehrer, and select your place by lot. And no face-to-face with Doppelgängers, as you have ordered."

Sieg Heil! – and the tiniest ghost of a shadow-message laughing up Heydrich's black sleeve.

"I haven't time in my life for these games." He rapped the glass behind His chauffeur. "Go!"

Gates, guards, dogs, barbed wire and lights. Rolling down the Salt Mountain, with its hairpin bends, the way the Fool came two nights before, but this night there is no manic Siegfried ebullience, only dark Hagen depression. He sat beside me and said not one word, until we got to the Grand, by its Hänsel & Gretel fountain, and the Fool leaned forward to be ready to get out and He said, "*Nein.*"

And the Fool said, uncertain, "But Herr Wolf, my luggage. . . . ?"

And He replied a savage "*Nein,*" again. "*Ihre Schwester!*"

In a swirl of falling, golden leaves, swinging out onto the new Munich

Wolf-road. Bloody Sister! As two escort vehicles close in from some-where, Brother could wring her neck – but then, being Piscean, the Fool rationalised. . . .

Halfway to Munich: at Rosenheim, the town of The Meeting. This time only a grunted, "Through Miesbach – the old road."

Mainly west, still, but south. A sign in the headlights:

Tegernsee.

With our first Hunding Hut and a madman crying. Now silent again, He watches trees whip by like ribbons in the Föhn's gusts, but before the lake, said "Bad Tölz" to the driver, and then, "South, through Murnau," so that the Fool thought, at last I know where we're going – back where we started, where our paths first crossed in the stars:

Oberammergau.

The moon is up on a sign: 10 Kilometres, and Christ's next return not due till 1940. Now, speeding on small border roads, with non-electric Austro-Hun villages casting only a coaching lantern's glow over the sign of an inn, and a last customer rolling home like Old Rhino-Hide to beat the wife and kick the urinating dog. Unfamiliar territory for the Fool, with no landmarks. Only this silent man, nailbiting in the night beside me. Silent until a fart – that makes Him bite more furiously than ever.

How do I roll down the window?

Even a crack will be betrayed by the screaming wind outside.

Is this why He always has the top down?

The meteoric odour dissipates with horrible slowness into leather and petrol. For the first time in my Fool's life I felt sick in a car.

"North," He said.

Christ, we've driven already 200 miles! A hamlet flashes by, with a great tree toppled onto gravestones by the wind, and now climbing a road as steep as that other one built by a dreamer up the salt mountain, Memory stirring. Climbing and twisting, with pines and fir trees swaying in endless waves like a forest sea. And then a snow-white wall in the headlights. A drawbridge. A moat. Portcullis of gilded steel like solid gold. And carved into the white stone, seared into it by a man's suffering:

Neuschwanstein

Journey's end. Mad Ludwig's New Castle of the Swan.

"Mad? – how can anyone call a man mad for wanting all the beauty money could buy? How much beauty would there be from the Wops like Leonardo without popes' money, may I ask?! Keep those cars outside, I'm going to walk with Herr Edwin alone."

The Mercedes and Black Order draw back and crouch beyond the drawbridge. An old gatekeeper, roused from sleep, stumbles to find switches for lights. He strides by, regardless. The Sleep-Walker.

"I know my way blindfold. I've studied these plans a hundred times for sets of Parsifal and Lohengrin. Mad? – what greater legacy could a man leave the world than Wagner's music and a place like this? Without Ludwig I'm convinced the Master would have killed himself. Definitely! Can you blame him? Scorned and reviled everywhere – not good enough for polite society. Mocking – like your sister! – as though Ludwig scattered castles like this in every village. (In fact there are only three in all Bavaria.) And only one that's perfect. Where we're standing." The entrance hall, with banners of fiery Fafner-dragons, couchant, and virginal Parsifal Knights rampant. "How can a man be so misunderstood? Of course, to the filth-mongers he was an 'invert', but what do such Yid-Science terms mean? Don't we all have split natures? The men that had him committed should all have been shot! Without exception! Thank God at least the poor devil took his chief tormentor with him into the lake. I've read the autopsy report – the marks on the throat of Gudden, the head keeper-swine, were definitely from the King's nails, holding the brute under while he drowned. It takes so little time. Less than a minute without oxygen and it's all over for us." A vast oil painting shows Kundry crouching in Klingsor's garden with the whore-flowers nude and fading. "Crumpling, decaying – I used to think that, looking at my Mother in her agony with the Krebs horror gnawing at her. One minute, and it can be ended. Euthanasia is the only answer for a civilised society – done without pain, it goes without saying. An injection, or perhaps gas, like the dentist, a peaceful sleep ... For two pins those shaveling Arschlöcher would have denied him burial in hallowed ground! Ludwig. Of course they came to their senses quick enough. The people would have risen in revolution if they'd known how their King was being treated. And then where would I be today? How strange Destiny is. One can't help feeling it work in a place like this. As

369

though Ludwig was watching us, every step. The poor wretched devil –
he never even got to sit on his so-magnificent Schwan Throne . . ."

In the Swan-Throne's Room: Gold and azure, with scarlet, and
angels, and archangels' busts protruding with swans from every valance
and sconce between the floor and the vaulted ceiling, lost eighty feet in
the darkness above.

"He was pilloried for extravagance – " Wolf-striding across the tiles
and up a winding stair behind the golden throne – "exactly as the
economists attack me for building roads. 'There's no money, we can't
afford it!' But I've done it. 'As Ludwig did it,' I tell those Ministry oafs.
'This castle of his which will stand for all time couldn't have cost more
than three or four battleships – that could have been sunk in an hour on
the Dogger Bank!'"

Off the winding stair into a gallery. He throws open a door.

"The Festspielhalle in miniature. His last thoughts here were of
Isolde. I know that absolutely from the letters. '*To be dissipated on the air,
among the floods of the voluptuous sea, in the resonance of the aerial waves, in
the universal breath of the All, drowned, absorbed.*'"

Oh, Oblivion, Joy supreme . . .

The overblown words, yet in that strange, guttural voice, so moving;
the unreal place, this gaudy temple for the Music perched high above
the waters of the Swan's Sea, so beautiful; the night, with the Föhn wind
howling, so –

Abruptly, He broke off His contemplation of Ludwig's private opera
hall, and opened another door to another winding spiral stair. A chill
draught rushes out with an echo of a madman's nightmare cry.

"They locked this door, on the morning they were coming to take
him, when all he wanted was to end it here, at the foot of his greatest
creation – a king's corpse smashed with its brainbox out on the cobbles!
– see the bastard-keepers explain *that* to his people!"

Round and round, and up and up, higher and higher: until an empty
room at the top of that great tower. Through a slit gothic window behind
Him the full Bayern September moon etches out the Castle of the Swan,
snow-white with blue-black moon-shadows, ecstasy in stone two hundred feet below us. And a thousand below that, the Lake of the Swan,
rippled by the howling wind of madness.

"And all for her! For our Isolde." The flush high on His pallid

370

cheeks shows the effect of His exertions. "You must tell her, Ederl. And if not, then I'll kill myself. Is this understood?"

"Ah – not exactly *completely* clear, Herr Wolf. Was it that if I don't tell Ettie that you were hurt about her not visiting with –?"

"Hurt? A man doesn't threaten to end his life, you fool, because he's HURT! I'm offering your sister what your noble mother dreamed of. The link between our countries. And if the Berghof isn't good enough, she shall have this. Neuschwanstein! Now, am I clear?"

And then –?

The Fool takes the Coward's way out and sends her His offer on a postcard from Budapest.

And then –?

She reads it aloud at a cast party for the Boris Godounov – and laughed and laughed.

And then –?

Subject 'A' lashes back with an open warning – at a secret meeting.

> *'I'm not going to challenge my opponent immediately to a fight. I don't say 'fight' just for the pleasure of fighting. Instead I say, 'I will destroy you. And now cleverness helps me to manoeuvre you into such a corner that not a blow will be struck until you get a thrust into your heart!'*

My Lady Greensleeves . . .

371

Second Movement
Fifth Passage

[tremolo]

Where are the Yeomen, the Yeomen of England?
In homestead and Cottage they still dwell in England!
Stained with the ruddy Tan,
God's air doth give a Man,
Free as the Winds that fan the broad breast of England!

... *In Spandau.* Another attack in the night: again the skeletal Hand squeezed & rattled that tremulous organ called Old Edwin's Heart – but his Russian Friends were ready with Helden measures. For a 2nd time, all the armoury of modern medicine was brought to bear on Number 7's frail Cold-War frame. Our Quadrille continues, and like thwarted Waring, my Birds hover: 3rd time lucky ...?

"We have to keep you happy, Kamerad. You like Wagner so we shall listen to Wagner."

An East Berlin record of the Dutchman, who doesn't age either. It seems the trio share a love of music: the young Soviet Lieutenant, ancient Number 7, and his ageless partner in schizophrenia, Edwin.

"For decades these great works have been perverted by Fascism in the West. The underlying reality of the Wagnerian Class Struggle with its hopes and exploitation of the Masses has been obscured. But today, thanks to Soviet scholars once more we can see the true aims from 1848."

The Master, children, resurrected as card-carrying Left-Winger? Gedanke also – she's moulting ...

373

"What are these scars?"

We had dozed off. Our arm had flopped. Our tube of life-supporting Potion had pulled out. The concerned Lieutenant was examining our Old Fool's wrist. Irony on irony: not 1 question asked of Hess's massive, missing, chunks of thorax – only the stark evidence of what Foolishness happens when Half-Cocked Eddie runs off on his own.

... *En route King Henry's East: Feb 5th, '37.* First mistake: it's Uncle Joseph's now, and guarded more zealously with Forms than it ever had been by Halberd & Mace for a Tsar. Edwin applies, through channels, from Paris. Sister was in London. We were separated as much as I had wished. Already I missed her more than I had dreamed.

Eddie the Fool sends postcards. No word comes back. He blames Europe's posts and makes increasingly elaborate arrangements for forwarding any dead-letter replies. Edwin the Scholar gets turned down again by the Abbot of Avignon and the King of Romania – also the Journal of the Royal Society for Archaeology:

> The work submitted, *Historical Vestiges in the Transit of a Grail*, shows some originality of vision but its completion, in the opinion of the Jury, is unlikely to be realized.

... With a *Post Scriptum*, by some donnish petty-f***ing hand:

> Not least through the hackneyed nature of the subject and a *paucity* of academic support!

Paucity! Edwin swore, and drank himself to the Comrades' Embassy in Paris which had swallowed his application for Kiev. Notice will now be given by the Comrades perhaps in 6 weeks, perhaps 10. A copy of *The Times* at a kiosk outside the Embassy advises that the Hon Edwina C-P's much anticipated London performance as Isolde has been cancelled because of a prolonged cold.

Brother almost telephoned ... then drove south. Then Exclammed! in desperation from Lyon:

GO PORQUEROLLES WILL WAIT TOULON WITH RILEY STOP
LOVE EDDIE.

And then hung around Toulon for a week, being importuned by naval rating matelots with acne in their striped jerseys and, when it was obvious she wasn't coming, bought one sailor, who seemed genuinely sorry, a supper, with good wine, but when he touched me the Fool fled to Hyères in the Riley, and then across with Deaf'n'Dumber on the *Cormoran* to the safer comfort of Mathilde.

... *On Porquerolles*: *"Mon enfant,"* hugging him to her fat, black-cottoned breasts, "so thin and pale! You've never been alone before. Not on your island. Won't I just give that creature a piece of my mind!"

But the creature never arrived. Eddie never had been on our island without her. Our Birthday – came and went, apart. Eddie telegraphed flowers from Hyères. No scent of them came back. I tried to compose – but every major chord came out as a diminished scrap of Wagner. I was emasculated even in my music. And at night I tossed in my dream of my Tower by the obsidian beach, with the flames, and a figure, a woman; from the back, black-robed as Mathilde, but when she turned, from the front she was white as Ettie. But with no face.

"Too much walking," said a practical peasant Mathilde. "Lie in the sun by the Lobsters and get brown."

Eddie lay alone, for three weeks past Easter among the portulacas, and imagined Ettie was there, an arm away, with her golden hair attracting bees, like honey. *Or her Venusberg thighs, catching men. . . . Like our lost friend, Pawel . . .*

More like some new friend. Some lounge-lizard rat-tenor bastard in London!

"Go to her," said Mathilde. "Bring her back. That's the best for both my darlings."

Edwin's peasant-mother loads him with hams and breads to take across the water to the Riley she cannot comprehend, any more than she could Him, or Bayreuth, from only seeing pictures.

"Come back to Mathilde soon, in one piece, my treasure. . . ."

Who waved with the best intentions as our blue Mediterranean moved between us, and her dumpy black body that loved me was reduced to a rock on the shore of our golden island. But on the road, on the continent of Europe, Dame Sorrow regains position. And no visa for Kiev from the Comrades in Paris when we got there. Perhaps in another 6 weeks, perhaps 10 . . .

Maytime in Europe. Rehearsals shall be starting at Bayreuth. *If she doesn't have another, inconvenient, cold! She knows she can't possibly do a Bayreuth hat-trick without us.*

She'll probably be at Triebschen, waiting. Michael Rau can find out. Edwin sets the Riley on course for Zürich and throws Bitch Sorrow overboard.

But Rau is away again, ruining his father's business in America. Also in Switzerland and Germany by the look of it. Advertisements appear in the Hun-Swiss papers for sale in Berlin:

> FREE PASSAGE: Be warned: popular opinion to the contrary, the undersigned advises that the Lohengrin of modern times, Adolf Hitler, will invade the Soviet Union and/or destroy the Jews of Germany (with those of Austria) commencing no later than 1939. First Class Sea Passage to Palestine will be provided for all applications received by September 1st, this year. (Estate brokering included at no charge.) Baggage limited to *two* (2) steamer trunks per adult or child. Any parties interested Contact: MICHAEL RAU In Care, The Mercantile Bank of Zürich.

The Föhn must have blown a gale over Switzerland. Say there are half a million of Them in Hunland. If 1 in 10 takes up our friend's insane offer Rau's mission in life will be accomplished with a vengeance. Edwin's mission was thwarted. Without Rau he was forced to telephone the Parrot-Sisters for an on-the-ground report from Triebschen. After a deeply suspicious maid, he got little Eva: like so many of her generation she is merely paranoid on the 'phone.

"Edwin? The Gräfin's boy? Is that you?"

"Yes, Frau Eva, it's me."

"How do I know this?"

The Gräfin's boy, after some thought, says, "I own the cottage underneath you."

"Go outside and wave to show me." Proving there is considerable logic to be found in any form of mental illness.

"I'm not there now, Frau Eva. I'm in Zürich. I want to know if my sister's there."

"Why don't you ask her?"

Edwin trapped, said lamely, "If she's outside she wouldn't hear the telephone, Frau Eva. I thought you could look."

"We are not spies!" Her parrot-tone was sharply accusing.

"I didn't mean to imply – I meant, if you should happen to be glancing through your telescope."

"Did Winifred put you on to this calling?"

"I haven't seen Aunt Winnie since last season."

"Aunt! Hah! Is that how she calls herself outside the family. That Man will be calling himself Uncle next! Well Daniella isn't here, if that's what she's after. My sister was deeply hurt not to be asked back again for the Parsifal costumes. And there can be no question about any money from the Museum!"

The sound of 2 parrots, whispering battle plans, denies the absence of brown/blue-eyed Daniella. Eddie said, on firmer ground, "I'm sure they don't need money at Wahnfried at the moment. Frau Eva; what about *my* sister, Ettie? Can you see – ?"

"It's truly too bad of you, Edwin. I have always thought you were a nice boy, despite certain rumours – ?"

"And we never spy – !" cuts in parrot Daniella – "ask Mausi."

With which the line to the cage goes dead.

In desperation the nice boy takes the Parrots' suggestion at face value and calls their niece in Bayreuth.

"I want to get a message to Ettie, Mausi. Could you ring Triebschen for me?"

"Of course I could, Eddie."

"Thank God!"

"But I don't know why I should, when she isn't there."

"She isn't?"

"Rehearsals have started. She's at the hall, wheedling Tietjen over Kundry as usual – for next year. Germaine Lubin's here for this year. From Paris, two days ago. It's marvellous. The Lubin can't speak a word of German and she's got a great buck Negro chauffeur for her Hispano

Suiza – he's the first Negro we've ever had at Bayreuth, except one in a circus in 1910! All the Wolf Maidens are cutting Lubin dead – and killing each other to dance with her black man at parties. Only, next to his French mistress he likes English Ettie best because she speaks the Frog lingo like a native. They were out half the night on a champagne picnic. She's promised to take him to your island. When shall I tell her you're coming back?"

A big buck, on our island.

With a nigger's miraculous, black, sexual organs! They're longer, and thicker. And they never grow empty.

Plunging-and-foaming, with a piebald Push-Me-Pull-You and a bumper of all-black and creamy Oskar Wildekuss to finish, in the back seat of a Hispano Suiza!

"I won't be coming back, Mausi. Goodbye."

"Goodbye, Eddie."

... *In Zürich*: Grennier's, the tobacconist's, is next to the hotel. Briar pipes, and cleaners, and pouches of supple pigskin for gentlemen. And brushes of badger-bristle, and little wooden tubs of saddle-scented masculine soap for shaving. And a straight razor, from Thüringen, with a blade in an ebony handle, as long and deadly as a Negro's gleaming prick.

"And a strop, Monsieur?" asked Grennier's.

"Isn't it already sharp?"

Please God, now I'm ready, don't deny me that!

"Sharp? But Monsieur must be joking. From Thüringen? It is to set the edge, after the using."

"I won't need a strop."

"Twenty old franks, Monsieur."

Five pounds sterling. The cost of a life without a value ...

The instrument of Death comes in a pretty box of rosewood, with brass corners and tiny hinges set in with screws so fine that they need a jeweller's glass. In Edwin's hotel room he studies them, box and hinges. Then I took out the knife that bites.

The blade extends – *snick!*

378

The bite of it feathers a testing thumb. So light is its touch that blood is impossible. Yet blood there is! One ruby drop, which is shed for Thee . . .

Ettie's blood also. Shall I leave her word?

Everyone leaves word. Make our Sister-bitch suffer.

But the terrible blade from Thüringen scared the hell out of me. Edwin put it down and went to the bath for his safety razor.

Coward! Play-actor! Wagnerian Fool!

The Safety Razor, by its name, is not built to harm. Less than a sixteenth of an inch of edge extends past its guardian shield. Enough to nick a chin, no more. The Fool proves it by drawing it across his wrist –

Scarlet.

The impossible is the colour of the cloak linings of the Three Maries, wrapping my wrist, my arm, my palm. Spurting and gouting, faster and faster, with the racing beat of my coward's heart.

Sweet Jesus no!

Christ-crucified yes. Dripping from my fingers, not drops, a stream, a flood. I stand and watch it, spreading out from me into the Swiss hotel's white wool carpet. My blood, Ettie's blood, from her bed as a girl at Trevelly; from her womb as a woman in the bath at the Griesbachs'.

Go on. Feel it. It's slippery, Eddie . . .

The Fool tries to stop it with his fingers, but it is sly, and wriggles free. A tourniquet! But when the Fool let's it go it spurts faster!

I don't want to die!

Panic's voice, screaming, into a telephone incarnadine with blood, filling the small holes of the microphone.

"Say this again, mein Herr?"

A human voice, clotting and sticky in my ear from a lobby desk. Salvation.

"An accident. I've cut – Dr Jung lives here."

"Herr Doktor Professor Jung, yes, he is here. More clearly please."

"Not here. He has a clinic in Zürich. Help me!"

"No, he is here."

"*God in heaven I'm dying. Call his clinic. Jung –* !"

"This is Carl Gustav Jung, old chap. Be a little calmer and tell me who you are?"

The God:
He had been in the lobby, but at this example of synchronicity – or from lack of blood – Edwin fainted.

"Only from shock, old chap, not loss of blood," Jung said in his gentle voice, after he had arrived, and coped, with the aid of the hotel's house doctor. "It takes more than one wrist for a young healthy animal."

"Will I have to be put in an asylum?" as I was placed on a stretcher.

"Is that what you want, old chap?"

"Never. I don't know. She doesn't need me. She doesn't love me." Sobbing, as an ambulance carried me somewhere.

"Your mother doesn't need you, old chap, but she still loves you. That part of her that's in you."

"Not my mother. My sister. It's a sin – I can't tell you."

As the ambulance was slowing, turning in to a drive and a small Swiss garden, with a number and address. 228, Seestrasse, Küsnacht, Zürich. And a legend carved in Greek letters into stone above a door:

Called or not called, the God shall be there . . .

"There's no sin you can't tell Jung, old chap – and when you have told him, then it won't be a sin any more, will it?"

He smiled at me kindly, from his vast height, but his kindness, and his riddles, were too much for me to cope with. I had summoned Death from the black beach of my dreams, and not found it wanting. Shock, and shame, rendered me mute. Jung didn't seem surprised, or to mind. He had me put to bed in a room of his house looking southeast to the source of the Rhinemaidens' river, with a window open, and no bars. And no locks on the doors. For a month this freedom was to be my prison.

"I don't want you to tell Ettie," the Failure said, that first day, as Carl Jung was leaving. "She mustn't be upset while she's rehearsing."

"If that's what you wish, old chap."

He raised his hand in a universal benediction. He closed the door. The river chattered to itself, and me, outside the window. *What we wish,* said the river, *is to show Her our blood, and have Her here, in our bed.* But it did not say, for many days, what Jung knew from the start: that the *she* in the bed of the river is always our mother.

Mama.

The God's Wife:
Emma Jung introduces herself to the Patient, next morning. Of middle height, still slim after 5 children, vivacious and attractive: the Patient thinks she looks an ideal wife and mother.

"You're looking better already," Emma Jung says, producing a breakfast tray, and speaking English. "You probably don't feel it, or like eating, but I'll leave the tray anyway, and have a cup of tea with you – unless you would rather we had coffee?"

"No. Thank you. I much prefer tea in the morning."

Shame for yesterday's action makes the Patient's speech horribly stiff and stilted, but Emma Jung doesn't seem to notice. She extends the legs of the tray and sets it on my bed and sits on a chair and pours tea in 2 large cups with ivy and gnomes on them.

"My husband's at the clinic, seeing patients. He makes an early start so that he can get back to go on with his village. Milk and sugar?"

"Yes. Please." And then, desperate for something, anything, to say; "He treats patients in a village as well as the clinic?"

Emma Jung laughs, a nice sound for a May morning, and passes the Patient a gnome-cup. "Not medicine. He's building the village – by the lake, just outside your window."

The lake is the Zürich See. Why had the Patient thought it was a river? Why had he slashed his wrist? He said to the builder's wife:

"I didn't realise you had so much land. It looked like a small garden when I arrived."

"It is rather," Emma Jung said cheerfully. "May I have a slice of your toast if you're not going to eat it all? With our early start I get peckish by mid-morning."

Peckish. Again as married couples do, she had picked up her husband's old-chapisms of English speech. "Of course you can have a slice, Frau Jung." Out of habit, polite Patient passed the plate. Bringing it back, and watching her crunch a bite, out of habit he crunched one himself. The butter was melted, with the almost rancid tang of farm-made.

"Oh God, I feel the most awful fool."

"Parsifal is," Emma Jung said. "At least he inspires awe in me. Innocence combating evil seems especially precious in our modern age."

"I suppose. Frau Jung – "

"Frau Emma, please."

"Frau Emma." And we smiled, as friends do, with the 1st first-names. "I had no idea that I'd be disturbing you in your own house. Your husband was probably being kind because of my mother, but I can't allow the inconvenience to go on."

"The inconvenience, Edwin, my dear, would be if you left us and I lost an expert on the Grail."

"You're interested?" The Patient is, despite a throbbing in his wrist.

"A fanatic," said Emma Jung. "I had hoped we could make an exchange. You and I telling each other what we know about our addiction, and in between, when my husband isn't busy, he can explain some of the things that make living with Richard Wagner's music so difficult."

"It's living with my sister. Or not – I haven't seen her for seven months. I hoped on my own I could make some real progress on the sites along the route of the Grail. What I think is the route. No one else does. I just got a stinking letter from the Royal Society. It's like Wolf, or Schliemann with Troy, just because you don't have a formal qualification the so-called experts, who've never thought of your idea before, look down on you. And Ettie, after all I did for her with accompanying, and arranging travel, and listening endlessly to her terrors before every new role . . ."

The Patient finds that he's crying. Tears dropping, plopping, and congealing the butter on his soggy slice of toast.

"Loving another human being is a painful occupation," said Emma Jung, "but perhaps less painful than trying not to. Do you remember in Malory, when Arthur's dying and he makes Sir Bedivere take Excalibur back to the lake where it was born? And you realise – for the first time after so many childish readings – as the sword sinks into the waters, with a terrible sadness you know that the whole magnificent structure of the Round Table is going to crash with it down into the Dark Ages. It's like that at the moment for the spirit of Western man. You and your sister have been living at the heart of that darkness. Don't be surprised or ashamed, because you're now aware and afraid. With awareness, and love, and my man Jung, it is possible to find the splinters and bring the Table back to the centre of a sane existence. I'll have Nurse come in to

382

change the dressing on your wrist when you're finished with your tea."

So began our task of gathering the splinters of Self awareness. Emma Jung left. Nurse changed the dressing and inspected the stitches, and gave the Patient a sedative which made him drowse for most of the day, until he heard a clink of metal on stone, repeating in a rhythm like Alberich's and Mime's anvils, and curiosity drew him to the window. Carl Gustav Jung was below me, building his village. Cottages, a school, a half-completed church waiting for a steeple.

"Hullo, old chap." He straightened his long back and waved a masonry trowel in my direction. "Emma tells me you're going to help her on the Grail. Perhaps when you're stronger you'll give me a hand out here with my village."

The construction site is only Lilliput. This giant of the human mind plays with houses for dolls! Granted they were made from stone.

"It's the closest we frail men can come to a forever," Jung said, with his wire specs pushed up, owlish, on his forehead, "working in stone. I do it for the little creature spirits of the lake. I think it's important at a time when the Zeitgeist is getting rather out of whack for ordinary folk, what with blokes like Einstein, who's turned Newton's apple on its head, that we have something *real* to focus our attentions, don't you?"

"I'd like to help," the Patient said, "but I'm not much good with my hands."

"Don't worry about skill, old chap – it's surprising what we can accomplish by piling one rock on top of another."

The Village:
It *is* surprising. Stone by stone, splinter by splinter, with Frau Doktor Emma in the sunny mornings, and her man Jung in the late May afternoons, the spirit rises like the Lilliput church we build together in the garden at the edge of the lake. By the time the steeple points, the Patient understands the basics: that each of us is Wotan; that at least one woman hides in every man, and a man in every woman.

We did not talk about a brother physically getting inside his sister! The Jungs didn't ask, and the Patient didn't tell them. We talked of his castle dream instead, and he learned of growing up – *individuation* – which is what his fleeing the castle meant. And my nudity on the leaping

383

horse signified my readiness for adolescence, or manhood; and the pursuing figure in the darkness was the shadow, Old Ego – or more likely, lost Our Father – with the women in front, half black-robed, half-white, as Mama and my split feminine nature. And the black obsidian beach was the boundary of life itself.

"And the flames?" the Patient asked Carl Jung.

"They separate you from the water of the sea. Your Self has been afraid of looking into the water in case it gets out of its depth – a jolly bad joke but we *are* all afraid of what we might see when we look deep inside; that's why we reject it. Particularly for us men, recognition of our feminine anima."

Wolf, Roehm, Waring, Eddie: homo-eroticism makes strange bedfellows. And love at first sight is our Self's mirror image. "I think I am beginning to see," the Patient said, "but why are the flames that terrible colour like my blood?"

"You've answered your own question, old chap. Although no interpretation is an absolute, the flames this time I should say *are* your blood. The symbol of renewal, and rebirth – it brought you to the knife, which brought you to me."

True. Except that I hadn't told him about Ettie, and the blood at Trevelly in her nursery bed. One thing was left in the dream.

"And finally, the tower?"

"Ah yes," said Jung, "the tower. Well that's pretty easy to explain."

"A phallic symbol?"

"Too easy. Leave the phallus for my friend Freud." Jung chuckled, as professional friends do, when they aren't any longer. "The tower is your consciousness waiting for you to finish building it, instead of running away from it. When at last you come to it, and climb it – when individuation's complete – some day you will see your life whole, and your place in it."

" 'Childe Roland to the dark tower came.' "

> *Once more the waters, yet once more!*
> *And the waves bound beneath me as a steed*
> *That knows his rider.*
> *But hush! hark! a deep sound strikes like a rising knell!*
> *And there was mounting in hot haste.*

All ashes to the taste.
The castled crag of Drachenfels
Frowns o'er the wide and winding Rhine.
To fly from, need not be to hate, mankind . . .

"That's it exactly," said Jung. "Poets know these things instinctively, but each of us has our own tower waiting somewhere, although most of us finish our journey without coming close to finding it. But you've made a promising start, old chap. I'd say you're a good third of the way home."

Visitor's Day:
In the Patient's 4th week, as he's slaving in the Lilliput village, shaping the church steeple, Michael Rau unexpectedly drops from the sky.

"I flew from Le Havre. That's a change of pace for an archaeologist, Eddie – building up something new, instead of tearing it down to get at the old."

"I'm enjoying it, Michael. I mightn't have started building if you'd been here in Zürich when I arrived. I suppose you've heard of my stupidity at the hotel. The whole town must be talking. I was simply the most colossal ass."

"The whole town," said Rau, "is talking about your Little Fellow's wedding to Frau Simpson. What about supper? I've found a new place here in Küsnacht."

"I'll have to ask the Jungs," the Patient said, evading. "I don't know if I can leave the village before the church is finished."

But Jung was at the clinic, and Emma was making a copy of one of my maps of the Grail route to be worked in embroidery as some mysterious present for her husband. "Edwin, dear, you're not seriously suggesting the village is a prison?"

"Only of my own creation, I realise that now, but it doesn't make it seem less real. I'm afraid if I should drink with Rau the feelings might start again."

"I can almost promise you they won't," she said, "and even if they do, just tell yourself, 'I have to help Jung tomorrow, and with my fair complexion, I don't need to shave this evening!' Enjoy your dinner."

Emma Jung waved the Patient away with a kiss, and he did enjoy it, once I got over the idea that the whole world was looking at my wrist.

The scar was extra livid against the whiteness of dress cuff.

Rau said, "Wear your watch on that side, Eddie – I'm having another helping of this crayfish soup. Tell me what it's like being part of the Middle Ages with old Jung. I hear he's gone off on alchemy and astrology now."

"Not literally, about lead into gold." Edwin was a new disciple, and defensive. "He means the transformation of one state of mind into another. I don't fully understand it, but the decoding of the old alchemists' books is fascinating. They all formed a sort of secret society under the noses of the church to keep what they were doing from the Inquisition. And if we're talking about going off on things, I saw your advertisements – you're as potty as I am. Apart from Wolf killing the Jews of Germany, you can't seriously expect your father to pay for all of them to take a First Class cruise to Palestine."

"It won't be all," Rau gnawed flesh from the carapace of a crawfish tail. "So far, I've had an even dozen replies, and half of those backed out after they thought about it. 'If you hit us, do we not bleed – *please!*' Can you think of anything more masochistic than to tell the world you're the chosen people, without a standing army to back it up? I only ran the advert as a bit of a giggle, as the delicious Edwina might say. Besides, her friend the Blond Moses will be paying in the long run, not my father. He's moving to America."

All true. Heydrich and the Black Order are financing mass emigration of *Them* – the fly in the ointment being that They pay for it, through confiscation of Their property.

"And serve the fools right," said Michael Rau. "Edwin, old friend, you wouldn't believe it – even though I offered, as part of my experiment, to arrange valid sales at no commission and have the funds set up here in our bank, my fellow Juden won't touch it. 'He takes no commission?' they say, clacking their damn phylacteries. 'Oi, what kind of a goy trap is that, Abie?!' Eddie, I wash my hands of them." Using a finger bowl and hot towel, before a course of venison in blood and madeira gravy on a Saturday.

Rau's anti-semitic Father-games have always been a mystery – and a lot of wasted effort – but an attempted suicide is in no position to cast stones at irrational acts of others. To whit:

"Putzi?" 2nd Surprise: a vast shadow fell across our table.

"Eddie-pal!"

The Management of the place provide an extra-sturdy chair. Edwin's Giant friend looks happier than he has in years.

"You're dead right I'm happy. That bastard Goering tried to wipe me out! Right now I'm on my way to London with Egon, I've got him in at St Paul's to finish his schooling. The Mitfahrt's responsible. She really is a 'fellow traveller' now – a positive shadow to Adolf, although that won't get the lady what she's looking for between the legs. I hear she stands nude on her head for him – anyhow, a few months ago yours truly made the mistake of saying to Unity Mitford on a yacht that, with all due respect to the gallant dead, in the next war I'd rather be in the front lines than stuck in New York like the last one. She rushes back to the Good Soldier, and the balloon goes up! Me with it. Let's have champagne to celebrate!"

As . . .

3rd Reich Productions Presents

PUTZI'S GREAT ESCAPE!

Script & Direction by Fats Hermann

FADE IN ON:

AN EXTERIOR SCENE:

> MUNICH, *the Hanfstaengl House, and we –*
> CAMERA THROUGH *French Doors to –*

AN INTERIOR SCENE

> *The* LOBBY *with the* red-and-green Picasso
> Woman.
> *Under her 3 heads and 6 eyes, we* HEAR a
> TELEPHONE. PUTZI HANFSTAENGL picks it up.
> He's astonished *as a* Personal Message *arrives
> from –?*

THE LEADER'S VOICE
(for it is indeed He! – curtly barking)
Mister Hanfstaengl, you must fly to Spain

immediately! Our Press correspondents there
are in danger! Don't worry, I'll send Bauer,
my personal pilot.

> PUTZI
> (*astonished*)

Danke, mein Fuehrer – but I have on only my
cutaway and striped diplomatic trousers!

> LEADER'S VOICE
> (*briskly*)

Never mind. I'll have Ribbentrop give you a
false passport. There are shitbag enemy
patrols in the most unexpected places!

CLOSEUP of PUTZI'S FACE – *dubious is the
word, before we* –

> CUT TO

BERLIN. A STAG PARTY *at the Finnish Legation.*
PUTZI *is attending, as – a* MERCEDES *car roars
up for our giant from his jolly rival!*

> CUT TO

HERMANN HERMANN, *Reichspräsident and
Feldmarschall, Chief of Forces of the Air!
The door* OPENS . . . *and we are inside* –
HERMANN'S HEADQUARTERS OFFICE.

> HERMANN
> (*welcoming/hearty*)

Ha! Putzi, my old friend – watch those
Carmen gypsy bitches when you get to Spain.
They're always on heat. Half my boys in blue
have clap already!

As our PUTZI *forces a laugh,* HERMANN *pushes
himself up, and waddles around the desk.*

> HERMANN

Your cover name is August Lehmann, and

you're an interior decorator (*Makes "queers" flouncing gesture*). Check your chute! Good luck, and Heil Hitler!

HERMANN *chuckles, and we —*

CUT TO

A LUFTWAFFE AIRFIELD and a HEINKEL BOMBER.
No seats. Only hand-grenades *festoon the ribbed metal walls. Parachute straps are* not *made to fit a giant! Two* BLACK LEATHER MEN *(with a Leika camera) are along for the ride . . .*

CUT TO

TAKEOFF . . .
Followed by a mystery summons for PUTZI *to attend the* PILOT.

PUTZI
(first shock)

You're not Bauer!

PILOT FRODEL
(for it is he)

Captain Frodel, at your service.

FRODEL *gestures,* Close the cockpit door! PUTZI *closes it. Then,* conspiratorial.

PILOT FRODEL

Aren't you Dr Hanfstaengl?

PUTZI

Of course I'm Hanfstaengl.

PILOT FRODEL

I thought you were Hanfstaengl. It says you are Lehmann but I've seen you in pictures.

389

Deeper puzzlement: if there's another man in
Germany that looks like Putzi Hanfstaengl, der
Fuehrer's a monkey's Onkel!

PILOT FRODEL

What, Herr Doktor Hanfstaengl, may I ask
are your instructions?

PUTZI
(*resigned*)
I am to go to the Grand Hotel in Salamanca.

PILOT FRODEL
(*now* he's *astonished*)
Who said you were going to Salamanca?

PUTZI
(*rolling eyes*)
The Fuehrer said Salamanca.

PILOT FRODEL
(*worried*)
Herr Doktor Hanfstaengl, I have no orders
for Salamanca.

PUTZI
(*exasperated*)
What orders *do* you have Captain Frodel?

PILOT FRODEL
(*after a* significant *Pause*)
To drop you over the Red lines between
Madrid and Barcelona.

PUTZI
(*astounded*)
You must be mad! Frodel, this is my death
sentence! Who gave you such insane orders?!

PILOT FRODEL
(*stiffly*)
They are signed by Goering's person. Two
minutes before takeoff in a sealed envelope.
Herr Doktor, orders are orders. I was told you
had volunteered for this deadly mission.

PUTZI
Volunteered?!!!

CUT TO

OUR PUTZI'S FACE – *outraged. He is* imagining
– A SPINNING NEWSPAPER HEADLINE: *As it
stops we see it's in* Der Völkische Beobachter

FOREIGN PRESS CHIEF
HANFSTAENGL LOSES LIFE
ON SECRET MISSION

CUT TO

Pilot FRODEL, *he is a* good *German, a decent
man. Moments later – to* PUTZI'S *alarm –*

ONE ENGINE COUGHS *fortuitously, and fails.*

PILOT FRODEL
(*urgent, to* BLACK LEATHER)
Emergency! We must set down!
(*but* winking *at* PUTZI!)
Waldpolenz, just outside Leipzig.

CLOSEUP OF PUTZI'S FACE – *relief! Then
scheming...*

CUT TO

A SMALL CIVILIAN GRASS AIRFIELD, *deserted,
in thick pine trees. Our giant friend spies a
donkey cart, with an old* PEASANT WOMAN.

391

PUTZI
(jumping in, cart sags)
To the railway station, little mother!

THE DONKEY *staggers off* —

CUT TO

LEIPZIG PLATFORM: *Where — Horrors!* PILOT
FRODEL *and* BLACK LEATHERS *are already
waiting!*

CUT TO

PURSUIT SCENE:
Over PLATFORMS, *through* COMPARTMENTS,
in TAXIS . . .
races our wheezing giant, PUTZI, *telling lies and
badly frightened.*

UNTIL, *finally,* 5 *hours later* —

LAST CUT

ZÜRICH, *from the* AIR, *with* PUTZI, *rejoicing
with his son,* EGON, *as church bells ring and
pigeons fly up past a Madonna and* —

BLACKOUT.

ENDE DES FILMS
Followed by
The Cartoon

Office of the Air-Minister,   BERLIN, W8
and Reichspräsident.   File 6841.
19 March 1937

Lieber Hanfstaengl!
    According to what I've been told today, you're now
in Zürich, and do not intend — for the time being — to
return to Germany.
    I assume the reason for this is your recent flight in
Saxony. I assure you, dear fellow, the whole affair was

392

intended only as a harmless joke. We wanted to give you an opportunity of thinking over some rather too-audacious utterances you have made. Nothing more was ever intended.

I consider it vitally necessary, for various reasons, that you come back to Germany straight away. I assure you on my word of honour that you can remain here amongst us as you have always done in complete freedom. Forget your suspicions and act reasonably.

With friendly greetings,

Heil Hitler!

Hermann Goering.

P S. I expect you to accept my word.

...*At the Village:* The Patient takes the Hermann Letter at face value – a Marx Brothers' custard pie paying off one-too-many Adolf stories – a prank of power, but not truly lethal. Putzi will be back in Nibelheim when the wind turns. It's the Patient's own return that concerns: how ever to meet again the sister who doesn't give a damn?

"I miss her terribly," the Patient confesses to Emma Jung, with black coffee and Dame Sorrow, next morning. "It isn't just being hung-over from champagne. Listening to Putzi gossip, it all came back. His house in Munich where we had such fun so many times. Frau Emma, she hasn't written one word! With this Negro chauffeur she doesn't care if I live or die. I knew I never should have left the village to go with Rau last night."

"That certainly spreads the blame nicely. Why should your sister think you weren't going to live? You deliberately refrained from sending her a note about your accident, as I recall. Of course, it's much more satisfyingly painful to hear such things of our lovers at second hand."

Like a Black on our Island, from our friend Mausi!

"You can't call brothers and sisters lovers," is the Patient's blurted reply.

"You can," said Emma Jung. "My dear, you have."

A speckled thrush perched on top of the Lilliput-church steeple, and sang its spring song. Summer's. June has started. The morning sun is

393

hot. Perspiration breaks out on the Patient's brow, beneath his arms, between my legs.

"I can't talk about it."

But as Emma Jung is silent, the Patient does – disjointedly, as in a Wolf monologue, bouncing back and forth as words connect to a thought . . . to an Ash/Elm tree falling on a bath; to Blood in a nursery bed which ends a babyhood – back to the bath! with the horrid blood in the white soap froth,

"With her wanting me to touch it – "

Or worse.

But the Patient did not say that to Emma Jung: what *worse* might be, if menstrual blood is mixed with Push-Me-Pull-You! He stopped short of mentioning even the Latin names of its 2 heads – what I had told was more than bad enough.

"In England we could go to prison. In Germany too, I suppose, except that Wolf would never do that to Ettie. Oh God, Frau Emma it's awful."

"Complicated," Emma Jung said; "this time there's nothing that inspires awe. If two healthy, extremely attractive and intelligent children are left to their own devices on a desert island listening to Richard Wagner's music, the result seems pretty straightforward to me. Edwin, you're not seriously worried about going to prison for making love now and then with Ettie?"

"It's breaking the law – and whenever she happens to be between her latest Nicholas Baers is hardly now-and-then."

"You're afraid of prison, but you want her to stay faithful to you."

In sunlight, the dark mysteries of Sex appear as ridiculous as its positions. "I don't often think of prison," the Patient admits to Emma Jung; "but why does she have to be so cruel to me when she has a new flame? Why can't we stay friends at least? She admits, the rest of the time, we *are* each other's best friends, but when she's got a new man like this nigger in the Hispano Suiza she says these horrible things about me running off after boys and men. All because of Roehm and the swan episode, and that fat swine at school with Waring, the Darling."

Which needs a week's sessions of coffee by the lake to even begin to sort out that mixed bag. And in our afternoons in the toy village Jung never alluded to the Patient's morning conversations with his wife. Then, one day a fortnight later, when the Patient had convinced himself

394

that Jung was completely without interest, he hung a little wooden gate on its hinges by our Lilliput church, pushed the wire owl-specs up on his head, straightened his long back and said, "There. That's done. But before you leave, old chap, I want you to take another week to read with me at Bollingen."

CURED!

But Jung refuses to answer any questions about what-and-where? His favourite mason's tools are gathered and put in an old portmanteau, with Edwin's travelling bag, in the back of the Riley as Carl Gustav Jung won't drive a car. We scrubbed down the Lilliput church with acid to remove mortar from the yellow stone. We said farewell to Emma. This next stage of a Fool's journey is to be with Jung alone.

"Good digging, Edwin dear. Come back in good time. Goodbye."

Emma Jung kissed me, and stood waving under the house legend of the God being there, called or not, as the Riley turned out on to the road.

"Frau Emma pretends so convincingly to believe in my Grail," Edwin said to Jung, "I almost think I do again, but there's still nowhere anywhere on the whole damn route that I can start to dig."

"You're not ready old chap, that's all. There will be when you are."

He sounded so sure. But it was I who had to wait. "I don't see how I can – surely there's a limit to waiting for anything?"

"Only when you don't want it. We take the next turning on the left and follow the lake."

... *Bollingen:* A small stone house, like one from our Lilliput village, grown-up, is planted square by the shore; like that first Hunding's Hut . . A stone embankment wall below it holds back the lapping waves. Other stones are placed here and there in the grass and trees; obelisks and crosses, with runic inscriptions carved in them in Latin, or Arabic, or Chinese, or Greek. Or Wagner's punning Hun –

Are there good Runes in Gutrune's eyes . . . ?

"Did you build all this too?" Edwin asked Carl Jung.

"I helped to resurrect it, old chap. The spirit of a dwelling had been here centuries before me. When we feel an immediate affinity for a place

395

I think it's always because someone else has stood having the same feeling, and seeing the same view. And if the feeling is especially strong they have shared the same wondering for life."

Beside us, a particularly large stone was set half into the ground. An inscription from the Mithraic Liturgy began:

> *Time is a Child –*
> *Playing like a Child –*
> *Playing a Game upon a Board –*
> *The kingdom of the Child.*

And above it was carved an eye, fairly crudely, and within the eye, on its pupil, was the reflection of another, and when I turned to see what the eye within the eye was facing . . .

"My tower!"

On a hill behind the house with trees about it: the tower of my dream, three stories, with small windows and the roof of a lighthouse to show the way across the board for playing the game of the child's life.

"No," said Jung, "it's not your tower. I built it. It's mine."

He said it sharply, savagely, as a child would say it, in a tone so different to any he had ever used that I looked at him in astonishment.

"Do you think you get to your tower without working for it, boy? I'm sixty-one years old. This is my work of a life. Find your own!"

"Yes, I'm sorry. I didn't mean. I will – "

"You did mean," said Jung, but much more kindly. "You thought you could settle in because the spirit feels familiar to you, as I knew it would. You will always be welcome here, old chap, as a visitor, but it is not the tower where you will end. Now let me show you your room, and we'll talk about what I want you to read."

Once more he's the normal, friendly Father Jung, Eddie has always known. Father Abraham, his schoolmates called him as a boy when he was starting out on the board. He leads Eddie into the house – the most wonderful house Eddie's ever been in. Every small room is decorated and painted and carved with images and legends from history and dreams.

"I want you to read Goethe," handing Eddie 2 books, "and Shakespeare – *Faust* and then *Hamlet* – and then we'll talk, but until then we shall be silent, except when I'm cooking in the kitchen, and then

396

we won't talk about the reading."

Like a religious Order. Eddie sees nothing odd in that, but the choice of reading matter surprises: the School's Boy-versions contained nothing about the Grail. Eddie can't see what's worth going back for. Nonetheless he reads both works dutifully in a little bedroom beneath the roof, fantastically decorated with winged creatures with emerald claws and ruby eyes – yet friendly, so that when Eddie falls asleep they don't return in nightmares to carry him off. Jung sleeps apart, up in his tower on the hill. The wind off the Alps strums the trees, like the Nornstrings on Erda's harp.

Three days it took to read the Prep assignment with some understanding. By the time I finished, the weather had turned. Grey rain fell on the lake and blackened the warm stones and their inscriptions. Inside the house we lit a fire with logs that Jung had split himself.

"Why these two?" I asked him. "Why Hamlet and Faust?"

"Because you've got one foot in England and one in Germany, old chap. Your English foot, Hamlet, with its mother's denial of a father's existence, made you as a child. Your German foot, Faust, is kicking you as a man. The devil exists and you're afraid of Him, as part of your nature."

"But my mother never denied my father. She even went to spiritualists to talk to him."

"But the 'father' she found, and brought back, and kept in front of you, old chap, was not the real father. By keeping her whole life for that pale imitation she shut off her children's father's life. The murder in Shakespeare's play is a *spirit* murder. That's why father is a ghost, still haunting you. And numberless English postwar sons like you."

My life between the devil and our deep blue Mediterranean ghost sea. "And what about daughters?" Edwin asked Carl Jung. "What about Ettie?"

"You know that, old chap. Your sister is your mother's ghost – in the sense that 'ghosts' are a foretelling of the future psyche that is to come."

"I don't see what that has to do with Faust. Unless you mean Wolf?"

Jung shook his head. The specs fell down. "I have given you Faust to read, not because every bargain with a devil is evil. Often it's the only road to equilibrium – but you must recognise it *as* a bargain. You must know the price. Then either accept it or reject it. And I don't say you're

397

going to understand all this, or do it either, after a single visit to two old duffers on a lake in Switzerland. Or a single reading. But you've made a solid start for a first innings."

For the rest of that day – all about Incest & Guilt & Love & Hate: about Wagner's music. In the evening, Professor Jung sets Eddie a final prep; written out in the Professor's own hand, and decorated also by him with illustrations like those on Eddie's bedroom roof. It contains Genius's private thoughts on a number of subjects – not to be published. It was called, as Cosima had called the Master's first collected thoughts, *The Red Book*.

When Edwin packed the blue Riley the next morning I believed in Carl Gustav Jung, the Father of spiritual alchemy, and in the absence of co-incidence – in Synchronicity.

"And there's one last thing I want you to do, old chap. I want you to go to Steckborn, at the head of Lake Constance. You can take a river barge there, to Basel – and then a steamer – because I want you to sail with the Goethe, through Germany, the length of the Rhine, reading, and thinking, before you make any decision about the Grail, or you and your sister. Will you do that, old chap?"

"Yes – but couldn't I forget the barge and go straight to Basel?"

"No. You should see it from the river. That's how I saw it for the first time. In a dream, mind you. God was shitting from a great height on Basel Cathedral. I've always wondered what He disliked so much about poor little Switzerland. I'll be seeing you."

The workings of Great Minds, children, are part of His mystery.

The Rhine Journey:
Edwin sails down the Great River: all the way, following the reverse of Dietrich's route in the Nibelungs' epic. He sails past its islands & castles & dragon's lairs & Germania statues & Roman encampments. He looks up at its bridges and towers and Lorelei mountains that gave Wagner his own pilgrim's inspiration. He sees the might of modern Nibelheim flexing in *His* forges, spewing gases. He sees Lohengrin swans fly over Byron's Drachenfels and Hermann's bombers roar over Cologne Cathedral. At Düsseldorf, a middle-aged man on the steamer tried to seduce me: but when he saw the look in my eye, desisted. The cure was working.

I made my bargain. I would search for the Grail, but only with Sister's blessing, between her lovers. I had been wrong to leave her. Between lovers, she was the only person in the world who loved me. My task from the devil was to love her even in those black, temporary moments when she abandoned me. Finding, and holding, love was more important in our time in the human game than a tin pot – Whoever might once have pissed or shat in it!

To leave the great river at Rees would have been to cut my pilgrimage short, so Edwin stayed on the steamer and went a few miles too far, to a raw, new iron bridge beyond Nibelheim's border, at the typically dull Dutch town of Arnhem.

Our Swan Boat

... *At Bayreuth:* Brother arrives as the Season for '37 is starting – without Sister. Eddie found her, wan and frighteningly haggard, huddled like Wolf in a chair with a blanket in full summer, upstairs in her room at the Griesbachs.

"Ettie, my God, my darling, what is it?"

"Pneumonia." A harsh raven's whisper. "It was, for a month. Now it's strep. It won't leave my throat – and the Mitfahrt's with him. Oh Eddie, thank Christ! I thought you'd never come back."

Brother puts her to bed. He flies immediately to Tietjen and Winifred at the Hall. Both also thank God he's back. The Specialist brought from Berlin at the Festival's expense says, in those days before Wonder-Potions, there is nothing more that he can do.

"The malaise of your sister is more spiritual than physical, Herr von Perceval. I have suggested recuperation in the Alps, at high altitude, but this too she has refused."

Brother takes her to Triebschen on the lake, without a murmur. He keeps her in the sunshine and doses her with Mathilde's meek-Wolf recipe: lemon, rum, quinine, 5 times daily. And whipped fresh egg concoctions with cream, and herbs from the orchard garden. After a week she could even take the acid of strawberries, and speak. We were out on the grass, by the sweet water, with most of our clothes off, in the sun.

"Darling Eddie, the treasure of it! I never thought I'd live. Why have you changed your watch to that wrist?"

"I found I was banging it on things when I was building the village with Jung."

"Being Jungianised doesn't sound much better than being Addled – what a cracked pair of eggs we are." She pulls his hand, with her hand, to her mouth, and kisses it on the palm, cupping it to her chin, so that the wrist is vertical, and the watch slips down, and she sees: and stopped her kissing, and looked at the livid line with wonder.

"For me, Eddie? A knife, because of me?"

"A razor, actually."

"A razor?" She shuddered, in what was now less sad, than strange excitement.

"A safety razor. The whole thing was just damn stupid. When I heard from Mausi about you and Germaine Lubin's Negro chauffeur."

"You old idiot. La Lubin would have the eyes on a plate of anyone that tried to even *see* her nigger's Thingee, let alone – Eddie, did it hurt? What was it like when you actually did it?"

Her tongue crept up to the livid line, and licked at it, with little snake flickers.

"I don't remember. It was a mistake. I hardly touched it with the bloody razor. You aren't supposed to be able to with a safety blade."

"Bloody," she said, "I bet it was. I told you you'd like it, but you wouldn't believe. All slippy."

"Ghastly," Eddie said. "It wouldn't stop. I was terrified, Ettie. You can't imagine."

"I can," she said, "Oh, darling Bro, yes I can. Be a love and get my makeup box."

"You don't need warpaint, just sunshine."

"Not for my Phiz – don't ask questions. Go on. Get it."

Eddie went into our cottage, and got it. When he came out she had pulled down the top of her swimming suit so that her breasts were bare. "You'll catch your death."

"Nonsense. They haven't shrivelled too much, have they?" She looked down at them, and up at me. "Darling, did you miss them?"

"Yes. Here's the makeup."

"Did you miss *us*?" She took the box and selected two sticks, and a

400

small pot of white Ponds cream.

"Yes, I missed us. I love you, Ettie."

"Old goose, I know you do. Give me your foot."

She took it without permission and kissed it – tickling it, so that Eddie squirmed & wriggled & shrieked, as I did when we were children, and collapsed on the grass beside her. But man and woman, not children –

"What are you doing?" Asked with that choking, porpoising, pounding feeling, as she covered my foot with the white face cream. "We can't yet. Ettie, you aren't well enough. I'll give you germs."

"You mean you'll get them. Don't worry, I won't let you catch anything nasty from Miss Pussy. We'll make a swan for her, so she can go back to Lohengrin." She drew a dark beak on Brother's big toe with the black mascara. "I don't have anything gold, so we'll have to use red for the eyes, like rubies." She dotted them in, on each side of the bridge of my arch. Her fingers slipped the face cream all the way under, like feathers, caressing the sole. "My Wotan-Zeus, little piggy, come and kiss Leda – lean back against the tree, Eddie, like I am, so you can brace it."

She spread her legs apart, and leaned against an apple trunk, half naked like a figurehead. The creamy swan-face of my foot slipped up her thigh.

"Brace . . . ?"

The word was a gargle in my closing throat as I felt her foot on my thigh, and then her toes, wriggling where we left off, a year ago inside my shorts against my –

"Brace means so you can do it too, silly Piggy, when Miss Pussy says *meow*."

Her swimming suit has a curtain-skirt for modesty. Beneath, behind the curtain, a glimpse of gold; he feels his foot slip past the fabric, senses gold hairs curling around his toes.

"Now, Piggy – push, Eddie!"

Her toes, my toes. Her flesh clasping, mine leaping.

"Wriggle them . . . God. GOD! What does it feel like, tell me, Eddie?"

A live glove, perhaps. An octopus wrapping. *Le serpent, ma petite!*

"Oh Christ, I can't tell you. Oh, Jesus, Ettie – !"

Both her hands had my ankle, faster and deeper, to strangle the swan, for insatiable Miss Pussy and spent piggy. Our feet came out in the sun.

401

Her toe-webs were white again. Mine were the hideous colour of flesh and blood.

"I've killed you!" A new meaning for pederast. Visions of back streets and abortions. Of police! "This time they'll get me for absolute certain."

"Silly old Eddie, it's only my curse." She flopped off the apple tree trunk onto her back on the grass. "God, that was marvellous for a second best. I wonder if anyone else has done it?"

He stared at his foot as she slipped hers alongside it. Our pedestrian colours mingled like froth in the bath. Above, on the hill, I saw the glint of sun on metal.

"Oh Lord," said Sister, "you're not going to ruin it all by being sick!"

"Not me. The Parrots again. Just like last time. I'm positive they've been watching."

"Have they really? Now I'm better we must send the poor old poppets a special peace-offering invitation from Auntie to Lohengrin." She lifted my leg and waved the ruins of our bloody swan in the old spy-parrots' direction. "Now you're back, darling, I *know* I can do the hat-trick. 'Thirty-Eight's going to be simply our best ever!"

It never occurs to the Casson-Percevals, re-united, that it may not have been the feuding Sisters watching. Or, if it was them, to which long ear among the Green Hill cliques the Parrots may be reporting.

All the better to keep you dangling, my Dears . . .

. . . At the Singers' Table: One more, one last glimpse of '37 – after her Elsa in the Lohengrin – which never goes to tear open the Garden, because the Little Fellow is at Wasserleonburg Castle, over the border, getting a taste of being a No-Body, with 266 pieces of honeymoon luggage, instead of a Coronation! The Wagnerians provide one in lieu for the Honourable Ettie, with stamping and unheard-of whistles, because of her illness, and missing Brünnhilde. Eddie watched her Lohengrin, Max Lorenz, bring her down the steps to The Leader waiting with the rest of us as worshippers at the table. In the year of separation her face has acquired an even more refined beauty from loss of weight – a prima donna's joy: Strength through Suffering. The Mitfahrt's Valkyrie dreams of being in His Ascendant are rudely dashed by Herr Wolf.

"I've never heard a more glorious Elsa! You were so ill – why did nobody tell me?! Edwin, this is the last time you shall desert your magnificent sister. This is an order, most precious Fräulein Ettie. Absolutely!"

"I wouldn't dream of it – bothering you, Wolfi dear. You're far too bothered with hangers-on, already. Unity darling, I saw your pic in the Continental Mail the other day in Zürich. The way they can show one's teeth as though there are nothing but black holes – coalmines, like Alberich's! – you must have been livid."

The Mitfahrt's beauty ends at the skin on her teeth. When she opens her mouth it's like looking at a cobbler's file. Herr Wolf chortles at this fresh outbreak of His feminine war.

"I didn't see this photograph, Gnädiges Fräulein Mitford. You should only use Hoffmann; he does wonders with the new airbrush."

"I didn't have the chance to go to Hoffmann, my Fuehrer. I don't know what picture Edwina's talking about. It's so typical of our damned British gutter press." Because she can't smile – with the whole table watching?! – the remark comes out petty and sourgrapes, as it always does when the Mitfahrt bitches about things British – which she *always* does. "Oh, Lord, Edwina, I'm sorry. That lovely pale dress."

A cup of Austrian chocolate – knocked onto Sister! By accident! The brown stain clings to her thigh, spreads into her lap . . .

He was galvanised.

"In silk! Quickly – warm water with cream of tartar and vinegar."

Down on one knee, dabbing, with a napkin. Waving furiously for the head waiter.

"Really, Wolfi dear, you mustn't fuss and bother, it's only a last year's frock – " Miss-Pussy Ettie, meow-smiling across His black head at her English rival – "off the rack at Harrods, Unity darling, can't you just tell? Not even from Paris."

"Chocolate looks so disgusting – it's my fault utterly!" Her Suitor shoulders the blame with happy vengeance. "The bill for a new dress must be sent to me! I absolutely insist. At a party in your honour! And silk – the fabric is so delicate – exactly right for Elsa."

Touching the hem, rubbing it, feeling the knicker-silkiness between His bitten fingers, as the Wagnerians stare at the New Men's Leader on His knees for this stained woman.

403

"Wolfi dear, I wouldn't dream of allowing you to pay for it. Or Unity either. Accidents are accidents. I'll chuck it out, won't we, Eddie? Now please, or you'll make me cough, let's all enjoy this lovely party."

Triumph so complete makes one (almost) sorry for the Mitfahrt. Through the remainder of the evening Herr Wolf can't keep His eyes off the brown stain in Sister's lap, and when E & E go home to the Griesbachs a Mercedes is waiting with the back seat filled to the roof with red roses, and a note:

> *You MUST let me pay!*
> *Your repentant Friend –*
> *"Wolfi."*

"Lord how he does go on," said Ettie. "Eddie pet, we'll make love in the morning. Throw this rag away."

Brother carried the silk dress downstairs and put it in the scullery dustbin in the alley off the kitchen leading to the garage – padlocked. Our Leader is in Residenz! I went upstairs to kiss Ettie goodnight. Outside the open window there was a clank of a dustbin lid. She was already asleep, with a smile on her lips for her lovely party. In the alley, a shadow moved past the locked garage, and through the laurel hedge hiding the Grave in the Hofgarten.

One *Heil* . . . and then silence, on the Magic Mountain.

Second Movement
Sixth Passage

[crescendo!]

❦

... *Korsetts, Mein Herr!* You can't imagine, children, what Knicker-Games are played in Nibelheim by Mr Wolf that autumn with Young Edwin's Sister's cast-off Dress! On his card to E & E that '37 Xmas:
"For the first time in living memory I have enjoyed myself!"

He gives Himself a present of the armed forces. (After Generals von Blomberg & von Fritsch have "fingers wagged" – chucked out for marrying a prostitute-poseur for pornographic pictures & tapping the b*ms of Wolf-Jugend with a ruler, respectively.) At the last meeting of a Mowgli cabinet, He names Himself Commander in Chief – and confirms Captain Fat Hermann in the rank of Feldmarschall as consolation.

... *At the Gerbers': Bleak Mid-Winter.* Alternating between Munich and the Griesbachs' to get Extra Coaching for Ettie's unheard of attack on the triple peaks: Kundry, Brünnhilde, Isolde.

"After your illness," Brother said, "adding only the Kundry would be more than enough."

"Darling, I'm going to be *thirty*. God, just saying the word!"

405

"Say glorious maturity."

"Say Hag. Wolf can't stand his women getting old – look at Winnie – I have to do the Isolde, or he'll run away to the Cow. He's got the common creature in his henhouse most weekends as it is, since he kicked Sister Raubal out."

"I don't know where on earth you hear such things now Putzi's gone."

"From *His* appalling brother, darling. Or half – in that squalid restaurant he runs for the thugs on the Wittenbergplatz."

Number 3, just off the Kudamm, in Berlin. Bruder-Alois's decor is Wienese Gauche (yellow-lace borders to the table-cloths, my dears!) but not squalid. The runaway from Braunau's rhinoceros whippings has come Up in the World as they say. Those with a mistaken notion of Wolf-Family ties use the place for ditto.

"Not only thugs," Eddie said, "Leni Riefenstahl goes there, and Magda Goebbels – and Eva may be ordinary, and not terribly bright, but she isn't common or a cow, Ettie. You could afford to be nice to her; no one else is."

"I can't afford a bloody thing except Kundry. You be nice to the Cow if she's so damned special. Although – " as brother was leaving – "one wouldn't have thought it was asking too much for just a little loyalty through your sister's hat-trick. It isn't as though you were still farting around with your ridiculous Pot. We can thank old man-of-the-mountain Jung for something!"

And Eva.

. . . *At the Carlton:* Since her off-hand lover sent the giant Hanfstaengl fleeing in 7-League boots across the borders, the inferior Fräulein Braun has become the Boy's sole confidant in Munich. At the centre of the Circle, both are alone – both needed only for one purpose: to stir the Sex-potion. Boy & Girl have an agreement to meet on Thursdays at the Tea-room when Herr Eddie's in town and He isn't. This late February day her corner place was empty and I thought He must have turned up unexpectedly, but a waitress had other news.

"A telephone number for you, mein Herr."

Tactful Edwin called from a public booth. "Hullo, this is Eddie Casson-Perceval."

"Hullo, this is Gretl." Eva's sister, cashing in on free rent, as part-time chaperone. "Eva can't speak at the moment but she wants you to have tea. Can you come round to the house? Number 12, Wasser-burgerstrasse, in the Bogenhausen District. You have to cross the Isar."

"I know the way, Fräulein Gretl. Put the pot on. I'll be there in twenty minutes."

Her Own Little House:
Sits on a slight slope, behind a wooden fence and laurels: an ugly, almost perfect cubic, stone and stucco box. Eva loves it as fiercely as any Josephine her Malmaison. Fresh snow made driving tricky, and Edwin went slowly for the Riley's sake. Four o'clock struck when we turned into the street. A lorry full of workmen drew away from the curb as we arrived. Changes are in progress: a head-high masonry wall is being built to replace the fence. The bricks are blanketed with straw to stop frost entering the mortar. There are far more bricks stacked up than completion of the wall requires. Also, re-enforcing steel, and a great heap of dirt excavated at the side of the building. Eva's doggies barked furiously behind a temporary barrier of netting: a golden-tan Alsatian that was also new, and two black, hairy Scottie-schnauzer creatures called –

"Stasi and Negus! – stop that noise for Herr Eddie, you bad boys. Don't you know yet who's our Friend? I'm sorry I couldn't speak earlier, Herr Eddie, I was on the throne. Welcome to my very own little Braunhaus."

Eva giggled, as she chattered her greeting and held the front door, but the forced – suggestive – gaiety, and her hasty powdering around red eyes showed she was terribly unhappy.

"Come in, come in, we'll both freeze. As I couldn't go out because of the weather I sent for some of these chocolate cakes of His that you like so much, from the Türkenstrasse."

With both hands tugging the Boy across her sill to the parlour.

"It is cold, Fräulein Eva. My car should be wrapped in the straw like your bricks. You seem to be building a whole new house."

"Only the cellar. And the wall – because the bad dogs bark so at the neighbours. Doggies, you can come too, if you will be good – not you, Basko, you have to stay and see no one steals our bricks." Basko is the Alsatian. Stasi & Negus rush in, bumping legs, as Mistress closes the

407

door. "Basko, is a half-brother of Blondi – He just sent him, with strict instructions about the bricks. I got some English tea as well, from the Berghof, last weekend."

"Before it snowed, Fräulein Eva?" – meaning, she's known for a week that the foolish Friend shall be coming.

"You should see the Berghof in the snow, Herr Eddie. They have to carry every kilo up there in tanks, with those tracks. Let me take your coat."

Her hands brush the Friend's neck as they take the collar.

"Is Fräulein Gretl not joining us for tea?"

"No." Eva stretches on tip-toe to hang the Friend's coat on a hook. The hem of her skirt rises with the stretch to reveal the silk-stockinged back of her knees, and a sensual dark crease of perspiration. "Gretl's taking a course in shorthand writing. Two hours from four till six, twice a week. Shall I take your jacket also? You are dressed for the Berghof, Herr Eddie; you'll roast with that pullover underneath."

The Friend surrenders the jacket also, and inspects. 1st: the Red Divan has been transferred from the Prinzregentstrasse. 2nd: the furniture – better than His own apartment. 3rd: lots of pictures – landscapes of Fischbach and Wax, portraits by Gallegos, and a large one of the little Braunhaus's Provider, done by Bohnenberger – but without those hypnotic eyes from the Salt Mountain bedrooms. Pride of place, naturally, is given to one of His watercolours, "The Assam Church," above a mahogany chest.

"Isn't it lovely? Professor Troost himself designed it. I'm so lucky – oh, Herr Eddie!"

And she flung herself, weeping, onto the Friend's woollen chest.

"Fräulein Eva, what on earth! You mustn't cry. Please. I haven't got a handkerchief. Oh never mind. Eva, dear, tell me."

It is, after all, transparently what the Friend is there for; and he knows a little by now himself, of the terrible anxiety that claws at Wolf's women.

"You are both English, you have to help."

Both? Her head was below my chin. Her hair was darker at the roots than Ettie's, but not enough to mean peroxide. "I will help, if I can, but I have to know what I'm helping about."

"Her dress. It's so cruel. I just won't wear it."

New sobs – and her breasts moving the straps of her lingerie beneath the blouse stretched under his hands across her back, make Friend a dull boy. "A dress, Fräulein Eva?"

"It's not even my size, I told Him, but He said I can fix it. A Stitch in Time, as they say – you know I used to make all my own dresses to save Him money. And you must have seen it." Her hands clutch Friend's pullover. "We had a terrible row. I told Him anything else, but I just *wouldn't*! – not in *her* dress, never! I'd kill myself first. Herr Eddie, you know her so well. Tell me I was right to say no about Die blöde Mitfahrt's!"

"*Mitford's* dress . . ."

Thank you God! – she doesn't think it's Sister's!

"You agree, it's a scandal! I thought first – forgive me – it's Fräulein Edwina's, but at least she's a great artist. She gets her own gowns from Paris, gorgeous; this one of the Mitfahrt's is machine sewn! From some London shop off the rack! And so badly stained, it will never come out. Can you imagine!"

What acts shall be performed in it?! (The Chicken-Farmer's sewer-records, from Waring, show us that Fräulein Braun has to have an operation after the convent because her vagina is too small! For a Wolf's organ? Or His pederast-swan-foot? Or a Wolf-baby's monstrous head?) Horrific prospects. Don't tell me!

"I forgive you completely, Fräulein Eva – do you think perhaps now we should have tea?"

"Yes, yes, at once. I don't know what got into me."

Eva produced a watery smile and went into a tiny kitchen to blow her nose. A gas cooker with jets for only two pots hissed blue flame from one of them at a black kettle. In the parlour room Friend Eddie sits on one of Professor Troost's chairs. Across from it, facing the Red Divan, is a stranger piece of furniture: an oblong box with a round glass lens, like Cyclops' eye. An anti-macassar embroidery drapes it, surmounted by a white hothouse lily in a pot. The Braunhaus is too hot for the lily which is wilting from the heat of the stove. The effect is Middle-Class-Funereal.

"Here is now our tea." Eva is again bright and happy, as women are when they've thrown a damper over everyone else. "It was so good of you to listen, Herr Eddie. The Fuehrer is right – so often I'm just a silly little goose. Have you guessed what it is yet?"

As his hostess sets the tray by the lily on the Cyclops box, her Friendly guest observes a loudspeaker grille, with knobs. "Possibly a Professor Troost wireless aquarium? Although it's got almost a touch of art nouveau, so perhaps not."

New Art being a touchy subject in the Painter-of-houses-Land.

"It's my 'Fernsehapparat', Herr Eddie – there are only three in all Munich! *He* was given it by the Telefunken firm. Shall we see if they are putting out a picture today?"

Eva pats the Red Divan. Her guest obediently sits beside his hostess. She turns a knob. The Cyclops eye becomes spattered with dots of snow that expand until it is solidly milky-white, then grey – that darkens to a black object appearing as a Hamlet-ghost in a fortune-teller's ball.

"Good God . . ."

His Face. The portrait from the Salt Mountain. It hangs, disembodied, staring with the hypnotic eyes, and then begins to speak.

> "I am pleased to make this inauguration 'Fernsehen' special experimental broadcast to you in Munich from Berlin. Soon, all our People will be able to see, as well as hear each other, and know what they are thinking – like the little Gruenwaldvogel envisioned by the immortal genius of Richard Wagner to inform our hero, Siegfried – no matter in what part of our Greater German forest they may happen to be. Sudeten, Danzig, or Vienna. Guten Tag, Deutschland."

The ghost-face withdrew back into the snow, and transformed itself into a Mowgli, snapping over the Chancellery with *Über Alles* from a scratchy orchestra somewhere behind.

"Eva, that's incredible, a miracle. In pictures, all the way from Berlin."

"Not truly, Herr Eddie, the Fernsehen picture is only here in Munich. The Fuehrer at Berlin was taken in a movie, on a film, by Goebbels – who I just hate! – and then they take another movie. What

410

will be a miracle is when they can show us Clark Gable and Snow White. Oh, why do the Austrians have to be so stupid! Herr Eddie, I can have a movie palace of my own downstairs for what it's cost."

"A cinema in your cellar, Fräulein Eva?"

"A shelter, Herr Eddie. All in case some Austrian Fanatic drops a bomb. Of course, it shows He cares for me, in a way, I suppose. There is even to be an escape tunnel to the back lane. That's why so much dirt. Come and look."

Déjà vu – but still frightening to look back, and Realise: cold concrete with rusting steel, dim light flickering from a generator, sighing pumps for dank air, a chemical "throne" with That Smell already from a workman – the future of Munich, & Eva, & Stasi & Negus, & Eddie – in scale model, this far ahead of His peace in our time . . .

"It won't be so bad – until the Fanatic comes I can use it for preserves." And once more above stairs, "Herr Eddie, I have a radio-gramophone also, and my new record – 'Der Vogelhändler', you must know – 'Schenkt man sich Rosen in Tirol', with wonderful Max Hansen and Lizzi Waldmüller, it's absolutely my favourite song."

> *If you give each other roses in Tyrol*
> *You know what that's supposed to mean.*
> *You don't just give the roses,*
> *You also give your heart.*

To a Bird Seller? Don't tell me! Mechanical canary warbles, and absolutely the most awful Marietta oompah-bilge, and yet . . . as she sings the foolish words . . . and her bosom heaves beneath that sleek silk blouse . . . the hurdy-gurdy, light-tuney little thing does get a Boy.

"Oh, Herr Eddie, I knew you'd love my Red Roses too. We must listen again, and sing it with me, and cross our hands like your Auld Lang Syne."

> *If you mean it thus, you understand me,*
> *If you mean it thus, then promise your love,*
> *If you mean it thus, then console me,*
> *Give yourself to me, together with the roses.*

"But not red ones, dear Fräulein Eva?" said the pedantic Boy.

"But they must be, Herr Eddie. I call it my 'Red Roses' song because

411

that's what He always gives me."

Our Bird-Dealer in caged spirits . . .

"Once more, please. The ending is so happy that it always makes you cry. Oh, Herr Eddie, if it's still snowing will you come for tea with the doggies and be our friend again next week?"

"If Ettie doesn't need me."

"Oh thank you, thank you. Dear Herr Eddie it's so wonderful to have a real Special-friend."

And there, in the flickering light above a tomb, hands crossed, Eva Braun kisses her Special Friend, on his lips, passionately. And the next week, again with our inevitable Red Roses playing, touches him. And the 3rd week, as the bloody record sticks, *lets him!* – in her overheated parlour, but sedately, with no swan or knicker games, face to face on the Red Divan. Once. To prove a point:

She can damn well copulate with Another-Man if her own won't visit. And her Friend can reciprocate with A-Woman-who-isn't-Sister. And enjoy it! (For operation or no, Fräulein Braun's vagina *is* deliciously – boy-ishly – tight!)

All the better to grip . . .

Because in the 4th week, children, with the barking of Doggies & a state of High Excitement, in an unannounced Wotan-flit, the absent Other lover arrives late for the Performance, in the middle of the Act!

TWO BAD DOGGIES

or

THE NAUGHTIEST MARIETTA OF THE LOT

THE CUE: *That Voice! Outside the window!*

MR WOLF [*hearty*]

Mein Baskerl, so like your sister, noble creature!

THE FRIEND [*beyond appalled*]

Sister! Lord it can't be . . . !

MR WOLF [*chuckling*]

You're happy, little ones, your Onkel Wolfi's here?

Delirium's the word! Through Bayern *muslin curtains, above The Friend's* buttocks, *Eva can see it is indeed – !*

OUR EVA [*whole body constricting*]

Ach, mein Gott der – !

MR WOLF [*a flattered owner*]

You still remember your old master ? !

On His Red Divan ? ! !

Where Miss-Pussy's claws *dig in.*

THE FRIEND [*terrified whisper*]

Ouch ! Eva, you're pinching – and He's supposed to be in Berlin about Austria.

MR WOLF [*hurt/disappointment*]

You noisy ones thought he was never coming, when he promised ?

But on the Red Divan our Eva's Inferior Feminine Anatomy [shaven, *clean as His whistle !*] *is* locked in spasm. [*The Friend's Male Appendage already died in shrivelled shock ! ! !*]

OUR EVA

Get *off* ! For God's sake Herr Eddie quickly !

THE FRIEND

I can't – oh Christ ! Eva dammit let me go. I'm trapped !

MR WOLF

You're asking Uncle Wolfi to open your cage, is that it ?

Our Eva pushes The Friend's torso *frantically UP with her arms – while slyboots Miss Pussy* clamps his shrunken nethers [*like a homeless hermit crab !*] *between her thighs.*

OUR EVA

Herr Eddie we *have* to ! Make it go – !

MR WOLF

Down ! Down I say !

THE FRIEND

It *is* down – it's you ! Eva, you simply must relax !

413

MR WOLF

Ja, Onkel will have you all out of there in a moment.

OUR EVA

Relax how can I He'll kill me oh I'll *never* ever get another little house all my own . . . !

> *At which prayer [in God's mercy, and Eva's frenzy, children] our twin-backed Couple fall off the Red Divan to the floor ! With an uncorking* Plop . . . *Eva and Friend are* apart ! ! !

MR WOLF

Now, admit, this feels better.

> *The Sound of Onkel's kindly soldier's hand upon the door ! [We aren't out of Vienna's woods yet !]*

OUR EVA

He has a key, I must go ! – be quick and explain –

THE FRIEND

Oh Jesus Christ to my sister !

OUR EVA

She won't mind she's so sweet you're so clever Herr Eddie !

> *Eva* flees *through Kitchen with her clothes* – less her Knickers *which drop; and The Friend's* Underpants, *grabbed up in a trade with every last gibbering stitch of his cleverness, savoir faire, and Self control . . .*

CURTAIN

And then –?

Off with his head! Or a bullet in hers? In these domestic Wolfish situations the mask can flip from Marietta-Farce to Hamlet-Death with the speed and crack of Donner's lightning. And dear dead Christ, what *of* Sister, when she gets the news? As she must, because while our Don Juan stuffs the knickers in his trousers' pocket and scrabbles at his flies with hands that are all thumbs, the round-shouldered silhouette is right against the curtains, turning the door handle -

And then the God who shat on Basel sent a true Three-Maries miracle:

"Scheisskopf! Damned rascal dogs – see what you've done!"

A ton of bricks for the wall fell over with a crash. Those 3 dogs must surely have a place in heaven – with the inventor of the zip fastener! Our Don Juan's flies in 1937 have 6 buttons and not one will fit its hole! While outside, despite more crashing curses, any moment the Leader must toss aside the last of the shitbag bricks –

But He wasn't tossing. He's *leaving*!!! Half-furtive, with hunched looks for the neighbours; half-raging, with a futile kick at the gambling Stasi & Negus.

"Blasted little black swine!"

An unmarked Mercedes is backed into the gateway to hide from passersby: not far enough to hide the snout, because of a pile of builder's sand. The latest Maurice leaps to hold the door. *He* gets in. The chauffeur says something and points across the street. In black and white Nibelheim the Riley sticks out like a blue thumb . . .

He knows.

"I promised I was coming." He had told the happy-go-lucky dogs. And Eva, the stupid cow – playing with my life and hers, some deadly Anima game to gain His attention – she must have known too.

But as the Mercedes left, spitting sand at the saviour, traitor dogs, and me, racked with terror for my sins against Him and Ettie, I didn't know, not for certain . . .

So young Edwin dangled, like the Austrians, waiting all that ghastly weekend to be eaten by His twisted love, at the centre of His web.

That very afternoon the Bad Giant Hermann sent His ultimatum to Father's land; this time backed up by Fafner's clanking tanks massed along the border. It was also the day that I noticed for the first time that the Riley was being followed.

Marietta was over.

. . . *At the Gerbers'*: "It serves you right to be followed. I suppose you were making goo-goo eyes at one of the Carlton's waiters. I thought old Jung had talked you out of that."

"Why do you insist I'm homosexual when you know I'm normal? And it wasn't a waiter. It was a Black Leather car – one of your friend Moses bloody – "

"Normal! The Leather Men don't follow people having tea at the Carlton. You don't even need the Riley for the Carlton – what's that bump in your pocket?"

Die Underpants – panic-stuffed, with a relieved-nerves giggle as her Special Friend left, on top of her knickers, by Eva.

"A scarf - " offhand – "and I took the Riley because I had to do some shopping. And I know damn well I was being followed."

"They probably thought I was with you. It's rather flattering really. Your scarf's already on the hook, let's see – "

Quick as a snake she struck at the pocket – and had the evidence out in the open.

"It wasn't a waiter," is all he can think of.

"A whore? You've been to a brothel? Catching God only knows what, and you come back to me with it?"

She dangled the pants and the knickers with fastidious disgust, pinched in her fingers.

"It wasn't a whore."

"An ordinary girl? Oh yes, I forgot, you're *normal*." Flinging the knickers at his face. "Well sniff and enjoy, darling. I'm sure she's still on them, little unwashed Münchener slut. Only don't expect to come poking at me whenever she's cursing."

"She won't be. And she was not only washed, she shaved it. And I'm not going back – *if* it's any of your bloody business. My God, what do I know *you've* caught? – with all the men you've had since Nicholas bloody Lizard-rat Baer, and doing damned bloody cunnilingus!"

"You never would, when I was bloody – why aren't you going back, dear, if she isn't a whore and you're normal and she *shaved* it?"

"She's married."

But the blurted little red lie only sharpens Sister's appetite. "And he caught you doing it. My runaway Don Juan, down the back stairs with the knickers. How delicious. Someone *shaved* you've met in Munich, like one of those Godawful Brown House statues – ?" eyeing the quality of the knickers and their label, she considered – "from Dortmann's, imitation silk, it must be musical or Mowgli – not Helene ex-Putzi?

She's a little long in the tooth, but not hairless. You need them to be motherly."

"Don't be absurd. It's none of your business – and anyway they're not from Munich. Her husband's Austrian and they've gone back."

"Austrian? Salzburg? Someone we met last summer at the Festival?"

"You're cold," Brother said, too smug for our own good. "I'm going to have a bath."

"Cold – ?" Her eyes sparkled with icicle points – "Austrian . . . good God Almighty. Brown House! – you've been poking *his* cow."

"I haven't. She isn't."

"She shaves it and he caught you! How utterly disgusting and humiliating!"

"He didn't."

"You realise you've ruined my career."

"Rubbish. You told me to be nice to her."

"He must have been absolutely livid. Did he see you naked? The Cow would never have been on top; your little bourgeois *Fräulein* isn't the sort. Or were you behind as usual? – doing Doggy, so he'd have heard you slurping and slapping. It's too horrible to contemplate."

But she was – enjoying every close-shave minute of it as Brother strips for the bath. "You never worried about the Parrot-Sisters telescoping at us in the boat, at Triebschen. Or anyone listening. Or the whole of Hunland talking, for that matter. Eva's dogs knocked over some bricks. Wolf went away without seeing anything."

"Except the Riley – my car – and now we're being followed. I won't ever have a scrap of privacy."

Or a little house all my own . . .

"You're hardly inconspicuous without the Riley. You can't expect to be the top Helden soprano and invisible at the same time. I'm sure Wolf doesn't know. Just forget about it."

Brother locks himself in the bathroom and runs the taps. When he turns them off she says through the door, in her voice from the magic time when we were little, "Do you really think I am, Eddie? – the top soprano?"

"Yes, I do, Ettie. And so does He, and that's all that counts."

And so it is. 2 days later, while His tanks invade Father's land – peacefully, without a shot, on a Saturday morning – He sends a begging,

417

handwritten message through Anna-Rudi Hess for the unspeakably Gracious & Noble Fräulein Edwina to sing at the Command Performance in Vienna on the Sunday night of His Anschluss coronation. And that a Grand Duke's Suite has been put at her Ladyship's disposal on His floor of the Hotel Imperial looking out on the Ring!

(Eva Braun, in disgrace for her doggy behaviour is trimmed back to a single room, one floor up, next to the lift, shared with her mother, looking down at the back court by the kitchens.)

But first – We have to Get There.

STATIONS OF THE CROSS

Of all the car rides Edwin took with Him – manic or depressive; under rainbows or through storms; hurtling up or down His great salt mountain; smuggled to funerals across borders; commanded to fairy castles of madness; weeping for deaths of a mother, or Geli, or finally – *no!* None was ever the equal of that processional triumph.

They went in the Riley, Ettie & Eddie – you must have seen them, children – one car back from His Mercedes in the black-and-white celluloid convoy that left Munich that Saturday at noon. Seen but not noticed: all eyes are on Him, and all cars are grey in black and white; the C-Ps don't stand out unless you know your radiator emblems. *He knows* – and so Ettie naturally refuses mein Hesserl's proffered State Mercedes and insists on the Riley.

"But dammit," Eddie said, outside the Gerbers, "He *saw* the Riley, across from Eva's; I told you; He's bound to remember. Talk about rubbing salt in the wound!"

"Yes," she said, wrapping a fox fur for the March weather, "hurry up, or we'll be blocked getting across the Isar to the Prinzregentstrasse."

The assembly point is under the corner balcony of His apartment. Edwin is sullenly stubborn. "I still want to go in Fräulein Anna's Mercedes. If you don't care about me, what happened to ruining your bloody career?"

"That was yesterday – I wonder what I should sing in Vienna? It doesn't have to be anything demanding now poor darling Frida's gone

... Gawd what a herd of cars – Eddie, dodge us in there behind Fat Hermann. Queen Emmy isn't with him. I do believe I'll be the only woman."

"No you won't. Leni Riefenstahl's filming."

"Blonde, and the right shape but, even if she shaves it, she can't sing, darling – this'll do us nicely." Edwin's Sister produced an Honourable smile at a theatrical angle for her rival's camera.

"I shouldn't bother," Brother said; "the director gets the final edit."

With which Miss-Pussy mewing, and flags waving, and sirens screaming, the cavalcade departs from Munich along the very route of the Putsch past the Bürgerbräukeller – and I wondered what He was thinking as That Head turned for a glance in the direction of His first wild starter's pistol shot at the ceiling ...

And then, at speed down the Wolf-Road to Mühldorf, one hour away from His starting point across the River Inn.

Braunnau – 1st Station:
General von Bock, all heel-clicking now that the dreaded worst (Wop Intervention) is over, comes up. "The way is almost clear, my Fuehrer. Another thirty minutes and Guderian's tanks will have reached Linz."

"Thirty minutes? Bock, this is absurd! Why so slow?" demands the wildly impatient, yet by no means certain of the outcome, Leader.

"The flowers my Fuehrer. The peasants insist on presenting them to the tank commanders."

"Excellent fellows. Don't wait for Guderian, General – "

A flight of Flying Fafner roars low, drowning out the new Napoleon, but His gesture is that of every conqueror, unmistakable:

Forward!

But using the old Army adage – Hurry-up & Wait! Our Pilgrims' progress is choked by thousands upon thousands of the faithful, increasing with every yard towards the border; all Jerusalem has turned out to see the Wotan-Christ. The worshippers have lit fires for warmth, and as we pass them they raise brands and wave them in our direction, so that His way is marked by a column of smoke by day – also, from stalled tanks broken down between the bonfires. Mechanics lie underneath them, oblivious of the Leader, working desperately with spanners and covered with oil.

2nd Station:

But Passau, with Frau Fai-Fai Kraiburg and her ribbons and blueing for her Dolferl's bruises, has *not* been selected – so we went through Hafeld instead, with its white wood farmhouse and straight-carved stream through a green field with first daisies open for the sun. And then Lambach – although not to the Mill where the Child-Wolf fibbed, and climbed apple trees; and the Miller was, like Frau Fai-Fai, long gone. We did stop at the Abbey, and the monk, Brother Groner, now Abbot, came out to meet us, sparer, and whiter in his tonsure, but seemingly pleased to greet his famous pupil. Abbot and Leader stood together outside the arch by the great glass windows of Parsifal's silver spear –

Observe the fenestration, Children . . .

I heard Mama's clear voice as He looked up instead at the gateway arch, with its first Mowgli mandala, and shook His head, and chuckled – until Abbot Groner points at the river, with a swimming gesture. The Leader-Wolf turns His back on its wet memories, and strides to the Mercedes and waves again tersely – Forward!

. . . *To Linz:* But Our progress is slower than ever. Edwin counts 50 tanks dead beside the roadway – not much improved since we rattled along it in Mama's rented cabriolet with Gust'l Kubizek.

"He did sweat so," said Ettie, "those guinea-pig pouchy types always do, and so many of them are tenors; it's really the worst part of singing as a job. Why in God's name didn't we take the train, Eddie? – at this rate we won't be in Vienna this month."

The Procession enters Linz in the Wiegener district (Father's death) without stopping, and then to Leonding . . . where Mutti died, with Krebs Cancer clawing at her breast as the Yid Doctor Bloch poured his scouring solution to burn out and scourge the Wound. Her only begotten-surviving Son went into the apartment building, with its stone balustrades like Trevelly's gardens, entirely alone; and again up to a third storey with its view across the Danube to Kürnburg, the Nibelungenlied castle . . .

And then – ?

As dusk was falling, to the Rhapsodie Hotel with its lobby of stuffed animals where the efficient police had routed out Mein Gust'l for

420

Mama. They are no less efficient now. The arrivistes meet Moses Heydrich in the lobby, allocating rooms for the Leader's Party.

"The Hotel manager has been pleased to offer his own quarters for your use, my Fuehrer – the Minister of the Interior will meet you there."

Seyss-Inquart, about to take a promotion. Herr Wolf trips over the polar bear in the manager's quarters and finds himself face to face with a *Negress!* – a large, not well executed, likeness of Josephine Baker, en deshabille.

"In Austria!" exclamms the astounded Leader-Wolf. "Can you believe! Tomorrow Vienna – what a day!"

And then – ?

As further evidence of synchronicity, the C-Ps are given the very room they had occupied 15 years before, with the same feather beds and even the same pigeon cooing, all fluffed up for its bedtime, on the window sill.

"It can't possibly be the same," said Ettie, "or anyway I don't think – how long do pigeons live? I'm positively whacked – get them to send up some tea and gin."

"Kaffee und Schnaps, Mein Herr" arrive with a tear-stained maid to light the fire in Brother & Sister's room. "I apologise to be late with the coals – I saw our Fuehrer! He will speak at the Rathaus. Our very own, from Linz!" Leaving, the child begins to cry with incoherent happiness again. Sister has a double schnaps. The plumbing at least has been modernised since our previous stay. Brother runs a bath.

"Do you want to go first?" with our usual politeness.

"No, darling, I'm boozing."

"You don't want to catch a chill if we're going out."

"I have no intention of going anywhere. I've had quite enough of stinking humanity for one day."

"Not even if He asks you? We are His guests."

"Especially if he asks – oh Eddie, for God's sake stop being such a crawling bloody nag. One Reich, One Folk, the same old Wolf buggering his vocal chords – no thank you very much!"

"Well I'm going. It's history."

"Meaning the most indescribable bore. You really ought to have been a don, flapping in one of those crow-gowns with crowds of peachcheeked boys. Well go on and leave me – it doesn't matter that I'll have to eat alone."

"I'll be back long before suppertime."

"Not if he makes a speech."

Sister drank, and Brother bathed – while the Leader–Wolf, euphoric, 4 doors down, trips a 2nd time over the polar bear & makes one of his spur of the moment Decisions & tells Seyss-Inquart that He is going to gobble-up Father's Land whole into the Reich – and then Edwin went alone into the seething, singing, drinking, hysterical mass of men, women, and children surging through the streets of Linz, as night came to the city that had cast Him out.

... *To the Rathaus Square:* From the Rhapsodie Hotel is only a few hundred yards, but it takes Edwin a quarter of an hour. And halfway there, despite the crush of the crowd, the realisation that once more I was being followed.

At first only by a shadow – from the lighted resin torches and straw bonfires burning in every window and stable doorway's arch. Then a shadow at a stationer's shop – with a sign carved as a huge, white quill-pen poised to drop a carved drop of ink, black as the Danube – and then I saw my shadow was a man, reaching towards me, forcing his way through the river of humans. A man in a long, dark leather coat with fawn suede facings like the snowy white ones Giant Hermann wears. They gave the man a military air, but he hunched too much, like a bird of prey, and his face was drawn with a mouth turned down from too many secrets. Police. One of Blond Moses' undercover men.

"Herr Casson-Perceval! Wait!"

As the law-abiding do, Eddie turns. Two accomplices appear from an alley behind the Fawn-suede man. Black Leather and hats. Why should three of them need me? Why hadn't they called at the hotel? Heydrich himself had put me up at the hotel.

"Achtung! You must wait!"

Fanatics? Anarchist bombers? Pan-Slavs or Germans? Patriots all. Who knows what combinations are roused and abroad on a night like this? The crowd sweeps Fawn-suede towards me, separating him from his fellows, throwing me out into the Rathaus Square. For a moment there is space. My ribs expand – until a bonfire by a bandstand crackles with wet wood like a pistol shot and my heart contracts. The police station where Mama sent for the Inspector to find Kubizek is to my right. A uniformed constable, moustached like His father in peaked helmet with eagles on the badge stands guard to hold out the New Men's mob from the seat of law and the old order. I move into his protective arc.

"Stay there. I'll reach you."

Fawn-suede too is in the open. The Black Leather pair are still locked in the crowd, hidden on the far side of the band stand. The uniformed constable turns at the end of his patrol and walks away from me. I follow.

"Stay for God's sake I beg you!"

No Heydrich man begs. I stay. He runs the last fifty feet, gasping. He is old. His face is blue in the police station light. His lips bloodless. My evasions have already half killed him.

"What do you want?"

"Take it!"

He thrusts a parcel, wrapped in brown paper.

"What is it?"

He is fanatic. Can a bomb be so flat?

"To the West. Take it. I advised your mother wrongly. You must publish."

"Advised my mother – who are you?"

"Mack, the notary, God help me! Publish in London. Goodbye."

He reels away. He may only be drunk – but he is dying. Spit flecks his stubbled chin. His nose is no more hooked than Dwarf-Goebbels. His speech no more of a whine than Mime-Himmler's. If you scratch us, do we not bleed?

If you are one of Us, must we not die?

The Black-Leather men are around the bandstand. Out in the open lunging like pointers for the smell of a Yid. A black van stands with its back door open, waiting, engine running. A white fog-plume of exhaust rises into the night. As Black-Leather reach Fawn-suede he collapses to the cobbles. Night and Fog. The crowd surges . . .

. . . And when it surged back, both colours and the van were gone. The son was left with the parcel meant for his mother. Under Austrian police protection and blue light, he opened it.

Brown Morocco binding, pages tipped with shiny gold – but more of them than I remembered. And attached to the first page, in her perfect copperplate, an Edwardian's letter, Capitalised and *underlined*:

"Dear Herr Mack:

My *proof* Copy, for your kind advice as to *local inaccuracies* of my little work, & *Libel* under Austrian Law in publishing the medical file attached as Appendix, at the rear, of *Genius* described as '*the Subject, A*'...!"

No longer a *subject*! Mama my darling: Wotan the god. His likeness stared at me over the Nibelung flames of the torches from every lamp-post – even from the fatherly Austrian policeman's doorway. Now sixty millions are *His* subjects – and all of them seem to be packing and fighting their way into this Linz town square.

And then – ?

The roar, howling and building, rattling the windows, the very cobbles of the square.

Sieg Heil! Sieg Heil! Sieg Heil! The sound shall never end.

And then – ?

He stands on the balcony above us. And with His arm raised, blesses us.... Tomorrow's world. Today. For all around Him are His Marshals and His Knights of the New Teutonic Order. All below Him are His sturdy Hunding vassals. And hidden in the darkness His Alberich slaves in fawn-suede caftans and yellow patches, and filthy pipe-stem trousers, crouching ... and Edwin, trembling, heart thumping, by a bonfire with the nightmare file in my hands – for on that torchlit balcony was my mother's daughter.

"What do you mean, I wasn't going? Darling, I changed my mind."

Anima's prerogative. Children, our minds are changing all the time! Eddie looked away from Him and mad Sister to the final page of Mama's Brown Book. A different hand, masculine, but just as neat. The writing seared as I held it for reading to the flames:

"The impelling power of the perversion is so strong ..."

... *In Mama's Shadow:* Eddie is frightened. Not understanding – yet already knowing – as a little braided Wolf-Maid of five is led forward to give flowers. Surely – utterly! – Sister at this point must be frightened too?

But Ettie only looks bored stiff, Mama.

"Edwina always will, Eddie dear, when the applause is not for her."

I know, Mama – but, please, you've been Freudianised and Jungianised and Addled – what on earth is *"Passive Sadism"*, or *"Coprophagia"*?

Or *Ultimate Extreme*?

And where will it lead Us?

Oh, Eddie – ask Wotan the jealous god, you silly: read His file.

This is Thy Blood that must shed for ME.

REPRISE REQUIEM

Der Alptraum

Fifth Clinical Observation

Nothing to observe. With countless numbers from Germany's military hospitals, and madhouse wards, and prisons, my patient, **A** *is gone, lost in the stream of broken beings that is our nation. Sooner or later, thwarted in a wasted life the "Fuehrer" personality will break free. For some young woman, there will be a reckoning.*

> *So much for God !*
> *For Germany !*
> *For Us !*
> ***Damn Him . . . !***

Third Movement

Ring of Aire

Overture

Frau Cosima's Final Prelude
being
HIS Transformation Story!

Götterdämmerung

Children, My own Dearest!

For how well I feel I now know you! – Such a *long* word in German our Title is! – & with what Trepidation you are now waiting for the End of such a Progress as our Siegfried's & Brünnhilde's!

But we shall *not* be Afraid, Children, as we enter His *Twilight*, for Richard Wagner guides Us. The Words & Music of His Genius sustain Us & shelter Us as our World spins in our small place in the Heavens – for that is how the last story of His Ring opens: the Three Norns, wise women who weave the Web of Life, are spinning –

In woe they descend to Erda, our Earth Mother, who awaits all of Us ... & we are with Siegfried & Brünnhilde, in Love upon their Mountain!

... And one Other.

This third person is named *Hagen!* And all about

this Creature is *Black*, for Children, he is not merely wicked, or cruel –

... He is EVIL in human form!

All Hagen seeks is Dominion & Power. He conspires a *Dreadful Plot* with honest & simple Gutrune & Gunther. They shall welcome Siegfried, the Hero, & offer him a Potion. He drinks. And then – He *forgets* his Love, Brünnhilde!

So their Plot transpires. Siegfried leads fearful Gunther through the Fire. Brünnhilde starts up in terrible Amazement. Later, in the Great Hall, Siegfried tells the story of His Adventures, & starts to Remember ...

But Hagen takes Him away on a Hunting Party. And while Siegfried turns His back –

... Hagen plunges in a Spear!

And then – as our Ravens, *Gedanke & Gedächtnis*, (our old friends from *Das Rheingold*, "Thought" & "Memory" – *do* you remember, Children?) fly ahead to tell Wotan, the body of Our Hero is borne back to Brünnhilde (in the stupendous *Beerdigung*, Funeral Music of Richard Wagner.) His Hero's Corpse is laid upon a Bier of logs from the Great Ash Tree.

Brünnhilde leaps on Grane's back & bounds into the massive Flames of the Funeral Pyre. The whole Great Hall catches fire & is consumed (in a so-wonderful *Red* light you shall see at Bayreuth). Even the mighty Rhine *floods its Banks* to weep in Remorse & drown away such Villainy. The Ring is dragged into the Depths. Hagen follows after it. All is laid waste ...

UTTERLY!

Third Movement
First Passage

[moderato]

Let thou and I the Battle try,
And set our men aside.
Accurs'd be He, Earl Percy said,
By whom this is denied!

. . . *In Spandau* – Waring is not to be trusted. A little bird pops that thought into the Old Edwin's brainbox. Gedanke, freed from Motherhood, has learnt to grasp the pen in one scaly, Feldgrau-isch-yellow foot, and so assists in the rendering of our cautionary tale! Gedächtnis, as Critic, splatters his droppings whitely at random on my accumulation of Mowgli-Marietta reference works – courtesy of Waring.

Methinks Gedanke is right: Jeremy has been too damn cool of late. Scarcely a rise out of him even for Our Eva's *shaven* Miss Pussy and the Doggy-Knickers playlet! – remembering lemon-Yellow Street, as Gedächtnis makes one, this blasé attitude to sex for sale, my dears, does *not* Ring True.

"Well it isn't as though you caught him with her, C-P. That's the sort of thing we need to get some proper cash flowing. One didn't tell you earlier but the Press have been stung rather badly since we started." (Bogus Wolf-Diaries *one* gathers are the wasp eating into our golden apple.) "Exactly. Once bitten, a chap has to come up with something stronger than gold. They've had treasures in lakes up to the gills. The Deathcamp vein still isn't worked out though."

Atrocity stuff. You must have something on that?"

HIM AT BELSEN!!!

... At the Rhapsodie Hotel: She doesn't come back from that Rathaus balcony in Linz until three the next morning. Five hours since the notary, Mack, vanished in flaming Night and Fog and a Black-Leather van. Five hours in which Edwin has read the file, and read it. Has first dreamed the young Boy-"A's" dreams as composer and poet; and then shuddered with Dolferl-"A's" agony and terror as those rat-trap jaws *snap* on the defecating, howling, puppy-Fox'l's penis; and then flushed with His Adolescent-"A's" shame for those laughing fat whores squatting, and grabbing, under the bridges of that harlot city, Vienna. And *then* realised that the first reckoning for a young woman had been one I thought old.

Had been Mama. *Then* was my *mother.*

And her reckoning, the dark waters of a mad March canal, and Richard Wagner's Death in Venice. And ashes ascending in a daytime nightmare past a white cupola with a Dome ...

And *then* – ?

Before *then*. The Rumoured One, Putzi's gossip-One from the earliest days on the Thierschstrasse.

And *then* – ?

Mitzi. The Henhouse-Girl, with rope & lake, (and a weak-kneed Help-Me note!) who failed Him by missing her ferryman's ride across the great river.

And *then* – ?

Geli. Who Made It. (Whether it was His hand or hers that pulled the trigger on His Desperado's revolver.) And is now Immortal, and truly loved when the mad wind blows over her bronze coffin on the Salt Mountain.

And *then* – ?

Martha, the American Dodderer's Daughter, another Failure.

And *then* –?

Renate Müller. Eddie's friend, and talented actress, with her haunted laugh implying the final Act's disaster – and happy landing. With one laughing leap from her Adlon Hotel window Renate made it. She is on

432

the far shore, waving. *Come over* . . .

And *then* – ?

The In-Between Girl, so far another Half-Hearted rider. Our cow-Eva, just getting her feet wet at the edge of the river. Not impressive. We must wag a finger!

And *then* – ?

> *Adam & Eve & Pinch-Me*
> *Went down to the River to bathe.*
> *Adam & Eve were drowned –*
> *Who do you think was saved . . . ?*

Quite right, old Chap, our nursery rhymes tell it all. You were a rider on the Rhine ferry too. But I think we got you off in time.

Edwin was saved, thanks to Carl Jung and his Emma. So far.

And *then* –?

"Bosh." Sister tossed the Notary's file aside with scarcely a glance. "Lord, what a night. Provincial! Eddie darling, you can't imagine – oh yes, and you'll never guess, Wolf's guinea-pig chum showed up. First impressions are always right. I loathed Linz with Mama and the Guinea-pig; this time was even more so. I'm going to sing Mozart tomorrow for Vienna. The Countess – what do you think?"

"Ettie, you *have* to read it. I've told you – it's *why* Mama died. The missing part from her Brown Book. You've been to this Head man of Adler's. You could understand the Freudian parts much more than me, but I don't think it's safe for you to egg Wolf on as you do. Please, Ettie, read it."

"And then drown myself like Mama. Thanks very much."

"So you agree she did it because of Him."

"Nothing of the sort. It's amazing anyone survives in Venice. The steps of those canals are coated in sewage. The stench alone would kill a stoat."

So it went. As she undressed, Brother implored her (which she loved rejecting) and when he tried to read her bits aloud she fellated him (in preparation for the Countess). Sister's joy is doubled, but Brother's fight for her soul continues. He leaves the file by her bedside with her sleep mask and ounce of brandy under the lamp (for when she wakes and parts keep on in her head), and in the morning still persists, while

433

the convoy for Vienna, city of dreams, is forming up with honking and loudspeakers under Heydrich's expert direction, and thrusts the file right before her narrow-bridged, self-blinding *nose*!

And then – ?

She got in a rage and tore the pages across, and again, hurling them on the glowing coals yelling, "For God's sake, Eddie, I don't *care* about Wolf's shitting dogs and drunk fathers and bandaged rats in Steyr and trapped Viennese whores. *He* said he was going to *be* the bloody Fuehrer and he bloody *is*. The damned analysts are the mad ones – as you should know after Mama and that crazy old Jung. For *once* in our lives don't be such a fucking fool!"

F*****g! The first time she ever used that most forbidden of nursery words to him: what a distance has been travelled since *b*m* was smuggled from Cornwall. Not used – screamed, in a Heldenmezzo that all Linz can hear, even over the honking.

But in the Riley, Eddie, sharp as a whip, sets the trap on *her*.

"I didn't read you the part about the rats in Steyr."

Or bandages, anywhere else ...

And then – ?

A pause, as His Mercedes rolls forward with His plans for rebuilding Linz as a mausoleum for *his* mother in the shadow of the Nibelungen-lied castle.

And then – ?

Ettie said, in her quiet voice, icy, the one for climbing mountains:

"This is the year I'm doing my hat-trick. If you don't want to help me you can go to hell."

Snap! Her trap is fool-proof.

Ultimatum.

... *Vienna: He* proposes to her again: in the Grand Ducal Suite at the Hotel Imperial, on His knees, head-in-lap, with tears when she rejects Him – but dried when this time she gives Him a new hanky, a bandage-wisp of lacy cotton with her initials, E C-P, delicate in green satin thread in one corner, to carry into the lists of Munich to joust for Peace as her Knight-Parsifal. So Vienna is not an *exact* reprise of the Berlin night in Eden. There is forward movement! If Wolf-"A" cannot

434

have more than a ribbon, the Fuehrer will ravish Czechoslovakia.

And Brother, after letters to Jung, does not desert her – although the frustration is fierce and the Self-doubts take him close again to the razor's edge. Closer, after a party for the Berlin Opera world given by the Dwarf under a silk parachute canopy, donated in a rare display of mutual goodwill by the Bad Giant's Luftwaffe. In fact both of them were there, a Goebbels and a Goering, opera lovers, side by side, smiling and joking – limping & clanking! – Laurel & Hardy of the Party. And by a bar set up in one silken corner, in a smart, dark green uniform with gold epaulettes and lettering on the shoulders being ogled by Mrs Dwarf – Magda Goebbels – an old military friend. From All Saints College.

"Ettie, look. For Heaven's sake – Pawel!"

She needs no urging. In a tent-full of good-lookers from Stage & Screen, Pawel is handsome. "You've filled out, Pawel dear," in English, as she kisses him, on the lips, to keep it private in full view of Magda; "it suits you. Green's so complimentary to the Slav complexion – whatever you're doing in it."

"What *are* you doing?" Eddie asks his friend, "you look fearfully grand, but whose army does it belong to?"

"Free Russian, we have our HQ in Potsdam. I'm General Pershkov's Two-I-C. Miles early but that's Sandhurst for you. Now tell me your news, Eddie – what about the Grail?"

"I've given it up – more or less – but even with a General Staff you can't really mean it? Free Russia? That great green mass on the map?"

"Not yet." Pawel smiles with those perfect white teeth. An enigmatic smile hinting at military intelligence. "And we've got more than a staff. About twenty thousand recruited so far and half a platoon coming in every week now they know we're open for business."

"Well you can book me at the Bolshoi any time, Pawel darling." Sister reclaims him. "I learnt heaps of lingo for my Boris – 'Da svidanya, Comrade-Frau Reichsminister.' " And she swirls her catch away from the tongue-tied Magda to an ice Swan-boat-full of caviar. Away from Brother.

"Ah, Herr Edwin, the sun seems to go quite half out when our golden Festspiel twins are separated."

The Dwarf slid himself into the opening, gratis. In uniform also: his white ice-cream salesman's, complete with white shoes (the one built up) and fresh silk socks from France. Slippery shades of Lizard Baer – who was across the parachute with Bad Giant Hermann and Queen Emmy.

"I understand your so beautiful sister has taken up Mozart," said Goebbels. Slyly, watching his wife.

"Yes, the Fuehrer dislikes it," Magda restates the obvious, happily, watching Brother. "He has not asked the Fräulein Edwina to sing for him since Vienna. Of course, her voice is still recovering from her breakdown last year."

"It was pneumonia," loyal-Eddie, always, in public. "And Herr Wolf knows she's limiting her engagements because of her triple roles at Bayreuth this Season. He's very understanding. We had supper with him last evening."

"Very understanding. Naturally, he is the Fuehrer. Last evening." Magda's face sets for a last supper. Her husband cackles with delight.

"We too are waiting eagerly, with the Fuehrer. Herr Edwin, you must see that your sister gets plenty of rest. And we must get together for a dinner – if you shall be visiting the Fuehrer again while you are in Berlin I have a small proposal on the new Arts Theatre you might give him?"

From Mime to Alberich and back again, the little devil, with his jab at Brother/Sister *resting*. And then the gall to slip in for a Wolf-favour!

"We never discuss politics." Our Golden Rule. On stiff-Eddie's blind side anyway. Our Wolf can speak for himself. "If you will excuse, I have to join Edwina, that officer she's with, we went to school together . . ."

She wasn't just with Pawel. The Giant half of the act had joined them: Hermann and Emmy (another damned actress) – the first time we had met since Putzi's great escape. The Fat One has put on another few stones of weight around the middle and more on his fingers. Their colours of refraction give the iced caviar a glittering iridescence.

"Ah, Edwin, my old young friend – I thought we'd lost you to the Little Doktor for the rest of the party." Showing off his good English – and no love lost between them. "Ten marks says he was trying to steal Edwina for his new theatre."

"It was mentioned, but more in connection with Herr Wolf than Ettie."

436

"Our Fuehrer," Queen Emmy reproved the Boy, with a soft-steel purr to her well-trained voice. "Even among old friends. Even my dear Hermann and I may no longer allow ourselves to use Adolf."

"We never have," said Ettie, too sweetly. "Eddie, you must tell Hermann your meeting-Putzi story. Come and dance me off my feet, in your lovely green, Pawel dear."

. . . For an instant, it's Mama gliding forward with that strong arm around her waist, swaying and swooning to the music, with those white teeth smiling down at her, and that olive skin gleaming with the same irresistible appeal. But then it was just Pawel and Ettie. And Eddie stuck between 2 rival giants. With a glittering ham of a hand, the Bad One manoeuvers the youth into a quiet corner of his parachute.

"Edwin, you've met our friend Hanfstaengl? Why this is excellent news! Tell me how he was – where he was – the foolish fellow. I just can't imagine that he took a prank so seriously – some chaps from my old squadron? Really, we must get him home."

"Yes, he showed me your letter."

"Exactly. I gave him the word of an officer and gentleman, but of course he doesn't have that sort of background, no military service, but he must come back; we all miss him. The Fuehrer was saying just the other day – perhaps he mentioned it to you, when you had dinner last night?"

He can't bend to tie his shoes, but the Bad Giant's ear is close to the ground. "No, Herr Wolf hasn't mentioned Putzi for ages."

"Ah well – now look, Eddie, you and your sister hear all the chit-chat as you call it, on the English circuit, how do you think my visit to Buckingham Palace is being received?"

"Ah – I'm, ah, sure the King will be delighted."

"That's excellent news – Lord Halifax tells me the same. Eddie, do you think when next you see the Fuehrer you could mention . . .?"

. . . And when the Fool looks around the parachute tent, Ettie and Pawel are gone.

"In a staff car, Herr von Perceval," from one of the footmen, dressed up in more parachute silk. "They did not say where. It was under the flag of the White Russians' general, but he was not with them."

Brother located the Russians' Mess in Potsdam. There was no sign of them. No word at our hotel – again, the Eden. Not that night, nor the next day, or night, or day, or forty-eight more hours. It was the fifth day when she came back: sleek as cat with cream. Sated Miss Pussy.

"I've been Ukrainianised," she said. "Darling, order us up some tea and gin."

"Get it yourself. Where the hell were you? I've been worried sick."

"Tegernsee. What harm did you think I could come to in Pawel's strong hands? Eddie, don't be a grouch – I'm utterly parched; I must have some gin."

"At Tegernsee."

"Yes. That little place of Putzi's was up for grabs for the weekend, so we grabbed. Utter heaven."

Our honeymoon heaven.

"You took him there! Hunding's Hut. Our special place."

"Darling, if I'm not allowed to go anywhere we've been naughty, Europe isn't big enough. Anyway it was only two nights. We went to Munich after that. The little Gerbers have sold out. A rather ghastly sausage man's running it now. We bumped into Wolf at the Carlton – doing a flit in the middle of all this Sudeten fuss, so it can't be nearly as complicated as the Yellows shriek. I introduced him to Pawel."

Rubbing His nose in it as well as mine.

"You deliberately upset Him. Truly, Ettie, I think you're mad."

"Only a little sore, my pet. Besides, *He* had the Mitfahrt crawling along behind – in a dress like mine last Season, with a Geli-doll sash and that frightful hyena laugh she has. And she's peroxiding her hair. I had to do *something* – Eddie, don't be cross. Pawel's away on man-oeuvres and rehearsals start next week and I know I've bitten off impossibly much with the three roles. And my first Bayreuth Kundry. It's like going to prison."

"No you haven't. You'll make it. You'll be marvellous . . ."

So quickly can the Wurm be turned, children. And hug Her, & get Her gin, & run Her bath, & massage Her feet & the back of Her neck – every day for the next 6 weeks. To say nothing of Her Mandrake Treatments!

438

OUR '38 SEASON

War-scares are everywhere for Czechoslovakia, and His black mandalas in the Festspiel Square, but the Wagnerians assemble for the dance in their hundreds, and their hothouse finery, unimpaired. Not unafraid – fear raises the temperature deliciously in the hothouse. All talk is of the '14 Season. All secretly desire to be part of The Last Season Before The War ... Liebestod Legends In Our Time ...

She did not sing the opening cycle. *He* did not attend.

And the first 2 houses have been sold out to the Strength Through Joy organisation: Let Siegfrieds & Brünnhildes be unconfined! Much coupling for the Leader is accomplished under the lime trees, but they are not a discriminating audience, my dears. The Wagnerians dine on imported foods and save themselves for Edwina C-P, the Pure of Tone, and Noble, trying for her hat-trick; and the Melchior's replacement as Our Hero, Max Lorenz.

The Leader-Wolf waited for the house lights to go down for G-D, Act I – then He was there, for Her, in the Box beside me. No jackboots. No announcement. No Goerings or Goebbels. A single young adjutant on His left hand. The Norns span. The Thread snapped.

> *"How would I love you, did I not let you go forth to fresh deeds, dear Hero?"*
> *"More you have given me, wondrous Woman, than I know how to husband."*

My sister, His Brünnhilde.

> *"You select my combats, my triumphs reflect on you; astride your steed – Heil, radiant Star!"*
> *"Heil Siegfried, victorious Light! Resplendent Life!"*
> *Heil! Heil! Heil! Heil!*

His Horn is heard. She waves Him rapturously off on His Rhine journey ...

And then – ?

439

Afterwards, in the Festspiel Restaurant, the Honourable Unity Valkyry Mitford finds she does not have a seat at the Fuehrer's table.

And then – ?

The second hat lands in the ring: Isolde.

And then – ?

Die Mitfahrt falls ill. At first no one notices. The girl coughs and is pale, haunting the Festspielhaus. The Family doctor is summoned by Auntie Winnie. Fräulein Unity Valkyry has but a mild bronchitis. No more.

And then – ?

The third hat. The last in the ring. Kundry and Parsifal. But can even Sister cap such previous triumphs?

"I can't," she said, sprawled legs akimbo, undressed, upstairs at the Griesbachs'. "Oh Christ, Eddie, the words have gone. The notes. They're all the same. I tried my Expiation, it came out just a croak, like a crow."

Like a raven. Nevermore.

"I'll get the doctor," Eddie said. "It's been too much. I did tell you, Ettie darling."

"Sod the doctor. I *have* to do it." She pulled at her hair and howled like Mama when our Father died. We had no brown bottle. "Only Saxon schnaps! Sweet Jesus, what sort of a brother can't even get a drop of gin in Bayreuth."

"You said you wanted schnaps. Ettie, you must try and be calm. I'll get gin. I'll go down to the Anchor – "

"I don't want blasted gin. I want you to suck me."

"I can't."

Not if life depends on it. She's Cursing.

"You mean you *won't*, you selfish bastard. My whole career at Bayreuth's finished. Anywhere. With a war I'll never sing again just because you can't bear the taste. After what *I* have to taste!"

"It isn't the tasting. It's thinking about – "

"*Think*? Since when did you *think* with your thing in my mouth?" She had it. Was squeezing it. Hurting it. Damnably.

"Ettie, please, I'll try and make love but not Push-me-pull-you."

"Damn and blast we're not in the nursery. The word is *cunnilingus*. Say it!" Slapping his face. Hard. "Say it!" Harder. "Like *cunt* – !"

"Ettie, God in heaven, the Griesbachs – "

Her hands in his hair, yanking him DOWN to –

"Say it, damn you, say Lick my cunt, damn you, lick me, damn you, Christ why won't He love me – "

But after C**t, what Nursery barriers are left to be broken?

She pushes him farther and pulls him closer. Her kimono is parted. Her tears fall hotly on the back of his neck. Her body shudders. Her torment racks him. She is Sister. Brother has bled for her, once, with a safety razor: now through the deadly blood he must save her.

So I loved her. In the way she wanted.

And then – ?

Kundry. Crouching. Her eyes glow out at Him across the hooded black pit. She sings like an angel and howls in her snakeskin like an Alsatian bitch. He hunches. The lustflowers open in the garden. The Wagnerians tremble in their hothouse passion. The grail descends, redly, throbbing. Now He trembles. The hothouse is shaking. The first panes breaking. Crystal smashing, and errant Parsifal Knights rampaging. The Wound is open. Beside me, He bites His lower lip so that it bleeds. And in the Interval He does not leave the box to hear the trumpets, but sits alone, with the curtains drawn, licking . . .

And then – ?

Telegrams pour in from Wagnerians all over the world. Herr Wolf breaks the Nursery Rule about No Clapping After Parsifal, at the Singers' Table: *and* sent her one more 100 red roses with Anna Hess, in Mama's Mercedes. For remembrance. She gave Him back a box, wrapped in tissue and green satin. Inside was part of her snakeskin Kundry girdle.

And then – ?

Unity Valkyry Mitfahrt is found standing by an open window, in her thin night-dress, soaked with rain, and coughing, as she pours her medicine out into a bed of waiting rhododendron bushes, to allow the pneumonia to worsen, before she is rushed to a Clinic, where He sends her His physician for these occasions, Doktor Platte, and an auto-graphed picture. Which she gives away to the ecstatic nurses while she averts her peroxided head and waits with the caftan-millions for the ferry across the great river of Nibelheim . . .

He comes back for a second helping of the Parsifal, and afterwards, at a private Family supper, complains that He is being poisoned – via His Special Beer, a dark concoction brewed at Holzkirchen, with a teetotal 1-per-cent proof of naughtiness. The young Adjutant is sent packing to bring more brown bottles: one is opened at random. (Picked by Lucky Eddie.) The Adjutant sips. Survives. Good dog! Master was satisfied. With the Adjutant dismissed until the next attempt, to a captive feminine audience (Winnie, Mausi, Ettie, Eddie) He expanded:

"Parsifal is the Masterpiece – I have to say it – but for special occasions only. In fact, after these extraordinary performances I feel more strongly than ever that it should be kept only for here, at Bayreuth, with people like ourselves who can understand its real significance. The Emperor Joseph had this identical problem with Mozart stirring up the masses in the wrong direction – and only with a fraction of the Art of Richard Wagner! Also, he was disgustingly foul-mouthed – Mozart – but with a highly developed faculty of recall. I have this myself to some degree – Ederl, tell me, was Frau Goebbels smoking when you met the other day? Are you sure? She has the habit of hiding them under the tablecloth. She thinks I don't notice. We shall have to wag a finger. Such a disgusting habit, defiling the mouth. The gums are all important – especially in pregnant women. When you come to Berlin I must show you Speer's model for my rebuilding. The Dome can contain three or four St Peters! Once we get this annoyance of Czechoslovakia behind us. As usual the old Welshman was right – what was it he called Beneš? A filthy lying little swine! Precisely – one could say, rat! – Beneš, of course, went out of his way to make the criminal Versailles proposals impossible for this Country. Well we don't hold grudges. In fact it would be hard to find a more generous people than ours – excuse me, most gracious possible Fräulein Ettie, but we think of you and Ederl as one of the family – and you could do worse than follow Frau Winifred's example. There's nothing I should like better than a formal union between our countries to start a united Europe – it can't possibly be left to the mongrel races or the Latins. The Italian Royal Family is totally decayed. All the old Queen talked about on my visit was Verdi! And applauding every squalling aria – how can there possibly be any sense of involvement with such constant interruptions? Wagner saw it so clearly – but this is the loneliness of Genius, to see the way ahead, and have to

442

lead so far in front of all the others. Sometimes it's quite intolerable. Obersalzberg for example, oppresses my spirit more each time I go there. The apparatus of security has destroyed the place. And it used to be so glorious, walking on the mountain, in those early days, when your so-noble mother visited. Do you remember our little picnics? So simple, and jolly. How I long to go back to such a time. Another year, one more Season, that's the goal now I've set for myself, then Goering can have it. He's let himself run to seed, but his approach is sounder than Goebbels'. Yes, the productions that Hermann puts on at the Berlin State are altogether better. Now, what shall we have our Ederl play for us ...?"

Too late for suggestions from His ladies: Mausi growing fatter in rebellion, openly snores; Aunt Winnie – not getting any younger! – shoots daggers at her daughter, then catches herself yawning! Gracious Ettie, who hates sharing, went half an hour ago to powder her nose.

"And never came back," Eddie said the next morning. Crossly. "You can't imagine He didn't notice. He may be repeating more often, but He isn't slow – and there's no excuse for being rude in Winnie's house."

"Aren't we a proper little gentleman. The gums are all important and the Wops are decayed. It isn't even noon. Go away."

Sister pushed her boiled egg aside and rolled over in her bed.

"I don't care about the Italians, either," Brother said. "It's what He told us about being German. Wolf can be fearfully pushing with a bee in His bonnet."

"I have no intention of becoming a bloody Hun. We're Swiss. Go away."

"We aren't. That's the point, Ettie. We're us – English, and if there's going to be a war, as you said – "

"There isn't, and I didn't, and we aren't anything, really. We're Wagnerians, darling – now do please bugger off."

The covers pulled over her golden head.

"You did say there was going to be a war. That's why you made me – before the first Parsifal – "

"Made you what?" Sex at least, can gain her attention on a prewar Sunday morning. She sat up. Naked. Her breasts were showing.

"I don't want to talk about it," Eddie said. "The passport thing is much more important – but one couldn't help noticing after the analysis, he does go on about rats. And now building this colossal dome."

"A proper little anal-yst. It's bilge, Eddie – but if you're so frightened, take me to Triebschen and make us Swiss."

... *At Zürich:* A world above the World: land of safe-nursery milk-chocolate and Alps. And Carl Jung. The Patient-Edwin goes to see him again in early September when the leaves are once more turning on the ash trees and the Sudeten pot coming to full boil.

Called or not called, the God shall be there.

Without appointment, Jung, working in the village, was: but his dear Emma, at a conference in Denmark, wasn't – and our village had grown to include a Rathaus, for Council Meetings of the invisible inhabitants.

"There's nothing there," the Patient said, "and yet it feels so like home."

"Nothing that we can see, old chap. But that doesn't mean that the houses and the church are empty. Shall we have a cup of tea?"

"I'm terribly worried about Ettie and Wolf."

"All the more reason." Jung poured milk-first into the familiar mugs with their ivy and gnomes. "Even *Furor Teutonicus* backs down a little in the face of a good cup of tea. You must break away soon from your Wolf. There isn't much time. Have you had the next dream?"

"It isn't me. It's Ettie. Even after Mama's Brown Book, she won't see the danger."

"Few of us ever do see our dangers, old chap. I came late to the Teuton one myself. Tell me about this book of your mother's."

So her son does. As much as he can remember of rats, and traps, and puppy-Fox'l, and the laughing bitches in Vienna – *but not a word about my bleeding sister.*

"An early Freudian," Carl Jung pronounces, at the end, in deep thought, with the tea long cold, "with such unswerving trust in the power of developmental fixations – but the analysis sounds like Wotan springing to life all right."

"It's Wolf I'm worried about," the Patient repeats it. "And Ettie upsetting him. She's always done it deliberately, and nothing ever happened, but suddenly it all seems awfully dangerous."

"It always has been – but only for the rest of us, old chap. When your sister teases the god, he must assert his masculine nature. Your mother's

Brown Book confirms that things are concealed in the background which we can't imagine yet, but we must expect them to emerge. Wotan's awakening is a sort of stepping back, or reaching back. The river has been dammed up and has broken into its original channel. But the dam will not hold forever."

Freudianism becomes child's play against such riddles. The Patient, riddled with uncertainty and fear for his sister, can only say to the tall friend from his childhood, "So there will be a war."

"A cataclysm. The man in your Wolf's clothing in one more Season will be fifty: the god will be battling for his soul. All the facets of his multiple personality – anima and animus, *and* their shadows! – must be consumed in such a struggle. But not by drowning, as poor feminine Ludwig was. For the Wotan-Wolf it must be transformation by fire, in my opinion."

"And Ettie?"

"When Valhalla burns old chap, Fricka, and Freia, and Brünnhilde go with it."

"But that's make-believe," the Patient cries, passionately. "We learnt it all in the nursery. For God's sake, *Wahnfried isn't real life.*"

"It has been your life."

And Sister's. And Wagner's. And His. Tales for little folk . . .

"Is there no way out?" I asked Jung.

"Floods and rivers must run their course, old chap. In 'real life' your sister might be safe if you perched her on her rock up here with us milk-chocolate people for a little while."

"But she couldn't sing up here."

"She could yodel. And she might hear the sound of her own voice more clearly in the echo."

"I don't think I can tell her that."

"You *can*," Jung smiled his most owlish smile.

Another Place:
In Zürich, Michael Rau is lost in a huge blue-leather chair, behind an enormous Louis-Something desk, shirt-sleeved and happily destroying the last of his father's Prague holdings. He threw a final gilt-edge in a waste-paper basket and jumped, or rather, bounced from the blue chair, and out around the desk.

"Eddie! Marvellous to see you. The old boy has nothing left in Czechoslovakia and it's almost time for supper – we'll find a place."

"I'd love dinner, Michael, but I want to talk business first. Ettie-business."

"Can I guess? Mr Wolf's huffing and puffing has sent you packing for a strong stone citizenship for your lovely sister."

"Yes – I think we have to, if she intends to keep singing in Europe with a war on."

"Which of course she does, or she wouldn't be our luscious Edwina. She feels Wagner is going to be popular in Europe – after Mr Wolf blows their straw houses down – does she?"

"I don't know. What do you think?"

"There'll be a full house in Prague to play to by the day after tomorrow. My father's not even selling short on Skoda."

"Seriously? Even with Chamberlain and Daladier flying all over the place for the peace talks?"

"You know a good Jewish son never jokes about his father's business." Rau beamed his broadest beam and slipped his short thick arms into a jacket. He had grown another chin in his pursuit of places.

"Michael – for Ettie's sake, I think we'll have to do it and become Swiss on our passports. Can you make the arrangements for us?"

"Consider it done, Eddie old friend."

"Just like that? I thought there were waiting lists of thousands?"

"My father's just become an American – taking his secretary with him. I'm to have a new mother my own age. The Casson-Percevals can have their places. Now come on – with all this excitement I'm almost starving."

Just a Rau-isch turn of phrase. It's "A" Who is slavering . . .

In the restaurant, Rau eats 7 courses and gives Eddie more than he asked for on his plate. It starts with an innocent's remark:

"This place is excellent, Michael – as usual. Our favourite spot in Munich has changed hands unfortunately. Ettie says the Gerbers have sold-up to a Hun-sausage man."

"I know." Rau hacked and stabbed some half-alive sea-creature. "I offered to buy them out in 'Thirty-six. Now I suppose they've lost everything."

"What on earth do you mean? Why would you have wanted to buy the Gerbers?"

"To prevent what's happened – Expropriation, dear Eddie. I keep an eye on all your Jewish friends – of course it hasn't done the slightest good. Your Bayreuth couple are equally pig-headed."

"We don't know any Jews in Bayreuth. Michael, you aren't making any sense."

"You've been paying them rent for fifteen years."

And so another penny drops.

"The Griesbachs? Jews?"

"It doesn't seem possible next to Wahnfried. That's what they think. Well they may be right, as long as the Festival is international."

Free of Illusion, I name my house . . .

"As to the Gerbers' situation," Rau said, "I'll get in touch with Heydrich's office. If they've been put in a camp we can buy them out."

He swallowed the sea-creature in a gulp, happy to be of service.

"I don't know what to say," said Eddie. "The Gerbers, in a prison. And the Griesbachs, Jewish."

"And they seemed such ordinary people," said Rau. "There's one other thing I could do in the light of the Czechoslovak situation. My father holds the mortgage to an old pile of stone at Třeboň. It's no use to him and it has one of your tin-pot stories associated with a haunting. All nonsense to a non-believer but it would give you a place of your own – to start digging."

Which quite banishes the plight of *Them* from Eddie's potsy-turvey mind, children, and sends him hot-foot home to Ettie with the momentous news – by way of the black-red city from his childhood map: the one with the tower. Where his blue Riley is stopped, and his mind further addled, by a blond beasts' parade.

. . . Nürnberg: Thinking of the implications of being able to *DIG* anywhere, Edwin hasn't realised it's Rally Week in Hans Sachs' Town or he would have avoided it like the Plague, as they say. The city is crammed within its walls at the best of times: at these others, with a thousand trains arriving, and a million men marching, there isn't a spare inch of room for Eddie or Riley to park for a night or to drive any further. We were stopped by the Wörder See – and a thousand

447

taut-buttocked boy-gymnasts, golden-shaven, rehearsing – when we were arrested.

"You cannot be stopped in this place!"

A shouting Party policeman, temporarily recruited, is our traffic warden.

"I'm stopped because I can't move."

"You cannot drive a Restricted Route without Passes!"

"I have a pass, from Bayreuth."

"This is Nürnberg!" Irrefutable logic. "You cannot stop here."

But the Riley was. Forever it seemed.

"I don't want to stop, but I can't get through – "

"You cannot drive a Restricted Route!"

"I understand that. I didn't know it was restricted. The pass is signed by General Heydrich."

Magic name. They recoil – until – "This is not a German vehicle! How did you get this signing?"

The spell was working backwards. Edwin said, without his Mama's gift for handling Officials, "God in heaven, General Heydrich signed it. Look – it's his damned name."

"You have forged this. You are now arrested."

The Riley is left to be ogled by the dispersing gymnasts. Its driver is put in a black Maria that smells of Black-Leather and Fear. We pass this way but once . . .

At the police station, in an office with browned yellow paint, and buzzing flies hatched and trapped by September, a similar Teutonic interrogation. The flies dash themselves against the panes. The voices bark. What has always seemed obtuse but comic in the Hun character, is now no laughing matter.

"You are English. What are you doing with General Heydrich's signature?"

The 100th time.

"Ask him – he signed it."

And being German they took this at face value. The Prisoner was left alone in the locked office with the flies and photographs of wanted men. The sun dropped. The flies dropped with it, only fitfully buzzing, crawling along the ledges with tiny feet, like hands. Their stalk-eyes can look for danger in all directions, yet find no escape from this heart of it.

Few of us do, old Chap . . .

Boots in a passage. Much Heiling & Stamping. Bolts sliding back. *He* is coming – no: only His Blond Moses. It was good enough.

"Herr Edwin, this is regrettable, but the Fuehrer speaks tonight. He's arriving with the Imperial First Reich Relics from Vienna. Our Security nerves are a little on edge."

Don't tell me! "Je ne regrette rien," was Isy Heydrich's motto. Once more Edwin detects that faint sneer (which upon closer scrutiny seems only Devotion) behind the Imperial Relics news.

"I can go?"

"Immediately. A formal apology will follow from the Reichsminister."

"That's very decent – but what about my car? I left it on a restricted route."

"All details have been attended to. Your sister's blue Riley is removed to the Hotel Stadtler. It has a Nuremberg pass. You have a room – driving tonight would not be possible. As I recall, you and Fräulein Edwina stayed with your mother?"

Je recall everything!

"Thank you again, General."

"It was my duty. I have rooms there myself. We'll go together – I wouldn't want you to go off the rails twice in a day."

"Thank you." Again. Proper little toady.

"And also – " those dreaded Teuton *also's* (meaning Therefore's) – "the Fuehrer has personally awarded you a place at the Rally."

"Herr Wolf knows I'm here?"

"Nothing escapes Him."

With which enigmatic reply the prisoner was released, leaving only the flies, and the black smell of fear waiting for the next object of His omniscient attention. Heydrich talked of Ettie's achievements during our brief ride to the Stadtler; not the Leader's, or International Affairs, or Security. He even had a favour to ask: that in exchange for Brother's swift freedom I should persuade Sister to allow Tristan-Moses to accompany her in private recital upon the violin!

"With yourself on piano, naturally. My instrument's too harsh for a solo. I've often wished I made it the cello. That gorgeous tone always reminds me of a jewelled scarab trapped in amber."

The poetry of the beast! Trapped Eddie barely has time for a bath to wash off the prison before On With The Show. Another interchangeable Black Order Captain has been sent to escort to the rally. A special route is cleared of all civilian traffic. A spare million men line it, Wolf-saluting like battalions of dominoes as our car passes with Blond Moses' Skull & Crossbones flying.

The Stadium:
The sun was set, the torches already flickering with their bandit shadows, the eagle banners hunched over the black mandalas, ripping beaks extended, talons gripping. The stadium was filled, but that says nothing, a mere few hundred thousand – la crème de la crème, my dears – for outside the stadium, ringing it, are the rest of the million. This is not Rosenheim, with sausage salesmen and fist fights in the cheap seats. This is Discipline, and there are no cheap seats: standing-room-only, and the cost of each is the standee's life.

The Black Order Captain leads Edwin through a section of the giants' stadium, down low on the ground; not up in the air where the giants live. Hermann, the growing-fatter one is already there, with the Dwarf beside him, barely as high as his elbows, busy Sieg Heiling the shadow men. "Working the crowd" the circus barkers call it. Or Empire-building.

The legions of Fafner are silent. It spoils the show to start it early. Edwin sees one familiar face at his level: Leni Riefenstahl, directing a camera installation – once more Young Eddie is to be immortal. *Or is he, too, lost in that final edit? Down on the floor with the other snippets of flesh and blood – sneezers, and fainters, and His farting – that made the beast human. Myths & Gods cannot fart, Jung's Basel dream notwithstanding.*

Speer's searchlights came on. You have seen it. I cannot describe it. Stupendous. Ice walls of the greatest of all Grail Temples, five miles high to Valhalla above us. The spine rippled. The Fafner legions flexed their scales. The very blocks and concrete of the stadium rumbled.

He is coming . . .

Not yet. A Wagnerian knows it, because there is no motif, children, but the hundred thousand in the sloped seats – the lucky few from the Strength Through Joy who were not fobbed off with Bayreuth, but got in to the main production – they think with the lights and the Über Alles that He *is*! – and begin to howl their ragged, untrained chorus. But the

450

Fafner legions know what Edwin knows and wait with the fire banked in their bellies until they hear it.

> *Make us the Mirror image of Thy power*
> *Hear my deep and fervent Plea ...*

Rienzi.

That shallow early work about the jumped-up Roman tribune. Shallow and early, yes: considered not worthy by followers of His Ring. But here it sounds, and sounds, from ten thousand bandsmen, brazen, the cry of the Dragon! Fafner unleashed! The bellow! The bellow!

He has come. He is HERE.

He lives – for I see Him – therefore I am. But so small, for such tumult. So why am I His, to kill or command? Why am I roaring with the five hundred thousand? Where am I going with this marching million? Marching, marching, onwards and on as the Dragon winds past me and Knowledge comes to me as it does at Bayreuth when the Wound descends: for now I know, absolutely, utterly, more surely than sexual passion's Self-gratification – with such a Million, such a Dragon, at my back, even this one puny, inverted, aimless and Sister-dominated male creature, a pale dot so small as He is: He-Hitler, I-Edwin, together can recover our lost and true Grail.

INTERMEZZO

[Or Footnote to History]

Late October. Tea with Our Inferior Eva. The world is happy with Peace in its Time. We meet at the Carlton – not taking chances! – Eva is looking much smarter, in a nutmeg tailored suit and a chocolate pillbox hat.

"I get them from Amyot's, in Paris, Herr Eddie. He lets me buy anything I want now the Mitfahrt's no longer with Him. He's never been so kind. Shall I tell you a little secret about what He did? The old Chamberlain was here for the last visit – you know the one at the apartment, Prinzregentstrasse? – and He let me hide in the bedroom while He talked to the old man! What the Eye doesn't See, as they say. It was so funny!"

"Yes, I'm sure, Eva, it must have been."

"Oh you English. Herr Eddie – it was where the old Chamberlain was

451

sitting. To *sign.* Can't you guess? Our Red Divan!"

Yes children! *He* had moved it back from His cow's so-dear-little-house-all-her-own for the so-Special Occasion!

(And you still thought He had no Sense of Humour)

[Foot-Foot-Note:]

Mausi, the rebel-Wagner, sick & tired of His jokes ("and those awful marathon Fox'l stories!") has a *"colossally huge* row with Mother!" – and runs away from Home! ("Come and see me, Eddie. I'm staying with Frida in Zürich – and her husband.")

The Last Straw. To desert Him for a filthy, caftan-Y*d!

Third Movement

Second Passage

[fast]

It was a Lover and his Lass,
With a hey, and a ho, and a hey nonny no,
That o'er the green cornfield did pass,
With a hey, and a ho, and a hey nonny no.

... *On Porquerolles:* First day of another new year – redolent of Mediterranean promise & excitement for our heroes. The marvels of Technology have come to our golden island: a telegraph office next to the épicerie on the Place. It has bakelite-and-brass fittings but still keeps Porquerolles hours (Pas ce soir! – or Sundays, or when the mackerel fleet's in) and thus is seldom quicker than word from Hyères via Deaf'n'Dumber on his chugging *Cormoran*.

Winifred's telegram had sped from the Green Hill 2 days before the C-Ps got it (brought the last suspicious sandy mile by Mathilde, trudging with bread and nunnery butter).

CONFIRMATION RING PARSIF TRIST AND FIRST HOLLAN-
DER EXCLAM STOP SENTA OF 39 IS YOURS STOP HIS
REQUEST SIGNED SENTA OF 14 SAY YES DOUBLE EXCLAM
STOP

Yes, Children! For Caballerian-Wagnerians, with their Fad nursery-arithmetic, the Dutchman's inexorable cycle has worked round:

453

1939 *minus*1918
Equals?
21 Seasons
Or –
3 Times His Lucky 7!

"Of course *yes* is the answer," Eddie said to Ettie, "How nice for Winnie after the Mausi business. I'll take it back to the telegraph office for you now."

"Ta," said Sister, stretching in the portulaca sun, "I'll write it out."

"I do know the address," Brother said. "What else is there to write?"

TO SENTA BAYREUTH YOUR SENTA YES ALSO BRUNN
KUND ISOLD SIGNED LOVE ETTIE PORQUEROLLES STOP

No Exclamms!

"But oh Christ. Ettie, you can't. We can't. Not again. Not four."

"We can. I shall."

"Winnie won't possibly let you."

"He won't let her stop me."

"Then you'll do it alone, because I shall be digging."

"You don't mean that," she said. "My own brother, after everything we've done and I get the chance of our lifetime. You won't really go off for some pot in Bohemia?"

The Boy should have been warned by the lack of hysterics. The flat note of reason – flat as the ears on a tigress, thwarted!

"It's my life too, Ettie. Třeboň Castle is on the salt route – which is the Grail route. Graz, Avignon, they're all connected by salt. The Romans even had pans at Camargue – "

"You've told me, darling. I'll send the telegram myself."

She did. Hoisting the final storm warning, but Eddie thought nothing of it – just thank God that at 30, half a hag and fully a woman, at last She's seeing Reason. Letting Me Go! So we each laid our plans in the sun, and made love when Mathilde was gone for the day, without aberrations.

While snowbound, on the Salt Mountain, Wotan-"A" decrees a race law sweeping in its generosity: the Mischlinge, *those shadowland half-Nibelung, half Volsung, who have only 1 Caftan grandparent are exempt! – and thus spared merciless Alberich's whip.*

454

. . . En route Třeboň: Edwin goes for the 1st time in mid-March, an early spring, a good sign for Digging; the snow is thawing, though log jetties still protect the bridges from the ice in the rivers. There is the usual talk of War, at the borders, but the Scholar ignores it, crossing at Cheb, and then by way of Praha, called Prague by some, where the Astronomical Clock tells off our hours – and months, and minutes, with Vanity & Avarice passing with the Twelve Apostles. And skeleton Death, bearing an hourglass, emptying . . .

The Scholar went questioning to Golden Lane in Prague, the Street of Alchemists, and by this Jungian direction was sent on under the potters' sign (of Adam & Eve, both made of clay) to the Town Hall Archives for maps of Old Třeboň. The Town Hall sent me to Strahov Monastery – a library before Gutenberg for the Kingdom of Bohemia, with a great leather globe, 15 feet in circumference. Big enough for the Norns to sit on. I found the maps I wanted.

The Castle of Our White Lady of The Grail

It is inhabited by an old one – Old-old, over 90, and living on alone (except for a servant) in 70 silent, icy rooms. The Scholar reaches her as dark is falling – *it always falls as we end a journey, that is part of our human nature: the bats come out as we go in* . . . the old woman's name was the Countess Maria Eustasia Vok-Rosenberg. Another tick on the clock of hours: *Eustasia*, children, was our Scholar's Mama's name. And the Countess had *met* Young Edwin's Great Grand-Mama.

"At Windsor, yes, oh so long back – she wedded that man in the basket chair. Such a fuss at dances. I remember – but you are going to dig up the courtyard, you say?"

"Not until I've investigated the cellars, Countess. And subject to your convenience, of course."

"Ninety is not a convenient age, boy. It's not my house any longer and my husband is buried with St Vitus at the Cathedral. Dig where you wish – but spare the long flower bed under the North Tower. There are aconite bulbs in the Spring, and I may not see another."

It was not her house, but Rau was letting her stay on until. Even for bankers it must seem slightly ridiculous to foreclose on a Castle! The

455

Scholar hires an extra servant in the town (the Countess Vok-Rosenberg's maid was as old as her mistress) and begins instant survey of his territory. There have been 3 castles, one upon another: the last, the living quarters, was a chateau; the middle was 15th Cent, with turrets and battlements, still fighting fit; the first, visible only above ground as foundations and a moat, was 5 centuries older. And under that?

The ground is rock hard. Dame Sun is needed as an ally. The Scholar retires the first night impatient but happy.

"I wouldn't sleep in that room," says the Countess's old maid. "Herself sleeps there with her gloves on."

"Your mistress, the Countess?"

"Herself – the White Lady."

"The room has a ghost. Well I don't mind, it has a nice stove to keep the chill off. What's wrong with her gloves?"

"Nothing be wrong if they be white, sir. But if they be black, thou'll sup with Old Nick."

The Scholar dismisses the crone graciously – like Sister – and keeps the candle burning. There is no haunting. In the morning the sun is shining on Czechoslovakia. Icicles melt onto the out-of-bounds aconites' bed beneath the North Tower. The would-be Archaeologist stands watching them after breakfast. On the Astronomical Clock the skeleton rattles for the Ides of March. In the courtyard, a black car with chains on its wheels roars up spitting chipped ice and gravel. Two stern men inside.

"Herr von Perceval?"

Hun is not unexpected in Czechoslovakia. Nor that Officialdom shall know our name:

"Yes, I am Casson-Perceval. Who is asking?"

"The Government of the Protectorate of Bohemia and Moravia. Please come with us."

A long title for a small town, but the sun has much melting work to do and the Scholar has time. But we were through Třeboň, beyond it, heading north and my officials were still silent.

"Where are we going? Where are you taking me?"

"To Protectorate Headquarters at Hradčany Castle."

456

"But that's Prague. It's hours. Really I must protest. I called at the Archives at the Town Hall. No one said a word – "

"The Town Hall is not aware of policy by the Protectorate. There have been developments. Do you wish to relieve yourself? Food will be provided on arrival."

The Sudetens have more politeness than native Huns, and the same sardonic hint of something up their sleeves as Heydrich.

"No – I don't want anything."

Except to be taken South again ... Sunday in Prague, the city is sleeping after church. The Street of Alchemists is unchanged – only His Battle-flag flying over the seat of Czech government, home of "that little swine Beneš" reveals the degree of political transformation.

"There's been a coup?" the Scholar said to the sardonic men. "Does that mean I can't go on digging?"

"Not a coup, Herr von Perceval. We are now proudly part of Greater Germany."

The black car swings up the hill of Saints Wenceslas and Vitus. The cathedral of the latter forms only a centrepiece of the enormous quadrangle formed by the outer walls of the Castle. As though the Houses of Parliament contained St Pauls, with room left over for the Tower and the Abbey. Under the flagstaff flying the Mowgli, we halted. 2 Black Order sprang forward.

"We have brought Herr von Perceval," said his pair.

"There has been a change of plans. He is to proceed to the village of Sedlec."

Sieg Heil!

"This is nonsense – I demand to see someone in authority."

"It is another hour. Do you wish to relieve yourself?"

Relieved, but not for long, because the Black Order follow in a second car to block the prisoner's escape. We struck west through the rolling hills of Bohemia, through Kutná Hora, seat of the Second Kings, and a silver mine for coin of the realm. In fits of religious zeal miners tossed dissenters down it. At a hamlet called Lidice the car of the Black Order passed us.

Another hamlet: Sedlec. A crossroads, an inn, hutch-cottages, an abbey – Cistercian from its fenestration. Snow covers its gravestones.

457

The lane to it is muddy. One set of rutted wheels has preceded us. One set of footprints leads away to the door of the abbey. The Black Order car stopped. Ours has to.

"Out, if you please, Herr von Perceval."

Now the Scholar could have welcomed the question. My bladder was bursting among the gravestones.

"He is to proceed inside." The Black Order's use of the impersonal *he* is chilling.

As *he*, the Scholar walked up to the door. Skulls for its handles faced me, grinning. Thigh bones for hinges squeaked their gross humour. Rib cages made little lantern lights and windows. All once human. Inside were thirty thousand more – and that was just the altar. A charnel house for Christ. In His Service.

"Edwin," said the Wolf of Bohemia & Moravia, "it can't go on. It's quite impossible. You must see that."

The Charnel Church:
But all I see is Him, standing there out of nowhere against this impossible Christian consecration of thigh bones and skulls, of fibulae and tibiae, of scapulars and pelvises flavescent as parchment, or grey-green with mildew, and every lost eye staring with the obscene gravity of black gloves on a white lady. . . .

"No, Herr Wolf, I'm afraid I don't see."

"You don't?"

He swings from His study of the skulls to face me. In the amber light from the rib cage chandeliers He has not aged a day from the fortune-telling glass table at Frau Steiner's, with the coloured plates that showed our destinies. His expression has the same intensity – and now it is that the Fool's mind locks in the raven's wing of hair.

"No, Herr Wolf. I've just come from Třeboň. I'm starting on digging for the Grail. No one's told me anything. Not even that you wanted me."

He grasps me by the arm – the elbow, and I still feel His skeletal fingerbones shivering my funnybone as He claims me.

"Now this is the selfishness of youth – to do only what we want to – well one doesn't blame you. All those of us with the artist in our temperament are occasionally impulsive so I'm not going to raise my voice, but I do have to wag a finger. For example, where would I be if I gave in to every whim of self-interest? – one of the endless provocations offered to me by the Czech rabble under the little swine Beneš? It would have been premature. A 'Naughty Marietta' time, as the so-gracious Edwina tells me you call it – you see! I know you, my Ederl – every thought inside that golden head of yours. . . . Look at these around us – there, that one with the bullet hole from Austerlitz, and this, slashed by a claymore – and these. All twenty-seven of these came off with the headsman's axe! Protestants. Yes, protesting in the rising against the Habsburgs that led to Wallenstein. Destiny has sent me as the new Wallenstein for this unhappy people. I'll make you a wager that I get ninety-eight percent of the plebiscite in favour. As a minimum. The people know. Their hearts in these frail cages cry out for the Leader to put their lives in order while they still have them. As I finally told old Chamberlain, an end, even with terror, is better than terror without end. In two weeks the gutter-press world will have forgotten the name Czechoslovakia – and this absurd hypocrites' outcry about *Them*, because a few windows are broken?! Windows can be mended over-night, but when Krebs creeps in it leaves nothing but these empty sockets. Treachery and deceit, and lustful depravity. Don't tell me! I simply cannot have the destiny of Germany, everything I've worked for, all these years of blood and effort, the resurrection of our Western Civilization put nowhere because a selfish boy – even an artistic one – won't help his sister when she needs him."

He stopped for breath – or to treasure some shattered brainbox!

"My sister?" as the skeletons rattled and rocked with laughter. "I'm here because of being selfish to Ettie?"

"Good fellow, you admit it, that's the ticket! Goebbels whined on for an hour about his damned actress – as though Lida Baarova was something special after a thousand others – I finally had to be exceptionally firm. In your case, it's quite simple. You can dig up this ramshackle castle of yours to your heart's content – I'll even get Hess to find you some labour. Now we're in charge, there's no shortage of hooligans who could benefit from a day's digging – up until the Bayreuth rehearsals, and after the Season. You need have no fear of anyone stealing a march in between. I'll have Himmler see that no one touches a pebble. So that's settled – although I have to say, Edwin, I was surprised – even disappointed, when our so-gentle Fräulein Ettie told me. The hurt she was feeling at having to tell a tale. You two have a so-marvellous family loyalty. An example for one's own to envy, I freely admit. I know what it cost her, but I can see why she felt she had to tell me. This is a truly magnificent task she's undertaking. The finest artist, at her peak. The utmost demands of performance. In our lifetimes as Wagnerians, '39 is going to be the season – Senta! . . . The first time we met was on the deck of the Holländer, remember? – I don't count that foolish excursion of Hess's to examine the stars in Oberammergau; we hadn't been introduced at that point. Astrology and Passion Plays! What mediaeval shithead nonsense! Come back with me to Prague and we'll call and give her the good news together."

A birthday present!

Mountain Climbing:

The C-Ps' Family happiness in person is postponed until the end of April – *His* birthday, on the 20th, His dangerous Wotan-50th – the precise moment when the Scholar had discovered a level of cellars extending out below the moat. They are filled with detritus, but every speck is precious. It can't be touched without the Archaeologist's attendance. He has to leave the White Lady's walls unbreached. A Black Order car rolls up, by chance, on the day Eddie had told Ettie by letter that he was leaving.

All the better to Trust . . .

. . . At the Griesbachs': "If that isn't the bloody limit," Brother said before they were even on the upstairs landing. "You don't even trust me to do what I've promised! As though Wolf wasn't enough, you crawl and toady to that bloody Heydrich for your machinations. Well you can drag me here – I suppose I'll even have to play the bloody piano – but you can rot in hell before I lift a finger in any other direction."

"Machinations? – how archaic darling. I suppose it goes with Potting. And as you've still got a tongue, we won't need the finger."

"That's what you think. Let's just see you run blubbing to Wolf because I won't suck you."

"I never blub – priggish little bastard!"

Oh they were adult, children! The atmosphere between them worsens hand-in-hand with the International Situation. Even among the rehearsing Wagnerians that's all anyone talks about – except Sister, pursuing her mad assault on the Four Roles. Brother frets for his cellars, and reads the headlines out of desperation during her endless rehearsals. During intervals – when I wasn't getting coffee, making at least that much public gesture – I corresponded with Rau by telephone on our Swiss citizenship.

"Not yet, Eddie, but I'm doing as much as I can, don't worry."

"Easy for him," snapped Sister, undressing at the end of a boiling Bayreuth summer day, "saving his own skin first, no doubt. How typically Jew."

"How what? How dare you! – after all Michael's done for us."

"Sodding in squalid restaurants. Speak for yourself, dear."

I struck her.

On her mouth, backhanded. The knuckles cut her. Blood started.

"Do it again," she said; "that's all you're good for with a woman."

He does it. On her cheek. A fist. There will be bruises.

"Again," she says, crying, "that's the hardest thing you've got."

She kicks out at his parts. Her nails rake him. He strikes her breast and gets an erection. Her tears shine, drop as pearls. She falls backwards before him.

"You shit," sobbing. "Appalling little arse-licking depraved shit- nothing I hate you. Go on and rape me then, why don't you!"

Her legs are open. Her wound gapes wetly. Redly. She strikes his shin with a hairbrush. He plunges on her. She covers her breasts. He stabs into her, he strikes her arms, her ribs, her shoulders. I don't feel the flesh she's tearing from my buttocks – only the furnace heat of her blood and its taste from her lips as she kisses me, slipping her tongue through the bleeding, around mine, drawing it back – and bites down. Sharp as a razor.

We cried out together, and then it was over, except for the throbbing.

"I'm thorry, oh Ethie – "

"Oh Eddie. Don't be. My fault – "

"Mine. We won't ever again."

"We won't ever have to, darling. You still love me."

"Only you, Ethie. Alwayth."

Always . . .

And then – ?

461

The peaks of the Four Roles are upon us. Mounts Kundry & Isolde are scaled with no problem. Ettie & Eddie play the Adam-&-Eve-&-pinch-me game again before Mount Brünnhilde – play-pinches, no tears or bruises, just happy giggles & squeaks, and then a Glorious-Maturity Immolation Scene. The Wahnfried kind, not Real-Life.

And then – ?

UNBELIEVABLE
POLISH MEGALOMANIA ! ! !

(The headline Script, prepared by the Dwarf. Nibelheim trembles, Europa too in these August dog-days, but in the Hothouse the Wagnerians clutch at their Programmes, and sit tight. She is coming! Backstage, before the Dutchman: Michael Rau, from Zürich, by Telephone!)

RAU

William Tell, you've made it! Quite a struggle, Eddie, believe me. All the rats are leaving.

EDDIE

Thank you, Michael. More than I can say. You can't know how much it means to Ettie.

RAU

Just keep the luscious Edwina singing for all of us, and beautiful. I suppose you wouldn't like to buy some of my father's shares of Krupp? I'm having a sacrifice sale?

(Dreadnoughts with Cannons move out of their harbours. In the Hothouse, the soaring masts appear in the dark of Bayreuth for the first time in port for 25 years. The canvas spreads o'er the boards where in normal times Siegfried treads. Sailors dance hornpipes where Rhine Maidens play. Fishergirls spin instead of Norns. Seamen, not Volsungs, sing and drown.)

DER HOLLÄNDER!

Ask in every Quarter of the Ocean,
Who knows this Ship, the fear of Godly men!
Now hear the Fate from which I will protect you.
To so dreadful a Doom am I condemned ...

*(And where Brünnhilde on brave Grane leaps,
instead, into the Whirlwind! along the Seacliff!
above the Vortex! to the Fourth Peak of –!)*

SENTA!

A Woman will keep Faith!
To the Pallid Man redemption shall be Granted!
Your Angel praise, Her Promise too!
Behold, till Death have I been True!

*(She hurls herself into the Sea. The Dutchman's
vessel sinks immediately and vanishes with all the
crew. The Sea swirls up and eddies down again. In
the glow of the rising Sun, the Transfigured Forms
of Senta and the Dutchman, in close Embrace, we
see emerge from the debris of the Wreck.)*

ENDE DER OPER

And Season, in a mish-mash blur of goddess-triumphs for Ettie, leaving
behind small human disasters & rumours of war for everyone else. And
through all the performances *He* moves with the Assurance of a
Sleepwalker, as they say; relaxed, cheerfully making His Wolf-jokes in
the House of No Illusions (more Harmonious with rebel-Mausi gone),
while at the gates a constant stream of His Generals and Mowgli Men
flood in, and swirl, and sweep away again: none of them, or Us, or His
Opponents, any the wiser of His intentions beyond Nibelheim's borders.

The Fool got the Word first, but was too stupid to know. It was the
long night after Sister's 4th triumph. The Wagnerians, happy and sated
beyond even their extravagant demands for Emotion, have finally left the

463

Magic Mountain to the small hours, and only 3 of us: Wolf, Fool, the Black Swan piano.

"Play Lohengrin, for me – the Prelude, and King Henry's arrival at the Field."

The Fool plays. The King hums, in that scratchy, pitchless singing voice of His, following the original Master's Score with one bitten index-claw.

> *I did not make this Journey idly;*
> *Let me remind You of the realm's Distress!*
> *Need I tell You of the Affliction*
> *So often wrought on German Soil from the East?*
> *To Me, the Kingdom's Head, it was a Duty*
> *To contrive an End to such outrageous Insults!*
> *As the Battle's prize I gained a Truce . . .*

Which, even as the Fool slams the chords in pale imitation of lost Putzi, in Moscow the Ribbensnob is concluding – with the iron beast who shall become the Old Fool's next jailor – The Pact of Non-Aggression.

> *. . . And used it to the realm's Defence;*
> *Fortified towns and Castles had I built,*
> *Men of Arms I trained for the Resistance.*
> *That term has Ended, the Tribute been Refused:*
> *With wild Threats the Foe prepares for War!*
> *Now the Time is come to guard the Kingdom's Honour,*
> *East and West – all of Us share the Task!*
> *Let all who are German be prepared to Fight!*
> *Then none will e'er again Affront our German Soil!*

"Glorious," He said, "so glorious. Just one more. The Swan-boat . . ."

And Fool obeyed, like all the Others – for had He not been named Our Fuehrer?

"Danke, Ederl. You played beautifully. These are long days. Good night."

"Good night, Herr Wolf."

And then – ?

A Wahnfried Lunch:

He throws it in Ettie's honour to tie up the '39 Season: her principal opposite players, Winnie, and the Prussian Tietjen.

"I will only say this about the noble Fräulein Edwina's so-exceptional performances for us, her admirers, in this landmark season. The Master envisioned a Festival which would have only pure-German singers and musicians for this purest German Art – but, meine Damen, meine Herren, if that had been so we should never truly have glimpsed Valhalla – without this, our English Brünnhilde. I know there is anxiety about our relations with England. Let me tell you as long as there is breath in my body I shall seek only peace between our countries. To that end, I hereby grant, on behalf of the Government of the Reich – so that she may stay by our sides on our Magic Mountain forever! – Honorary German Citizenship! – with the fullest freedoms and privileges! – to the Honourable Fräulein Edwina Isolde Casson-Perceval. And her brother, it goes without saying . . ."

With which afterthought the applause shakes Nietzsche & Schopenhauer, and Richard & Cosima, and all the other treasured Relics in their Gilded Frames on the Satin walls.

"Oh you dear Wolfi," Openly! As She *kissed* Him! On His Pale Cheek! In almost *Public!* "How terribly sweet – but Eddie and I have just been made dull little Swiss."

And then – ?

The blood rushes to the cheek, the violent colour of the Maries' cloak-linings. A sexual suffusion.

And *then – ?*

He rushes out.

And then – ?

Explosions in Berlin. And Moscow, London, Warsaw, Paris, again Berlin, at the Kroll Opera House, with the Bad Giant and Mein Hesserl as terrified as Eddie for the consequences of Her action. Terrified as Eva when her Friend meets her outside a cloakroom, all alone, twisting a French handkerchief.

"Oh Herr Eddie, it's so terrible. He's going to fight those stupid Poles who have been shooting us and He'll go away and whatever is to become of me? And before He left Munich I know He saw the Mitfahrt, after I thought she was gone – He *did*, Herr Eddie! – at the Prinzregentstrasse, and again yesterday, and now He's sent this Ultimatum. Oh my God I'll have to kill myself!"

And then – ?

A rare Blut Aurora Borealis appears over the Alps, the first in a lifetime, to stain the snows of Charlemagne's Mausoleum, and the Salt Mountain crimson as the Rhine.

And then – ?

The Declaration. War on the Wireless!

And then – ?

The Englischer Garten in Munich, with the teahouse where Mama took Us when we were children, before the shot was fired at the ceiling in the Bürgerbräukeller. Now, a tall, thin, pretty girl with bad teeth and bleached hair, a second-rate Valkyrie with no identification, walks slowly through the bronzed September beauty of dahlias and chrysanthemums, and finds a bench, of German oak, from German forests, and sits, and looks at the German Kinder playing around her with their toys and hoops and dolls; and takes out a toy revolver, Party calibre, 6.24 millimetre, and puts 2 toy bullets in the recesses of her Brain, poor creature . . .

And then – ?

He is told. And shown her note to Him. And leaves His generals and His war to ponder Love & Death. The aristocratic victim-patient, an Enemy on paper, is put in the Room of Mystery, Number 202, Nussbaumstrasse Clinic, under utmost State Security with the finest Hun doctors – even Dr Morell, the Leader's Quack – while He instructs Our Inferior Eva to purchase linens, and toilet waters, and take them with her own hand to where she lies, this fallen rival, fading out of the picture . . .

And then – ?

Nothing. The Phoney War Intermezzo. The grounds of the White Lady's Castle freeze again. Brother plans – and naturally sticks by Sister, now the English are in danger – while Europa, naked and defenceless, waits to see where Wotan's Will shall wander.

Upstairs, and downstairs, and in My Lady's chamber . . .

Mama (or Mutti) *und* Mitzi *und* Geli, *und* Martha *und* Renate, and now, Unity-Valkyry . . .

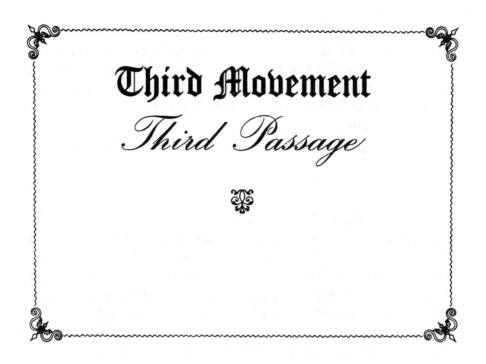

Third Movement
Third Passage

... *On Porquerolles:* Nothing has changed, yet all is different, this winter-to-spring of 1940. Peace is War. Friend is Foe. Youth is Aging. *Sweet Christ above us, Eddie will be 30.* Next year.

But it's this birthday that reality strikes: Old. Out of our Twenties. The golden days are gone forever. Yet they seem still around me on our golden island, the only sign of change being oil freshly applied to Annabelle's and Berthe's and Charlotte's steel shutters. There is to be a Season – if somewhat truncated – of Ring and Holländer, and Ettie is to sing at it, Brünnhilde & Senta. Naturally Wolf-Rejected has forgiven Her, abjectly (after His gratifying visit to the stricken Unity in her secret room at the clinic) in a crawly letter.

"I told you he would – he's sending poor Mitfahrt Home on a train from the Red Cross in Zürich. Eddie, my idea of us being Swiss is dull but it's working marvellously. I don't mind a bit scaling down after the Four – and I wouldn't have a note at Bayreuth if we'd stayed as ourselves."

"We are still ourselves," said Eddie-the-logical. "And it was Rau's idea."

"I mean English, darling. How absurd it's all been – like the Goat getting his hackles up, for a handful of Poles and some Huns in Danzig! If you ask me they'll all be back to normal with their feathers down by the Festival anyway. Tristan Heydrich says Fat Hermann's working on peace frantically behind Wolf's back. He's asked us for supper by the way, going through to Zürich."

"You can go but it would give me the creeps having supper with Blond Moses."

"I've already accepted."

. . . The Horse dream is back, with the Cliff and the Castle, and the Flames on the Obsidian beach, fiercer than ever – but now there is a hill rising in front of me, out of the flames, higher and steeper as the horse and I-Rider plunge through the fire and struggle in desperation upwards. While behind, and down below me, is now a tall, tall stranger in a long blue Maries' robe, but with a hat like Wotan's. And no matter how fast my horse, he stays with me, the Stranger, hand extended, beckoning with Charnel-white fingerbones to the Tower – for at the summit we come full circle, horse and Rider. The Tower is always waiting, and over the sound of the waves under the cliff, a harsh, cold croaking . . .

"I'm here, Eddie, you've been – " but no! What loving Sister truly says:

"Oh Lord, can't you take an extra guzzle of gin before you sleep and stop this god-awful moaning!"

Supper at Karinhall:
A Musical Evening. Much laughter and good eating. Rank hath its Privilege: beneath the thatch of his manor roof, Squire Hermann plays with his toy trains for Us. And Mucki, the wedding-day cub grown to adolescent-lion estate, now claws at a Gobelin instead of Union Jack.

"Mucki," said Queen Emmy (now a proud Mother), "precious, I wish you wouldn't do that. Hermann dear, he's a bad example for little Edda, say something firm to him."

Yes children, little Edda, Eddie & Ettie, all together in the Goering nursery – The Bad Giant was amusing and stopped being Fafner, and Emmy dropped her Queen for a Day and was just another member of the Company. Concerned for Art and her small daughter's future.

"Of course the Fuehrer had no choice in the face of the Poles' intransigence, but it's all become such a horrible misunderstanding. I look down at Edda's crib – but Hermann is trying with England, this man from Sweden, aren't you my darling?"

My dears, why *is* it that Actors & Actresses, exposed to Perfection in the written word, vent their own so erratically? Fat Hermann hugged his actress-wife to his acres of green-gold velvet bosom (a smoking jacket, specially constructed, with re-enforcing, in the colours of Chief Huntsman of The Reich) and poured himself a quart of one of the better brandies.

"We shall have peace shortly, there's no doubt about that whatever, but it's a delicate thing, negotiating – it can't possibly be left to that stuffed ass Ribbentrop! His understanding of the British is quite abysmal – and he wouldn't know a Modigliani from Mucki's litter box! However one has to tread carefully. Eddie, would you be prepared to help on the journey back to normal relations?"

"Anything," said the Fool, "but I don't know what I could help about."

"You could meet Peaceful friends, in Zürich, say, and tell them directly what we're thinking. You speak the language, isn't that the expression? – I really don't think an Englishman will ever trust a Swede. Two such pig-headed races – with exceptions made to you and my dearest Karen's memory."

"Strindberg," said Emmy, with a shudder, "such gloom. It took me months to get over Miss Julie."

"I don't really have any English friends in Zürich at the moment," quoth Foolish-Eddie.

"But you could write," said Fat Hermann "to that secretary of Lloyd-George's, for example. And suggest a meeting – with someone on our side at the highest level, if you take my meaning. Don't post the letter inside Germany ... "

Because Death's-Head Mime is watching. Little and grey, and jealous as Hell of his prerogatives, at the mouth of the cave.

... En route the Green Hill: The C-Ps bid farewell to their ample host, and travel their neuter way through Greater Nibelheim, avoiding the Capital with its rationing, for the rustic pleasures of the Black Forest, & coaching Inns, & crackling fires, & smoky hams & fresh brown eggs,

469

where, on a bright April morning, close to the Fool's Day, evil Mime, travelling also, by chance finds them, Eddie & Ettie, playing Hänsel und Gretel.

Centre stage, Heinrich Himmler – and scarcely seen since Geli's funeral, but even Eddie is aware of the Chicken Farmer's darkly increased Reputation – the latest of the gang to be strangely drawn to the Leader's golden lad.

Gentle Jesus, meek and mild, Look upon this little Child . . .

How mild he was, the Skull & Crossbones butcher – and affable, and Self-controlled. A simple lightning knock on the door was his idea of Terror.

"It's coffee," said Ettie, stretching, "with that sluttish child-maid. Well never mind me, go and let it in, brother dear."

Not sluts: Blond Moses, crisply-creased and Lightning-barred.

"Good morning, Herr Edwin. I don't wish to intrude, but the Reichsminister presents his compliments and requests the pleasure of your company at breakfast."

Frankly pointing that Fox-snout past Brother at reclining Sister.

"Oh it's you," she said, graciously. "I never eat breakfast in public, ever, and if Eddie's going to leave me and guzzle I want my bloody Kaffee first."

"I shall see to it myself, Fräulein Edwina."

The blond beast smarts with pleasure under her Korsett lash and leaves Us. "I don't want to have breakfast with Himmler," says Eddie, "but how can I get out of it?"

"Pick your sodding friends more carefully."

"He isn't – "

"A sod, or a friend?"

Mime Fodder:

The Chicken Farmer has gained weight. His chin is even weaker and his eyes more hidden behind their Tojo glasses. Mouse-grey Mongolian cat's eyes with tiny whites, red-rimmed to show the killer-mongoose in him – and slurping thin porridge in the most revolting fashion – but he greets the ageing young Edwin politely.

"Please, Herr von Percreval, beside me if you would. Today is my meatless day, but you of course must order anything you wish."

470

Another Fleisch-less Faddist! – they make Fat Hermann seem normal. Edwin tucks into his holiday ham and eggs. Isy Heydrich can afford no dietary risks and has nothing.

"This is a momendrous day for Germany, Herr von Percreval. You shall not have heard but I may tell you – the Fruehrer has despatched frorces to Scandinavia. They are already restablished and welcomed by the population."

Momendrous? Fruehrer? Mime-Himmler's speech tumbles out past his rat's teeth in a rush, while his small, indeed delicate, paws wave his dripping porridge spoon for emphasis.

And the whole of Europe fears him.

"That is momentous, Herr Reichsminister. Thank you for telling me." No sarcrasm, children: manners have always made our Eddie.

"Not at all, not at all – there is another reason. Frortune is an amazing thing! When General Heydrich informed me of your passprorts left with the innkeeper I said to him, 'Heydrich, we have to meet Herr von Percreval again.' These researches you are doing in Bohemia, Herr von Percreval, and elsewhere into the Holy Grail, are of extreme interest to me. Such a discovery might have immense effects – particularly in our relations with the Vatican, but also with Greek Orthrodox populations. If I propose that my Deprartment assist you in a frormal manner, what would you say?"

So was my devil met, as Jung had warned me he would be, sooner or later in His Country. At the Black Forest heart of it. Should I blame myself for my surrender, when even Caesar lost that struggle?

"What sort of assistance, Herr Reichsminister?"

"Whatrever is required." The red eyes gleamed. He knew he had me. "As the Fruehrer has already suggested, labour for excavations, naturally. Then scientific resrearch and exprert's advice. Money also, but for the present that is in shorter supply."

"It doesn't really need money. It's more a problem of getting people to let one just *look*, if you see what I mean? There's an old Abbot at Avignon, for example. He's awfully nice, but he simply won't be budged. And that's the other thing, most of the places I'm interested in aren't part of Germany."

"Start with those that are," said icy Heydrich. "For the time being."

471

"I suppose I could. What sort of scientific chaps were you thinking of, Herr Reichsminister?"

"You shall see for yourself, Herr von Percreval. General Heydrich shall arrange it. In this way we shall both sides be re-rassured, yes?"

Such re-rassurance! Oh my dearest, dearest children . . .

. . . Upstairs: Brother rushes hot-foot to Sister. All he has ever dreamt of! Beyond his wildest imaginings! Fame will be his, and Frortune! The Grail's finder shall be Immortal!

"On our Easter holiday? You're going to drop me here with these peasants in this bloody awful forest a thousand miles from anywhere?"

"Half a day from Munich. I'll take you there first. You can stay at the Gerbers – all right, you can't stand the new sausage man. We can make it the Carlton."

"And what about when you start looking good and proper for your blasted Pot? Darling, there's a war on. I can't travel without you. Eddie, what's to become of me?"

Darling reveals the depth of her anxiety. But the selfish brute says, "You're sounding just like Eva. You'll go on exactly as you always have. And I have to be back for rehearsals because I promised Wolf."

"Like his *cow*?"

"Two days, Ettie – that's all. And when I go to the White Lady you can come with me. The Countess would love to meet – "

"Bugger and sod your bloody countess. You can Fad-off now but I'll pay you back, Eddie. You'll be sorry."

I know, Ettie darling.

. . . At Sans Souci: Edwin's first Scholarly steps into the quicksand seem innocent enough. A plain stone building near the park; Lime trees opening their new leaves; a brass plate on a varnished beechwood door:

> THE NAVAL INSTITUTE
> FOR
> SPECIAL STRATEGIC STUDIES

The Scholar ascends 7 stone steps and rings a bell.
The door is opened by a smartly turned-out naval rating, saluting.

"Casson-Perceval. I have an appointment through General Heydrich to see your Director."

"Jawohl, mein Herr!"

Ship-shape, we march along a gleaming hall with naval ensigns and whited knot-work – Edwin has always been impressed by sailors.

"One moment please, mein Herr!"

Halt, one-two! And waiting . . . at a glass office door. A tall shadow approaches it – and becomes a uniform with 4 gold rings. An omen.

"My dear Herr von Perceval, an extreme pleasure. Kapitän von Maser, at your service."

As tall as Jung, with a black patch over one eye, and 4 duelling scars, and a limp that shows a wooden leg, and many medals. A sea-dog, from battles on the Main, and Eddie was here for witchcraft? Don't tell me!

"How do you do, Captain. I'm not really sure why I am here, actually, I feel a bit of a fool, but Herr Himmler seems to think you might have some scientists who could help me?"

"Possibly. You have been the subject of much comment. We shall proceed by the companionway to the upper deck and meet my technical people."

The Pendulists:

Past charts and barometers, and a periscope, cut-away, and a gyroscope in sections: the apparatus of modern sea war. *But please, sir, I want to find the Grail. . . .*

At the top of the stairs. Another glass door. Chart tables. More instruments. Serious men in white coats hunch over numerical compendia, with purple India ink and special pens, meticulously recording. Head down, the blushing Pot Scholar slinks in behind their briskly limping Kapitän-Direktor.

"Gentlemen, may I have your attention." Heads come up, reluctantly, drawn by the Fool from their vital War work. "Thank you. Let me introduce that person for whom we have been eagerly awaiting – Herr von Perceval, who is researching for the Holy Grail."

Fool is led forward, Exhibit 1 in lunacy, to meet a greybeard clutching a measuring device.

"Professor Doktor Frein, ballistics – Herr von Perceval."

"How do you do?"

"And Bergmann, and Bosch – both in meteorology."

"How do you do."

"And Klauss – Hans – you may have heard of for his advanced work in the Faustian pentagram incantations – is our leading Pendulist?"

At which Fool thinks, Have I heard aright? And says, "Ah, no, not actually."

Or of Brandeiss, a Cabalist, red hot on the *Tattwa* – "the Aryan Indian branch of Pendulism, you will recall?" – or Morgenstein, "a Spiritual Sensitive for the Beyond", or Grossberg, the "Dowser Through The Mercury Transmission Process for Petroleum Reserves". Mama must rest happy: her Fool in Numerology has met his match.

"I shall leave you with your peers," said Kapitän von Maser, who by neither blushing nor apologising was clearly mad as all the rest. "Until luncheon they shall wish to corroborate your findings, and if all goes as well as I expect, after luncheon we shall have the pleasure of a little drive."

... The Experts of the Institute grilled our Scholar to a turn on Pentateuch Yews, & Salt, & Templars' consumption thereof, & why Kiev? & the correspondence of Gitanos' travel routes to mighty Charlemagne's. And at the end, so worked up were they, that one exclammed, "Miraculous for Germany!" and had a little faint over his pendulum.

"I had no doubts from the start," said Kapitän von Maser, 1-eyed over lemon-grilled sole ('twas the Friday after Easter, my dears, Narvik was burning) "with your intimate connections at Bayreuth, and then of course, as a practicing phrenologist myself, I had but to look at your temple planes for their alignment into archaeology – however, such is the nature of that modern curse, Bureaucracy, that for the Reichsminister's approval, and scientific confirmation, we must apply the final test. But do not be alarmed. ...."

And off they drive, Fool & Phrenologist together, through the springtime countryside of the greenwood Hartzwolde, to a broad Estate belonging to –

"Kersten, the Swedish masseur who has worked such wonders for the Reichsminister and the Reichsmarschall with both internal and spinal problems. We maintain a small establishment here with auxiliary

474

colleagues, who unfortunately require a measure of supervision in their movements."

FUHLSBÜTTEL

A plain sign for those who enter in.

"An annex to Ravensbrück," said Kapitän von Maser, "but somewhat more lax in discipline."

But the names mean nothing to a Fool: the budding, golden-yellow Laburnum and sweet mauve Lilac screen the mouth of the black cave, and disguise the stench of the breath, and distance mutes the smoking bellow of dreadful Fafner.

. . . At a country house much like Trevelly, the Travellers stopped. And went inside, and into a small drawing room, whose only oddity was a small sign, "Astrology":

"With someone waiting to produce your chart, one of our finest practitioners, Herr von Perceval may I introduce now – "

"We need no introductions, Kapitän. On the Cusp, I remember. I have met before, your Piscean."

Frau Marthe Steiner:

Then a name, and now a number. In Oberammergau, in the 'Twenties, she was Old – she must have been forty – and grey. Now she was sixty and looked no older, or greyer; only, perhaps, from memory, or prison diet, thinner. Her superior, the naval Captain in charge of Quackery, is positively ecstatic at such an auspicious Sign.

"How the circles of life close, do they not!" von Maser cried. "That your astral charts have already meshed must be the final seal of approval for your venture, my dear Herr von Perceval – but the niceties have to be observed. If Frau Steiner will be kind enough to fill in the forms in duplicate, I shall see that they are transmitted to the Reichsminister's office myself, by hand, so that there shall be no delay."

He hobbled away, chortling, all 6-foot-6 of him, with his wooden peg thumping on the carpet. We were alone, Frau Steiner, the Reader, and I.

"Do you really remember me?" Edwin asks her, this time able to speak as equals, in German. "After so long – you must have seen so many people."

"You remember me, mein Herr."

"But that's different. I was young – it was very special, having one's fortune told."

"This is not a word I use for it. I remember, mein Herr, because it was not every day I received an English golden guinea, or that the hair of three people matched the metal of their currency, or that the chart of a young noblewoman showed her to be the Neptunian dominating all aspects of the chart of the man already sitting at my table."

"I remember the table," Edwin said. "The glass plates you used. The colours. I remember every detail vividly. That was where we first saw Him, Herr Wolf, sitting at your table."

"Is that your name for a Taurus with Libra rising – Herr Wolf? A savage name for a savage man. I curse the day he came to my table."

"He isn't really savage. Not when you know Him."

"Oh I know him, young man," Frau Marthe Steiner smiled sadly. "Mars, conjunct Uranus in Capricorn was your sister – with him it is Moon-Jupiter. All death and sex. Scorpio on the lowest level. With Saturn in his Tenth house, the same as for Napoleon, but the Frenchman did not have the Pluto aspect in his sensual nature. As you are here, I suppose your sister has not been able to keep away from him?"

"She has – at least – Frau Steiner, I have to say I really don't know what on earth you can mean by that remark."

"Do you not, young man?" She looked into my eyes, and I found I could not look aside. "Has she not sent him presents of an intimate nature? Does she not flaunt herself in front of him, then whisk herself away again? Has he not asked her to marry him – not once but three times over? And has she not rejected him, but kept herself a spinster, living in unnatural union with you, her brother?"

"Good God. How can you – no! I won't allow – it simply isn't possible. Oh of course, you must get records from Heydrich's office . . ."

The Fool's babble tailed off. She *knew* – because the fault, dear children, shines not in our stars but in our eyes.

"You must not blame yourself, young man, for God's purpose."

476

"How can you believe in God," Edwin whispers, "when you know everything? A necromancer doesn't need God. If you can see all that, you *are* God."

"If I could see, my dear young man, I should not be here. Now what is it that I am to tell you for Kapitän von Maser's forms in duplicate?"

"But if you know – " still persisting – "then you *know*."

"Oh yes, young man, I know . . . but my time is not yet."

"When? I mean, what's going to happen? With this war? With Him? With me and Ettie?"

"I think this is not what the good Captain requested."

Frau Steiner patted the Fool's hand gently, and then moved to a secretaire by a chintz curtain at a window looking out at a bed of yellow aconites . . . for my White Lady.

"I'm going to look for the Holy Grail. He wants – I want to know if I'm going to find it."

"An ambition so large should show some reflection."

She pulled a blind and drew the curtains so that the room grew dark, and took from the secretaire the same coloured glass plates. And the sides of the secretaire folded down. And within it was the clear glass table. Frau Steiner set a lighted beeswax candle under it.

"Place your hands on my table and tell me again of your existence on our planet."

1911 Toulon, 1:30 in the morning.

"A Sagittarius moon," she says, as the red light moves across my fingers, "to be much involved with men, yes. And your Sun in the Third House of Mercury, yes, the victim, yes, it all comes back, and your mother, the Virgo, yes, with that sweet autumn sadness, she died in nineteen-twenty seven, at your birthday, yes?"

Now the green light is on me. The light of the label from Mama's brown bottles.

"Yes," her son whispers, "just after our birthday."

"So. Well I see no Holy Grails, but we would not expect that."

"I had hoped to."

"Dear young man, we are not telling fortunes; we are looking at the strength and weakness of human nature. There is much strength in your chart for the next cycle. See, from the amber light, the colour of a great corn harvest, a crop is being reaped – "

477

"The Ukraine – could I be finding it in Kiev?"

"If you persist in fortunes you must answer your own questions. I only see a Sun rising for the first time over a horizon. Neptune opposite the Sun creates illusion, entrapment and confinement. When both your Suns rise upon the harvest I see one last possibility of altering the circle. See, here, at the confluence of the boundaries."

She slides her coloured glasses. Red moves towards amber . . .

"In thirty months you shall be under a Jupiter Return, a rare occurrence. At such a time all things are possible. Seize your opportunity, young man! For your Wolf at that same time has his Saturn in transit conjunct his Uranus. This is the peak of his power over his victims."

Red floods amber! Blood on the Sagittarius Moon for all of us Victims . . .

"And is that all you can tell me?" Edwin Fool asked Frau Steiner, in childish disappointment. No more cake at our party! "Only this Jupiter business? Nothing more specific?"

"I have told you enough for one lifetime, young man, if you make use of it. But do not be alarmed, I shall make the forms for the Reichsminister look safe enough. That is the least I can do as my part to stop the wheel."

She blew out the candle, and opened the chintz curtains, and put away her coloured glasses and the table of mystery. The room contained only a secretaire, and a sofa, and a puzzled, not-so-young man left with more riddles instead of answers.

"Just like Carl Jung," he moans to the Pendulum Captain, as they drive away from the mouth of the dragon, back to Berlin. "I simply don't know what one is to make of it all."

"Dear Herr von Perceval, to each his own discipline – that is why the Reichsminister employs experts. Professor Jung's new work on the Alchemical is of the utmost fascination. Transmutation of Elements, think of it! I have written several times begging him to address us at the Institute – which reminds me, I wonder if before you leave for the field you might consider giving a lecture on your theory of correspondences between the Parsifal Myth and the Salt Routes, and how you have attacked them with the scientific method?"

Scientific? Mad as Hatters, children.

. . . In Spring-Time: the only Ring-Time. April, 1940. The Scholar

478

lectures his peers in Fad madness. Frau Steiner's report gives the chicken-farming Mime "the greatrest satisfaction!" And Good Luck! The red light turns green. Petrol & Hooligan-labourers are put at the Archaeologist's disposal.

MY OWN EXPEDITION!!!

Eddie did not go back to Ettie – she had her own plaything, a crack at the deported Manon Lescaut with the Paris Opera. Yes, so late they were still planning on performing! For each Company there is a Season. Europa, naked on her bull, pretends not to see its B***s – and waits to be ravished.

... At Třeboň. Last week in April – 1st week in May: the most momentous of my Life! *I WAS DIGGING!* Or to pick a point, the Hooligans are: a raggedy gang of 20 Moravian misfits who half-heartedly scrabble at the muck in the cellars while the Expedition's Swiss backer watches until it is too much for his nervous stomach and he grasps a spade himself to set the loafers an example! And at 6 o'clock each evening, having started a scant 12 hours earlier, they escape to their hot suppers!

"I suppose they can't stay longer," Eddie said to the co-ordinating official from the Death's-Head office, (a condescending-sniveller type), "but couldn't they perhaps work in a sort of watch arrangement, like the navy?"

"We are the SS. Also, this would mean extra rations, mein Herr."

"Oh dear – I tell you what: I'll call the Reichsminister's office."

Mime-Himmler spoke himself to his myrmidon – and after that there was a doubled group, 40 Hooligans, and enough of whatever it was they ate, and no sign of condescension by any Black Order man towards the Expedition's Leader.

Even under this arrangement the work stopped at ten – 2200 hours, officially. After they left the Scholar would sift through their screenings, and scratch some more himself until midnight, and then it was impossible to fall asleep in my haunted room. Not because there was ever a sign of the Lady – with either pair of gloves – but because for every foot we dug, my mind was a hundred leagues in front of it. And then, at the back of the first cellar . . . a hearth! And pots! And 2 leather belts with brass studs in an arrangement that is clearly 9th Cent!

Oh ecstasy! And then, in the cellar under the moat, beyond – a chapel.

At first the Scholar Edwin refused to believe. The stones must be a fallen arch, not an altar. But then there was a Cross. Bronze again, a crude casting, set with cheap, semi-precious pebbles, not jewels – but Religion was Here. Christianity passed this way, heading East – and earlier by two centuries than anyone had so far charted.

And then there was the accident. A wild cry, and one of the labourers disappears from my sight at the far corner of the cellar. Dust fills the chamber. Coughs and screams from the frightened others.

"Back!" their Leader shouts at them. "Get more lights. Let me through."

The ceiling has partially collapsed. The Leader has to crawl, dragging a rope. The space decreases. The sound of sea waves in my ears. The cave at Tintagel, with the wizard-fox watching. But no, the sound of my own blood, merely, pounding with my heart when another rock tumbled. The lamp was crushed.

"Another. Quickly. Quickly."

They provide it. There is a new respect for Edwin – a first respect, ever. Heady stuff. But the cost was a man's broken spine. The labourer lay twenty feet down, in what seemed to be a tunnel, stretched terribly across a boulder.

I called for a ladder, and went down to him, my first dead man. His blood marked the rock, red on white.

On white. It was salt. The tunnel was a mine-working that connected to the great salt caverns stretching east from Třeboň towards Brno, then called Brünn, and beyond it, Slavkov, which history calls Austerlitz, where, in a transit of Saturn, Europa suffered her first conquest by Napoleon.

And then, beside the warm corpse the Scholar saw a blackened silver serving plate.

This is my body . . .

Dented, an impure sterling, with a "C" etched, and an "R", and a two-headed eagle scratched, of slight archaeologic value – to be consigned with a tag to a museum back shelf for cross-referencing, *see,* "Charles the Great", or *Charlemagne* – but to me, priceless. For it was Confirmation.

That is Exaggeration, Edwin.

I admit it – but there was a pillar of salt, Mama, and there was a chapel, and it was old; a sign of the Fish instead of the Eagle – the same initials and I can have a Grail.

The New Edwin let his Hooligan labourers leave early, although the Black Order guard said there was no need to.

"Surely they'll want to have a funeral," said the Expedition Leader, "even this sort of people."

(And because, while we are being Truthful, the lad was considerably shaken up from the experience of finally Setting a Good Example.)

"Well I can't say I mind the excuse to pack it in early, mein Herr – God knows we have something to celebrate today."

"Indeed we do! The relic!"

"Of course, mein Herr." A smile. That is Condescension, Edwin. "I was thinking of the Blitzkrieg's triumph in France."

"Blitzkrieg? France?"

And as the Fool said it, may God save me, all I thought was, *Avignon.*

Third Movement
Fourth Passage

[in march time!]

When e'er we are commanded to storm the Pallisades
Our leaders march with fusees, and we with hand grenades;
We throw them from the glacis about the Enemies' ears;
Sing tow row row [etc] British Grenadiers.

Olde Booke 14 – 2 lucky 7's! – but Gedanke has spoilt it by freshly disgracing herself with a crapulation on the pips of Old Edwin's Coldstream Major's shoulder. A Bird-hanging was only averted because Waring was here, and for some reason my compatriots respect – no, revere, him: Man of Letters, and namby-pansy today in an apricot cravat the colour of Ettie's Rat-Baer knickers. Our Jeremy's are in more of a twist than usual because of DUNQUERQUE – or Dunkirk, as he now calls it. Yellow Street believes its *own* myths. We must say nothing which will detract from the glory of The Great Embarkation. What is there to say? He came. He saw. He allowed the Fellows to Fad off to Dear Old Blighty because of Ettie –

"Oh come, C-P. – pendulums, and Eva Braun being forced to look after Unity Mitford is one thing, but Dunkirk and your sister is totally irrational. You can't possibly expect editors to believe ..."

Says Waring. Who never played a bloody note – or sang one since Yum-Yum – and who, after this cell-full of scrawlings and the best efforts of crapulous G & G to keep Old Eddie *honest* – idiot Waring still hasn't got it into his pointed brainbox that: *He Wasn't Rational!!!*

483

But He wasn't MAD either, the favourite celluloid myth. The yellow editors would buy MAD quick enough. As we have seen, my dears, He was an Artiste. Also, a Sensitive (infinitely more-so than any of the quacks in the Pendulism Institute) who could read messages in the waves of the Aether that Ordinary Men were cut off from. Not women. The female of our species got His Moon messages –

Dunquerque. Very well, children: if someone is offering you a better – a *rational* – explanation, buy their yellow rag. Otherwise, hear what uncomfortable words our Wolf in Eddie's clothing saith and form your own bloody opinions.

. . . *At Třeboň.* Wolf-Klingsor, wizard of Battle, sends for His Fool when the Dunquerque Pocket is closing – and just as a 3rd cellar was discovered in the White Lady's castle!

"I simply can't," cried our petulant sorcerer's apprentice to the unheeding Black Order emissary sent to bear Eddie to Him through the air. "Not now. It isn't even Bayreuth, and He never wants anything important. She must have done something. Oh bugger and damn."

. . . And but 5 hours later was approaching a rocky defile in Flanders' Marches, Brabant's country. A pleasant village called Brûly-de-Pesche on the Belgian-Frog border, with cuckoos cuckooing, and cows softly lowing in green meadows with daisies – and then bellowing in pain as their udders swelled to bursting because not one peasant had been left behind to milk them when the habitations were cleared to make way for Klingsor's Fortress.

WOLFSSCHLUCHT

Wolf's Gorge. The name was in the open and "A" was in his Wolf's clothing, the corporal's Feldgrau of his 2nd Fox'l days. He was pacing in an obviously hastily prepared wizard's garden: clumps of wilting-hothouse-transplant marigolds with freshly laid sods as a checkerboard-quilt between.

Keep Off the Grass!!!

A message from the Hun Heart, on a 2nd Gothic painted sign, and so

He walks (on Teutonic gravel paths forming perfect right-angles) with only 1 companion at a time (because that's all there's room for) while the Volsung Military Machine hovers at the intersections, or jockeys in elbowing pairs an anxious 20 paces behind. Now and then our Klingsor-Wolf will jerk His head or twitch His nibbled fingers and a frantic scurry then occurs in the gravel as this echelon departs and the next takes its place – all without damaging the greensward and marigolds. (While thousands of tons of high explosives rain down on everything else.)

The Fool waits at a neutral corner of the board, jumping at the muted thumps of bombs & cannon, and wondering for the thousandth time How Bad Is It, what Sister's done?

"Ah-ha! My Ederl! Good fellow, come and join me. Jodl you won't mind – and make sure Group A doesn't try any funny business. No mock heroics from those Panzer rascals!"

The Knight-Marschall thus addressed looks frantically for some way to clear off without leaving the gravel. The Fool solves the problem by walking directly across the grass. At which feat the Might of Germany hisses a collective breath.

"English common sense. That's exactly what I'm looking for. In fact I'm counting on it – Linge, clear out of our way, for heaven's sake – I can't stand being listened to over my shoulder, it's like having a parrot on a perch waiting to crap on it. Also parrots carry lice, I don't care what anyone tells you to the contrary. Ederl, do you remember that one of Frau Cosima's the little ones buried at Wahnfried? In the Hofgarten, near the gooseberries?"

"Yes, Herr Wolf, I remember."

"What a long face. I suppose you've been listening to the news. Worrying for your gallant countrymen. Well you mustn't. The Frogs have been typical – but your Tommies are professional soldiers, and we expect a bit of rough and tumble. They'll be home soon enough and then they'll brag about it. 'There we were on the beaches – !' yes, I assure you, Ederl, 'The best days of our lives!' they'll be saying to the end of them. And some will be prisoners; but being dead is a damned sight more final than a week or two in prison. Don't tell me!"

"Two weeks, Herr Wolf?"

"You know one's little exaggerations. Actually, I give it six – two

485

months at the maximum. Of course I can't let them take their playthings home as well. I'm not completely mad, in spite of all these gentlemen's opinions! I've had a lot of trouble with Goering – but one expects that from the Air. Our Hermann's never been in the trenches – and now he couldn't be! The man's simply colossal! – but there's nothing more demoralising for a good infantryman than to have to leave his rifle and gaiters behind – and his little personal treasures, mother's letters, pictures of sweethearts. Oh, yes, those 'chaps' have to know they've been in a scrap – more to the point, their idiot English leadership have to know. That raddled old rogue Churchill – the very worst type of prostitute-journalist! – it's easy for him to blow off steam on the BBC about bleeding and sweating, but when the soldiers come back and sit in the ale-houses – what is it you call them?"

"Pubs, Herr Wolf."

"Pub, yes – tell me, what does it mean?"

"It's short for a Public House, Herr Wolf. Like a Wirtshaus – "

"That's *exactly* what I want. Public! Let's have the story of these Dunquerque beaches out in Public Opinion between rounds of ale, and that will squash the drunk Churchill flat. We'll have the peace treaty by the end of the Festival in August – with honour. Which is more than those poor Tommies have any right to expect – we didn't start this war, remember. Right, off you go then."

With a warm pat on the Fool's shoulder.

"Go, Herr Wolf?"

"And see for yourself, boy. That the Crazyman's let them off the hook on purpose. I want an impartial English witness. Talk to the American Press in Paris – and tell your sister. Yes be sure of that. Tell the most gracious Fräulein Edwina from me personally that her dearest friend and warmest admirer has behaved to England in a way your so-noble mother would have approved. And we'll have a Gala when I come to Paris myself – I want to hear this Manon-whatever-it-is of hers. She made absolutely the right decision about Switzerland. Above the struggle on both sides – and able to sing for all mankind. What a talent! What a woman! Jodl will give you something suitable to ride in."

Exit Fool, overwhelmed. Over wilting grass, trespassing on Genius . . .

On the Beaches:
With no choice in the matter, Edwin went – or 500 yards back from them. And lay on my stomach, and felt like a traitor. The grey tanks of the Panzers were a similar distance behind me in a ring, with their immense barrels pointing like one of the spiked collars waiting backstage in the Festspielhalle to be worn by the giants. With their crews not believing it: *TO SIT?* when in one slithering, clanking lurch Fafner could be on Nibelheim's enemies, devouring them? And all the time the Stukas roaring and banshee-screaming with those sirens so casually mentioned over luncheon at Wahnfried – because the Bad Giant never lets up, no matter what His instructions, but ineffectually (because sand cushions high explosions, this I assure you). And smoke, blacker and oilier than any stage-Klingsor's, roils over the little Sunday ships, plying and sinking; and over the figures lying like me in the salt, and black-oiled, and excremental, and evisceral fouled sand of the beaches, and then mingling its stench with the fog, as midsummer night is falling.

For now it is summer fog that saves them, more than His clemency, or the Sunday Sailors' gallantry. And when the fog lifts, and only the smoke still drifts across the sun ... Edwin went walking, and there he sees Dame Sorrow's two faces of War, whose names are Defeat and Victory.

> *But have you seen a Ship at Sea,*
> *With blood-red Sails and blackened Mast?*
> *High on her Deck the pallid Man,*
> *Her Master, keeps His endless Watch ...*

Walking on the beach, Eddie sees the playthings left behind by Tommy. *He sees guns with their breeches spiked, and others in perfect working order, with rounds still unfired in their breech chambers. He sees the Gibich Vassals, rushing forward for the best looting – and pausing, when they see some of the bodies half buried in the French sand are German. And Edwin saw the dead Tommies, his boyhood compatriots if not his Class-mates – until he came on a face with the back of its brainbox missing, and the front of it from School. An ordinary boy, neither pervert nor bully, once I had played tennis with him. Now the sand flies had him. And I saw the mementoes left, the message He wanted: the letters from Mamas, the pictures of Etties who were sweethearts and sisters – if not in the sinful sense that We were. Some of the pictures sank, with blood and oil and shit caked to them. And some, as a breeze came up, after the little Sunday ships were gone, some loves floated away, Home, across the great river, to maritime England . . .*

> *How the Wind howls!*
> *How it whistles in the Rigging!*
> *Like an arrow He flies, without Aim,*
> *Without Rest, without Peace . . .*

Wolf-the-Dutchman has an Aim, perhaps a true one for remorseless History, but Edwin did not serve it. I did not go to the American Press, but to Ettie, staying in Boulogne, sleeping-in, on a gorgeous Sunday morning, while refugees milled, thinking there was somewhere they could run to. And I told Ettie what I had seen as His impartial witness. And she was not silly about it.

. . . At Paris: "Eddie darling, it is dreadful, horrible. But it should never have happened – not for Danzig. Who's ever heard of Poland? But now it's over. We started it, foolishly – the dear old Goat never would have! – and now Wolf's won it, because although he's peculiar in lots of ways he really must *be* some sort of genius. Just thank God that *because* he is one it's all over so quickly. Now they can all be sensible and have another Versailles or whatever they do on these occasions, and we can all go back and get on with the important things. Eddie pet, I don't want to drag you from your old pots, but now you're here anyway, do you think you could perhaps possibly stay with me for my Manon? The Parisians really are pretty frightening and Louisiana sort of seems their territory."

"Sort of. You know I will! Oh God, Ettie darling, I do so love you."

"I know you do, darling."

I'll make you pay for it . . .

But not until after:

THE PARIS GALA
A Party Piece

(By Our Special Social-War Correspondent: E C-P)

Celluloid Ettie & Eddie & Wolfi,
Went down to the Triomphe to wave;
Ettie was drowned *in Applause, my dears!*
Who do you *think was saved?*

It was a *marvellous* party. Nicholas Rat-Baer was there –
yes he was, Lizard-conducting away simply like *mad*,
with the whole Philharmonic, on *top* of the Arc! (and
doing all sorts of naughty knickery things to French girls
under it!) – and Wotan's little Speer, Albert, he was
there, goo-goo eyed, to be shown the Opera, and the 1st
Corporal's Tomb, & how spiffing they were – only not
nearly big enough, Albert liebchen – you'll have to do
better than *that* to stay in Master's good books; and who
else? Well the whole cast of Manon Lescaut – which as
Wolf pointed out was really *pinched* by Puccini from
Massenet, so He went down terribly well with a lot of
the Frogs (who were feeling pretty *piqued* by perfidious
Albion, for shooting at their battleships). And of course
there were a few silly ones – I mean there always *are*,
aren't there, at a really good do? Two old crones
escaped from Bedlam, or left over from knitting in front
of the Bastille, who met Him in the street and positively
shrieked & crossed themselves against the Evil One, if
you can believe. (Wasn't that just too like our darling
Mathilde?) And there were simply *oodles* of presents.
The Frogs gave Him *twice* as much as they tried to steal
at Versailles, & in return He was so grateful He let them
keep half their country, and you really can't beat that!
Except, Yours-Truly could have, because when he
made a flying trip down to Avignon (in the wrong half)
the old Abbot was just as selfish as ever about not
digging up the Yews! (And Eddie's going to be 30! –

489

my dears, it isn't *fair*). And then we all went home to Auntie Winnie's at Wahnfried for the next binge, the first of the Season, before opening Rheingold. Just Family. Just like always . . .

Except – NO MAUSI!!! Yes, the rebel Wagner, her lovely father's daughter. Why? I can tell you, dears – but *whispers*. Because she'd had this simply *fearful* row with Mummy on the platform in Zürich.

"For the last time, Friedelind, I ask – your brothers command you – return and spare them such disgrace. You have a choice. Come home and be kept safe for the duration, or stay in neutral Switzerland – but you absolutely must stop talking about Him like this, or – "

"Or what, Mummy?"

"Or if you go to enemy territory the order will be given."

"What order, Mummy?"

"Austilgen und Ausrotten!"

Which must be utterly the *wildest* exaggeration ever heard by a hysterical runaway daughter weeping wildly & bumping into Yours-Truly on the platform. *"Destroy and Exterminate"* a Wagner? By her own Mummy? Don't tell me! What in God's name is Our world coming to?!

DESPATCH ENDS!

(P.S. Of course, Auntie *is* at That Age.)

DESPATCH *ABSOLUTELY* ENDS!

. . . *At Wahnfried:* Exit Mausi, a strong character, if misguided. Her two brothers, Little-Wolfi & Wieland are in the Grey Army, youngest Nickel is at school with nuns, out of temptation. Ettie & Eddie are the only children left for 1940's Season – and it is one, even without Parsifal.

"I agree with our Fuehrer," says Winifred, "there has to be some sacrifice with our sons in the field."

"We can't possibly have all this turning-the-other-cheek business

490

with our men's backs to the wall in the heat of battle; it would give quite the wrong impression ..."

... Is His way of putting it. But a Ring at Bayreuth is a Festival in itself and there are many non-combatant Wagnerians to attend, and still Great Bockelmann to sing Wotan and the Holländer for them. Indeed, our Rudi Bockelmann is greater than ever now as the Bayreuth Artistes' leader of the Party – my dears, quite chucking his weight about.

...At the Griesbachs': "I can't stick him when he's such a pompous fart – Eddie, you'd think Bockelmann had won the bloody war. I actually overheard him yesterday in a corner going on to the Waltraute, what's her name, about us still being English."

"Whatever did you do, Ettie?"

"I waited until he was getting his Korsetts off and then opened the dressing room door by mistake to one of The Riefenstahl's nosy cameras," said Big Sister on the morning following her big Valkyrie scene with Wotan, "*He* proposed to me again last night – why can't you play him something placid for a change?"

"I've tried to get Him on to Schubert for years but He says the name reminds Him of Mozart. Why don't you say yes and marry Him?"

"Say yes?" She stared over the sheets, and her coffee, with incredulity –

"Yes."

"Me marry Wolf?" – and a secret touch of discomfiture.

"Yes. Why don't you?"

"*Why?*" – that instantly became hostility. "And do *It* with him? A man that bites his nails and farts in public uncontrollably?" Followed by her short, shrill laugh, when things aren't funny.

"I'm serious Ettie. You wouldn't have to sleep with Him. He'd do anything you tell Him to. You could have separate bedrooms. He's the most famous man in the world and He worships you. I should have thought it was ordained."

"Two years ago, darling, you 'thought' he was going to kill me."

The etching acid in that *darling*.

"That was before Dunquerque, Ettie. Before lots of things. I agree with what you said then – He's *done* it. And now He's making a whole new peace for a single Europe for the first time since Charlemagne. And

491

He's over fifty and He's won His battles and He's made up for Versailles. You'd be like an Empress. Like Cosima and old Wagner."

"It's that bloody Charlemagne isn't it?"

"I beg your pardon?"

"You *ought* – mock polite little swine. Wanting to fob me off so I'll stop singing and you won't have to accompany and can just dig for your sodding pots all day. I've never heard such selfishness in my entire bloody *life*!"

The coffee cup whizzed – but Eddie had been in battle and ducked. Shattered remnants. Brown stains sinking into the Griesbachs' best wallpaper. Heaving breasts, flashing eyes, golden hair flung back across her shoulders, waist-long – by God, she was magnificent! Also, terrifying – and out of bed, naked, advancing, grabbing up a paper knife –

"I didn't mean anything like that. Leaving – "

Backing Eddie into a corner in his light summer raw silk pyjamas.

"You bloody *do*, you worm. Just in Paris you said you loved me."

"It's true, I swear – "

The knife is tortoiseshell, pressed to my heart.

"True what? True loving or true leaving?"

Entering my ribs, carving my soul.

"True loving Ettie. I don't ever want to lose you. I couldn't bear to think of you doing it with Him. Not ever. Horrible. You're so beautiful."

"Oh bugger." The tortoiseshell snapped cleanly. Death was only a tiny scratch. Below my nipple. She licked it. "You love me and you'll swear – that's what you said."

"Yes, I swear." Anything. His groin was rising.

"Not now. I'm dress-rehearsing Dutchman. Tonight. Make sure we've got champagne. After Götterdämmerung."

"Tonight, yes. Champers. Oh God Ettie – "

"And don't dare waste a drop on any knicker games in between."

"I won't. I promise."

But no sooner is she gone to Dress-rehearsal than the lying, ageing little gold swine creeps to her laundry hamper – and found that she was bleeding.

Desire became ashes. The sun darkened, literally, in one of Bayreuth's thunders to set off Donner's in the Festspielhalle – and those

492

others just beginning to drop from the skies above England . . .

Out of mind. He hates any part of it when she's Cursing, and what she most wants is impossible. *And I promised.* Getting the champagne early is part answer.

"You've been boozing." She picks it up at the Singers' Table.

"Only a sip."

"You're not going to get drunk on me – goodnight darlings – " to the wartime worshippers, "I've got this simply splitting head with all the thunder, you'll have to excuse us from the party."

Back to the Griesbachs in the Riley. Petrol is rationed, but the C-Ps' war-work is vital. Upstairs at the Griesbachs', the bath water, tinted.

"Ettie, don't make me – "

"Don't be such a coward. Open the champers, I'm not going to bite you."

"Do you mean that?"

"Do you love me?"

"You know, more than anything – but can we just do it the ordinary way . . . ?"

Like Frau, and Herr, good bourgeois missionaries.

"Of course, ordinary, silly old darling. Just as long as I know you love me."

Totally. Oh Ettie, utterly . . .

Normally. With such relief at not having to do anything funny peculiar like Push-Me-Pull-You, that the lad outdoes himself.

"Lord pet, Big-Sis is positively dripping. Scusi for a second – mind if I borrow the champers?"

Anything. Ettie darling, absolutely . . .

Lying, sweated and exhausted as she vanishes with glass and bottle, streaked with their lusts into the bathroom. Water running. Once again the thunder crashing. Coming out, all smiles, Rhine-gold re-cleansed with a topped-up bumper of bubbling champers for little brother.

"Now we'll swear, darling. Say you won't ever leave me."

"I won't Ettie. Not as long as you need me."

"For always. Say for Eternity and always."

"For Eternity and always."

"I promise."

"I promise."

"And swear on our two bodies."

As she bent and gently kissed him. There, and there, and *There*.

"I swear on our two bodies."

"And now drink together, out of the same glass. You first, Eddie."

Raising the bubbles to the light. To his lips. Pearls before swine. Precious beyond rubies – *because the sparkling Champagne by a Klingsor-miracle is changed to Burgundy; carmine-tinted, slightly swirling, with jewelled globules, milky white.*

"Oh Christ what have – ?"

"You promised. Drink it."

"I can't. Oh Jesus Jesus Ettie – "

"You swore, you bastard. On our bodies. For eternity now drink it or I swear I'll get Wolf never to let you dig and I'll never ever let you see or touch me for the rest of our lives."

Our Wildekuss or Lose Me.

He drinks. She drinks.

I-Eddie, You-Isolde. To the end of Time . . .

Third Movement
Fifth Passage

... in Truth, a step aside from the main Work,
for a few bars of the Pure Baroque,
more correctly to be called, my Dears:

A GIGUE

being

The Strange Dance of Mein Fräulein Anna

A *gigue*, children you shall recall, being from the Scottish & English branches of our musical Family, composed in lively triple-metre Form, and frequently employing the *Inversion* of our Theme!

Employed now at Gedächtnis' insistence – the rude bird of Memory will not be put off another second! – perhaps the dark-cloaked creature is so insistent on the Hess Flight because of the links to his thieving raven brothers in the Tower of London. Bird, thy time is not yet. Eat thy stolen crumb and allow Old Edwin to forget that previous revolting scene ...

... Třeboň. As day from raven-night, the Young One flees from Sister and her Potion, to the safety of the White Lady's cellars, where, observing our youth's perturbation, the ancient Countess Vok-Rosenberg kindly invites him to share her supper.

"Blood pudding and tapioca, dear boy. It is nourishing, if not exotic. Are you sure you shall not join me? You mustn't hold back out of scruples for my ration. These sparrow bones need practically nothing, and you look pale."

495

"No, Countess, thank you; I dined in Prague, and I always feel a bit shaky after a long drive. I think I'll go down and see if they've cleared away the new door under the moat."

"As you wish, dear boy, but do come to tell me of the Festival before I retire. I passed through Bayreuth on my honeymoon Tour. There was not even a hut for music. Only a somewhat muddy hill and an oppressive climate."

Plus ça change, Comtesse.

The 3rd Cellar:

Work begins below ground, unbothered by approaching winter. The work goes more slowly – the young Leader's Hooligan ration having been cut by a sudden bureaucratic demand for factory labour in Bohemia's battle-smithies. (For no good reason: is the war not ending?) There was only dirt coming out of the cellar but the same care had to be exercised; that umber clump of muck could be rusted armour of a Knight Parsifal. 14 hours a day the Expedition Leader watched them digging, his Hooligans, and at night thought how hopeless it was and useless. His whole spirit cried out – Avignon! (Also, Kiev, but even Eddie knew that was wishful-dreaming.) The war *is* ending: He has said so. The maddening part is that France is in His orbit, or at least most of it, anyway the important chunk of it, Paris. How can a provincial nowhere town producing stinking bottled water hold up Edwin's Destiny?

The Fool had just decided to write to enlist the Chicken Farmer's aid on my problem – when Assistance appeared to drop from the skies:

Early one morning,
Just as the sun was rising,
Eddie heard a loud whining,
On the fi-eld below . . .

A Messerschmidt with 2 engines and skis on its wheels. Stellvertreter Anna Hess was its only occupant.

"Herr Rudolf. What a surprise. Is this an official visit?"

"Only a training flight, Herr Edwin. Each of us must keep himself in

496

readiness for the Call in our nation's service. I had heard of your work at Třeboň when I was at the Institute for Strategic Studies. How fascinating to think that the Holy Grail may have rested here at one time in history. May we talk privately?"

"We could use the Countess's apartments. Would you like coffee – I have some from Zürich?"

His Deputy sets a stiff example: "Stimulants affect the valves of the heart. Sergeant, post a guard on my aircraft until I return from Herr von Perceval."

Mein Rudi didn't need a stimulant: he was keyed up, marching in quick stiff strides, with little tosses of the head and clapping of the hands. When he pulled off his flight helmet the winter sun caught the small scar on his brow. The Countess was still in bed. Hess sent her old servant packing.

Ho-ow can you tre-at a po-or Mai-den so!

"This is a delicate matter, Herr Edwin, but I shall come straight to the point. The Fuehrer is determined to make peace with the English. All possible avenues are to be explored – but naturally He cannot be seen to pursue some of them publicly. As His Deputy I can take greater risks on His behalf – He can have my life! – thus I am making contact with Englishmen at high level abroad. Only through accommodations with England shall Germany have security, of this I am more totally convinced than ever. The Fuehrer, in His Genius, holds other views about the dominance of the Heartland, through the Caucasus Plateau Island – but this is for another time. Herr Edwin, I formally request that you contact Lloyd-George for me."

Re-member the vo-ows that you ma-ade to your Le-ader!
Re-member the bow'r where you vo-owed to be True!

"I suppose I could write a letter, Herr Rudolf. Perhaps to his secretary. I could post it outside Germany."

This seems to be the preferred route when dealing with the Mowgli kitchen Cabinet.

497

"Excellent! You may say that I am prepared to have a personal meeting – preferably in neutral territory, but this is not essential. You have visited Herr George at his house in Kent, yes?"

"At Churt. Once or twice, with Ettie, we have."

"Then perhaps you may prepare also for me a sketch plan of this estate – the larger fields, buildings, surrounding hills – it shall not need to be a work of art." And as Deputy and Fool-Surveyor march back across the crunching snow to the aircraft, "Herr Edwin, these are such difficult times, so delicate, we *must* be successful. There can be no second chances. I thank you for the plan, and for the Fatherland! Auf Wiedersehen!"

Thus sang the poor Mai-den, her so-orrows be-wail-ing,
Thus sang Fräulein Anna, in the valley below:
Oh, don't de-ceive Me ... !
&c.

The Messerschmidt, with "2's" and "5's" and "6's" in its fuselage number (but no Lucky 7's) ascends as a lark into the blue air, in 4/4 time. At great personal sacrifice the Expedition Leader leaves the Dig and makes the trek to post my note in Switzerland. This time there is a direct reply: but not from the Goat's Secretary.

... *1st Week in March:* The 3rd cellar has produced nothing. The Scholar takes refuge in witchcraft and journeys to the Pendulists' Institute to ask if there's any point in continuing at the White Lady's castle. Such things cannot be rushed, Edwin! He leaves his precious plans under suspended blobs of various metals and walks for lunch at a small restaurant near Sans Souci. A Black-Leather car pulls alongside. The Chicken Farmer is in the back seat, adding "r's" and beckoning. For anyone (in Nibelheim) other than the Fool, a sickening gesture.

"May I roffer you a ride?"

"Very kind, Herr Reichsminister – but I'm almost there. On my way to lunch at Gottfried's, it's only around the corner."

"Ride anyway. It's a cold wind."

A burning one for Rothers, when that fringer beckons. The Fool takes the hint, and while being overwhelmed by cheap cologne observes that

498

the Reichsminister has cut himself whilst shaving – right cheek, half a centimetre above the lip.

"One understands that Herr Hess visited you recently, Herr von Percreval?"

"Yes, he did actually."

"Was this a social visit?"

"Well we chatted, you know – and I offered him coffee, but he can't drink it because of his heart valves. It was more of a training flight than anything, I suppose. To keep his hand in."

"Training for what – do you suppose?"

The edges of Mime's eyes are redder than ever from reading all those deadly tiny records.

"I don't really know, Herr Reichsminister. In case Herr Rudolf was called to defend the Reich, that sort of thing was how he put it."

"Herr Rudolf, yes, you have known each other for so long. Called by whom – do you suppose?"

The Chicken Farmer's Mongoloid eyebrows cover the lids of his Aryan's eyes. It makes his Oriental questions deceptively bland.

"By Herr Wolf, I imagine. It did seem a little Quixotic, now that you mention it."

"By our Fruehrer, yes. And what else did you chat about in this so Quixrotic fashion?"

"My digging. Nothing very much. And then he took off – "

"But *something*. I should like to know, no matter how little."

The Chicken Farmer's temples puff out strangely – like mushroom knobs – rich food for Kapitän von Maser, phrenologist.

"I'm afraid it was in confidence, Herr Reichsminister. One can't betray – and Herr Rudolf is after all Herr Wolf's Stellvertreter, isn't he?"

"The Second in Crommand of our nation, yes – and he talked to you of peace with England."

Not mushrooms. Like a Crobra – striking!

"It was in confidence," flutters the sparrow. "I really don't – "

"There can be no digging without my Deprartment."

"I realise. I'm very grateful."

"And I rappreciate your sense of honour. I would never ask you for the contents of your privrate convrersations. Or letters. Unless they

499

concerned the fate of the Nation. In future, telling me only that Herr Hess has called will be sufficient. But do tell me quickly. I understand you shall be joining your sister, the Fräulein Edwina on your French island for your brirthday as usual – ah, here is Grottfried's. Enjoy your lunch – and weigh the dangers of coffee crarefully, Herr Edwin."

See how they dance the jig called Treason: our Fafner-Hermann, and Mime-the-Frarmer, and Fräulein Anna – His transvestite Freia, leaving the Twilight dance when the flames have barely started!

Edwin saw Himmler once more on the ballroom floor that spring of '41, when the Peace Quadrille was still whirling. Leaving Fuhlsbüttel, he was just coming out with a Black Order flunky, and the always polite Fool said, "How do you do, Herr Reichsminister?" And got this blank look back, and realised that the mushroom temple bulges weren't the same.

"Ein Doppelgänger, Kapitän?" from astonished little Eddie.

Seadog von Maser thumps his peg-leg, chuckling. "The fellow quite had you for a moment – and you know the Reichsminister, so that's excellent. I'll pass it on in the report. As you can imagine it gives our great men some rest at night when there's corroboration of effectiveness."

"You mean they're actors, trained deliberately?"

"Trained, certainly, and some were actors one supposes, but appearance naturally is the most important factor. Most are drawn from the criminal classes – and damned lucky to be so. Full rations and good quarters for the Duration – I'm sure they thank their lucky stars. A turn of phrase, not meant to slight members of the profession. ...."

Which has no firm answers for Edwin's White Lady problems, and the pendulae are all being used to find the *Bismarck*. And so:

... At Porquerolles: The Day of Leaving. Us, on the stone jetty waiting. Deaf'n'Dumber approaching in the distance. Us kissing Mathilde, being engulfed by her. The *Cormoran* bumping gently alongside. A matelot jumping off. Our first bags down. A low noise from Mathilde. Somewhere in the chest. No, the heart.

"*Comment?*"

"*Rien, mes enfants. Au revoir.*"

Collapsing to the stone bench.

"It isn't nothing, Ettie."

"I know. But I have to go. There's only the one connection to Milan. What do you think, Eddie, shall I cancel?"

Colour coming back to the old cheeks. Breath a little easier.

"No, go on. I'll stay, and meet you in time to hold your hand."

"If you're sure. Mathilde, darling, do take care. I'll come back after Tosca. Oh I hate the bloody wops."

Brother, watching the *Cormoran* sail away with Sister, Mathilde's angel, down from heaven. I had a pony and trap take her massive frame back to the villa and sent to the nuns for the one with medical knowledge. Mathilde is just overweight, "Like too many of us on this island, monsieur. Bed rest, and clear fish broth for a week and she'll be kicking up her heels like a young thing again."

Eddie fed her the fish broth for two days, and on the third she died. Just a small noise, early in the evening, and when I went in she was gone. And the golden times with her. Eddie sat through the night beside her gross old body and wept for the days that never come again. And in the sunlight, amid the pines waving in the breezes from our Mediterranean, with the nuns' help I buried her, and left mimosa and fronds of tamarisk. And went home alone through the maquis, to the Villa of the Casson-Percevals, although Madame de la Verendry begged me not to.

Attention! Le serpent, mon petit . . .!

Hot tears, a cool breeze, the slight scrape of a fisherman's lap-strake and keel. The mosquito net waving. The tears and the netting distorting the stars.

"Mr Casson-Perceval, sir?"

So English-crisp the voice in the head. So at odds with the villainous shape it sees: a black face, all grimaced-teeth-and-eyeballs through the mosquito netting.

"What on earth – ?" Edwin, exclamming!

"I'm terribly sorry, sir, but I'll have to ask you to come off with us."

"Come off?" Silly Eddie, not understanding.

"Yes sir. No noise please, and leave the house exactly the way it is. Of course you can lock the doors."

*Ignorant f*****g foreigner!*

"We never lock the doors."

Under the Sea:

A rubber dinghy in our Bay of the Lobsters. A submarine-serpent lying off. 2 days & 1 night to Gibraltar. Diesel stink and frightful noises. And not one answer to the Fool's questions – with the most awfully nice Naval Politeness – so I gave them up. And then a flight by moonlight from the Rock, out over the Atlantic and the Bay of Biscay-O (Old Song 7 – Don't tell me!), hour after hour into a gale and no one in the mood to be polite even if they could have heard the idiot's questions. And then Home. A landing field Somewhere in England, as they say. And out of the aircraft, legs so cramped that the clot couldn't stand and fell in the English rain and blackout of a hideous English May three-o'-clock morning and a voice said,

"Yes, that's him. Casson-Perceval, good day – thank you for coming."

You miserable worm. And Piss-pot-Percy said unto this, his bent-pricked, red-headed tormentor, verily:

"Cameron! May I ask just what the hell's going on?"

Traitor's Gate

We are never free of those shower-bag tyrannies, and dorm-wakeup scandals, and coarse-Games' squire-archies, and all the thousand other humiliating reminders of when our world was filled with giants with lifelong memories about the Time you Peed after Rugger in the Shower you little Snot – and in Cameron's foul case, back even further: to the Beginning of Time, with The Aunts, tiny-booted Athene, and great Boadicea – spying on Boys Being Boys with Pawel's Sprouting Genitals, from behind her beads at the Bath-Time door.

"You'd like a chance to wash up first," is Cameron-Present's cryptic rejoinder, "and then a spot of breakfast. Did you have a good flight?"

Still enjoying tearing wings off flies.

"Bloody awful," said Edwin-as-Eddie. "Cameron, I demand to know why I'm here. Am I under arrest or what?"

"Arrest? – old boy you're a Swiss national," with that solicitous old School smile behind the Fagmaster sneer. "All will be suitably explained after we run up to Town – now I'm sure you want to get squared off."

Suitably-solicitous my arse. Squaring-off takes place in an arched hut made of galvanised metal with RAF roundel markings over the lav, but the water was hot, so that was a *pleasant* surprise, dears! – and brekker was old England's B & E, so that's jolly-d too! With good old Cameron talking of You-Remember-Old-This and Old-That, as an Air Force steward shuffles the plates around – and no one else comes near at all. Our Eddie is a very special baby . . .

Dawn was starting when we left the arched hut with the roundels, and the rain stopping, and a black Austin with hoods on its lights, and Eddie & Cameron in the back, chatting. No handcuffs. Upstairs, or downstairs, Mama is on the Other Side, sister in La Scala; there is no lady's chamber, no hiding place anywhere for Eddie in this England, waking in its spring greenery and freshness, unblemished, not like poor smashed Brabant-Belgium and fair cousin France ground under His heel for declaring His war for Him.

"From reading the Zürich papers I'd thought there would be more sign of things, Cameron, but I suppose the press exaggerates as usual."

"Had you, Casson-Perceval?" Producing the sneer-smile again, which makes that long Scotch face more saturnine than ever. "I think I can promise you the odd sign fairly soon."

. . . *Somewhere North of Reigate:* The signposts are taken down, but that doesn't fool Edwin. A row of cottages with the centre one gone, and beds left hanging, and a line of craters leading to and from them across a pleasant field.

"Just a mistake," Cameron observes. "Jerry lightening ship on his way home – but I forget: being Swiss of course you don't think of Germany as home."

How's that ?! Not bad for a cricketer's kick in the groin, old Boy.

And then – ?

Croydon, where the whole house-row is gone, but only a row here and there, where the craters missed the aerodrome – understandable inaccuracy when aiming from high level.

And then – ?

Town proper, coming up through Herne Hill and the Elephant and Castle, and the signs Eddie had asked for, of His War-Father's wrath in the battle for Britain, are everywhere for the Fool to see. . . .

503

He sees the space where Rotherhithe docks should be, and their cranes fallen,
chopped off at the knees, gaunt wading birds crippled, necks drowned, under
water, taking great ships with them. Hulls submerged, as expected; and some on
dry land where beyond all rational belief or calculation the blast had set them.
And he sees Cockneys in the demolished streets around, still doing business; and
some faces are sad, and some are happy, and some urchins were as rude as ever,
shouting "Wotcher!" at the passing Austin, with its whiff of Edwardian
Privilege. And then he sees the parts that mattered, over the river, in
civilisation. Mama's Little Flat, south of the Park, gone. And Charlotte Street
where we dined upstairs with the Goat and the Fanny Woman, gone. And the
Nag's Head, for drinks with the Pill-Man doing a flit, gone. And the brick
flower stalls with the narcissus and violets, of Covent Garden, gone – but not
the barrows. Life in the old girl yet: with London Pride.

And then, as he passed along the yellow street, the Fleet, half gutted
and good riddance! and realised that it must be deliberate, this route of
agonised, devastating loss that we were taking, the enormity – then I saw
St Pauls, still standing, and Cameron just sitting in the back seat, with
one long Scotch finger, infuriatingly tapping, until Eddie said – no,
yelled at the long Scotch bastard, "All *right*. I *see*. But *we* started it, and
we're still doing it, and it isn't much different in Berlin."

"But on nowhere near this scale, unfortunately old boy."

– before Dresden dwarfed it, and Hamburg melted into the crucible
for all the forges that fed the fury of His war.

And then – ?

Edwin came to another Tower, a White One also, in the heart of
London, and I said, but quietly, "Stop playing games with me,
Cameron. I am Swiss. You have no legal right to arrest me."

"Why on earth should we want to, Casson-Perceval?" as the
portcullis rises, and then falls with a clanking thud behind me, and 5
croaking ravens fly up in front of the black Austin, to perch above a
doorway leading into my new tower by the green steps from Traitor's
Gate, by the great river of England's past deceits and sometime
glories . . .

Along a hall, with antique Beefeaters carrying modern gasmasks; and
up a flight of steps worn by traitors' feet, and the many innocent; and
policemen now – 2 stalwart, truncheoned London bobbies, *Nah-then,*
nah-then, we-can't-have-this-'ere! Observing some lunatic bureaucrat-

nicety about the Geneva Rules of Confinement, before giving way in their turn to soldiers, machine-gunned, clacking to attention for Long Scotch Cameron and his kidnapped Fag-prisoner. And then a door, bolted and studded swung back, squeaking, into a whitewashed cell with iron rings in the walls and an electric fire, and a plain table and bed like the ones at Hotel Landsberg, and a man, with a plaster cast on his leg, and a black eye, and a leather flying suit.

"Do you know this chap, old boy?"

And Edwin, dropped by childhood into the old School patter, cried aloud as though he was chattering to Ettie, "Christ – it's Fräulein Anna." And then, swift little lad, "No it isn't. I say, it's one of the bloody Doppelgängers."

Because the brute had this completely stunned look in his black eye, at seeing Yours Truly, my dears – and no beer-mug scar above it – and began to shout positively hysterically, in a silly Mock-Rudi voice, in appalling English, "Enough of such games. I demand once more to see the Churchill." Which was quite the last thing on earth any of the Treason-dancers ever dreamed of, children. That raddled old whore of a journalist? Don't tell me!

"Sure?"

Said Cameron to Eddie, almost languid, he was so damned excited.

"Of course I'm sure. But take his shirt off if you don't believe me."

"One doesn't doubt your word, old boy." One was, after all, at School. "But as it's rather important we will just check it out. Guard, remove the prisoner's shirt if you please."

Which makes the poor mad fellow fairly roll his eyes in agitation, children, but it was For His Own Good – and of course he didn't have a mark on him, my dears, front or back.

"And what about this?"

A picture of an aircraft, crashed, with a cow and 2 rustics, prodding with pitchforks.

"No. Hess owns a different kind of Messerschmidt – it doesn't have those fuel tanks and the number has twos and fives in it. I have a sort of a thing about numbers."

"Thank you, Casson-Perceval."

"But where on earth did you find him?"

Cameron, curtly gesturing: "Guard, you may dress the prisoner."

Out in the passage, right-turn! – *not* the way we entered! – up another flight, and another, and another, to a room at the top of the tower, with no electric fire, bitter cold and damp, looking out at shattered London.

"This is where I'd put you if I had my way, but the Prime Minister directs otherwise. Sit down. We're going to have a chat, Piss-pot Percy you wretched snot."

Now that's more like it.

... *On the Nature of Treason:* A long chat. Hour after hour, with every word recorded by a mouse of a woman with stockingless legs, knees blue with the cold, and stubble showing on her shins. When did you meet Mein Hesserl? Why? What's this about a map you drew? And in heaven's name why old L-G, when the Goat's completely past it?

"Because they all think of him as the peacemaker," Edwin said, "still. And not just Hess. Goering and Himmler. And I know him, Lloyd-George, particularly his Secretary – believe me, Cameron, their peace hopes are genuine. The real Hess wants to fly to Churt, I'm sure, although he never said so directly."

"In Kent – so why do you suppose the German High Command would send a lunatic double to parachute onto the Duke of Hamilton, at Dungavel House, in Scotland?"

"I haven't the foggiest. Why don't I drop a note to Rudi and ask him?"

"Don't be snide with me, you worm. Swanning around Europe with your sister while our best chaps are dying and we're half-seas under. My God, talk about living in a dream world – you must be the only man on the globe not to know that Hess is gone."

"I'm not myopic – gone where, Cameron?"

"Flown the coop – 'Felsennest', or whatever they call Adolf's current pigsty. As to *where* precisely, I suggest you enquire of your fat friend, Goering. His man Galland's squadron downed a certain aircraft off Texel Island. With suitable celebration at Luftwaffe HQ I'm told. Or try that loathsome beast Himmler. When you go home you'll find the bastards have all pushed each other's arse one step up the ladder – if that isn't too crude a definition of promotion for a man of your artistic sensibilities."

506

"You mean I can go? And I've said, I don't think of Germany as home. And how will I get there?"

"The way you came, snot – and I only wish you'd go west en route. You'll be landed somewhere along the Côte d'Azur. Bereft and in grief you sailed there by small boat after your frog Nanny died. We've arranged the missing boat. You just get your revolting body back to Hunland, and stick like glue to your bastard Herr Wolf, and when you're in Zürich go to this address with whatever latest madness of his you happen to know."

"You expect me to be a spy? I have no intention – "

"Don't you love your sister?"

So simple a question. Of infinite complexity.

"Not Ettie," Eddie whispered, "Cameron, you wouldn't do anything to Ettie . . ."

But of course he would.

"If you should fail to co-operate, the appropriate security apparatus in Berlin will be notified of her involvement, with sufficient documentation. By our reckoning there have been two dead women in the swine's life already."

The Number is 5, know-it-all, if we count Unity-Valkyry; and 3 attempted.

She sleeps 'neath the Green turf
Down by the Ash Grove . . .

Third Movement

Sixth Passage

[scored for Cannon, with full ensemble]

ffff

WOLFSSCHANZE

Wolf's Lair, Rastenburg, East Prussia, and our wheel has turned to that shortest night, the longest day, the Solstice – when Dame Sun splits Arthur's altar at Stonehenge – the 21st of June (see all His lucky 7's!) in the year of Our Lord, 1941.

The concrete smells wet; the walls of the Fortress are still curing, so rushed is the pace of His furious construction. The piano sits in the innermost room, but one (the white room with the ribbons), our old friend the Black Swan brought as a talisman to keep Us company. The Marschalls of Parsifal pace without surcease and wait on His whim and the morrow. But in the same sanctum is Business As Usual with Wolf, and Wagner, and the Fool summoned as expected without warning.

"Endless plains, Ederl, one only has to look at them to know it's right – horseshit and hovels! The human animal must have air! breathing room! it's the same for a nation. Tolstoy hadn't the slightest understanding of Napoleon, yet the moron-intellectuals call him a genius. A century and twenty-nine years ago tonight he stood like this to cross the Nieman – and it's exactly a year since I settled the Versailles criminality at Compiègne, the best thing I've done in my life was to blow up that train! Of course he wasn't a Frenchman, Napoleon, people forget that. How easy it is, the idiots imagine, to wheel an army into battle, not thinking of the line of mothers and orphans who stand behind the commander's shoulder from the very first moment ... France was child's play compared to Russia – we're not moving into the cradle of civilisation with the higher virtues to be protected like the Paris Opera – and wasn't your sister glorious as Manon Lescaut? I'm not saying it's changed one's mind on the Latins, no! – but it can sway the emotions. I hear she was truly stupendous as Tosca in the torture scenes – I had a special memo from the Duce; he wants to come to Bayreuth this season. It's going to be nip-and-tuck whether we'll have taken Moscow in time – or whether we can get you to Kiev before your noble sister needs you. The sheer distance of this horseshit country. Do you know that ninety-nine per cent of Russia has never heard of the water closet?! Poor poor Hesserl – he really made my mind up for me – they've locked him in the Tower of London, they say – the ghost of Anne Boleyn walks with her head under her arm, and he's affected by such things, mein Rudi. You've seen the letter he wrote me? – no? It's truly pathetic in many ways – after all, he's offered his life for me, a man can't ask more than that. He didn't expect peace from your English, but he was prepared to die for it; that must be worth something when we come to Judgement. A true romantic – the proof? – Ederl, our Rudi read novels! Ask the orderly if the bed is turned down, there's a good fellow – and the coverlet! I can't tell you how many times the oafs forget the coverlet ... You know I have the very first ribbon she gave me – yes, from the Dutchman's stage: cobwebs, then that shaft of sun struck through and lit her hair. And she sang ... dear God! And while I'm on that subject, you missed the Tosca opening night. Oh yes, I heard – I almost sent for you – but the Balkan Campaign had to be won, and then Heydrich told one about your old Nurse dying, and of course how instantly *I* understood – alone in a little sailing boat on the Mediterranean, how perfectly right! – yet how tiny few so-called human beings ever do, or can understand. Never mind, never mind, the dear creature has gone to her reward and they say she didn't really suffer. My Ederl, once again, my most sincere condolences. Through our dark night, play the Swan Boat for both of us old fellow . . ."

UKRAINE

. . . With the Troops: As a matter of fact, children, Old Eddie has told a little white lie, to make a ripping yarn better! He didn't ride with the Black Order: I went with Pawel and his Free Russian Cossacks – or Kozz – but it's still in the van of His army. Scholar Edwin has thumbs-up from the pendulists for Kiev! – and this ride isn't bleak and frightful like Dunquerque, it's cups of fresh milk, and strewn flowers: we are Liberators, not the Conquering Horde. The peasants come to Pawel, and kneel in the dirt of Ukraine churned up by his tracks, and kiss his hands, and the hem of his dark green jacket. (Even Ettie had been swept off her feet by that dark green, with the gold shoulder flashes.)

"Hejtman!" The peasants call out to him, "Ukraine lives! You have saved us!"

"Just like you promised, Pawel," from his friend Eddie, truly awed. "At the Aunts, but I never for a minute believed you'd do it, free Russia. How extraordinary life is."

"I don't care about Russia, Eddie. A free Ukraine is enough."

And at night when we bivouac, Pawel's peasants bring him plucked chickens, and crusty bread, and ikon pictures of their sort of patron saint, wrapped in coloured scarves, which appeals no end to the Romantic in Edwin.

And darker presents . . .

"*This Jew was the worst commissar, Hejtman! This Jewess was his informer!*"

A stream of small darknesses, building to a river, washing loose in every village, and swirling to the rear with the other prisoners in the care of the Black Order, His chosen people.

And then –?

A special Storch 'plane from the Fuehrer's Flight arrived to drag the Fool away for the Season!

"Bloody hell," cursing futilely to Pawel, "there's absolutely no need. It's only Ring and Holländer again, and she knows every bloody note. At this rate you'll be at Kiev in a week."

"Six, if we have all the luck and the Reds don't get a successful guerilla action going in our rear."

How our Slavic brothers simply *adore* their Pessimism, my dears.

...At Bayreuth: Brother says as much to Sister on arrival in the world of Illusion – and didn't half get a flea in his ear.

"The one real man you can call a friend out of your limp-wrist crowd and you stab at his back with that pansy whine. All because of Tegernsee. Pawel's got a certain measure of *realism*, which is more than we ever get around here, listening to the bloody Dwarf lying his drawers off on the wireless. There isn't a snowball's chance of Wolf getting to Moscow by Christmas. I'm not at all sure I'm going to sing in Hunland again."

"A snowball has every chance, there's nothing but – and *realism*, from you, Ettie? Well don't hold your breath for a call from poor blasted Covent Garden. We don't know how well off we are. Just count yourself damned lucky to have no bombs in Switzerland and Bayreuth."

"I hadn't heard the Garden was bombed?"

"It isn't – I mean it wasn't – "

"What do you mean?" With her look that means She's on to him. "Eddie, you've been acting strange since Porquerolles. What's the matter?"

"Mathilde. I loved her."

"We both loved her. No, you've got some sort of a secret. Something to do with not going to my Tosca, I can see from your face – you went to Toulon and mixed with the sailors! That's where you heard about bombs. Confess, you can't hide anything from me."

"Perhaps that's where I heard it. Ettie, I didn't mean to miss your bloody Tosca."

"I know you didn't, darling – and truly, I do know how you felt after Mathilde; I don't blame you for a sailor – anyone to take our minds off this ghastly mess the war's turning into."

"You think about all that?"

"Pet, big Sis isn't completely addled."

And she opened her self to the returning traveller; but after, in the moment of tristesse, when the world can be seen without the blinkers,

512

when Eddie should have taken his advantage – taken her in that flash of common sense from the Green Hill and its tentacles *instantly*! – instead . . .

"I don't think we should rush any decisions, Ettie. Wolf says once Russia falls even old Winston will see reason. And it makes perfect sense – we'll still have the Empire, and Wolf will have a sort of United States of Europe. He's been right all the way along. And we're stuck with this Season, and it can't make much difference to go on this way till Christmas."

"That's true," she said, reflecting, "and I can always change our mind if Wolf takes Moscow."

OUR '41 SEASON

Only the most diehard foreign Wagnerians brave the hazards of His war to attend the Festival, and their appearance has the mothballed seediness from that long-ago re-opening in '24. Gowns & Tails stored in the same tissue, with the same mothballs. Only the Parsifal uniforms of the Black Order look smart. The War-Wolf still finds time to attend – still comes in when the House lights are down, not to disturb the worshippers, although for many, if not most, *He* is now the only god to be worshipped: Master of Europe, soon of great Russia. Trills Ettie-Brünnhilde:

> *Think of the Vows that unite Us,*
> *Think of our mutual Trust!*

"The magic never fails," He declares, at the first Interval, "Ederl, what a gift your so-noble mother brought to Germany. I shall not fail her memory now – and I've just found out that Franco's a half-Jew, so that explains Gibraltar! – but how vast that manure pile is to the east. Thank our stars for Blitzkrieg!" Booms Manowarda-Hagen:

> *The world becomes for Him a mere wood, in His restless quest*

513

even to Gibich shores He roams from the Rhine. As if with
idle hands He drives the boat swift against the current . . .

And then, from a Waltraute whose name even Eddie can't remember,

> *With a silent sign He sent the Nobles*
> *Of Valhalla to fell the great world Ash.*
> *He summoned the Council of the Gods,*
> *By His side bade them sit, fearful,*
> *In rings and rows the heroes filled the Hall.*
> *So He sits, silent, solemn on His sacred Throne.*
> *He sends His two Ravens on their travels,*
> *If ever they return with Good Tidings*
> *Then once more, for the last time*
> *The God will smile into Eternity . . .*

"I estimate Kiev in three weeks at the most," He said, allowing a single uplifting note of business at a subdued Family supper that night.

"How we all pray, my Fuehrer," said Winifred; a mother with one Wolfi-son wounded from France, and returned alive to her, but another at the Front. And a daughter lost: Mausi-Friedelind may not be mentioned in the house of no illusions.

Ettie said nothing anyway. Playing the Ice-Maiden, more frozen and distant the harder He tries. Eddie played for only half an hour and was dismissed without being able to crack the happy gloom.

"He has enough on His plate without you being beastly," the loyal Fool said to Sister, reversing roles once more upstairs at the Griesbachs. "I have to go to Zürich but I'll come and see you again before I leave for Kiev. Just in case."

"Wolf's my affair – and you don't have to go, not for a non-existent pot. Or not so soon, Eddie – let Pawel at least have the place settled down. That's his job. He's a soldier."

"But I want to be there, Ettie. I can't explain. It's like Marco Polo with Kubla Khan."

"Oh sod the whole lot of them. And why Zürich? At least you could save that part of the holiday for me."

"We'll go to Triebschen, then I'll only be half a day. I have to see Rau

514

about our investments."

"You're lying again – and there aren't any sailors in Zürich – you've got a new little friend."

"Only Michael, and we've never been to bed. He's in love with you, you know that."

"Haven't you? Is he?"

... *In Zürich:* The House of Treason is found to be *under* the oysters' "place" – run by an ex-monk married to a quondam-nun! – so that after betraying His trust, little traitor-Eddie has no appetite.

"A small helping really, Michael. I'm not hungry, and I've got to get back to Ettie at Triebschen. Did she call at your office, by any chance?"

So quickly doth suspicion breed.

"Alas no. You should have brought the beauteous Edwina so that I could tell you both my plans – try and guess?"

Eddie's dearest friend grinned as he slurped his oysters down.

"I can't – unless you've finally driven your father bankrupt?"

"No such luck. He's richer than ever with Lend-Lease. I'll tell you, Eddie, I've stopped fighting it. If your Mr Wolf takes Moscow, I'm going to New York to head the business."

Gurgling with delight, Rau summoned up a fresh tureen.

"A tycoon? Helping your father? – so all along it was only a game?"

"So it seems, old friend. He will have deserved to win – Herr Wolf, not my father. I did my part, but the fools wouldn't listen."

Rau had stopped laughing.

"You mean it wasn't a game? Michael, I don't think I'll ever understand you."

"That's why we find each other such good company. Your old Goat's chemist-chum, Weizmann, safe outside, has declared war 'with all the resources of International Jewry!' – and now Heydrich's shooting Kikes in the Ukraine instead of selling them. Can you wonder that I'm going back into business? – we Yids weren't born to be saved. No more arguing, Eddie, I don't care how much you object, we're having the pheasant next."

The putative monk had that ready too.

"I was just in Ukraine," said the Fool, "with Pawel, and I didn't see any Jews being shot. The peasants were pretty worked up over the ones

515

that were Commissars but that's understandable. And Heydrich's a cold fish but he isn't a butcher. In fact I should have said he's a pragmatist."

"Wanting to play the violin for the luscious Edwina? Tristan to Isolde seems hardly pragmatic – but then I'm non-Wagnerian. Heydrich does have a Jew's head for figures, though, we worked well together. Over three-hundred-thousand dragged from the wreck in spite of themselves – you can't sneeze over that. Except – Eddie, there's something I should have told you. Your hotel friends from Munich could not be included. They died of influenza. But that's absolutely genuine. Heydrich produced the medical certificates, and good Germans don't lie about things like that. I'm sorry. Believe me, Eddie."

And when we were finished, and hugging good-bye, and Eddie said, "Thanks for what you tried to do, anyway. I only wish I understood your kind of game."

"And I yours, old friend. Don't get yourself killed in Kiev looking for something as common as a Grail."

And laughing he strode, or rather rolled, on his merry Way, to a New World. . . .

The Golden Gate:
Is not! Children, Kiev's monument of legend is a pile of blackened stone, with hinge-pins rusted like Annabelle's, and a triangle of grass kept trimmed in peacetime by peasant cattle-women kneeling and tearing it by hand, in handful-clumps, but not trimmed when our Fool sees it because there is too much other public trimming to attend. And winter comes early in Ukraine. . . .

Fighting is heavy, but still they get there, the Wolf-Men, with Pawel leading his proud little army of Free Russians – which no Russian ever has been – and a safe distance following (it wasn't *my* bloody legend) on September 21st, I, Edwin, entered Ukraine's capital. Wolf's Victory, Mama's Birthday, the Equinox after Solstice, the first day of Autumn, divisible by 7.

Our golden Youth is attached – gazetted, should be our Edwardian term – to the Interior Ministry of the Greater German Reich, through its creature, the pendulists' Strategic Institute, and *its* creature, The Sub-Section for Special Psychical Research.

Edwin never eats with the killers. Nor saw them that I know of. All the

516

Black Order have skulls and crossed bones – it's not my job to find out how they use them. Kiev is a city in chaos. Between the trembling Iron-Man's hysterical scorched-earth orders of Retreat, and Wolf's of Attack! little stands unmarked. The Scholar's 1st intended starting point, the Church of the Nativity, had been dynamited in 1935 (because it was also a shrine to the poet Schevchenko) and is now a River Pumping Station – with Beverage Kiosk, surrounded by iron railings, plastered with Stalin's visage. Wolf's eyes in posters always had that air of the dreamer, hypnotic, otherworldly. The eyes of Stalin were of this world, the frozen one he hacked from the blood and spirit of a people: the eyes of a bland brute, squinting.

Tosh:
Pawel finds Eddie an interpreter-assistant, a girl with blond hair & blue eyes (so *that* was all right) and a hopeless last name (which we never use). Tosh (ie, from Natasha) speaks some peculiar French, and Eddie has his little bit of The Aunts' All Souls Ukrainian, so this is our so-simple common pigeon-tongue. Tosh is an admirer of the excessive Tchaikovsky (then considered the height of reactionary daring among the Comrades, my dears) and of Pawel, with whom she slept for the week before he crashed onwards, and then told her new friend all about it.

"So like a roche, all the times! – but such lovely soft skin. Would you like to amour me now he is gone, Monsieur-Gospodin-Eddie?"

Free Amour is her only Progressive tenet. She hates all the rest of the Comrades' Gospel with Slavic passion. Nor does she shave her legs, which was peculiar for Eddie when lying against her (almost masculine); nor under her arms – and certainly not anywhere else!

"This shall be so obscène," Tosh says, giggling, while gently parting the gold fluff on her magic molehill, and eyeing Edwin's safety razor. Which he kept away from her: we all know what trouble you can get into with one of those. And with blades so devilish hard to come by.

"I think you're awfully nice," said our lad, on that 1st occasion of offering, "vraiment – but actually Tosh, I simply must get started on finding a cleric."

"But I am trained to take notation, Monsieur-Gospodin-Eddie. Because of notre red Cheka monstres you think we are sauvages, nyet?"

Prettily pouting.

"Nyet – not at all, Tosh. I mean clerical like a priest – un curé – or a monk. Damn it, even a bloody vestry cleaning woman. I haven't been able to find anyone religious at all."

"No," Tosh said happily, "they were all shot for being Rasputins. They have used to do things to girls behind the curtains. And many with garçons – such is the truth. If I find you one like this will you love me tonight, Monsieur-Gospodin-Eddie?"

"Sooner. The minute you produce him. Or her."

An "it": a cripple, with its left leg gone above the knee, and outwardly a male, because it wears a man's clothes, but it has no beard, nor need to shave, and a strangely pitched voice. Because of these 1st War mutilations, the poor devil has been spared. Tosh introduces it as Old-Blov:

"It is sixty years and hates also the comrades." It-Blov's entire tribe having starved to death in Stalin's famines of the early thirties – to solve *his* Ukrainian problem.

Old-Blov is a Godsend to young Edwin's. Le garçon-Blov had served as an acolyte (behind the curtains – before his pennies dropped) then been apprenticed a stone-mason directly to the Bishopric of Kiev, under the Bishop's tender eye doing repairs on all the churches, until made redundant by the Bishop's departure in war and revolution. Old-Blov's greatest asset is that he knows other half-men with secret ecclesiastical links.

"Yes, your Worship. Most from the laity, but I know two priests also – if your Worship is sure Stalin won't be back."

"Les Boches shall be chasing l'Ogre over the Urals by next month," said Tosh firmly. "Come back demain morning with the names, Old-Blov – Monsieur-Gospodin-Eddie has secrétaire work for ce soir. Da svidanya."

With which the rougeant couple repair à toute vitesse to Gospodin-Eddie's forward base of operations: a ravished room in the former Peter-The-Great Hotel, re-christened the Oktobre by the departed comrades, and now Der Blitzkrieg-Palast. My tower of babble. The whole building stinks of garlic and human excrement. Some Hooligans have been recruited to scrub it top to bottom with disinfectant – ineffectually. Another small problem with Tosh is that she doesn't seem

518

to notice. And, after Edwin has gone to immense pains to get hot water, is scandalised at washing in a bath, daily!

"It kills the skin, Monsieur-Gospodin-Eddie! Shall I ride the Huss-cock like with your cher ami, General Pawel, all night?"

Product of his Sandhurst training! Eddie is less roche-like and succumbs after a mere 3 rides, bareback: also saddle-sore. In the morning a fresh pile of ordure has been left on the carpet at the head of the passage stairs by one of the Hooligan scrubbers. Stinking and steaming: there's no heat in the building.

[reprise]
Winter is Coming . . .

Hard frost but a bright sky. For the first time the air was free of the thunder of heavy artillery. Occasional bursts of machine-gun fire from the outskirts completed "mopping-up". Old-Blov has Edwin's 1st key to the city of death.

"A priest who once was from St Cyril and All Martyrs, your Worship. Father Konstantin – he also was with the Death Of Our Lady when she was buried for safety in the Skulls' caves."

The most sacred relic in Ukraine! Reputedly more than 1000 years old. Who could dream of such fool's luck so early? What else may not be stored with such a treasure?

The crippled wretch begins to hop in an agonizing fashion off along the pavement.

"You can't possibly walk. I'll get a car."

The Logistics people are happy to oblige: any young friend of the Chicken Farmer's is a friend of theirs. Old-Blov creeps with his canes into the back seat as though entering heaven. The trio drive east at his direction past a decapitated statue of Lenin with the head gazing balefully from a carpet of curled yellow birch leaves, another Baptist's on its plate, garnished with crab apples.

"The pig," says the beautiful Tosh, "I piss on his mother."

"Uh, where exactly are we going?" enquires young Edwin, as OIC of the expedition. "Which district of Kiev?"

"To the ravin de La Dame Ancienne, Monsieur-Gospodin-Eddie –"

in almost a whole unilingual sentence.

"Old Lady's Ravine – the Ikon, Old-Blov?"

"Bless you, no, your Worship. It has the name for a Jew witch who was burnt for putting one of her spells on the mayor's wife. Long long ago – no one remembers what mayor, or what was the spell for. They only remember the witch. When the cold is worst in the Christmas moon you can see her walking with a bright blue shadow on the snow when every other shadow is black in Babyn Yar. The new sewer is being run there now."

Edwin's guides to this officially atheist land cross themselves for their old-wives' tale. Their OIC has eyes only for the church appearing in front of the Black Order's car.

"Here is your St Cyril's, Monsieur-Gospodin-Eddie. The finest spires-gothique en Kiev – but then the monstres knock one down to put le radio up."

One spire was collapsed into the street, like London's cranes. The church windows were boarded over. The standing spire had a wireless antenna with a stork's nest on top. A tall, elderly Ukrainian with jet-black hair stood at the door. From the way he held his hands, downwards, folded one upon the other, thumbs locked, sheltering the Host – here was my priest.

"Father Konstantin," squeaked Old-Blov, simultaneously bowing so that he dropped one of his canes. Polite-Eddie retrieved it.

"This one is not a Boche."

"No, Father, from England. Was this your church?"

"Once I was part of the life of it. Come inside, young man, and see what is left of it."

Konstantin took a large black iron key from his threadbare jacket pocket and unlocked a small door, at the side of the building. Tosh borrowed Monsieur-Gospodin-Eddie's white silk scarf for her fair head. With Old-Blov clacking behind, our quartet entered.

The transept. There were no lights, all was dirt, yet I could see that it was beautiful. An elaborate Iconostasis, or Image Screen, cut off the altar from our vision. Apostles in niches kept vigil across the top; a Last Supper was painted above the centre gate; the Christos was to the right with angels; the Mother of Mary was to the left. And to the extreme right, the most useful sign: a torn gravure photograph, hand painted.

"You were Uniates, Father." Forbidden Catholics, mourning the exile of their leader, once a bishop of San Francisco in Michael Rau's new world. "The banished Patriarch," the Scholar said, "His Holiness, Tikhon."

"You are right, young man. What is it you wish from us?"

"I wish only to help set up the Dark Lady, your ikon, once more in the place and church established for her in Perchersky Lavra, the Monastery of Caves, which some call the Community of the Skulls."

"Not only. Some other cause brings you to Kiev?"

"One other thing, Father, it is true, but I cannot know that I shall find it in Kiev. All I can do is hope. I search for the Holy Grail."

"Armies have searched. Perhaps you should pray, young man."

"Perhaps I will, Father. Shall you help me?"

"I would, sir, but we Uniates have vowed to keep our Lady hidden until Ukraine is free once more."

"You are, Father. Free – I came here with my friend, your Hejtman."

"You know our Hejtman?"

"We went to school together. Its name was All Souls College."

"Then you have been sent from God – but still I may not lead you to the Skulls without our Hejtman's blessing."

And stubborn, stiff-necked bastard, he wouldn't – no matter how much Church drivel the Scholar trotted out. In a fury of impatience Edwin drove back to the Blitzkrieg-Palast.

"So smart, Monsieur-Gospodin-Eddie!" Tosh, undressing in a twinkling, with a virgin's wide-blue innocence, "All about churches, I was étonnée! We ride the Huss-cock now you find your priest, nyet?"

"Nyet! We find that bugger Pawel – toot sweet!"

Gospodin Eddie joins a convoy leaving in the afternoon. Dead machines and shit-makers litter the frozen fields. With the frost, Fafner's tanks can move even faster. Where Mother Russia's winter stopped Napoleon, it seems she is but another of His allies. Mile after mile after mile – the distance of Berlin from Paris, and still only half way from the Dnieper to the Don. . . .

"Christ, Eddie – " a tired Pawel, dragged from mid-briefing for yet another battle, for a few more hundred thousand square miles and men – "you can't possibly expect me to sort out a politico-religious squabble in the middle of action. Those bloody Uniates can babble on for years and Stalin's *running*, man! Edwin, there's never been anything like this in all the history of war."

"Well a letter then, if you can't come yourself. Surely you can manage that?"

"I have twenty divisions wheeling for the pocket on each side of me. Jesus – "

"I'll write it. If you'll just sign it?"

"Stubborn arse. Get hopping. We move out in an hour."

Eddie wrote, Pawel signed – and even sealed, using his signet ring and some special wax employed on secret cryptographic papers by a machine like a typewriter, but with telephone dials.

"That's why we're winning," Pawel says, with a wink. "Our little enigma. Good luck Eddie – and by the way –" over his shoulder as the tanks grind out into a Ukrainian sunset of incredible glory shining on ice crystals in the grain fields – "keep in mind that religion is really Heydrich's baby ..."

And when these Slav sparrows fall, even by their millions, children – in this vast black land who will ever see? Or know ...?

Back to Kiev – against the traffic, with all the troops thumbs-up and grinning from their conning towers and turrets, and by God I have to tell you it was infectious. To think that I, Edwin *know* Him. Hell, He wants to marry my damn-fool Sister.

"She's mad," Eddie tried explaining it to Tosh, from his wasteful bath in the Blitzkrieg-Palast, "she could be the Empress of Europe. I'll never understand women."

"Perhaps he is no good for riding the Huss-cock, Monsieur-Gospodin-Eddie, your Wolf – oh vitesse, vitesse! you look so *pink*!"

And then –?

Back to the Church of St Cyril & All Martyrs, with Old-Blov, hopping, and Konstantin waiting. *And through the birch trees, just over the green hill that shelters the Old Lady's Ravine, still the sound of light gunfire, to a Fool's ear still just a rearguard action, good insurance, mopping up in Babyn Yar.*

"Goodbye Commissars," cackled Old-Blov, "and their Jew-women. If only that arch-devil Lenin could be here to go as well."

"Vengeance is mine, saith the Lord," boomed Konstantin, reproving.

"Well, young man?"

"I have it. From Pawel. That's his seal."

The priest inspected the letter from the battlefield . . . with apocalyptic gravity . . . and slowness . . .

And then –?

"Meet me here again tomorrow, young man, and you shall have our final answer."

Back to the Blitzkrieg-Palast, driver! And waiting – always bloody waiting. First for this damned do-nothing priest –

. . . And now for yet another tank to pass the Fool's car, sitting in his blind impatience with his sexually obsessed Huss-cock-woman. A tank with a large blade welded on for moving earth in sewer excavations. Moving over the green hill and through the birch trees to the Old Lady's Ravine called Babyn Yar.

But the next day I had it!

"Yes, young man, Konstantin shall lead you to the Skulls to recover the Dark Lady of Ukraine so that she may be ready when our Hejtman re-takes his throne."

King Pawel the First, and Eddie his 1st official court Fool.

"Can we go now, Father? In my car?"

"No, young man."

"Why not for God's – Tosh, I simply can't take any more. Ask the idiot why can't we go?"

"Because Perchersky Lavra is destroyed from the top, he says. You have to go in to the cavern of the skulls from the bottom. But not me, Monsieur-Gospodin-Eddie, c'est religieuse et pas de femmes."

"But I need you Tosh."

"I can't," she said. "I am afraid of the dark."

So I went without her into the Community of Skulls. I went following Konstantin the priest down a stair into a crypt, and then through a door hidden in a wall, and then along a passage leading east, under the green hill and the new sewer and the tank for moving dirt in the ravine called Babyn Yar.

I SAW NOTHING!

RIEN!

Nyet?

I swear on my mother's grave.

. . . In the Community of Skulls: Edwin's 1st face-to-skull encounter is a collection crudely cemented together with mortar, blocking the mouth of a cave. The priest had brought a hammer and chisel, and when he produced these tools Old-Blov with a shrill squeak of excitement threw down his canes and grasped the hafts, then fell on the interstices and delicately severed enough heads to let us pass. To another passage, not a cave, and more heads, and more, and more – 4 broken walls all together, with others to either side: dozens, hundreds of damned holes!

And there is Avignon, untouched, and the White Lady's Castle, unfinished, and the starting point of the vessel's wandering, the Three Maries – not to mention sites only vaguely considered so far within Nibelheim itself, like Drachenfels or the salt mines below Salzburg in the shadow of His Salt Mountain. Even the Fool was daunted.

But swiftly revived.

"This wall next," booms Konstantin, and no sooner has Old-Blov attacked it than our lamps reflect a tiny hint of gold, "Praise be to God! She lives! Ukraine lives! Young man, on your knees!"

The Black Lady – because the ikon is black with age – shows the Virgin transported in death with a halo of golden wire knitted around precious stones, and her Son watching with a single giant diamond above His rubied, bleeding head.

"Holy Mother," squeaked Old-Blov, "bless your Worship, we can die happy at last!"

But Edwin was most un-happy – because even behind the relic's grotto there were more skulled-up spaces leading off to endless dark.

"Our Lady must be taken to St Cyril." Bloody booming Konstantin.

But *He* hath other plans for Her. Because, children – when Fool & Monk & Cripple emerge from Erda's underworld . . .

"Class One Artifacts become the property of the Reich," announced that foxy bastard, Reinhard Heydrich. "Herr Edwin, I'm leaving the Ukraine tomorrow. Have supper with me tonight."

No question about it.

"Impossible!" The outraged priest thundered. "I defend Her with my life!"

"That is not required, thank you Father." From droll Isy, with that ostentatiously invisible sneer. "I am aware of your relic's patriotic significance. I shall see that the ikon has full security until the

524

restoration of some form of semi-autonomous administration for the Eastern Region. You have my word. Captain –" to a Black Order acolyte – "take the thing and provide a receipt."

"Judas!" Roared the priest – at Eddie!

"At seven," said Heydrich. "Without your ladyfriend."

Blond Moses knew Everything, my dears, about Everyone, Everywhere.

. . . At the Blitzkrieg-Palast: Tormentor & Victim dine in a private room – on battle rations, for Good-General Heydrich always sets the personal example for his men.

"As does our Fuehrer, but you know better than me, Herr Edwin, how Spartan he is in his diet. Even so, he has been having trouble with his stomach – perhaps you've heard?"

"No, General. I haven't been with Herr Wolf for some weeks."

"What a misfortune. I regret that tonight as recompense I can't allow us to enjoy the gourmet delights one could, oh, let's say in Zürich, for example?"

Oh let's! Fool's gut lurches violently. Its owner toys with a slice of dehydrated gristle and manages a choked, "Yes, the food is good in Zürich, General."

"And you still manage to enjoy it often."

"I am a Swiss citizen."

"And your sister, as I don't need reminding, Herr Edwin. A great disappointment that I couldn't be at Bayreuth this year."

"We must hope for next season, General, after the war's over."

The rebellious mess slides across Fool's plate.

"There is many a slip, Herr Edwin, but when this war is over I hope we shall both be there to admire your sister. I notice that your feasts at Zürich follow your simpler meals with the Fuehrer – but I apologise, my chatting seems to be stopping you from eating. The quality of the rations has deteriorated sharply since we've been cut off from Argentina by the Royal Navy."

"Actually, General, I'm not terribly hungry. I think it's the sight of those skulls in the caves."

"A soldier of the Grail needs a strong stomach, Herr Edwin." For a moment Heydrich drops the hidden sneer; he seems to contemplate

525

caves of his own ... "The Royal Navy is a remarkable organisation, it does so much more than just blockade corned beef. Admiral Canaris always had the greatest admiration for its Intelligence operations – the Admiral and I played in a quartet, you may remember?"

"Yes, General, I do remember."

"You have a good memory, Herr Edwin, an eye for detail, both so necessary for gathering information – for your Grail researches – and it's good also that we keep in touch; we'll be able to have many more dinners together."

"Shall we, General?"

"Oh yes, when you're at your war-work in Třeboň, now that I'm to become the Fuehrer's Protector in Bohemia. A magic opportunity – I've always idolised Wallenstein, and I don't mind confessing that I shall be greatly relieved to be spared from this difficult task in the East. And now, I'm afraid I see my driver waiting. My compliments to your sister – your present ladyfriend isn't a patch on her, but when the cat's away ... Also, I haven't bothered to inform the Reichsminister Himmler of your dining habits in Zürich. That can be a little secret between us – for now. Goodnight, Herr Edwin."

Foxy bastard killer swine. And on top of all that – moral scruples. He never cheated on his wife. Except with Ettie.

Third Movement
Seventh Passage

O – that a man might Know
The end of this Day's business 'ere it come,
But it sufficeth – that the Day will end,
And then the End is known ...

Is Old Edwin going mad?

Over G & G's raucous objections the question must be faced: who *is* Eddie? – when he pretends to be old Cosima? or climbs into Wolf's dreadful scrambled head? Waring hates them, the Cosima Bits, and all Superior Edwin's skilful Playlets and wee musical Dance Games.

Our Jeremy is jealous – it goes without saying! Those 'Thirties novelettes had not one spark of *invention*, my dears:

"C-P you can't possibly expect editors to put out their readies for your half-baked ideas. You promised them sex."

I promised them Wolf & Ettie. And half-baked? Oh yes, children: Hänsel und Gretel's first crude ovens are building by '41's turning Season.

Trapped in the snow, Fafner flailed; all seemed black in pure white on that Infamous Day of December – yet another 7. And so, on the Salt Mountain, half a world from Pearl Harbor, on that same date F D Roosevelt's Yids' bill was presented from Rheingold *for payment, by Head-Waiter Hagen:* His Nacht und Nebel Law. *Through dread Night, Fog – Smoke. Resembling No One,* They *shall vanish. Utterly.*

527

(Another co-incidence. And see, Children, how so-skilfully our Fool-isch Old Eddie has evaded the Question!)

A *Divertimento* . . .

. . . *Out of our Doldrums:* Even Russia's winter ends. Fafner's tanks gird up again; special new oils are rushed to development by Wolf-Wotan's little Speer, and I.G. Farben with its workers' concert halls. Work has never stopped in the skull-tunnels beneath Kiev; now Edwin leaves it in the unimaginative, but undeviating, hands of a Deputy provided by the Chicken-Farmer, and returns to his White Lady for the Next Step:

DRAIN HER MOAT!!!

. . . *En route:* "What in God's name for?" said Sister, visited in Vienna. "Eddie, I honestly don't think you have the slightest shred of *reason* for any of the damn Potting, while I have to cope with the most appalling inconvenience. I've only seen you once since Christmas."

"Schliemann didn't have a reason, Ettie – he just knew there'd been a Troy, and roughly where. And a private railway coach is hardly pigging it, and I make all the arrangements for grub from Zürich. Who else in Germany gets real coffee?"

"That isn't the point. I want to see more of you. Our birthday, and we're not on Porquerolles and it's hellish lonely, you've no idea. Darling brother, I *miss* you."

"You don't think I enjoy spending my life in caves full of bloody skulls and no one to talk to except peasants?"

"You don't spend your nights in them."

"Of course I don't sleep down there. We're billeted in a hotel. It's quite ghastly."

"You're billeted with an *'assistant'*! – don't lie to me. Trash something; Tristan Heydrich told me, a farm slut from a Ukrainian hovel. I bet she doesn't even wash between her legs."

"She does. And it's Tosh – she's a friend of Pawel's. And that bastard Moses promised – "

"Pish and Tosh – now you're lying about Pawel, he has far too much taste to take a slut. Oh, hell, Eddie, I'm sorry – " grabbing his hands, squeezing them to her breasts – "Eddie, you don't love me even a tiny little bit any more, do you?"

"Ettie, you're absolutely everything – "

"No I'm not. You swore our oath, but the first moment you can, you break it."

"I swore about us – I risk my life every day for you."

Out it popped. Cameron's death-sentence. Then, mercifully, not tears: an eyelash, which requires all her attention with a tweezer.

"What on earth are you talking about? Your life?"

"About travelling to see you. Battle zones, air raids – and we didn't swear about not having anyone else. It doesn't mean a thing, you've had hundreds."

"Not since we swore. I can't stand Huns any longer."

"This girl isn't German, and I've only had one, and she isn't a slut. She's rather like you in a way – well not *like*, but sort of blond hair and our eyes."

"And does she shave it? – like the Cow? – who makes two by the way."

"I haven't seen Eva for ages. Wolf keeps her out of sight at the Berghof."

"Cows don't mind." Sister snorts, and dabs scent behind her knees. "You didn't tell me if this Trash person shaves it."

"Because it's none of your damn business."

"So she doesn't. A proper little proletarian Trash." Sister giggles – and traces her thigh with a finger. Upwards. And whispers in her Baby-Ettie voice, "I have . . . I did it specially for you . . . a birthday present."

"Did what?" Even Eddie can lose the flow in their mad conversations.

"Shaved her. Miss Pussy. Aren't you dying to see?"

"Oh Lord. Oh Ettie – "

The secret room. On the outside, snow-white, without its gold-leaf fluff, our magic mountain, sleekly powdered: inside, rose-red – Lipsticked! – *and opening, for the first time the full flower, every swelling petal revealed in the Kundry garden.*

"Oh poor darling Eddie, I'd no idea you'd get so excited. Oh God, don't waste it . . . rub darling . . . rub, it stops wrinkles, oh God. Oh *GOD*!"

529

So Edwin stays in Vienna. But when she begins cursing he flees the premises with shallow excuses, and fresh Guilt-feelings: After All She's Done For Me.

"But I'll come back soon, Ettie, I promise – or why don't you come up to the Castle and visit? I know last time you said sod the Countess but she's really a sweet old duck."

"All right. I will. I'm singing for Reinhard in the Prague Festival next month. After I've finished this latest bloody Figaro. Now Wolf's locked up Parsifal I don't know why he doesn't ban Mozart."

"Why do you sing it, if you don't like it?"

"Darling, how many singing jobs do you think there are in full companies at the moment? The alternative is the back of a lorry with an untuned upright going to some godawful Rathaus – or Sweden. I'm even reduced to Nanny-Goat country, and trolls, at Stockholm in the autumn. Or is that Norwege? I never can remember?"

But I do, my Darling. I do. I DO . . .

. . . *At Třeboň:* Spurred off the deep end by Sister's open display of love, Brother attacks the moat. This is not a waste of time, as Ettie implies: a delightfully embossed halberd being brought to light for the 1st time in 6 cents., & a mace, & 3 carcasses of ruptured bones with shot in them from the time of the First Protector, Wallenstein.

Which produces the 2nd. A great tank of a Mercedes, dark bottle-green, with a pennant of some kind flying, glides to a halt on Fräulein Anna's landing strip. Heydrich got out, dressed as Tristan in his Black Order suit but without the cap, to show it was a friendly visit.

"Good morning, Herr Edwin – I've come to see if these remains of yours belong in my museum."

No one is fooled. The flunkies fall about Heiling in all directions. Fool pales.

"Good morning, General. I hadn't heard that you were now a collector."

"It's part of my scheme for elevating the Czechs' opinions of themselves. There was such a success with the competition for the set designs of 'Rusalka', and next month I'm having the re-opening of the Rudolfinum. Your sister is singing for us at that."

530

"Yes, Ettie said. She's asked me to accompany if I can get back from Kiev in time."

"I'm sure you can." The Fox-mask's sneer leaves no bloody doubt about it! "I'll arrange an aircraft. It would give me the greatest pleasure to have both of you as my guests. It will be my last opportunity – I can tell you, just between ourselves, that I'm going to France. I've just finished working on the administrative statutes. Bohemia has been a dress rehearsal, you might say."

"You're going as Protector of occupied France, General?"

"Vichy too, yes. I really don't think these fellows of yours are much use to the museum."

The tall devil turned a skeleton with a gleaming boot and looked no end pleased with himself. But all Fool heard was Vichy – which means *Avignon.*

"I'll make sure to get back for Ettie at the Rudolfinum," promised our tunnel-visioned little toady. "And we'd both love to have supper."

"Good. Let's say seven, at my residence. I try to keep myself for the family as much as possible these days. My daughter's coming along marvellously on the piano, she'll be overwhelmed to meet your sister. How are your dinners in Zürich, by the way? They seem to be less frequent recently?"

"I've been too busy with the excavations, General."

"Nose to the grindstone – well the times call for extreme effort from all of us. And you haven't visited our Fuehrer either?"

"For the same reason, General."

"I'm sure of it. Good day, Herr Edwin."

The bottle-green Mercedes ran over a shinbone while it was leaving.

"Throw this rubbish back in the ditch," ordered Edwin-the-easily-terrified, before going back to the castle to be sick.

And before you scoff, cruel children, you didn't know the beast. You weren't there. You didn't see those slit eyes look down that nose. *Understand me*: Blond Moses Heydrich had ordered (despite his business-side's objections, and his artiste's own delicate and heaving gut) the real deaths of the hundred-thousands – and they weren't even traitors. Not one of the poor sods ever played the Black Swan for Our Leader and ran off to Zürich with His table-talk droppings.

531

Edwin left the moat, with the damned skeletons, to drain, and fled Bohemia for the safe rabbit holes of Kiev, to put as much ground as possible between excavator and France's next Protector: from Wallenstein, to Napoleon, to – even a Fool can guess at the next station marked out by that huge ambition. Our Wolf isn't getting any younger with His stomach cramps.

"What is the matter, Monsieur-Gospodin-Eddie?" from a sulking Tosh. "You don't like to ride the Huss-cock avec moi, not even après I waste a bath?"

"I have a lot to think about – responsabilité."

"It's those cavernes, you should not go down so much. They make your head funny. I have some vodka from General Pawel – stay and amour me, Monsieur Eddie."

"Pawel was here while I was away?"

"Da," she said happily. "Riding tanks isn't like cavernes. Like a roche, all night. Perhaps the cavernes have made you a half-man like the It-Blov, nyet?"

And when Cuckold-Eddie tries to prove he isn't, he can't. And next morning, leaving the Blitzkrieg-Palast, gets a worse shock, if that's possible, when *He* drives by, not 10 feet from me, bowing-and-waving to all the Sieg-Heiling – and then with enormous relief realising that it was only another of the bloody Doppelgängers popping up like Punch-&-Judy.

"The Fuehrer himself," informed the Chicken-Farmer's flunky who was Edwin's co-ordinator for Hooligans & Rations, "has just completed a lightning visit to the Kharkov Pocket before returning to his Headquarters, where, Herr von Perceval, by priority signal you are requested."

"But I can't. Oh Christ, look I just got here. Say I didn't get the message."

"From our Fuehrer's own person?"

That's the trouble with working for a god; all the little conventions, (like white lies, or moral scruples) the things that make life bearable and society run smoothly fall by the wayside.

"But it's fifteen hundred kilometres. I can't get transport."

"But this is the good news, Herr von Perceval – the military situation goes so well that our Fuehrer has moved his headquarters to join us in the field. At Vinnitsa.This is only two hundred kilometres!"

Close enough to drop in for a cup of His bloody raspberry tea!

... *Vinnitsa:* No hills, only a flattening in the endless plain, almost a swamp, with malarial mosquitoes; a suitable hatching ground for that loathesome Toad-Bormann, meeting the 'plane in person, crawling to the top of the ladder. But also bright flowers, and wild onions, and birdsong, and some clumps of soft scrub willow and white birches, although not enough to screen the bunkers, or the chalet of pine-poles set on one side of a spot of nowhere.

WERWOLF

And the same gravel paths and smell of wet concrete. The same air of enormous happenings, that all things are still possible. The same frantic activity, of Parsifal Marschalls leaving and arriving. The same tiny island of calm at the centre, cut off from more than one opinion at a time to concentrate on His desire of the moment: Defeat The Bear. This is not the place to consider those swelling mounds, and sewer ravines, or the dragon's-blood liquids of I. G. Farben. They belong to the country of the mind, which no man visits, except the owner; or glimpses, except Mime-Himmler, the Chicken Farmer responsible for racial cultivation, on those solitary God-to-man walks of revelation when the Voice speaks in the forest or on top of the Salt Mountain; or with Edwin the Fool, who digs up skulls and plays Wagner on the piano ...

He walks straight to me, both hands out to grip both my elbows.

"Ederl! How truly wonderful to see you! I can't say how much I've missed you."

He looks older. The bags beneath the eyes are puffier, the whole skin greyer, but the eyes are even brighter – dazzling when He lights them up specifically for my person. Any one of the entourage would die for one of these dazzles.

"I'm sorry it's been so long too, Herr Wolf. Ettie sends her love, by the way."

Little white lies? Don't tell me!

"Does she? What I'd give to hear that voice again – and see her, of course, in the Festspielhaus – but we've got Ivan on the run now, the collapse could happen any day, and then Moscow's definitely going from the map. She didn't send anything for me?"

"Ettie?" O what a web – perhaps life *is* better without lies. "No Herr Wolf. She didn't know exactly that I was coming. What sort of thing were you expecting?"

"It doesn't matter. She mentioned at our last dinner that she would remember with a small token, but you know our ladies – how their minds leap. Join me for a walk with Blondi. I've taught her new tricks since your last visit, three metres up a wall, it's quite astonishing. Go away, Bormann, and leave me with Herr Edwin – I don't mind telling you, Ederl, Bormann's an excellent fellow in most respects but he will insist on mothering me like some monstrous hen. He's made himself irreplaceable since Hess left me – but we won't talk about that, the man was ill, it's the only logical conclusion, some form of breakdown. I don't blame him – God knows one came near enough to it oneself at Christmas. At first – after Roosevelt and his Yids – I told Jodl we'd lost. It just shows that there is simply no possible substitute for the Will. And if *I* doubt, think how easy it is for the others, the General Staff man looking at casualties, or the footsoldier looking at those fallen comrades in the field. . . . And all one has to support him is the golden image of your sister – yes, I mean it! – with the unquenchable fire in her singing, trapped on her rock, betrayed by the potion and Gunther's stupidity – like some people in Berlin that we won't mention! – alone in the flames but never defeated. I tell you, no human has ever had a more glorious inspiration! Not all the shaveling shithead nonsense laid end to end since warfare started on this continent could begin to match it. The image of her lying there. . . . But I've said, that's over. Any minute we're going to see the Rhinegold gleaming under the water in the Moskva – if one can see it for sewage. Do you know, they didn't have a w.c. even in the Kremlin until fifty years ago! And today these Slav swine still just pour their shit out of the wall into the river – where the Red oafs get their drinking water! But I don't underestimate Stalin – any man who's killed ten million human beings and all his generals and still commands a hundred divisions must have something to him. Fate has always ordained this struggle – it's nothing to do with Roosevelt, Siegfried has to battle a bear. But the bear *lost!* that's the main thing. I've often

534

wondered whether I shouldn't have made the Ring obligatory for NCOs and above qualifying for promotion – but you can't teach new dogs old tricks. They'd disregard it as they do one's own works, for that matter. One mustn't complain. Just think where I'd be now if my opponents had actually read what I wrote?! I can't imagine what I was thinking about to publish – mind you, the money came in handy. If it hadn't been for that, and your so-noble mother – her dear memory comes to me more and more as I grow older. If I had been who I am today . . . I don't blame your sister for forgetting her promise. Will you tell her I forgive her? I understand she's singing for Heydrich at some function in Prague – the man's getting positively soft-headed about his Czech rabble! – his hop to the Frogs will sort that out. We're meeting at the end of the month – your name came up, yes, some amusing story he has to tell me. About your bone digging I shouldn't wonder. I almost came to see your skull caves, but you know my problem with claustrophobia. Come back and play for me tonight after the briefings – and don't stay away so long in future, my Ederl, or I shall have to wag a finger. . . ."

And as if that isn't close enough to Edwin drowning, in the General Officers' Mess with Toad-Bormann watching, Fool finds himself by chance next to a typically bland Swede, swilling vodka and peddling ball bearings, who manages by chance to walk with me for a breath of air in the birch woods and mosquitoes, and says in the most casual manner, "A mutual friend from London is worried about your health. He doesn't think you've been getting enough to eat in Zürich recently. He wonders if he should send a parcel?"

"No," Fool said to the bland Swede, "I'll be having supper in Zürich on my way home."

But if playing Wagner on the piano, or being companion to His monologues required the least degree of attention, our Eddie would be a dead duck, children.

And consider our Self f*****g lucky!

. . . *Zürich:* Another visit to the House of Treason. The Traitor waits till dark – but knows Heydrich will see – and then tells the little blank Swiss who lives under the defrocked monk and now-pregnant nun all about Heydrich, and my dinner engagement, and the funny story he was going to tell Wolf at my expense, and I said, "You can tell Cameron that this

535

simply has to stop, because I'm going to kidnap my sister if I have to, but she's getting out of Germany."

And the little blank Swiss said, "But you shall still be there – or are you abandoning your search for the Holy Grail, mein Herr?"

"Damn you and Cameron to everlasting hell."

But it was the sort of remark one expects, my dears, from a blank race of cuckoo-clock makers profiting from everyone else's misfortunes.

"I shall pass on your message, mein Herr. Enjoy your oyster stew upstairs."

And Rau, the only soul who could have provided consolation, was gone from Zürich. "And I'm afraid," said his secretary, "we don't yet have Mr Michael's forwarding address."

Which leaves Jung.

... *At the village:* A May evening. The light leaving, shadows cast by the tiny steeple; long enough shadows to light the soul, and his Emma, standing, smiling, welcoming. The Traveller returns to a spot of illusion in yellow stone; the closest the Young Edwin knows to a home.

"Hullo, my dear."

"Hullo, Frau Emma."

"I'm sorry I missed you last time. My man Jung told me that you'd abandoned our Grail."

"He said I'd return to it, and I have. I'm digging all over the place."

"But you aren't close to it," says Emma Jung.

"I think I may be. Frau Emma, I have so much to tell you. I'm excavating the Skull Community in Kiev, I'm absolutely positive there's a connection between the Grail and the ikon, Death of Our Lady. Her robes are identical to the ones on the effigies of the Three Maries, in the Camargue, and I know I'm going to find a similar link at the White Lady's Castle – that's in Třeboň, in Bohemia, I only came to it by accident, through my friend Rau. The link is salt. Life's so extra-ordinary."

"For some of us it seems to be." Emma Jung smiles, but gently, at such enthusiasm. "You won't find the Grail in Russia, my dear. That society shows no flicker from the lamp. Do you want to stay with us for long?"

"I wouldn't dream of intruding."

"I'm sure you have." We laughed together. She said, "Perhaps a cup of tea? Jung isn't here, I'm afraid. He's gone to the tower for a birthday celebration."

"At Bollingen? I don't have much time – I won't bother him on a special occasion. Thank you, Frau Emma."

"Why not let him decide if it's a bother? Have you dreamed of the tall stranger? – Yes, I see that you have. Go and visit him, my dear."

"How can you know so much?" Edwin asked, with that creeping-spine feeling. "It's astounding. Frau Emma, it's frightening."

"No my dear. It's a normal progression. Take care of yourself on the journey, and give my man my special love."

"I will. I shall – Frau Emma, may I say that I love you also? I mean – "

"Yes you may say it. And thank you, Edwin, I know what you mean. I'm so glad you've been spared going to prison for your sister. Bye-bye, my dear. Come back soon."

"I will – and thank *you* – if I have time. If I can."

"We always can," said Emma Jung. "It's if we want to. The road is getting dark. Run along."

. . . *Along the road:* Only a single window lit; arched, with a stained-glass picture in the centre, of a golden apple in a ruby bowl. Jung is in his kitchen. The Traveller approaches it. The Great Man is wrapping lamb chops – in a child's birthday-paper! Furry-Friends & Little-Bo-Peep. With bloodstains and little fatty bits sticking out.

"*GO AWAY!*" Roars Carl-Gustav. Peering out with his owl-specs, at the night through the bowl-window. "Bloody boy. I told you this is *my* tower. It's my party. You weren't invited. Don't stand there – *Go to hell away.*"

The Fool trembles.

"I'm frightfully sorry, I shouldn't have, I should have remembered, but Frau Emma, of course, I will, at once, my taxi, goodnight –"

No taxi. Only tail-lights red as the bowl – as the eyes of a dragon – vanishing, leaving a ten-mile bloody walk. Edwin-the-Meek begins it: tripping almost immediately on one of the blasted inscriptions set at precisely the right elevation to stub the toe and smash the shin.

"*Oh-Christly-shit!*"

Echoing across the black mirror of the lake. Followed by rich Jungian

537

laughter, and, "Now that's more like it. Don't be an idiot. Old chap, come in, *come in.*"

"You're sure?" Hobbling and rubbing. "I don't want to spoil your party if it's private."

"Stop chuntering," said Jung, completely filling the kitchen's door, "isn't that a good word? I've just learnt it. This isn't my birthday, it's Uncle Sam's. Have some wine with him while I finish his present."

Uncle Sam sits in a Jungian-carved chair with griffons for legs, and sphinx-paws for arms. Uncle Sam is grey – also white, brown, and black, with the ears of a spaniel, the curly coat of a poodle, the legs of a beagle, and a face that might have started as a Pekinese.

"Use his own language, old chap, he's American." Said the Genius.

"Hi Sammy-pal." Said the Fool.

Uncle Sam scratches his stomach, revealing the genitals of an Irish Wolf Hound, and looks towards the Bo-Peep chops with the eyes of a saint at the end of Lent.

"He's stuck with me for the Duration," Jung explains, as Eddie-pal pours. "Do you think he'll mind if I don't finish this part by the bone?"

"No. I don't think so."

"Good. Then you can give it to him. You'll appreciate with your Numerology, this is a special time for Uncle Sam, reaching three – multiplied by seven for a dog, so he's actually twenty-one, or I shouldn't have gone to so much effort. And *you* are thirty-one, or you wouldn't either. Bearding the old shit-head in his den. I can be very tiresome can't I sometimes?"

"I think you're wonderful," gushes the Traveller, "stupendous – both you and Frau Emma, but I'm afraid I never understand a quarter of what you tell me. Do I take the paper off first?"

"I don't know, old chap. Ask Uncle Sam."

Who solves this riddle at least by lunging across the table, and then growling in the most fearsome manner under it, with tearing noises.

"So," Jung says, "Emma sent you."

"Yes. With her special love. She knew somehow, amazingly, that I'd had a special dream – about a stranger."

"Of course she did; that's her job. Was he tall?"

"Yes."

"Tall as me?"

"Yes. In a blue cloak. With a huge hat, like Wotan's, when he's turned into the Wanderer."

"Well I don't have a hat, so that's who he was all right. The Wanderer – a little early, but you've always been a precocious sort. You Arthurians are."

"But what does it mean? He has skeleton's fingers, and wherever I ride on the horse he gets there first, and he's always pointing at my tower. And now that's always at the top of an enormous hill that I have to gallop up for hour after hour, with the flames around the bottom. And there's always this croaking noise. Almost like harsh laughing – but sometimes it's more like crying. What does it mean?"

"*How is your sister?*"

"Ettie? – why, she's well."

"Then it means nothing." Turning away. *Turning his back on me.*

"But it must mean something. You knew in advance about this Wanderer."

"I asked about your sister. I'm old. The Western world is dying. And you come here, to my tower, with your lies and evasions. That Wolf monster has gathered you to his fold. Leave before I strike you."

The ferocity staggered me.

"I thought you'd help. Frau Emma said –"

"You don't need help. Your sister's well. You are both happy with your incest. Electra and Oedipus, blind as bats. Go from my house. *Go!*"

"You don't give me a chance. There's no one. Heydrich will kill me. Then she'll be helpless. She won't marry Wolf when I've begged her. Cameron lies. Nothing could save her. *Christ why won't you listen?*"

"This is the first time you've spoken, old chap," said the real Carl Jung. "You want to destroy your sister. I hear you. Now tell me."

But only silence in the tower – except for growlings and clicks and whines from the mutated beast gorging on its nursery chops beneath the table.

"I don't," Eddie whispers in horror.

"The last time you tried, it wasn't a great success as I recall. I'm still waiting. *Tell me.*"

"I'm a spy."

Jung stared through the specs – for a minute, an hour, God knows.

And then laughed so hard that tears fell on the lenses and dripped from the stainless rims.

"Is that all?" Clutching his ribs. "My dearest fool I couldn't go five steps in Zürich without bumping into a spy. Now be sensible. Wanting to destroy your sister is perfectly understandable – and vice versa – it's only your modus vivendi that's a little peculiar. This serving her up to Herr Wolf for his butcher's breakfast. And now that the Wanderer's arrived on the scene. Yes, Emma's right, as usual – it will be much quicker if you just provide the answers by talking. You read the case history on Wolf-man 'A', you told me about it, so there's no confusion there about your actions. Why don't you start with Heydrich? Except for our Fuehrer, Teutonicus Heydrich's the only one that's interesting."

"I can't talk about Heydrich if you think I want to kill Ettie. It's monstrous. Of course, I thought Wolf as 'A' – but that was then, before He was fifty. Before he was winning. He's got everything now, or almost, and then there will be peace. Churchill makes all the noises, but that's just Winston's way. There's a constant stream of people going backwards and forwards from Stockholm with various peace plans. It only needs Russia to cave in. I told Ettie she'd be like an Empress."

"And you think Wolf 'A' is winning in Russia?"

"Absolutely. It looked pretty bleak before Christmas, with the counter attack. I was in Kiev for that and everyone was damned dodgy."

"In Kiev – you didn't go back to your sister?"

"No no. Ettie was safe as houses between La Scala and Vienna. They positively drooled over her Tosca. Of course I joined her *at* Christmas. We spent it together at Triebschen."

"That was when you warned her about your friend 'A'-the-Wolf?"

"No. Why should I? I've explained."

"But you said he was losing?"

Simple questions. Fool's answers. Jung stares over the tops of the owl's glasses.

"Yes, but not really. Only one battle."

"If he lost more, you'd warn her?"

"Of course. I'm trying now, with this business about Heydrich."

"How many?"

"Sorry – I don't follow."

"How many battles must be lost?"

540

"I've no idea. It doesn't matter. He's winning all of them. Look at Rommel."

"You'd warn your sister if Rommel loses?"

"Not necessarily. That was just an example. And he won't. He's a tactical genius."

"So if he did lose – Rommel – it would be much more serious?"

"I suppose."

"And then you'd warn your sister?"

"Yes. Look this circling is ridiculous. I love Ettie more than anything."

"More than 'A'? – just as an example."

"Love Wolf! God, he's far too terrifying."

"But if he wasn't terrifying?"

"He always is."

"Always?"

"Well of course not *always* – there are occasions when He's good company. Sometimes quite marvellous actually."

"But you still hate 'A'? – when he's marvellous?"

"Of course not. That would be stupid."

"Even though 'A' killed your mother?"

"He didn't. Oh I know I once said – but not actually. You can't call writing a letter, killing. You have to use common sense, surely."

"Which is why you fear Heydrich – it's common sense?"

"Bloody right! He can have you shot just for looking cross-eyed at him."

"On whose instigation?"

"On his – well the Chicken Farmer's. That's Himmler."

"Heydrich kills people for Himmler?"

"Not *for* – if you don't mind my saying, you simply turn everything. It's state policy as it would be for any government. Cameron would be exactly the same I can tell you, and I went to school with him, the red Scots swine."

"But to stay with the point – Heydrich kills for the state?"

"Yes. Like any soldier."

"Or the SS? – the Black Order, as you call them?"

"Yes."

"Who swear personal allegiance to the Fuehrer?"

541

"Of course. Everyone knows that."

"So Heydrich kills for 'A', to Heil Hitler?"

No answer, then or now, by Edwin.

"And now perhaps you see," said Carl Jung, "why I don't bother, old chap, with simple questions. But let me ask you one other – Heydrich is the most powerful figure in the Teutonic Empire? – perhaps excluding your friend the Chicken Farmer?"

"He isn't a friend. I can't stick Himmler."

"But Heydrich –?"

"Yes. He's the most powerful."

"And if *he* was lost – just to take another example – then would you warn your sister?"

"There wouldn't be any need. If bloody Heydrich was gone we wouldn't have a problem with Cameron."

Jung sighed and picked up the chewed scraps of nursery paper. "The mind has long since prepared its answers, and closed itself to the difficult problems. Which is why I rely on my numinous symbols – the ones that have life-giving and illuminating powers, like birthday parties and your Wanderer – even if your sister does think the old bore of Zürich's mad as a hatter."

"Ettie's never said that." The youth lied. Lamely – then swiftly, to make up for it – "I see a bit about what you mean with me and Wolf. I suppose because I never had a father. Can you explain the wanderer in my dream, the stranger – in your normal way. Not the questions."

"The important steps in life don't need them. The stranger is the next Individuation stage, your Self's progress. He arrives at the watersheds – hence his blue cloak. And the hat is to aid his deliberate blindness in the face of distracting temptation. To keep us on the upward path – which is why your tower now is on a hill, hardly surprising during a catastrophic war when everything combines to pull us down. Especially our Selves, we are always our worst enemies, that's why we can only survive if we learn to respect the subconscious."

"Like Wolf's Voice?"

"There is no respect in a one-sided conversation," said Carl Gustav Jung. "You can have your old room for the night. It smells of turpentine because I'm in the middle of painting a new dragon from a particularly striking dream a month ago – but I won't bore you with the details. Good heavens, I clean forgot. We never did Happy Birthday for Uncle Sam."

So Fool & Genius sang it to the oblivious hound, gnawing his gifts beneath the table. And in the morning, as his fool of a patient was leaving, Jung said, standing under the Eye of his child's game inscription:

"Rescue your sister, old Chap, if you can – for when the beast in 'A' is at his most human, and loving, there will be much killing, and we don't want hers on your conscience – but as Michelangelo tells us, 'Whereas death killeth all men, yet the thought of it hath made many.' I'll be seeing you."

Third Movement
Eighth Passage

"Summer Is Icumen In!"
WHO NEEDS WARING?
[to be sung *brightly* as a Round of 4 parts]

"Not I!" croaks our Spy.

Old Edwin is no longer a fool. G & G are all the help that's needed, (with some slight conveying by a friendly guard) and reborn-Nibelheim's so-efficient postal service, to speed a simple missive to Yellow Street. And then watch the carrion-vultures hover, those print-devils! Rending each other for every last drop of Wolf-Through-Eddie.

> *Ewe now bleateth after Lamb,*
> *Loweth after calf, the Cow,*
> *Merry sing Cuc-koo!*

Exit Jeremy.

. . . *At Hradčany Castle:* They have a row about S*x, before Dinner-with-Heydrich, Brother & Sister. We are staying in some other Arch-Duke's quarters, beside St Vitus' Cathedral, with a magnificent view over Prague down to the river. Re-union had been warm in Vienna because Figaro had been intermezzoed by the Royal Air Force, striking at

Kinder or Kultur with equally dispassionate tympanic precision.

"A school Eddie. That little boarders' place run by the nuns, behind St Stephens, across the Ring. I sang on through the worst of it, and most of the Wieners stayed put, give them credit for that, and then we came out and there was this little red bundle and it was a little girl with no legs. I mean *none*, Eddie."

"Ettie darling, how frightful for you," taking her in his arms. "But it isn't just our side dropping these horrors – it's every bit as bad in London."

"But we don't have a bloody side. That's the point. It's all so utterly eff-ing point-*less*! Mama was the only one with any common sense – and anyway, we don't know about London. You can't possibly believe the yellow Beaverbrook's press. Make love to me, Eddie, for God's sake. No games."

And so the horror withdraws, until next time, and the sun brings out all the horse-chestnuts in the most glorious profusion, and driving through the green countryside in our old blue Riley you'd never have known there was a war on – if your petrol was provided by special Chicken-Farmer vouchers, and grub by your special weekly hampers from the Épicerie Diplomatique, in Lucerne.

She was the very best Ettie – and on top of that, Eddie still hasn't got used to her being *shaved*.

"Better, darling. I got electrolysis from an old hag in the Bundstrasse. It was rather peculiar doing it, but just look."

"I daren't. Show me. Oh Ettie, so smooth, and you can see, I always wanted, oh Lord, oh *now* . . . !"

A marvellous aphrodisiac: even so, barely enough to take Brother's mind off the coming ordeal with the butcher-Tristan running this beautiful countryside. Why is he inviting me? Why the toying references passed on to 'A'-the-Fuehrer? What will happen if Heydrich *stops* playing? And my every effort to make Ettie clear out, she resisted more firmly than ever after the RAF bombing.

"You can't seriously expect me to run away now, Eddie – just for my own skin when people need music the most desperately?"

"There's still the neutrals."

"Goat-milking and trolls, thanks very much."

"All right – America. We could join Michael. The Metropolitan's

546

been hounding you for years. You're too special, Ettie. It worries me dreadfully."

"I can see, and I'm grateful – we've got the afternoon before this do at Chez Tristan; come and play. I feel like being extra specially nice to you darling . . ."

With tongue games at the back window, and the shaving, almost unbearable. *Worth anything.*

"You're liking it, pet, aren't you? *More* than anything. Except now like this? or this? If I stick it all the way in will you do Big Sis a tiny little favour?"

"Mmm. Doesn't matter. Whatever. More please oh Christ Ettie . . ."

And then, lying drained and exhausted, the weakest moment for surrendering to payment on demand. All bills due.

"Will you do it now for me, Eddie, before I bathe?"

"Just say, but I don't feel strong."

"You don't have to be, silly – it's only tweezers."

Finding them, by chance, all ready at hand beside the bed, and then rolling over, up on her knees, splayed wide as possible, puckered and humble, at Brother's mercy.

"No, not hurt you, Ettie, I won't do that."

"It won't hurt, only a tiny bit; it's just awkward or I'd do it myself. Go on, take them."

"Awkward? Do what?"

"Oh don't be obtuse, darling – pull the hairs out around my bum."

Brought up short against the target. His bull's eye. Perhaps a dozen small wisps, fine as always but a touch darker than gold closer to the surface.

"You can't be serious."

"I wouldn't have asked, and you've promised."

"But why? There's no need. You're sleek as cream, everywhere."

"Not there. I looked in the mirror. I want to be super clean for you, Eddie. I want every last one of them gone. Now."

"No. It would hurt, and it's mad."

"It's my arse, and you promised. Do it."

"No. You don't need it."

"Damn and blast I stuck my bloody tongue in yours – and you promised lying little sod."

A heel lashes back, smashes the rise of his pubic arch.

"Ow! – bloody bitch what –"

"You promised. Do it or I'll kill you."

And then realising – it *will* hurt her! "Is *that* what you want?"

Wince, no sound, but puckering tighter, gasping, convulsing. "*Is it?*" A whimper. "Or *that?*" The other sharp end of his instrument slipping, "Or *this?*" stabbing into her most delicate parts.

"Please . . . thanks . . . Eddie, don't be cross."

Crying now.

"I'm not cross you stupid *cow* –" only one curling Rheingold strand left. "Now go to everlasting hell it's *done.*"

Throwing down his torturer's tongs.

"Let me see," she whispers. "The hand mirror . . . oh yes . . . oh Eddie it's got you excited again . . . kiss me better. I only wanted it, darling precious, for you."

Damned Fool!

Chez Tristan:

The Protector's personal bottle-green Mercedes comes to collect his guests. The Casson-Percevals, Aryan perfection in a couple, sit in the back, immaculately groomed & evening-dressed.

> *Bullock starteth,*
> *Buck now verteth,*
> *Merry sing, Cuc-koo!*

A pair of farm labourers trudging home turn to gaze in awe, then tug their forelocks to the Mighty's car (one lucky yokel with a crude wench, lounging and groping on the parapet of a bridge at a hairpin turn by a stream in Holešovice, does not pay his respects!) – but now bullocks drinking . . . and smoothly the last few miles through dusky woodlands and a rustic-wedding village to a white-painted brick wall, and the roof of a manor house over the top. "Panenské Břežany" engraved on the gateposts. A Black Order detachment standing guard. Inside the grounds a beautiful château, modern but after the style of the Loire, in parkland, and 3 golden children, 2 boys and a girl, playing as others just like them at Wahnfried twenty years before.

Moses Heydrich has changed to civilian dinner dress. "Silke," he calls to the golden girl, "come and make your curtsey to Fräulein Casson-Perceval."

A not unattractive little creature drops her Knicks, and says, "I think Fräulein Edwina you must be the finest singer in the whole world."

"Adorable," trills the object of such adoration, "Tristan Liebchen, I'd no idea you'd got yourself such a Louis Seize setting. Is there a laiterie for your Antoinette?"

"Only a small summer house. My wife is waiting for us there with the drinks."

"Oh lovely."

Said Sister, but it shall be a more equal contest than our beauteous Edwina's used to. Lina (née van Osten) Heydrich being Blonde, Danish & Noble – if from a family on the way Down, but our Isy's progress soon fixed that! "Frau Heydrich, how delightful – I can't think how we've missed each other for so long."

"I'm a home body," replies the Protector's lady, "and my father was a village schoolmaster, and after what the Admirals did to Heinrich I've never had any use for the backbiting social circles one finds in Berlin – will you have strong liquor, or chilled hock?"

With a smile that quite melts the cockles of Brother's foolish heart – except that Hubby's watching down that yard of butcher's snout.

"Ettie will have her gin and Italian. I'd love the hock – I could pour, if you like." Anything but sit under those slit eyes. "Do tell how you and the General met?"

"At a dance on a ship. And the next day Heinrich just arrived at my village, with his violin in a box under his arm, like Blondel." The romantic sod. "Thank you, Herr Edwin, pour by all means. What a treasure to have such a brother."

"Isn't he just?" from the Fräulein E.

"You've just returned again from Zürich, and visiting our Fuehrer – " our implacable host, now playing solicitous. "How did you find his spirits? I see him tomorrow myself, at the Chancellery, before I go on to Paris."

"You didn't tell me you saw Wolf," Sister drawled, in her don't-care voice, meaning cross-as-hell. "I suppose he talked his usual twaddle.

Really, Frau Lina, I find at Wahnfried it's almost more than one can stand – but as lucky-you doesn't mix in social circles, you're spared all that."

Dear! A servant announces dinner. The happy party repairs indoors, with Brother trying madly to mend the wreckage strewn by Sister and his tormentor, her sometime lover.

"Herr Wolf was in good form, with the new offensive going so well. He's taught Blondi to jump a ten-foot wall, and He was expecting some sort of a special present from you, Ettie, that He thought you'd promised – and actually General, I went to see Carl Jung in Zürich, and his dear Frau Emma. They're the most marvellous couple when one has any sort of problem."

"Then how fortunate that you know them. Please sit on my left, Herr Edwin – Fräulein Edwina, here to the right, although placement doesn't mean much when one has a round table. Some guests think it's the excessively romantic streak in my nature, but I call it an excellent device for solving the foolish problems that seem to come up on such occasions. Not tonight, it goes without saying. The foie gras is a gift, sent from old Pétain . . ."

Fox-bastard. Keeping Eddie-on-toast for 5 courses until the Welsh rare-bit!

"I don't follow the various schools of psychology," said the schoolmaster's daughter. "What particularly do you learn from Professor Jung, Herr Edwin?"

"Not nearly as much as I should, I'm afraid, Frau Lina. He uses so many riddles, and the rest's mostly mythology – this time about Electra and Oedipus blinding each other, although I don't think they did, but I'm hotter on Teutonic myth than the Greeks. You can't really say it has much relationship to ordinary life, but occasionally it shows one a different way of looking at things."

"I didn't promise him a damned thing – Wolf –" said Sister – "certainly not special. I think he's a little gaga, these days. And Electra, dear ignorant brother, wanted to kill Mother for doing-in Father. At least one's spared the worst of Freud's bosh when you get Addled."

Quite overlooking the small gasp from her hostess over the "gaga". Which leads to the *coup de foie gras* from host-Heydrich as the guest couple are leaving after the delightful musical finale, for Voice, Violin, & Pianoforte.

"If your sister can spare you for a day, Herr Edwin, I'd like you to come with me to Berlin for a word with the Fuehrer in the morning. I'm piloting myself, but that's no more hair-raising than those daredevils of Goering's. Fräulein Edwina, I assure you your brother will be in good hands. 0945, mein Herr – my car will collect you from the Castle on the way by."

And then –?

Back through the twilight woods and fields – the sun sets late, the month before mid-summer in Bohemia-&-Moravia. . . . Sleepless hours, tossing-and-turning for that ride on the morrow with the ex-Protector of Czechoslovakia. Sister, uncaring, sleeping-in, plucked clean-shaven as the infant that first explored the nature of Sin on our golden island. Now their House is the Citadel of Praha, Hradčany Castle, with Brother doing a St Vitus's dance under the flapping flag of His empire, for the torturer to take the fool to Him for our final confrontation. One last horrific finger-wagging-spit-storm and then the solution to the Traitor-Eddie problem. . . .

And then –?

The Fool dresses – while the bottle-green Mercedes growls at the door of the mock-château from the Loire, waiting for this Teuton-Louis to take leave of his Danish Marie-Antoinette.

And then –?

Kisses, bending down to little golden Silke . . . before out of the gates leaving Wife and Kinder waving; and so off through the woods, and over the bridge, and turn the hairpin corner . . .

And then –?

Find them standing, those 2 yokels, with a machine-gun that jams, and a Mills-bomb that doesn't. Presents from red Cameron in London to make up for Pétain's foie gras.

And then ?

Explosions! Shrieking shrapnel! The Hero of the Empire leaps out, terribly wounded, and in the finest tradition of His Black Order still pursues his assassins, firing all his revolver bullets before collapsing, and being taken in a bread-van to the surgeon's knives . . .

And then –?

Septicaemia, poisoning of the blood of the god who was sometimes called Blond Moses, & sometimes Isy, & always Tristan, a romantic, the right-hand of Wotan struck off:

Well singst thou, Cuc-koo,
Nor cease Thou ev-er now . . . !

Exit Reinhard Heydrich.

Codetta

Edwin did not go to Him that morning: did not go until after the lingering spread of the poison, after the stupendous Siegfried State Funeral, under the gargantuan Teutonic Cross, and the flaming bowls on the burial pylons, and the day-and-night playing of the Beerdigung music for the death of the Martyr of Prague. Although the Fool went down on his knees and gave thanks beyond expressing, he did not attend or observe any of that. I did not go from my sister's side until all that was left on this earth of her once-lover was part of a legend, and only a burnt patch to show that there had ever been a village called Lidice. . . .

Saved by Fate – *again*! – this Fool was summoned to the Salt Mountain, on a gorgeous June morning, and in the late afternoon escorted by a phalanx through the solid rock, and as evening was falling, upwards, but now utterly alone, through a copper shaft that gleamed like the red-gold that lines the passage approaching Alberich's harsh anvil; and upwards still, to the peak above the summit, where I found them together in Death: staring down on their world.

Olympus

"To hold death in one's hand, this is the extraordinary thing. Look, yes look at him. Ederl, tell me what you think of that."

He stood in the centre of the Kehlstein, His Eagle's Nest at the very top of the Mountain: with the clay Death Mask of Heydrich in His soldier's bitten-fingered hand. The arch-sod wasn't gone at all, but was still staring at his victim down that immensity of nose; and that mocking sneer on those thin, cruel lips, still knowing. Everything.

Ettie & Eddie & Pinch-me . . .

"I don't know what to say, Herr Wolf."

552

"Quite right. The turning points of history render a man speechless. For days I was unable to concentrate my mind on the problems of war – all I could think of was this incredible stupidity of the Jews."

Blond Moses gleams, caught a last time in the light. Outside, the sun sets into a bed of summer clouds above the peaks – the deepest cerulean still in one gap beyond Charlemagne's ice mausoleum. God's glory in man's folly.

"I can't stand this place, I never have, it's too grandiose altogether! I hold Bormann and Speer jointly responsible. Look down over there, at what once was our green island of peace when your so-noble mother helped me to have it – there, that's Goering's palace, did you ever see a greater monstrosity?! And over there, Ley, and now Goebbels is planning; they've all got to have them! At *my* expense! It's insufferable – how can a man possibly escape? How can I *think*? And that elevator shaft, one can't stand it. One has to close one's eyes – I wanted to blow it up but Bormann says the Party's put in too much – money! Trapped by the filthy curse of it! The one thing I can't match in my opponents, their unlimited cash with all the Yid-world behind them. This murder of Heydrich is only the latest example; the verminous louts don't care how many lives this war costs! That little swine Beneš in London – and Dear Christ how right the old Welshman has been in everything! Why has Fate chosen an animal-thing like Churchill? with a syphilitic father? The madness is contagious; it's passed on through the blood. Do you realise that they *sat* there in their holes in London and cold-bloodedly calculated what would be the nature of my reprisals?! – to induce an uprising. I couldn't believe the British would ever permit such a thing. In the first heat of the moment I ordered ten thousand of the Czech rabble done away with, but then I realised that wouldn't equal one hair on this irreplaceable man's head – I know, it makes one shudder! Also, it would be counter-productive. There is only one answer: the complete eradication of the cancer, and standing here it's just come to me – sometimes it requires an event of this appalling magnitude to shake these ideas loose in our heads. Once the Stalin-gang has fallen and I have access to the northern wastes of Russia, we'll ship the whole ratpack up there – the Caftan crowd, their own country. Heydrich's old chestnut of Madagascar, but infinitely more useful because there are tremendous reserves of minerals, and so forth. Two countries in reality

553

– they'll be divided down the middle: males east, the brood-females west. Unable to spawn, the breed will be gone from our earth in a single generation, and far more humanely than anything the forces of International Yidry propose for yours truly, may I say. If one had ever had children and then lost, can you imagine the barbarity? There would be only a single option for anything one loved, and we certainly don't want to face that! Praise be, I shan't have to. The armies fight with even greater dash and brilliance after this affair. Rommel – I've been reading the Punic Wars again, and Carthage – I sent him the original battle routes along the coast; it's amazing what a feast history gives us if we know where to pick her fruit. And then it's definite that I'm leaving. Yes! – it goes back to this monstrosity of a shitpile, Beethoven was absolutely right. 'I thought he was a god, Napoleon, but he's only a man – like all the rest of them.' After he made himself Emperor. Now, Ederl, I'm going to share a confidence with you – and even though we know each other so intimately I must ask for your word as an English gentleman – may I have it?"

Under the fallen sun, and the Twilight blazing and dying all around, only a giant's spear-throw south and east beyond Heydrich's death leer in His hand, is Cameron-the-assassin-master's Zürich . . .

"Yes, Herr Wolf, of course."

"Good fellow! You know I never doubted, but I'm so tired of explaining to that shithead Bormann – there has to be *one* soul in this world to trust and nationality doesn't enter into it – anyway this concerns your sister."

"Your secret, Herr Wolf?"

"Exactly. You see over there?"

"Your mausoleum mountain?"

"That's it. Six years ago, after the old Welshman's visit, I bought some land – a few dozen hectares, and since then I've picked up a few more, for greater privacy – no problem now because the rest backs onto one of Ludwig's estates – curious how all the right things always turn back on themselves. When I resign after the peace treaty, which I estimate will take six months past Christmas, so that's one more year, we'll get the Dome finished in Berlin, but I intend to live the way your so all-seeing mother always intended. There's already a perfectly acceptable small house, although we'll want running water – we can hardly expect our so-graciously beautiful Fräulein Ettie to live completely like an unwashed peasant can we?"

The purple twilight wraps the death mask in a pall for Caesars.

"You think Ettie, with you, in a hut . . . ?"

The lips of Heydrich seem to draw open on the small teeth, to laugh and laugh – but it was only the night wind from the Alps getting up.

"Precisely, Ederl – oh, at first it seemed ludicrous to me as well, when one's offered her Neuschwanstein, the whole country! – but that's the very thing. The Napoleon complex. A magnificent woman like your sister, with your noble mother's simplicity, doesn't want all this toadstool rubbish that's sprouted on the Berghof. We're *artists*! Siegmund and Sieglinde – like this place you both have at Triebschen that Heydrich told me so much about, with the old Parrot-sisters and their telescope. We've had some laughs over that, I can tell you. Poor Heydrich apparently was bringing one of those special anecdotes for me when death took him . . . No more gloom. The man's immortal, an inspiration – I'm giving him a postage stamp, the highest denomination ever! He knew what he was doing, the risks he was taking – driving himself, the top down, no shitbag Doppelgänger and outriders for him! Go like a soldier when one's called. Magnificent. His only mistake was trusting Czechs – and listening to these vile slanders he was part Jewish! Not a shit-particle of truth! I've triple-checked it. Now, Ederl, you know my secret. In the coming months I want you to look at the place, and sound out your sister – but gently, no bull at a backside. This is one's last chance for her to take one seriously. But not a word to a soul about our little plot. Only my personal adjutant knows – I had him swear on the Blutflagge, in front of me. And my Ederl, just between us, I have a name for it – *Wolfrest*. I shan't come up to this horror ever again. Now, one last time for our gallant Heydrich, play our Siegfried's Beerdigung for me. . . ."

He gave Brother a map, drawn in His own artist's hand – to be guarded naturally with my life! The first obstacle the Fool has to smuggle it past is Bormann, crouched in his toad position at the base of the lift shaft, literally beside himself with jealousy!

555

And then – Eva, hovering behind the muslin of the bedroom wing by the grotto of Geli's bronze coffin, clutching black Stasi & Negus. All in the family.

"Herr Eddie, come and have tea and tell me, How is He? Since Heydrich, I've been so terribly worried. I say to the Doggies, it means it could happen – and we've been so happy recently. Truly I think He loves me, even if He still hides me from the Goerings. Oh Herr Eddie, quickly, what did He say?"

"I'm afraid I can't, Eva dear. You see I gave my word."

"I'll tell Him about us."

"You'd never!"

"No – I couldn't, I know, but you could give me a little hint, dear Herr Eddie?"

"You don't need to worry. He's pretty well got over Heydrich. It was mostly about after the war."

"Oh thank you, I'm so relieved. When you are here it's like fresh air. And He's away so terribly much. Herr Eddie, why don't you come to see me more often? Please?"

Good doggie. And ride the Horse-cock all night. Opposite His Hypnotist Portrait? Don't tell me!

. . . *En route Wolf's Rest:* In real life the mausoleum mountain of Charlemagne's legend is called the Untersberg – over a salt hill, under this one. There is no name on the lane leading up from the valley, just massive twinned oaks arching, with a mass of wasps buzzing for the sticky new growth, and then aspens and pines, mixed, and then meadows with remnants of orchard and all sorts of flowers – orchis and birds' eye daisies, chiefly. The lane is unpaved gravel, graded since winter by some machine. Only its heavy tracks are visible on the surface: Master does not come this way often.

The Riley needed second gear, the hill was steeper. Off to the left, the roof of a hunting lodge briefly visible – Mad Ludwig's retreat? – then it was gone and we were out on to a levelling for paradise regained: chalet, log-porches, cross-hatched windows with vines climbing, birds nesting, a small stream burbling into a pond with sedges; 2 wood-ducks swimming. No human being for miles – 7, *as the raven flies, across the*

valley to tiny white blobs that show where the Guard changes and our Eva
watches night after night ...

No electricity. And outdoor privy. The key to the chalet's front door
was on top of the beam where He had told me. A kitchen cum dining,
two bedrooms – 1 whitewashed, with cot; 1 feather four-poster – and a
possible 3rd in the attic, reached by a pull-down ladder. A large parlour
with fieldstone hearth, and there has to be the Piano: the 100th
Bechstein. In tune. I opened a window and played it – and a fallow deer
came out in the orchard and listened. Paradise indeed.

Edwin closed it up and came away.

He does *not* tell Sister her new role as the Goose Girl. Rehearsals
have started for our '42 Season – but only Ring and the Dutchman
again; she knows it with her socks off. Brother sneaks flying visits to his
diggings. By conservative count there are still 300 skull-grottoes sealed
in Kiev and the Hooligan-force is sullen, taking no joy in the great
Work.

"Can't you explain to them –?" the Expedition leader pleads with
Tosh – "like Tut's Tomb, there'll be books and films, not just me –
they'll all be famous when we find it?"

"They are pigs, Monsieur-Gospodin-Eddie. All they say is not
enough beets in the borscht. I shall have to have my hairs done. You see
how you are a whole man again now you stay out of the cavernes, nyet?"

With Heydrich dead, the Boy's performance has improved, 'tis true.
Also, his friend General Pawel is off at the back of beyond on the
endless plain, brawling over some collection of hovels called Stalingrad,
before plunging on across the Don to the Volga and the end of Europe.

... While, at the southern end of the Salt Trail, the White Lady
produces nothing for me either. The moat drains to reveal only the
foundations of a blacksmith's and his cottage – roof timbers perfectly
preserved. In a fit of childish spite Eddie has them burned and then goes
to see the same thing at Bayreuth. A life of rich accomplishment.

OUR '42 SEASON

The true Wagnerians are fewer, the American variety having abandoned play – but no one has taken them seriously anyway: "Have you heard? – Melchior's in Movies!" being their emotional Peak, honey!

But the Nibelheim specimens snuffle more easily in the Death scenes, so *they* are happy – even if they won't admit it and talk constantly in corners about Mad Rudi's Betrayal & The Eastern Front.

Only Edwina C-P provides any Table spark at all.

"Oh by the way, everyone, tomorrow I won't be doing Senta."

"You're ill?" From Winifred, seeing the box office receipts.

"The stress of the most glorous Brünnhilde of my life!" From Wolf, reaching across His grey-brown bowl of barley broth, to pat her paw – and touch her napkin.

"You never said – I would have got you something." From Brother, who wasn't even asked this time for a Mandrake Treatment.

"It's none of that. I'm just not going to sing again until the war's over. Anywhere."

What Yellow Street calls a "bombshell", darlings.

But we three who knew her best, all knew she was joking.

Except that she wasn't.

And no matter how He pleads, first going pale, and then red in the face; or how poor Auntie, trying to keep as cool as though she were dealing with runaway Tosca-no-no, invokes certain obscure contractual clauses; or Brother says, "But Ettie darling you can't simply sit around." (Although he was secretly *thrilled* to be left entirely to his Digging devices)

"I'm sorry, and I love you all for asking, but I'm going to be silent as well as Swiss for the duration. I've made up my mind."

Which rather puts a damper on the closing celebrations.

And then –?

He takes the Fool aside.

"Did you see the place? What do you think?"

"I did, Herr Wolf. It's awfully nice. Just like the old –"

"But your sister, man! What does she say?"

"I haven't actually asked, Herr Wolf."

"You haven't?"

A spit-explosion? Don't tell me!

"I've been sort of waiting for the right moment."

And shaking at the knees.

558

"Thank God." Understanding one is past our mortal comprehension. "Yes, I'm delighted! You must understand, Ederl – Fate has made this the moment. It's why she has decided to retire. We do all these things with the subconscious. Ask her this evening and fly to tell me in Vinnitsa. In person, mind – don't be put off by Bormann – I have the most positive feelings of my life!"

...*At the Griesbachs'*: a Proposal by proxy: the stand-in Swain, rather than kneel, sits on the edge of her bath, both parties naked.

"Ettie darling, there's something I want to ask you."

"Me too, pet – pass me the tweezers – you first."

"I will – but before that, I want you to listen, Ettie, seriously." Balancing the instrument of torture in his palm, Fool speaks. "It's utter nonsense, I realise, but we have to be super tactful. I have to fly to Him specially with your answer. I mean it's wonderful that you're finally going to stay on the sidelines in Switzerland, but if He has a fit He could stop my digs."

"There's nothing in any of them anyway." Examining her own entrance. "I thought the damned electrolysis lasted longer. Tell Wolf to win the bloody war. Now, be a special love before you go, and do my bum."

Presenting it for inspection, the puckered little eye-within-the-I. There is no greater trust than this: Now, for Doctor, Open wide.

"Ettie, please, this is extremely important. Can I at least say *when* He wins, then you'll think seriously?"

"Say what you like. I can't splay myself all night – get on with it, Eddie. The job should be easier than last time, only about half have grown back."

A frilly gold lace around the window – *porthole*, dears, for all our sailors.

"There's no point, Ettie. You can't even notice."

"Then why are you so excited? Pet, you're positively gushing. But we mustn't do it till after, or the tweezers won't grip."

And then –?

After. Brother did what Sister wanted, their newest form of mad togetherness, a little pain for perfect pleasure.

And then –?

559

Eddie sighed, and said, "That was marvellous. I suppose somehow I'll tell Wolf – but what are you going to do in cuckoo-clock-land? We'll have to find something for when I'm away, if there isn't going to be singing. Perhaps the Red Cross – "

"Are you mad? I'm not milking goats on a hill. I'll go with you, of course."

"Not to my diggings? You can't. There's a war. He'd find out immediately."

"Bosh. And I don't mean go down the squalid things. Just see a bit of the country. For the first time in our lives have a proper holiday. I've wanted to do Russia ever since the Boris."

As though it was Mama, junket-planning a Fad with Thomas Cook's. And then –?

A succession of Ghastly Scenes: Fool-with-Wolf, Fool-with-Sister; Wolf-with-Parsifal-Marschalls, with Fafner really losing! Pawel-retreating; Monsieur-Gospodin-Eddie-with-Tosh, screaming; a Desert-Fox, invincible-Rommel, frying and running; an Arctic von Paulus, standing frozen and dying. Ettie brawling with Eddie, but shipped back to Switzerland, finally, thank Heaven! Half a million Volsung vassals trapped in a Bear's pocket, starving. Kiev Hooligans openly laughing at the Expedition leader in the skull tunnels. Edwin thinking, Christ, life is over, I'll never find it, my Grail, and getting Pneumonia and staying through Christmas – no visit to Sister – not to waste a single minute. The Tenth Anniversary of Siegfried's accession. Circles huddled around wireless receivers in the Blitzkrieg-Palast, listening to a broadcast from the hovels at that place across the plain, called Stalingrad. But the sounds really-truly, children, coming from the Dwarf's underground transmitters at home in Nibelheim. A telegram arriving, carried via Fafner in a secret enigmatic code known only to Wagnerians:

BRUNN HERE CMA WOTAN ALSO CAN DO NOTHING COME
AT ONCE EXCLAM STOP SIGNED SENTA BAYREUTH PS AT
ONCE DOUBLE EXCLAM STOP

...At Wahnfried: Edwin arrives at midnight, on the 2nd day of February, of the year that will be the '43 Season. Still with an aching chest and light head from the pneumonia, and travel conditions aren't easy, even

with the Chicken Farmer's passes, and Winter is relentless, howling snow on a north wind at thirty degrees of frost.

Please God, she hasn't! – not guns or ropes or drownings; not like Mama, and all the others.

"Where is she?" Screaming it at Winifred over the screaming wind tearing the Hofgarten. "I should never ever have left her alone all this winter. And Christmas –"

"Eddie, dear, we must stay calm. She's in the Festspielhaus, please listen . . ."

But Brother was gone, back into the whirling white waste blanking out Mad Ludwig, and the blackness of the Grave, and the thorns of Mama's roses as I ran into them, and rushed on, heedless, past the hidden gate in the wall leading to the old Spy-Sisters, through the laurels where little children played mock Funerals & Twilights, over the space of the square above the Wagnerians' Restaurant, deserted of shadows, endless as Russia. Dimly looming, the dome of the great Hall built on the Magic Mountain, the small side-door, the tunnel-passage to the stage, set once more for the Dutchman. The sails stretch up, and away, to the top of forever. And at the base of the mast, not lashed for safety to the wheel, but clutching it to her as some sort of anchor – Ettie. She stood, staring out across the pit, but in the light of a single silver spot, her eyes were not Senta's, for leaping into the vortex, but Kundry's, leading us into temptation.

"Ettie, oh darling darling – you are all right? Swear to me – it's so utterly my fault. Getting Winnie's telegram. I can't tell you how worried. I'll do anything. *Anything*, just say."

"Thank you, Eddie pet. I'm sorry you were worried, and dragging you from your old tunnels, but now we have to save him, you see, so run along to the piano, there's a lamb."

"The piano, but why? Ettie, it's one in the morning, Christ I've travelled all day. I've had pneumonia. I'll play for Wolf in the Sieg-friedhaus tomorrow if He wants –"

"Not for Wolf, darling. Poor Wolf can't tell if he's coming or going. And I know you must be wiped out, but you have to be a love if I'm going to help him – and don't put the reading light on; you don't need the music and it would spoil the mood."

561

And still the Fool doesn't grasp. "Mood? For whom? Ettie, I'm absolutely whacked!"

"He's here. Eddie, just do it."

Out There, across the Hood, beyond the empty cane-pews of the vanished worshippers, behind the Family Curtain, in absolute darkness, in His Master's Box – Hagen is hiding.

No need to be told, but she says it anyway:

"Liebestod – and when you're playing, Eddie darling, imagine it's me."

And then –?

No, *then*! The moment this Fool was born for.

Imagine . . .

The Song of Edwin

... *Mild-und-Leise* - how Gently-&-Softly
She smiles,
How Sweetly!
Her-words-&-My-words
Her-arms-&-My-arms
Her-heart-&-My-heart
I-Eddie-&-Tristan, She-Ettie-Isolde . . .
But only my piano?
There should be Sweet Strings, a hundred, crying . . .
And liquid
Bass-Viols in equal Count, throbbing . . . and
Brass shining-&-surging, and
Organ for Her Passion's crescendos, curling-&-cresting –
For OUR Love . . .!
Oh God! see my Ettie stretching, Oh Christ hear Her singing!
Who hears such singing really-truly never-ever shall die.
Singing-*and*-saving, Holding-*and*-having – only please, God
Me-not-*Him* in Her arms
Not the Monster
Entwining-enfolding . . .
Shall day waken Eddie?
Nevermore Ettie-darling! We have Our day's Menaces sweetly

Defiled! Ever We flee It . . .
But Oh, Ettie-my-own-dearest-Darling – does that day's
Dawning never affright Us? Oh never-Eddie!
For Our Night lasts Forever
Banishing dread-&-sweet-death so Yearned-for,
So longed-for . . .
Death-in-love in *your* arms precious-Ettie
Far from the Sun, golden-Eddie
From that Day's parting Sorrow
Free from Delusion, gripped by Our Yearning
Free from our fearing Ettie – Only sweet longing Eddie
Free from our Languishing, Free from our Sighing, enclosed in
Sweet darkness, no more Evasion, never more Parting
Only breathing to choking, perception enkindling, endless
Self-knowing, Do you not SEE it Eddie
His heart swelling with Courage –
Christ-sweetest-torn-Christ-Ettie! Not *HIS*!
ETTIE LISTEN –

> "I am yours, my Fuehrer."
> She said the words.

And then –?
Collapse. By brother, with blood from the rose thorns on the white
keys.
And then –?
Hallucination (which you can tell, children, had already started! Did
you ever read such drivel?) with images of the Box curtain parting; of
Sister running down off the stage to the piano; of Him, standing on top
of the edge of the Hood, looking down in the pit; of that hypnotising pale
face caught by the single silver spot; of a shaken Black Order adjutant
sent packing for help with a stretcher; of being carried to the Griesbachs
through the blizzard, and being settled by Ettie; and hot-water-bottled;
and fed Mathilde's lemon-and-quinine, and kissed.
And then –?
Brother, deserted; creeping, tottering from his bed, looking down
from the windows, watching Sister disappear in white snow and a green
cloak to the little Siegfriedhaus, just like her mother. Me, stealing down

the Griesbachs' back stairs, like Eddie smuggling Putzi from imagined danger, and out again into the blizzard; to the window they had peered through when we voyeurs were only children.

And then –?

The face of Madness – or rather, fever's over-wrought Imagination, because it pretends it sees Him lying, with Sister squatting, splayed, wide-open and hairless. But you *see* – that is *fact*. That is why we played the Tweezer Game, silly! This is what He has been expecting – His "Something Special."

And then –?

Penultimate nightmare. From the *Alptraum* file – after simple Impotence, and Auto-Erotic Visual Gratifications: Coprophilia & Coprophagia & Coprolalia & Undinism – which in the Nursery we would have called Being-Naughty & Making-A-Mistake. Or, You dreadful, Girl – how Frightful!

As Jung was when he dreamed he saw God the Father shit on Basel. "Except that it's Ettie, Mama! And she isn't only doing Biggies on Him – she's peeing like a nun!"

All golden on His smeared-white face that flushes crimson, loving it.

That is Utter Revulsion, Edwin!

"No, Mama, truly! Under Ettie – that man's *eating* it! And *drinking*! Number 1 and Number 2!"

Except the Stench, Herr Hauptmann Analyst: and the Taste.

Which can only be eradicated by I.G. Farben's Zyklon-B . . .

The Fool:

Fled, and blacked out in the snow . . . but is found again, and really-truly very ill this time, so that he is taken to Wahnfried, and put in old Cosima's last bedroom on the ground floor, and the Leader-Wolf's own quack arrives, gross Dr Morrell, with monkey-gland extracts instead of Mandrake Roots, and Ettie nurses me around the clock for a month, and spring arrives for Our Birthday, and a super-marvellous present to celebrate me being well.

"Mime's here," she said. "The crawly Chicken-Farmer simply insists, so I've told him ten minutes – and then don't worry, pet, Big Sis will come back and throw the ghastly creature out."

Considering Stalingrad, and losing his right-hand Blond Moses,

Himmler looked well: you might say, thriving. A merciful release, losing a rival. It was the first time of meeting since the death of Heydrich.

"You've been through a bad time, I hear – but then so have we all. Howrever, I think I can lift your spririts further. If you had your choice where would you most like to continue your resrearches for the Grail?"

There is only one answer.

"Most, Reichsfuehrer? At Avignon – but since that's not possible with Vichy, then Dietrich's Fortress, on the Hungarian border."

"Good. Finish getting well and you shall have both. And if there are any rothers you think of, pass the names along to Kapitän von Maser at the Institute, for vetting. Labour shall no longer be a problem. Good mrorning, Herr Edwin."

And then –?

You damned vroyeur idiots! What do you bloody think? A Mriracle! The Fool frorgot his bloody kiddy-nightmares, and took up his bloody bed and walked !!!

Third Movement
Ninth Passage

[grace notes]

... No other Land could nurse Them
But their Motherland, Old England!
And on her broad Bosom
Did they ever Thrive!

... *Tick tock:* irregular rhythm. Gedanke & Gedächtnis once more saved Old Eddie's life: the black wretches' hopping and croaking brought his Grenadier guards (G & G wanted only to peck out my eyes). But after all that nursery excitement, small wonder the old ticker missed a tock!

The other thing that revived Us is Waring: my dears, Our Jeremy is in the most delicious twist at being freshly locked out. He suspects the worst – that we're finally getting to the best parts – and so billets-doux arrive with the Prison gruel:

> "Forgive misunderstanding over style, C-P. Street people now recognise advantage of Period flavour. Cash no longer a problem."

Bribery after Corruption – J.W. & Yellow Street shall sniff not a whiff until It is Finished. Or I am. Tick-tock. Even this small expenditure of spleen drains the account. But not long, now. Come, winged messengers, flutter old Eddie's brainbox, shake the fool's next page loose. ...

... *At the Griesbachs':* Brother can't let go of the nightmare with a month's bedrest and Swiss rations:

"But *why*? We finally got you safe in Switzerland – it was *your* idea to give up singing – and now you're doing it again and Wolf's definitely losing Africa and half of Russia. And you wouldn't take the whole world when you could have had it on a plate, with Neuschwanstein to boot! Ettie, *why*?"

"That pile? – I thought you were the one with sensibilities. Besides, darling, I'm not singing again – the Liebestod was an exception to cheer Him up – and anyway I have a house now. When you're really well – and since you don't love me enough to take me on your miserable Pottings – Sister's going to be a Goose Girl for the Duration as you wanted."

Sensibilities! Christ!

"I *do* have them. And it's only because I so desperately love you – that's the part that's so frightful. Ettie, you can't mean it – you're not going to come back and live with Him in Bavaria."

"Once He gets me hot water. Brünnhilde draws the line at not being able to have her Friday night bath. Now, eat your brekkie, pet, it's special this-week's butter from Lucerne. Poor Winnie's cook was absolutely green . . ."

And then my devil arrived with the ultimate temptation.

Avignon

The old Abbot is standing in his doorway for Edwin as though he's known for all these years that this would happen.

"I see you have a piece of paper. I suppose that means my yews are going."

"The Papal Legate's signature is on the document, Father, and the Nuncio's Office has countersigned. We have the blessing of the Holy See. I'll save the trees if we possibly can. And any relics will be treated with absolute veneration, the same as at Camargue. After all, if we find the Grail – "

"Rome blesses the rape of Camargue as well? You are in league with the devil, but perhaps this means God's Will be done. While you are here, do you wish lodgings in the Abbey?"

"Thank you, Father. That would be most kind."

"We shall see." The Abbot turned away from the hot sun, into the shadow of the doors – then back. "Unless Rome's papers bless them also, the Barbarians with you are not welcome in our house."

"No, Father. The guards have lodgings in the town."

And every morning tramp sur le pont d'Avignon – the New One, in the lee of the old Roman, burnt by the Huns – and every evening march back again, escorting Mad Eddie's Hooligan-force to its place of slumber. (An abandoned quarry, which the Expedition Leader does not need to visit.)

Reprise: I SAW NOTHING!

But Edwin did try to save the Quincunx Yews. A dry moat was dug around each dark-green ancient, with each left standing on its small island, under my Mediterranean sun, to die, indirectly, as that other One did on *His* cross, of thirst. . .

And then –?

Hot-foot to Camargue! to Li Santo, my town of the Three Maries. No scruples here – no old Abbot; and the scruffy, soutaned priest who charged cash on the barrelhead for Ettie to sing for our abortion had long moved on.

Edwin-the-Leader swiftly commands the removal of most of the north wall of the vestry to get at the crypt.

"That bunch over there –!" barks the Death's-Head sergeant – "over here, on the double!"

A ragged operation. The sergeant, a career-man, shudders.

"Six months of basic training, you couldn't instil discipline into these Gypsy swine. Mein Herr – are you ill?"

Pretend it. Sway a little. Avert the head – because half Edwin's Hooligans were once Eddie's Gitanos. The one in the centre column, third from the rear, with the eyes of a free man, was once a King with the wild white horses.

"Only a touch of the sun, sergeant. Don't push the men too hard at midday."

> *I saw Esau,*
> *Sitting on a See-saw!*
> *Esau saw Me, I –*

Rhymes of childhood. I saw Sevastyani, crowned King of the Gitanos.

He saw Edwin; and because he was regal, he did not spit or curse me: he merely forced me to look him in the eye.

The Death's Head laughs. "The bastards should be on their knees to your lordship – giving them a holiday on the Riviera when they could have been shipped East with the NN Brigade."

Gather together the Outcasts of Israel . . .

"I'm sure you're absolutely right, sergeant."

. . . At Dietrich's Fortress: The Black-Order Kondor lands the Expedition Leader half a continent distant. Disembarking, he sees at once that in Hungary, heat is not his problem, but delayed torrential spring rains. A squelching quagmire, the 'plane's wheels hubdeep in grey-yellow clay, my feet also.

"We were lucky to land," said the pilot. "For going on to Kiev, I won't be able to lift her off while it's like this."

"Kiev can wait. There's plenty to do here."

The senior myrmidon marches up; an Engineer Herr-Major with a broken left arm and stiff neck. Leader & Major slosh through a tour of inspection. Tarpaulins have been spread over the roofless cottages to provide Hooligan shelter for this latest pampered group.

"It involves less canvas than tents," says the Engineer-Major, "and we uncovered a primitive latrine ditch to dispose their wastes outside the perimeter walls. Call it the Hotel Imperial for this crowd."

"They can stay for the time being – in fact it'll put them closer to the work. Now, Herr Major, the experts in Berlin give the east quadrant their highest rating, so I want us to start excavating from that wall – then extend the dig back in layers to these living quarters. Once we reach them, you'll have to find somewhere else for the workers. Meanwhile, ask if any of them are stonemasons – holes will have to be breached in the parapets at convenient intervals to expel the over-burden or we won't have space to breathe. The dig-layers should be three metres thick. With the work force you've got, how long will that take?"

Out slide-rules! – the Engineer's stiff neck has thawed appreciably at this display of Edwinian expertise.

"Quite a proposition, Herr von Perceval. Say two months to the layer, if we can find an efficient method of expelling the water as we drop the level. We'll be below the foundations, and if it keeps on like this for the summer that's a monumental quantity of pumping."

"I've done some thinking about that, too," said the Grail's genius. "I was rather wondering whether we couldn't use the well in the central Keep."

"Until it fills – it is all of ten metres from the top at this moment. That should give us all of half a day."

Junker hog-sarcasm, my dears.

"That isn't quite what I meant, Major. I thought sappers – from outside they could tunnel in at right angles from the base of the hill, and as we go down from the top, at each layer we'd lop off the existing shaft. We'd have a sort of giant bath siphon. There's an old gypsy camp that looks about the right spot, but that's just guessing. Naturally, you'd want to confirm with your instruments."

"Jawohl, mein Herr!"

So that was all right. Edwin's well scheme proves out. The ground is hardened. The Kondor waits.

"We shall have re-enforcing wire laid at once," said the Engineer as the Grail-Leader was leaving. "It shall not hold up the work again."

"Thanks very much, Herr Major. Sure you've got enough men?"

"This is the least of our problems, Herr von Perceval. For more bodies we just ask our local King of the Jews. Best of luck in Kiev."

The young Leader was well pleased, and flew off, all golden into the morning sun.

. . . *On the Roundabout:* Kiev, Carmargue, Avignon, Dietrichstein, White Lady at the centre: a new quincunx has been formed, and it seems the Expeditor spends as much time in the air as below the ground. And on top of it has to find time for Ettie – and Zürich!

"You must make Cameron understand," Edwin literally begged the smug, blank Swiss under the ex-monk's restaurant, "I don't know anything of war value. I'm an archaeologist, pure and simple. I had a breakdown this spring. My sister's even given up singing at Bayreuth. And every time I come here I'm putting my head in a noose."

"I am sure that Colonel Cameron appreciates your position, Herr Perceval."

"If they've made that bent prick a colonel, God help the British Army."

"With their success in Sicily, it would seem He does." The Swiss smiles as only a neutral who lives with his arse glued to a bank, can. "London asks specifically to be kept informed of the whereabouts of your sister. It was noted that her name has not been announced for this year's Festival."

"London can go to hell."

"Quite so – but if a reply is not passed by the end of July, then the package which arrived this week will be forwarded to the appropriate office in Berlin."

"You loathesome little dropping."

"*And –*" blanker & smugger than ever – "her position is to be updated monthly, but a letter will suffice for that. Using indirect wording. And under the circumstances, Registration would seem wise."

Brother capitulates. Lying a little. Hating completely.

"She's staying mostly at Bayreuth. We may be having a holiday week at Triebschen next month if I can get away."

"Thank you, Herr Perceval. This war keeps us all so busy."

. . . *Back to Sister:* "She is not with us, dear Herr Edwin," said little Frau Griesbach. "Fräulein Edwina is gone, she said, to the country since three weeks. One wonders, might my husband and I also speak to you about a certain subject?"

"Of course, Frau Griesbach. Any time – but I have to make a trip for a day or two. Can it wait till I come back?"

"One shall only hope, Herr Edwin."

"Good. We'll have a nice chat then. Auf Wiedersehen, Frau Griesbach."

"Auf Wiedersehen, dear Herr Edwin. And always our love to dearest Fräulein Edwina, as well."

. . . *Wolf's Rest:* The vines bloom above the door; the grass in the orchard is waist high, mixed with flowers; bees drone; fruit forms; the ducks on the pond have raised a family. Ettie as Goose Girl is furthering their education.

572

"Hullo, Eddie darling. I'm seeing if they'll recognise names – but they're not terribly bright. Have you found us a Pot?"

"Not yet, but I've got a frantic amount going. Ettie, you look marvellous."

"Do I?" she said. "I never bother with a mirror and the fans don't care – do they, silly duckies?" Who hide their heads in shame, b*ms up. "Well, brother darling, don't just stand gawping – come and kiss me."

"I was thinking how lovely, in such a simple dress."

"Wolf got it for me. The Cow makes them apparently – or used to. I had to take in the waist a mile – but don't let's talk about the Cow. Kiss me, fool."

Always . . .

"I carry your picture everywhere," Brother said, "look at you last thing every night, but still I forget how everything wonderful you really are."

"Darlingest Eddie, how sweet." Giggling, stroking his face. "So Big Sis will tell you a secret – I don't wear a stitch underneath."

Clean for His whistle.

"Come swimming," Ettie said, afterwards, "and then we'll do it again, only longer."

"I don't have bathing dress."

"After we've been doing It out here in the grass? Idiot, we're a million miles from civilisation – who on earth do you think would ever see?"

. . .As a tiny flash reflects from some coming-or-going on the Salt Mountain across His valley. And it all floods back! His frightful face, with the stench, the smearing –

Nonsense! It was all hallucination. And even a telescope can't – not this far – Can it?

Sister obviously doesn't think so as she leads her Boy out on to a bench of rock, glacier-smoothed, moss-cushioned, with a blue view into the next world.

"Austria anyway – it's quite my favourite place. What would you like for lunch? I'm not much at cooking yet, but I could do us a salad."

"Lovely. But how do you get things without a car?"

"I grow the veggies, myself; don't you think Sister's getting clever? – and an old gaffer comes up with the rest in a trap from the village on Mon's and Fri's."

"Don't you get terribly lonely? What do you *do*?"

"Do you get lonely down your old holes?"

"Constantly. I miss you dreadfully."

" 'That is Exaggeration, Edwin!' " which it is, and can only be laughed at, remembering other Mama-isms. "If you're ready for a shock – Big Sis reads."

"Books?" Little Eddie can't believe his ears. "Left-over Karl Mays?"

"Our claws are showing, dear. One reads, as they say, eclectically – I'm just finishing Pawel's *Brothers* as a matter of fact."

"What did you think of it?"

"Dull darling. I'm going to wade through Goethe next." Then changing registers, into her Naughty-Ettie voice, all throaty, "Eddie before salad, while I'm still slippy, let's play the Swan-boot game again. . . ."

A 2nd tiny flash across the valley, and the Duck Family quack at their Goose Girl's glad cries. And then we have cold-drumsticks with her veggies out on her rocky bower. And after, inside for Ettie-&-Eddie's Rest, a Proper One, to be ready for the next game, Push-Me-Pull-You, on the 4-poster feather bed. And then in the evening, singer's-throat lubricated for the dust-dry words, she read the *Brothers* to me.

" 'Love all God's creation, the whole and every grain of sand; every leaf, every ray of His light. Love the animals, love the plants, love everything. . . .' Eddie, darling that's so exactly what I feel up here in my hut. And today, with Us, I've loved *you*, so it's absolutely perfect."

But it was His hut.

And in the morning . . .

"Does Wolf come up here often?"

"Not once, so far. He must be winning again in Russia."

"But He gave you Eva's dress?"

"Sent it – accidentally-on-purpose, c/o poor Auntie – although I think she's forgiven me, because they're only doing Meistersinger this year, and she can get a hundred cow-Eva's for that."

"Shall you be going? Even if you're not singing?"

"Are you mad?"

"We've never missed a Season."

"You can't call Hans Sachs a Season, Eddie – and you hated Stolzing from the beginning. Anyway, with the war, one couldn't possibly listen to a bunch of howling Huns."

"So you still really do feel that we're Us, Ettie – English?"

"Darling idiot, what on earth else?"

"Traitors."

"Eddie, we're *artists*. Our little tribe gave Papa in one war, surely that's enough. And to be purely legal, we're ghastly Swiss."

"But being so close to Wolf? After the war, you don't think some will rub off on us?"

"I hope so." Her laughter peeled across our dell. "Brother dear, if He wins we have to listen forever to Blondi conquering Russia – but if Wolf loses, we'll go to America for our memoirs and be enormously rich."

"But seriously . . ."

"Everyone knows it's going to be a stalemate. Franco's got a peace treaty practically in the bag. Now, how much longer is Sister allowed to have you with her?"

"That depends."

"Not on me, my pet. Ettie hasn't been a bitch once. You can stay forever. So depends on what?"

On so incredibly much: on the tip of my tongue, from the back of my mind, waiting to spill when the floodgates open. That awfulness. The stench. I KNOW YOU DID IT ETTIE! But a raven flew over from His side of the valley, *craank-craanking* our peace, and Brother-&-Sister both looked up – and the gates stayed shut.

"I can hang around another day, but then I absolutely must get back to Kiev. I have this nightmare all the time: I'm just about to find something significant – tremendously! – and then the Front collapses. And I can actually see the Grail, almost touch it, but the Reds cut me off."

"Don't you dare stay in Russia." Grabbing his hands, pulling him close. "After that frightful business with the Poles, in the forest, in that ditch? You won't take chances? Promise?"

"Promise."

"Good darling. It isn't worth it. Not for an old pot that never existed. And not when we've got us. Remember, 'Love everything', Eddie – and me, we'll be like proper Brothers."

575

2 more paradise days. Brother-&-brother love each other more completely than ever in their lives.

"I'll drop in each time I fly, if I can," the male one swears, "but August for sure. Oh, and the Griesbachs send their love. She had something she wanted to ask. I rather think the poor old things are hard up for cash and want to rent our rooms. They could, if I knew when you were going back."

"I won't be."

"You mean for September?"

"For always. Eddie dear, Sister doesn't intend to meet Wagnerians again for as long as she lives."

"'That is Exaggeration, Edwina'."

But she didn't laugh. Only said with her Driven-Ettie look, "No it isn't."

"Then I won't argue – but where will you roost for the winter?"

"Darling fool, I'm staying put."

"Here? All alone? You'd be completely marooned."

"No I shouldn't. My old peasant has a sleigh, and I'm going to learn to ski. Love everything, Eddie, remember . . ."

. . . And leave her, waving, talking to her duckies . . . His Geli canary. . . . The Riley was past the object in the grass on the way down to the valley before the mind said, *That was a Templars' cross!*

Stop the Riley. Walk back, into the aspens and pines to find an overgrown clearing, with a rusted rail, and a handful of graves, ancient, with great trees splitting the stones up through them. And beyond the graves, on Charlemagne's Mountain, a cave, with its entrance collapsed, and a tiny stream trickling out, down over the gravestones, forming miniature stalactites and stalagmites of white crystal. The staff of life and taxes: common salt for the table of serf and Emperor.

. . . *Roundabout: September,* '43. 1000 Hooligans now in Kiev; the same at Graz; 700 split between Avignon and Camargue, as needed, and about the same again at the White Lady's in Třeboň – three-and-a-half-thousand men digging for the Fool and their lives and nothing to show for it except some inferior Frankish burial bracelets, and ikons of less value in the skull grottoes. With still a hundred to explore, and the Eastern Front crumbling; all the unpronounceable names that Pawel

576

charged through so bravely, now toppling back into the nets of avenging commissars.

"And when they get here, Monsieur-Gospodin-Eddie," from a weepy Tosh, just starting her damned curse, on my first night back at the Blitzkrieg-Palast, "the Red pig-swines will kill me and violer moi toujours all night, nyet?"

"I'm sure we won't lose Kiev," yawns Eddie, "and if we do, Tosh, I've said I'll take you with me so stop crying for le bon Dieu and let me bloody sleep."

... While the Hooligan-force underground is stroppier than ever. The next morning Leader-Edwin's Black-Order adjutant tells him he fears "the rabble may even attack the guards! I have ordered them doubled, so that no man patrols alone in a gallery – and they shoot to kill."

It goes without saying ...

"And then we're down another pair of hands. Surely you can maintain discipline in some more effective way."

"A bullet's the only discipline these Slav oafs recognize. What method, Mein Herr, did you have in mind?"

"Well, sort of personal example. You know, pitching in with them."

"Crawl on our guts with these swine? Herr von Perceval, let me make it clear – all my good men want is to shoot this backstabbing filth-collection of yours, and go up in fresh air to the front for the Fuehrer, and hold the line!"

Which was clearly Insubordination, Edwin! – and should form the subject of a report to Mime-Headquarters, but a Wolf-Summons intervenes.

Baltic Vortex:

> *Oh! Have you seen a Ship at sea,*
> *Blutrot die Segel, schwarz der Mast?*

Blood-red her ensign, black her crosses, His grey-ghost warship prowls offshore, guarding-&-watching under brightness at noon. The Baltic tide is out, the beach stretches hard-packed for miles in two directions, East-West. To the north lies the grey ship's element, deceptively passive for late September, lapping at a soupy skim of weed in froth along the edge of Nibelheim's finest, most expensive, holiday strand. To the south, pine trees, bent to the wind's order,

577

irregular and cramped like old Frau Fai-Fai struggling for a crippled footing in the dunes. In time of peace Kinder play here with spade and bucket to make their little dream-domes and castles; basket changing-huts and canvas chairs available for hire by their elders, and hanky-panky for Mothers with their lovers, with Father detained by faraway monkey-business in the towns. In war, the beach is empty, except for a single set of Robinson Crusoe prints.

Edwin follows them. Far ahead, down the beach to the west, a dot on the sand; the tracks to it wear size 8 shoes, small for a man – petite for Colossus.

"Ederl! You're here – but I had Bormann send the message days ago; what took you so long? Never mind, never mind, tell me how you are?"

"Well, thank you, Herr Wolf. And you're in good spirits."

Our Pale Man is positively bubbling, children.

"This magnificent rescue by Skorzeny of the Duce! On top of a mountain, right under our enemies' noses! One realises again anything is possible! In the finest Heydrich tradition! It's been a difficult time, but there's always this spot in a battle. Defeatism?! Don't tell me! Ask Caesar! – and one missed you at the Festspiel. Oh, I know your opinion of the characterization in Meistersinger, and in some respects one agrees, but you might have been there to support me, to maintain the international flavour; you know I've never agreed with the purely German approach. How could one! You realize where we're standing?"

But Brother can see only that small mouth in the pale face, the gold-capped mole-teeth repaired at such expense. *All the better to eat . . .*

"Not precisely, Herr Wolf," fleeing the nightmare. "Mama always found the northern resorts too cold, so we never visited."

"That marvellous woman, more and more she sustains me! One can see so much of her now in your so-noble sister – and how can I ever thank you enough for your help in getting Fräulein Edwina to take care of Wolfrest for me – but we aren't here to talk about resorts, foolish fellow. Out there! The very spot on the sea when the storm first struck! The courage it required in those days to make a sea crossing. Life itself at risk every time – the wind shrieking one's name in the rigging; the monsters we all fear lurking in the deep. The inferior Minna spewing her guts out – one can't fault her for that, I've suffered God knows! – and bravest, truest Robber never leaving our Master's side. . . . Mein Fox'l, Blondi, there's never defeatism from a dog, only men let you down. . . . Imagine Wagner standing – lashing himself to the masts to face the furies. The terrifying lightning! Planks cracking! Any normal mortal would be on his knees, cursing fate, crying for the shaveling's version of heaven to save them – but Genius, it goes without saying, Wagner doesn't whine and cringe: he sees the example of a mere dog's courage and nobility, and from that we get the Holländer. So! – I've decided to act. First, a statue, here, where the Dutchman sprang from – something truly magnificent and elemental – even the idiots who never listen to a note of the music will have to be impressed by the scope of the man! – and then the new weapon. There, just along the beach at Peenemünde." Swinging the uncomprehending Fool to look in its direction. "I'm sorry, Ederl, I can't tell you any more for the present – it isn't a question of trust, but I never allow myself to accept these things until I've seen for myself that they work. But I can promise you it's truly going to be my Wotan's Spear – warfare will be stood on its head overnight! And it's not one of those Yiddish magic-box tricks that so many so-called experts are constantly badgering me about. One can't imagine why the fools on the Staff are so blind! This atom business in particular – you don't have a scientific understanding so I shan't bore you with detail, but it seems a pint of this seawater beside us could blow up London! Marvellous news – although you know I was determined at the outset to save it as we did Paris, but Churchill the syphilitic struck first, and now the Americans with Rome. Absolute barbarians! But getting back to this Jew 'atom' weapon. What commander from the beginning of time wouldn't want it? I said to Speer, give me the facts and figures, only a fool doesn't learn from his enemies; that's the secret behind all successful campaigners. Well! My dear Ederl, they said to me, these shithead so-called graduates, that if – that little word of ours – *if*, we took all the manpower of the Greater Reich, and all the money, and all the industrial and scientific brains, and did nothing else for a mere ten years, then there was a *one-in-five* chance that this infernal device *might* work! Imbeciles! – I used the term to their idiot faces – Immobilize our entire effort? and bankrupt our nation?! Through *debt*?! Christ on the cross, can't they *see* – this is *Their* ultimate weapon! Against *us*! Classic! Naturally I've cancelled all work on such a project. Only thank one's stars the minds of that cursed race at least are so completely predictable."

579

Whee! Like an arrow He flies,
At random, nor rest, nor respite ...

... At the Blitzkrieg-Palast: After all the months and tons of digging –
one small gleam in the dark: a model boat, with beaten gold on its
bottom planks, and containing an effigy of the Three Maries, all
identical to that of Li Santo's in Camargue, is found in a skull-grotto of
Kiev!

"Tosh! They got here!" Whirling her round that marvellous night.
"My Templars! All along I was right! Fifth Century! Mediterranean!
Oh God, it's fantastic – and there are still thirty grottoes left. It could be
there Tosh, just waiting!"

"The Reds are waiting – only fifty kilometres. Monsieur-Gospodin-
Eddie, je suis effrayée of the raping. You fly Tosh soon, peut-être?"

"You know I'll fly you. Don't be a silly girl. The armies are just taking
up their defensive lines for the winter. We'll be safe as houses."

With a quick Huss-cock ride squeezed in to keep her happy, before
rushing away again down to his skulls. And finding in the tunnels, beside
the normal reek of sweat and faeces, now fear; because guard and
Hooligan alike knows what will happen when the Bear gets his hug on
them.

The Leader just didn't have a minute to think about it, dears. Pawel is
back, ready to fight to the last Kozz-Cossack for the capital of their free
Ukraine.

"Now that you're dug in, Pawel – I mean Leningrad held for years, we
must be good for the winter, wouldn't you say?"

"Christmas is what I'd say – an All Souls' Christmas, not Orthodox.
Ukraine never stood a monkey's hope in hell of being free, Eddie – not
once your 'Chicken Farmer' butcher got his squads pig-sticking. Stay
and be skewered by Ivan in a cellar, if you like, but pull all the strings to
get Tosh out right away."

"Surely it isn't that bad," the Fool protests. "There's talk of a new
weapon, and Franco has peace proposals on the table. Pawel, I still need
Tosh for translating – even if she is a bit erratic – and with my passes I
can always get us a 'plane. If it's going to be Christmas, we can at least
wait another month. I can't possibly leave when I know it's *there*. If you

want I'll send Tosh along to your room. I'm simply too busy to keep her happy."

Admits the pimp of All Souls.

"The Aunts would turn over in their graves. I must remember to send them a card. You laugh, Eddie, but I haven't missed a Christmas yet. It doesn't seem the moment to start."

"I'm not laughing, Pawel. Just thinking of Mama – 'the sisters of Sappho'. I didn't know the old things were still alive. Give them our love too, I suppose, although Ettie and I never did at the time."

And then –?

Full Winter, even for blasted Russia, a month early, locking up Kiev and Ukraine. Shells landing in the suburbs, but on the opposite side of the city from Perchersky Lavra, so the work keeps driving forward in the Community of Skulls. Only 10 grottoes still left to open – *It has to be there* . . .

And then –?

Mutiny in the tunnels. A Hooligan-uprising, on a day the Grail Leader is topside pulling strings for Tosh's aircraft. To no avail. "It isn't a question of a ticket, mein Herr! No 'planes are flying!" And underground, 30 mutineers – simply dragged into an empty grotto, and sealed, to become part of the next idiot's collection. 7 grottoes left unopened. Our lucky number. "Sod waiting for new stonemasons! – dynamite the bloody thing!" Bringing half the roof down, but that being the least of one's worries: above ground there are no roofs left to tumble.

And then –?

Two hours of half-sleep, with Tosh crying, and clinging to Gospodin-Eddie's limp roche, like a bébé, seeking Mama's breast. *Nyet! Troy existed – there has to be a* . . . dodging bullets, falling buildings, to dive back underground, still reeking of cordite, the fumes making the eyes weep – That is Frustration, Edwin! "Blast the next one – forget the damned safety regulations!" Idiot Teutons, going by the book when the world's ending. "I'll do it then. Give me the sodding plunger! Misfired? Christ Jesus what moron –? Clear out, the lot of you, I'm going in myself." But the Leader knows his life is being saved for a Special Purpose. The hurtling rock misses him. "I told you so – bring the lanterns. I need light, damn you!" Another squeeze, another chasm . . .

581

The last grotto.

And then –?

Only this bundle of paper? scraps of parchment? illegible scribblings? A Fool could weep, even if his eyes weren't half blind with dust and nitric fumes and fury of frustration. The salt tears drop and smear the rust marks on the parchment. A melting mixture as polyglot as any Tosh translation: a mish-mash Rosetta stone of Cyrillic and Latin words and symbols: Place names, King's names, columns of sums with initials at the bottom: "C.R." Salt tears. Salt tax, collected for Charles Rex.

It's all been done before . . .

I've come too far – but It *was* here! They brought it in the golden boat with the Maries, the Heart in the Grail, and must have taken it back again, in the 2nd of the Holy Roman Empires, for Charlemagne, and somewhere along the salt routes, lost it. At one of the places whose names are now in my hand!

And then –?

Escape from the rat-trap becomes the only object – with the precious bundle, "And you, Tosh, da, but I've got to round up something to ride in first."

"You promise me, Eddie. To come back? – tu promis, your Tosh, nyet?"

"Promise, Tosh. Hang on here at the Palast. I'm going to find Pawel, and get us a tank."

And then –?

Then children, for the first time in Russia, he – Edwin – sees:

The Fool sees Kiev's ruined Gate still standing, waiting to fulfil another legend. He sees the long guns with rounds frozen in the melted barrels, exploding. He sees Cold that freezes the trunks of men so quickly that they stay standing, like the headless statue of pig-Lenin. He sees men with their penises locked to Russia with a bridge of yellow ice – and sees what happens when they try to break it. He sees coils of bowel that extrude from anuses when men's wastes form a second frozen bridge – and Stabbed-in-the-Back takes on a new Slavic and terrible meaning, when partisans fall on their fellow creatures in that frightful position.

And he sees – I saw – Pawel fall.

My friend from All Souls, with the last of his Cossacks, by their own

582

hands, before Stalin's, and I saw Pawel's lips move, to form words – but must only have been animal grimaces, in extremis . . .

And then, blocked by a machine-gun nest above a frozen river, I saw Fafner, the very heart of the Beast, somehow, incredibly, gathering its brute strength for one last flail of its muscle armour to break out of the rat-trap.

Yes: I was There. I saw the columns of the Black Order forming, as they had when I made my pact with the devil that night of searchlights in the city on the red-and-black map: Hans Sachs' Nuremberg.

Honour your Volsung Masters . . .

As twelve abreast, they form up, in their best – their last – uniforms, His Black Order Legion that bears His name on their Death's Heads and Lightning Bars. Twelve abreast, His Knights, jet black, without great coats in the white snow. A Million then; now, His finest mere Six-hundred, marching by me, in their butcher-stepping boots, waist-high and gleaming, and their drummers in front, six of them, drumming, the beat of Rienzi, Tribune of Rome.

And the Partisans falling back! Terror-struck, their guts to water at this sighting of the last true Dragon of Europe, marching in its Order, singing His name as it goes about its dying. Down goes the first rank! – but three drummers are spared, the beat becomes Lohengrin's *– and still It keeps marching! Down, the second rank, the third – but the Mandala is high, they are over the river! Half the ranks gone.* Siegfried! *Only Three-hundred, but His name on their lips, & still they go forward. Upward – almost at the ridge! The Partisans are breaking, running, from the dragon. Only Two-hundred Knights left marching – for a fallen* Parsifal, *the name We give Him, the drum-beat His Drummer – yes, only One, now plays Him: the sound of my grail, a beating heart – as now the Bear's tanks roll over the crest across the river, their proletarian barrels turn, humming . . . but still His Parsifal-One-Hundred are marching, & the Flag is still high, though frightfully blooded, & the Drum is still beating – though muffled – the boots are still stepping, the Lightning still gleaming and flashing for Donner & Thor. Now Fifty: five ranks only – but still with the Drummer, & His colours flow forward over the snow: beat Black for Death, our Liberator; Red for the new faceless brute fording the river . . . the Last Knight falls – it was the drummer: unarmed, but still clutching at the End, beside the drumhead, His mandala; the flag We thought was only Silly Marietta.*

583

And then –?

I fled Russia, without Tosh, without Pawel, with only my idiot's Bundle; brute Bear knew the Fool would be back.

Third Movement
Tenth Passage

The North Wind doth blow, and We shall have Snow,
And what will the Dormouse do then, poor Thing?
Rolled up like a Ball, in his Nest snug and small,
He'll sleep till warm weather comes back, poor Thing!

... *In Spandau.* Old 61 – adding up to 7, for the young Fool's miraculous escape from the rat-trap ice of Winter's Russia. The 1st escape. The 2nd seemed more of a miracle when it happened, I assure you, children! After 40 years wandering the gulag, it takes the faith of Jesus to believe that the gate of hell has opened – really-truly, Eddie! – and these nice Cheka men are putting you in this comfy motor car for a lovely ride through Chekhov's country, and when you wake up you'll be all better, you'll see ...

The Nice Men who once extracted Drugged Eddie's nails – that our boy always took such pride in, neatly clipping (so as not to pinch Ettie in their Delicate Moments).

> *First drink, Hero, from my Horn;*
> *I spiced well the Draught for You*
> *To waken clearly your Memory*
> *So that the Past shall not slip your Mind!*

As though it could, ever. Unlike Hagen, the Red bastards did their nail-pulling not to annoy – Eddie being of the Masochist Persuasion, they know it pleases. I deserved my future torturers. I left Tosh to their forerunners' mercy.

. . . At Love Cottage:
"But darling, you didn't. You tried everything."

Says Sister, bringing Brother hot buttered brandy & lemon, in front of her hermit's fire, for Xmas.

"I didn't try hard enough, Ettie. I should never have left her. I ought to have taken her with me when I went looking for Pawel. Oh Christ, what those butchers will have done – "

"Stop it, Eddie. Stop it now. We can't change our pattern. We can only go on as part of Nature and love what's left all the more. As I do. You'll be astonished – Sister has two tame deer that know their names, and four squirrels, and a thief of a magpie – you'll meet them all tomorrow. Now, drink up."

St Frances of the Untersberg. The New Ettie, filled to the brim with Love. No light cotton hand-me-downs of Eva's for this visit; for the mountain winter, Sister was all soft-&-cuddly in angora woollies, and sheepskin booties, and her own skin was its pure pink-&-white perfection, and her hair its richest gold.

"Not a drop of peroxide, and I'm almost as ancient as Mama when she left us – isn't that incredible?"

"You look straight out of heaven, after Russia – Ettie, come to Porquerolles with me? Just for a week, anything to get away from ghastly snow. Please."

"I can't darling. You know I have to be here in case Wolf needs me – He's suffered even more from winter and Russia – but you must both learn to love snow, as I do. And icy mornings, because they make it all the more wonderful to have the stove, and hot drinks, and the trees, all covered in their quilts, and little birds feeding from the houses I've made them. And in the evenings, marvellously clever books – people have said things one never imagined. Eddie, the Pot's such a waste."

"But Wolf never comes here." Brother attempts to stick to the main bone of contention. "You haven't seen Him since September. Ettie, come out of this damned country and go somewhere it's safe."

"Darling idiot, you just said Porquerolles – which could be a battle at any minute like Sicily. What could possibly be safer than here on my mountain? There's some other reason. Eddie, you're hiding a secret."

"Only that the war could go badly. If the Russians invaded – "

"They wouldn't stand an earthly. This isn't peasant Ukraine with everyone revolting. Besides, Kiev's a thousand miles. And if you truly haven't got a secret, it's because you're utterly bushed, come to bed."

So they undressed by the fire in their Hunding's bedroom, and stroked each other's bodies, that was like loving themselves, with their fingers tracing out the delicate places – their only difference: her's is still smooth-shaven.

"And Miss Pussy's lips are a little fuller, Ettie," he whispers, "sort of wider and softer."

"Do you mind, Eddie?"

"Oh God no, she's even more gorgeous and luscious."

"Darling I'm so glad. She was a little frightened you wouldn't – " as they slip to the floor, with the flickering fire – "precious pet brother, Sister *does* have a little secret – " as he slips inside her, in and in – "Eddie, that's so lovely . . . are you listening? Yes more, darling, more – oh God, oh please! . . . oh my best-ever-lover your Ettie's going to have a baby."

"You?" flopping off her. "Us?" staring at the mute nether lips smiling for him, wide and dreamy as her others. He lay and stared blankly at the ceiling. The enormity in wartime. The time lost from searching.

"Another abortion? I don't know a gypsy in bloody Bavaria."

"Silly old Eddie, I mean *have* it. How could one possibly kill Baby now we know all about Love?" Her fingers tracing again, my forehead, my ears, my eyes, "And naughty Thingee, and Ballees – because of course it's going to be a boy. I wonder how much he will look like us?"

"How much?" Sitting up. Head in hands despairing. "It'll look *completely*, woman! Now the whole effing world – "

"Darling, don't be so histrionic, you have to be loving when Sister's in her Condition. Besides, it's heads or tails he'll be dark."

"Rubbish. Mama's side are all blonde – and Papa was, even if his wasn't. Ettie, what on earth does it matter about our hair colour – they come out two-headed! Or at best idiots – I'll have to find you an abortion and you'll have to do it. Oh Christly blast bugger and damn."

Getting up and storming to the window. Across the valley, no light shines on Alberich's Salt Mountain because of the bombers.

"Eddie, you'll freeze it off by the window, and I want you again, snuggly inside me. Come back –" reaching with her new all-loving self – "they hardly ever have idiots, really – the Church just says that, I've been reading – and it isn't nearly certain about the blonde. It all depends which one of you got there first, and as far as eyes, His are blue too."

"A Wolf-child?"

Was that a flash, across the valley?

"Who knows?" Her little-girl giggle. "That's the delicious part. Although, if we're speaking frankly, I'd be surprised – "

"Oh please. Do be frank."

"You don't have to get all snotty. At Wolf's age, and being so tense, with all the drugs the quacks feed Him, it isn't conducive, and you were closer to my time of the month. It's all rather complicated."

"Surely not."

"If you're going to be snide and beastly, I'm sorry I told you. It's bad for Baby – they know. That's why it's so important they feel us being loving. Come back inside me."

"You're mad!" This time her screaming brother really means it! "You've always been. But I'll bet you haven't told *Him* he's going to be a proud Papa."

"How could I when He hasn't been for a visit since? I was happy to leave it as a surprise, but as my own brother's been so horrid, you can do it."

And the peculiar thing was, children, that the Mad Woman of the Untersberg had never looked more normal. Radiant, even, despite her present crossness which she tried to hide because it spoiled the Being Loving.

"You expect *me* to tell Him?"

"It would be kind. I can hardly use my old peasant."

"Any particular time or place? Announcing in *The Times* might be a little dodgy."

"Sarcasm's un-loving; Baby can hear, too – but there's no hurry. The next time Wolf sends the broomstick and you meet, just say it. He'll be delighted. What could be more wonderful? – The Cow obviously can't have one with the wrong-shaped Miss P – if you'd learned an ounce of psychology from crazy old Jung you'd realise the logical thing is that Wolf will want to make peace right away."

"Logical – if it's blonde-and-blue Eddie's baby!"

"Really, you're going to make me quite cross and ruin everything. For God's sake – He'll *expect* it to look like *me*. I look like *you*."

The old Ettie, for a moment.

"So either way he'll never know?"

Yet Eddie could swear that was a flash, across His valley . . .

"My brilliant brother. Talk about blue – poor Thingee's dying. Now come back to the fire and we'll make him all warm."

. . . *At the Strategic Institute:* But not Berlin. The Pendulists have moved camp to the retreat at Fuhlsbüttel (it's proximity to Ravensbrück providing a safe umbrella. The Allies should Risk Innocent Lives?). No sooner is Edwin inside the building than he hears the welcome whine of a dental drill. It comes through a door on this side of the Astrology parlour, marked: **Der Zahnarzt**.

Bormann was in the chair, and from the swollen twist to his Toad face, suffering even more than Yours-Truly – so that was a 1st gratification – except that his glazed lack of comprehension means it isn't real-Bormann, only another Doppelgänger from the Acting Studio, 2 doors down. The Zahnarzt, a middle-aged man with spotless white coat and kindly face, briskly turfs the mock-Toad out so that Eddie can sit.

"My dear Sir, that's a nasty impaction. Be brave for one more moment while I get the anaesthetic. Fortunately we still have a supply, but naturally we don't squander it on riff-raff."

"Ank-oo," mumbled our Hero, "ver'kin'."

"Relief of pain, old fellow, that's what we're here for . . . and just a quick pin-prick – good! Now, you sit quietly for five minutes while that takes effect and I just pull my temporary off this Polish swine. Don't worry, he doesn't understand a word we're saying."

Although the poor sod pretends to writhe in agony as the infernal device is yanked out. Eddie positively blanched, and closed his eyes.

"Secretary Bormann's impression is somewhat wider than the double's," the kindly Zahnarzt explains, to fill the time, "so I have had to squeeze the fit, but for only a pair of window crowns, simple enough – although I don't suppose you share my professional interest at this moment, poor Herr von Perceval." The Pole moaned. The Zahnarzt prodded some mechanical horror back in the wretch's mouth, before continuing his exposition. "The Fuehrer's requirements however were a true artistic challenge – his advanced paradentosis requiring major extractions, upper and lower, from the substitute, you understand, before the replacements? For the first fitting I wasted novocaine although the individual concerned was a Jew. And how any of them can complain when they're getting gold work in wartime is beyond me. Now, my dear Herr von Perceval, let's make you well. If one may say, I'm a worshipper of your sister."

The unfortunate Pole staggered away looking every inch a Toad, and so twice cursed. Eddie got better, with heavenly swiftness.

" 'At's 'underfu."

"Don't try and speak, there's a good fellow. Rest the jaw overnight – I'll give you pills for sleep, and drop in to see me before you leave in the morning."

The Phlegmatist:

Edwin leaves the kindly Zahnarzt's office, to find further comfort, though it, too, is disguised. A monstrous apparition filled the hall; fatter even than Giant Hermann, with a thyroid swollen face and piggy little eyes, almost hidden; and purple lips; and bloated hands, mottled and pinpricked with white scars, yet – as it extended the right for introduction – the apparition moved with silent swiftness on small feet.

"Edwin, if I may call you so informally – Felix Kersten."

The Swedish absentee-host of the unfortunates at Fuhlsbüttel. A "Doctor of Manipulative Therapy" by label, in the kingdom of quacks. Also, children, quondam dish-washer, and film "extra" for some of The Riefenstahl's lesser productions. The Chicken Farmer swears by him.

" 'Ow'doo'doo." Mouths Edwin, resenting such 1st-name familiarity.

"I see you've been suffering. Yes, there is excessive tension in the neck. Allow me." Kersten's voice was gentle, yet somehow menacing. His hands were repulsive, his body odour not fully masked by expensive cologne. He performed magic.

"I can't believe it's so much better," Eddie marvels. "Do I pay you a fee?"

"Only my regards to the Herr Reichsführer Himmler, when next you see him. And please have dinner with me tonight."

"I'm not sure I could eat. The whole right side's numb."

"My chef will allow for that. Your bedroom is on the second floor. Rest now, Edwin, and join me at eight."

The second floor was uninvaded by any of the inmates allowed to wander below. The Repaired Fool found a coal fire glowing, a private bath, with hot water, steaming; pleasant view over snowy fields & spinneys to a wood. Like any other half-decent country house. *Except for the smell when a Guest opens his window.* Sweetish, musky, a mixture of tanning and peat. It came on a light breeze from beyond the dark wood.

It came from Mama's cupola in Venice. It came from burning death. The Guest closed the window.

I smelt nothing . . .

. . . En route to dine, Eddie meets peg-leg Kapitän von Maser of Phrenology, stumping briskly.

"My dear boy! Delighted to see you safe from your Russian adventures! We have some remarkable findings on your Kiev material, but you're a day early."

"I wanted to allow time for travel. I'm spending the evening with our host."

"A man of mystery." The Captain cranked his head down from his immense height, lowering his voice as he went. "A word of warning – by character assessment Felix Kersten can only be assessed a Phlegmatic, with a Sanguine touch – and we know what that means." And now, straightening, regaining volume, "Enjoy your dinner, my boy. I look forward eagerly to our joint discoveries tomorrow."

And away he hobbled, with his 4 Stripes & Medals, for a conference on Grand Strategy through Dowsing Confirmation.

(This is the meaning of Total War, children.)

Supper with Felix Kersten deals with ending it. The Swede comes straight to the point.

"I know you were closely involved with the Lloyd-George peace negotiations before Barbarossa. It seems to some highly-placed author-

591

ities in the Reich, who do not wish to be directly involved as yet, that these should be re-activated. Would you be willing, Edwin?"

"Well, ah, you couldn't actually call them negotiations." *He* would call them bloody High Treason. "One did write the odd letter. What do these authorities have in mind, Mr Kersten?"

"For the time being only the relaying of this information to interested parties that you visit in Zürich."

The Phlegmatic Humour implies sluggishness. Kersten, with his buried little eyes was as sluggish as an anaconda waiting for lunch.

"That's all? Just tell? Or rather –" the Fool blusters – "what do you mean about Zürich? I only go there for my sister's business affairs."

"So I understood from the late Heydrich. Don't worry, Edwin, I too have investments. If business is to continue as usual afterwards, the role of go-between is vital in all wars."

The gross Swede had dropped the casual air with the mention of money. His face was more purple than ever as he reached for my arm across the table – the Sanguine Touch getting the better of him. (Eddie having that effect on Certain Men.)

"I'll mention it to Zürich. Can I say what authorities?"

"One with agricultural interests."

"Christ! Himmler knows about me visiting – "

"Calm yourself, Edwin. We would hardly be meeting here if the Reichsfuehrer did not wish it. The jaw is troubling; I think you should retire – and allow me to apply massage again. It will bring on sleep without medication."

But not without dreams. The black obsidian beach, the dancing fire, no horse: I was walking, and no beckoning Stranger, only writhing shadow shapes, all with the face of the Pole who was Bormann, and a smell – but that was no dream.

The night wind has shifted. In the morning the whole house is filled with the sweetish odour, until an orderly from the Zahnarzt's goes around spraying dental disinfectant, which makes it worse. At the Pendulists' meeting, however, only the Fool seems to notice. The Experts are occupied with more important matters, fine-tuning their equipment.

Eddie's precious Bundle from Kiev is open and spread out on a table. A tripod of telescopic bamboo sections with brass ferules extending to a height of 5 feet, being already set up over the parchments. A small gold plumb-bob hangs on a fine-tooled sterling silver chain.

"Purity of the metals is mandatory," the leading Pendulist declares, adjusting.

"But what does it tell you?" begs Fool.

"Patience, mein Herr, the calibration cannot be rushed."

"I thought you'd already done all that."

"My dear boy, one must allow daily for the earth's precession."

Von Maser's humouring of Ignorance brings knowing smiles around the table. The plumb-bob shifts a millimetre to the right. A ceiling fan is shut off as extra insurance.

The bob hangs stationary; a third of the way down the place-names column of the 2nd parchment. Fool leans forward.

"One moment, my boy." Von Maser held him back. "To kill two birds with one stone, for our psychical division – which name, please? From your head."

"It has to be one from the Quincunx . . . Dietrichstein. At Graz."

A long sigh. Then a small round of applause, led by the Director.

"Yes, dear Colleagues, it is truly gratifying to have secondary confirmation – "

"Primary, Kapitän von Maser!" This jab from the Psychical Division, a waspish individual. "We have said before, there is no rigour to the metals' theory."

"Gentlemen, please, surely as experts and equals, we can agree to differ. In any event this site is not the primary information we have obtained."

"It isn't?" from Eddie. "What is?"

"The most important page is missing."

"Shit!" It was not scientific, it should not have escaped. I regret it. "But bloody hell," cries the Fool, "after all that horrendous effort."

And Tosh. And Pawel. I had to turn away from the quacks.

"Dear boy, all is not black. The good news shall be that what you brought to us is only a copy. And the best news – the original exists! We have located it in the Vatican Library."

Enough to make a man a Christian. Almost –

"A slight problem, dear boy."

"Why on earth should Rome object?"

"The problem, mein Herr," snipped the Wasp psychic, "is that Rome does not know it owns the document. Nor does my Division show such a thing. We have only the half-baked work of these Metals' believers."

A general outcry from the expert affronted. Incredulous beyond rage, the Fool says, "You mean you only *think* it's in the Vatican – just from your bloody pendulums?"

"Herr von Perceval, this was a massive effort. All instruments! Even withdrawn from the North Atlantic ...!"

Edwin walked out on the quacks.

"Have faith, dear boy," confirmed Von Maser as the Riley started. "Overtures are being made. The page is there. We shall find it."

Or what's a grail for?

... To Camargue: But at Li Santo the Hooligans have found nothing in Leader-Eddie's absence – not helped by a collapse of part of the east wall of the transept where Ettie had sung.

"The shoring gave way," from a thoroughly browned-off Black Order. "These gypsy dogs can't be trusted an inch – not even when it's their own useless hides. We lost a dozen at once, and as many again have been on half shift ever since. Damned malingerers, the lot of them, and labour's getting tighter every day. They can thank their stars I'm not a superstitious man or I'd have shot that old Gitano bastard King of theirs for his curse. At least there's some justice in heaven – the wall got the old shitbag first. They'll be having a new coronation any day."

The Expedition Leader broke the rule about Not Looking. I went to the place allotted as the Hooligans' sleeping quarters; an assemblage of rush huts, and worn-out fishing-smack sails, and a handful of roulotte wagons, stripped of paint and anything burnable. My Provence sun shone, but the mistral was blowing, cold from the north with dust that stung the eyes so that Edwin was weeping before he found Sevastyani. The old man was propped up against a saddle in one of the roulottes. Once brown-skinned, black-haired, a King in his prime, now he was sallow, grey, bent in the middle like a sailor's hammock, his barrel chest was crushed.

"Sevastyani, I'll see you get a doctor, a proper place."

"No need, young lord, this is my place." His voice was hollow as marsh reeds in autumn when the pith leaves them.

594

"But medicine, Sevastyani, you must let me do something."

As though the Fool has not caused everything.

"Do not blame yourself, young lord. God in the stars orders our leaving." Pausing, for more of the desperate hollow breathing. "Does your sister still sing for His favour?"

For some idiot's reason, I felt impelled to tell him the end of our equation.

"She's going to have a baby, Sevastyani. This time really. Perhaps she'll sing again afterwards."

"Perhaps, young lord." Weaker and weaker, as though he had only been waiting. "Any child can change destiny."

"I believe that, too, Majesty."

"When she sings, young lord . . . ask her for one song for Sevastyani."

"I shall, Majesty."

"And one for yourselves," though now the Fool can scarcely hear him, "one for young lord, and lady . . . and one, Camargue horse . . . and one, Gitano . . . and one, all of us . . . Lost world . . . Europe. . . ."

Exit Sevastyani, perhaps of Atlantis; & Tosh, translator of the babble of Europe; & the Gerbers, hoteliers who minded other people's business and so lost their own; & Pawel, my Cossack friend who also loved horses; Nibelungs all.

And then Avignon, with 5 more deaths on his conscience: five brown shadows 1000 years old. The Quincunx yews stand on their gravel islands and weep sharp needles, dry as slivers of bone onto my head as Edwin walks by below the ground – trying not to see the Abbot standing at his door, watching men dig for nothing under a blazing sun.

And then, Eddie standing down in the trench with sweat pouring off him, working as hard as he demanded from any of them (if not for quite as long, and on Swiss rations – but then he *was* the bloody Expedition Leader!) which was the understanding he reached with himself in that hell-hole in the ground:

"Finding the Grail is nothing to be ashamed of, Father." Defying the power of that heron-figure standing over me, in silence. "Even if men have died for it. I risk my own life with them, and look at the tens of thousands who died on the Crusades which your church made saints of. My search may be the only enduring thing to come out of this whole damned war. Which I certainly had nothing to do with starting, but if it allows the means to *look* – why isn't that God's Will?"

"God does not show himself as a skull on a helmet, my son."

"Then how do you explain, Father – I've seen churches where He showed Himself as thirty thousand corpses of Black Death?"

"And did you find Him there, my son?"

The Grail Leader has more important things to do than argue standing on the yew trees' heads of pins. Logistics & Manpower are overriding problems here too.

"The French are rotten workers, mein Herr, we've always known that. In-breeding – but Vichy's scraped the barrel for this lot; they've given us half a madhouse."

A line shuffles by, some hang-dog, staring at the ground. Some head-in-air, skulls vacant already for a new owner – one moron in particular, there, in the middle, smiling his idiot head off as ever.

"Deaf'n'Dumber!"

That is a chosen Vessel of our Lord, Edwin.

"The Frog bastard looks moon-struck, mein Herr – but half of them are acting. Don't you worry, we have a dog he'll hear when it barks."

But this time Edwin acted. Dear Christ! don't tell me you didn't expect it?! Not save Ettie-&-Eddie's childhood companion? What do you think I've come to?

Brother went straight to his Abbot. "Will you look after the man for me, Father? Some light duties? Perhaps if you have vehicles, he used to be a sailor, on a steam launch called the *Cormoran*."

"I shall do what I can for him, my son – but should he not stay with a shovel and become a saint?"

... *Next Station:* The White Lady at Třeboň: yet another black funeral, the old Countess Vok-Rosenberg's (who died of being 100, so don't blame *that* on the boy).

The night after her burial. Edwin lies in his room in her castle, legally Michael Rau's, lost on the other side of Atlantis. The winning side – even this fool can't block that reality. How much longer? It doesn't need an Allied victory – just mutual exhaustion, like last time: with Peace of any sort would come collapse, the death of all my hopes. Do I go on, racing the Clock at all 4 locations? Or trusting in the Pendulists' madness and the purity of metals, plunge the whole damned lot on Graz? One huge concentrated effort, as Schliemann did for ...

Awake!

Screaming. The nightmare is still with me. *A woman in a virgin's gown, blue with a red lining, advancing to my bed. She wears a hood, the moon is shining, but her face is hidden. Eddie shouts,* Out! Get back! *– It's Tosh under the hood, I shall know that laugh anywhere.*

"*Da. We do it with gloves on, now, Monsieur-Gospodin-Eddie. So much passionnant, the Huss-cock ride with les gants. The boy wears these white rubber ones, les blanches, pour délivrer bébés – and leaving your Tosh in the red snow, nyet? And she shall wear these ones – see Monsieur-Eddie, les noirs, the black silk, like a horse's Thingee, like the ones you saw buried at Babyn Yar.*"

I didn't! I saw nothing, you bitch! NOTHING! RIEN!

But she had left. And the blue on her robe was not the Virgin's. It was the blue of the shadow of an old Jewess-Witch, burnt at the stake. The first of her race.

... At Fuhlsbüttel: The Pendulists agree with the Grail Leader's sudden decision to abandon Třeboň – flattered by his request for their expert opinion. Material is transferred to Graz. Discussions for the missing page of the Salt List are continuing with Rome. All at the Institute feel a new wave of optimism – from the published forecast of the Swedish Sensitive, one Gruenberg, in the Norwegian yellow press: Defeats, Struggle, but (although postponed to the '48 Season) Final Victory!

"The only trouble with this prediction, Edwin," said that Phlegmatic fellow Swede, the gross Kersten, on a quick Roundabout meeting in Munich, "that which makes it less than totally convincing, is that Goebbels had it planted." The Dwarf, still very much up to his old tricks. Felix Kersten, with a hand on Eddie's arm, turned Sanguine. "It is, of course somewhat amusing, Edwin, to know that Frau Magda is carrying the forecast in her purse, as an omen. You may tell Zürich that we have a second interested party, by the way. One who soars above the earth."

Also with Swedish connections; a fitting description for our Blimp-Giant, Hermann.

"You mean the Reichsmarschall's changing horses again?"

"Testing the track. Edwin, these tendons to the carpus feel tense,

597

allow me to give you a body massage before you continue driving."

Politely refused, my dears: we don't want another bloody Darling episode. Instead, Eddie got Eva at the Carlton, looking every inch an Honourable, in her Parisienne haute couture (mainly robin's-egg shot-silk, cut on the bias over the hip, with a muff of silver fox) but underneath, the same little bundle of bourgeois worries.

"Herr Eddie, I just never see Him. Oh, I have the whole Berghof – do you know, the Staff call me 'Chefin', now? Yes! Even Bormann, although he doesn't mean it; he knows I'll never be the Chief's proper wife. You can't make a Silk Purse, as they say . . . I hate Bormann. Even when the Fuehrer can be with me – and *He* calls me His Tschapperl almost all the time, except when the Russians are being too unbearable – but even then the horrible Secretary is there, calling me Mutterschaff and controlling every penny. I can't stand his coarseness and sarcasm."

"I loathe Bormann too – Ettie and I call the bugger the Toad."

"This is so right, Herr Eddie!" The Chefin's giggle brings whispers from gossipy Müncheners in the tearoom. "A horrible squat Toad-bugger, this is what he shall be from now on. You know in his letters to his 'Mummy Girl', Gerda, he calls himself 'Daddy Darling'! Oh Herr Eddie it's such fun to be with you. Just like the old days. Instead of here at the dull Carlton, come and have tea with me and the Doggies at our little Braunhaus."

"Do you think that would be wise, Eva? Now that you're Tschapperl?"

This grain of common sense because Black Stasi & Negus have suddenly appeared to guard Mistress's honour; more effectively than last time, with their leads twined round her so-attractive legs under the table.

"Herr Eddie, now we are both mature – and the only reason I come to Munich with the Doggies is that we all get so homesick for our own little house." Her bright face clouds. "It won't be good tea, I'm afraid. We can't get your English any more."

"That's all right. I always carry some with me in the car."

Once burnt, twice as foolish, being Friend's motto, barking & laughing, off all four drive across the Isar. Eva's district is still spared bomb damage. At the little Braunhaus the shrubbery has completely hidden the air-raid shelter – so ahead of its time.

"Now everyone has them," the Mature-Eva muses. "Whoever would have thought the world could be so silly over the Poles? At the Berghof the Toad-bugger has men digging escapes all the way down to the mines. Doggies, you stay out and play in the garden while Herr Eddie and Mutti have their tea."

Like last time, Doggies. Inside the little house not a thing seems changed. Sister-Gretl, away at war-work; the muslin curtains – that hid His face at the awful moment; the Fernsehapparat, with its blank Cyclops eye – that once transmitted it; His paintings, with the detailed heads on the tiny people: a doll's house, frozen in time – no: one so-familiar item is still missing.

"Our red divan, you still remember Herr Eddie?" Shall we ever forget? Mature-Eva has another little giggle and drops her silver fox muff on a velour replacement. "He keeps it at the Prinzregentstrasse to remind Him of what He did to the Old Chamberlain. Now I must powder my nose. Put in the tea when the water boils – One-for-each, and One-for-the-pot, as they say . . ."

Eddie-&-Eva, Darby-&-Joan, Trouble-&-Strife, what the world calls Domestic Bliss. Edwin spoons out the leaves, One-for-each, & – these triangular thoughts turn inevitably to Sister, next on the visiting list. And the growing image swelling in her belly. She simply cannot stay up there and have it squatting in the wilderness.

"And how is your so dear sister? We never hear a word these days of Fräulein Edwina." Psychic-Eva, nose-powdered, has taken off her suit jacket to reveal her breasts – through what her Friend could swear is the same translucent chiffon blouse. "Wherever are you hiding her, Herr Eddie? The Toad-bugger says she has become a nun – is this true?"

"Not exactly. More a hermit. Ettie's taken up nature in her old age. She's staying at a little place we have in Switzerland."

"How much one admires her," as the Mature-Eva sits, beside her mature Friend visiting, on the velour replacement, "and how kind she always has been," as a breast, reaching to pour, brushes. "When you see her, give my special love," and fingers touch, passing teacups, "and His also, it goes without saying," sipping wistfully, leaning against His Ederl's mature shoulder, "English tea is so delicious. And how I agree about Mother Nature, when I look at what she does for us in our mountains," with our thighs pressing, and skirt rising – and our Eddie's

mature-Thingee! – "I plan little hikes and expeditions we could take –
the Doggies, and me, and our Fuehrer," with our teacups down, &
knickers, "of course He says He can't any more, although He used to
always," as her hand slips – and stays, guiding lightly, maturely, "but
often I see Him looking so wistfully through the binoculars at the
opposite – Herr Eddie, we shouldn't!" – but we do, and this time the
Doggies *are* good, and Mistress is better: even more boyish-deliciously
tight in maturity than Friend remembers – but like damned women of
any age, totally one-track minded! – "I peek too, through the glasses,"
before Edwin has even stopped gasping, let along begun thinking of
what she's prattling, "and there is this so-adorable tiny little cottage,"
the Chefin's mature hand tries to hang on to her falling pleasure, "with
sometimes smoke, so someone lives there, only it's too far to see them,
across the valley," trying vainly to stuff aging pleasure back inside her,
"do you think, Herr Eddie, I should ask the Toad-bugger to buy it as my
present for the Fuehrer?"

"Good God no!" finally grasping, "I mean, Eva, if Bormann did, you
and Wolf would never have a minute's privacy."

"How right this is. Oh Herr Eddie, you're always so clever, and don't
you agree getting mature is better?"

"Yes, it was lovely."

"Because we are true friends. I think perhaps you are my only real
friend ever, Herr Eddie."

"That's terribly flattering, but surely not?"

"Yes. It's a fact. And your hair is so gold – will *you* buy it for me?"

The FAIR sex? Don't tell me! The deceit of Woman! The Cow has
known where she was heading from the bloody beginning at the Carlton.

"I could look," croaked Friend eventually, "but what about money?"

"It couldn't cost so much, a little cottage, and I have been saving up
my dress allowance."

"These legal things take time. It needs lawyers."

"Oh, thank you, thank you, Herr Eddie. What we're now doing shall
make our Fuehrer so happy!"

And to celebrate our 3-way union ... the sirens go off – and Eva
rushes out half-naked to grab bloody black Stasi & Negus, and then
bombs begin falling (in Cameron's first deliberate daylight raid across
the Isar, but for once Edwin actually thanked the bent-pricked bastard –

600

for taking her mind off it!), and then all the good doggies troop down to the shelter His foresight of Genius had provided for them.

... *Zürich:* The blank Swiss in the House of Treason receives the Kersten news about the Peace Feelers without the slightest interest. All the chocolate sod wants is Ettie!

"London is not satisfied with 'Rural Bavaria' as a location. They wish specifics."

"But I've told you, these overtures come right from the top, Himmler and Goering. It doesn't make sense – no, I'll go further – this personal vendetta of Cameron's is madness. It so happens that my sister is with child – and that's why her whereabouts are secret, but if the Scotch bastard wants reports on her personal life, I'll make it bloody personal. I'm going to send a letter about this peace business, and yours and Cameron's blocking of it, and I'm going to do that tonight, directly to Churchill."

Which *we* know is a so-little white lie of Eddie's, because the absolute last thing our Fool wants now is Peace, at any price, but the Swiss, lacking our imagination, children, finds the act convincing.

"Now we have a reason for your objections, Herr Perceval, I am sure London would be satisfied with a general indication. Is she in the northern or southern half of the country?"

"North, naturally, to be near Bayreuth."

"In her 'secret condition'?" Sharp enough to cut himself.

"The village is completely isolated. They think she's a war widow from the Eastern Front."

"And who is the father? When is the child to be born?"

"That's none of your damned business."

"We shall see. Good day, Herr Perceval."

"Go to hell."

... *At Love Cottage:* "Why in God's name couldn't you have just gone on singing?" Brother demands of her. "Or looked after orphans, if you *had* to do something with children?"

"Don't shout. Baby has complete ears – put your hand here and feel him moving."

"I want nothing to do with it. Ettie, I beg you again, come with me to Triebschen."

"You know I can't darling. What did Wolf say when you told Him?"

"I haven't seen Him." Expecting an outburst, but she said mildly,

"Good. Actually I've changed my mind. It'll be better if He sees it after – He gets so excited about little things, He'd only want me to move, or bring up a mobile hospital – or send the Cow to visit. These days I look rather a cow myself."

"You certainly don't. You've never looked better –" taking her hands, on his knees, imploring, "be reasonable, Ettie, you can't stay here to have it. How can we possibly get a doctor?"

"Silly old Eddie – Nature doesn't use a doctor. When fawns arrive it just happens, all beautiful in the bracken, and dappled. But Sister isn't completely addled, my dear; a crone from the village does midwifing; she'll come and stay when it's time."

"And when *is* time?"

"That's a little vague, pet, but sort of Mayish June."

"And what if the midwife sort of isn't here?"

"Then I'll have to find some bracken and muddle through. Oh, Eddie, don't be such a worry or I won't let you visit. Baby has to be tranquil. It's been marvellous through the winter; days and days with absolute silence. Eddie, come to bed."

Where Baby-makes-3. Little Mother lay back, and peeled off her nightie to reveal a mountain.

"How can we possibly, when you're like that?"

"Big Sis will show blind Mr Thingee his way."

Which worked out rather well, all thingees considered – with a certain excitement at the thought of a 3rd party lying so close to our lust. Indeed, feeling its small life move at the tip of him, Edwin quivered in a brand new way – until the After, when the guilt was worse than ever.

"There's no earthly need, Eddie. It was lovely. I told you it would be."

"It wasn't our making love. I was remembering a nightmare."

"Tell me," she said. "You know it helps to talk them out."

"Mathilde always said dreams come true if you tell them."

"And Mama said by opposites. Go on, Eddie, what was it?"

"You were both being injured – quite horribly. Please, I don't want to even remember."

"Darling brother, you see, you do care about Baby. Can you try and be here when I have him?"

With a big-Sisterly kiss for Mr Thingee, to bribe the simple-minded.

"Of course I'll try, but I can't take off a month. Couldn't you be more precise about the date?"

"Not really – and Eddie darling, I'm not starting a row, but now I've given up singing, don't *you* think it's time to be honest finally about your mad old Potting?"

Another outbreak of New Maturity – between licks of old Eddie – and she meant it, children! Lying there, naked and distended with her bi-fathered bastard, which might still be 2-headed from incest, in a shack in the woods, talking only to squirrels – and yet the Grail search, backed by all the scientific and logistic genius of the Teuton people, *that* was madness.

"I won't begin to argue seriously with you, Ettie, but I've a list that makes it all but certain – and the Vatican's about to provide final confirmation; I've got manpower Schliemann never dreamt of – and there *was* a Troy. There will be a Grail. What more can I say to convince you?"

"But you haven't actually found anything, have you?"

An extra-special big lick. The bitch was *still* pretending to be loving!

"You don't *listen*, Ettie. This Salt Tax list is proof positive."

"But it isn't really, is it, darling? Eddie precious, you're not being grown-up."

At which Edwin, full 3-and-30, lost his temper, and immaturely drew to her attention the logical inadequacies of the female's gnatlike mind.

"For the last time, Ettie, the Grail legend is myth; but the foundation of all myth is *real* – and if you can't even grasp that trifling distinction I simply give up."

"If you're quite finished – and I'm not going to get cross, because of Baby – at your age, since you can't be married like a proper man, or have any actual relationship with a woman because you're so threatened, and so deathly afraid of letting yourself be properly queer that you can't have a best male friend either, perhaps you need your tin-pot for –"

"*How dare you?* And you call this being *loving*? As for my age – women of yours die in childbirth. I don't give a damn if you lie here and *burst!*"

And stormed down the mountain; & halfway, got a flat; & got out, &

603

kicked, & cursed, & screamed aloud to heaven; and then squatting beside the Riley, saw the tombs, freshly emerged from the retreating snow, with their icicles of salt; and remembered Eva baaing on about Daddy Darling digging shelters all the way down to the mines; and thinking, Charlemagne! – buried under the mountain, which he isn't, because he's at Aix la Chapelle –

But Something Is!!!

Third Movement

Eleventh Passage

[for full chorus]

TO ROME!

At the high celebration of God's Grace
Humbly shall I expiate my Guilt;
Blessed be he who is Steadfast in his Faith:
Through repentance shall his Redemption come.

Though not with Minstrels & Glad Cries does Eddie Tannhäuser make his Pilgrimage to the Eternal City, but squeezed in the rearmost bucket-seat of a lurching Heinkel troop-carrier ferrying Black Order parachutists for the Last Ditch. May's weather over the Alps is appalling. When the stinking Heinkel lands even the most battle-forged Death's Head would have gone on his knees to kiss the ground had the drill-book allowed. Instead, Eddie's flight-companions are marched off, green as goose-shit about the gills, but briskly-stepping. A 3-wheeled grey Fiat, the size and shape of a clockwork mouse, arrives in lieu.

"Signor Cassoni-Percevale?"

"Si, Edwin Casson-Perceval."

"Aspetta per una machina?"

"Si, aspetto per una machina."

"You are wishing to speak Inglese?"

"Rather. Or French or German. I'm afraid I never got past the guidebook in Italian."

"Inglese, perfecto for me, having been spend two winters in your country. Please to accompany my own self, Signor Cassoni-Percevale."

The odd side of this conversation is a tiny grey friar of some obscure Oblate order. The Fiat has only a single seat, centred, in front, so that the mouse-car's driver can be blinded by a flapping Vatican standard. Edwin, as Pilgrim, perforce rides behind, with his bag and a breviary discarded (from its open state apparently in some haste) by an earlier passenger. Also, a strong smell of ground coffee mixed with petrol, almost worse than the Heinkel. Portions of each substance are on the rubber floor mat.

"I think perhaps you have a fuel leak, Father."

"Only because there is no the cap, Signor Cassoni-Percevale, please be not worry, and I am Brother Pietro, for naming. Cigaretto?"

"Grazie, no – I say, do you think it wise –?" too late! A match already flares! ... but rather than immediate conflagration, Mother Church chooses the on-going torture of Brother Pietro fanning a small red glow ahead of the fumes. "I'm surprised you still get proper coffee," the Pilgrim essays, in a somewhat forced conversation.

"This is from being diplomatico. I am myself collect all type of parcel for the Mission, and sometime Library, as now."

Brother Pietro turns to smile at parcel-Eddie. The mouse-car almost rolls over. Brother Pietro, prevents this with a practised gesture, casually inhales, then touches the glowing cigaretto to a dangling medal of St. Christopher. The journey continues in this fashion. The petrol smell grows stronger, the floormat wetter. Brother Pietro lights one cigaretto from another, before blithely discarding. The Pilgrim observes little of Rome.

"So beautiful in May," puffs Brother Pietro, "we are all praying there shall be no explosions from bombing through the liberation. Here is the Franciscans' Chapter House. You are our guest of Monsignor McGuire. Arrivederci, Signor Cassoni-Percevale."

The House of Franciscans

Has high sunny windows, and smells of garlic, and sedentary males with higher priorities than washing under their extremities.

Monsignor McGuire, with a purple dicky, is Pilgrim's height, but stocky, with that Irish mouth that looks like a shut drawstring purse, and a pointed, thrusting chin bred for confrontations with The English.

"Mr Perceval, sir. We can tell you haven't altogether enjoyed your ride with our little Pietro."

The plural, yet singular Monsignor, clearly speaks for all of Us.

"It was more the aircraft, Monsignor McGuire. I was in Graz when I got word that I could come to the Archives, and I've been bouncing for most of twenty-four hours, but I'm more than ready to start."

"Well that'll not be today, sir. Our man you'll be needing is elsewhere, receiving instruction, but your Grail has waited long enough, it can stand a little more."

"If I may say so, Monsignor McGuire, you sound a little doubting. And perhaps American?"

"You may, sir, and we are, on both counts, seven years in Boston that's a fact, and your not being of the Faith, another – but our doubts are neither here nor there. Higher powers have decreed that you shall be looked after as one of our own, and it's looked after you shall be. You'll be having a room looking at the White Sisters' Garden. We hope it's to your liking."

Sure and isn't it a be-autiful room, me darlin's? – with fresh flowers cut, and best lavender soap, and young Edwin not being one o' the club, as you might say, doesn't think it too passing strange that a man a-wearing o' the purple should be acting as a page and all. Not that our Boyo ever meets another living soul except our Monsignor McGuire; not at meal times (which are laid out by buffet, in a private dining room), not even when the pair of us are out a-walkin' on an evening – and a breath of a one it is too, and that's a fact, with night-scented jasmine against a brick wall warmed all day in the sun.

But the Pilgrim *did* think it just a trifle odd when he got up in the night to go for a pee and found a Swiss guard in the absurd pantaloons outside my door, and odder when the guard paced the hall beside me to the loo, and took station while I was occupied, and paced back when I wasn't. And the next morning when I went out to the White Sisters' enclosed garden a pair of the Swiss by chance were there too – always strolling between me and the gate.

"I take it I'm some sort of a prisoner." Eddie confronts Monsignor McGuire when lunch arrives and the Archives haven't. "May I know why?"

"Now whatever could have been giving you that idea, sir?"

607

"Guards on the lavatory, actually."

"A diplomatic nicety," dismisses Monsignor McGuire, "Vatican City being perched on a needle's point in these parlous times, you'll surely appreciate that."

"I do, but I wanted to be *in* the Vatican, not escape from it, and if approval was granted for me to visit the Archives, why can't I still?"

"A matter of departmental protocol, a slight thing, not to be worried over, but if you'd like to be keeping your mind working, we'll arrange for the library to send over some books on your speciality."

"That's very kind, but I'd much rather go there myself."

"And wouldn't we all like this war to be over? and Godless Stalin not in power? but we're not free agents in these matters, Mr Perceval, sir."

"Agents – you can't believe I'm a spy!"

"Belief's a tricky business at the best of times," replies Monsignor McGuire, "even for an agnostic such as yourself, but rest assured your stay with us won't be unduly protracted."

"I hope not. I could have been in Provence. The work at Li Santo has run into flooding by the sea, apparently – and I'm by no means agnostic, Monsignor McGuire. You can't search your whole life for the Grail and believe in nothing."

"Most reassuring, Mr Perceval, and what would that be in your case?"

"I'm a Jungian. I believe in a greater Being, but one that's revealed as our inner Self, call it a soul if you like. But free of shibboleth and mumbo-jumbo – and of course I'm not saying a hierarchical church doesn't have a function for the lower classes, or more backward races, the Ukraine, with the Uniates, for example. But unfortunately, with the commissars back in the saddle that chance has gone again."

"So you're not a Marxist by philosophy?" McGuire's tone has changed, the slight derision Romans reserve for the faithless is gone. Our purple shaveling is a politician.

"I loathe Marxism," said Edwin. "It represents the death of Art."

"And Fascism the resurrection of it?"

"Hardly, it's too one-dimensional, but it doesn't turn wonderful old churches into Pumping Stations – and I'm really not political, Monsignor, I want nothing from life except to find the Grail, and the Right side of the political fence has let me try. When I'm successful, the world should be grateful to Germany, but it won't be – their Leader knows that only too well."

"Ah yes," said McGuire, "now isn't that the most interesting of all, your friendship with the Fuehrer? Mr Perceval, sir, have patience; we feel that we're a deal closer to our Archives than we were. We shall be after sending you some books, and meet for supper."

An encouraging turn in our conversation, but our Swiss guards stayed in the garden. The Pilgrim sat in the sun and watched our pigeons flying above our great dome of St Peter's: a midget's dome by Wolf's standards . . . and by "A's"? the swelling womb? – which brings in Ettie, and Eddie's frightful remark to her on leaving, about bursting, and thinking of her all alone if a midwife doesn't get there, and Complications, which is all a man hears of, about childbirth; imagining the unimaginable, rippings, and unbearable pain. Brother-Edwin will have to go to her from Rome.

But my crypt of the Three Maries has flooded, dammit! – and Avignon's just really starting; and Dietrich's Fortress only down to the 3rd level, with at least 4 to go and the Bear drawing closer; and God may send a miracle once we get to the Archives . . . by which time the apricot evening has closed on Rome, and Sister's pain receded. Brother-Eddie bathes, in a vast marbled bathing hall with ten tubs, all but his own empty, and the Swiss guards outside it. And then down to dinner, to find a note from McGuire, that we're detained, and Sure would Mr Perceval-Sor mind eatin' without us in our Church prison?

And then a truly wonderful experience: 2 books, set out on the sideboard; one being a gorgeous illustrated Bestiary of the Pelican Legend, whereby the bird, at first excessively devoted to its young, when they reach rebellious adolescence, strikes back with its wings, killing them, and then itself, piercing its breast, and pouring out its life's blood over them, which resurrects them. Sure-&-Begorra – *A wonderful Bird is our Pelican / Whose beak can hold more than its Belly can!*

And accompanying this crude parable of the Godhead, an 11th Cent forerunner of de Troyes' *Quest*, "The Story of Perceval's Sister", in the Greek, with illustrations of her shaving her hair, her crowning glory, ie, children, that naughty word, V*******y; and then she too, like the pelican, after presenting Galahad the sword, offering her life blood to redeem Sinful Eve.

Which makes the old Adam in Eddie wonder what the hell sort of nursery-game damned McGuire's up to in our land of Machiavelli?

The Monsignor arrived as Edwin was looking a second time at the rare Pelican, with its lovely colours, still fresh as yesterday after a thousand years, and not daring to think what else Rome must have in its cellars.

"Ah, Mr Perceval sir, we feel you've enjoyed your reading more than our little Pietro's driving, and sorry we are not to have been with you for the meal, but we might share a cup of coffee and a glass or two of port upstairs?"

"I'd like that. The books are wonderful – shall I bring them?"

"Best not, but we'll see they're sent along to your bedroom."

"You're very kind."

" 'What doth the Lord require of thee,' Mr Perceval, 'but to do justly, and to love mercy, and to walk humbly with thy God?' Our Book of Micah."

"I'm afraid I haven't bothered much with the Old Testament God."

"Let us pray it isn't mutual."

But that slight Roman derision says, *We don't mean it.*

At the head of our stairs McGuire turns into a gallery blocked off by more Swiss. A solitary bell strikes for some faraway observance. We open a door between the portraits of 2 dead cardinals. The room within is a small refectory, converted to a study, with 2 carved chairs and a painted ceiling, and an inlaid screen, that reminded Pilgrim of Jung's tower. Our coffee waited in a silver jug on a low table, holding also our decanter. The floor was bare, and echoed when we walked on it. The air was close, the smell stronger of vanished generations of unwashed males, with stale incense from a brass and gilt censer hanging on one wall below an anguished crucifix: like the bleeding pelican, the Church lives for Death.

"Now then," said McGuire, "won't you take a chair, Mr Perceval, while we do the honours, and say a word-or-few more on your political fence-sitting vis-à-vis the Grail?"

"That's the point I was trying to make, Monsignor. I don't see accepting the resources of a particular State, in order to recover an object of world-wide human mythologic value, as having any political connotation at all."

"Mythologic? ah yes, your being a Jungian," McGuire passed a demi-tasse of coffee, and then the port decanter. "We always think a gentleman should pour his own wine – you don't see recovery of the Grail as a religious act?"

"Not for me," as Eddie took port. "For practising Christians, of course."

"And what if the Grail had a relic inside it?"

"That seems highly unlikely, if you mean a heart – but if some organic matter was contained, then it would be up to science to establish age and race, etcetera."

"And if it was empty? – the Grail, that is, as you expect, Mr Perceval?" McGuire sipped, surprisingly abstemious. "And say it was discovered under the auspices of a particular regime, your German friend's regime, you would not think that carried an implication?"

"Divine Displeasure?" Edwin laughed, and poured another delicious glass. "How could it, Monsignor McGuire? Empty or full, the Grail would have been wherever and however it was before there was a political Europe."

"Or a modern Perceval." McGuire studied the blood-shade in his glass against an ivory panel in the screen. "As a Jungian, do you also subscribe to Professor Jung's recent espousal of re-incarnation?"

"In one's own case, no. As for Jung's, I don't think he means it in the literal sense of the Indian fakirs – more for its allegorical part in the transformation of the human personality."

"Which you called a soul."

"In a way it is, yes."

"So you, yourself, are close to being a religious man – " McGuire again studying the glass, this time against the upper fretwork section of the screen. "But to return to the Grail, if it was discovered under the aegis of a Bolshevik regime –?"

"But it won't be, damn it. Monsignor McGuire, excuse my language, your wine's strong, but one of the reasons I'm impatient is that every minute I waste here, the Red Army gets closer to Graz. And if they should overrun it, Stalin would blow the place to kingdom come before

611

he'd allow a relic with the Grail's significance to see the light of day."

At which point, children, there came a gentle coughing, more a sighing, from behind our screen – except that Edwin thought we must have been imagining, because McGuire completely ignored it.

"Mr Perceval, sir, you're saying it's necessary to sup with the Devil, in the face of a greater evil – which the sweep of Europe by Jewish Bolshevism will be, the Church would agree with you on that score – but we do still have a divergence. On this business you call 'organic matter' – the Church could never allow such a relic to be carved up like a chop on a butcher's slab."

Through the fretwork Pilgrim caught a glimpse of white, the butcher's apron? No, a handkerchief, dabbing. No – signalling!

"The Church is suggesting some form of quid pro quo, Monsignor McGuire?"

One dab for, Yes!

"Certainly, Mr Perceval, if we were to grant access to our Archives, we should expect to have an observer present at the site."

"I don't object to that, but even with whatever I may find from the Salt List it won't narrow the field down to a single site."

"Sure, and it would be no problem for us to provide a man at each."

"All right – but it couldn't be opened or moved without my being there also."

Again, the white flag capitulated.

"Eminently reasonable, Mr Perceval – and vice versa, naturally."

"Fair enough. But scientific measurements, and photographs as well."

More coughing, but no flagging. Our sticking point? The Pilgrim waited through the worst moment of our Life for . . .

Success! One more white signal.

"As long as there is no desecration," said McGuire, "and the final resting place is Rome."

"Agreed. Do I put it in writing?"

"An English gentleman's agreement, surely, Mr Perceval, is as binding as the word of God. But we do have one last small consideration."

"Yes, Monsignor?"

Our inevitable *And then*; the so-little last-words Pilgrim has been dreading. Yet all my life wanting.

"*Mein Sohn*," for the reply came in German, and not from McGuire, through the screen, commanding, "you shall have to become a child of Mother Church."

Are you sleeping, Hagen, mein Sohn . . . ?

But that dream-scene of Wagner's by the Rhine, is all in black, while Pilgrim's at the Tiber is white, this Hamlet-ghost he's been awaiting. A white man, in white gown, with white buttons down the front, and white skin, and hair – although that was more grey, but so hidden by the skullcap that the impression was white – even the lips of the vision seemed bloodless. The only things coloured and human about Our Machiavellian Holiness, as he came around the screen to meet our newest martyr, were his papal shit-brown eyes, and ruby ring.

"I agree, Holy Father." Instanter!

"On our knees," said McGuire.

And kiss our Ring . . .

"Then I accept you, my son, and baptise you, with the name, Edwin, in His Service."

Fully. At last. Amen.

Converting:

The mechanics are trivial after the Fact: McGuire, that Irish trickster, kicks off our Catechism en route to our Archives; the Vatican spies assigned to each Grail location shall Instruct our hero in his subsequent lessons of the faith in the field.

"You're a quick study, Mr Perceval sir, and no mistake. We'll have you through it in a month, and resting all the easier in the air-raids for the comfort of first Confession and forgiveness of all past sins."

Which is enough to give an incestuous lad hot flushes, but McGuire thinks it's the excitement of the shelves opening before our New Boy's blue eyes.

"Quite a moment it must be, after a lifetime's search. We'll be leaving you with our Clerk of Records for the morning, and we'll have our second Instruction after lunch."

Lucky Eddie.

But oh, children, entrance to the Archives *was* a moment! Say only that against the hidden stacks of Rome, the Burghof's in Wien, the British Museum's, are as nothingness. For a day I, Edwin, walked with the recorded gods of man.

Although the spark originally igniting this excitement, the Salt Tax List, when reached, proves depressingly dim. The missing page is there, and the year looks promising: 847 AD ($7 \times 121 : 21 = 3 \times 7$) – but no place-names ring a bell; small villages, tinier hamlets, they had vanished a millennium ago. The Convert has a photographic copy made, for the Pendulists, grasping at straws, and joins the exodus streaming from the Seven Hills in the oncoming face of Liberation. Brother Pietro despatches both packages, Eddie & Photo, in a volatile petrol haze, smoking happily a cigaretto and driving off unscathed in the clockwork Fiat, between craters, as the first bombs fall.

"Jesus Christ we can't stop now," said the Convert's sky-pilot, caught mid-runway. "Pray you bastards back there. *Pray!*"

Holy Mary Mother of God, steering us sinners through smoke, explosions, chunks of concrete smashing the fuselage, blast-gases hurling us upward ... then down! – a church in front! a cupola! – vanished, literally the 'plane flew through it! *Pray for us sinners*, and now our own supporting groundfire – but we were so close to the muzzles, no detonations! the fuses weren't set! Instead, Allied fighters screaming in on us. The Convert saw their cannons blazing, straight at me, and felt a sudden draught on my legs, and I saw the legs on the man next to me disintegrate in a red spray.

And so once more the Fool survives, like little Pietro, working out His special purpose.

> *Magnify Him that rideth upon the Heavens*
> *He is a Father of the fatherless*
> *And bringeth the Prisoners out of captivity ...*

... Roundabout: The Convert gave thanks, and took the Salt Copy in my own hand across the smoking skies of Nibelheim to leave with the Pendulists at Fuhlsbüttel, safe as ever next to Purgatory-Ravensbrück, for Scientific Analysis, or to Save Lives, depending on our idiot-perspective.

And then, without time to think, south to Li Santo, to see for myself how bad was the flooding.

"Tricky to start," reported the Death's Head sergeant, "we lost three by drowning before it was plugged. It was a tunnel to the sea – half those damned olden-day priests were smugglers – but it washed out a couple more of those model boats you're interested in. Another of your ill winds, mein Herr."

Blowing of all things, in this southern extremity of France, a Russian Ikon, 13th Cent, which proves that they made the journey all the way back. "And much later than I'd thought," said the Grail Leader. "Excellent work. Keep at it."

With a moment to reflect on friends in Ukraine who didn't get back ... before Avignon, to tell the Abbot the good news, and take a lesson.

The Tabernacle:
"Joining the Faith, my son? At the hands of His Holiness? Five old trees must seem a small price in Rome to gain a soul."

"My sailor-chap, Father –" the Converting Edwin chose to ignore an inflection which came precious close to blasphemy – "old Deaf'n'Dumber, have you been able to find useful things for him to do?"

"Not in everyone's opinion. Doubtless you shall form your own, my son. You will find your friend behind the stables."

Revealed by the sounds of wedges driving, and wood splitting, and the smell of resin and cedar curing under the Mediterranean sun. Deaf'n-'Dumber smiles happily at Eddie, and lifts another plank into its allotted position in a shrine he is constructing.

"To the memory of our fallen innocents," says the Abbot, arriving uninvited. "A chapel in miniature. As you see, it is entirely of the yews' wood. On this cross there will be no nails."

The Convert has built his own church in miniature, a whole village. He knows the difference between reality and illusion for the human spirit. This chapel of Deaf'n'Dumber is large enough for a dozen human beings to actually sit in, and contemplate their actions, and God's re-actions.

"Any relic that we find, Father – short of the Grail, which has to go to

615

St Peter's – but anything else can rest here, in Deaf'n'Dumber's tabernacle."

"You will not find such an object here. We already have God's purpose. The old trees would have died at some time, warming one pair of hands at some cottage fire. Now your sailor's work will warm countless hearts. When you wrestle with the guilt of your actions, my son, be comforted by that."

Damned shaveling impudence? Don't tell me!

"Furthermore," grumbles the Avignon supervisor of Hooligan material, "this gravel's like quicksand. Herr von Perceval we need every scrap of shoring timber we can get."

But even Yours-Truly-Fanatic refused to cross that line. My dears, there *are* limits.

Aren't there?

. . . *On the Clock of Hours:* Time's passage whirls faster. With no word from Ettie . . . Eddie agonises . . . then flies to Dietrich. The scale of the work is truly impressive. A half-mile wide hole, by 40 feet deep, surrounded by the fortress wall, and every scrap of dirt has had to be expelled beyond it. And it hasn't ever stopped raining! The fortress is besieged by a skirt of mud, making further rape difficult for her ravishers.

"Some damn priest has shown up to get in everybody's way," the Engineer Major reports. "Otherwise, we've moved the labour force out as required, and your idea for the drain with the well was first class, but shifting the new excavated matter in this weather can't be done. As fast as I get a roadbed started we have a landslide and away it goes. The dormitory area too, but that isn't so important – at least it hasn't been, but now we're needing every pair of hands."

"Can't we get more? We have the highest priority from Berlin."

"Don't think I haven't tried, mein Herr. I've waved the Reichsfuehrer's order at the local people till I'm blue in the face, but it's the most unbelievable thing. Now the Jews are formed in these zonal ghettos, the Central Authorities have given the allocation of labour for tasks to *them*. Herr von Perceval, the inmates have taken over the asylum! – and if the lunatics in charge want to call their mob 'tailors' instead of 'diggers', we suck the hind tit. I myself was reduced to bribing their local King of the Yids with schnaps – and got two one-armed grandpas for it. But you're a persuasive man, Herr von Perceval, and not being German, well all one can say is good luck."

King Yid:
The Convert reports to his field-catechizer for quick instruction, then leaves the astounded/disgusted Engineer with his mud-disposal problem and sloshes off towards Graz, some ten miles' swim across the plain. The Hooligan force is billeted in Margaretsberg, a quaint walled-suburb, once a separate town, with fenestration, the Scholar was interested to observe, dating it from the Wallenstein era. But now, alas the antique buildings have been allowed to tumble into disrepair. Accommodations that once suited five-thousand inhabitants admirably are being simply wrecked by ten times that number – burning the most delightful window-frames and doors with no regard for their aesthetic value. Increasingly Edwin finds himself loathing the modern age.

A Black Order patrol mans the Ghetto gate. Two Yellow-Stars share this duty with them.

"Excuse me – I'm in charge of the Expedition excavating the Fortress at Dietrichstein, and I wonder if you could be kind enough to tell me where one might find the person responsible for labour allocations?"

"Certainly, mein Herr!" With a smart Wolf-salute.

"The Elders' Committee Room," in a whine, from one of the Gelbsterne, pointing, "at the top of those stairs. Over the tannery."

"Marked as their synagogue. You can't miss it, because of the stink."

The Black Order gives the Grail Leader a knowing grin.

"Thanks very much. Oh, one more thing – I gather there's a Committee Chairman; I'd like to be able to ask for him by name?"

"We run on numbers here." Yellow-Star number 2.

"Don't listen to the insolent swine, mein Herr – and don't take any crap from the rest of them. Just hold your nose and ask for King Yid."

The Grail Leader leaves the gate detachment to sort out its disciplinary problems, and proceeds to the tannery.

The smell over the stairs is of sewage, not tanning. Outhouses, unattended, have filled to overflowing: how can men allow themselves to live in such conditions? At the top of the stairs an elderly specimen sits at an orange-crate.

617

"Your Committee Chairman, please. I don't have an appointment, so if he's busy I'll wait."

"You will, mein Herr?" Surprise, but as Mama says, It costs nothing to be Polite. "One moment only, mein Herr."

The old clerk uses a carved door that has escaped the vandals. Two other Elders peer out, interchangeable with their Orthodox full beards, and shovel hats, and gaberdines, and mutter some Yiddish, not one of the Scholar's tongues. The Clerk shuffles back.

"The Chairman regrets he is busy, but he shall soon be available. If you will give me your name, please, mein Herr, and where you are from?"

"Casson-Perceval. I'm in charge at Dietrichstein – "

"It was meant your nationality?"

"Swiss."

"Thank you, mein Herr. Again, one moment."

Clearly these politenesses are the games the Engineer-Major encountered. But Patience is a Virtue, Edwin. Compose ourself to sit this out. Laughter now, from the group inside; the phrase, "Der Engländer!" more laughter, but Albion's Race is used to the mockery of lesser breeds. The door re-opens.

"You may go in now, mein Herr."

All 3 Elders trot out.

"Thank you. May I please have your Chairman's name?"

"We use numbers here."

"I'm aware – but I should prefer a proper name. Otherwise all I've been given is a nickname, which would make me equally uncomfortable."

Generating more Yiddish confab. Crooked smiles.

"The Chairman is pleased to be addressed as His Majesty, mein Herr."

"Then never mind."

Enough is enough! The Grail Leader pushed past the mockers. Their inner sanctum had been a storehouse; hooks and pulleys still in place. Now it was laid out as an office; stark, two planks on trestles for a table, three dying chairs; not a picture, not a rug, not a scrap or stick to make it liveable. A door, partly ajar, beyond the table; pushing forward the hinges squeak; music from a wireless, *Lohengrin*; walking on a thick

618

carpet, past walls of a thick flock-paper, with lamps, exquisite furnishings, oil paintings; below a cut mirror, a dining buffet piled with food, an ice bucket with wine. A man in gaberdines stands by it, his back turned in deliberate rudeness; on his head a child's paper party hat, cut out of yellow paper, in sawtooth jags, a nursery crown. Edwin is dealing with Dementia.

The mad king tipped its crowned head back so that the face was reflected in the mirror. Full black-bearded, phylactery on his forehead, but the mouth was wide-open, smiling an insane smile, as though every calling stranger was its closest, oldest friend.

"This long it's taken you to get here! So doesn't King Mick rate even a bow, already?"

"Dear God ... Michael ... what have you done?"

... *In the Throne Room:* "Eddie, old friend, why such questions?" The same Rau shrug, and smile, and hands-out gesture. "Booze, grub, nice things – I'd say I've found the most fantastic of all our places – but tell me all your news. The Pot-hunt? the beauteous Edwina? – and for heaven's sake put away that long countenance. Dear man, this is a celebration."

The Rau laugh was unchanged too. Edwin laughed, I couldn't help it.

"That's more the old Eddie. Have some of this wine, it cost an arm and a leg to get, and I have to make sure it's finished in time."

Eddie drinks Rau's wine – *because if I ask instead, Whose arm? What time? the whole fabric will unravel.*

"It is delicious. You're doing yourself proud. Better even than my Swiss rations."

"Keeping body and soul together. Cheers! – now come on, Eddie, what of you? And your noble and gorgeous sister?"

"Cheers! – not much. I'm converting to Rome. She's going to have Wolf's baby."

Which made Michael Rau positively *howl*, children.

"Dear friend, how I've missed you. That's been the worst part, Eddie, sitting here waiting, with just that pig-necked Junker Engineer – no matter how rude I was to him, he was too stupid to notice. Your Wolf-Man should have picked a Master race with a sense of humour. Is Edwina truly pregnant by him?"

"Vastly, or at least she thinks so. It's rather embarrassing actually. She took up Love of the Earth when she dropped Wagner." Eddie explains to his Best Friend about Sister playing Goose Girl. Partly! "She's more baffling than ever. I mean, she gave herself to Wolf after Stalingrad – in a fashion I couldn't even begin to tell you – and now she lives in a hut He bought for her, which He can see by the way, with glasses from the Berghof, and so can Eva, although she doesn't know – and now *she* wants me to buy the bloody place, to give *Him*, it's madly involved – and yet Ettie won't say a word to Wolf about her being pregnant, and He never goes there. They haven't met since the creature was started. Michael, she's stuck up there, utterly alone, no proper clothes – no adulation! – yet she's *happy*. More than she's ever been in her life. Genuinely. And Wolf, who wanted her more than even getting to Moscow, now that He's got her, doesn't want her, and she doesn't even mind *that*. You explain it."

"Simple, Eddie, it's like my party hat. They save each other for special occasions. At the next Stalingrad, they'll be back in each other's arms – have some of this cloved ham with me, it'll only go to waste."

"You still eat ham, wearing prayer boxes?"

"I'd hate my closest friend to think I'd given up all my values." Michael Rau refilled both our plates with meats and sauces. "And you still haven't found the Pot, Eddie, or you wouldn't be here – or turning Catholic. Tell me about that interesting byway."

"I don't know when I first thought I'd go Roman . . ." which takes Eddie through the 2nd helping, and Rau through his 4th. "Perhaps it was Mama always rather putting them down, or that first time at Bayreuth seeing the Grail – not that I take the witchcraft side seriously, but I've always been drawn to the symbols."

"The ash-tree and the cross, a marriage of convenience. Will the Wolf-child be baptised?"

"I shouldn't imagine. I'm going to Ettie as soon as I leave here, and stay with her until – if she hasn't popped already. Look, Michael, I'm horribly embarrassed to ask, but about these labourers you have?"

"Eddie, what a hopeless old moralist you are. There's no embarrassment. Just tell me how many you want."

"As many as I can get – another five hundred?"

"Done. Lime sherbet before the cheese?"

"Lovely – I'm afraid conditions at the dig are pretty grim. In constant mud, under canvas."

"Stop flagellating yourself before you're an official member of the club. Edwin, dear friend, if these Yids of mine weren't bitching and whining in your mud, they'd be going East in the morning to be the dragon's hot breakfast. Tell yourself you've prolonged their ignorant lives. These are real limes by the way, smuggled from the Crimea."

And he chuckled, and green cream melted from his bearded lips, and he kept pressing sweets and drinks and kindness on me: so all that was like the old Rau, but the expression in his eyes, under the nursery crown, that was crucified, and new.

"Didn't you go to America at all?" Eddie asked, maudlin as usual after brandy.

"Would I lie to my best friend? Yes, I went."

"And?"

"And I ran my advert in the New York Times, for a few months in the spring of '42, and when no one bothered, I couldn't waste any more time, and so I came back to do business with Heydrich instead."

"How could an advert for Jews escaping, work in New York?"

"It wasn't about escaping. The ad was on the mass killing – although Roosevelt's office-boys censored most of it for National Security. Who can blame them? There are more Yids on that side than the New Deal can handle."

"But your father was one of them."

"So isn't there always a silver lining?" Rau searches for it in his brandy. "To be honest, I was tempted to stay. There seemed no point coming back; the old man had no remaining assets on this side – and then, as the Americans say, Bingo!"

"He had *you*," Eddie whispers. "His son."

"Yes, siree-bob! The only begotten – in whom he was not well pleased. But Heydrich was instantly ready to be partners – your friend Blond Moses never approved the killing of Kikes, so inefficient by German standards, using up good bullets and trains just to feed a dragon."

"But you let them die here, your Jews."

"While I live like a King." Rau nods, the crown shifts. "But they die more slowly, old friend, and if my business luck holds there'll still be

621

enough of *Them* left for a last supper after your Herr Wolf takes his curtain call. A dozen should be ample. I forget exactly how he wrote it in The Book – but do we not breed like rats in our sewers, already?"

"I won't let it happen," said Eddie. "I won't let you kill yourself. I'll see Himmler – no, Wolf even."

"The kiss of death," said Michael Rau. "Dear Edwin, the man *loves* your sister, if you want to ride a white horse, charge off in her direction."

"I've tried Michael. Everything, but she won't go – and if she did, there would be no more Grail. I'd be denounced. For three years I've been a sort of spy."

"And you worry for my neck? Eddie, in this production Parsifal loses. Give up the Pot, rescue Edwina – and smother the Wolf spawn before it takes a breath."

"Murder? How could I ever?"

"Pretend it's one of your diggers."

"Christ that's cruel. You said you didn't mind – "

"I said, old friend, I was not embarrassed. *Minding* is a different matter. *Minding* is standing on the platforms at the loadings. *Minding* is having to croak for these pathetic, spineless specimens all around me who wouldn't take a free ticket when I handed it to them with two steamer trunks, first class. *Minding*, is hearing them bleat because they're only allowed one cardboard suitcase for the ride east with the diamonds up their arseholes. *Minding*, Eddie, is having to cut out a fucking paper hat when some idiot Yid burns the last one. Edwin, I *mind*."

"Yes, Rau, I won't take the labourers. I'm sorry."

"You fool. Since we first met, in the Hofburg Reading Room, twenty years or whatever it is, in all that time I don't think you've understood a word I've said."

"Perhaps I haven't, Michael, but we're still friends. Aren't we?"

And Rau's answer? Why, a big kiss, children. Wet lipped, bearded. On my foolish mouth. Now our love only lacks the pieces of silver.

Olde 75
[to be sung sweetly]
Saw a Youth, the morning Rose
Blooming in the Heather,
As her dainty Leaves unclose,
Straight to gaze on Her he goes.
'Twas in Summer weather.

. . . *En route Love Cottage:* Goethe penned it, my gentle Franz composed:
Eddie, flying, hummed it, suddenly consumed by an overwhelming
sense to be with Sister. His companion on the last leg into Munich, that
glorious early June, appears to be a recruit for the Pendulists' Brigade:
tall, 1-armed, 1-eyed, scarred & twisted, with an abstracted air, though
well-born, a Colonel, with all the prerequisites – save that he seemed
rational.

"Count Claus Schenk von Stauffenberg, at your service."

"Edwin Casson-Perceval."

"Ah, the Fuehrer's Bayreuth circle."

"One was, rather. When there was a Season."

"I see him today at the Berghof. Shall you be meeting for this
season?"

"I doubt, it's only Meistersinger again. One week in July, and my
sister doesn't sing. It isn't the same."

"What is, Herr Casson-Perceval?"

The Count fell into a brown study of despond and gazed out at
smashed Munich with his one good eye. Edwin hopped off and found a
Black Order car among the ruins. The first five miles of autobahn is one
continuous patched-up crater. Brother arrives at the Untersberg and
ascends the winding lane with increasing excitement. *Has she . . .?*

At 50 yards it was obvious she hadn't. Once more in light cotton she
sat in a bower, big as a house. Her golden head was framed by clematis.
Her legs stuck straight out in front of her. One hand rested on a book,
with the other she scratched, through the dress, most indelicately.

"Eddie darling, marvellous! – but Sister's got a simply godawful itch
on Miss Pussy and we've run out of calomine."

"I've got some. Ettie, thank heavens you're all right. Flying in to
Munich I had this tremendous premonition, the oddest feeling. I was

623

sitting by an army man called Schwenk-Schellenberg – no Stauffenberg, one of those Junker families, without the neck. Or much else, he ran over a mine – "

"Pet, that's fascinating for your memoirs, but give us the bloody lotion before I die."

"Sorry. I will. Just have to find it – the other most extraordinary thing – here's the bottle. I met Rau."

"In America?" She took the lotion. "Hold the cap for me."

"In a ghetto." Brother held the cap; she pulled up her dress. "A sort of refugees' camp outside Graz. Michael's got himself up as the king of the place, in the real sense, even wearing a cut out crown – Ettie, that's frightful!"

Fiery-red, pustulant, where once was snow-white and golden.

"A slight infection. Ladies get these things." She upended the bottle. "Damn, it needs three hands and I can't see over the top. Eddie, be a love."

"You want me to hold up your dress?"

"Fool, I can do that – I can't *see*, not without a mirror. Just pour some on and rub it in."

"Shouldn't I wash first?"

"That depends what you've been touching, darling."

"Nothing, but after travelling."

"Not even King Michael? Oh never mind – use the pond. And don't frighten the duckie-babies. And *hurry*!"

5 new yellow powder puffs scatter. Ma & Pa quack weedily. A cuckoo sings as it murders someone else's baby. Rustic idyll. Glaring infection. Eddie dabs a little above the swollen lips. There was a most unpleasant smell.

"Ettie, it's nasty." Working the white cream liquid in with his fingers. "It needs a doctor."

"Rubbish. Oh God that feels a million times better already. Work it down under."

"You'll have to open your legs more." Running the cream around her edges, catching the drips. "I'm sure it comes from that damned shaving."

"It comes from being summer and not being able to see what I'm doing. It makes one feel like those awful fat men who get enemas on

Jermyn Street and can't do up their shoes. Gawd, Eddie, how I wish it was over."

"You haven't said Gawd for years." Brother capped the bottle and pulled her dress down. "It will be over – but with this infection, Ettie, I've decided. You can't stay here. I'm going to take you to a clinic."

"Sister's big brother. Very manly." She giggled. "Look who's woken up, playing doctor. Poor Mr Thingee – shall we kiss him better too?"

"Don't be ridiculous. It's a reflex. I wouldn't dream of letting you."

"Liar. He's juicing. Eddie, I don't mind. But I have trouble kneeling. Stand here, beside me . . ."

Leaning his back against a rustic post, clutching her head, his face in the flowers. Such was his strength of character.

"Mmm," she wiped her chin, "shades of getting ready for a last dress rehearsal. Do you miss our frantic old days, brother darling?"

"No. Ettie you shouldn't have. I feel dreadful. Oh Christ, and next week I'm booked for my first Confession."

"I don't know why you've never just been able to enjoy without the mea culpa. What do you mean, booked? You aren't finally getting yourself Addled?"

"Not that sort of confessing. I may as well tell you. I've gone Roman."

Which momentous news, however, does not surprise her. "Only that it took so long. Now you'll have a permanent stock of lovely choirboys."

"I'm not taking Orders. It was partly political – a condition of getting Vatican help with the Grail. At the Very Top, one might add."

"Pius the Fraud? Really-truly, Eddie? Well I'm damned – but you're not lugging me to a bloody clinic, and that, my dear, is that."

Brother-&-Sis had a tiff, a bloody Mother & Father of a row, actually – him trying to lug her to the car; her, sagging – then terrifying him that she was bursting. Finally a draw was called: by unanimous decision the sibling pair shall have supper, then Edwin shall drive down to the village for the midwife who shall live-in at Love Cottage till things are accomplished, that She is delivered.

Even in her Condition the Earth Ettie has planted her this-year's veggies. Eddie strolls out and plucks leaf-lettuce, and new fennel, and baby-finger carrots to be eaten with eggs, and fresh bread and a selection of cheeses.

"I must say," he said, "it does make life simpler for meals, giving up the butcher."

"When you think of springtime, and all the lambies it makes you quite ill. Tell me about meeting the Fraud Man while we have coffee."

So Eddie recounted his Little Pietro cigaretto-stories, and devious Irish McGuire, "but the Holy Father isn't a fraud, Ettie. A canny politician, I grant you – but that's part of their job, isn't it?"

" 'Holy Father'? You were bound and determined to say it some day."

But she meant it kindly, so they laughed, and were nice to each other, until the time came for Brother to kiss her forehead, and say, "It shouldn't take me more than an hour, both ways." And she replies. "Don't hurry on my account." And he kisses her again, because she looks so innocent – such a *Madonna* – and went out to the borrowed Black Order car, and climbed in, and checked the handbrake, and depressed the clutch, and pulled the choke, and reached for the key – and had to go back inside and explain, "I must have left the bloody thing in a pocket, probably in the bedroom." But can't find it in either, and gets quite furious at his own stupidity, and hurls things, until she says tranquilly, "Darling, what exactly are you looking for? Let Sis help."

"The sodding key! What do you bloody think?"

"I thought something important. Pet, don't worry about the silly key, you'll never find it tonight."

"I bloody will if it kills me."

"It might. Eddie darling, I threw it in the pond, and it would spoil everything if you drowned."

At which the Explosion, children, was truly Impressive – loud enough to be heard across the valley!

"Then –" at last, between clenched teeth – "I'm going to effing walk."

"You'd be half the night," she replied, with a little moan, and slight gesture to her diseased groin.

"I don't care how long, you theatrical devious bitch. I'm getting the midwife."

"But I'll have had it." Cleverly biting her lip. "Eddie, all alone."

"Dappled in the bracken – Better stuff a cork in it."

And out he strode; hardening his manly heart to her "Oh God's" and "Oh Eddie's" – with a kick for the sodding car on his way by – but scarcely registering her affected, muted sobbing which followed him past the duckie-babies going bye-byes, and into the lane at the end of the ruined orchard, where the forest began, where the dragon lurked.

"Eddie-Christ-it's-started! I've burst!"

And racing back! Knowing she HAS! With all my If-I-hadn'ts! Let today's sex happen. Shouted. Shaken her –

... If I had never loved her.

> *But the Youth impatient cull'd*
> *Rose among the Heather,*
> *Rose stung sharply as he Pull'd,*
> *But her Days, alas, were told,*
> *Wounded both Together ...*

Her blood, her pain, the shrieking, my terror. Too soon I rushed for hot water to boil, when I needed cold, to bathe her. Too late I held her hand, when she needed a skilled surgeon. Hour after hour through the hideous night I prayed, knowing there was no God to hear me. Birth is real: life after death is rubbish.

Life with sunrise, is the miracle.

"It's coming, have towels, Eddie ... can't stand pain ... get knife with the lettuce."

"No knife, darling Ettie. I'm here. You'll be all right. I know it."

"Knife's for cord, idiot."

I got the knife, and laid it shining on the bedside table. And watched Life coming, descending, thrusting, pulsing, smeary black-headed and squirming, not breathing. *How many heads?*

"Smack it, Eddie."

For It's Own Good. God lives. Ettie pants, still bleeding. Eddie's terror mounting: *only* 1 *head*! Now We are 3.

"Cut the cord – tie it."

In a bow? A reef? A granny? The end slithers through my fingers. It bleeds too, poor worm. Some kind of crude half-hitch stopped it.

"Wipe its face, Eddie. Clean its mouth. It mustn't choke."

How could it, with this ghastly non-stop screaming?

"Give it to me Eddie. With the towel."

Against her breast. Swollen. Waiting.

"You didn't tell me, Eddie."

"Tell you what, my precious darling?"

"What it is?"

"Oh that. It's a girl, Ettie. Just like you."

"Is she really, Eddie?"

"The spitting image. I can tell from her fingers, the same shape as yours already. And her ears, the lobes have your dip in them. And blue eyes of course, and she's going to have the same brow, one can't tell about the skin when she's all like a lobster. The only difference is the dark hair."

The *only*!?

You Fool – *WASN'T IT ENOUGH?*

"It doesn't mean anything," blasé New Mother says; "they all have dark at first before they lose it. What shall I call her?"

"What do you want?"

"I hadn't thought. She was going to be a boy. Nothing Wagnerian. Something English and loving. Countrified."

"Rose," says Brother – no longer Father?

"That's rather common."

"One of the new princesses was Something-Rose."

"That's what I mean. Every barmaid in Clapham."

"Not with Casson-Perceval – it doesn't sound bad, Ettie, and it's June, and everywhere outside you can smell them, quite the nicest part of summer. We could add Mama's to make it formal."

As though We are the only parts to the equation. Self-contained. Rude shock; there comes the noise of an engine outside Love Cottage.

"The midwife, Ettie, thank heaven."

"We don't need her, you've managed – besides, my peasant doesn't drive. It'll be Wolf, oh damn. You know how soppy He can be on these occasions and I'm weepy enough myself at the moment. And you're hopeless with Him. Eddie, I don't want Him rushing us into any half-baked Wolf decisions. Go and let Him in, but you're not to leave us alone, and if He starts being stupid chase Him out again. And be firm."

Yes, Mama.

He was not alone. The young Adjutant (Ederl's battle-replacement, straight-shooting, non-musical) was with Him; but so-tactful, already stepping away from the Mercedes to take station with the duckies at the lane's corner; the Adjutant's role as Wotan Stand-in is simply – if any

Outsider intrudes back-stage – to lay down his life for our Principal Player's.

"Ederl! – how long it's been! Almost a year! Is your so-most gracious sister stirring at this hour of the morning?"

"She was, Herr Wolf; actually, she had a rather disturbed night – and it hasn't been a year, only nine months."

"Months! – this past winter has seemed a century – and sleep? I haven't closed my eyes for twenty-four hours. The most momentous development of the war – the fools have landed! That's why I'm here, I must see the Fräulein Edwina. Take me in and then give us a moment together, there's a good fellow."

Whatever the duration, He has aged years in this Interval: the skin has greyed further, and sags from the lower eyelids so that now the whole cheeks are pouched. The eyes, though, are ablaze with all the old fire of a virtuoso performance. Two paces past young Eddie, and up the steps, ducking His head for a strand of clematis –

"Herr Wolf, excuse me, one moment, I'll check with Ettie, if she's got her face on – who did you say has landed?"

So managing to be through the door before Him, to slow progress through the parlour.

"Face nonsense! She knows I hate cosmetics – her English skin is her greatest glory, like your noble mother's. It's come in Normandy. Obviously that's a feint, the crudest possible – but do you think those cretins on my staff believe it? The human constitution can only stand so much. I walked out on the whole ratpack of them. By the time the smoke clears they'll come to their senses. We'll have firm intelligence – Edwin, am I dreaming or was that a baby?"

"As a matter of fact, Herr Wolf – "

"She has hired a maid with a child, I understand. In the rural districts such things are commonplace; when one was younger, it was the norm. Don't tell me! The Fräulein Edwina can't be sleeping through such a racket. The mother should put a drop of schnaps in the milk."

"A good idea, Herr Wolf. If you want to sit down for a moment, I'll tell her."

"And pack the creature to the attic. Infants! – night and day screaming their damned heads off. One could never hear oneself think."

"Yes, Herr Wolf –" thank God, it's stopped! – "I won't be a second with Ettie."

The foolish optimist slips into Sister's boudoir. Baby Rose is drinking, little kitten mewlings and kneadings, at her breast.

"Dammit," Uncle Eddie whispers, "couldn't you have done that sooner? He thinks she's the maid's. Ettie, what in Christ's name am I to say?"

"Tell Him not to shout; we mustn't be frightened or it curdles."

"It must be cheese by now. I'm terrified – what do I *say*?"

"What on earth do you think? I've had a baby."

"Not *a* – *His*! And the Allies have invaded Normandy; I'm going to lose Avignon. This is quite frightful."

"You're being upsetting. And horribly selfish. Rose is yours just as much, even if she isn't – and remember what I said about not leaving. Let Him in."

A worst-moment-of-my! . . . Definitely in the Top 3 of life's most difficult! Children, our Child's hair was *black*.

"Herr Wolf," bracing oneself once more to the parlour, "Ettie's looking forward to seeing you, but she isn't exactly herself, this morning."

"Hardly surprising, given your sister's artistic nature, with that brat squawling – or perhaps diet? Something she's eaten?"

"No, Herr Wolf, the vegetarianism's worked wonders."

He can see for Himself, Edwin.

The door open. Mutti & Baby, blooming. Shades of Klingsor's garden. The look on His face. Waiting for His rages.

"Eddie, don't stand there gaping; can't you see dear Wolfi and I need to have a private moment?"

"I'm not. You said – "

"You just don't *listen*. Private. Run along."

Gladly, Mama. Uncle went outside and sat with the duckies who splattered and dived. Aircraft flew constantly, to and from the Salt Mountain. The young Adjutant saw the 'planes and Edwin's slightest movement, but never moved a golden muscle in his hiding place down at the lane's corner. Fearless. A dragon slayer.

Not like Uncle, dying a thousand deaths waiting for the spit-explosion.

What's she telling Him?
YOURS, our Baby-Wolfi? Or HIS, my Incest-Eddie's?
Both bastards. The parent ducks' feet steering, their beaks shovelling; they swim underwater seeking treasure with their jewel-eyes open, diamond necklaces streaming upward from their nostrils.

> *Dame Sun, send us the Hero*
> *Who will give us back the Gold ...*

The ducklings twirled on the surface, Woglinde, Wellgunde, Flosshilde, waiting for the grownups, splashing, refracting the crystal. Something glittered in their mirror.

> *Rheingold! Lustrous gold!*
> *How brightly you once shone,*
> *Wallalaleia, Wallala ...*

The key to my car! Edwin reaches down into the water – the ducklings rush! thinking it's edible – but like Siegfried, selfish Eddie kept it. In the pond's mirror, saw his own reflection.

> *So handsome!*
> *So strong!*
> *So desirable!*
> *What a Pity he's a Miser!*

Or Queer! – and too late for Pity, children; because not from Rheingold, with its promise, this ducks' chorus:

> *Let us leave this Madman!*
> *He swore Oaths – and does not Keep them!*
> *He knows Secrets – and does not Heed them!*

(They swim, greatly excited, in wide circles close to the shore.)

> *Stubborn man, a proud Woman*
> *Today shall inherit your Treasure;*
> *She shall give us a better Hearing.*
> *To Her! Wallala, Wallala ...*

Clever-Eddie having defeated Sister's key-trick walks across to his borrowed car to try his luck further. Invasion or not, there is no need to be hysterical, Edwin. Herr Wolf is a Genius. The trench-line held 4 years in Papa's War. The mindless deaths of a few hundred-thousands is all that's needed by his son. With angels & ducklings, confess our sins: pray for Stalemate for my Grail.

"You, imbecile! – Lunatic come here! This instant, Idiot! Her own brother?! Cretin, I can't believe it! By God in heaven, this time I'm going to wag a finger!"

Expelled by the gunshot violence of His rage, the ducks fly up in all directions; even the fearless Adjutant is caught off balance for a moment and pulls a revolver wildly, before seeing that the threat to the State is only a devastated Fool.

"Silent are you? I don't wonder! White with the shame, and so you should be! – unbelievably despicable behaviour! – leaving it for the woman to shoulder, the worst kind of coward! By rights she should be dead already – yes! Dead! – that's the word, that gets to you! – what you've done! The enormity! – and behind my back, while one has to hold together a whole world. I count you as responsible. Don't dare to argue – the man's always responsible in such situations. The woman knows it's wrong but she's ruled by her instincts. 'Nine months', you had the gall to tell me! – and not a word when one might still have done something about it! Now, at this stage of the proceedings? You may still lose her – and tears won't help. Brace up, man! Poisoning of the blood, one's seen it too often – but she's strong, thank your stars; you don't deserve such a woman, and now the afterbirth's come away at last, cleanly without too much bleeding. Yes, boy, you heard me! *Placenta!* You never thought of that! What could you have been thinking of to let her go through it alone? For the sake of your absurd idea of honour! It was horribly immodest for her, having to allow me, but I said, this is no moment for that sort of bourgeois claptrap. I've seen births, and guts spilled. Such courage she possesses – your truly gallant sister could have had an abortion at any moment, like Goebbels' women, but I can understand why she didn't, once the father was fallen – at Lvov, apparently – his memory becomes sacred, the child shall be a re-incarnation, the warrior stock – if it wasn't female. But you? – I say it again, Fool! you could have killed her! Hiding her up here just to be away from Munich gossip?! What's gossip to people like us? To a Wagner – an artist like your sister? or Frau Cosima in the same circumstances? We rise above it. Where would I be if I listened to the filth *Their* Press peddles? Now pay attention – we can't beat about the bush any longer. A young man of your age, such ignorance is pitiful – although one concedes, one's Orderly experience, running the ambulance parties – Edwin, your sister has a vaginal infection, and a slight tear to her rectum, but Mother Nature will heal in an amazing fashion given co-operation. I shall send my Adjutant back for Morell with the necessary supplies – against my better judgement, she really should go down to a clinic, but if you've come this far we must try and salvage your precious idea of family honour. What could be more honourable for any child than a father fallen in battle? – there's no disgrace to being a bastard under such circumstances – Wagner again – a girl, if she's pretty, can always make a marriage. With your noble sister's resource she could take a prince! 'Die Rose' – a little rosebud. She's going to be adorable, the image of her mother, and superb racial stock from the father, one has only to study the features. They're both resting quietly. It's extraordinary, one came here, not knowing what one should find – Now I don't have a doubt: it's *not* Normandy! It isn't in the British character, or the whore-Churchill's morbid fascination for the wrong view of history. Calais – that's where the crossing will come. The best panzers are still in reserve – and when the rats do land, those that aren't drowned – because the casualties are going to be fearful – they'll make Churchill's bloodbath at Gallipoli seem a Sunday school picnic. Wasn't Dieppe enough for them? *Men never learn.* Well, Roosevelt's Yid shitbag are going to this time! Once the West's tidied up, I shall reach accommodation with Stalin – he only wants the Baltic States and a warm water port somewhere in the Balkans – then I'm going to concentrate on Linz. I've decided to move the Dome there – not Berlin, the city's squalid roots could never be hidden. Linz is altogether a finer site. Clear off the river front, incinerate the waste, set the Dome – it'll look truly stupendous. And across the river, facing it, thrusting up, Kürnberg, the castle that began it all, our destiny. Now, go to your sister, beg her forgiveness, promise her that these year-long absences for this Grail rubbish have stopped. You're too old for such childishness. There's a war on. She needs you. And I expect your word on this – the afterbirth is wrapped in a towel, by the way. When you bury it see that you go deep enough – and put a rock or two on top. The habits of animals are sometimes unspeakably vile. Am I clear?"

633

"Jawohl, Herr Wolf."

End of Term! Xmas! The Happiest-Moment-of –! . . . because, children, He's still going to *win*, and:

HE DOESN'T THINK IT'S MINE!!!

.

Third Movement
Twelfth Passage
[Last verse]

God save our King, and bless this Land
With plenty, joy and Peace;
And grant henceforth, that Foul debate
'Twixt noblemen may Cease.
[Reprise]
"Who needs still Waring?"

Gedanke puts once more our question, with inverted Teuton vehemence & yellow nibbles at the Old One's ears – taking *her* payment in advance, the witch, before the Eddie-fleisch falls from these bones. Gedächtnis, meanwhile, exhausted from so much calculated remembering – of *Chevy Chase* (Olde 16: 1 plus . . .=7!) – has built himself a cosy nest in the leaves following Stalingrad's surrender (by Sister) and broods on Human fallibility. Also, gathering stubs of pencil, a button of Prison bakelite, and Waring's sepia snap "To Yum-Yum, from Eddie C-P", pushed under the door with our gruel to trade on Chummy Good Old Days. This hysteria induced after the Ravens & Yours-Truly fed him Wolf-with-Afterbirth. This, it would seem from the scrabblings & implorings is finally up Yellow Street's alley!

The vagaries of Sex. Have I made a huge mistake? Is broody Gedächtnis the *female* of the species? Strange things do happen in the breeding process – not only mixed identities, that staple of Wagner as well as G&S.

"Who *was* father?"

635

That, for Yellow Jeremy, *is* our burning question, children.

Stay out, damned Waring! Let the sod suffer.

THE '44 SEASON

When He was gone (to wait at Calais, like Caesar, for the other Winnie) – there was a slight argument at Love Cottage. **Diminuendo**, because our Rose is sleeping.

"I simply can't believe it," with Foolish incredulity, "that you let Him actually *see*, while I was here, and after you swore I wasn't to let you be alone, for even a second. And having to bury it, and the appalling terror thinking He thought it was *me*, and then your cock-and-bull about the Hero of Lvov. Ettie, the damned Adjutant had his gun out – I really thought Wolf was going to have the young brute kill me."

"You do talk the most utter nonsense, Eddie; the boy's anything but a brute, compared to the thugs a perfect pet, actually. And so far as the ghastly after's, what was I supposed to do, push it back in the bottle? Wolf can be amazingly practical and resourceful at times – you could learn from Him."

"I suppose He's learnt all He wanted from you, anyway – numbers One, Two and Three, it's beyond describing how disgusting His fetish is, and that you actively encourage and abet it."

"I beg your pardon?" Edwina the ice-maiden. "I don't know what you think you mean by that filthy remark, but I never want to hear anything like it near my daughter ever again. As for her fathering, if Wolf wants to keep that part our secret, for our own protection with assassins and maniacs in every direction, it's none of your damned business."

"She may be *my* daughter."

"Hardly, darling, she has only one head and behaves far too normally. Why do you have to be so insanely jealous and ruin every single happy occasion? Now you've given me the weeps again. Oh go away and leave us, blast and damn!"

Which keeps mock-Uncle tied as her abject slave for a whole extra week, with no word from the fronts about diggings or battles, but thinking, Even if they've landed some people onto a beach in Normandy, I would have heard if they'd done the real thing at Calais – which is confirmed when the Grail Leader finally clears the mountains. Driven Back! Every Day the Channel is Crimson! Enormous Losses! Which makes it a shock to be greeted by peg-legged von Maser when one reaches the Pendulists' Institute:

"Ah my dear boy, just in time for the meeting. We are re-establishing priorities, given the altered situation. The Sensitives still feel the Americans' cutting of the Cherbourg Peninsula will fail with the turning of the moon, but given your ventures in the south of France, you may wish to be doubly re-assured with a reading from Astrology as they're the real experts."

"The whole peninsula? However many Commandos did they land in the raid?"

"Numerology confirms not more than half a million." The Kapitän slaps Edwin's shoulder to emphasise the re-assuring nature of this news. "The pocket will undoubtedly be closed by the Fuehrer with the next neap tide – a complete inability to land supplies, do you see? Furthermore, my boy, we have the first results from your Vatican labours. A triumph. Three new sites, by far the most promising to date, and all within our borders! What do you say to that?"

Grasping at Straws, Edwin!

But Faith is Contagious – and so easy to be lulled by the Experts, when those silver needles swing, and the Advance stops at Caen; or the Mercury drops, and Storms sweep the Channel. As Cartography points out, Cherbourg is four hundred miles from the Camargue, mein Herr! – which may be only a hop in brute Ukraine but in a war between the civilised men of Europe shall keep them busy for years.

"I'm sure you're right," the Grail Leader replied to von Maser, "but I'll leave right away for Provence, to speed things, in case. What are these new sites? – although I don't think we've a prayer of finding labour for anything fresh at the moment."

"My boy, your lateral occipitals make it all too easy for you to fall into the trap of pessimism. I think when the Reichsfuehrer hears one of the names at least, you may be pleasantly surprised." Von Maser clamped his optimistic claw upon a map string and pulled it down. "Because the villages on the Salt List have been lost to time, we have indicated by region their modern equivalents. The figures to the side indicate Numerology's assessment from the metals – the order is inverse, thus

637

the Wartburg, at 6, has least probability; the region of the lower Rhine at 3 is promising; the valley of Bad Reichenhall, with 1, is outstanding – but these have to be set against the radius of the areas involved. When that adjustment is made – "

The black glove covering the steel hand fell with a solid *thunk* on Hero Country.

"Drachenfels," said Edwin, "Mama's last Dragon in Europe."

"Exactly, dear boy. Our Reichsfuehrer will have to be a superman indeed to resist the Lorelei."

"Have you told him yet?"

"As he inclines to the Melancholic, no. I have been waiting for the right Characteristic moment. Something to boost the spirits further when events are already on the rise."

"I appreciate that, Captain – but about these numbers: it looks to me that if you narrowed down the starting point then Bad Reichenhall would get the nod?"

"That is correct. Do you have such a starting spot?"

"While I'm in France, put the needles on the valley immediately to the north of the Untersberg."

"Obersalzberg, my boy? Ah! The fields augmented by the Fuehrer's presence! Yes, this could be."

"I was thinking of one much more longstanding: The Great Rex."

"Ach!" exclamms the Institute's Direktor, "Charlemagne? Mein Gott!"

... *Roundabout:* A month of riding the whirlwind: Camargue, Avignon, Graz, Fuhlsbüttel, stopping at each only long enough to hear the latest horror story about Labour Shortage or Desertion, in France; or the Wettest Year in recorded history at Dietrich's Fortress. Thanks to Rau, manpower there is not a problem. The Grail Leader wants to visit – but news comes that Caen has fallen.

... *Back to France.* By night, in a lightning storm above the Alps, and then caught again by Allied fighters who seem now to roam at will. Edwin escapes with bullet holes in his tail, our still-so-lucky little Wilhelm Tell.

638

"What do you think?" he asks the regional Black Order commander at Avignon.

"The Northern movement is all to Paris, but we could lose our Camargue base of operations overnight from an amphibious strike. Here, we shan't have a problem until they land in strength for Marseilles."

"Will they do that?"

"Wouldn't you?"

No more Foolish questions. By armoured carrier to Li Santo to think of the Three Maries, the start of the Journey. The Grail had landed at this spot, and gone inland: it had not come back. But there may still be a clue in the undisturbed ground beneath the first graveyard with the Templars' Cross.

"Bring in the bulldozer," the Expedition Leader ordered his Death's Head sergeant, "one more pass through, to a depth of two metres, if you don't strike water – then get yourselves out."

"All the tombs. With no exceptions?"

"Exactly. Why do you ask?"

"Only that the new one, mein Herr, where you ordered us to put the gypsy . . .?"

"All the tombs. With no exceptions."

Sevastyani's soul is safe in Atlantis. Safer than mine.

. . . *Back to Sister.* To keep a promise – but not because of Ettie: Rose.

Dying to see her, by chance Uncle Eddie rides through the sky a 2nd time with the 1-eyed, 1-armed recruit for the Institute.

"Count Stauffenberg? – Casson-Perceval, we met last month."

"The Fuehrer's Bayreuth circle, I remember. I myself am going to the Wolfsschanze. Shall I give him your regards?"

"And from my sister, that would be kind. May I help you with your briefcase?"

"Thank you, no, Herr Casson-Perceval. I am accustomed to the weight."

Always be kind to the Crippled, Edwin.

Mama, I *tried*!

639

... *At Love Cottage:* Rose is blooming. Also Mummy, under Quack Morell's care.

"I don't know what he sent me, Eddie, but whatever it was it's done the trick. All the gaps are mended. Being a mummy works wonders for feeling naughty."

"You're not suggesting that we? – in front of Rose?"

Yes, under her button-nose! Uncle's own at the Venusberg, repaired; thinking, *His* eyes saw This, torn & bleeding – expelling! the filthy perverted bugger.

So you see, children, our Edwin isn't *completely* a victim of Repression. Only Guilt – when he squeezed in a visit to Zürich. Now We are 3, the risks are unimaginable.

... *At the House of Treason:* "My sister's had her baby," Eddie informs the blank Swiss; "under the circumstances London can't possibly continue this blackmail. She has to be allowed to live quietly. Surely even Cameron doesn't go in for torturing widows and orphans."

"A widow," said the Swiss, "so you know the identity of the father?"

"I don't. My sister does. It's entirely her business; I shouldn't dream of asking. The man was killed at Lvov, apparently."

"A German father?"

"A half-Swiss orphan. You might remember that when you're selling my niece out to the highest bidder."

"No money changes hands as a result of our transactions, Herr Perceval. She is still near Bayreuth, is she, the Fräulein Edwina? – the northern region?"

"I would have told you if she wasn't."

"We hope you would." The Swiss stared his cuckoo-stare, blankly.

... *To the Village:* Out along the lake – but both Jungs are away. There is no health in us ...

... *Back to Munich:* For a connection to Vichy. A barking Black-Leather comes up as the Grail Leader shows his passport. "Herr Casson-Perceval! The Reich has been combed for you! The Fuehrer commands your presence! The highest priority!"

This time, He must know what I've done – mustn't He?

640

... *At Wolfsschanze:* His lair on the edge of Russia still smells of fresh concrete: a new 10 metres' thickness has been added to the roof; bushes, grass, small trees even are being planted, and watered by Hooligan-gardeners, in a vain attempt to hide the whereabouts of Klingsor from the air. (You only have to look for Blondi's doghouse, children, with her exercise run and special jumps.) The usual frantic activity: today's special on the menu, a visit by the rescued ex-Duce – Mussolini's presence is not required as urgently as the Fool's, so the Italian shall arrive by train. A red carpet is being unrolled as Edwin drives past the platform and joins the pacing throng on the gravelled walk outside a temporary wooden nest being used while the principal residence is re-decorated. 1-eyed Count Stauffenberg is there with his briefcase, looking pensive and abstracted, but saluting back when Eddie waves, before being summoned to the Presence inside.

"Could you tell the Fuehrer I just got here," Fool asked the young Adjutant; "I gather it's important because He sent the Storch."

"I shall tell the Fuehrer, Herr Casson-Perceval, but the conference for the Counter-Offensive is just starting – you'd better be prepared to wait."

When it's Our Bayreuth Circle? – the young whipper-snapper should know better! The Fuehrer-A emerges. The Fool is pushed to the head of the gravel.

"Good morning, Ederl. What brings you all this way?"

"Good morning, Herr Wolf. You sent for me."

"Ach, my mind's going! Yes, I've telegrammed Frau Winifred but I've no other means of getting word to your gracious sister. All our spirits need a lifting after this Normandy fiasco. She absolutely has to sing one of the Eva's at least – tell her that, with one's love and respects – and I don't expect to hear any argument about rehearsals; she knows every note of the role by heart."

... And get to the back of the queue, Fool.

Other petitioners surge forward, but He is already back in the temporary bunker. Count Stauffenberg marches away briskly, sans case, but Fool walks slowly to the car with His summons for Sister. *He's* doomed to disappointment, which should keep Him happy.

I remember having that thought with crystal clarity – as the windscreen of the car flew out and hit me.

641

And then −?

Heat, on the back of the neck.

And then −?

Concussion, from the reflected wave off the concrete.

And then −?

Screaming, from the young Adjutant, without an arm! − and from others imagining other bits missing. And barking, from Blondi, suddenly in the middle of the bedlam, lunging forward, single-minded, which is more than can be said of any human present − I saw her diving in the wreckage, and that was the second thought: She's going to pull the Body out! − because it doesn't require thought to know:

He must be dead. No one could survive it!

Smoke pouring from the entrance, flames running up creosoted wood, Staff-Generals wandering in circles on the gravel, a siren sounding for an air-raid after the event.

That's it! Stalin's done it!

And then −?

Hopeless confusion. Some Black Order men dying. Some standing, sobbing; all of us staring at the smoking death of the Dream. Death in tattered trousers; Death with its hair on end; Death with blood streaming.

And then −?

"Ederl − your so-noble sister − you haven't left to tell her yet?"

Because it was not His time. For the injuries were all to the *front*, or the right *side*, and we know, children, if we know anything, that when Death comes it will strike where there is no shield of Dragon's Blood −

In The Back.

And then −?

The Fool flies away in the Storch, to carry the news to Ettie and Winnie in person − and if I can find a moment, to imprisoned cow-Eva who will be frantic − and land at Munich, and climb out to be met by the Black-Leather:

"Herr Casson-Perceval, in the name of the Reichsfuehrer, Heinrich Himmler, I must request that you accompany me, to assist the Ministry with certain enquiries."

Which in Nibelheim, my dears, can only mean torture for Yours-truly, before His certain execution.

642

On The Anvil

The Prisoner Edwin was taken to a cell in the dungeon of a castle, although they called it a Regional Headquarters. He was left there through a night in which all he heard was screaming – or sometimes, more horrible, sudden silence. He himself was not interrogated, but nor was he fed, or watered, or allowed to shave next morning when he was taken without a word from the cell and marched along a passage, and out into a courtyard, and stood against a wall, facing a line of men along another.

A volley of fire. The men fall down.

The Fool clutches his heart and is taken to an airfield and flown to Berlin.

The city has changed in his absence – half of it is missing – but he doesn't notice details, being intent on his own problem:

What will they do to me?

Not, Why? – they need no reason. He finds himself in a street he recognises, in the district of Dahlem. He went through another courtyard of bodies, freshly lying. I felt sick, weak, filthy. I was pushed into another cell without a window. This is the point they want: Tell them Anything.

Half an hour, an hour, I don't know. The cell door opened. A monster entered – taller by a head than Putzi, heavy as Goering, but solid ham-muscle.

"Kaltenbrunner –!" this Death's-Head Major-General bellowed: "tell me your part in it, you English piece of fag-shit, before you die."

"Part of what?"

He struck me.

And then –?

I fall down.

"You're not dealing with Heydrich. I don't fuck your sister. Get up."

Brother stands. My mouth is bleeding.

"When did you first meet Stauffenberg?"

"Three weeks, a month –"

Kaltenbrunner kicks my thigh with his boot. I fall down.

"Next time I'll step on your nuts. I'll tear your prick out by the roots. I don't play the fucking violin either. When did you first meet him?"

"I've told –" *but his boot is lifted, coming down at my groin, steel-heeled! I soil my trousers. Screaming.*

"That's quite enough of such tactics."

The voice of our saviour. Another Black Order beast stands in the doorway. Another General. This one has a gentleman's face – *please God?!*

Kaltenbrunner spat on my face and left, treading on my little finger.

"Walter Schellenberg." The new beast speaks English. "Mr Casson-Perceval, I bitterly regret the treatment you've received, but you can understand that in the circumstances, given the nature of the crime, feelings run high. I'll send an orderly to help you clean up, and then I'd like to have a few words in private."

In the Fool's humiliation, he wept for such kindness. That is the object of the Game, children. (Now, Edwin speaks as a Professional of Interrogation, but then he was a rank gentleman-amateur.) After the laundering, Eddie was taken above stairs to the grownup part of the house. Walter Schellenberg's office occupied a corner of the building at the end of a passage on the 2nd floor. His gun-ported desk had a clear view of the entire length of it.

"Please, sit down, Mr Casson-Perceval. As I gather you haven't eaten, I've ordered breakfast. I'm in charge of Counter-Espionage."

"Thank you very much, but can you tell me why I've been arrested?"

"Through confusion, Mr Casson-Perceval. We shall get to the bottom of it – although the conspiracy is extremely wide-spread. As an Englishman with close links to the Fuehrer, naturally you've long been an object of considerable suspicion to certain thick-headed members of the Party. Do you know a woman called Frau Marthe Steiner?"

Schellenberg passed a tray of rolls and coffee across the gunports.

"Yes. She's a fortune teller, but I haven't seen her for years."

"Stauffenberg saw her the day before he tried to assassinate the Fuehrer. He asked her to align your two horoscopes. Why should he do that?"

"God knows. Obviously it didn't work. It never does. It's always evasive – utter rubbish."

"But it brought you all three together at the right instant. Why was that?"

"*He* sent for me. To ask about my sister singing again. It had nothing to do with astrology."

"Was your trip to Zürich immediately beforehand, also an astrological co-incidence?"

"Yes. I go regularly, for business reasons, and to collect rations – it wasn't about the Kersten business if that's what you mean."

"What do *you* mean, Mr Casson-Perceval? But take time to eat your breakfast."

I never did, not a bite. Just as a mouthful gets into position Walter Schellenberg manages to ask another of his random, penetrating, gentlemanly hellish-trick questions. He is especially kind and polite while asking about the Chicken Farmer's Swiss business.

"And your Vatican visit? the Reichsfuehrer arranged that too? Most interesting. I'm obliged, Mr Casson-Perceval – where would you like to be taken now, by the way? As your trip was interrupted."

"Munich, please. I have to see my sister."

"We can take you directly to Bayreuth. That is where she's staying, I remember? – from your conversation with this British contact in Zürich?"

"I'll get myself to Bayreuth. I have a car in Munich."

"As you wish. And Mr Casson-Perceval – let me know when you make further trips to Zürich."

Off with his head!

. . . At Love Cottage: The duckies – adolescent now, no longer babies; waxy apples on the old trees, warming; buzzing bees passing among the flowers, over Rose, lying in her wicker crib on the grass beside her Uncle; perfect little fingers, perfect little toes; perfect peace in perfect heaven.

But her hair is still dark.

"You've had a frightful time, darling," said Sister, stroking his forehead, "but think about Wolf. The poor man's going bonkers – even without this ghastly bombing. What could He possibly be thinking of, asking me to do an Eva for Him?"

"I tried to tell Him, but you do know the part backwards, and Winnie's agreed. It would show we're still behind Him. Won't you

645

reconsider? They won't have to know about Rose in Bayreuth. I'll stay with her at the Griesbachs."

"While she starves to death? You may be swish, pet, but you haven't got a bosom – and I have no intention of hiding our treasure when we go there."

"But you've just said you *wouldn't*. For God's sake, Ettie – "

"I said, singing. If Winnie wants a little inside supper to show she still loves Him, of course I wouldn't dream of not showing."

"Do you love Him?"

"Idiot, sometimes I wonder if you even think at all about human beings, you ask such foolish questions. Your damned old Pottie fixation. Of all of us, you're the one who probably should have been Addled. You know we've always loved Him."

And then –?

THEIR LAST SEASON

Only a handful of Wagnerians gather on the Magic Mountain – the House is sold out, but the crowd is not Us. Instead of our mothballed tailcoats and the last century's lace, the audience wears uniform: the Dwarf, in white, & the Bad Giant, tin-medalled; Wolf-Jugend & Mädchen, in Dirndl & Hosen; black Parsifal Knights out of armour, on crutches, from the Front, with wound-leave, for Inspiration before going back for their last transformation; the Strength & Joy brigade, looking neither in farm overalls, after 4 years of war-rations. The Pan-Hun houseful the Master dreamed of, but never imagined.

And talking of houses, my dears, the Casson-Percevals' first shock comes over their accommodation. Uncle-Eddie had expected a fuss – now We are 3 – but it wasn't about Rose.

"Not these days," said Great-Aunt Winnie, distraught with last minute arrangements and cancellations, "if your sister lost a soldier lover, that's a badge of honour in decent people's estimation. I'm afraid it's rather more embarrassing, and you obviously haven't heard – Edwin, there's no way to beat about the bush: the Griesbachs were expropri- ated. It was an accident, one of those red-tape nightmares in wartime – if the dear foolish little people had only *said* something, I would have had

646

the Fuehrer stop it in an instant, but the pair of them simply sold up and crept away like mice in the night. One gathers they held off while Ettie was singing, but then, like the rest of us, they needed the cash. You'll stay here, naturally, with baby Rose. Isn't she the most adorable little thing? Every inch, her mother."

She's going to be a raven beauty, if anything, more striking than Mama – only joking, my dears, we know *that* isn't possible!

> *Mirror mirror, on the Wall*
> *Who's the Kundry of us all . . . ?*

Wolf-Klingsor arrived on our 2nd Wahnfried evening, and huddled in the Siegfriedhaus.

"It's shell shock," said Winifred. "I don't know what His doctors are thinking of. He should be completely isolated and resting. You warned me, Eddie, but I wasn't expecting. He almost fell when He stood to welcome me. The poor, poor, man. He's got this terrible fear of people seeing Him in public, yet He's forcing himself to do it for the Festspiel. His courage is phenomenal – but then we've always known that. And He's lost that young Adjutant He so relied on. Edwin, I know your feelings about Meistersinger, but I'm going to ask you to escort Him to and from, and be with Him in the hall – people won't think it out of the way to see you taking each other's arm."

No, Auntie. Or rather, yes.

And then –?

Hans Sachs, or rather, Bockelmann, singing for all the old virtues – the Little Men of Nibelheim standing up to the godless East's faceless State. They didn't stand when He first arrived, because as usual He came in with the house lights down, and then sat half behind His curtain, with Ederl to run for cold chocolate with whipped cream in the Interval, to give Him strength for His big moment.

Honour your German Master.

Uncle Eddie sat in the Family Box, with Ettie, flanking, and baby Rose in a cot behind, in Ludwig's private Fürstenzimmer, as the song contest ended, with Eva to be married, and all on stage happy. I felt Him tremble as the chorus started, and the audience joined it, two thousand voices. . . .

And then – ?

The Fool joined them. I stood. I sang it.

May God forgive me? I doubt it. A spotlight swung, at Winifred's urging, out from the vast stage, across His singers, across the hidden players, across the great hood hiding their pit; across the Wagnerians – or the ignorant, it didn't matter; across the cane seats of exquisite discomfort; across the black curtain half hiding Us; across Ettie – not singing, still as a statue, white and golden; across me, flushed from singing, weeping, choking:

"*They want you . . . my Fuehrer.*"

May God forgive us, thus spake Our Ederl, before His last battle.

And then –?

After the spotlight caught Him, and the 2000 sang the chorus for 4 encores, We went as always to the Singers' Table: Ettie on one side, Eddie on the other – but no Goebbels, no Goering.

And then –?

Ettie broke her vow (as always) and sang, while Eddie accompanied (as ditto): everything but Liebestod; in public she was all His heroines save Isolde.

And then –?

In Privat. The nightcap at Wahnfried. Only 5 of Us in the drawing room with Master & Cosima, and the disciples looking on from the satin walls. Before walking slowly with Him, supported now by only Brother & Sister, across the lawns, past the Grave, to the little house of Siegfried.

And then –?

At the door. Ettie saying, "Eddie, look after Rose, there's a love, I'll only be a minute."

And then –?

Back to the Wahnfried Nursery, vacant since Mausi & Nickel & Wieland & Wolfi & Ettie-&-Eddie gathered for our first Fox'l Stories, where I held Rose to me, and tried not to think of the little house beyond the Grave, or hear the noise of Ettie, when she came home, retching, and gagging, as though she was dying. Or the sound of water running and running, all night it seems, as though she can never, never-ever, wash off some invisible filth, and unspeakable smell.

And then –?

A message in the morning:

I fled, stop. *At once!* EXCLAM.

A New Page. Old Edwin was going to start the next Passage – but put it off because of the Number: 13.

Stark horror from Numerology. What else, pray, does the prevaricating Fool think he has to look forward to? My dear children, be warned by his example: now We are in The Book of Hagen.

Really-truly.

. . . At the Chapel of the Yews: The same chaos as Ukraine, plus disbelief by the winged messengers of Blitzkrieg at the speed of Nigger-Jazz advance; every Parsifal Knight for himself; disintegration. The Grail Leader fights his way against the tide, and arrives at Avignon to find Marseilles already taken. Which means also our golden island; once more great Annabelle and Berthe, and Charlotte fall silent.

"What the hell brings you here?" from a Death's Head Major waiting in a fever while a last tank gets its tracks fixed. "We have orders to regroup at Orange, across the river – the *maquis* swine mutilated two of my men – dressed as priests, can you believe it?! I've given the bastards something to remember us by. Thank Jesus! – my driver's got the bitch running. Don't be an idiot, von Perceval, get on board!"

"All my records are in the Abbey. I have a car. I'll catch up. Leave without me."

"You dumb arse – the place is charged!"

But the tank engine is roaring, and the Fool doesn't want to hear him. Our earliest Hopes are in this building.

Run, Edwin! – over the scaffolding, bridging the dry moats where Quincunx sentinels once stood. Past the wicket gate, through the plain window of the vestry – see, the Abbot, waving! Wave back, Edwin. We'll get our records and say goodbye, but when our war's over we'll return, we'll sit in the fierce sun, and talk about the old –

But before I could say it, the Abbot and his Abbey were gone.

They came down in a Trinity – Nave, Transept, Chancel, leaving only dusty rubble. All that's left for the fire to consume is . . . a tabernacle of Yew-wood, a hand-cured morsel. Only the growing crackle of Fafner devouring the little chapel, and a rhythmic thumping like a beating human heart. *My heart?* Too loud, but the rhythm *is* human. It comes from inside the chapel: a human hymn to a deaf-&-blind God – Hear Us, thy servants,

Sweet Christ, get them out!

The doors are too well crafted, made to withstand the southern storms that blow from Africa: I cannot budge them. The gold hairs on my Fool's hands, singeing, the little windows of the Tabernacle melting; within, 4 Hooligan-shapes writhe, twisting, all tied – all but one, gagged. That One's mouth opens but no words come out.

And being deaf, like God, he cannot hear my oaths, or prayers, or cries . . .

. . . At the Pendulists' Institute: Eddie again presents his compliments to 1-eye/legged von Maser.

"I'm just out of France, Direktor, on my way to Dietrichstein – have Metallurgy given us a reading yet on the Untersberg valley?"

"Indeed they have, my boy! An inspired judgment on your part – Communications has been trying to catch up with you for the last week. Gold gives a reading of One-point-eight. Silver, even better: point-six-five! You shall see, with labour so scarce, losing Avignon will prove a blessing in disguise."

But even our little master of the stiff-upper, had to be struck dumb by that blind faith in silver linings.

For Deaf'n'Dumber SAW me . . . as the fire crackled . . . and the true idiot tried too late to put it out . . . and my Provence is a dry country . . . Yes! He saw, with a master-mariner's eyes from those far-off days of sailing on our blue Mediterranean; of ferrying small children with piping voices, and wooden tea-chests, and music, and toy donkeys and chunks of marble wearing silly hats; and somewhere he is waiting, that Chosen Vessel. And in that Place he will sing with the tongues of angels, for Vengeance is –

"Von Perceval, dear boy, sit down. This constant travelling, you've been overdoing it."

"Only a touch of the sun," shrugged-off the gallant young Leader. "On the matter of labour, have you asked the Department?"

"Ah – " said the Captain, (meaning, No, Edwin) – "one has thought

650

of the matter, and the request to the Reichsfuehrer, dear boy, coming from you – the personal approach is so much stronger. The Reichsfuehrer will be pleased to receive you for breakfast, tomorrow."

... At the Bergwald: Mile after mile of unpatched craters until Edwin is deep into South Bavaria, still untouched by Cameron's bombers for some obscure strategic reason. Mime-Himmler's cave lies at Aigen, outside Salzburg, Bayreuth's rival. Eddie nurses poor Riley, aging but valiant, up a winding horror of a track that could be blocked by a single mounted knight at arms. An enormous pair of wrought-iron gates bars final entry. Also, numerous Black Order, in a concrete blockhouse, Wolf-Saluting madly.

Pass, Friend! Fool is recognized. My knees are rubbery and tummy watery. Through great windows in the dining room, far distant is Charlemagne's peak, and Sister's Love Cottage. The sun is just striking it. *Rose will be waking ...*

"Herr von Percreval, what a pleasure, we're just starting, come and join us."

Us, was 3 young Black Order, the very finest specimens, and 2 young ladies the same, with startling bosoms. Through a slurpful of grey porridge these latter persons were called "My Srecretaries" by the immaculately dressed Chicken Farmer. The face was not immaculate: puffier, greyer, matching our Real Leader's, but with the shadow of a beard already sprouting and a boil, enflamed and ugly, on Himmler's lost chin. This did not stop the "Srecretaries" from gazing worshipfully.

"Although one can have no objection to eggs," said the Chicken Farmer, "my feelings to ham have grown much stronger with the wartime presrervatives that are used. How is Kapitän von Mraser?"

"He seemed well, Herr Reichsfuehrer; it's amazing how he manages, considering his injuries."

"An example to us all, is our Kapitän ... "

And after the baronial hall with the Knights & Srecretaries, Kaffee in the study. Mein Host furtively locks both the doors and slips the key in his tunic pocket – patting it.

"Herr Edwin – I hope you don't mind such framilirarity when we are alone? – first let me say how distressed I was to hear of the accident of your rarrest. Were you mistreated in any way? Was there any conduct by

651

any of my men that was in any way rimproper? You must tell me."

"To be honest, Reichsfuehrer, your General Kaltenbrunner was pretty rough, but General Schellenberg made up for it."

"I'm glad to hear that – and I prize honesty above reverything. The problem with Kraltenbrunner, Herr Edwin, is that he doesn't attend enough of our Meditations – I have a dozen of the top ranks for a weekend, to sit in communion and simply pronder the state of the world. You've seen him since the bombing, how far would you say the Fruehrer's health has weakened?"

It is the Interrogator's art to drop such unrelated questions – but to hear them from the Grand Inquisitor's own lips was a curious sensation.

"He was a bit unsteady – but remarkable, considering."

"Naturally. Our Fruehrer is remarkrable in all ways – but if there should need to be a change of government, no matter how distasteful the prospect of such a change shall be to me prersonally – will you tell the British authorities you meet in Zürich, as a Swiss national, that I stand ready?"

"Ah – " said Edwin.

Meaning, Christ! Because what's a Trerror for, if not to strike from the earth the carrier of such blasphemy?

"You are reluctant because of your long friendship, Herr Edwin, but it would be – if it should come – an act of kindness. The Fruehrer has served long and faithfully the Nation, and our Rorder. But we are all human. Frankly, the problem is Brormann – this Toad, as I have heard you and your sister call him." This appealed to the Mime in Himmler. He actually laughed, showing bad teeth, sloping inwards. "I wonder, Herr Edwin what you call the rest of us? But seriously, tell Zürich – and inform me whenever you meet the Fruehrer, how he seems at such times. Remember discretion is the better part of vralour, as they say."

"Certainly one would be discreet, Herr Reichsfuehrer."

"Thank you Herr Edwin. It is a sad thing for a nation when the Leader is too isolated from the people. Shut away in private castles. Do you know it's more than a year since I was myself invited to the Brerghof!"

Heinrich Himmler searched his tunic, having forgotten which pocket he patted, but eventually drew out the key and unlocked his study door, and gazed positively wistfully past the boil on his vanished chin at departing Eddie. Poor little grey Mime, master of Trerror . . .

Until realising, Bloody hell I never asked about the Untersberg allocation!

"How can there be any question, Herr von Percreval? – the Grail's discrovery clearly can affect the whole War's outcome. Your quest has the highest priority. The necessary rarrangements for labour shall be made by my staff at Mauthausen."

But our Fool has never heard of it. (Really-truly, not once before that moment.) He took his usual coward's way out, and went instead to paradise.

. . . *At Love Cottage:* the ducklings are full grown; summer's apples fallen, fat wasps eat them, and get drunk, rolling on their backs, legs waving. Rose the same – not drunk, but full-fed and gurgling up at Uncle Eddie with eyes that match the end of summer's sky. Her black hair has a curl in it, one and a half twists, making a priceless ring on Uncle's finger. Ettie, as Mummy, sits in her bower, one breast barely covered, maternally slicing the last runner beans for our supper.

"You're simply going to have to get away," Uncle says; "the whole of France has fallen, and I saw Mime this morning to obtain his approval for my next dig – he shares your opinion that Wolf's bonkers. I'll drive you and Rose to Triebschen before I get started. It'll be just the same, but you'll be safe."

Rose gurgles a small bubble at Uncle from ruby lips. Mummy wipes them.

"It won't be anything like the same, Eddie, and I never said Wolf *was,* I said He was going – and I'm not. How could I possibly take Rose to be spied on by the Parrots? – I want her to grow up in our mountains."

Rose waves a tiny fist towards them – then thumps her Uncle Eddie, just hard enough to prove he's losing.

"Switzerland's nothing but bloody mountains. Ettie, we'll sell Triebschen and buy somewhere you like better."

"Why?"

Rose loves Mummy's tiny questions best because Uncle dreads them.

"I've said a hundred times – because of the war. Because of the Berghof across the valley; they'll start bombing. It's too dangerous."

653

"Rubbish." Mummy exchanges bean tops-and-tails for daughter. "There's another reason. I don't know why on earth you still bother to lie to me. Your face is utterly transparent and always has been." Rose nods, she loves all shining objects. "It's your damned Potting! You're going to tear up Love Cottage."

"Don't be absurd."

"Prove I'm wrong. Where's this new dig happening?"

"It's part of the Bad Reichenhall district."

"That's practically next door to us. What part?"

"Metallurgy haven't determined exactly. The north end of the valley."

"Our valley?"

"Well sort of. The salt mines."

"They run everywhere." Rose waves and laughs. Silly Uncle, but clever Mummy's on to him. "One comes up here."

"It's miles away. Right at the bottom of the hill. I don't know if there's even a mine-working."

"*I* know! Honestly, Eddie, what a hopeless sod you still are. All this bilge about worrying for Rose and you're going to blow our little home off the map."

"You're being paranoid. I haven't the least intention – "

"After you've just spent half an hour of solid lying? I'll tell Wolf, it's His property, then we'll see who's paranoid."

"You silly bitch, I'm not going to touch His damned property. And I don't spew all night because of Him, either."

Which blows the lid completely off. An awful silence . . . before the most frightful sound.

"You utter spying swine – you've made our Rose cry. Beastly, beastly. Come with Mummy, darling."

"I'm sorry, Ettie, you know I love Rose more than anything. I shouldn't have said – it isn't my business."

"You obviously love her more than me."

"It isn't true. I worship you. It's only because I do, that I worry so much. I won't mention it again."

"Promise? Ever?"

"Promise. Always."

"You'll break it."

"I won't."

"Yes you will – it's not your fault, you just always do."

"Ettie, I swear. Rose can cross my heart – " taking her tiny hand, tracing the points of His cross with it – "there, it's done, and hope to die."

"That should last for this evening, anyway. Change Rose; all your shouting's made her wet."

Not only that – but as it was clearly bad Uncle Eddie's fault he held his noble nose, and cleaned her, and while doing so heard Mummy, Uncle's sister, in *His* kitchen, for no earthly reason, retch her guts out before supper.

That is a Conditioned Reflex, Edwin.

We know, Mummy.

Now we have our own – and hope to die . . .

Third Movement
13th Passage

Children, clever Gedanke has an Idea: a verse from
Dear Old 20 – to take our minds off the Other Number!

DOWN AMONG THE DEAD MEN

[in 4/4, Firmly]

Let charming Beauty's health go round,
In whom celestial Joys are found;
And may Confusion still pursue
The senseless woman-hating Crew;
And they that Woman's health deny,
Down among the Dead Men let them lie.

It's almost over! – Our Quadrille; that mix of 4, locked in a square, with
5-figured Popular Lays & Operatic Airs – *Isn't it? Isn't 3-Score-&-10
Your allotted span for torture?* Old Fool! There is no Statute of
Limitations. So today Edwin enters the 2nd half of his 8th decade, still
nailed to the Great Ash Tree, in which my 2 black friends hop so gaily,
mocking lost Eddie at his cell window:

> *Down, Down, Down, Down,*
> *Down among the dead men let Him lie!*

That unutterable Toad bastard. Read, children, and weep.

Autumn:
Of the last season: men die at Boulogne; and at that dreary spot on the
Rhine called Arnhem; and at Warsaw, where the Bear sits on its
haunches across the river and laughs its head off. After all, my dears, as
Eva & Ettie say, those idiot Poles started it . . .

. . . *At the Ghetto of Graz:* The rains of winter, spring, and summer have
given way to the Flood of autumn in the wettest year on record; the

657

quaint walled compound at Margaretsberg is awash; sewage floats out of the Hooligans' latrines and into the ground floors of the antique buildings where they rest from their labours; the Death's Head brigade at the gate are sodden, on half rations, overwhelmed by the stench – of their job.

"King Yid? The fat arsehole's still pigging himself up the stairs. If those swine of his were human they'd have had his guts for garters years ago. Yellow bastards. Follow the empties, mein Herr, you can't miss the pisstank."

A wine bottle floats past, pointing up the message. The Grail Leader waded in its wake, then climbed the stairs. The gaberdined Elders in the outer office are thinner, and fewer. Their skins as yellow as their stars, the whites of their eyes, ditto.

"From an outbreak of hepatitis, Eddie. This wet weather's played hell with our hygiene, even though we're down to less than five hundred. Come in, old friend, and get warm."

Michael Rau, embracing, is plumper and fitter; his skin is cheerily red – bottle coloured; his breath and his rooms smell of liquor, mixed slightly with smoke from a cheery fire. A large oil painting hangs over the cozy hearth.

"My Breughel," Rau touched the painting, a loving gesture, stroking. "I picked it up from a Vienna contingent. It's the Peasant Breughel, as you can tell – almost as great a satirist as Bosch. Of course, Eddie, I would have liked 'Massacre of the Innocents', but beggars can't be choosers. Our Pieter made a good living from the Inquisition – as a sectarian he should have been burned. Dear friend, forgive me – you're the expert now."

"Hardly, but I have joined the club." Eddie breaks the momentous news. "I was Received today, and I had an idea."

"Two excuses to open a new Bordeaux. I hope you don't mind mutton; beef's getting scarce." Smiling Michael Rau takes a dusty bottle lovingly from a crate warming near the fire, and decants wine into crystal, on a table set with silver, as a scarecrow in gaberdine rags brings in a platter and sets our feast before the Breughel. "Tell me the great idea."

"You see, you're laughing already, and I agree it seems too simple, but I'm dead serious." Eddie clasps his friend's warm hand, for emphasis – and finds it trembles, slightly: Rau is cracking. "Why don't you *all* say you want to convert? Everyone in your ghetto. Ask for a priest to be sent for Instruction and I'm sure I could get it backed by the Vatican, right at the top. I had breakfast recently with the Chicken Farmer – he's wracked with contradictions and he wants Rome's help. I'll bet you anything he'd listen."

Michael Rau smiles kindly, and pats his other hand on top of Eddie's – to hide the trembling. "I'm a poor man, old friend. You know I got rid of all my father's holdings. The meat really isn't too bad with enough Rosemary on it."

In Remembrance of the Old Rau the two friends eat, and drink . . . until Eddie cried out,

"I knew you wouldn't take my idea seriously, but damn it, Michael, why the bloody hell not? You want to save your people – that's why you play this whole mad game of pigging it while they starve. You have no religious convictions, you hate the old jealous God – for the sake of just *saying* it until the war's over – why *not* ask to convert?"

"Dearest old Eddie, come with me."

Michael Rau pushes himself up from the table, and takes the remains of the carvings on the platter, and walks past the Breughel, and through the outer office of Scarecrow Elders, slavering, and to the head of the stairs up from the yard. At the foot of them, creatures huddle; huge-eyed, yellow-starred. With his trembling hands their mad King flings the mutton scraps down on them. The flesh and bone lands on bald heads, and bounces into the water making iridescent rings of grease.

"If I offered them, Eddie, to your Cross of Rome – and they'd accept, my poor sheep-heads, I don't doubt that – they wouldn't be Chosen, would they?"

"I don't know. I don't want your bloody riddles!"

"Then I'm twice as sorry, old friend. Forgive me."

Rau swung away from the scrabbling mass and rolled his way back to the civilised comfort of his rooms, and brandy, which he poured and passed in complete silence until he said: "Eddie, there is no riddle. I'm playing this 'game' to make the bastards outside the wire – the ones shouting the loudest in America and London – make them face up to their conceit; so that they will finally get it through their grotesque mishapen heads: the Yids are *not* His people. They are as good, or as bad, as all stinking humanity and they suffer because they love it. Catholic, Nazi, or Jew – in Manhattan, or Palestine, or this ghetto – Jehovah doesn't care a floating turd of shit."

"But you *want* to save them," Edwin shouted, "you told me last time, even if it's only a dozen – enough for a last supper."

"It's not up to me to save them, Eddie. Or the Pope, or your Chicken Farmer – my sheep-heads will have to be saved in spite of all of us, to prove me wrong."

Tears rolled down from Rau's eyes; he was very drunk.

He must be. Mustn't he? Because if he wasn't, then he was bonkers – which made Eddie cry too, for all our old days, and unforgettable places.

Because one other thing perfidious-Fool hasn't yet admitted: his best friend had abandoned King Yid's yellow-paper crown for a black skull-cap.

"Naturally it was my father's," said Michael Rau, beaming, with one of his childlike sudden mood-swings. "I pinched it from him. Come on, Eddie. No more tears. Drink up."

Yes, Papa. In Remembrance.

. . . After the Hangover: Loathing came on Edwin the next morning – for Dietrich's Fortress; hatred for its bottomless acres and wasted effort that could have been spent where it might really have mattered. Shining visions turned to mud, and nothing to show for it but a note of congratulation from Monsignor McGuire on clever Eddie passing his exams.

Reality has to be faced: the Bear is going to get here anyway. The Expedition may have a month left of wallowing. The Grail is God's work: He must send a sign.

"If there's nothing solid in seven days," the Expedition Leader instructed his Engineer Major, "we'll turn off the pumps. You've done a marvellous job; I want you to know that."

"Don't thank me, Herr von Perceval. I'd have been dead long ago if I hadn't had the luck to catch this train to the madhouse. If you really want to show your gratitude, can you put me on board for the Untersberg project?"

660

Which was Irreverent, Edwin – but the man *was* a damned good Engineer.

Leader-Eddie went out in the endless rain.

... Look down from the battlements. A helpless face stares back, horribly contorted – then vanishes, swept away in a ghastly sucking. Fool sees what he's been doing at Dietrich's fortress.

He sees a space the size of the Green Hill, enclosed by the walls of a prison. He sees a great pump crushing a bent man's fingers. He sees blue-clay mud so viscous that duckboards cannot rest on it, and he sees the old fuel tins and the horses' bloated bodies used to support those planks, and the sheep-figures crawling over them – and I saw a thousand human souls, saw them carrying slop in pails yoked on their ulcerated shoulders to pour on slop already so high against the outside walls that it was already oozing in again. And I saw the place my thousand slept in, under shreds of canvas, and lacy-rusted corrugated-iron, with no side-walls to keep the mud out, and I saw the mud sweep rag-mattresses and cooking-pots before it, stirred in the ghastly soup with the figure who had cried to me for help and vanished . . .

God had sent His sign.

The sobered Expedition Leader closed down Dietrich's Castle 1 week early and sent a Black Order message to the Chicken Farmer's Headquarters:

GRAZ COUNTERPRODUCTIVE THIS DATE STOP REQUEST
RE-ALLOCATION DRACHENFELS TO BE CALLED LORELEI
HIGHEST METALS READING CLN GOLDEN PROSPECTS
EXCLAM STOP.

And then –?

Why then, children – with a prayer to his Maker that he-Edwin was not mad, thank God, like Michael Rau – our Uncle Eddie flew home to Rose.

(And Ettie, naturally. Some things surely go without saying.)

. . . *At Love Cottage:* Rose remembers! It was unmistakable, the gurgling chuckle, the grasp on Uncle's little finger – *my* finger. My Rose in the snows, for the first fall had cloaked the mountain; our snug harbour was

661

silently perfect, except for a bright gray and blue jay, and Rose's tiny laugh.

"I told you," said Ettie-as-Mummy, "no one's ever cross, or gossiping, or all the hopeless things we used to be, and do. How could anybody ever want to leave? If you had any sense, Eddie, you'd chuck the Pot completely, not just Hungary, and stay and read the Bible to Rose for the winter."

My dears, she *was* – and not the nursery one with the pictures of all the chaps looking soppy: Mummy had acquired a Gutenberg version, reworked in Heidelberg, circa 1848, a red-letter Wagner year.

"If you were going to start," said Uncle, miffed, "you might at least have used an English one so you'd see where the quotes come from – but since you've been bitten, can we get Rose baptised now?"

"Are you mad? Condemn our precious to a lifetime of Roman mumbo-jumbo?" Rose waves 2 round legs, with perfect toes, and stares with disbelief at Uncle. Grownup Mummy said, "I'm reading the damn book for its literary qualities, darling, not for my soul – which is doing very nicely, with Nature, thank you."

Rose accepted a last kiss and fell asleep. Mummy & Uncle also went to bed – as Brother-&-Sister and rather frantic, as they hadn't for some time! – and picking her moment with exquisite care, after, as Eddie lay inwardly bewailing his Manifold Wickedness, Ettie said,

"But if we're talking of religion, how did you get through the confessing? You've been rather naughtier than most new boys."

"When one takes instruction as an adult, the Church expects a full plate of sin – after all, one's a heretic anyway. One makes a general breast-baring, as it were. My Confessor was very decent; he didn't try and pry."

"And what if one gets one that does? After now, for instance?"

"I shan't go for a while. I'm not a fanatic."

"But when you do?"

"I should say I'd had relations with a woman."

"That's true, one can't be more relationed than us." Sister's hand traces its familiar path across Brother's groin. "You wouldn't say it was me, then?"

"Good God! Never!"

"But that's the point, surely – " freshly moistening her fingers,

662

slipping them wetly into his corners, "God *sees*. He knows you're lying. He's looking now, while we do this . . ." with our tongue, "and this . . ." our mouth – and more of both, and more! while the fool squirms, torn in two now, by Anima & Holy Mary – in 3, counting Ettie; who went on to make a complete balls of it, and then lay on her back, laughing.

"I mean, it is funny, pet, doing Push-Me-Pull-You with one's Sis – however many beadsworth is that?"

"We love each other, wholly. I don't call that sinful. I told you, I don't believe in everything. It's more mental, a state of mind – like you and Nature."

"As long as you do mean that, because I'd hate to think every spotty little priest playing with himself in a cupboard knew it *was* me, or that you had to burn in hell forever –" as she kissed with sticky lips – "night-night."

. . . Until the morning, when, for our sins, the Convert found just how closely He watches over Us.

I Spy:

Rose led Uncle to it: she was crying, too early for breakfast, too fretful for our treasure. Mummy stirred. Eddie said, "You stay, I'll go and bring her."

The little face was puckered, the little hand brushing angrily. She rolled her head, this way, back again, cried again. A drop of water from the ceiling had landed on her perfect button-nose.

"Never mind," said Uncle, "it's just Mr Snowman, melting, on the roof, 'cause it isn't proper winter yet. See," holding her, and pointing, "there's a crack in our ceiling; we'll fix it before our Rest."

After Uncle's coffee: the practical fellow climbed up in the attic – not an easy task because the pull-down ladder had jammed but eventually, with a precarious balancing of apple boxes, he made it to the opening and found that the cord had just caught on a nail, so that was simple. We never used the attic bedroom; the floor was dusty, cobwebs framed the window, but the leak wasn't there anyway, the water dribbled in from the space behind, under the eaves. A hatch opened into it. Eddie went back for a candle. In the kitchen Ettie said, "It'll be my squirrels, they go for the bark on the rafters. You're not to disturb them. I'll move Rose's crib."

663

The rafters are whole saplings: there had been squirrels, the trunks were neatly peeled, and an entry, squirrel-sized, leads out through the hand-split laths that form the roof under the tiles, but no nest; now only old wasps' combs hang down, converted into flats for spiders. The bricks of the chimney warm them; the candle shows the water coming from behind it, under a roll of motheaten bird-netting for berries, and some clay pots, "and seed flats," Eddie calls down to Ettie, "and an old car battery of all things, and another – a third! It's quite mad what peasants collect, you should see all this stuff. They're harnessed together in a positive cat's cradle. Shades of Mama, not letting us have electricity for the wireless." And pulling aside the netting, "there's even an old gramophone."

... a wire recorder, actually; leading to a microphone that hangs above a knothole in Mummy's bedroom (& Uncle-Eddie's); with a box-camera suspended also, an expensive Leica, focussed narrowly on the comings-&-goings: the lens shutter is activated from the recorder: *All the better to –*

"Eddie, you're being ages, and a little drop simply doesn't matter – come away, you'll disturb their hibernating."

Uncle ripped off the wires from the terminals, and exposed the film to the light through the cobwebs, and stuffed the netting back, so that Mummy shouldn't see, and went downstairs as though nothing had happened.

"You look as though you've seen a ghost," she said.

"A touch of claustrophobia; it goes back to that time I was trapped in the cave."

"Too much time in tunnels isn't healthy. Eddie darling, really, stop the Potting – and stay here with us."

"I can't, Ettie, I'm just getting the Lorelei started." And adding, casually, "I couldn't find the leak – does your peasant ever come up to do repairs? Or anyone else from the village?"

"Not a soul. My ancient's the only man left for the Duration and he could never manage ladders. No one invades us but you, my pet – and Wolf's new adjutant, once, just finding the way after that other poor boy lost his arms. But the new one isn't the squirrelling sort – Mum's-the-word, and Wolf-salutes – even Rose couldn't get a smile." Rocking her, to show silly Uncle how we tried.

"Ettie, I'll make a bargain: go with Rose to Switzerland and I'll give up Potting."

"Would you?" Rose stares with Mummy, 4 wide blue eyes, wondering. "No, you wouldn't. Poor darling, you were born with absolutely the wrong kind of phiz for a liar."

Rose agrees: Uncle's long face is the funniest thing ever!

... *After lunch:* Faithful Riley took him down the snowy track, cautiously, with chains on, away from his Snow White & Rose Red, both waving and calling, with the blue and grey jay screaming, and fresh, soft flakes falling and melting on their fair faces, and gold – *but no, one is still raven-haired; dark as the brooding pair that fly a mile high above the valley, south to north, ahead of the Fool.* So that it should come as no surprise to see, at the junction where the road splits in 3: for Bayreuth, or His Salt Mountain, or the far Dragon country – a black Mercedes waiting, and in it, disguised as a squat grey toad, the Secretary to Alberich and black Hagen – and Herr Wolf, on the good days, it goes without saying.

But it was a surprise, to see the thug-form of Daddy-Darling, and to hear, "Herr Edwin," in that coarse, farm-labouring Brunswick voice, "the Fuehrer heard you were driving in the region. Please come to the Berghof. He has something to show you."

How did He hear? *How did He ever? A big bird told Him.*

... *At the Salt Mountain:* Eddie & Riley follow the Toad's Mercedes through massive steel blast-doors that rise electrically into an underground garage. Three banks of Death's Heads guard it. Death came too close with 1-eyed Count Stauffenberg: almost in the family. The Fool climbed out of the Riley. A skull-guard ran a metal-detecting wand over his person.

"Leave your luggage," ordered Bormann, "it shall be checked separately before being taken to your room."

"Am I staying the night? I have an appointment in the morning at Drachenfels."

"We can arrange aircraft. This will depend."

With the incomplete threat, the toad-bastard strutted ahead like a gutter Mussolini (the Duce always considered himself a man of culture)

665

to another steel door, smaller. It opened to a lift. Fool entered, expecting to rise. Instead –

The lift drops, swiftly, leaving the Fool's stomach to follow with his luggage. Several floors flash by, of solid rock. The lift stops. The door opens. A small dark room: a sloping floor, a red light sign, *Ausgang*, above a second steel door leading out for emergencies. Four theatre seats are arranged two-thirds of the way back. A small table holds a bowl, empty, that once contained sugared Kuchen. The air smells like Eva's shelter, as though someone has made mistakes in a dark corner.

"Be seated, Herr von Perceval. The righthand, if you please."

Playing with his wedding ring, slipping it up and down, obscenely, Daddy-Darling sits beside the Fool with his thick thighs touching.

"You said I was to meet Herr Wolf."

"I said the Fuehrer had something to show you."

The thug raises his squat toad-arm, and stabs the wedding finger upwards. A curtain pulls back on a faintly whining motor. A film projection beam comes on behind the Fool's shoulder, a screen shines whitely. From its glare the Fool sees a plate glass window covered by a shuttered blind in the wall beside him. 10 feet away, no more. Then numbers in a circle, counting down;

9

8

7

No titles. No music. Not a Riefenstahl production.

6

5

4

Lines and flickers, the print has been run many times, like the Little Tramp's that came to School from the Women's Institute.

3

2

I

A Gothic sign. The film is in colour. Black-on-Red. Don't tell me!

THE PEOPLE'S COURT

SOUND:

But scratchy, too treble.

A VOICE:

Male, barking, hysterical, screaming:
"Loathesome Swine! Verminous Scum! Extermination is too good for all of you!"

A FACE:

Round, weak, apoplectic, wearing a floppy cap like the Master's bust, far away on our island.

A FULL IMAGE:

A Hanging Judge, standing in a sort of pulpit.
"You know your sentence. I leave you to guess with your Maker at a suitable form of execution."

A GROUP IMAGE:

Eight MEN, unshaven, ashen, civilian-clothed, but no jackets, no braces or belts for their trousers. The Fool gasps, recognising three from his walks on the gravelled paths, but cannot put a name to them.

BLACKOUT:

No, only a cut in the film, poorly spliced, producing momentary blackness, broken by a brief yellow flash with some red dots, then a white room, out of focus, coming in. Lines on the walls, now, crisply, the joints of tiles, and curved lines become pegs. A games changing room from School? No, the pegs become hooks, and the hooks are too large for any except a giant's clothing, Death's Heads stand waiting, rubber-booted, rubber-gloved.
The Fool said, "I don't want to see this."
The Toad-bastard grunted, "The door is locked."
The wedding ring slipped faster, up-and-down that thick finger.

THE GROUP IMAGE:

But now the Eight Men are naked. They cut poor figures, stooped, flab-sided, droop-bellied, anything but Volsung Heroes. They cannot hide their genitals; their hands are manacled behind them; their ankles shackled. The shackles

667

make a noise; the men are trembling in unison. Alberich's anvil chorus in flesh.

THE FIRST MAN:

Is led forward. The Fool closes his eyes. But there is sound. Sound has been this Fool's life, perfect pitch. Rising, rising, too high for the male range, the sound from castrati. The Fool blocks both ears with both hands. He leans forward, rocking in his darkness, choking –

Ice cold water! In one's face. Spluttering. One's eyes wide open.

A FIGURE:

Hangs from a black iron hook. Something glints at its neck – the wire from my life, my piano. The body twists. The wire bites. Blood spurts – from the neck, the tongue, as half that organ falls to the tile floor, bitten off, to be joined by other matters, that ejaculate in spurts, and stream and splatter, sliding down the legs and over the shackles as the body twists, and jerks in unbelievable muscular contortions, jack-knifing to the waist, with blood-and-brown dripping from the buttocks . . .

CUT TO:

THE HEAD:

Where the eyes start from their sockets, resting on the cheeks, perfectly balanced, half-through their eyelids – and then the silver wire of my piano – *His Rat-trap* – cuts through the wind pipe and the tune is over, with a last spill of vomit to fall into the other.

THE OTHER:

Because that is the most dreadful: that the others have to wait there, watching, hearing, in their anticipation adding to the smelling,

7

6

5

4

3

2

Until there was only One, the Last Man, left, waiting, and the Fool sat shuddering, and retching, his gold head turned away from that Toad-

Face to the glass wall beside him – *where the blind shakes, as a trembling hand moves it back in place again. A small, feminine hand, with its private soldier's grip, and bitten nails. The hand of Hagen.*

"So now," said the bastard toad-brute in the seat next to the greatest Fool that ever lived, "and for the future – with these visits to Zürich, and your sister, and the child, we all know how we stand, von Perceval."

And how We fall.

The wedding ring slipped off completely. It dropped and lay at Edwin's feet. Daddy-Darling picked the ring up, licked it, and slid it back on his thick finger, wetly.

. . . *Upstairs, tea-time, His private quarters:* Just Eddie and the Chefin of the house – with black Stasi & Negus, scratching by Mistress. Our Host was absent.

"Yes, still on business; He works so hard. Oh, dear Herr Eddie, it's so lovely to see you." She kissed her Friend on both cheeks to prove it, then looked around as though they were conspirators. The reunion was being held in the small parlour-dining room. "You must consider this your home whenever you get out of those old mines."

"Thank you, Fräulein Eva, but I'm terribly busy. As well as here, we're just getting a dig started at the Drachenfels."

"But you must have some time, and we are in Berlin so much. In the awful bombing, I can't have the Doggies – dear Herr Eddie, forgive me, you seem sad also. Has something happened? To your dear sister?"

"No, nothing, I'm just tired – it's probably the air raids. They make driving difficult."

"I can't bear to go to Munich – to see what they've done to our beautiful city. And the fog-machines here on the mountain are horrid – but enough of being down in the dumps, you must stay for the night at least. The Fuehrer insists – you are to have your old room, He says, from the long ago, before even I lived here. What so-long special friends we are, Herr Eddie – oh, good, here He is coming now to join us, He so wanted to be here to meet you. And Herr Eddie – " putting a finger to her lips – "pretend you don't notice about the shaking. It's in the mind, Morell says, from the horrible explosion. We have to be extra cheerful for Him."

The shaking is minor, a tremor of the right arm that can be controlled by a hand in a pocket: the limp was the big thing, almost peg-legged now, thumping like von Maser, as He came across the pine planks and then the braided oval of the carpet.

"Ederl, my dear fellow! Forgive me if we don't shake hands – too much lye in the soap again. I've had a special committee at Farben's looking into it – the full resources of the chemists of this country and we can't get a wartime soap that doesn't skin one alive? Don't tell me! Now, let's look at you."

As though He hasn't . . .

For that is the hardest part, to stand, in one's normal Foolisch posture, with one's slight English diffidence (that He & Eva find so-charming); one's golden head tipped slightly down and to one's side; one's perfect lips slightly smiling, one's perfect teeth barely showing – with my eyes averted, because there Edwin can't hide it, the knowledge of the cellar. Nor can He, because He looks away at once, here-there-everywhere – yes, one of Our manic moods, children.

"To begin with, I haven't thanked you properly – it's reprehensible, but I've had a full plate this autumn, preparing the Counter-offensive. The grand slam. Excuse me if I sit, while we let our Chefin pour our tea."

Eva helps Him to a rocker. Edwin says, "Thank me for what, Herr Wolf? – or I should say, my Fuehrer."

"You should certainly not! After twenty years? Perhaps in public, that's a different matter, but in our private moments, one would be hurt deeply – to thank you for saving my life, naturally. I've told people a thousand times. If I hadn't gone outside to greet Herr Edwin – I wasn't even told, that's the extraordinary thing, because Bormann was playing his old tricks of keeping things from me – for my own good, the man always says, and of course he's right, one gets a million demands on one's time, there has to be some screening – 'But not the oldest friends,' I told him, 'there aren't so many that it's too much for your thick Brunswick head to manage.' One has to be firm with Bormann, even wag a finger – the fellow's like some dogs, they're faithful enough but they have that stubborn streak, they get a bee in their bonnet – you flying with Stauffenberg. One knows that a dog like Blondi is yours, body and soul. The other kind get jealous, they're often the ones that turn and have to be put – Where was I?"

670

"My last visit to the Wolfsschanze, Herr Wolf."

"Ah yes! The bombing – the Voice said it: Ederl's here. As clear as a bell – anyone who hasn't the gift would never believe it. We have all our miracle machines and weapons – the rockets are devastating Britain, I'm sorry to tell you, but Churchill has never listened. I doubt that he can, now the spirochaetal infection is sufficiently advanced into the central system – I've been speaking to Brandt about it, because of these headaches – modern science is achieving wonders, but the brain is the miracle. I suspect that the Voice, as I call it, because it comes at such rare and special occasions – only a handful in one's lifetime – it must be a marshalling of all the brain's resources, much as the mobilization before a grand campaign. Every cell and fibre massed for that plunge forward to avert catastrophe. In extremis there really is no limit to what the human mind can do – *if*, our little word again – *if* the human that owns it is prepared to obey his instructions. Perhaps it takes a soldier, someone who's been trained to respond instantly, unswervingly, to orders, so that when the summons comes, you just move forward. Like my rebuilding, or moving the Dome, immense thought and concentration have gone into the decision for months before the offensive. Take the counterstroke I've got up my sleeve for the Nigger-jazz brigade. I can't tell you where, but you can guess that once more I thank Caesar. That has to be the difference between us – Churchill gets his inspiration from the bottle, Roosevelt from *Them*. The stupidity of such men can't be believed! – building on dregs when all history is there to support us. Perhaps in the last analysis that's the Voice – the accumulated wisdom of the racial memory, refined and focussed through one especially gifted individual – and I don't say that in an immodest sense, it's nothing to do with oneself that one possesses a certain type of brain. One could just as easily have been a cretin – or had Churchill's syphilitic background. The line is razor sharp dividing the halves of humanity – no, it isn't just the brain, it's what the human individual does with it. A specimen like Bormann, for example, is admirable as my secretary, one couldn't get along without him, I freely admit it – even Himmler in his own way, although I can't stick the fellow personally – but neither of those men has the spark that would drive them. *There are no limits* . . . yes, this is the single lesson life's taught me – if the mind *believes* that, then anything is possible. With Himmler – I can't be specific, but like all the others he's already attempting to countermand certain of my most vital orders on the ground of public opinion! God in heaven! Be guided by History by all means – but *opinion*? Whose? The Yellow press? Your enemies? Stalin's Reds? *Them*? Ha! Remember Napoleon and Cromwell needed centuries – and they didn't have the Caftan-crowd on their backs to contend with, owning the printing presses of this world. But history goes beyond all that – history is in our stars, it circles and returns in its own time. Those are the cycles of time the Chosen man must think in. It isn't easy – being singled out never is ... Tschapperl, what are you thinking of? You've let our tea grow completely cold. Herr Edwin hasn't touched a thing."

So the Fool wrestles through raspberry-tea and sugar-Kuchen, and the rest of the evening when a film is shown – in the main drawing room, with the blackout curtains drawn, and a screen to block the fire in the massive hearth – and what does one watch, my dears, in such a setting? Why, 2 harmless interludes, to take one's mind off things: from the land of Nigger-jazz we watched *Snow White* & *The Reluctant Dragon*.

And then –?

Why Musik, naturally, liebe Kinder. Kultur, the highest Europe has to offer; The Master's, played 4000 feet up the Magic Mountain; Edwin's Special for these occasions, a medley of 49 motifs. Seven 7's, to get one through the rest of the evening without more talking, or thinking, just one's hands moving across the keys in Sister's songs – *but I can't stop wondering, Can she hear them? Can my Rose?* Which proved one was sane, until Eddie remembered: *She has His hair.*

"Once more," He said, "your last – Siegfried's Rhine Journey. Ah, my Ederl, so much depends ..."

And then –?

Why Bed, children, naturally. Bye-byes, in the Privat wing with the hypnotic eyes of the Portrait, and the composite nude, and the bronze catafalque for Geli, where Eddie, unable to sleep for some fool's reason, saw Him at three in the morning, hunched, with that trembling hand on the casket, drumming.

And then –?

I closed the door, to shut Him out: but not the sound of water running, in a basin, with scarifying lye soap from I.G. Farben, for endless washing.

And then –?

The Ardennes! Caesar's Battle Route! – a 2nd time, providing a last flash of illusion that Klingsor's black magic is working – but Edwin didn't see that trick. The coward fled again into the bowels of the earth, which he still thought, being a Fool, could hide him from His madness.

Refrain:

> *Down among the Dead Men,*
> *Down among the Dead Men,*
> *Down, Down, Down, Down –*
> *Down among the dead men let Me lie!*

... *Winter, the last season:* The Last Campaign fails. Nigger-jazz triumphs – and comes howling through the gap in the Ardennes, borne on the American military wireless even to the Drachenfels; a Lorelei called Peggy Lee, she drowns out the Wagner which the Grail Leader has played over loudspeakers in the diggings to encourage the Hooligans to one grand final effort.

The rival songfest worked! My dears, a chapel was discovered, 10th Cent, high up on the rock above the Rhine, & a sepulchre, with lovely bones, & armour – and deliciously macabre touch, a second skull beside the body.

"But loved or hated, my dear boy, who can say?" said von Maser, peering past his eyepatch. "Your remains are Chivalric, which is promising. The Sensitives will have a group session over them once we are relocated."

Things were getting too hot for the level heads of the Institute (although Ravensbrück is still not bombed by Cameron) and the Pendulists were moving from Fuhlsbüttel to cooler quarters in the south.

"Astrology," added the Kapitän, departing in haste with his 1 eye-and-leg, "sees a stalemate in the late spring. They say the Enemy's line will go through Berlin, but Bavaria will remain to us. Your woman, Frau Steiner, is really most positive. It seems that Saturn has completed its malign pattern. But just between you and me, dear boy, be prepared to lose Project Lorelei. Put all your eggs on Charlemagne – and make sure you take extra travel vouchers, the petrol situation has gone beyond all bounds of reason."

The Grail Leader stays at the Drachenfels to the last minute – any day now. The Bear rolls into Silesia. The Allied Mental Defectives (Wolf's description) meet the Bear's slit-eyed Keeper at Yalta. On the Feast of St Valentine, to prove their own toughness, the stern Western fellows out-Fafner Fafner and coolly parboil Dresden (after ensuring enough refugees are present to make a meal).

Beside himself for the safety of Rose – and Sister – Fool drives Riley in appalling conditions of snow and bombing south to Love Cottage.

His plan is nothing less than to *kidnap them*! (by putting a Sleeping Draught in Ettie's chocolate) and thence to Triebschen, without any of her idiotic questions. Can you imagine?!

Once clear of Munich, the bomb-craters stop: we enter the charmed circle, the Plan is feasible – until the Riley got me to the foot of the Untersberg. The lane was guarded by a Death's Head detachment.

"Herr von Perceval? – ah yes, you are on Obergruppenfuehrer Bormann's list. You have permission to proceed."

But only after a complete search of car, and luggage of driver. They drove up the lane, Eddie & Riley, until we were clear of the troops, and then Edwin stopped beside the tombs to think, and looked out over the valley. Complete stillness, white tranquillity. No sign of the black horrors on the far side in the cellars of Mama's chalet, or of the 1000 human moles her son has toiling in the salt galleries.

The Idea!

Comes out of the white nowhere.

"The mine," the Fool shouted to his dear old Riley. 'We'll find the branch coming up to the tombs, and take Rose out that way – and Ettie."

So bucked was the moron by this mental activity that he reversed without even visiting Love Cottage, and sped past the guards to the Chicken Farmer's castle (the Pendulists having taken refuge in one of its towers).

"Here are the plans of the known galleries and workings," the Grail Leader addressed the Senior Practitioner, "and this is the Army Survey of the Untersberg. You'll see I've marked the location of the cemetery in the red circle, on the north flank. There are salt deposits in a cave by the tombs, but none of the known workings runs closer than three kilometers. If your needles could find any positive indication, there's still time to move the labour force to that side of the valley."

"*If?*" the Senior Practitioner was offended, "in this hour of the nation's fortune, Herr von Perceval, there can be no question of *if's*. Not a moment can be wasted. I shall consult Astrology at once for the most auspicious moment to align the instruments."

"But that could take months."

"My dear young man, calm yourself. We are dealing here with Science. The metals cannot possibly be suspended without considering the magnetic influences of the Moon – under the circumstances we can forego the planets. This means twenty-four hours at the most – if I may suggest, fill the time by arranging your labour force. Science cannot help you there, but the Survey sheet gives off an excellent aura. My hands feel exceptionally positive about the whole thing."

(The Senior Practitioner's hands had found the aura of the *Bismarck*. Too late to stop it sinking, but the Institute can hardly be blamed for that.)

Edwin descended from the tower to find luck running high. The Chicken Farmer is also in residence: in his study, looking wan.

"Herr Edwin, sit down. I wish I could be more chreerful, but I have just received word of Lrorelei closing. I had such hopes for it. The national situation is so prerilous."

"I don't think we need to abandon hope yet, Herr Reichsfuehrer." The Fool enthusiastically outlines the work set in train for the Charlemagne side of things, less personal motives, it goes without saying. "The problem as you can see will be one of manpower. I talked to the regional overseer by telephone, but between the Secretary taking people for air-raid shelter construction, and the Reichsmarschall for some Museum Curation scheme, there's hardly anyone left locally for the Grail."

"This is nonsense." Himmler snapped out of his Mime-lethargy. "Brormann's being deliberately obstructive, he hates Charlemagne for butchering the Saxons – but this is an emergency. As for Groering moving his rart collection, that is of no consequence whatever. Herr von Percreval, my Deprartment will furnish new recruits. But first I have to swear you to secrecy – may I take your word as an English gentleman?"

"Of course, Herr Reichsfuehrer."

"I'm sorry that I have to ask, but as this involves an order of the Fruehrer –" for a moment Mime's resolve weakened; he looked up at an oil of a Siegfried vessel dashing itself against the rocks, then decided! "So be it." He scribbled on a paper. "I shall place my raircraft at your disposal, and a warrant. Proceed to this location. Establish with the Commandant how many trades he has that would be of use – miners, drillers, and so frorth. Also the fittest general labourers – this may even include prohibited groups, the warrant will so specify. Tell him that rail transprortation shall rarrive commencing tonight. All movements are to be complete within two days. How is that?"

"I don't know what to say. Marvellous."

"I should thank you, Herr Edwin. It's such an enormous relief to be able to *act*! For a positive purpose. It's strange, but from the first, despite Brormann, knowing the legend of the Untersberg I have always felt that Charlemagne would provide the final key. It matches so well with the Fruehrer's main vision. How tragic that he no longer sees it clearly. First the assassination, now this frightful horror at Dresdren – it would never have happened if we had been able to pursue matters through Stockholm and Zrürich."

. . . *At the Cave of Fafner:* The Fool's approach and descent by Storch co-incide with a night raid on Linz so that the bomber fleet, with its fighter screen, is above him, and the defensive gun batteries below. The murderous charges aimed by each at the other explode at half-way house. The searchlights stab, blinding: the tiny Storch twists, madly evading through banks of fog; the side-walls of the cleft are brilliant as quick-silver, stygian-black, crimson-and-yellow as a bomber falls, trailing a comet's tail of flaming fuel, then, two-thirds down the cleft disintegrating in a sun of man's making. After ten thousand feet riding Death's shoulder, the cleft ended. The Storch landed.

The Fool steps down, in the fog and blackout no one can see him shaking. The mouth of the cave is framed by a great gate, with a name, and a legend, but so high overhead, scarcely visible, illegible. A staff-car with dimmed blue lights arrives. The gate opens.

"The Assistant Commandant – my superior's compliments, mein Herr. I'm sorry to be late for your arrival. The raid upset things. One understands you have a special warrant for labour allocations?"

"Rather a large one, I'm afraid."

"The more the better from our point of view. Trying to wind an operation this size down in a hurry is a hell of a problem. Forward, Driver."

Through the great gate, another, a third set of jaws closes behind the car with blue lights. *Inside.* The cave at first seems empty, barrack blocks stretch in rows; not a light shows anywhere; no human figure moves over the deserted ground – only dogs, their eyes caught green by the car's blue, loping and prowling. Faithful Alsatians: good Blondi.

In the Commandant's Office there is coffee, only ersatz, but it's hot; the ritual helps to put the terror of the flight with all the others.

"Herr von Perceval, I'm the Commandant. Welcome to Mauthausen." A Death's Head colonel, a tired, thin man, quite short, with a harried high-pitched voice and receding hair – a clerk, more than butcher, with manicured hands. "I've only just got back myself, another Crisis meeting in Berlin. One has to wonder how long we can keep up the flights in these conditions – what is it exactly that you want from us?"

The Toll House:
No more escaping it: now the Fool knows the Cave's name.

"People with mining, or quarrying experience, ideally, Herr Commandant, but I realize one can't ask the impossible. Any able-bodied men would do."

"At this stage most certainly, mein Herr. They go down like flies with typhus, and all the other communicable diseases they bring with them from their sewers. We can deliver, but how long they'll last, we don't promise."

"I understand. I'd like a thousand."

"Scraping the barrel, but it should be possible." The Commandant turns to his Assistant. "The Reichsfuehrer's warrant says time is of the essence, we'll dispense with formality. Take Herr von Perceval directly to the Senior Capo. The man knows up-to-date conditions better than we do. Muster a roll-call and load them directly."

"Thank you very much indeed, Herr Commandant."

Can we believe? In Fafner's very jaws, the Fool still spoke so effing politely! The Commandant smiled, thinly.

"Wait till you see what you're buying, Herr von Perceval. At least if we can ship the product out tonight you'll have a head-start on tomorrow's bombing. Some may arrive at Berchtesgaden in one piece. What the hell is the world coming to?" But the Commandant knows that these days there's no answer to such questions. Our yesterdays were better. "I once was privileged to hear your sister. I visited Bayreuth as an aide to the Reichsfuehrer – it was the 1939 Season, before all this started. The Fräulein Edwina sang the part of Kundry, in *Parsifal*, I have never forgotten it. She must sing again, when this is over. Will you convey my compliments when you are next with her?"

"I will, Herr Commandant. And again, thank you."

"At least, don't blame us. Gute Nacht, Herr von Perceval."

Back into the fog, with the Death's Head Assistant. The car with blue lights drives past more of the dogs' green wolves' eyes, and the endless rows of faceless buildings, to stop at one that is smaller and separated from the others in a compound.

"The Boss Capo probably won't be here, but I'll check before we go further. I suggest you wait in the car, mein Herr, it's warmer."

A heater gives off diesel fumes, but scarcely raises the temperature. The Capo's Palace is the size of the little Siegfriedhaus; its windows broken. The Assistant comes back smacking his hands against his upper arms for circulation.

"God, are we going to get spring this year? It was as I thought, the fellow never sleeps. Forward, Driver!"

The blue-lights are useless in the fog, the car creeps slowly. Spring is delayed, but day is coming – bad news, Fool thinks, given the Commandant's ominous remark about losses from bombing. Ahead, over the barracks a faint red glow colours the fog to form a morning skyline. Stupid Fool. It's midnight.

"Poor Linz is buying it again. I should warn you, Herr von Perceval, things always look worse in the dark. I only wish we *could* stop operations after sunset – the glow makes us a perfect target – but thank God, for some reason the Allied idiots never seem to take advantage."

In the fog the glow is brighter, deeper, redder, boiling and swirling like The Master's steam curtain in the Festspielhalle. The car with blue lights turn a corner. The Fool blanches.

"The disease situation would be hopeless without it," is an Assistant's observation.

"Driver, stop!"

THE OBSIDIAN BEACH

I saw a man take a steel baling hook. The hook was twelve inches long. The curve, eight inches in diameter. It had a cross-handle of wood. The tip of the hook was bright. The rest was caked with co-agulated matter, like the man's clothes. He swung the hook at a naked corpse. The corpse was that of a young girl, that might once have been a sister. The hook sank into the girl's body. It made a plopping sound. It entered through her abdomen, which was swollen as though she was pregnant. It was a yellow colour. Then the hook came out through her vagina. Her cunt. Her pubic hair was blonde: it was not only Them who fed His oven. The body slid down in front of me. And then the rotten flesh ripped apart and the whole hook came out. And with it the entrails. And the blood-shit-slime covered my shoes. And a cloud that stank beyond anything a mere viewer in a cellar could ever, ever, ever, imagine, sprayed upwards into my nostrils.

"Hold your nose, Herr von Perceval, and wait again here."

A second hook caught the girl's body under her left breast. It slung her up onto the fire. Her shaved head lolled, out and down. The eyes opened. Blue eyes. Mama's eyes. My eyes. And she had been pregnant. But the true horror was —

in that new criminal reality the Myth will not turn off! The play keeps on. Figures dance along the glassy shoreline: the Nibelungs, toiling. They lift and heave, they drag, they stack objects, with gelatined petrol for ashlogs. An I.G. Farben funeral pyre. And beyond the Obsidian Beach, the hill of my dream: only a mound, but it looms like a mountain. The Nibelungs attack it, with shovels, with bare hands; gases flare out when they do so, in jets like a Roman candle. The Nibelungs drag more oily objects from the mound with hooks, like those in a cellar. Part of an object falls off, to be lifted by hand and —

NO OBJECT.
STOP THESE GAMES WITH WORDS, YOU CRIMINAL.
CONFRONT IT. SAY WHAT YOU *SAW*.

I saw her arm bend at the elbow. I saw it rise, like Siegfr–

NOT STAGE DIRECTIONS, *REALITY*, DAMNED FOOL.

I saw her fat melt. I saw it join the pool. The SS Assistant strode along
its edge. His boots matched its mirrored surface. From each crisp
heel-print new flames sprang up, of the girl's burning fat. Actual Loge's
flames, that shone off the silver-bones and made real Donner's
lightning-bars. The SS man stopped beside a Jew directing others at the
burial mound. They walked back side by side. The Capo was scrawny.
He came up only to the SS man's shoulder. Then the fog rolled down
and hid them. The driver of the car with blue lights sounded the horn.

Synchronicity:

"Good evening, mein Herr."

> *Blow, bugle, blow, set the wild echoes flying,*
> *And answer echoes, answer, dying.*

Poems are reality. There is no co-incidence. Michael Rau bowed to me,
obsequiously. He wore no crown, no cap; his beard was gone, and his
three chins; his head was shaved; his face was hollow, in the light from
the pyre – a skull, already.

"Hullo Michael."

"So you do know this rogue, Herr von Perceval. War makes strange
bedfellows. Capo, this must be your lucky night. Excuse me, gentlemen,
the camera-crew have over-exposed the film again. I'll leave you both
for a moment."

The SS man walked back to the fire at the edge of the lake of fat. Two
stick-figures with a tripod were filming the nightmare; choosing artistic
angles, and measuring the light.

"For a voyeur in high places, with special tastes, mein Herr. The
Commandant's Assistant is graciously allowing us to set a price. Do you
wish to open the bidding, or shall I?"

Two frames of madness: Adolf Hitler's cellar in high places. Rau's by the ghastly lake. Because Rau *was* mad. To see and hear him, an onlooker would swear Rau had never met me in his life.

"Michael, for God's sake, at least say my name."

"This is not permitted by regulations, mein Herr. However, when Aryans and inmates meet in such circumstances, it's customary to exchange a skin for something of value, for the sake of the old days."

"You mean *your* skin, Michael? Thank Christ! You damned pig-headed – I've been trying for a year! You didn't have to let it get this far – to put yourself in here, but we've been over all that. It won't cost a penny to leave, you old idiot – you'll come as the first man chosen for my Untersberg group. I'll see you're freed the instant we arrive."

"I am afraid, mein Herr, these transactions have to be in Camp currency."

Rau bowed again, with that moronic formality. The SS man walked back.

"All done then, Capo?"

"Not quite completed, Herr Assistant Commandant. The gentleman wishes to visit the bank."

"You damned rogue – you've really found yourself in gravy. Herr von Perceval, don't be bullied; we can soon get the bastard's price adjusted."

"I can take care of myself. Whatever he says. Let's just get on with it."

"Very well – Capo, complete your transaction while the siren goes for roll-call, and not a minute longer. Ride back with us in the car."

The fat-lake and its beach receded. The flames in the fog subsided. In the car with blue lights there was silence. At a building like all the others, except for its name, Special Administration, the SS Assistant stepped into an office and threw a switch. The banshee-wail of the siren mercifully drowned out the crackle of burning fat – *but in reality it continues, louder and louder AND LOUDER*. Rau took a key from a board stencilled casually, Verboten. I followed him down a passage. Through a window, skeletons in their stripes flooded from the Night and Fog. Rau unlocked an ordinary door.

And then I saw all the backstage props from so enormous a production – disgorged from the railwagon gullet of its dragon: the clichéd bales of hair, the lingerie and shoes, the prosthetic devices, tiny ones, from children, in a bin, marked, Krupp For Smelting.

"And what you really have to see –" said this terrible, mad, play-acting Rau, as the siren screamed: "Nothing less than the heart of the Treasure of the Nibelungs – from our teeth, mein Herr, and believe me, when they come out, we bleed, already."

And then – only then – a criminal fool released his rage.

"Do you truly think that I ever doubted it? Did you never think, ever, in any of our places, that I accepted you, Michael, as my own flesh, as Ettie's?"

"Not quite, mein Herr." The skull-face smiled, and for the first time there was an echo of the old Rau. But so faint. "I loved you, Eddie, old friend, that was the difference."

"But you *knew*, Michael, that I did too – I just couldn't say it. Does that mean you have to let yourself be killed? I'll say it now, if that's all you want."

Shout it, loud enough to drown the siren.

I LOVED YOU MICHAEL – LOVED LOVED LOVED !!!

"You idiot, I still do!" And I grabbed him. I shook him like an insect – which was appalling; his robust arms were matchsticks. The siren stopped. We looked at each other. We heard each other clearly.

"Saying it once, would have been enough, Eddie, but you were always over enthusiastic about some things. Here's the price, old friend – when it's over, save me my baker's dozen, that's all."

"You know I will. I'll save more. Hundreds. I get extra rations."

"Just a dozen. Do you promise?"

"I promise."

"Even if it means losing the Grail?"

"I promise."

Two best friends walked back past the Jews' hoard. One, always an outsider, locked the thin door that guarded the squalid treasure. The other said, "Michael, do you really have to?"

"You know I do, old friend."

The lock clicked. One cried hot tears, scalding.

"Eddie, be happy for me, old friend. After all our years I've found my real place."

Exit Michael.

682

Down, Down, Down, Down . . .
Among the dead men the flames roar upwards, the fat melts, the arms rise,
the skeletons dance on the Obsidian shore, but the yellow gold is indestructible
and still shines.

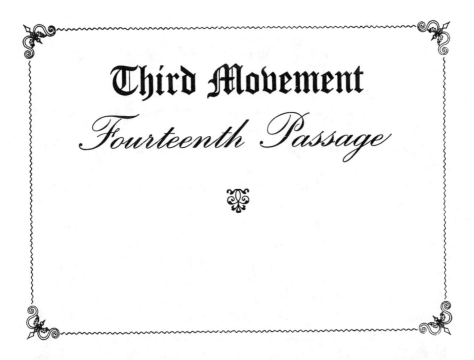

Third Movement
Fourteenth Passage

Without introduction: it is enough that we start on the Upbeat – 2 lucky 7's; that the Prisoner with that number has survived this replaying of the frightful 13th; that the broken heart pumps, the cripple's hand scrawls.

. . . *In Cloud-Cuckoo-Land:* The sun is warming Zürich, but the snow has not yet melted, ice still locks the lake beside Edwin as he drives by taxi to the house of yellow stone. With each mile the fears mount: How do I tell them? What if he isn't home, my magician? It's the Swiss's bloody fault, they're the mad ones, living like cabbages as though nothing's happening outside their bloody door! As though the stench stops at the borders when the wind of madness blows! I hate them, I've always loathed them, smug, soulless bastards with their tick-tock hearts and bloody watches and buggering their milk-chocolate sodding goats.

. . .When the Fool *knows*, my dears, that Jung is Swiss as Swiss can be. And dearest Emma. And here they are . . .

Carl Gustav was splitting wood, with wedge and hammer, wearing plus-fours of a ferocious purplish plaid, with wide scarlet braces, and thick socks, in an almost Real-Siegfried yellow shade, while his sweet wife sat on a bench on the sunny south side of the stone house, pouring tea into the gnomed-and-ivied mugs.

"Edwin my dear, will you join us? I've got an extra?" as though she had known.

"Shitbag wood!" Roared her husband – a wedge had bounced and fallen. "But my fault entirely, the grain is never wrong. Old chap, how are you?"

"Immensely better just for seeing you both. I dreaded you wouldn't be here."

"Poor Edwin," said Emma Jung, "you must have a honey muffin while it's hot, if things are so bad."

"I never leave at the spring solstice anyway, old chap, I'm sure I've told you that." Her husband set down the sledgehammer and wiped sweat from his owl-specs, and gulped a great gulp of tea. "All the spirits of renewal for the year start on your birthday – in our Northern Hemisphere, it's different for Australian aborigines – that's why I was so drawn to you and your sister from the start of our acquaintance."

"But you've never met her," said Eddie, "not properly; that's part of the problem. I have to talk to you about Ettie, and this time it's most frightfully serious, but when I say it in so many words, I always end up seeming the one of us with the problem."

"Don't use so many, then, Edwin dear." Emma Jung spread butter already half melted from the sun. "Your sister won't leave Germany, how's that?"

"Precisely, Frau Emma, but you can't imagine why."

"She has a child of a German father."

"You frighten me," said Rose's uncle. "How can you possibly know? – and why would it make any difference if the father's German, if he's dead?"

"It wouldn't. So I presume, old chap, he isn't dead." Jung crams a honey muffin whole, into his mouth, and then chews, a dozen times exactly, before he swallows, and all the time watched Eddie in that owlish way, so that the fool can hardly wait for the next riddle. "Is he German?"

"Ettie says so." Which is no lie – exactly. "The baby's a girl. She's called Rose. The most perfect thing you ever saw."

"What a relief for you both." Emma Jung smiles at Uncle Eddie. "I take it, that you stand in as the surrogate father. Do have the last muffin;

they have to be eaten once they're cut open."

"Rose," Jung ruminates, thumbs on red braces, "Dante with Beatrice, the image of everlasting love, the woman's view of Eros in her life, ascent to heaven – what's in a name indeed. How did you come to select it, old chap?"

"You make me utterly transparent," Eddie protests. "I chose the name, yes – but it was nothing like that, just a song I used to play at school. It was June, the dog-roses were out and smelling heavenly, it simply popped into my mind."

"There you are then – heavenly!" Jung snaps the braces an enormous *snap*, quite immoderately pleased for such a small riddle. "Now, old chap, if you're going to stay the night you must help me do the wood for the tower."

"I'm sorry, I really couldn't. I've got a bit of a phobia about fire at the moment. Even the thought of stacking wood, you can't imagine – no one can. It's so gorgeously tranquil here, and I'm responsible. For Rose, for Rau, for all of them – oh my Christ Christ Christ . . ."

. . . *& Tosh, & Deaf'n'Dumber, & the Griesbachs, & Sevastyani* – and those are only the ones with' names: so that Emma Jung puts her arms around the weeping Fool, and her husband stops snapping and splitting, and both together, between them, help their patient around a corner of warm stone to place him in a western-facing conservatory under glass, massed with spring flowers forced in pots, where, with complete incoherence it emerges: the threatened horror in the cellar – and the endless hand-washing; the filming by the damned, for the damned, of the burning-melting Obsidian lake of Edwin's nightmare – and Sister's ineradicable stench, and her retching; and the chapel of the Yews, burning, and the conversion of Rome – only as a condition for the Fool's searching; and his latest farcical pretend-scheme for continuing: by kidnapping His loved ones! – all adding up to utterest defeat. And only God and the Jungs know what else spewed from the depths.

"Edwin dear," said Emma Jung, whose calm reassurance is the next thing remembered from that hot-house breakdown – and that her husband had left us to go back to his splitting, because the relentless sound of hammer on metal followed thunk and crack as the ash-logs parted and fell asunder, regular as Swiss clockwork: "Healing will take years, you have to accept that, together with your guilt of the death of

687

your friends; but you have also to keep guilt in perspective. You were not alone in being drawn to the perversion of Adolf Hitler – and infinitely far from being the most important, you know that – Lloyd George and my own dear stubborn man to name but two of the more exalted. Edwin, you believed longer because you were so much closer to temptation. If we are in the very heart of a cyclone, let us imagine the storm of the Flying Dutchman – if we can stay there, and move with the pace of the storm, all will seem like blue sky to those on deck, and even if you turned to someone beside you, let us say, your sister, she too would see the blue sky, and the sunshine, and so would all the other passengers. And of course psychologically, my dear, they have to – because what is the alternative? If they leap off the ship the great storm will engulf them. And on board the ship there are only two things they can do: trust in the captain – or mutiny, and find another Master. In your own life, Edwin my dear, you have been coming closer to mutiny, but rather too late, I'm afraid, for this wartime voyage."

"But Rau," the Fool cried in his agony, "Frau Emma if you had *seen* him. His eyes, as he looked at me –"

"You have been terribly blind to all your friends' needs, my dear, but you did not kill them – and you risked your own life with them, that's important when you come to weigh the balance."

"So I'm to plead not guilty? Frau Emma, I can see your face. You know I shall never be clean. Not ever."

"Edwin, my dear, no thinking being on this earth is free of guilt, that is a condition of existence, and until humans hatch out of a laboratory bottle it will be – and even then they will probably look back and quite irrationally hate a particular retort or a test-tube for getting them on life's shelf in such a muddle."

"We didn't use a test-tube, Frau Emma. Oh God, I can bear anything except that Rose would grow up to hate me."

"That is just a last remnant of your infantile, sibling death-wish. You resent Rose for arriving. All parents go through it, for a man at your age the stage passes very quickly."

"I didn't say I was a parent."

"No, you blame Adolf Hitler's perversion for that too. It's unavoidable. Your friend Herr Wolf has become Laius, king of Thebes for the

688

world's Oedipus Complex, and will be for a whole generation."

"Frau Emma, it isn't only in my head. Rose has *black* hair. Ettie says Wolf really could be."

"The Father? My dear, dear boy, of course she does, but it will take a miracle to save your poor sister. She is, I am afraid, too completely identified with Brünnhilde – but the *Ring* is my husband's department. He wants to see you about it when you feel strong enough."

"I suppose it had better be now. I have to go back tonight. Michael Rau's people are arriving for the Charlemagne, if they got through the raids – oh Lord, how mad that sounds. Everything does now about the bloody bloody Grail."

"Not to me, my dear," as she kissed the Fool, once, lightly, on his forehead, a crowning-anointing. "From this moment, dear Edwin, your personal Quest is truly starting. Now, come into the kitchen and have a good supper before you go to my man Jung."

A family kitchen – because that was another thing the younger Edwin, in his blind selfishness always completely lost sight of, Emma Jung, besides being wise, and kind, and beautiful, was the mother of 5 children.

Last Supper:
Food smells, of onions and herbs – and dog: Uncle Sam, that American lost soul, curled up in a basket, still waiting under the table for the Duration; almost over, to hear the BBC's version. Which got the Fool trembling again, so that Emma Jung raised an eyebrow at her lofty husband who reached a yard of arm over his wise-owl's head, without looking, and switched off the wireless.

"An advantage of wearing my specs in the up-position, old chap. It allows me to show off in the consulting room – or did, when I consulted. By Jove, doing wood doesn't half work up a bally old appetite."

Not for bally-Eddie, already given enough food for thought to choke him. Yet in one scrap from Emma there was comfort: it was not the Fool's fault to have been brought close to Genius – and there was another excuse: close-to, Carl Jung, and that faraway Other, seemed still, in their kitchen or under their Storm-Troop chandelier, Ordinary Men – with the odd quirk, it goes without saying. Washing hands to the bone, or dreaming that God shits on Basel.

"If you'll excuse me," Edwin said to both Jungs, "I really must get back. I don't think anything can be helped by more talk, and I couldn't cope with a tower session. Perhaps later, if there is a later, but for now it's my mess, I accept that. I'll just have to dig us out of it."

"That's the ticket, old chap" – with his kindest old-owl smile.

"I'll call you a taxi," his wife said. "Edwin dear, pour my man his coffee while we're waiting."

"Certainly, Frau Emma. Thank you." Not noticing how artfully, by leaving, she had converted her kitchen to his tower. The Fool said to Jung, "Honestly, how long do you think it'll take me to get over this idiotic new fear of flames and burning?"

"Honestly, old chap, I've been given a case of most marvellous Oporto as a present from a bit of an ass in Lisbon – we'll open it and toast a happy conclusion to the last act of your Ring's cycle."

His strong woodsman's hand brings down a crystal decanter etched for the occasion: Volsung vassals in horned helmets, and Grane, the flying horse, with a Valkyrie, her hair flying, and a castle across a drawbridge, waiting.

"How is it that you always have exactly the right thing ready?" the Fool asks his magician. "Whenever I'm here, a book, or an archetype on the ceiling of the bedroom you give me, or the cups we drink out of, when you don't even know in the first place that I'm coming?"

"Life's only a waiting game, old chap, and we only read the entrails we wish to notice. You like the decanter; another fellow might see his fortune in my knives and forks. I say, just look at this colour – worth its weight in gold, as my Portuguese benefactor went out of his way to tell me."

The magician poured his potion, and tested it to the light. The Fool mused,

"It's the colour of the lamp at Bayreuth, the Grail descending. In the patterns of *my* life I can't ever get away. I didn't mean to imply you were ever dishonest, you must believe me."

"How could I help you if I didn't, old chap?"

A magic smile this time: perfect wine, a true Jungian moment.

"You can help me by telling me the unvarnished truth about myself, for once. No riddles. How can there possibly be a happy ending to this

690

mess? Ettie won't leave her Love Cottage, and if she would, she's locked up now by Bormann, as a hostage near as damn it, for some game he's playing, and my own chances of finding a way through the salt galleries with only the quacks' bloody pendulums are next to hopeless." And with another glass inside ... "The damned Ring was never *meant* to be happy. It was never meant to be anything – except sixteen hours of egomaniacs caterwauling to a hallful of hypocrites. On the most uncomfortable seats ever made, one might add. And look what it's led to! Without Wagner, I honestly believe none of this would have happened. People say its Nietzsche and Schopenhauer, but they're nothing, no one reads a word – it's the damnable music. And my fault for playing it, because it was flattering, with Wolf – although I always knew I wasn't a quarter the pianist Putzi was. Hanfstaengl's chording was utterly stupendous. Mine's always seemed like a child's by comparison. I can't imagine why Wolf got rid of him."

"Because the ousting of Fasolt is essential, old chap." Packing his magic Meerschaum pipe, with a calloused thumb, "and if we're to be freshly honest with your Self," and taking a match – *Please God, don't strike!* – "you thoroughly enjoyed playing Loge, the trickster, worming your way in for Hanfstaengl's position. The fear of fire isn't new for you by the way – " putting down the match, *thank you!* – "it hasn't been since your mother's death in 1927. Freud would have said since the Zeppelin fell into your London house as a burning penis – not to speak ill of the dead; the man turned my life, and his own ending was grievous, poor fellow. Now have another glass, and listen to me." As the wine rolls from the Valkyrie's crystal, thicker than blood, luscious as velvet. "We have reached Parsifal at the Easter Pool – and I'm not telling you this to be unkind, but some things have to go into that golden head of yours straight, or we may never get you out again. Old chap, you must brace yourself. The story of your life has been the confusion between two stories. You have thought yourself part of the Ring – done everything to force yourself to the heart of it through your incestuous alliance with your sister, and almost incestuously, with the Wolf-man, with whom she so long delayed consummation. Old chap, that Ring is over. Others will replace it, the cycle plays eternally, but Mr Wolf's turn at it is done. I grant it has been a striking production, one of the greatest when seen in historical perspective, but all that is of no account. You know the legend:

The hall must burn. Siegfried must die."

"But Brünnhilde," the Fool pleaded, "for God's sake, not Ettie. I must save my sister."

"We cannot say whether she will be needed by the immolation," the seer in Jung replied. "As Brünnhilde, she is not singular but part of the collective with all the other women that surround the Monstrous Father – the Minotaur, as you once accurately described him. That the subject, 'A', as we may call him, in Freud's terms desires her death by burial in shit is not the point, of course he does, with his mother and all other women he has ever loved, or men, for that matter – oh yes, old chap, your own danger has never been more acute than it will be in this last phase of 'A's dementia. But I, Jung, am not concerned with Vienna's narrow vision of the single person. Here we are looking at the whole board of the human race – that is what is being played out for us by the cast from Bayreuth, and the Great Myth may not care whether it obtains the death of your sister. After all, old chap, several other victims balanced on the horns and lived to tell the tale – the ones with some sense of humour, I should imagine. Shit is only our nursery returning. Nothing is more farcical, when it stops being terrible, than sex."

"Ettie does have, she always has – " the Fool grasped this last reed frantically – "well not too much at her own expense, although she's getting better as she gets older, even if she won't laugh at a fad when it's fresh – but with the Ring, you really think there is still hope that I can drag her out of it?"

"It doesn't matter what I think – but you took my thoughts off their rails, with this discussion of your sister. You, old chap, are my concern, as Emma's patient. Your role in the life theatre as I said is not in the Ring, but the pure fool's Quest. You have always known that, and accepted it – but you thought you were already living it. Old chap, the unhappy news I have to tell you now, is that your drama comes *after* the great ring is completed. Once, I sent you down the Rhine, but that was only a shadow voyage. A forerunner, to give your spirit some advance warning. Your true life-journey, with all its cruel demands and un-answered questions, is only started. It begins, I would say, with this terrible unresolved question of your sister's safety."

"And Rose," the Fool whispered. "Please, don't tell me Rose – "

"I did not use the word, *terrible*, lightly, dear old chap. Parsifal's journey is within, that is why for Wagner it had to follow the Ring. So far in your production you have only seen the external facets of Wotan's personality. In *Parsifal*, the Wanderer must find himself – and the vital question he must ask for the wounded Amfortas, he must ask *himself*; and the strength he needs to battle evil Klingsor he must find *for* himself; and the magic power of the spear must come *of* himself; and the wound he must heal is the wound *in* himself – and whether one human lifetime is sufficient for that is always the great imponderable. But Emma and I send you in the God's care, old chap, and wherever the journey takes you, know that called or uncalled, He *is* always there."

And then –?

Carl Gustav and Emma Jung stood at the door of their yellow stone house, with warm light pouring from the open doorway of his kitchen, and the tall trees, leafless, surrounding his tower, and the snow covering the tiny houses of our village, all except the steeple, peeking like a snowdrop, or first crocus, because its point was gilded; and the Eye-within-the-eye watched him, as they waved him off, that Fool, upon his journey – and what was the last thing that Carl Gustav Jung, that great man, said to me, Edwin Randolph Browning Casson-Perceval?

"*I'll be seeing you.*"

The words of a child, to a child, because,

> *Time is a child*
> *Playing like a child*
> *Playing a game upon a board*
> *The kingdom of the child.*

And then –?

Edwin came to the first square on this new board, where the game had now to be played dead-earnest. The square was still marked as it had been in the past, still located at its old position, beneath the restaurant of the ex-monk and former nun – but the player waiting on that square was different. Aye, wee bairns! The Swiss is gone – with any luck Transformed by a bullet, the blank bastard!

... *At the House of Treason:* "Sit down, Casson-Perceval, I've a deal to say to you."

693

In Zürich, Edwin's nemesis, his Fag-master, is still red-headed (though greying prematurely at the edges, my dears, and *thinning*!) and still bent-pricked, to judge by his foul disposition; and more Scots-if-you-don't-mind than ever from his rolling "r's", and "a-deal-to-say", indeed! So how, you ask, was this colleague from All Souls different? He had only 1 eye, the long Scotch sod. What had been the left eye was covered by a brown leather patch, like von Maser's black one, but whereas the Pendulist-in-Chief was made romantically piratical, Cameron looked more coldly vicious and predatory than ever. As though he had nothing left in life to stare at with that harsh remaining orb but Your-Truly. A scar ran upwards from the patch, still livid. The wound was recent.

"I'm sorry about your injury, Cameron. Is it, ah, permanent?"

"Sorry are you? – for flying glass from your swine's rockets? Aye, it's permanent."

That "aye" was clearly Affectation, Cameron – but Rose was waiting.

"I'm sitting," the Fag said, "that's what you wanted. I'm pressed for time, what do you have to say?"

"You're pressed? I've cooled my heels a month in his benighted place. You were ordered to report more regularly since Christmas last."

"There is a war on."

"Don't try and play your queer games of speech with me, you Quisling fag worm. Men never change, that's the most depressing fact of life – and if you care a jot about your sister's, you'll stop thinking of your own pansy skin for once, and listen bloody carefully.'

"What about my sister?"

"I'll ask the questions. You just think twice before you lie about your answers."

"I won't say a damned word if you won't explain. You know already I care about her safety more than anything. You spend a day with a Kaltenbrunner stepping on your fingers, then you can talk."

"Did he do that?" The prospect pleased Cameron: that nasty cold streak that enters the Scotch heart up the kilt. He produced papers from a briefcase chained theatrically to his wrist. "It'll be more than your fingers when the Russians get hold of you – or your sister, for that matter."

"The Russians have never heard of me, and Ettie never sang there.

694

I've spent half a day with Carl Jung's riddles, I'm tired, talk some sense, man."

"The Yalta Meeting's decided there's to be a Four Power tribunal established for War Crimes. You're on Moscow's list for acts in the Ukraine. The penalty for your category of particular beastliness is death. Does that not sound sensible enough?"

"I don't believe you." Brave words, but in Cyrillic characters the family name is a mouthful that sprawls clear across the page. "But not Ettie's – it doesn't mention her. And I'm a Swiss national. I have no intention of going within a thousand miles of that appalling country for the rest of – "

"Look at the map, man." Cameron thrust one. Huge curving red arrows from the East. "Our Soviet Allies are only four hundred miles from where we're standing, *now*, in Switzerland. They'll make Vienna within three weeks. How many miles is that from your magic dung-heap?"

As the raven flies? Croaking distance.

"Aye, that's given you something to bite down on. Well add this for good measure. If Ivan gets to Bavaria before Tommy or G.I. Joe, it'll be a quick thrill for Eddie up the arse with a bayonet, and the other for your sister."

"You unspeakable swine. How dare you use such language!"

"Because it's the kind that slave drivers and whores of tyrants understand. *But* – " red Cameron abruptly produces a cold-blue revolver as Brother Fag lunges across the table – "*if* you don't bring your disgusting body another half-inch closer, and give me the distinct pleasure of ending a useless, parasitical existence, aye, that's better – " as the attacker subsides, white-faced, beside himself – "much against my own inclinations, Casson-Perceval, I'll tell you what Higher Authority in its wisdom wants to save your fag's carcass for, or rather your sister's, and this brat she's spawned – have you heard *him* speak of Operation Valhalla?"

"Never. What is it? If you didn't have a gun I'd – "

"Shut up!" Snapping it. " 'Valhalla' is the plan for defending the Southern Redoubt, the Elite Leibstandarte – what about from Bormann? Himmler? there must have been some mention?"

The Last Stand . . .

695

"Wolf's spoken of such a thing, but never seriously. He covers a hundred similar topics in a conversation. Himmler's certainly in no condition to lead it – if you're all so bloody prescient in London why in God's name didn't you take advantage of the peace feelers I sent to you?"

"The terms are Unconditional Surrender. Bugger your feelers. I ask you again about Bormann, has he approached you?"

"The brute knows I come here. He showed me films of executions after the July affair. He's practically holding Ettie and Rose a prisoner."

"Oh good man. At last. I knew it."

Inexplicably, Cameron sank back in his chair, exhaled, became human. Old School Chums with Eddie.

"I don't care what you know," said Uncle, "with the Russians coming, and my sister – little Rose, I've seen what Stalin's Neanderthals do."

"Keep it in mind if you start to waver." Cameron withdrew another map from the briefcase. "Show me exactly where she's located."

"She isn't. I told you near Bayreuth, a village –"

"Start lying again and I'll shoot you in the leg. *Show me*."

"Do you promise that you'll save them from the Russians?"

"That depends on you, old boy."

"How?"

"If Mr Wolf throws in the sponge soon enough our side will be down to Bavaria before Ivan. If not . . ."

Silence . . . except for goat-bells, and a million tick-tocking frosted Swiss hearts, and a small voice from a trapped Fag, asking:

"What do I have to do, Cameron?"

And then –?

Cameron told him.

And then –?

Piss-pot Eddie flies back to Rose, and Ettie, to make the most of the time remaining . . .

. . . *At Love Cottage:* The 1st day of Spring and new hopes; a late snowstorm has freshly blanketed the mountain, and early-bird Edwin has been up to check for leaks – cum recordings – in the attic. All's well. Now Rose lies snug-as-a-bug in bed between Mummy & Uncle, object of happiness and adoration. There are curls on the sides now, not just in

696

front: satin-soft, black velvet – and perfect eyelashes, matching, when she bats them at Uncle to break his racing heart.

"We're going to speak any day," Mummy says, "aren't we, my brilliant poppet – we read to her in both languages – make a bet, Eddie, what it'll be."

"Her name, I suppose. Often they use pets, apparently, but you don't have one. Ettie, wouldn't you like to have a dog, for protection?"

"Against what? My deers? A horrible brute from the village last summer ripped out one of the fawn babies."

"You might be grateful. There's going to be chaos. You could get any sort of thugs coming up here."

"Bosh. Men of that type are far too idle to hike up mountains."

"They could be sent up."

"Listen to melodramatic Uncle Eddie –" tickling Rose's latest dimple – "who's ever going to waste time on precious Us, Mummy's poppet?"

"The Russians. They're already almost in Vienna. They think Rose is Wolf's. Can't you imagine what that means if they caught her?"

Mummy rolled up on an elbow and became Sister to stare at Brother's eyes, above her daughter's. "The Russians couldn't possibly have heard of Love Cottage. Or Rose. Or me for that matter – not after only my one crack at Boris. The man who came to listen from the Bolshoi, I remember, was quite hopeless with the double-barrel in the name. I had to write it out like punishment lines, twelve times on the back of a programme."

"They learnt the lesson, Ettie. I'm listed as a War Criminal because of Kiev."

"For robbing a tomb? Eddie darling, aren't you ever going to stop being such an old worry? No Russian peasants in smocks and sickles are going to come storming up here because of your Pot. Pure Chekhov, isn't he, our Uncle Vanya-Eddie, Mummy's precious."

Rose agrees, all arms and legs waving; Uncle's terribly funny.

"The charge is using slave labour. Ettie, I've seen the document. It's serious, frightfully. The penalty's hanging."

"Better not let the nasty men catch us – "

"Ettie *listen* –" grabbing her, roughly, over our Precious. "The Reds take whole families, that's part of the Terror. You can't laugh it off – not for Rose."

"All right," she said, "see, I'm not laughing. Drive us to Triebschen."

"I can't. It isn't that simple. There's something else I haven't told you."

"You amaze me, darling." Her coldest oldest-Ettie voice. Hell hath no – as Mummy threatened. "Tell me now, Eddie."

"It's Bormann. I can't drive you out because he's got troops at the bottom of the lane. He's holding you hostage."

"That arse-licking Toad? He's just a secretary."

"He used to be. Now he runs everything, at least around Wolf."

"So drive over to the Chalet. Wolf will stop it in a moment."

"He isn't there. He's in Berlin, He practically never leaves."

"So we're stuck?" she said. "All this hysteria you've started, and we just have to sit here until the Toad goes, or the Reds get here with their bayonets? Oh, bloody wonderful."

She pulled Rose to her: The Women versus the Idiot Male.

"I told you because you have to understand how serious it all is. I do have a plan, but I don't know when it'll be ready. You simply have to trust me, and be ready to go with Rose at a moment's notice. No luggage, just you."

But there was interest in her suspicion: "What sort of a plan?"

"I can't tell you that either."

"I bet! You haven't hatched it yet."

"The plan isn't just me. Outsiders are involved; the last details are still being worked on. Ettie, be ready, and trust me."

"Shall we, Precious, trust him?" Rose is dubious, but loving Uncle, gurgles permission. "All right, we will, but Mummy's taking our bible."

A small price to pay. "All right, the bible, but nothing else. Just be ready."

"And what are you going to be doing while we wait for this bombshell?"

"I have to keep busy with the Charlemagne. It's important that no one thinks there's anything different."

"So you can go on Potting to the very last second. We might have known."

"But I'm going to be close. And you mustn't worry – there won't *be* bombing, that's the whole point."

"Mummy's Precious," with each word a kiss for Rose's black curls,

"Uncle's definitely, this time, stark, selfish, bonkers – but we love him."

"I'll be able to get away from the diggings to see you practically every night for supper. I'll bring bacon or something for the rations. Three of us again, it'll be almost like Porquerolles."

"Bacon suppers?" said Sister, "you're not going to expect me to cook meat in Love Cottage?"

Single-minded in that family? Don't tell me!

"There's just one other thing," Brother said, "but we'll do that after breakfast. You'll enjoy it. You can help me."

"Why not before breakfast?"

"I'm not talking about sex," said Uncle primly, "we have to build a beacon, for a signal fire."

Which they did, laughing, and forgetting – because they were young, by the standards of Old, and it was sunny, and pink-cheeked, and snowy – easy to forget the task's grim purpose.

"Why not now?" said Mummy, with That Look, "Rose is resting."

"Why not?" said surrogate Eddie.

So they did, extra-special, toes-to-nose, under Rose's, for their Birthday's present. . . .

. . . In Erda's world: There is no division between Day & Night toiling among salt, because the walls of the mine are white. The Erda Leader's battalions work and sleep underground – the weather does not flood or freeze, and bombing can't matter. Only 500 of Rau's Gelbsterne thousand have survived disease and their rail journey; the end of the line for Labour, each sub-human body is now suddenly precious. Forays are made by the Reichsmarschall's Art Curators, and Toad-Bormann's slave-drivers, but the Chicken Farmer's paper-powers are still strong enough to ward them off.

April's Fool's Day: a belated extra present. The Senior Pendulist's magic hands produce the aura of a mine-working in the right direction. Four frantic days of effort later – Break-through!

But the Bear hugs Vienna.

For 7 Days:

The battle against time rages. Erda's tunnel beyond is choked from a fallen ceiling. Every stick-prop is dragged from the existing galleries.

699

April 11:

That twice-singular number. Break-out! – into a vast Erda's chamber.

But the Bear breaks Vienna.

Von Maser comes hobbling with the news, crouched double in the tunnel. The Erda Leader cries first, "You aren't going to believe – we've got masonry, a wall dividing the space completely across. It's enormous."

"My dear boy!" Peering, 1-eyed, past the lamps on the white walls, flaring, "We all knew, it was only a matter of trusting. I'll report this omen to the top immediately, they need every scrap – and don't be afraid at this stage to use explosives."

An enormous blast. All the lights go off. Screams of panic from the Erda Hooligans.

The Bear swims the Danube.

Explosion. The salt dust settles, terribly slowly, reddening eyes for additional frustration, but at last –

"A tomb!" bellowing it on the land 'phone to peg-legged von Maser. "It's the size of a small chapel. This far under the mountain, never entered, I think we're really onto something priceless."

As all our old Dream, our Passion, floods back –

While the Bear rolls West.

"Never mind. I always had faith, dear boy – you haven't heard? Roosevelt died! Yes, after our yesterday's news. Berlin is euphoric. Keep on, keep on, there are no limits when Fortune starts turning. I should warn you, though, that the Art side are booby-trapping their galleries – apart from the historical waste, it could make things difficult for our working people."

"I'll have the sappers make us a new entrance, then we'll be independent. What do you think? – with time so precious dare I blow the seal on this tomb?"

"Only you can make so momentous a decision, dear boy. Good luck. Western civilisation rests with you."

A heavy weight for slender shoulders, but for the Grail, a feather. Into the breach –

As the Bear shits on Spital, the village Shrine.

Desecration-Explosion! More sore eyes – for another tomb, "Or chapel, or sepulchre, or whatever the bloody hell we want to call them.

It's Kiev all over again," Project-Erda's Leader glooms, abandoning bright hope to von Maser. "The effing things could go on one within the other forever."

"Drastic times, drastic measures, my boy." The Pendulists' Commander gazes around Erda's cavern, and pronounces, "We shall bring Mohammed to the mountain."

Every last Quack of them, with all their Ephemerides, & Lunar Tables, & Stellar Chronometers, to whisper and mumble of Trine Aspects & Inverse Force Fields.

All escape from the Legend is closed off. Linz falls.

The Bear squats in the Nibelungenlied Castle.

No Great Dome either.

The world of the old gods above is ending.

Jung would love it. Erda's Leader can't wait to watch it. The needles are split between 3 tombs that all have C R carved on them and, if the surveyors are right, lie in the quadrant of the cemetery below Love Cottage – but there are 9 other tombs, some even grander.

"Do you think –?" to von Maser, scarcely daring to breathe it – "could we have found an Arthurian burial ground? Twelve Knights, the circular arrangement . . .?"

Pacing from one to another around that vast rotunda, tapping the marble slabs at Erda's entrances, eeny-meeny-miney –

Lambach is gobbled. Only 50 miles?!

To a Bear on the rampage? It will need –

An enormous blast. All the lights go off. Screams of panic from the Erda Hooligans.

"Don't light matches – it could be gas!"

"Try the communications!"

"Dead!"

"I'll go and find out."

Erda's Leader stumbles back, following the narrow gauge of the rail lines to the entrance.

"Sorry about that," drawls an Art Curation type, "we had a premature detonation of one of our security devices. Only in French Moderns, thank Heavens. Have you heard, the Leibstandarte are holding?"

Madness under the earth. But on top of it, 12 abreast, black-and-silver:

701

The Parsifal Knights step to the Braunau-Passau Line.
The Bear, remembering, recoils.

5 hours' sleep. The 3 marked tombs are entered. Only more tunnels. The Pendulists say, This One. Or, perhaps . . .?

Flip a coin: call, *Heads!* – then take Tails.

And with this scientific method, for *His* 56th birthday, on the 20th of April, Project-Erda's Leader emerged into the sunshine of the Untersberg, His Mausoleum Mountain.

Edwin has *won!* – has beaten the clock, and the Bear, and Erda. Uncle Eddie can save Rose, and Ettie, free of Bormann.

So that it comes as somewhat of a shock . . . to find the Toadbastard's Skull & Crossbones brigade set in a new ring, at the very edge of the apple orchard; with nothing between them and Love Cottage but the vital small meadow – and the pond of the duckies, and the slab of rock with Sister's bower, and the beacon we had built there together for Cameron's signal.

To know that after all my effort the plan the old School chums had laid out in such cold Scots' logic was impossible.

A moment, children. Gedächtnis brought it back too sharply –

but there are no moments.

Not just my heart, the clock is racing, Gedanke shows that with her black wings against the moon – for I write this at night, these final days and hours – and every second wondering: Shall We be allowed to reach Our ending? to bring Them back across the River, at least on parchment, Eddie's precious ones?

Or will they get there first, flying ahead, the craaancking Raven bastards, and bar History's door still to Edwin with the lying Yellow Street version of How, and When, and Where Valhalla ended . . .?

On-on! Ignoblest English – there are 14 letters in Casson-Perceval! 7-on-7.

OLD-EDWIN SHALL MAKE IT!!!

. . . At Love Cottage: False alarm. Even while Brother was feeling that pole-axed sensation, Sister came out on the porch, with Rose, both waving. The Toad-bastard's Death's Head brigade is leaving.

702

"With all the village wives' rumours of Russians, mein Herr," the Lieutenant in charge confided, "one had thought the Frau von Perceval might be worried for the baby, but she says she isn't. However, to stay on the safe side, I'll move the troops halfway. There's a suitable bivouac around the bend – beyond those tombs, you know the place?"

"Indeed I do, Lieutenant. Thank you for your consideration."

The Black Order goose-march past the duckies getting ready for this year's family. Uncle's legs wobble him to the porch.

"Ettie, when I saw them here, I can't tell you – how's Rose?"

"My darling brother, you might credit Sister with being able to manage a little Lieutenant – " presenting our Treasure, "we're fine, aren't we Precious? We're getting a tooth."

Our First. Calling for special kisses, and Uncle's horny miner's thumb to massage the nasty angry gum. *And wonder – Will it be a mole-tooth, half-rotten?* But the stub is milk-white, perfect as a snow-drop.

"What else would it be?" Mummy croons, "with all our lovely veggies? We'll lose it anyway, won't we Precious, when we're a big girl of six."

"When . . . !" in an aching echo from Uncle's heart. "Every day when I leave you in the morning I wonder whether by the evening we'll ever – sorry, it's just the situation's so desperate. Ettie, one evening if I shouldn't get back – "

"Bosh. In a month we're having our first birthday."

"But if – "

"We won't let Uncle hold us if he's going to be morbid."

And Rose gives Uncle a tiny love-bite, as warning.

"I'm not being morbid – just facing reality."

"To have our Guy Fawkes day in May?"

"Purely for your safety. You light the beacon five days after I leave, if I'm not back. And you must keep the fire going for thirty minutes."

"Easy for *him*," to our Pet – and then as Ettie, "You can't seriously expect me to be exact over a half an hour, with the sun."

"What are you talking about?"

"Time, darling. We don't have a clock."

So Brother passes her his wristwatch. Which was a present from Michael . . .

"And for God's sake remember to wind it, if you expect Cameron to get the flight here."

Which was a Silly Thing to say.

"Cameron?" Every maternal hackle shot up. "The creature that tore wings off at All Souls? You're trusting Rose to a Cameron when you know how we feel about the Scots."

"For heaven's sake, that was a hundred years ago."

"Twenty-five, and people don't change – at least men don't. Eddie how could you possibly?"

"Because we *have* to. Bloody hell, the Russians are coming. There's no other chance."

"And what do you have to do for it, for Cameron?"

"Nothing. It's humanitarian."

"You're lying. That's why all the business about not coming back in the evenings. What do you have to do, Eddie?"

"I've told you – "

"Hold Rose."

Thrusting her abruptly into Uncle's arms. Precious loves the excitement – it means new kisses – but where is Mummy going?

"Ettie, what the bloody hell?"

She was running, with a match box from her Love Cottage pinny apron pocket, running to the beacon!

"You crazed bitch, I'll tell, it's to do with Wolf – Rose, oh blast, where can I put you? – It took us hours, woman, to build it! I'm going to Berlin to ask Him to stop now, for your sake – Rose, don't cry, *please*, Uncle Eddie doesn't mean – For Rose's sake, she's *His* daughter. That's why Bormann's been keeping you under guard. Ettie, I'm begging, we'll never get one with dry wood in time again."

Whistling in the wind. From thatch-tinder, to twigs, to resin, to pine boughs, to great branches of dead ash, Mummy does Guy Fawkes proud. The Fool's beacon goes up to heaven like billy-o.

And was answered. From across the valley came the wail of a siren. And my Sister's voice over it, rising and rising.

"*You trusted our Rose –?*" and her voice was truly Wagnerian – "*to Cameron and Bormann?*" – a Helden rage reserved for only the most monumental treachery, "*You bloody, bloody lifelong fool! It's HIM they're after.*"

And then –?

A rumbling, that grows to a trembling, that strikes a harmonic in the compressed structure of the Alps, and resonates deeper than any opening E Major that Richard Wagner ever contemplated – and smoke poured out all around Mama's once-past chalet that had become His Fortress; dense, roiling white clouds enveloping it as Klingsor hid the whore-garden and his castle at Bayreuth, but the bombers were non-believers. Sight unseen, their bellies opened. For the first time since the Prelude's curtain, hell and death came to the Salt Mountain.

And then –?

Mummy took Rose, without a word, from Uncle's arms, inside Love Cottage – leaving him with a burnt-out beacon, and a car arriving at high speed with the Death's Head Lieutenant who had been so obliging.

"Herr von Perceval, you are ordered at this instant, by Obergruppen-fuehrer Bormann, in the name of the Fuehrer, to Berlin."

And then –?

Without an extra shirt, or toothbrush, or goodbye to Rose, and Ettie, the Fool was roared away down Charlemagne's Mountain, not knowing when, or even if ever . . .

And then –?

In the car: the Death's Head Lieutenant, to prove he's a decent sort leans over, "We are proceeding to the Berghof for your flight – if we ever make it out with this raid. I have been instructed also to advise you mein Herr, the Reichsmarschall Goering is already under arrest."

You doubt Valhalla is shaking?!

And then –?

Up that steep and winding road, past the pill boxes, but not one tourist, choking on fumes from the smoke machines to find the Chalet scarcely touched by that apparent devastation, although the barrack blocks were hit, and of more concern, the landing strip, with a tiny black Storch skimming in between the craters.

And then –?

The Storch breaks a wheel strut on landing, but the pilot through superb skill stops safely – but there shall be a delay for repairs – while the siren goes again, and all troop down to the cellars dug deep in the Salt Mountain where the air is fouler from the smoke-fog machines than the bombing – and ironies compounded: Mrs Toad (Mummy-Girl-

705

Gerda) was cheek by jowl with Fattest Hermann and Queen Emmy.

"Edwin, you're going to Berlin, you have to tell Him," the Bad Giant's vast jelly-mould face was ashen. "I intended only to lead the fight if the torch was fallen. The fault is everything going through that swine Bormann."

Making sure that the swine's wife hears it. Poor Gerda: to be dead in a year of Krebs-cancer. . . .

The all-clear sounded.

The Fool is escorted to his pilot: a woman, can you imagine? The Storch is unscathed – but the bedroom wing, with the hypnotic eyes, and composite nude, and Geli's Edelweiss grotto has bought it. Two small black shadows run from the wreckage.

"Stasi! Negus!" Herr Eddie called them, for Eva's sake, but they ran away from me down the mountain. Poor Doggies . . .

"They're the lucky ones," says the Fool's brusque lady pilot. "It's going to be rough, say your prayers."

Nibelheim-By-Night:
Berlin is burning – only pinprick fires, but an infinite number, laid out by a random hand from bombing and shelling, yet from the sky forming, because of the blank parks and lakes in the centre, inevitably a circular pattern: an immense ring, flaming.

The Storch flies into it like a circus animal through a hoop of burning paper, the lady pilot is a tiger. Strangely, Eddie isn't frightened. Death is so obviously inevitable from the curtain of tracers that rise to meet him – in beautiful colours; orange, red, green, shades of Putzi's Picasso Woman – and there is even a certain exhilaration: go on, you bastards, *hit me!* A bizarre fascination to see them miss, those thousands of shells for this one small target, one drop of ink in the night.

All over.

The Storch was down. Somehow the Fool's lady pilot had found a spot without overhead wires, or rubble on the ground, without any aids to guide her except two pairs of blue car headlamps flashed for brief seconds – and each time they did so, producing a fresh concentrated barrage.

"Head down and go for it. Good luck. Tell the Fuehrer, Hanna says she's ready."

706

"I will. You were bloody marvellous. No one else could have – "

A phosphorous bomb halts idle chat. The Fool is standing light-as-day at the Brandenburg Gate. With his charmed life he strolls among the bullets to a crater where saner heads drag him down.

"Is it Speer again? Christ you're lucky!"

"Casson-Perceval, actually."

"Ach, the one for Bormann." The voices are disappointed-military, unimpressed by Toad. "Wait for the flare to finish. The sergeant will take you – are you under arrest?"

"I don't know. I don't think so."

"Never mind, you're in good company. Keep talking for a day and it'll all be over for the bastard. And the rest of us. Make the dash now – skol!"

No way to fight His war; the boys in field-grey have clearly been drinking in their fox-holes. Fool & Sergeant run like mad across the rubble to be met by boys in Black.

"Is it more snatches for the party?"

"For Bormann," grunts the unseen sergeant. "Over to you, I have to get – "

One of the Fool's bullets claims an alternate victim: Death is blind.

"Leave the body, man. To the Bunker. Get inside!"

. . . In Alberich's Cellar: This is the place where all the smells of all the lairs have collected: wet concrete & urine, farts & faeces, burning electrical insulation & armpit sweat – and ranker from the groin; and the unique contribution of haemorrhoid sufferers, second-rate Napoleons; and Josephines somewhere, with their Timely reminders; also dog shit & doggy breath, and high horsemeat for dog dinners – and human; and hot oil for overworked air-circulation pumps, and cordite fumes as a result; and tobacco, at its most unpleasant, from burnt-out tips of cigarettes, left wisping to act as the solvent of the smells, the binding agent, melding them into a blue-grey stinking, stinging, almost-liquid, fug.

No gravel walks, but all the familiar gravel-faces – those, at least, that have made it to the end of the path: some smile at the Fool, some grimace, some look right at him but don't see him, having gone over already to another dream-world from this one, via red-crossed cartons marked, *Morphine.*

707

"Von Perceval's made it!"

From mouth to mouth of the compos mentis, as though the War's turned, by the Fool's act. They even reach to touch his clothing.

"Are you from the South? By Panzer? Is von Manfred holding? Is von Manfred's Group *with* you?"

"Yes. By air. I don't know. I'm by myself, I'm afraid."

Afraid? Don't tell me!

The gravel-people drift away. That's the other difference from the other lairs – the drifting, where always there was that frantic coming-and-going, that urgency: the World is waiting for the Word! Now for –

"This way, mein Herr."

A tall Black Order corporal points the way:

Down:

3 flights of metal stairs, steep as ship's ladders. The gravel-faces of the upper level recede. On the middle, store-rooms, with more red-crossed boxes, and bandages, and shelves of Mama's brown bottles, for hallucinations – the sound of laughing? Female? Understandably hysterical.

Not this laughing: carried on two new smells – War's oldest, Dames Cunt-&-Booze. The store-rooms are crawling with surplus Parsifal Knights and whores dragged in from the streets – or respectable women, no one asks questions at this point in the garden of spread thighs, & dropped Black Order trousers, & Aryan slime on silver Lightning bars, & gaping Miss Pussys – dripping from 2 Knights for each flower. 3 – Christ, 4, in this corner! However many the ways Kundry's bitch-magic can dream up for turning both ends against . . .

The whining-mewling of *puppies*?

The sound of *children*?

Children *laughing*?!

"Blondi has produced a litter. Also, Herr Doktor and Frau Goebbels are in residence with their family."

The Corporal makes the last insanity sound normal. Only a Fool would be surprised – to find the Dwarf at the end where he must be.

. . . *At the Bottom:* Purity. Quiet and calm. Few faces, but the most familiar. His Women, nuns at their Wolf-Machines, their telephones, still spreading the Word. Still smiling. They trust Him.

And music is here, naturally. But not The Master's!

Schenkt man sich Rosen in Tirol, Weisst Du, was das bedeuten soll...

His 'Red Roses'. The shallowest operetta, with the artificial canaries, trilling, but muffled, from behind closed doors. Beside the telephone exchange, one opens.

"You?" says Bormann. "Those shitheads were supposed to hold you at the top. In here! Quickly, goddamn it, do you want the world to know?"

Toad In The Hole:

The Secretary grey toad-bastard lives with a grey filing cabinet, a grey metal bed, a black-and-white Portrait, a sepia oval frame of Mummy-Girl, and a small arsenal of weapons. The office bedroom is five grey paces square, no more. A plan of the cave-cellar spreads across the grey wall facing the Portrait. The bunk-bed is placed against the third wall. The fourth has shelves of books and files. A good carpet covers the grey concrete floor. Stolen-Flemish, from the pattern, and the room's only colour. There was one chair and the Toad plonked his fat arse in that.

"You took your bloody time," was his opening remark.

"There were raids everywhere. Hanna performed a miracle to get me here at all. Why am I under arrest?"

"You've got it backwards, mein Herr. You're here to make the miracle. If it's still possible. I had no idea *he'd* leave things so late in the game – marrying the Sheep. A proper honeymoon she's got out of it, playing that damned record! I can't do a thing with him in this mood. Maybe nobody can, but you're going to try, by God, or your sister's taking the high jump. You've got that?"

Tough words, but sticks-&-stones: sickly sweet cologne can't hide it – our toad-bugger is as terrified as the rest of us.

"I haven't got anything, Herr Bormann. I'm told I'm arrested – you say I'm not. You threaten to kill my sister – "

"No threat. I've signed the order." The bastard waved it. "And the child – and don't think for a moment I don't mean it. Only one thing in this world's going to save them – you get *him* to agree to join her. I don't give a fuck what lies you have to use – say the brat's his, that might help,

709

he half suspects, and he's always been afraid he wasn't man enough to knock a woman up the stump. Get him to the Untersberg, von Perceval, and I'll get us to Argentina, I promise you."

The bunker rocks in a massive explosion. The bookshelves sway – through 30 metres of concrete.

"How could I believe anything you tell me sitting here is going to work outside? You haven't the slightest idea what the streets are like."

"Streets, you moron?! I've spent a thousand hours planning this manoeuvre. Do you think we can drag Mussolini's wop's arse out of the mud on a mountain and not manage a damn sight better for ourselves?"

"But if Wolf's married Eva? What about her? And what on earth do you really expect me to be able to say?"

Another horrendous *whomp*. The Toad's desperate confidence faltered.

"The marriage was always a possibility – she never let up, bourgeois bitch, I allowed for it – but not that *he* would take it seriously. He's never been the same since July. Enough crap. It's done." The moment of Doubting Thomas was over. Daddy-Darling lifted his own arse from the chair. "No more fucking questions. You just pray for divine guidance."

Man schenkt die Rosen nicht allein, Man gibt sich selber mit auch 'rein . . .

"But I must ask – do I knock? I don't want to embarrass – "

"You think you'll find the love-birds on the nest? He can't stand being in the same room with that bloody record – smash it and do us all a favour. Now help me shift the bookcase."

The request is no more peculiar than the other scenes going on all around and above. A section of the shelving hinges at the centre. Fool & Toad rotate it into the room. The brute activated a switch by the Portrait. The wall opened.

The Secret Door

The one Eddie has been seeking since Tintagel, and the fox . . . ?

"Go down to the end and wait."

Lit by a blue light a narrow passage parallels the toad-hole. To the right, ending immediately at a steel slab; to the left, thirty feet only, then

710

more steel. Surprisingly, for such a confined space the air is fresher than the bunker's.

"Besides your normal gift of the gab there are two special answers to remember: you're using this way in because the top was blocked when you landed – and Himmler told you about it. The chickenshit gave you this plan of the installation." Another huge explosion. The Toad pressed a paper – his paw was sweating. "The rest will take care of itself. Or it won't. Allow five minutes, then push the red button."

"I don't have a watch."

"Count to three hundred. One last thing – He'll be surprised. Make the most of it."

And then –?

The Fool's tomb was sealed.

Ready-or-Not:

No nerves, Edwin. We are Numerologists, now, children.

We love magic numbers. Count to 21.

And try the steel door to the right, dear.

That's 49 – and it's locked, Mama.

… and that's 84, and our Eddie will be found after the Reich in 1000 years – *that's 105* – by some other Fool weaving mad conjectures to account for the Presence – *lost count, bugger and blast! was that 154?* – here lies a Fool who sought the G***l.

252 – it must be!

Turn. The passage is barely wider than a young lad's shoulders. Swiftly he walks it: the length 7, & 7 –

Fool's luck! 14 paces. The red button is purple under the blue light.

301. Ready or not, Open sesame.

Or not . . .

But *yes*!

. . . In the White Room: His shoulders are bowed. Below Mutti, He sits on the truckle bed; its rails are brass, and bound with ribbons, shivering, because His whole body is shaking. He holds a puppy in His hands, newborn, seeking for life, for milk at the trembling bitten fingers. He strokes it.

The mother bitch, Blondi, looks up as the wall opens, at the Fool, she

711

might have killed, torn the throat of, to protect, and instead wags her tail on the bare floor, thumping.

Her master is astounded – but not surprised.

"You heard. The Voice. And the dog knows. Mein Ederl. Out of all of them. You came."

"I suppose I did, Herr Wolf."

His palsied head looks away again, too filled with His own emotion to fix the Fool's lie. He gazes down at the mother with her other offspring, five of them, on a bed of sacking, beside Him, nursing. His sentences come slowly; completely – yet with gaps, and strokes of the puppy between them where there has always been that torrent of words.

"They aren't even pure-bred. It's the fault of a shithead adjutant's greyhound. Yet she could have whelped with the whole world for a nursery. What horrors the mating urge inflicts on Nature's creatures. What moments and places Fate picks for our turning points. This one is Fox'l. I've never allowed myself before to have another. A new Fox'l. What do they do by themselves, do you suppose? If we don't name them? They have a way of knowing. I've often watched in a litter. The mother will call and only one will answer. There are always favourites in a family. The male dog often attacks the bitch's favourite puppy. And how does the brute recognize it? Of course they have all our emotions. It never ceases to amaze me! The idiots like Bormann from farms think animals don't feel! As though we humans are unique instead of just one walnut on the tree of life – at the top, granted, for the time being, but that will pass too, the war proves it. Humanity doesn't deserve the legacy of genius handed to it. This modern age, you'll see, there won't be genius in it. This one is Tschapperl –" putting down Fox'l to take up another wriggling plump golden handful: His speech now more normal – *His* version of normal. "I've seen that she had exposure to the finest in our cultural heritage – Fräulein Braun, I'm talking about. Or rather, one doesn't know what to call her – I allowed her to tie the knot, as she puts it – yes, last night, a wedding of sorts. They like it to be on a Saturday for some reason."

"Congratulations, Herr Wolf."

"Danke, Ederl." The puppy-Tschapperl nuzzles a white ribbon on the brass bedrail. "These things mean so much to women. Their muslin curtains, and spotless floors, and hurdy-gurdy music – those synthetic canaries! with a crack, it drives one to distraction! yet how can a man deny a woman at her happiest moment? – I'm referring to marriage in general, not our particular circumstances ... There are three bitches and two males in the litter – the ratio in this country at the moment, but that gets made up in a generation – like rebuilding a city, thirty years, it never fails – even without Bormann's masculine contribution! You won't have had a chance to see our Mr Secretary, his behaviour has been erratic in my opinion. Naturally it was a terrific shock, losing Himmler as well as Goering to the traitors, but now with death ready to take one, it doesn't matter in the slightest. .... The man's name was Wagner – the official for the ceremony – isn't that peculiar? We played the Lohengrin, on record, without you. Those damnable Roses! – Edwin, go through and ask her to take it off for a moment, I have to have the dogs put down and it simply isn't suitable. I was going to order the act before her whelping but then it seemed von Manfred – " *a sudden flare of the old voltage!* – "and there's still a chance, if you, my Ederl, were able to break through!" ... the current fades ... "No, I can't wait any longer. She'll get attached to the puppies – you're such good friends she won't be hurt if it comes from you – Fräulein – mein Tschapperl, about the damned record. Give me five minutes, like a good fellow, and then we'll have Parsifal. The tone on the upright is hardly what you're used to, but we're under field conditions now. Use the connecting door – by the Dome."

"Yes, I see it, Herr Wolf."

A model of the great cupola for Linz, sits now by itself on a small folding table. The Fool walks past it to the door, to follow as ordered after the cracked Tyrol Roses, & also after Blondi, & puppy-Tschapperl, & Fox'l, to another lost pet....

The Blue Lady's Chamber:
Yet, she was not unhappy, our Eva, when the Fool walked in on her.

"Oh dear Herr Eddie, you didn't let Him down. You came to join us for the end."

"Ah, sort of. I hear congratulations are in order."

"Isn't it wonderful? You see, Herr Eddie, after so many years I found His Achilles' heel they used to tease me over. Please, sit down beside me." She pats the object she's sitting on: there's no co-incidence. "Our red divan, yes, from the old Chamberlain. Herr Eddie, *He* was so shy

713

doing it – I mean, saying it – at the ceremony." Girlish giggling, over the *doing it*, "Of course the affair was so simple, no priests or anything. I wore my garnets He gave me, that time we first met, for tea, do you remember, I was so down in the dumps, at the Carlton?"

"Yes, I remember. And now you're happy. I'm glad."

"You're always so sweet to me. Of course, it's sad too, about all our poor Doggies – I hear the Berghof's been bombed. I don't suppose, Herr Eddie, you know whether my little Stasi and Negus . . . ?"

"I'm sure they're all right. Dogs are very resilient."

Fool's lie: soothing balsam, from Parsifal.

"How I hope so." She faltered. "Oh Eddie, losing the Doggies, and everything *He* tried so hard for –" but her current was the stronger; she gave a rueful smile, "but We all have to go Sometime, as they say. And at least Not always a Bridesmaid. . . . The garnets were so cheap compared to everything else he's given me, but special. Just a moment, I have to wind up the record."

On a crank machine, from long ago. Everything except our *lignum vitae* needles.

"Eva, dear, that's one thing I wonder if I could mention?"

"You want to know what I'm going to use? Cyanide. It's very quick – no different than eating an apricot kernel. The same taste. I'll show you."

"*My God! Please no –!*"

As she reaches to the dressing table. A phial.

"I didn't mean *now*, poor dear Herr Eddie, I just meant to look at. You bite down once, that's it, and then so peaceful, in heaven forever, like the beautiful mountains I imagine, if you don't believe the hell that the English Sisters used to frighten us to death with. And they would never allow the Doggies, whereas that's the one part I'm absolutely positive about. If we go, they do! Why don't you like my 'Red Roses'? It has such a lovely melancholy don't you think?"

The Liebestod Phial is a small bronze bullet in her hand, with glass married to it; inside, the Potion. Amber. Drink me. All over.

"What I was going to say, Eva dear, about the record, it is a little loud, and the crack – He wants me to play some Parsifal."

"Loud? After thirteen years of Bayreuth and old Wagner? My 'Red

Roses'? But I'll stop – after we have one last crossed hands for the good times."

A one-time boy-and-girl stand face-to-face,

> *... Meinst Du es so, verstehst Du mich,*
> *Meinst Du es so, dann Lieb' versprich,*
> *Meinst Du es so, dann tröste mich,*
> *Gib mit den Rosen mir auch Dich.*

The boy and girl uncross their hands. She lifts the Marietta needle.

"See, I've done it. I suppose it's different for you and your sister, with the Wagner. I wish we could have met once more, I always thought the Fräulein Edwina was so wonderful and kind to me in the old days when I wasn't a Chefin, having to put up with the Toad-bugger. That's the one thing I really hope, that when we're gone, Eisenhower or Stalin hang up our Mr Secretary by his you-know-wheres! Now, dearest Herr Eddie, take this to remember her, and give your Eva a special kiss, and go and play your old Master's noises, and thank you always for being the poor Blöde Kuh's only proper special friend."

She turns her face, and passes a tawdry gem, the shade of a pomegranate, the namesake fruit of thwarted passion. . . .

I took the garnet earring, and kissed her, Eva Wolf, née Braun, sitting on our Red Divan, in front of her frilly dressing table, beside her cracked record of Tyrol's Roses: looking at her bride's reflection – which shows her looking at herself, looking at the apricot kernel in her hand, and a Fool of a man looking at her: with tears – which must damn him in the eyes of the English Sisters, and countless many others, for that eternity the Potion shows us is to come.

"Don't be sad, dear Herr Eddie. I have to be strong, because I'm sure I'll have to help Him, when it happens, you know how He hates hurting anything."

We know. Give yourself to Me together with the Roses. . . .

The damned Fool left the stupid Cow, and sought out once more Amfortas, by the Dome, which to the Fool's red eyes had visibly expanded, to make space for the newest arrivals.

The Dome

Is huge, but the white room seems empty without Blondi.

715

Now there is only the metal bedstead, and His braided ribbons, and a cooling space on the concrete floor that had been home to a faithful bitch with a wagging tail – and 5 new, blind, sacrifices, which, like all the others, ended the instant that He knew He loved them.

"Ederl, I have to say, thank God that a man was made into a soldier. Such decisions wouldn't be possible if one had been only the artist. Can you wonder they all go early, like Van Gogh? – even though that was the Great Destroyer, syphilis stares in every painting. Artists know so much better than their brutish fellows the state of our hideous world. . . . I had Linge, my valet, take the puppies – Linge is the only man who can be absolutely trusted – but I had to give Blondi the pill myself – to test it – the poison comes from Himmler's people, and at this stage one can't let the possibility of further treachery undo everything. It was so quick that one wonders why one ever put it off and endured so much misery from the filthy jealousies and innuendoes . . . Mad Ludwig knew – *mad*? Don't tell me! I identify with that poor man completely! More even than Wagner – it's true! because the King has the *power*! – to bring the artist's beauty to the people, and still the swinish herd reject him. Like Caesar, and Cromwell, it goes without saying, and Napoleon poisoned by his own entourage – there isn't the slightest shadow of a doubt about Napoleon! . . . We crossed the river on the same day, for Russia, did I tell you? Sunday, yes . . . I always choose a Sunday – for two reasons: because many of the hypocrite-fools of one's opponents are on their knees in their churches, yes! – or more likely not to be, after a night on the bottle, like the swiller Churchill! – but mainly because from one's earliest youth it was the special day. The Voice speaks on Sundays more than any other – although one didn't have anything to associate it with until I heard Parsifal for the first time. Please, yes, play it for me, now."

And so the Fool takes his place – beside the Dome, at an old mess-hall upright.

"The first time it was too much for a man to take in – Parsifal – even with *my* appreciation of Wagner! It wasn't until the Putsch failed – then I realised the sacrifice that always has to be demanded of the Leader. One realised that's what Easter *is*, make no mistake about it! the shaveling morons haven't the least idea! – Hacking and stabbing! Bodies rotting in the trenches! Heads coming off in gouts of blood. Entrails hanging on the wire – Christ on the Cross! that's Easter for the Leader! All year round! That's what he must expect from the moment he agrees to the devil's bargain. In exchange for Genius; the mountain-top first, then the barbed wire. The rat-trap, springing down – one used to watch it in the trenches – heads and tails, how they squealed! Oh yes! and as if betrayal isn't enough, there's the torture of sex, because he's a man but he can't surrender – all that is in Parsifal. . . . From those first sneering adolescent moments with priests, the sniggers of his fellow soldiers, or syphilitic stinking pimps in the Yid brothels of Vienna. Can we doubt for a single second that Richard Wagner suffered from them also, when we hear this music? The Master knows what's coming for any man who truly espouses the Cause. . . . That scream of agony from Kundry! – when I heard your sister give that frightful scream for the first time, like the rat-traps something almost snapped in me, I don't mind admitting it. She accepts the *blame* for our suffering – this is at the end, naturally, when she repents for the whores in the garden – she acknowledges what the bitches have done to men! Over and over and over. Endless oceans of blood and suffering because of women – this, Kundry *knows*. One could have gone on one's knees to her, right there in the Festspielhaus, in sackcloth and ashes – *ach*, given up everything! the whole struggle! And when she looks out . . . those enormous, martyr's eyes – how can a Leader allow such a thing to be performed in wartime? Any time! I would have surrendered without the first bullet fired, and gone back to my mountains, but your sister – even though she gave me her ribbon – this one, the green – that first time on the Dutchman's ship. From that instant she knew she had my heart, but she was too noble a creature to take advantage. Like your mother. The first woman in history to deny herself the Leader for the sake of the Cause – your sister, the indescribably gracious, magnificent, and gallant Fräulein Ettie. This shitting country never deserved her little finger! As for the Nigger-jazz crowd – just thank God they didn't get her. Imagine if she had given in to the Jews of New York's Woolworth Metropolitan? . . . But one should have done it, that Sunday one first heard her as Kundry, and the Grail descended. I should have crossed over the pit – turned my back on the whole shitting, backstabbing ratpack of them; Goerings and Himmlers and their thieving, sub-moron Gauleiters. *Sub-humans!* Try sharing a Bayreuth with those dumb bastards? Well, it's done. Finished. Mein Ederl, one last time, play the Grail March for me . . ."

And then –?

717

In the soaring Good Friday music, at the very height of it, the Fool said, in the part reserved for him, the part of the tongue-twisting Judas, the Jew's part:

"It isn't too late, Herr Wolf. Today's a Sunday. And Kundry is waiting – Ettie, rather, with Rose, your daughter. In the cottage you've always wanted, on your Mount Mausoleum. I've found the tomb underneath, it could be King Arthur's. Perhaps even of the – "

"Charlemagne's tomb . . .?" on a note of rising wonder.

"My Fuehrer, yes – that too is an outside possibility."

And then –?

The pale cheek flushes. Miraculously, the hand and head stop shaking. The eyes take on whatever indescribable aspect and shade it is that each observer thinks he remembers, and the Voice of A commands – BELLOWS:

"Anything's possible! Bormann! Bormann, damn you, Plan Rheingold is on! Get your arse here this moment."

And then –?

Why, the Tarnhelm Story, children.

. . . *Transformation:* After all the hours of waiting – the years! – of brooding, it happened so quickly, like Teuton clockwork.

The Toad-bastard, loaded with weapons, responded to the Call.

The Leader said in A's voice, "Linge, be ready, I must go through for the moment, to be with Frau Eva."

(So the valet was the only other soul on earth who saw this.)

Bormann, fortified also from a bottle, snapped at the Fool, "Wait in the tunnel."

The wall opened. So did the door to our inferior Chefin, on the Red Divan. Her Special Friend heard one last *Red Roses* . . . a small *crack* – which might have been only a broken record; he smelled a scent of almonds to mix with the stenches; in his pocket he gripped a small, semi-precious stone the colour of blood, from past affection.

Exit, Eva.

As we say, dear Herr Eddie, 3rd time Lucky . . .

"Step aside!"

Bormann again – thrusting past to jab the red button, thick-thumbed, missing once. But on the next, the steel slab swings at the left end of the tunnel. In a cell the mirror-image is waiting: call it Mock-A, the pride of the dentists, ein Doppelgänger, the face of Death. However sub-human

718

it was, the creature knew the fate that waited for it. The Toad-bastard stuck a Mauser under the double's ribs and forced it back from the tunnel to the White Room.

Blood sprays, and flows across the Dome . . .

A smoking pistol. A former Desperado's. The *crack* this time will be heard around the world – yet Real-A returns from our Eva's bedroom. His hand is shaking again – *but His face is flushed in the final release of passion.*

And the Fool, horrified, knew:

9th time lucky. After 8 attempted – *HE'S SEEN ONE DO IT.*

"We must proceed to stage two at once, my Fuehrer." Our Mr Secretary croaked in his toad-Saxon, "A moment only while I engage the airlock."

The tunnel is a Chinese puzzle of doors – no, a maze, the Minotaur's. A lost-count section of stone wall slides. A chill gust of dank air sweeps in from the dark. From Erda.

Bormann produced three strong torches. Each non-subhuman took one for his journey.

"You first, Herr von Perceval, then you, my Fuehrer, following. My duty is the rearguard, for counter-mining the tunnel."

Real-A shivers, and remarks, perhaps to the Fool, perhaps as footnote for History, "Do you remember our Demok-rats Bolthole? across the roofs, that day with Mausi? It had the same architectural dimensions."

"Yes, Herr Wolf, I remember."

And now the road to Valhalla is a sewer.

The Mauser's crack this time echoes, is deafening – but was heard by no one. The man called Wolf, or Wotan, or Real-A, or Adolf Hitler falls, unseen, into the swirling brown waters, joined by this other garnet-coloured liquid. There is no Dragon's blood. His own human nature wells up from the base of His neck, dead-centred.

Dolchstoss

In the Back. As it must be.

"One wrong move, von Perceval, you get the next one."

The 5th-rate Hagen, Bormann – still half-in, half-out of the blue-light's passage – jabs another black-magic red button. The steel slab sliding this time releases 2 more terrified doubles: 1 mock-Toad; 1

719

Other – plus the 1 in the sewer, plus the 1 with Eva – the Fool's mind can't remember which One was real.

Were any of them? Ever?

The Doppelgänger pair crouch, eyes fixed to the Toad-face in the torchlight.

"Hop, you fucking Polack swine or I'll have your nuts off."

The words can mean nothing, but the pair have perfect understanding. The doubles rush, splashing: our group is a Quartet conducted by a Saxon bastard-devil with automatic weapons.

"Get going, von Perceval. *Go man* – we've only sixty seconds!"

For half-slipping, half-swimming, counting the numbers by 7's, praying . . .

56.

The blastwave knocks the Fool forward – the doubles are on top of him, something in his mouth, unmentionably disgusting, vomiting . . .

"Arseholes! Get up!"

Tunnel, blue lights, red buttons, the corpse that was Real-A – all vanished. Or has it? The perfect likeness still stands at the Fool's side, with 2 toad-Bormanns. Of such is nightmare.

Alptraum:

"You lead again, von Perceval. There are steps around the corner. Head up them."

In torchlight things grow on the steps, whitish-greenish forms of animal matter. Yes! The will to Life is so precious that it grips and survives in even such places.

77 steps. An iron rail to cling to, but the mock-Wolf was created too perfect in His image. The 56-year-old creature is gasping, its heart bursting.

"You stay with the feeble swine, von Perceval – let us by."

TWO Toad-faces pass – remember, Edwin: the one with the guns is real.

Suddenly there was light, flaming, thunderous noise, monumental street battle.

"Nothing can live out there," yet the real-Bormann is exultant. "You, cretin, get moving – No, wait."

A thug-paw thrust a leather notebook into the mock-creature's pocket. A thug-boot in the back propelled it, outlined against the flares. The toad-double staggered forward, arms upraised, the universal signal of helpless I-surrender. The real-bastard took aim with his Mauser –

The mock creature falls. The shadow of a tank passes by it, over it.
"Down," bellows Bormann, "down! Fool – that means you!"
Meaning me, Edwin.

Only half the steps, down: 39 . . . is 3, 13's, a frightful number.

A dripping manhole cover of cast-iron has Imperial Teuton eagles embossed. For a sewer? the Fool thought – the Race is mad in the entire.

The manhole's other face is turned to the Underground – but not Erda's, or another sewer.

BAHNHOF FRIEDRICHSTRASSE

The Berlin Tube. Young Edwin used to come here with Waring, on his shooting stick, watching. Not tonight, Jeremy. With no electricity the station is stygian. With the rails live, thousands would die. The tunnel is packed with the Volsung Volk, escaping the carnage Unter den Linden.

"We have to get under the Spree," Bormann shouts on a wave of fear and schnaps. "Von Perceval, shine your light. If I use mine the mob will see this animal, and we still need its Polack hide."

God knows what for. The doors of Escape are closed.

Wotan is gone; the last act drops back to Teuton-Marietta.

THE RIVER CROSSING

A BLUT FARCE

The doors are Huge, *the diameter of the tunnel! A corpulent figure with* walrus moustache *and* brass-buttons *embossed* BVG, *holds a great Key and a Book. This Person is the* HERR OBEROFFIZIAL – *being consulted by the Army in the form of two* Feldgrau COLONELS *and a* Lightning-Bar GENERAL.

721

THE HERR OBEROFFIZIAL [*reading officiously*]
Between the hours of midnight and 0630, in
accordance with Berlin Municipal Transport
Company Standing Orders, these bulkhead-doors
may not be opened. Herr General, I repeat that these
regulations are signed in the name of the
Commissioner for Safety by Rail.

THE HERR GENERAL [*barely containing*]
But Herr Oberoffizial, there are no trains running.

THE HERR OBEROFFIZIAL [*obviously*]
Herr General, trains do not operate between the
hours of midnight and 0630.

COLONEL ONE [*exploding*]
Gott im Himmel! There are *no trains* you pig-shit
oaf!

COLONEL TWO
None anywhere!

THE HERR OBEROFFIZIAL [*on his dignity*]
Herr Colonels, may one remind, these Regulations
are not for trains. They exist in the name of the
Commissioner for anti-flooding.

THE HERR GENERAL [*doomed heroic*]
Reverse! There's nothing for it. We shall have to
chance the Russians!

THE TOAD BASTARD BORMANN [*groaning with terror*]
Ach, a rule book! Otherwise the plan was perfect.
Hunnishly he turns to follow his defeated army brethren.

THE ENGLISCH FOOL *deciding enough of Hieronymus Bosch*
Herr Oberoffizial, you can see I am escorting the
Fuehrer. Open these bloody doors or I'll have you
shot.

> *He shines the Torch on – THE IMAGE!!!...A*
> *moment of astounded silence . . . and then – the*
> *Key is turned! Our TRIO passes out of Marietta to*
> *the Other Side, after which their journey is –*

> [*To Be Continued ...*]

Third Movement

Final Passage

[flowingly]

On Richmond Hill there lives a Lass,
More bright than May-day morn,
Whose charms all other maids Surpass,
A Rose without a Thorn.

Old School's 49, cannot let us down. Seven 7's must see me to the end of it – *though the heart be frail, and flutter; and the blood be thin, and cold; though the eyes do weep, lips tremble – oh, Edwin! thou art OLD.*

Why go on?

Gedanke & Gedächtnis scream at the blasphemy . . . but no, it seems only a raven-mating in the ash tree. You effing fowls, the children of Yellow Street don't CARE. They never did. The world has spun with the Norns a million-million miles through the heavens since *He* fell in the sewer. Grail WHAT? Bormann WHO?

No more!

Leave your remaining black dredgings from Eddie's decaying brain for the feast you can have when the old Boy's gone. Eyeballs first, tongue for Afters. We torture no one but ourselves.

> *This lass so neat, with Smiles so sweet,*
> *I'd crowns resign to call Thee –*
> *Crowns? Life itself! My precious, my darling, my only, my all – that's the least I owe you. Take it, and eat: body & soul.*

725

But first, let me kill the Toad.

... *May Day: Across the River.* Not yet safe in the trees: as dawn comes for the Trio, all too early that May First morning, Morgengrauen, the waking rays of impartial Dame Sun light on hunter and hunted with equal pinkness – an absurd softness of colour for the harshest scenes imaginable. Rape of war takes on its literal meaning as the peasant Bear is loosed to dance in Berlin's society parlours & cellars.

Losing whole streets was the Trio's problem – with Fool's luck they saw no Russians, not one! At first there were the bridges for guidance, even though fallen, but once out of the Boulevarde Friedrich-List-Ufer, all was strange as the moon. The landmarks for the bastard-Bormann were only roofless shells and heaps of smoking rubble.

"Damn to hell, von Perceval, you can't lose a whole barracks. The Zossen HQ is concrete. Kick that cretin's arse. We *have* to find it!"

The Double looks more like the Wolf-original than ever: grey, shaking, bent over, coughing from dust and smoke and emphysema, the trainers at Fuhlsbüttel couldn't have hoped for better.

"Why can't we just let the poor fellow go? He's half dead, and if people see we'll have a riot."

"They won't see it when we find the blasted garage. Its skin is priceless for later. Is that Exhibition Park?"

The toad-bastard had murdered the skin that was priceless. *The Boy must be Put Down* ... our Mr Secretary can murder again without blinking those amphibian eyes – yet the Fool follows him through hell with blind devotion because he has one unswerving purpose:

SOUTH!!!

At any price. And South is Rose, and Ettie, and Safe-through-Cameron.

"You there! Brat – over here!"

A miracle: a ragged urchin boy who lived and played with rats – one of the Kellerkinder, the children of Nibelheim who came to maturity in a waste of ruins. Proud of his skills the Kellerkind guides the Trio under the rubble to the Zossen garage – in the western suburbs, the Good Side of Berlin, the side away from the Eastern frost.

And then –?

726

The next miracle. A Black Order panzer – a great Tiger tank, in running condition! With driver!

"Good man!" cried Bormann, "I shall never forget you!"

"The situation will still be touch and go, Herr Secretary, although so far the von Manfred gap is still open – Heil, my Fuehrer!"

Our Doppelgänger. It managed a weak Wolf-salute in reply. The Tiger-driver disappeared down into his conningtower. The motor roared to life. *Life!* The Trio embark: Double first, helped by Fool; Toad last – because the brute had unfinished business with the Kellerkind, but the nature of the exchange was mercifully hidden by the armour plating and the engine running. That Bormann's Mauser was out of its holster when he came down the ladder, does not prove more murder. . . .

And then –?

0430:

Magic numbers. They add to 7. With what he thinks is a conclusive omen The Fool waves goodbye to Berlin – remarking to himself on the astonishing survival of green trees, alive and leafing in a street of burning desolation.

And then –?

THE TOWER

The one of Fool's dreams. It is squat and grey, like the Toad, giving no hint to the unwary of its all-reaching function.

"What is that place?" the Fool asked the Tiger driver. "On the left, with the tower?"

"Nothing to bother us, mein Herr. Only Spandau Gaol."

We run in circles for a span, but every step is Synchronicity.

0630:

Rechlin, a last functioning outpost of winged-Fafner. A special Condor stands ready – through the tank's portholes the Trio can see the engines turning – before the bombs begin falling.

"They can't take off in this," shouts the Tiger driver.

"We can't stay," screams Bormann. "There's an Alternate, at Wittenberg."

"We might have fuel to make the gap. I can't promise. But for the Fuehrer – "

The Condor explodes. The Tiger swings on its axis for our Leader. one magic word for another.

SOUTH!!!

0800:

Only 2 hours more on that bright morning but Fool's luck seems endless. The gap *is* open. In a field beyond, a Storch, already waiting. The Trio climbs from the Tiger. The Double is almost unconscious from fumes, and the motion. Half-carried, half-dragged, it's still an object of veneration. Wolf-salutes from the Tiger driver, and the Storch pilot. The Trio bundles into the tiny aircraft: from the safety of 6-inch armour plate, to painted canvas.

"I haven't had a chance to top up, Herr Secretary. We can pass over the Americans with luck, but we won't make the Berghof for the Fuehrer – she only has radius for Saalfeld, perhaps Bayreuth."

Perhaps? Don't tell me!

The Storch squashes cow-pats in a bumping rush for takeoff. Behind, grounded, the Tiger driver who would never be forgotten was stranded without fuel. A sheet of flame comes out of the sun from a Katyusha battery hidden in a copse of linden and beech – the Battle of the Beech Tree is over for the Tiger. The Bear's infantry advances. A member of the Leibstandarte In-*His*-Name does what must be done: the Tiger driver goes down shooting, with one last bullet for himself.

They shall not know *He* passed this way.

1000:

3 lucky circles on that mad morning, Nave, Transept, Chancel – Sanctuary! A curtain-barrage from the Nigger-Jazz brigade is rendered harmless by Fool's magic. Saalfeld with the mad American player, Patton, is behind.

"We may even make Nuremberg, for the Fuehrer – damn! The gauge is falling! The Americans must have got a tank."

No *perhaps*: it will have to be . . .

From the deadly North, from the air, the sleepy town of the Green Hill looks still picture-postcard perfect. And on landing: cows, meadows, steeples, river, cobbled streets, the Anker Hotel, the Restaurant of Owls, the Square & Avenue called Wagner: in the Master's name, all war long, like Paris and Rome, bent-pricked Cameron hasn't touched it.

And oh, what memories, seeing that dome shining on the Magic Mountain, what emotions – but not for a toad turned into a Secretary.

"How long to refuel? Can you make repairs?"

For our Fuehrer? For Believers, even a mock-Wolf makes anything possible! But a heathen siren sounds. Defence is a thing of the past, like the great performances. Cameron's bombs come before the end of the first warble. Yet damage is light. The Anchor and Owls are intact.

Only the Storch and the runway are hit. . . .

"We'll be all right," said Bormann, but shaken, in a sandbagged gun emplacement. "You doubted the cretin's value, von Perceval. Now we'll see."

A closed Black Leather van was commandeered. The Double was stuffed in the back, with no more consideration for his new worth. The Fool was allowed the privilege of riding with him. The Storch pilot became the van driver – until the man passed out from loss of blood, which he had not reported, out of Loyalty. Dear Christ, the myth was potent.

"Arsehole!" croaked the grateful Toad, "von Perceval, you take over."

"This isn't the way to Nuremberg."

"Shithead! The house – what do they call it?"

. . . *No Illusion:* We know – every step, every cobble to Wahnfried. Still nothing was harmed on the Magic Mountain. The Festspielhalle, with the great stage, waited, with the golden wigs, and horns, and sails, for a new performance, just like Last Time. Once more, the Norns' God has found Richard Wagner: Not guilty.

This late, the Fool still clings to that illusion. Art is art, only.

And then –?

The van turned the corner by the garden wall of the Parrot-Sisters, and the hedge where we had all played as the Golden Children, and the Grave, where the Parrots, and Doggies, and Mama, and Genius, all ended – and the Fool saw the next result of Cameron's actions.

729

The Doppelgänger stared with dull incomprehension: yes, he saw the wall of Wahnfried torn away, but it meant less than nothing, for his was only the outward Form – the Brain was missing. It took a real Fool to see.

He sees ... the whole Garden-Room, and Cosima's, thrown out in the garden. He sees the great copper roof torn down like paper. He sees the gallery where Liszt's daughter walked, or was wheeled, abruptly nowhere. He sees one of Liszt's incomparable pianos, crushed, with the other lath-sticks in the wreckage. He sees portraits, of Mausi, before she got fat in rebellion, when they were all still a Family – with a Mama and Papa – and yes, he sees Real-Siegfried, smiling, in socks, and jolly Aunt Winnie, as Senta, looking at him adoringly, before she went to the first corner Rally. The idiot sees those other one-time Masterly disciples, Nietzsche & Schopenhauer, reduced to the sum of their frames and glasses – words proved worthless among the ashes. And on a radio-gramophone standing under the sky, under mad Ludwig's pedestal, I, Edwin, my Self sees a small bust, of marble, with a floppy cap, with a tassle, like one that came in a tea-chest, by a boat called the Cormoran, *to launch this Illusion.*

"Not here, Fool – the garage behind the guesthouse!"
Real-Siegfried's little house was spared. Heaven held him blameless – but the garage is locked. It still has the nursery notice about Not Starting Engines in the mornings. The Family are not in residence. So Bormann shot the lock off.
And then –?
Why, our Mercedes, Children.
Mama's very own. Yes, this flaming scarlet antique roadster was a toad's idea of going through Nibelheim incognito.
More practically, the thug also had a change of clothes, civilian suiting, cut for a heavier weight, of indifferent cloth, brownish, with a blue tie: thus arrayed he looked like Fat Hermann in hand-me-downs. The Game-keeper of the Flame, also. From a pocket of his ex-uniform our Mr Secretary took an envelope.
"The last will and testament, von Perceval – three copies, take one, it could be worth a bundle."

730

Ingratiating bastard. Nonetheless, well organised. The Trio adds drums of petrol to its luggage and leaves at noon. 1200.

Exeunt Bayreuth.

. . . *Early afternoon:* Smooth sailing. The Wolf-Road from the Green Hill to Nuremberg is unscathed, and both lanes are being used for South. No need to go in the opposite direction, it's Out of Season. But Hans Sachs' city within its wall is burning from a superfluous daylight attack of Cameron's. On the safe side, the Fool stopped and poured a drum of petrol. The Toad stood in a field of sugar-beet with the Mauser and watched the mock-Wolf defecate – another liquid process. The creature saw terror in every kindness. Bormann chucked it a beet and said,

"You're doing a good job, von Perceval, I'll never forget it."

The words made the Double's affliction contagious.

"Just a moment," said the Fool.

And then –?

The town with the tower first seen on Mama's black-and-red Thomas Cook map was left behind with the rest of the stinking mess.

"Step on it, von Perceval. We want to make Munich before nightfall."

Exit Hans Sachs.

. . . *Early evening:* To the heart of the wheel, central Bavaria, with fairy castles & English Gardens, & Peace-on-paper, & broken promises & hearts in tearooms; a kaleidoscope of memory as mixed and out of joint as Putzi's red-and-green Picasso woman.

And as though Cameron can read the Fool's thoughts and follow the worm Piss-pot-Percy by them, again the bombers arrive as the Trio does, so that the direct route is blocked and they have to detour over the Isar . . . in such a meander that there was no rhyme or reason otherwise why we should have passed both the Bürgerbräukeller with the starter's shot in its ceiling and Eva's little house all her own – but we did, directed up the slight hill that the dear old Riley would have known without its driver (*and where* is *poor Riley?*); past the spot where the pile of sand once blocked the Doggies' angered Master; and the high wall and the sheltering laurels where we got our first intimation of how it would be, how it is.

731

And then –

At the corner, as the Trio was turning back towards His autobahn, with Mama's red Mercedes, they passed a small black shadow trotting resolutely, sniffing this side, that side, finding its way doggedly, so that Herr Eddie braked, and called,

"Stasi!"

Or was it Negus? So lost, and small, and come so far looking for Home, and Mistress . . .

"For a fucking dog in a raid?! English idiot you'll kill all of us!"

Cameron dropped a block-buster to prove it was possible – and when the Fool looked back, once, over my shoulder, the little house was there, but no little black shadow, trotting and sniffing.

Exeunt Doggies.

. . . *Nightfall:* With each safer mile into darkness and towards the heights, the Toad expanded. Past Rosenheim, of the Meeting, the bastard becomes positively loquacious.

"Thank God, that's the worst of it. Von Perceval, you've done a magnificent job of driving, I don't mind admitting. I'm a lowlander but there's something about just getting back in reach of the mountains, a strength to them. Christ, how I tried to talk *him* into this move! If we'd stayed one more hour in that fucking bunker we'd have bought it, the lot of us. I bless the day I brought my precious family down here – please heaven, my Mummy-Girl has them all in the Tyrol through the tunnels, out of the reach of those bastard Ivans – creatures from the stone-age! The whole West can see that by now. The last thing he was right about – the so-called Allies will be at each other's throats before the month's out. It's just a hellish tragedy that he didn't take advantage of making peace when we could have. Christ knows I encouraged him, but he had that blind streak. I don't mind admitting now, he was more than a little peculiar on many days. I blame that shitfaced quack Morell completely, all those bulls' balls injections. How could he really imagine he was buying that property and keeping your sister and the child in secret? The man had a complete lack of common sense for cash and taxes and such things. He was an open book to me."

"Really?"

"Absolutely. Oh, I don't mind admitting there were days he could swing the lead and get one agreeing to a lot of nonsense – two months ago he had me convinced it was right that we should all go down together as Nibelungs – King Attila in the hall – but what's the point if we're going to turn around the day after tomorrow and be on the same side against Stalin? That pathological bitch Magda Goebbels, wiping out her own kids – you didn't hear? All six of them! It's unbelievable. But you know, von Perceval, whenever the cunt was next to *him* you could hear her damned ovaries rattle! As for the Russians, a forearm-stiff in the chops, like dropping a pig, that's the answer to Ivan. And he'll have to be answered double-quick. The Fellow-Travellers will be crawling out all over Europe, and we have the goods on them, every cell in the occupied countries – for a price. That's the gist of the deal I'm going to propose to London's operatives when we reach your sister, as you agreed with them in Zürich – our skins in exchange for the cretin back there, plus the Red Lists. And of course they'll take his child."

As casual as that.

"I never agreed anything with London," the Fool said, blanched in the night. "What do you mean about my niece?"

"Don't bullshit – watch where you're driving, man!"

An unfilled crater almost claimed Attila-the-toad and his idiot-driver, who imagined that he could control the wreck of the world. Let blood relatives survive? To start a dynasty? After Lenin & the Tsars? Don't tell me!

Mineshafts & pistol muzzles at the backs of necks. Children's.

"All right, she isn't really my niece, Bormann – but you know she isn't *His*. You know she's *my* daughter."

"No," said the toad. "I don't. With your own sister? What kind of a perverted swine . . .?"

The Question of the Fool's life. And answer came there

. . . In the Valley of the Shadow: Another night, but when was the last sleep? The marks of our lives flash past Mama's red Mercedes, the spokes of our wheel, the roads to Landsberg, to Linz, to the Swan Castle, to Oberammergau with the Passion – and the stars: Death occurs under a travelling Aspect, and he prefers a transit of Jupiter because it means departure from wherever we are on this astral plane. And the dark thread of violence with Pluto, for Edwin, and Saturn for Sister, still rising, so that Death is explosive, with hidden enemies.

Today, tonight, Mars lies on Edwin's Sun, and Mercury; winged messenger defend me. For Edwin's chart looks strangely positive – as though the Fool has escaped his dread and been liberated from some terrible influence. Tomorrow, the morning coming, Mars will be conjunct Ettie's natal Sun – to Frau Marthe Steiner, when she read it, that was astounding . . .

Next Mark:
Berchtesgaden, with Hänsel-&-Gretel rotating, and the legendary Mad King turned to stone on the heights, above – Obersalzberg: and the legendary Emperor of One Europe sleeping under them – the Untersberg.

Over & Under: Heaven & Hell.

Next Mark:
The twin-oaks, for the road to Love Cottage; trunks entwined in love's knot as –

"Christ's shit! Stop, man! Those tanks are Ivans!"

5, grouped in a circle, at the foot of the lane, gossiping.

"They can't be," Uncle gasped, braking, heart squeezing. "The Reds are halted at Passau. It was only two days."

"Look at the turret stars! Turn, damn you, fool! *Turn!*"

Red Stars in the Morning, Death is aborning. Braking & turning. Screaming & tipping, righting & wronging –

"Where the hell are you going? Fool, you'll kill us!"

"The diggings – the Reds can't get Rose – my sister!"

"You've got another route to the landing zone?"

"What do you think I'm saying?"

The ravings of maniacs. Only the cretin lost in the back stays silent. Death for him is a certainty either way. The Bear hasn't seen. Down again is the only answer.

. . . In Erda's World: Nobody home. The Nibelung rats have abandoned ship 2 days early. The lights are left on in the workings. The walls shine whitely. The Trio of Fool-Toad-Cretin pass as swiftly as the latter's condition will let them.

"How much further, von Perceval? You've dragged us miles."

"I thought the railway would be working."

734

"If you've been lying – "

"Honestly. It starts to rise once we get to the sepulchres."

The Wolf-double has gone too far already. The creature stumbles, its breath comes in short paroxysms, its pale face has purpled – the shade *His* was for a woman's dying. The Trio come to the round table of tombs that could be Arthur's.

Dead End:

"Oh Christ! How could they – the stupid, stupid buggers!"

"You've lied," the toad-bastard screaming it, raising the Mauser. "There's no way out."

"There is, but for some reason they've sealed them up again. Just give me a moment, I'll remember which one it was."

White-on-white? Salt-on-salt? Don't tell –

"That one!"

"You're sure?"

"Yes!"

The 7th one around the Circle.

"How does it open?"

"We used explosive – but then they were mortared. It's only pushed back now – a pickaxe should do it."

The Fool grasps one. The mock-Wolf sags on another tomb, ready for dying. The Toad stands by with the Mauser, glowering.

"It's not budging, Bormann – you'll have to help."

The toad-bastard *is* a game-keeper on days off. Solid under the flab. The entrance stone wiggles.

"Again, von Perceval. More under your corner."

The pick slips, holds, eases upwards.

"It's over the sill, up just another fraction . . ."

And then –?

Fool saw the small slight gleaming, just beyond the rusted iron of the tool, the twisted colours of a wire, so that he knew, although he didn't know he did, and was moving, though he didn't know he moved, enough that his usual Fool's luck saved him from the direct thrust of the explosion, which even so, hurled him to the next mark around the circle – but the Toad was caught: Bormann's right leg, trapped at the thigh, under the full weight of –

735

The Cretin was on him – with the pickaxe, lifted high . . . brought *down* – into that brute skull, at the front, so he could see it coming, clean through.

Exit Daddy-Darling.

And Doppelgänger: the work was too much for the creature's heart, but it died happy – in ecstasy, covered in the blood of its victim, if that word covers a holy murder. The Fool was alone, with only two souls hovering to their reward, or perdition.

His head was ringing, but otherwise there was only a sense of lightness, and well being, of imminent high adventure. He passed through the door of the passage of the 7th sepulchre, and walked upward – until it began to be dark and he realised that last time they had used torches, and he had to return to the killing ground and take a portable lamp from the salt wall, and shine it for a last time on the letters **C R**, that might stand for *Christus*, or *Charles Rex*, or neither, and re-enter the passage, and set off for the second time upwards, and turn the corner so that the light was gone from the rotunda – when hell broke loose in the earth around him.

1, 2, 3 . . . up to 12, the dozen Rau asked for; a ripple-effect of explosions, a super-Booby trap.

Oh Christ: If the Way be closed . . .

But it wasn't. There was the delayed sound behind him of a torrential rushing as some underground river's seam was burst open, then that too faded, or blended with the rushing in his ears, and he walked quietly out on to the mountain, by the cemetery, below Rose, and Ettie, and Love Cottage, early one morning, just as the sun was rising – Old Number 22, he remembered – and the air, though it chilled him, was sweet as only Life can be to the returning Traveller.

. . . *At the Bower:* He breathes it in, and stretches his arms, and thrusts his chest out, Proud as a peacock, as they say. Herr Eddie looks up to his loved ones who will be sleeping in downy nests of sweetness.

But they aren't – or at least Mummy isn't. Sister's up with the lark, busying herself with the tasks of the starting day: fill the kettle, light the fire.

But the fire she's lighting, my dears, is *outside* the cottage, by the bower. Wonders never cease – nor Woman's Nature:

She's rebuilt the bloody beacon!!!

And then –?

No! Then only – did it come upon him, at the same moment as a pair of jet-black Ravens flew high above him across the valley, craanck-craancking, in their harsh fashion, 2 Thoughts:

Bormann was right, Cameron will kill them.

&

She's lighting it to call him.

But these premises were clearly so antithetical, so only a mad Fool's way of thinking, that he said to himself instead, as the fire took hold:

It's only Ettie being Ettie, and called up to Her:

"I'm back. Put it out."

"I see you are. I can't. Good morning, darling."

"But you must. I can't hear too well; I've buggered my ears, but we have to talk before we light it."

"Poor poppet, that's something new, with the ears – is He with you?"

"What?"

"Is Wolf with you?"

"No. He's dead. How's Rose?"

"She's sleeping – SLEEPING – Eddie, I can't shout like this. Hurry and kiss me."

"Ettie, I'm terribly tired. Please – at once, put out that bloody fire."

"You look tired, poor pet," *for now they were close together & She could see him,* "come in and have tea while we're waiting."

"Marvellous, proper tea, you can't know how wonderful that sounds."

Because he couldn't hear the last part – or his addled brainbox wouldn't let him.

"I'll put honey in," *as She kissed him, ever so warmly,* "extra sweet. I got a new comb, for the most darling darling brave brother ever."

And once more, as he kissed Her back, he heard those harsh Ravens passing these moments into Memory, & he said,

"I'd adore honey – you pour while I put that fire out."

And She said, taking his hand, & leading him, again like a child,

"Don't be such an old fuss; it's almost out by itself, and anyway they'll have seen it. Now sit in the kitchen. I've got something serious to tell you."

Ettie's right. Silly Eddie – the beacon is almost out, because She hasn't

737

rebuilt a very big one & he watches as She stirs a dollop of honey in, & gives it to him, & he sips, & she stands against him, stroking his neck, & he gulps, & dear Mother in Heaven it's everything wonderful between them & he asks,

"What is it? – to tell me – because I want to see Rose."

And She answers,

"It's about Rose, actually, and us, darling, about us all *being*, if you see what I mean?"

And he says,

"Not too much, it's still my ears I think; there was an explosion. Is she in the bedroom?"

"No, but she's all snuggled; there's no need to worry. Eddie, pet, it's because after you left, you see I've been thinking, and of course it can't work, not again, darling. It was all too special, and there really won't be a place, not for us – even without the Russians' ghastly prison thing. So that's why I had to do it."

"Do what? Ettie, the room's sort of swimming. I want to see Rose."

"I know, pet, it's the honey, only to make you sleepy so you won't be frightened. Rose is in the bower. I wanted her to see the last sunrise."

And then –

he knew he wasn't frightened, although, after all the Chicken Farmer's games on the board, for the first time this is TERROR. And he stood up, with the room swaying & the noises in his ears rushing, like Liebestod, soaring & crashing & She said,

"They'll think Wolf is here anyway, and we'll all be together, like before, on Porquerolles, darling Eddie, with Mama, and for always."

and then –

he heard the greatest E Major opening in all the world, that means Cameron IS coming, & he went out – he rushed out, smashing against the doorposts, falling over the steps, sprawling through the budding vines & the crisscross railings stripped by the squirrels for their barknests for their babies, & the duckies flapping like monstrous bats leaving obsidian beaches, & he plunges through the remains of the fire, but not noticing the burning on his piano hands & noble face: only Rose, in her bower, infinitely more pink-&-whitely beautiful in the dawning over the Salt Mountain; Rose waving at silly Uncle; Rose laughing at Mummy calling

"Eddie, it's too late now, darling; we must be together."

& then

Rose crying! – at the thundering, mightier than Thor & Donner even, over the terrible Teuton blood-mountains, but not as Terrible as his rage at his Sister

"BURN IN HELL FOREVER BITCH
BEFORE I LET YOU KILL HER."

AND THEN

More running & falling!
More crashing! More bleeding!
More bursting!
More burning! – Love Cottage! – more thunder, more lightning!
And then Frozen

Postlude
After the Fire

... *In the Land of Ice* there is no Liebestod; only 40 years of wandering, waiting, wondering and suffering – but gladly, because Pisces deserves it, and even suffering is Life, and Where there's Hope, as they say ... even for a Last Survivor.

Which *is* his Hope, Edwin's, or Fool, however you call him, children – because I am *not* last. The line continues, whose name is Rose Eustasia Edwina Casson-Perceval – even if they Christened Her inevitable Gretel, those village peasant souls who clustered round me like Michael Rau's Breughel painting on that horrific May morning, as the Red Bear clanked up the hill to take me, and claw me to its hairy dreadful bosom: Uncle Eddie, that burnt offering for Rose; offering perfect Rose to her new parents – as I had to for the Legend, so that Siegfried may continue, the Golden One, that One who leads us Upward from our frightful animal natures. That One who hangs on the Cross for us, or from the Great Ash Tree outside a Prisoner's window, whatever our Number ...

Where I see Him now, smiling like Michael, haloed: and my black ravens, White and Shining, great wings beating, fanning the papers, slipping away from me, quill feathers lifting now, not scribbling ...

And She is there. Rose lives! I know it! She is my Grail, and I *have* found Her. For I knew by the End how to seek Her. But listen on the wind, my dears, as it reaches my Tower. Listen ... and She sings, like that Other inexpressibly, purely, magically, who died on Her Mountain, but rises again for me.

Edwin, Dearest, that is ... I know, Mama, but truly. I do *hear Her singing, and singing. And*

DAVID GURR emigrated from Britain to Canada with his parents in 1947, at the age of eleven. He went to school in England and to Naval College in Canada; he also read mathematics and physics at the University of Victoria. From 1954–70 he served in the Royal Canadian Navy. From 1971–80 he ran his own company as a designer and builder of houses. In 1976 he began to write. *The Ring Master* is his sixth novel. He lives in British Columbia with his wife, Judith, who is a sculptor.